THE GREAT BOOK OF KING ARTHUR
AND HIS
KNIGHTS OF THE ROUND TABLE

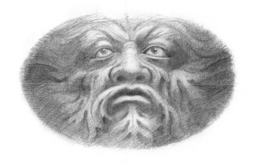

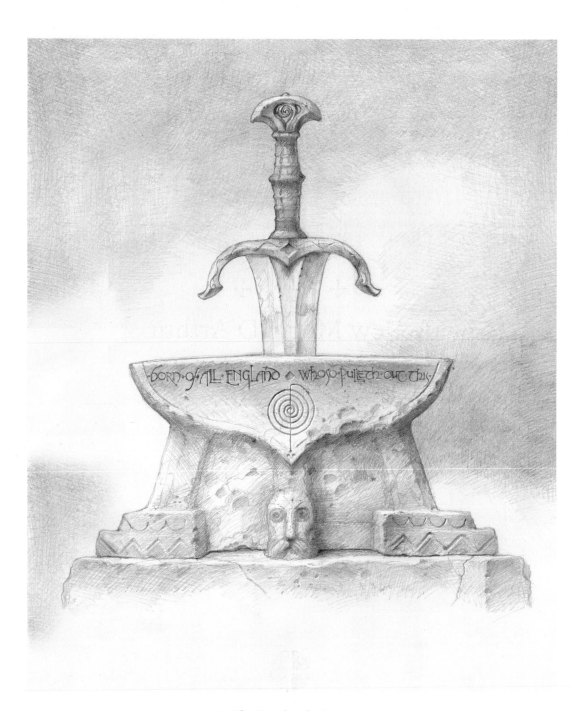

→ *The Sword in the Stone* ←

THE GREAT BOOK OF
KING ARTHUR
AND THE
KNIGHTS OF THE ROUND TABLE

✠ ✠ ✠

A New Morte D'Arthur

Compiled and Written by
JOHN MATTHEWS

Foreword by
NEIL GAIMAN

Illustrated by
JOHN HOWE

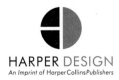

HARPER DESIGN
An Imprint of HarperCollinsPublishers

Also published in the United Kingdom by HarperCollins*Publishers* in 2022.

The Great Book of King Arthur. Copyright © by John Matthews 2022.
Foreword © by Neil Gaiman 2022.
Illustrations © by John Howe 2022.

HarperCollins books may be purchased for educational, business, or sales promotional use. For
information please email the Special Markets Department at SPsales@harpercollins.com.

Published in 2022 by
Harper Design
An Imprint of HarperCollins*Publishers*
195 Broadway
New York, NY 10007
Tel: (212) 207-7000
Fax: (855) 746-6023
harperdesign@harpercollins.com
www.hc.com

Distributed throughout the world by
HarperCollins*Publishers*
195 Broadway
New York, NY 10007

ISBN 978-0-06-324312-5

Library of Congress Cataloging-in-Publication Data has been applied for.

Printed and bound in Italy by Rotolito

First Printing, 2022

MIX
Paper from
responsible sources
FSC
www.fsc.org
FSC C007454

DEDICATION

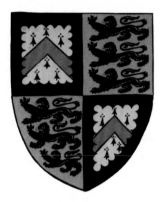

The Arms of Sir Thomas Malory.

———— ✠ ————

To the memory of Sir Thomas Malory, Knight,
born 1415 in Warwickshire; died 1471 in London.
&
To John Ronald Reuel Tolkien (1892–1973)
The greatest chronicler of the Ancient Days.

ACKNOWLEDGEMENTS

First, I wish to thank my wife, Caitlín Matthews, who has shared my long journey to the writing of this book and whose constant support and wonderful wisdom have made every page glow brighter than they would otherwise have done. To my two other readers, Dwina Gibb and David Elkington, whose comments have helped shape the contents of each story. Also, to the memory of two other great Arthurians, who taught me so much about how to form these fantastic tales: John James (1923–1993) and Peter Vansittart (1920–2008) who I like to think would both have enjoyed this book. To Neil, another of the truly great storytellers of our time, thanks for the fabulous Foreword. To my agent, Peter Buckman, for some rigorous comments at the beginning. And last, but by no means least, to John Howe, whose extraordinary art graces this volume. I have long admired his work, and for his willingness to focus on this text when he was already involved with many other projects, I shall always be thankful.

John Matthews
Oxford, 2022

CONTENTS

PLATES

FOREWORD

My first exposure to Arthur was a big hardback, with colourful paintings. The painting in the first chapter of the red dragon battling the white at the base of Vortigern's tower is seared in my memory. I was six. The book belonged to the Harris family, and I would go to their house and read their books. That was where I first read the Narnia books, and where, on Mr. Harris's shelves, I first encountered Dracula. That was where the good books were. I would read the stories in that book with awe and trepidation, amazed at the tales and glorying in the lushness of the art.

Roger Lancelyn Green's *Tales of King Arthur* was the second exposure, and the third was being taken to the cinema to see the, for me at that age, intensely disappointing film of *Camelot*. The people on the screen seemed under the impression that the story of King Arthur and his knights was some kind of love story, which to me at the age of seven seemed about as misguided as it was possible to get. I wanted white and red dragons locked in battle, flashing swords, giants bested and mysterious knights in coloured armour who never spoke, not songs and kissing and a sad ending.

When I was about thirteen, I subscribed to the Book Club, advertised in the back of a newspaper's Sunday magazine, in order to get the free two-volume complete *Oxford English Dictionary* (with magnifying glass), which I needed, I had realized, to read William Morris's fantasy novel, *The Well at the World's End*, which used many archaic words I couldn't find in any usual dictionary. I had to order an actual book from the Book Club as well, in order to keep the free dictionaries, so I ordered a beautiful edition of the *Morte D'Arthur* filled with medieval illustrations. I remember the joyous day the book arrived, opening it and tumbling into Malory's world. Reading Malory was easier than reading William Morris. I fell in love with Merlin, son of a demon, immediately. I became, well, just a little bit obsessed with Arthurian fantasy. I had already read T. H. White's books (in various confusingly different editions – I did not yet understand then that contradictory stories, and differing retellings of stories you have already read, lie at the heart of the Matter of Arthur) and I enjoyed the stories – while always wishing that things had gone differently for poor Arthur, whom I had liked so much as young Wart, and to whom I had wished only good things.

I wondered at the when of it all, and the why. The glorious anachronisms added to the joy, like Shakespeare's *Julius Caesar* with its clocks and books and doublets. The Arthurian stories were written down and collected at a time when everything existed in a glorious present, so a mythic age of high adventure and chivalry took place in Malory's own age of chivalry. Some of the stories, it seemed to me, were old stories, remembered, told and retold, and some were composed there and then, inspired by the old ones. Both kinds were marvellous.

I delighted in things Arthurian, although they were always in short supply, and in my teens and early twenties I took joy in each and every rare Arthurian sighting. It was there, the thing I loved, in *Monty Python and the Holy Grail*, and although that was a comedy it was a comedy that understood Arthurian Fantasy, and used it as a mirror to reflect the jokes; it was there in John Boorman's film, *Excalibur*, although that seemed uninterested in the characters as people and mostly succeeded, it seemed to me when I saw it, on the spectacle.

I don't remember what the first book I bought by John and Caitlín Matthews was, although I do remember that I bought it in a magical bookshop near the British Museum, and that its subject was (unsurprisingly for John or Caitlín) Celtic magical traditions. (Wikipedia and Google were no help when I went to find out which book it could have been: the couple have written so many books, together and alone.) What I mostly remember was how useful it was. The year was 1988 and I was researching magical traditions for *The Books of Magic*, a four-part comic I would write for DC Comics, and I was getting slightly discouraged. I had bought a shelf of magical books as research and found them dull, unconvincing, and often faintly embarrassed, as if the people writing them were unable to shake the feeling that what they were writing was fundamentally silly. I strongly suspected I could make up better and more convincing magical systems than the ones I was being offered. The book by John and Caitlín was the opposite of these. It felt grounded and convincing, was well-researched and well-written and was never less than interesting. It was one of the inspirations for the third part of *Books of Magic*, the one illustrated by the astonishing Charles Vess.

John, Caitlín and I shared interests – in Arthurian and Celtic tales, in the magical traditions of the British Isles (which are never as old as you might imagine, unless they are), in the work of the brilliant British novelist, John James. (His novels *Votan*, about a Greek trader named Photinus whose exploits inspire the legends of Odin, and *Not For All The Gold In Ireland*, in which Photinus inadvertently creates many of the finest stories of Celtic mythology, are two of the best things I've read.) The first time I talked to John and Caitlín in person, in 2013, it was about their work restoring James's unpublished final novel, *The Fourth Gwenevere*, and their plan to bring it into print.

John Matthews is an expert on matters Arthurian. He knows his stuff. He's written fact and he's written fiction, he's written for children and for adults. In this book, he has assembled for us a new *Morte D'Arthur*. He has taken some of the stories that Malory didn't retell, and has collected them together, to show us a whole new set of tales of Merlin, of Arthur and of his knights. In doing this he makes something new and unusual, as if we are allowed to step through a mirror into another world in which these are the famous Arthurian stories, the ones that have always been retold and evoked.

Like the best Arthurian stories, they contain chivalry, knights on horseback, swordplay, magic and noble heroes and beautiful women. But there is a feeling of freshness to them that I love.

What I enjoy most about them is that they do not in any way feel like the leavings, the stories that weren't good enough to make the final cut, the B list. These are tales, for the most part unknown to me, with the freshness and life of the best of Malory's retellings. Here we might encounter a young King Arthur in disguise as The Knight of the Parrot, or a young Lancelot on a quest for his identity which involves enough magic, high adventure, murderous tourneys and enthusiastic sexual dalliances to make *Game of Thrones* look positively anaemic. (And these stories also remind us just how much George R. R. Martin's most famous sequence of books owes to the *Morte D'Arthur*. The Arthurian tales are in the DNA of Westeros, just as much as the Wars of the Roses.)

John Matthews's authorial voice is well-chosen. It makes the stories feel old, which they are, but it is still cheerfully contemporary in attitude, while never sacrificing clarity for either cod-archaism or current phrasing. You will not need the two-volume complete *Oxford English Dictionary* to read this book. It is of now and of then, much like the stories.

They are old, but still they speak to us.

For, almost 600 years after Malory's time, these tales feel like they still exist in a glorious present, as if one could travel to King Arthur's Court simply by walking, and find oneself in Camelot, on a fine spring morning when the flowers are in blossom on the edge of the forest, on the verge of a fine adventure.

Neil Gaiman
January 2022

INTRODUCTION

The Forgotten Tales of Arthur and his Knights

Towards the end of the fifteenth century, a man named Sir Thomas Malory completed a book from his prison cell. This great work is known today as *Le Morte D'Arthur* (The Death of Arthur). It was not the title he had intended, but the printer, William Caxton, not only edited the book but gave it the title by which it is still known. It became an overnight success and is still the 'go to' source for all things Arthurian.

In the year 2000, in celebration of the new millennium, I edited the text for a new edition with stunning illustrations by the artist Anna-Marie Fergusson. More recently, almost 20 years on, I prepared a further edition, published by Chaosium Inc. in 2022, the first to include a running commentary of marginal glosses to help readers unfamiliar with Malory's work or his milieu to find their way through the densely packed pages of his great book.

Malory's chief source was a massive compilation, written in Old French in the thirteenth century and known as the *Vulgate Cycle* (or in its most recent edition, the *Lancelot-Grail*). This work, itself compiled by a group of Cistercian monks, consisted of stories gathered from many different sources. It was huge in scope and length, running, in its modern edition, to eight volumes. Malory himself edited this multi-volume opus to less than half its original length, cutting out vast tracts of theological explication and focusing on what were probably his favourite stories. Caxton further edited Malory's work, transforming what was intended as a collection of chivalric tales into what many consider to be the first English novel.

However, even at 500+ pages Malory could not include everything, nor indeed did he have access to tales written in other languages: Spanish, Italian, German – even Hebrew – which extended the range of Arthuriana several times over. As I worked on the 2000 edition, and more recently on the revised and updated version, I realized just how much Malory had not included. Here was no 'Story of Caradoc of the Strong Arm', no 'Jaufre', no 'Knight of the Parrot'.

Having recently commissioned some new, full or partial translations of several texts for my own research purposes, I began to wonder if there could not be a 'new' *Morte D'Arthur*. In this could be collected many of the stories excluded from Malory's book, such as those works mentioned above, written, as was his own, for a contemporary reader, with links between the tales to give the whole edifice a beginning, middle and end – just as Thomas Malory did in his own book.

Once this idea caught hold, I could not let it go, and the result is the book you hold in your hands. I realized early on that I needed a 'voice' for these stories, and into my mind walked the nameless cleric and storyteller who presents the stories as his own homage to the greater writer he so deeply admires.

In doing this, I was thinking of Caxton's own preface to the book he printed, in which he said that *'many noble and divers gentlemen of this realm of England came and demanded me, many and ofttimes, wherefore I [had not] made and imprinted the noble history of the Sangreal [the Grail], and of the most renowned Christian and worthy, King Arthur, which ought most to be remembered among us English men tofore all other Christian kings'*.

Thus prompted, Caxton went on to produce the book that was, more than any other, to establish the fame of King Arthur. Not only is Malory one of the finest prose stylists to write in English, but he tells a superb story with pace and flare. His consummate ear for dialogue, and his unerring ability to delete the prolix and dull from his sources, makes his book as exciting a read today as it was 600 years ago.

The selection of stories that make up this new volume span the whole range of Arthurian tales, from Celtic to late medieval. They include such tales as *Lanzalet*, included here as 'How Sir Lancelot Earned his Name', which offers a very different portrait of the great knight, to 'The Story of Perceval', which focuses on the quest for the Grail and brings out some profoundly different meanings from the story as we find it in Malory. I have also included several stories from the loosely knit cycle of poems and romances relating to the figure of Sir Gawain. Once recognized as one of the key figures among the Round Table Fellowship, Gawain underwent a steady and consistent demotion, until by the time we get to Malory's account, he is little better than a murderer and a womanizer. The early versions of his story represented here in 'Gorlagros and Gawain', 'Gawain and the Carle of Carlisle' and 'The Rise of Gawain', tell a very different tale, in which Gawain is the hero *par excellence* and gets into some truly astonishing adventures.

Then there are the Celtic tales, which have a quite different atmosphere. Here this earliest branch of Arthurian literature is represented by such epic stories as, 'The Tale of Sir Lanval', as well as what must be the most unusual –

and certainly the strangest – story in this book, 'The Story of the Crop-Eared Dog', a medieval Irish text which deserves to be better known. It is full of extraordinary flights of fancy – proving that the Celtic imagination was far from dead by this date. But perhaps the most intriguing of all is the medieval Irish tale called 'The Visit of the Grey-Hammed Lady' – hitherto unavailable in English – which marries the magic and colour of Celtic mythology with the proud chivalric tradition of the Arthurian epics. I am especially pleased to be able to include it here.

The versions collected here are not translations in any exact sense of the word but are rather retellings of the original stories into modern prose. Just as Malory 'edited' the Vulgate Cycle and other works into *Le Morte D'Arthur*, which was further edited by his publisher, William Caxton, I have endeavoured to make a similar collection of the stories Malory either never knew or chose to leave out.

In working through these stories, I have found there to be several common themes: chivalry of course, romantic love, the bravery of the errant knights who pit themselves against all kinds of odds. But by far the most potent and powerful theme is the continued encounters between Arthur and his knights with beings of the Otherworld. It suggests a kind of warfare going on, a rift between the worlds, which prompts otherworldliness to invade. Again and again we find scenarios that reflect this. It seems that almost every time either the king or one of the knights leaves the safety of the walls of Camelot, or Caerleon or Carlisle, the Otherworld awaits them – often just around the corner. If they, on the other hand, do not venture forth, the otherworldly beings are just as likely to force an entry themselves – offering games, quests, or challenges which none of the fabled Fellowship can risk refusing for fear of damaging their reputation as brave and fearless men. The story of 'The Elucidation of the Grail' (p. 309) told here gives a very understandable reason for this, and I have added my own internal references to the various stories to keep this theme at the forefront of the reader's mind.

It is through such story-making that we learn, not only of the rich and varied details of medieval life and spirituality, but also the dreams that haunted the minds of their makers – men and women who were certainly a great deal closer to the world of subtle reality than most of us today. It is this inner life that continues to inhabit the Arthurian tradition and enables it still to exercise such a powerful fascination over us today.

J.R.R. Tolkien, perhaps the greatest mythographer of our time, objected to Arthurian legends and literature on the grounds that they were 'incoherent' and 'inconsistent', due to the vast range of stories borrowed from each other and the huge pool of older material. This is certainly true, in one sense, of Malory. He had so much material to draw upon that he struggled to bring a coherent form to his book. However, despite some inconsistencies where, for example, characters killed off in one book reappeared later in another, Malory in fact succeeded overall in making his work tell a story that has a beginning, middle and an end. Argument still rages over his intent whether to write a whole book (hence the original title of his work, 'The Whole Book of King Arthur and His Knights of the Round Table') or a collection of separate stories. There is, perhaps, to be fair to each argument, something of both in the *Morte*. In compiling the present work, I have been aware from the start that there are inconsistencies of character and event in some of the tales retold here; but I have attempted to avoid this by excluding certain parts of the original works, just as Malory did, in order to arrive at a reasonably coherent narrative. This has inevitably resulted in some losses, which I have indicated in the notes at the end of the book, where omitted sections are briefly summarized for the benefit of those readers who prefer to know what they are missing. In most instances these are in part dictated by length. Some of the works, such as 'Sone de Nansay' and 'Sir Torec' are of considerable length, so that to include all would be to extend the present book into several volumes – hence I have curtailed them by excluding parts that stray from the main thread of the stories.

Throughout, I also kept in mind Tolkien's unspoken question proposed by Leonard Neidorf in his excellent paper on Tolkien's own Arthurian poem, *The Fall of Arthur*. 'If an author makes a series of correct selections from the available materials, modifying all of them where necessary, would it be possible to harmonize the traditions and produce a coherent narrative?'* I feel that the answer to this question is a resounding 'yes', and I have done my best to create such a narrative here. Inevitably, there will be places where ideas and beliefs seem to clash, but I feel that when we enter the Arthurian world, we are entering another place, where normal frames of reference do not always apply. Arthur's world is a world of Faery, where almost anything can happen, and frequently does. With this in mind, I believe the following epic is as close as one may get in our time to a work Malory himself, had he been granted more time and access to a larger library of Arthurian literature, might have achieved. I make no claim to be as great a master of prose as he undoubtedly was, but I have tried to arrive at a pared-down, direct language such as Malory himself used in his incomparable work.

The unity of the collection comes from the presence of the fictional collector and teller of the tales, who frequently interrupts the narrative with comments of his own. Malory himself does this from time to time, referring often to 'the French book', probably the *Lancelot-Grail*, which in fact tells the story of Arthur, Merlin, Lancelot, and the rest in a single vast, sprawling collection. As did most of the compilers of these tales, the collectors use a technique known

---

* Neidorf, L 'J.R.R. Tolkien's *The Fall of Arthur*: Creation from Literary Criticism,' *Tolkien Studies*, vol 14, 2017, pp. 91–113.

as 'interlacing', where a story would begin, get interrupted by another which would in turn be itself interrupted, often three or four times, before returning to the original tale. I have, for the most part, avoided this, as it can be difficult for a modern reader. Instead, I have allowed our collector of these tales to add comments and make occasional references to other stories – some included by Malory himself, others having links to each other, prompted by their author's knowledge of other tales. Another device of Caxton's editing was to add what we can term 'ends and beginnings' to each book: thus, *Explicit Liber Primus* (End of Book One), *Incipit Liber Secundus* (Beginning of Book Two). I have adopted this here to add to the links between Malory's book and my own.

In making my own tellings of these stories I have tried to find a style which reflects the original, while not seeming too antiquated. The rhythms of the works themselves, often written as poetry, are frequently hypnotic. I have tried to capture the best of these while keeping the narrative flowing.

Many of the original stories have nameless characters: 'a lady', 'a damsel', 'a knight', or 'a lord', being the most oft used. Since the characters are often similar in style and behaviour, I have given them names drawn from other Arthurian sources to make them recognizable.

To complete the vision of this 'new' *Morte D'Arthur* I was incredibly fortunate to secure the collaboration of my friend, John Howe, famous for his illustrations and design work on *The Lord of the Rings* book and films, to illustrate this epic collection. The results are as breathtaking as anything I could have wished for. They more than do justice to my words and I am forever indebted to John for taking on this task.

Towards the end of my work on this book I came across a quotation from the English poet John Masefield (1878–1967) whose own Arthurian poetry I had discovered many years ago and have always loved. In a collection of Masefield's Arthurian poetry (*Arthurian Poets: John Masefield*, edited by David Llewellyn Dodds [Boydell & Brewer, 1995]) I found the following passage:

> *Has not the time come for a re-making and re-issue of the epic [of Arthur] …? Is not the time ripe for an Authorized Version using old poems and fables little used by or unknown to Malory…? It is our English epic; we ought to make more use of it than we do. (p.8)*

This I have attempted to do. I hope that the many thousands of people who love Malory's original work will find my additions not too far off the quality of his own – though I cannot claim to be the master of style that he undoubtedly was.

John Matthews
Oxford, 2022

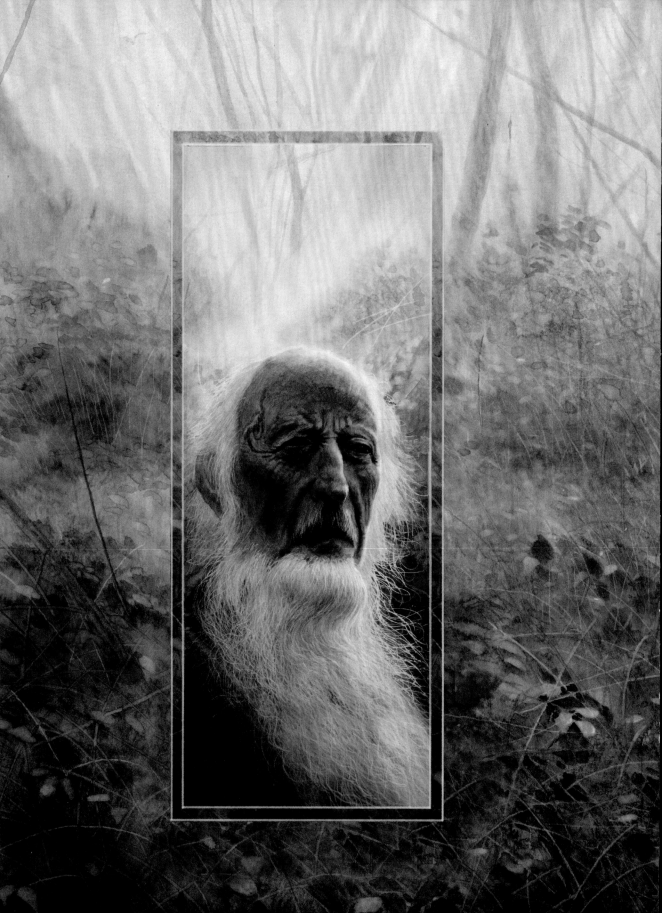

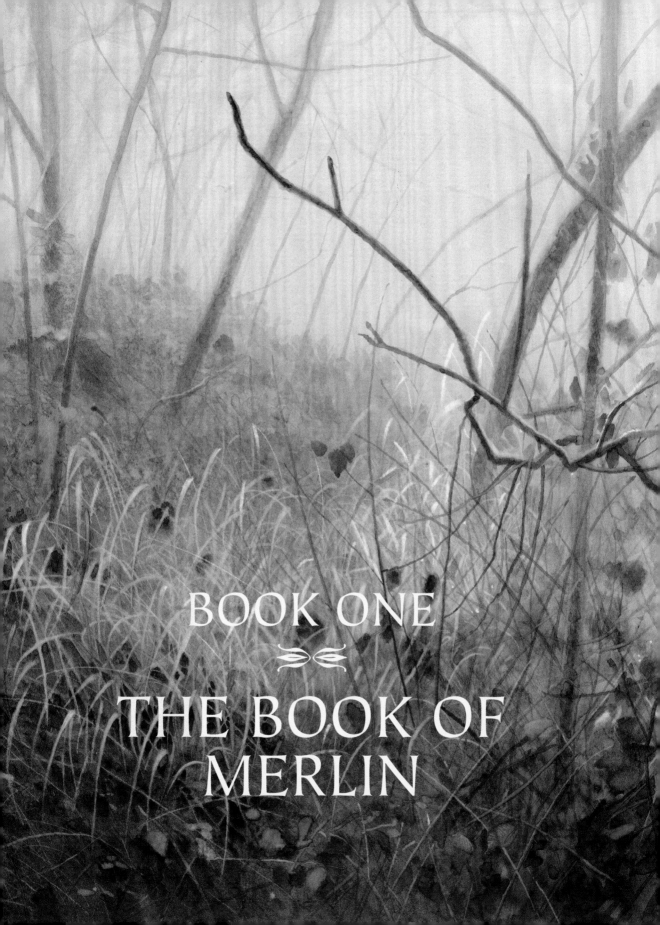

BOOK ONE

❦

THE BOOK OF MERLIN

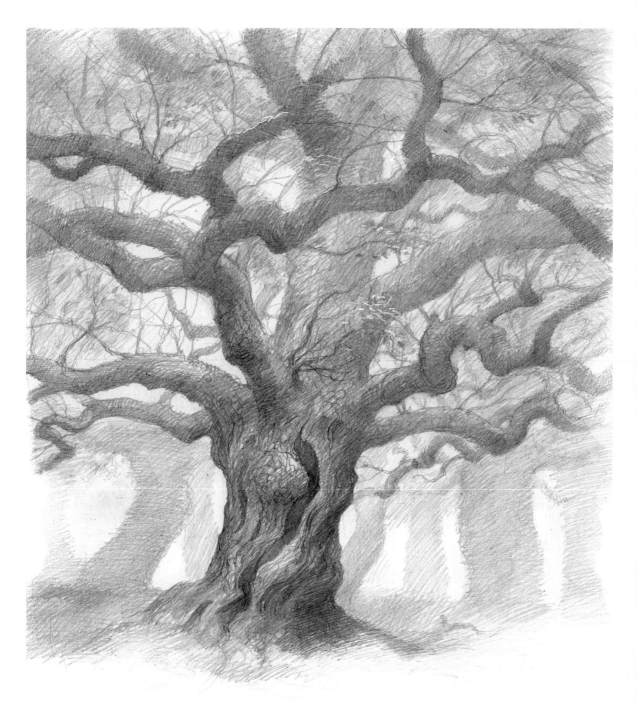

→ *The Mighty Tree* ←

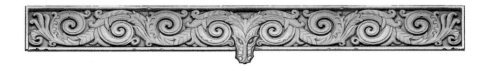

1: THE COMING OF MERLIN

✢

HERE, AT THE BEGINNING, MY STORY OF KING ARTHUR SHALL BE TOLD. A BOOK THAT SHALL TELL THE STORIES THAT MASTER THOMAS MALORY WAS UNABLE, FOR DIVERS REASONS, TO INCLUDE IN HIS GREAT WORK, KNOWN TO ALL THE WORLD AS *LE MORTE D'ARTHUR*. THUS, THERE SHALL BE A NEW BOOK OF KING ARTHUR AND OF HIS KNIGHTS, THAT MAY LIVE IN THE MEMORY OF MEN AND WOMEN OF NOBLE AND GENTLE MIND UNTIL THE MAP OF TIME IS ROLLED UP.

✢ ✢ ✢

IN THOSE DAYS King Arthur ruled over all of Britain from the city of Camelot the Golden. He held many great feasts at the Round Table, where one hundred and fifty of the greatest knights sat, as you will have heard. Sir Lancelot, Sir Palomides and Sir Gawain, the king's own nephew, and his brothers Gareth, Guerrehes, and Agravain were all there, as were many others, including the queen's Knights and the Heroes of the Grail.

But Merlin was first: long before the coming of Arthur. Some say he was the son of a demon, others that he was born, of no human agency, in the Great Wood that stretched from Camelot in the south to the barrier of the Roman Wall in the north. It was rumoured that even the old gods feared him. But whether this is true or not, once this island of Britain was known as Merlin's Isle, around which he built a wall of brass, and he it was who raised the hanging stones on Salisbury Plain, to make a tomb for a king. He made the boy Arthur King of all Britain in those far-off times; and it was he who caused the forging of the sword Excalibur and its gifting to the young king. And Merlin it was who brought the stone in which the sword was set, to a place of choosing, where the king and the land were joined. And after that he built Camelot the Golden – in a single night, they say.

Let us begin therefore with the tale of Merlin's birth, who became King Arthur's great counsellor, and wrought many strange and wondrous things in that far-off time. The story of his coming, and of the events that led to the appearance of Arthur himself, is less often told. So here I shall begin.

NO ONE CAN speak with certainty concerning the origins of Merlin. But one tale that is told, and that it seems Master Thomas chose not to include in his great book, tells how a certain princess of Dyfed was found to be with child, though it was believed that she had never lain with a man. When examined, she told how a most beautiful being had appeared in her chamber on many nights and that he had made love to her as gently as summer rain upon the earth. Each morning he was gone, vanishing she knew not where. Nor could she tell whence he came, only that he was kind, and that he seemed to glow like a candle in the dark.

Most who heard her story were quick to name her harlot, while those of a less harsh disposition believed that the one who came to her was a demon – since it was well known that demons always look fair when their true likeness is foul. But soon the child within her clamoured to emerge into the world, and when it was born the midwife turned pale as she saw that the infant – a boy – was covered in a thick pelt of grey hair. At once the Princess's father and mother demanded that the child be taken to a priest to be baptized – believing, no doubt, that it would vanish in a puff of sulphurous smoke. But when the priest poured holy water upon the babe's head, its furry covering fell away and dissolved, and it was heard to crow with delight. At the same moment there flew overhead a type of hawk that is called a merlin, and this the Princess took to be a sign and named him for the bird.

Those who tell this story say also that when he was ten years old, the boy was accused of being unnatural, and that he and his mother (who by this time had retreated to a nunnery) were summoned to appear before a magistrate. When they did so, Merlin astonished all by knowing more about the judge's scurrilous private life than any man could by ordinary means, and he spoke so forcefully and with such clarity, denying that his father was more than a man, that in the end he was set free, as was his mother. Thereafter people avoided the child, believing him either devil or creature of Faery – which I would say is the more likely thing. But one thing that is told, and that gives the lie to this tale (unless it be that the Princess gave birth to two children and not one) – for Merlin had a sister it seems, a twin, who at first showed none of his unnatural skills, but in time became known as a prophet in her own right. Her name was Ganeida, and though I know little of these matters, yet my heart tells me that neither Merlin nor his sister were of mortal stock but were born of the air itself.

Be that as it may, as Merlin grew to manhood, so good and generous was his nature, and so clever his wisdom, that in time most people forgot his origins, and when his mother's father, who was a king in Dyfed, passed away without issue, he was accepted as the heir to the kingdom and became its ruler, and though many remarked that his wisdom had a smell of the uncanny about it, yet none chose to challenge his right to rule. It was at this time that he married Guendolena, sister of Rodarch, lord of Cumbria. Few now tell of this alliance, save one account that I have found, by Master Geoffrey of Monmouth, who also wrote of the deeds of Arthur in his famous 'Historia Regum Britanniae'. There, Merlin was known as both a wise man, a poet, and a lawgiver, to whom lesser men came in search of knowledge. But as king he was also a warrior, who would lead an army of men into battle.

A time came when Prince Peredur, leader of the North-Welsh, and Gwenddoleu, King of Scotland, were at war with each other. Merlin joined the ranks of the Welsh, as did his friend Rodarch of Cumbria, who had married Ganeida when Merlin wed the king's sister. With them were Peredur's three younger brothers, who were very dear to Merlin, and these five fought side by side, until on a day when battle was joined with great ferocity between the Scots and the Welsh, the three young princes fell to the swords of their enemies.

When he saw this, Merlin lamented loudly, his voice rising above the noise of battle:

> 'How can malignant fate
> So cruelly take from me
> My dearest companions!
> Bravest of youths,
> Your courage has taken
> The years of your lives.
> A moment ago,
> You fought beside me;
> Now you lie on the earth,
> Fresh blood upon you!
> Who now will stand
> Beside me in battle!'

All around him the fighting continued. Men fell dead on every side. But the Welsh pressed forward and at the day's end held the field. Merlin ordered the princes to be buried, but nothing could console him for their loss. For days he wept, threw dust upon himself, and rent his clothing. Nothing could reconcile him to the death of the young men.

In the end his mind gave way before his sorrow, and he ran mad, fleeing into the great wood of Calydon, that lay to the North of the battlefield. Every day he rested beneath a particular tree in a grove of apple trees, plucking fruit from them and devouring it eagerly. There too he befriended a lone wolf to which he spoke often, believing it to understand him. But when winter came and there was no more fruit on the tree and little or nothing to be had in the wilderness, Merlin cried aloud:

> 'Gods of the earth,
> Where is the fruit I am used to eat?
> Who has taken it?
> Here in the wilderness
> The forest is leafless;
> There is no cover for me
> Since the winds took away the leaves.
> If I dig for roots
> Hungry swine and greedy boars
> Rush to steal them from me.
> Wolf, my old companion,
> So weak are you become
> You can barely cross the field.
> All that is left to you
> Is to fill the air with howling!'

Merlin's cries happened to reach the ears of a travelling singer who, when he heard the strange voice and its wild words, was drawn to a high place, where the woods bled dark to the horizon. There he found Merlin, lying in the grass, naked and wasted, complaining loudly to no visible person:

> 'How is it that the seasons
> Differ from each other?
> Why must the Spring
> Provide leaves and blossoms,
> The Summer give crops

And the autumn ripe fruit?
Then comes Winter
Destroying everything.
I wish there was no Winter,
That Spring was back,
That birds sang again
And springs flowed free!'

The singer, observing this, decided on a bold move. He unslung his harp from where it lay against his back and played a few quiet notes. For a moment Merlin's sight cleared, but as he raised his head and saw the singer nearby the madness overcame him again and he fled deeper into the woods.

The singer, having tried to follow him, gave up his pursuit and returned to the road. Soon after this he came to the court of King Rodarch, who had fought alongside Merlin and witnessed his descent into madness, and who was husband to Merlin's sister. Ganeida, having learned of her brother's affliction had, along with his wife Guendolena, sent men to search for him, but all had returned without having seen so much as a hair of him.

When the singer described his encounter with the naked madman, the light of hope sprang again in the eyes of those who so sorely missed him, and Rodarch ordered his soldiers to go with the singer and bring the madman home. The wise singer, knowing that the presence of armed men would only drive their quarry deeper into the forest, asked to be allowed to go alone. For, as he said: 'It may be that music will calm him, and that my words may cause him to remember his family.'

Rodarch consulted with Guendolena and Ganeida, who readily gave their consent. The singer retraced his steps to that part of the forest where he had first heard Merlin's wild voice. There, he once again unslung his harp and sang a song that he had made in readiness.

'*Mourning fills Guendolena.*
Once no woman in Britain
Was as beautiful as she.
No goddess white as she,
Not blackthorn, rose or lily.
Once, Spring's delight rose in her,
In her eyes the stars held sway.
Now she lies sick with sorrow,
Bewailing her lost husband,
Faded as a fallen star.

'*Alas too for Ganeida,*
Who weeps by her side,
Mourning the loss of a brother.
Wife and sister weep together –
Their tears a river of loss.'

At first there was only silence, then the sad and wasted figure of Merlin appeared and stood listening. As he did so his eyes once again became clear, and the madness drew its shadow from his mind. In a normal manner he greeted the singer and asked him to sing his mournful song again. When he had heard it, with tears in his eyes Merlin begged to be taken to Rodarch's court, where he might see his wife and sister.

But Merlin's happiness was short-lived, for when he saw the people thronging the streets of the city his madness returned, and he attempted to flee back to the forest. King Rodarch had set guards to watch for the singer's return, and when he heard of the wildman's distress, he gave orders that he should be captured and brought thither, and for music to be played to maintain his calm. But when Rodarch ordered the madman to be securely chained for his own good, as the fetters closed upon him, the light faded from Merlin's eyes and he spoke no more.

At that moment Queen Ganeida entered and stood looking at the wildman with pity in her eyes. Embracing and kissing her, Rodarch noticed a leaf caught in her hair and smilingly removed it. At this Merlin began to laugh, rocking back and forth in his chains.

Surprised, Rodarch asked that he reveal the reason for his mirth. But Merlin stayed silent, while the king, his curiosity piqued, began to offer him rewards to explain himself. Irritated by this, Merlin answered at last that he would only give an answer if he were set free and allowed to return to the forest. 'Gifts corrupt those they are given to,' he said. 'I value more the peace of the forest of Calydon.'

Rodarch hesitated, but at this moment Merlin's wife Guendolena entered and begged him to set her husband free. As the fetters were removed, Merlin smiled and said: 'I laughed when you took the leaf from the queen's hair, lord King, because I know how it got there. Just a while since she lay in a leafy glade with her lover!'

Rodarch's face darkened and he turned in anger to his wife. But she, hiding her guilt behind a smile, called Merlin's words the ravings of a madman. 'How can you believe one who does not know truth from lies?' she said. 'I can easily prove his words false.'

Then she called before them a youth and asked Merlin to foretell how he would meet his death.

Merlin said: 'He shall die by falling from a high place.'

Ganeida sent the youth away and instructed him to change his clothes and cut his hair. Then, when he again stood before them all, she asked Merlin to foretell the manner of his death. Again, the madman laughed and said: 'He shall die in a tree.'

All this time she watched Merlin closely, knowing how his wisdom worked within him.

'You see,' she said, 'if my poor brother can foretell two different deaths for the same person, how can you believe such an accusation against me? Watch a little longer and you will see what I mean.'

Then she sent the youth away yet again and told him to dress in girl's clothes. When he returned, she asked Merlin a third time to foretell the manner of the 'girl's' death.

'Girl or not,' said Merlin, 'this one will die in a river.'

Now it was Rodarch's turn to laugh, for he understood that Merlin had foretold three different causes of death for the same person, proving that he was truly mad. 'Let him be set free to return to the forest,' he said. 'Perhaps there he may recover his wits.'

At once Merlin hastened away from the court, filled with joy at being set free. Guendolena approached him at the gates to the palace and begged him not to leave. But he would have none of it and sternly ordered her to move out of his way. At that Guendolena fell on her knees before him, crying out that he should not go away again. Ganeida, who had followed him from the court, said: 'See how your wife kneels in sorrow before you, brother. Will you so abuse her that she must wait for your return for ever? Shall she come with you to the forest or remain here?' Then, knowing that a long absence and Merlin's madness would render their marriage vows broken in the eyes of the world, she asked: 'Shall your wife re-marry if you do not return?'

Merlin, wild eyed, stared at the women. 'Let her marry again if she wishes!' he cried.

'But tell the man who seeks her out to stay away from me. Let him take another road.' Then he hesitated, and for a moment it was as though the clouds in his eyes dispersed. Staring towards the sky, he said: 'When the day comes for her to wed, I shall be present. Rich gifts shall I bring to her.'

Then he departed again for the woods he loved so much.

Guendolena wept as she watched Merlin depart, and Ganeida too mourn-ed his passing, for though she feared his knowledge of her secret affair, yet she loved him still and bewailed the loss of his wisdom.

✠ ✠ ✠

MONTHS PASSED INTO years and the youth of whom Merlin had made his threefold prophecy grew to manhood. Then, on a day when he rode to the hunt, he started a stag, that ran before him over the brow of a hill. The way was unusually steep, and near the top his horse stumbled, and the young man was thrown from his saddle. He fell down the steep escarpment and caught his foot in the branch of a tree growing out of the hillside. He was left hanging with his head beneath the water of the river that ran beside the hill. So it was that he fell, and was drowned, and hung from a tree – proving Merlin's prophecy on every account.

Meanwhile the prophet continued to live in the wilderness, loving the forest more than he had ever loved life in cities and courts. One night, as he was sitting beneath the trees, gazing up at the horned moon and bathing in the glory of the bright stars, he fell to thinking of Guendolena and wondering if she still remembered him or had found peace in the arms of another. As he watched the stars, he saw signs that indicated that she was to marry again. And he thought back to his words at their parting, and how he had promised to bring her gifts, and this he determined to do.

Next day, he rose and went through the woods, gathering a great herd of stags and goats, does and she-goats, which he shepherded into a long line. He himself rode at the head of this strange column on a great stag. He set out for the palace where Guendolena was about to marry, just as the stars had foretold. As he arrived at the gates, he called out her name.

When she came forth, she was amazed at the sight of Merlin and the great herd of creatures he had brought with him. Her bridegroom, whose name the story does not remember, was standing at a high window. When he saw the ragged, hairy wildman mounted on the stag's back, he burst out laughing. Looking up, Merlin saw this, and sudden wild anger filled his heart. With terrible strength he seized the antlers of the great stag on whose back he sat and wrenched them off. Then he flung them at the window, so that they struck the bridegroom's head, crushing it and the life within him and sending forth his spirit upon the wind.

At this there was a great outcry. Merlin drove his heels into the stag's side and made off at full speed, pursued by soldiers. Such was the speed of the stag that Merlin would have certainly found refuge in the forest had they not had to cross a river. But there the stag stumbled, and Merlin fell into the water, striking his head, so that for a time his wits deserted him. In this way, his pursuers caught him and brought him back to the court to be placed in the care of his sister – for his wife no longer wished to see him following the death of the man she had intended to marry.

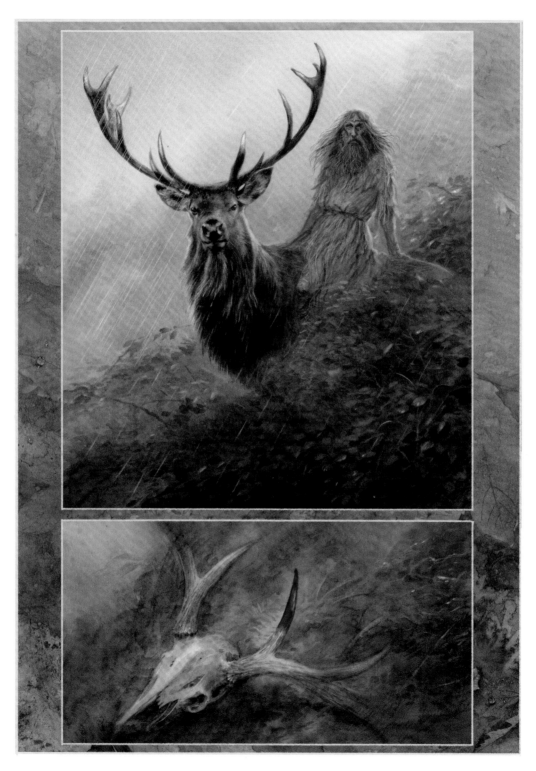

PLATE I: *'He himself rode at the head of this strange column on a great stag'*

Indeed, they neither spoke nor saw each other again, and not long after, Guendolena died.

Once again Merlin began to fade in the grip of captivity. He became surly and morose, refusing to eat or speak to anyone. Rodarch, seeing this, felt some pity for him, and commanded that he be taken out into the streets, under guard, and permitted to see the people thronging the marketplace. The king hoped that this would remind Merlin of his former place in the world and that he would be restored to a semblance of sanity.

In the market, people nudged each other and pointed at the madman with his wild hair and beard and ragged clothing, but he in turn ignored them, looking ever towards the west where the Great Wood lay. Then he caught sight of a man begging by the gates and laughed aloud at the sight. A few moments later he saw a youth carrying a new pair of shoes. Again, Merlin laughed wildly, and at this the guards decided to take him back to the court, since this showed that he was still mad. All the way he struggled against them and cried out to be allowed to return to his forest home.

When he heard the story of Merlin's laughter, and doubtless remembering the last time Merlin had laughed in this way, Rodarch wanted to know the reason for it. He promised that if the prophet would tell him, he would let him go again, and at this Merlin smiled. 'I saw a man begging by the road when all the time he sat upon hidden treasure. Then I saw a fellow buying patches for his shoes, but the truth is, he will never need them. He is drowned already and even now floats in the river.'

Rodarch sent men to enquire into the truth of these visions, and sure enough they found a bag of gold buried beneath the spot where the beggar had sat, while the body of the youth was found in the river.

When this confirmation was brought to the king, Merlin demanded to be allowed back to the forest. Ganeida begged him to wait until the frosts of winter were over, for the weather was already turning cold and she feared for her brother's life in the icy woodlands. But Merlin shook his head. His eyes seemed clear as he said: 'I do not fear the cold, sister. The hardships of winter are nothing to me.' Then he hesitated and to Ganeida it seemed that he spoke as he had of old.

'Food may well become hard to find through the dark months, so if you wish me to be safe, I ask that you have a house built for me in the Great Wood. Let it have seventy doors and seventy windows, so that I may watch the stars in their courses and read the secrets of wind and rain. There shall I perceive the record of the future, and if it pleases you to have scribes sent there, I will tell them what I see so that these things may be recorded. Come as often as you like, dear sister, and we shall speak of these things.'

With these words he returned to the forest.

Ganeida determined to carry out his wishes and gave orders for the house to be built. A great building it was, tall enough to see the horizon on every side, and with a roof that could be opened to allow a clear view of the vault of heaven. Afterwards it was known far and wide as Merlin's observatory, for within it he could see all that passed in the world and read the mysteries of the stars. There Ganeida went often to stay with her brother, and they spoke at length about future events. While Ganeida was with him he predicted the death of Rodarch, and a new war between Scotland and Cumbria that would follow. At this time also, he spoke of the coming of a great king, who should hold the lands with honour and strength and wisdom. It is even said, in the old books, that he made a song which told of the last days of Arthur, and other things that were still to come. Not all the words of this have survived, but I have sought out those that have, and set them forth here.

> *How mad are the Britons!*
> *Affluence will lead them to excess.*
> *They will fight amongst themselves*
> *And engage in feuds.*
> *The king's dark child*
> *Shall spread disruption everywhere.*
> *He cannot wait to seize the crown.*

In time, all these things came to pass, as the king's dark child, Mordred, did indeed seek to overthrow his father, as Master Thomas has told.

✛ ✛ ✛

ONE DAY, AS Ganeida prepared to return from the wood to the court, Merlin asked her to seek out the bard Taliesin and see if he would visit the observatory. 'For we have much to discuss, and I hear that he has but lately returned from Brittany, where he has learned the teachings of Gildas the Wise.'

When Ganeida returned to the court she found that Rodarch was already dead, as Merlin had predicted, and she mourned him greatly, paying tribute to his greatness and gentleness. But as she had promised, she sent word to Taliesin, the story of whose birth was full of strangeness and who, though still young, was reckoned the greatest bard in all of Britain, asking that he should visit her brother.

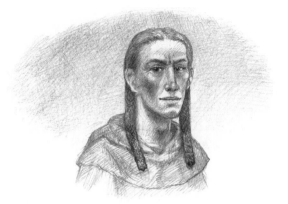

→ *Taliesin* ←

When he heard this, and knowing of the great wisdom possessed by Merlin, the bard entered the forest and found his way to the observatory. There the two seers spent many weeks together, talking of various matters, such as what weather is, and how the clouds are formed. And Taliesin described the shape of the land of Britain and named its islands and rivers, its mountains, and valleys, all of which Merlin recorded. Taliesin had learned much from Gildas the Wise, who some say was a Christian monk, while others speak of him as belonging to a more ancient faith – of this I cannot tell if it be true or not, only that Taliesin spoke of him with great kindness and called him master, though few there were that he would acknowledge in this way, except perhaps for Merlin himself.

In his turn, Merlin told of the creation of the world and how it was made up of circles within circles, and of the stars and planets whose influences touched upon all the actions of humanity. He spoke of the four elements, that were joined together in harmony, and how the air was made to capture sounds, and of the creation of the sea. Also, he told some of what he had seen of the days of the great king who would soon enter the world. These things Taliesin recorded, for he knew that Merlin spoke only truth.

While they were together, a man came by who told them of a new spring that had miraculously broken forth from the earth nearby, and that was even now forming a lake of water, and several streams that flowed through the wood. He said also that there were rumours of the spring having powers to heal, and when they heard this Merlin and Taliesin decided to visit the spot. When they came there, Merlin looked upon the water and tears came into his eyes. He cupped his hands and drank, and at once the madness that had plagued him for so many years passed from him and his eyes were clear at last. Hale and hearty, he seemed a man of lesser years.

Turning his eyes heavenward Merlin exclaimed: 'My senses are returned! I was carried off from myself and became like a spirit. I understood the flight of birds and the speech of animals – all of which pleased me more than any word or deed of man. Now I am free to carry out the work set for me.'

Taliesin stood amazed and gave thanks for the restoration of his friend.

Soon word spread of the miraculous spring, and many people came to speak with Merlin and to witness his cure. Many thought he should resume the kingship and lead them to victory against their enemies, but this Merlin refused, saying that the time was passed for such things. He declared that he had other work that he must carry out. 'For a great king is coming, who will need all my wisdom, and who shall unite the land and bring miracles in his wake.'

Thus it came to be, as all who have read the words of Master Thomas know. For though Merlin had already lived a long life, yet from the moment he drank of the spring he seemed younger. Soon he would walk abroad in the world again, leaving Ganeida to remain in the observatory and to begin her own life of prophecy. For it is said that, as his twin, she drew upon the same store of wisdom as he. But of this we will say no more at this time but turn instead to a tale concerning what happened after Merlin left the forest, but before the time of his first great prophecies to the world.

———— ✠ ————

EXPLICIT THE COMING OF MERLIN.
IMPLICIT THE STORY OF AVENABLE.

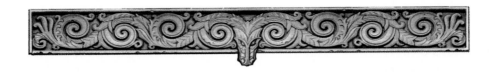

2: THE STORY OF AVENABLE

✠

FEW NOW SPEAK OF THE DAYS WHEN MERLIN WANDERED THE
WORLD BEFORE THE TIME OF ARTHUR. BUT THERE IS ONE
STORY THAT IS REMEMBERED STILL, IN WHICH ONCE AGAIN
MERLIN'S LAUGHTER WAS HEARD, WHEN A WILDMAN STALKED
THE DEPTHS OF THE TREE-SHADOWED WOOD.

✠ ✠ ✠

IN THE YEARS before Arthur ruled, the
Emperor of Rome was named Constantine.
It is said that his origin was in this very island,
but I can find no record of this in the old
books. The emperor had in his service at this
time a lord named Cador, Duke of Almayne.
This noble lord was disinherited and driven
from his lands by a powerful neighbouring
lord named Frolle, a favourite of the emper-
or's. But Cador had a daughter, Avenable,
who was as spirited as she was fair, and seeing
her father so evilly treated, she devised a plan
to help him. She disguised herself as a squire
and made her way to Rome. Calling herself
Grisandole, she showed her bravery many
times over, so that she came to the attention
of the emperor himself, who made her first
his personal squire and, when she had served
him for a year, knighted him, along with
other young squires, at the Feast of St John.

A great festival accompanied the celebrations, and the new-made knights set up lists
and began to joust with each other. Grisandole fared well, defeating everyone who
rode against her, and ended by carrying off
the prize. The emperor was so impressed by
this that he promoted Grisandole to be his
steward.

Soon after this the emperor had a dream.
In it he saw a great sow, the largest he had ever
seen, crashing through his palace, scattering
all before it. It was pursued by twelve young
lions who, when they caught her, mated with
her – one after the other. As he woke, sweating and crying out, the emperor noticed that
the sow wore a circlet of gold like a crown on
its head.

Much disturbed by this dream, the emperor
rose and went to Mass and then to dine. Still
troubled by his vision, he sat at the table sunk
so deep in thought that the best part of two
hours passed without a word being spoken,
and all who were present were forced to sit
silent also, and to refrain from eating.

It was at this time that Merlin came to a forest near Rome. He knew the nature of the emperor's dream, and its meaning, and wished to set matters right. He took upon him, by way of deep and ancient magic, the shape of a stag with a white foot, and in this form he ran through the streets of the city until he came to the emperor's palace and so into the very hall where the emperor sat.

Everywhere there was uproar. People chased the stag as far as the palace, where they waited, not daring to enter. In the hall pots and pans went crashing, and food and drink was scattered to the floor. The stag halted before the emperor and knelt down, laying its mighty head upon the ground. Then – as the story says – it spoke.

'Leave your pondering, Emperor, for it will not avail you,' said the stag. 'You shall never understand your dream until you capture the Wildman who lives in the forest outside this city. He alone can tell you what it means.'

Having said which, the stag leapt away through one of the windows, scattering shards of glass to every side, while all the rest of the shutters and doors in the room crashed shut. By the time they could be opened the stag had vanished, leaving a trail of bewildered guards and citizens behind it.

The emperor was so infuriated by this that he cried out that whoever brought him either the stag or the Wildman should have his very own daughter to wed and, if he was nobly born, half his kingdom and the rest upon his death. At once a number of nobles and knights called for their steeds and weapons and set forth on this strange quest.

Now at this time there lived many strange creatures in the forest, including many tribes of Wildfolk, who though they seemed of human stock, dressed in leaves, and lived together in houses built from the branches of trees. None knew if they were Pagan or Christian, or how they ordered their lives, but they were fierce and proud, and few dared seek them out.

Grisandole went with those who sought the emperor's favour through the finding of the particular Wildman. Most gave up within a few days when they could find neither sight nor word of the Stag or the Wildman, but Grisandole continued her search, wending her way, now forward and now back, throughout the length and breadth of the forest.

At length, as she took her ease beneath a great oak tree, the stag appeared before her and spoke: 'Avenable, you waste your time searching, for you cannot succeed unless you do what I say.'

'What shall I do?' asked the girl, wondering that the stag knew her true name.

'I shall tell you,' answered the stag. 'Get fresh meat and salt, milk and honey, and fresh baked bread. Bring with you four strong men, and a boy to turn a roasting spit. Make camp in the heart of the forest, where it is wildest, and set up a table with a linen cloth on it. Roast the meat and set out the table with milk and bread and honey and hide among the bushes until the Wildman comes – for I promise you he shall.'

Then the stag leapt away at great speed, leaving Grisandole to wonder if this were some evil trick that was being played upon her. Nevertheless, she decided to follow the creature's advice, and made her way to a nearby town where she obtained all that it had asked of her and hired the services of four men to carry the food, and a boy to turn the spit.

They repaired to the forest and finding a clearing amid the trees set up camp and laid a fire and set the meats to roast. Soon the savour of the cooking spread through the forest on every side, and Grisandole and her companions hid themselves in the bushes.

They did not have long to wait, for soon there came in sight a wild looking man, clad in leaves, with long matted hair and beard. As he came, he struck the trunks of the trees on either side with a great staff, so that the forest rang with the sound of its blows. When the spit-boy saw him, he was so frightened that he fled, half out of his wits, and the men who Grisandole had hired looked like to follow him; but she spoke sternly to them, bidding them not to be fearful.

The Wildman, meanwhile, seeing the fire and the table spread with good food, began to sniff and snort and finally sidled up, and snatching the meat in his hands tore at it furiously, dipping it in the milk and honey and slavering like a mad dog.

When he had eaten his fill and was stuffed near to bursting, the Wildman lay down by the fire and fell fast asleep. Then Grisandole and her four companions stole out of the bushes and bound him fast. At once he awoke and began to bellow and cry, but they ignored the noise and put him upon a horse and tied him to it. Then one of the men sat behind him in the saddle and set forth to return to Rome.

As they rode, the Wildman looked at Grisandole and began to laugh. When questioned he was at first silent, then at length he said: 'Creature formed of nature, now changed to another form, hold your peace, for nothing more will I say until we stand before the emperor himself.'

Grisandole hid her fear at these words, though she noticed her companions exchanging glances. When they arrived at the gates of Rome and passed within, word soon spread of their coming and the citizens crowded into the streets to see the Wildman, who snarled and gnashed his teeth at them in a most fearsome manner. The crowd grew as Grisandole and her small company approached the emperor's palace. He, hearing the noise, came out to see what was happening.

'Sir,' said Grisandole. 'Here is the Wildman you have been wanting to question. I give him to you and wish you joy of him, for to me he has given nothing but trouble.'

The emperor promised to reward his faithful knight and sent for a smith to put the Wildman in chains. But he, standing up straight and speaking in a normal voice, said that there was no need, for he would not try to escape. And as he did so the ropes that bound him fell away.

Thus everyone knew that this was no ordinary creature.

'Who are you?' asked the emperor.

'That I shall tell you,' said the Wildman, who looked less wild with every passing moment. (Here you shall hear yet another version of Merlin's birth, but I must leave it to you to decide which one you choose to believe.)

'One day as my mother was returning home, she entered the enchanted Forest of Broceliande. There she became lost and had to spend the night under the trees, and there a Wildman came and lay with her, and begot me upon her, for she was no match for his strength. Next day my mother went home, and in a while found she was with child. She carried me to full term and bore me and had me baptized. But as soon as I might I left her and returned to the forest, for such was the way of my father and I could do nothing else.'

'Well,' said the emperor, stroking his chin, 'I will not put you in irons as long as you promise to help me and do not go hence without my leave.'

To this the Wildman gave his word.

Then Grisandole spoke up and told how he had been captured. 'He said that he would not speak openly until he stood before you.'

'Is this true?' demanded the emperor.

The Wildman nodded.

'Then speak.'

But the Wildman shook his head. 'Not until you have called your lords and nobles before you. For I have much to say that they too will wish to hear.'

Frowning, the emperor sent for his privy counsellors and his lords and nobles. It took fully three days for them to assemble. Meanwhile the Wildman made himself at home and ate and drank well and washed and dressed himself in clean clothes so that he seemed more like an ordinary man with each day that passed. And when at last the court was assembled the emperor demanded that he speak. But still the Wildman refused, until the empress, a most beautiful woman who was accompanied by twelve maidens, were also present. All looked at the Wildman with curiosity.

He, in turn, looked at the empress, at her ladies, and at Grisandole, turning his head from one to the other in some amusement. Then he began to laugh.

'This laughter is not seemly,' said the emperor. 'Speak!'

Then the Wildman ceased his laughter and stood up. 'As you are a true emperor give me your word that no harm will come to me – whatever I say – and that when I have done, I may depart of my own free will.'

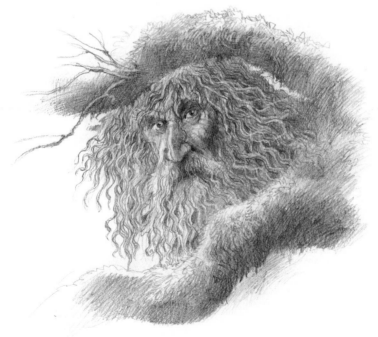

→ *The Wildman* ←

'It shall be as you ask,' the emperor said. Then he looked at the Wildman for a long while. 'I seek the meaning of a dream that has troubled me for many nights.'

The Wildman was silent for a moment, then raised his eyes to the royal pair. 'This is the dream in which you saw a great sow, crowned with a golden crown; and as you watched you saw twelve lions come and lie with her, one after the other. Is this the truth?'

The emperor nodded, while the empress seemed uneasy as she sat on her throne, her eyes turning to the twelve maidens who served her.

The Wildman held up his hand and the room fell silent.

'Hear the meaning of your dream, Emperor. The sow that you saw signified the empress, your wife here, and the twelve lions who lay with her signify her twelve handmaidens – who are not women at all, but men disguised – who lie with her when you are away.'

A great murmuring broke out amongst those gathered near, and the empress grew white and seemed as though she might faint, while the twelve 'maidens' cowered in their places and seemed eager to leave the hall. The emperor spoke no word for a while, then he turned to Grisandole and said quietly: 'I would know the truth of this. Despoil these women of their garments that all may see.'

Grisandole came forward, signalling to the guards to surround the 'women'. They were quickly stripped of their clothes. It was soon clear to everyone that they were men indeed, though they had grown their hair long and used an ointment that prevented their beards from sprouting.

Then the emperor was so angry that he could not speak for a time. Indeed, the only sound was the sobbing of the empress and the groans of the twelve men. At last, the emperor asked his counsellors and the nobles gathered there what sentence he should carry out against those who had done him such a terrible wrong. With one accord they declared that the felons should all be burned to death.

Then the emperor rose up and commanded that this be done and done swiftly. The empress and her lovers were taken to the courtyard, screaming and crying out their innocence. But a great fire was piled up, and all thirteen were burned to death in that place and so paid for their crimes.

And as the smoke from their fiery deaths rose in the air, the emperor turned again to the Wildman and thank-ed him for his wisdom. 'Though I know not how you came by this knowledge, I am glad of it, shamed though I am.' Then after a moment he said: 'I hear that you also laughed at Grisandole. Why was that?'

The Wildman paused and looked at Grisandole, who knew at once that the men she had hired must have spoken of this. 'Even as I laughed at the false women,' said the Wildman, 'I knew that this brave knight is also no man at all, but a woman, and nobly born at that, and as brave and true as any man here.'

At this a great silence fell. Then the emperor turned to Grisandole and said: 'Is this true? Speak now, for I am in no mood to be denied.'

Silently, Grisandole nodded.

Some at once cried out that Grisandole should also be taken out and burned, but the emperor told them to be silent.

'I bid you go from here and put off your men's clothing and dress yourself as befits a woman. Then we shall speak further.'

In a while Grisandole returned and

everyone gaped in astonishment when they saw what a fair and gentle maid she was. They learned then that her true name was Avenable, and that her father was the Duke Cador, who had been driven away by Frolle. All these things the emperor considered, then he turned to the Wildman.

'Now what shall I do?' he asked. 'For I have promised the hand of my daughter to the one who brought you to me. Yet I can scarcely marry her to another maiden!'

At this the Wildman smiled and said: 'This is my advice. The lady Avenable's father and mother, as well as her brother, who is a good and brave youth named Patrick, having been driven into exile for no better reason than the greed of your Duke, live now in Provence, in a town called Montpellier. It would be a good thing if you were to send for them and restore them to their proper estate, for they are true to you and have served you well in the past and will again. As to the matter of your promise, that is simply set right. You are in need of a new empress – why not take the maiden Avenable to your wife. I dare say she would not object.'

The emperor looked at Avenable and saw from the colour in her cheeks that she was indeed not averse to the notion. He turned again to the Wildman, who said: 'If you are looking for a husband for your daughter you need look no further than Avenable's brother. But that I leave to your own good judgement.'

Then the emperor, looking long and searchingly at the Wildman, asked: 'Who are you that know so much of the affairs in my Empire?'

'That I will not say, for there is no need for you to know,' replied the Wildman. With that he prepared to take his leave, nodding first to Avenable, then the emperor, then bowing to the rest of the assembly. No one attempted to stop him as he walked from the palace. But at the entrance he paused and raised a hand towards the lintel of the door. As he did so letters were engraved deep into the stone. I will tell you that I have spoken with one who stood where Merlin stood, and that he bears testimony to the inscription, which read:

KNOW THAT THE WILDMAN WHO INTERPRETED THE EMPEROR'S DREAM WAS NAMED MERLIN, AND THAT THE STAG WHO ENTERED THIS PALACE AND SPOKE TO THE MAIDEN IN THE FOREST WAS MERLIN ALSO.

With that the Wildman was gone, none knew where.

The emperor did as Merlin had advised and married Avenable, that had been Grisandole. He restored her father to his lands and rewarded him greatly for the suffering he had known. And last of all he married his daughter to the Duke's son. After that the emperor ruled long and wisely, as did his daughter and her husband, who came after him. But Merlin was never more seen in that land, having returned to Britain where the usurper Vortigern now ruled, and where the Wildman would soon prophesy many things that were yet to come.

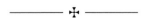

EXPLICIT THE STORY OF AVENABLE.
IMPLICIT THE TALE OF MERLIN AND THE DRAGONS.

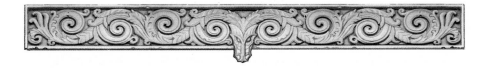

3: MERLIN AND THE DRAGONS

✠

BEFORE AMBROSIUS, AND AFTER HIM UTHER PENDRAGON, RULED OVER THIS LAND (AND AFTER THEM ARTHUR), VORTIGERN THE USURPER MADE HIMSELF HIGH KING BY HAVING THE TRUE KING, CONSTANS, POISONED. VORTIGERN THE FOX HE WAS CALLED BY MANY PEOPLE – THOUGH ALWAYS BEHIND HIS BACK – BECAUSE OF HIS RED HAIR AND HIS SLY AND SECRETIVE WAYS. OTHERS NAMED HIM TYRANT, AND SOON THE LORDS OF BRITAIN TURNED AGAINST HIM AND BEGAN TO MURMUR THEIR ANGER ALOUD.

✠ ✠ ✠

WHEN WORD OF this reached Vortigern's ears, he grew fearful for his rule and sent messengers to the leaders of the Saxon race, who raided all along the coasts of Britain at that time. Two powerful lords in particular – brothers named Hengist and Horsa – he sought to make his allies, offering them lands if they would bring their armies to fight on his side.

Knowing Britain's lands to be rich and plentiful, the Saxons agreed, and soon their dragon-craft nosed into the shore and sailed along the rivers to the great cities of the land. Vortigern made them welcome and gave them gifts of gold to secure their allegiance.

Hengist, who was a cunning lord, had brought his daughter Rowena with him, and when he saw her Vortigern could not disguise his lust. They were married soon after, and in this way the Saxons became part of Vortigern's family.

From this time, the incomers began to wield ever greater power in the land, riding abroad, stealing and pillaging and doing as they pleased. Thus, the murmurs against Vortigern grew louder, until they were heard throughout Britain, and the Lords began to raise an army to drive out the Saxons and remove Vortigern from his throne.

When he learned of this, Vortigern, who was a superstitious man, read the signs in the stars and saw that his life was under threat. He called his counsellors and druids to him and demanded that they find a solution. After much consultation they advised him to withdraw from Lud's Town (that men now call London), where he had built a fine palace, and make for the fastness of Wales, where he should seek out a place hard to access, there to build a new fortress with strong walls that could withstand a siege. From this place of strength, he could send forth men who would prey upon all who came near, and thus hold his enemies at bay until the mood of the people turned once again in his favour.

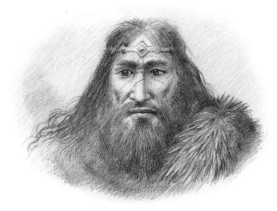

⇢ *Vortigern* ⇠

Vortigern listened to their advice, though his anger against the Lords of Britain was great. And all the while, Hengist's daughter Rowena whispered in his ear, filling his mind with dreams of recovering his power and wreaking red revenge upon those who had turned against him.

So it was that Vortigern, gathering those still faithful to him, left his city and rich palace and fled into the harsh wild lands of Wales. Several of the lesser lords stood against him, but Vortigern's army was still large and strong enough to overcome them, and soon he made a sprawling camp in a sheltered valley which lay at the foot of the place known as Mount Erith, where there had once been a fortress of the Romans. Here Vortigern decided to build his strong place, from where he could keep watch across the lands on every side and consider when the time was right for him to venture forth against his enemies.

Vortigern sent for his artificers, carpenters, stonemasons and labourers, who began to assemble materials to build the strong place. Trees from the dark forest of Arroy were cut down; stones from the quarries in Pembroke carved and brought to the hill, while other men began to brew vats of lime to anchor the stones. But each night these things vanished as though they had never been. Not a sound was heard, nor did the soldiers placed on guard see anything, but on each morning, stones and wood and all other supplies were gone – as though the earth itself had swallowed them.

Furiously, Vortigern summoned his advisors and druids and demanded to know the cause of these things. For hours the so-called wise men muttered and mumbled amongst themselves, then finally one was deputed to speak to the king.

'Sire,' he said, 'we do not know the reason for these things – though we believe it may be caused by ill-aspected stars – but we do know how you may prevent it happening again.'

'Speak,' Vortigern said.

'You must seek out a child born without a human father. Have him brought here and kill him swiftly. Then scatter his blood on the ground. This will make it strong enough to bear the weight of your tower.'

'How is this possible?' demanded Vortigern. 'Is this not against nature?'

A druid named Maugant shuffled forward.

'I have heard of such things. The Roman Apuleius in his treatise *Deo Socratis*, writes that between the moon and the earth live tribes of creatures known as *incubi*. It is said that they have the appearance of angels, though in fact they are demons. They lie with women and beget strange children on them. Thus, these infants are born without a human father.'

Vortigern bent his head and was sunk in thought for a time. Then he stood up and called to the captain of his personal guard. 'Go out and search the area. Find me a child born without a father. Do not return empty-handed.'

So Vortigern's soldiers went out, their red mantles burning like flames in the green landscape. For days and nights they searched, receiving only blank looks and the sign against evil in response to their questions.

Several days later they arrived at a town that was later called Caer Myrddin, and there as they watered their horses and took refreshment they saw a group of boys playing a game. Soon a quarrel broke out between two of the lads, one of whom was clearly of noble birth, while the other was a strange-looking youth with a shock of black hair. 'How dare you speak to me like that!' shouted the well-born youth. 'I have royal blood in my veins – who knows what flows in yours? Water or mud perhaps? You don't even have a father!'

At once the soldiers sprang up and surrounded the boys. Two laid hands on the strange looking youth and held him fast, while the captain questioned the one who had spoken out.

They soon learned that the boy was the son of a rich woman who had entered a local convent following the birth of her child. The captain at once summoned the mayor of the town and demanded that the woman be brought before them.

This was done and the woman, clad in the habit of a nun, stood before them with downcast head. When she saw the child, held by two soldiers, she began to tremble. Roughly the captain demanded her story, and here again we hear a story that we have heard before. Nor should we be surprised to find that the woman was a princess of Dyfed, and that her child was called Merlin – for she was indeed the very same whose tale we have heard and which I will not tell again here.[*] All that I will say is that the stories I have heard and read tell of a white beard. Yet here stood a boy of no more than twelve summers. How this could be I may only guess, though Master Thomas tells how Merlin appeared to Arthur as a boy when the king encountered the beast named Glatisant,[†] so that perhaps we may see this change in him as no more than a seeming.

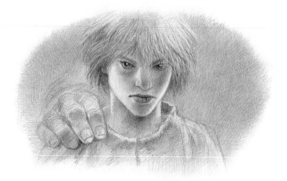

→ *Young Merlin* ←

When they heard of the strange circumstances of the child's birth, the soldiers knew they had found the one they sought, and though his mother begged them not to harm him, they bound him and placed him on a horse.

All this time Merlin remained unspeaking. Only as the soldiers prepared to depart, did

---

[*] See 'The Coming of Merlin' pp. 3–11
[†] *Le Morte D'Arthur* Book 1 Ch xix.

he say: 'Do not fear for me, mother. I shall not be harmed.'

The soldiers set forth at once with all haste to return to Vortigern's camp. On the journey the boy spoke not a word to them, and the men looked at him askance, several making the sign of the horns against evil.

Thus, they came again to the valley below Mount Erith and the boy was marched into the king's presence. A chair was brought forth for Vortigern, who seated himself and looked at the boy with some curiosity. Merlin, however, gave no sign of fear but stared back until the king dropped his gaze, turning instead to where his advisors waited.

'Is this the one you foresaw?'

'It seems so, my lord,' said the old druid, Maugant.

Vortigern turned to the captain of his guard.

'Tell me what you have learned.'

The captain rehearsed the story of the fighting boys and the tale told by Merlin's mother.

'Very well,' said Vortigern. 'You may proceed.'

At this the captain drew his sword, but as he did so Merlin spoke up.

'Lord King. Since you have had me brought here, will you not at least tell me the reason.'

Vortigern looked at him with seeming reluctance. 'My wise men have advised me that your blood should water the earth on this hilltop so that my strong tower may be built.'

Merlin turned to where the king's advisors stood together, sheep-like.

'By what right do you make this claim?' he asked.

'By the right of our wisdom and the truth that we read in the stars,' answered Maugant.

'Does your wisdom tell you the reason why the foundations will not hold?'

Maugant shook his head and his companions looked with fear in their eyes at the youth who stood so calmly before them.

Merlin turned again to Vortigern.

'Perhaps before you spill my blood you should learn the true reason why the building will not stand.'

'Do you indeed know this?'

Merlin turned to Vortigern's advisors.

'You have told your lord that only my blood will make the building stand firm. You are wrong. It is what lies beneath the hill that causes the stones and timbers to vanish.'

He turned to Vortigern. 'Have your men dig deep into the earth. There they will find a pool of water.'

Vortigern looked to where his artificers had gathered, looking on with uncertainty at the boy who stood before the king, showing no sign of fear.

'Proceed,' Vortigern commanded.

Reluctantly the builders set to, breaking the ground and digging down until water began to seep through the freshly turned earth. Soon a pool gathered and grew until they could dig no longer.

Vortigern watched them, as did his advisors. The boy Merlin stood silent and alone, and none approached him.

When the water had all but filled the delving, Merlin addressed Maugant again. 'Do you know what lies beneath the pool?'

'Nothing but more earth, I dare say,' answered the Druid, though in his eyes there was doubt.

'You are wrong once again,' Merlin said. 'Beneath the water is a stone chest. What is within is the true cause of the events you have witnessed.'

21

He turned again to Vortigern. 'Tell your men to drain the pool and you shall see.'

Again, Vortigern nodded, and his artificers set to work, making holes in the side of the hill and laying pipes within so that the water began to gush forth.

Soon the bottom of the pool was exposed. There, sure enough, was a stone chest, measuring as much as five men on one side and three the other. Upon it were carved strange symbols that few present could understand. Maugant alone showed his fear by the trembling of his body, for surely he could read what was written there.

Once again Merlin faced the king's advisors. 'Do you know what lies within the stone chest?' he demanded.

Not one of the supposed wise men answered. They looked rather at the ground and shifted their feet.

'Within the chest are two serpents,' Merlin said. 'One is red, the other white. They have slept and woken many times since they were placed there. Often when they wake, they struggle with one another, for they are ancient enemies. For this time the red dragon represents the British, and the white the Saxons you invited to this land, Lord Vortigern. Their struggle causes the stones and timbers of the tower to be sucked beneath the earth.'

Vortigern shifted uneasily in his chair, but he nodded and several of his strongest men came forward and with great labour and many fearful looks, lifted the lid of the stone box.

At first there was only darkness within, then the darkness itself began to move and turn and from within it unfolded the two serpents of which Merlin had foretold. Glad for their freedom they flew up into the sky, and hot fires were in their breaths. The shadow of their wings covered the land in darkness.

Vortigern and his advisors and his soldiers and artificers turned pale and covered their heads as if expecting fire to rain down upon them. But the serpents fell upon each other with such a great hissing and crying and with great reeking gusts of flame, that all those who watched forgot their fear and gaped at the struggle with wide eyes.

For a long time neither beast had the advantage, raging across the sky with screams of rage. But at length the white serpent began to drive off the red, giving it many deep wounds with claw and flame. Then suddenly the red serpent drew upon its innermost fires and struck back, rising higher in the air and falling upon the back of the white and biting its neck. Locked together, the serpents fell to the earth, cracking it with the force of their great bodies. Smoke roiled about them and then ebbed. As the air grew clear, the watchers dared approach. At once the red serpent raised itself and flew into the sky with a great screech of victory. Circling the hill once, it then flew off to the north and was seen no longer. Behind it on the hillside the body of the white serpent lay still, its neck torn open by the red, its hot blood scorching the earth beneath it until (it is said) nothing grew there again.

Silence fell.

Vortigern sat still in his chair, his eyes still reflecting the light of the battle. His advisors, including Maugant, had already turned their backs and were making a quick descent from the hilltop.

Merlin stood alone, his eyes upon the king.

'Now you have seen how these things will end,' he said. 'The Red Serpent will defeat and destroy the White; the Britons will overcome the Saxons and take back their lands.'

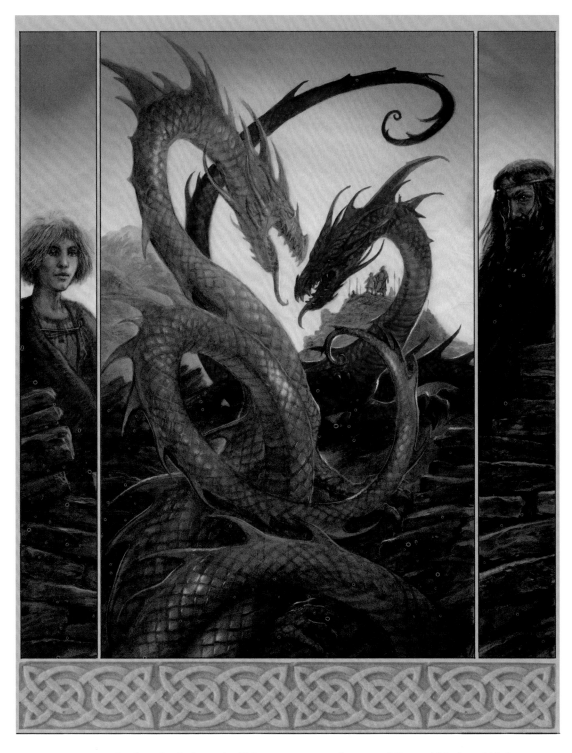

PLATE 2: '...then the darkness itself began to move and turn and from within it unfolded the two serpents of which Merlin had foretold'

As he spoke there was a light around him that had not been there before, and where before they had seen a child, now they saw a man of power, whom none dared approach.

'Build your tower, Vortigern. Though it will not save you.'

Then it was that Merlin spoke at length and gave forth many of his greatest prophecies. It is said that he wept as he did so, for the dark times that were to come. I have heard that Master Geoffrey of Monmouth collected these sayings later and set them in a book, but this I have not seen so I cannot include them here. What I have heard is that the youth spoke of many things, until the end of time itself, and that he foretold not only Vortigern's death but the coming of the Great King. Many could not listen to his words but covered their ears and fled away from there. Vortigern himself turned pale, for he knew that his time was growing short, and that he would never again rule over the lands of Britain.

And so it was, for the sons of the usurped King Constans, Ambrosius and Uther, brought their army to Britain and fought against the Saxons until Hengist and his kin were slain,

and the invaders driven out of these lands. And in the end the brothers came to the hill where the strong tower stood tall above the valley – for Vortigern had caused it to be built in spite of Merlin's words. There the brothers caused fire to be lit around it so that it was consumed, and with it the tyrant himself, along with his Saxon wife, just as the youth had foretold.

Thus Merlin made the first great showing of those that he was to make and brought closer the time when Arthur would be born. Of that tale, how Uther Pendragon came to be king and lusted for the Lady Igrayne of Cornwall, and how Merlin enabled them to lie together and beget the future king, Master Thomas has told, so I shall not rehearse it here again, for now it is time to turn to the stories of the Round Table that are not included in his great book. Here we shall learn more of Lancelot and Gawain and of many other knights whose names are remembered still, though Master Thomas did not speak of them.

Thus, at the end of the First Book, I speak no more of Merlin but turn instead to stories of the Round Table and of the great knights who were part of that mighty Fellowship.

———— ✙ ————

EXPLICIT LIBER PRIMUS.
INCIPIT LIBER SECUNDUS.

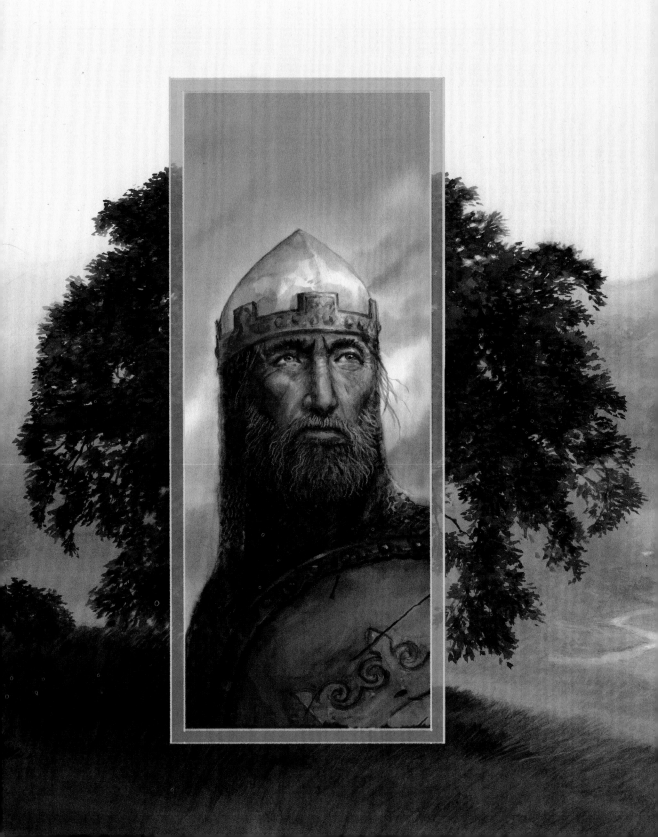

BOOK TWO

❧❧

THE BOOK
OF THE
ROUND TABLE

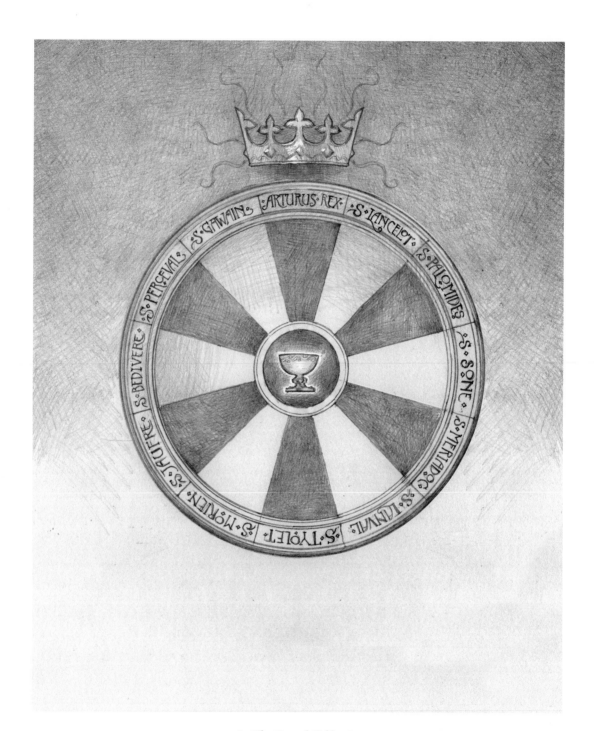

❖ *The Round Table* ❖

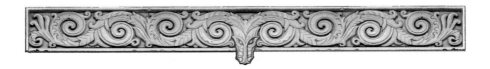

4: THE VOWS OF KING ARTHUR AND HIS KNIGHTS

IN THE TIME FOLLOWING THE WARS WITH THE ELEVEN KINGS, OF WHICH MASTER THOMAS HAS WRITTEN, THERE WAS A TIME OF PEACE IN BRITAIN. THEN IT WAS THAT KING ARTHUR FOUNDED THE FELLOWSHIP OF THE ROUND TABLE IN THE CITY OF CAMELOT THE GOLDEN. ALL WHO CAME THERE FOUND SUCCOUR, AND KNIGHTS WERE ABLE TO PROVE THEMSELVES AGAINST THE MANY DANGERS AND TRIALS THAT EXISTED IN THOSE TIMES. MASTER THOMAS WRITES LITTLE OF THE CREATION OF THE TABLE – EXCEPT TO SAY THAT MERLIN MADE IT 'ROUND, LIKE THE WORLD' AND THAT IT WAS IN THE LIKENESS OF TWO OLDER TABLES, BUILT TO HOLD THE SANGREAL. MASTER WACE IN HIS *CHRONICLE** SAYS ONLY THAT IT WAS BUILT AT ARTHUR'S COMMAND BY A CERTAIN CARPENTER FROM THE LAND OF CORNWALL. ALL THAT IS CERTAIN IS THAT THE FELLOWSHIP OF KNIGHTS WHO CAME IN SEARCH OF HONOUR AND ADVENTURE, FOUND IT IN PLENTY IN THAT WONDROUS PLACE.

✠ ✠ ✠

THERE IS A tale not included in Master Thomas's great book, that took place not long after the Fellowship was established, and which tested the strength of both the king and his lords. It began when King Arthur held court in the city of Carlisle, close to the Forest of Inglewood, where many strange creatures roamed. In the morning, a huntsman came to the king and told him of a grim boar that stalked the forest. 'Never did I see such a one before. I have broken more spears and arrows on his hide than I care to remember, and he has killed several of my hounds. He is truly great in size and strength: big as a bull, black as a bear, tall as a horse. His tusks tear up whole trees and he leaves a trail behind him like an army on the march.'

---

* Twelfth-century author of *The Chronicles of Arthur*

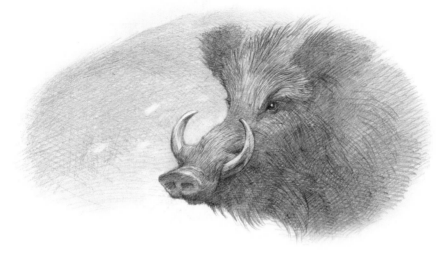

✦ *The Great Boar* ✦

'If this is true,' Arthur said, 'I would see this monster for myself.'

The king gave orders that no one else was to go after the boar save himself and three knights whom he would choose from among his best men. These were Sir Gawain, Sir Kay and a veteran knight named Sir Baldwin of Britain. Together with Arthur's chief Huntsman and Master of Hounds, they set out to track the beast to its lair.

First, they loosed the tracker dogs, then the hounds, and soon enough the music of the chase echoed through the forest. Yet when the great boar was cornered at last, it turned upon the hounds and ripped at them with its terrible tusks – killing them all.

When Arthur and his knights arrived, the huntsman awaited them.

'There lies the beast,' he said grimly, indicating a grove of thick trees and tangled bushes. 'But be advised and leave him alone, for I swear he will slay you all if you venture near him.'

Therewith the huntsman turned to burying the hounds that had been so savagely slain, then headed for home, since there was no more work for him to do. But Arthur looked to where the boar could be heard snorting and rooting in his den and said: 'Sirs, this is a great challenge, such as our fellowship was founded to address. Let us make this an occasion to swear separate vows, that we must not fail to carry out. Mine shall be that I will bring this beast down by myself and prepare him for the feast. Now, I command you, make your own vows!'

Gawain, ever ready to accept a challenge, said at once: 'I vow to keep watch at Tarn Wathelyn all night' – this being a place much feared for the apparitions that had been seen there.[*]

Kay said, roughly: 'I will ride through this forest from now until this time tomorrow and kill anyone who stands in my way or challenges me to combat.'

---

[*] See 'The Adventures at Tarn Wathelyn', pp. 260–5

28

All three looked at Baldwin, who laughed aloud and made this great boast: 'I vow that never from this moment will I be jealous of my wife, suspicious of any pretty girl; and that I will not refuse food to anyone that asks for it, or fear to turn aside from any road for fear of death.'

Having made their vows, the four men parted from each other, and each went his own way: Arthur turning toward the boar's den, Gawain toward the Tarn, and Kay into the forest. Baldwin, however, returned to Carlisle and went to bed.

✠ ✠ ✠

L ET US SPEAK first of the king, as is his right. He sent his own hounds into the thicket around the boar's den, but the fearsome beast soon routed them, and Arthur was forced to call them off. Then he heard the beast coming towards him, rooting up trees and stones as he came. The king leapt upon his horse and seized his spear and prepared to meet the creature. No one knew what its charge was like, since no one had ever survived it.

When the creature came in sight, King Arthur quailed. Red-eyed it was and bristled like a moving thicket. It charged with its mouth wide open. Flecks of foam flew from its jaws. Its tusks were at least three feet long and its hide was so thick and hard that when Arthur used his spear to fend it off the wood splintered, and the beast smashed into him.

The king fell winded from his horse, which was killed outright by the blow and Arthur himself received such a wound that he was to feel for the rest of his life. He struggled upright, leaning against the side of his dead mount for support, and uttering a prayer to St Margaret, drew his sword and raised his shield.

When the boar struck him a second time, the shield shattered at once and the king was knocked over again. The beast smelled like a kiln or a hot kitchen, and its breath so overwhelmed him that he was almost overcome by the stink. He leaned against a tree and strove to collect his strength. This time, as the boar approached, Arthur was able to dodge to one side, and he struck the creature so hard that it staggered. Quick to press his advantage, the king ran forward and struck again. His sword point went into the beast's neck and it fell to the earth. There the king dispatched it with a great blow, then he cut off its huge head and stuck it on a pole and set about butchering the corpse with all the skill of a professional venerer.

Until this was done, he would not rest, but when he had completed his bloody work, and strips of meat hung drying from the branches of a great oak, he knelt briefly and gave thanks for his delivery. Then, weary and hurt, and with no one to attend him, King Arthur fell into a deep sleep.

✠ ✠ ✠

L ET US TURN now to Sir Kay. As the day drew on, he rode by the twisting ways of the forest until he heard the sound of two horses approaching. Drawing aside he waited in the cover of the trees until he saw who came there. First rode a girl weeping bitterly, followed by a grim-faced knight who drove her on. As she came abreast Kay heard her cry out to be set free from this villainous knight. At that he rode forward, calling out to the man either to release the girl or turn and fight for her.

29

The knight reined in his horse and pulled the girl's mount closer to him. Staring hard at Sir Kay he answered grimly: 'I will be glad to accept your challenge – if you think you are ready for it.'

'I am ready to be sure,' answered Kay. 'But first tell me your name and how you come to hold this lady prisoner?'

At this the girl burst out weeping again, but her captor ignored her.

'I am Sir Menealfe of the Mountain,' replied the knight. 'I won this lady in a tournament at Liddle Mort, north of Carlisle. Her family are dead, and she has no one to support her. Therefore, she is mine by right of combat.'

'Then prepare to lose her again – to me!' cried Kay, and the two dressed their shields and, laying their spears in rest, charged together.

Menealfe was the stronger of the two, as he proved by knocking Kay clean out of the saddle. The fallen knight was so shaken and winded by this that he could not even get up at once. Taking this as a sign of surrender, Menealfe declared him prisoner.

When he had breath to speak again, Kay said: 'Sir, nearby is my brother knight, Sir Gawain, who awaits my coming. If we go to him, I am certain he will ransom me.'

Menealfe looked down at his fallen opponent and smiled grimly. 'I will be glad to do so. Let us go.'

They rode through the dusk the short distance to the edge of Tarn Wathelyn, where they found Gawain keeping watch. As soon as he heard them, he challenged them both.

'I could not keep my vow!' cried Sir Kay. 'As a result I am this knight's prisoner. Will you be so good as to ransom me?'

'Gladly,' said Sir Gawain. 'What should I give?'

'Will you run a course with this knight?'

'Why not?' answered Gawain. 'If he is willing...'

'That I am, and gladly,' said Menealfe, his eyes gleaming as he sized up his new opponent.

The two knights prepared to do battle.

Both were strong and powerful, but Gawain was the more skilled in the joust, and his first spear laid his opponent on the earth. Kay rejoiced, mocking his fallen captor, but Gawain helped up the fallen man and pulled off his helm to let the air get to his face.

Menealfe spoke quietly to him. 'Sir, you have ransomed this knight, who is so loath to let matters lie there. If you will allow me to rest for a while, I should be glad to joust with you again for this lady, who is my rightful prize.'

Gawain looked at the sad lady, who had remained silent throughout these exchanges. When he saw how fair she was, he said: 'I would be glad to do so.'

When Menealfe was rested, the two took fresh spears and mounted their horses and rode together again. Once again Sir Gawain was victorious, and Sir Menealfe was laid low with a wound to the head.

'Ha!' cried Sir Kay. 'Now you have lost everything, for all your boastful talk'.

'Good fortune never lasts forever,' said Gawain reprovingly, helping the fallen man to his feet.

'If we were alone,' Menealfe said to Sir Kay, 'I would make you eat those words.'

'But we are not!' said Sir Kay haughtily. 'And you have lost everything.'

'God forbid you should speak so to a man who has fought well and fallen,' said Gawain. Turning to Menealfe, he continued: 'I pray you not to take Sir Kay's words ill. Tomorrow, ride with this girl to King Arthur's court at Carlisle. Say that Sir Gawain sends you, and let the queen decide the disposition of this matter.'

Sir Menealfe swore upon the hilt of his sword that he would do as Sir Gawain asked, and that he would give safe passage to the girl on the road to Carlisle. Then, as darkness was falling, the three knights and the girl made a fire and settled down to sleep in the shade of the wood. None spoke much, for in his heart Kay was ashamed of his words to his fallen opponent, as well as at his failure to fulfil his vow, while Gawain nursed the anger he felt towards his brother knight. The tale does not say what Sir Menealfe or the lady thought, but it is certain that the girl was much relieved by the promise of ransom from either the king or queen.

✤ ✤ ✤

MORNING HAD SCARCELY begun when they heard the notes of a hunting horn. Both the Round Table knights recognized the king's particular call, and at once they set out in search of him. They came to where the strips of boar's meat hung on the tree and the fearsome head lowered from the pole on which it had been set. There they found the king, stiff and sore from his wounds and a night in the forest, and still without a horse to ride. They gave him the girl's mount and set her up behind Sir Menealfe, and the whole party set out for Carlisle.

As they rode, the king asked for an account of his two knights' adventures.

'I kept watch as I promised,' began Sir Kay, eager to tell of his adventure despite its outcome. 'But this knight won me and then Sir Gawain won me back, and this girl as well, and took Sir Menealfe prisoner.'

At this the girl began praising Sir Gawain.

Arthur looked with delight on his nephew. 'What is the ransom set to be?' he asked.

'In truth I know not,' replied Menealfe. 'This brave knight sends me to the queen. She it is who shall have the accounting of my life.'

'God be praised!' exclaimed Arthur. 'Do you ever fail in your quest, Sir Gawain? It seems to me you are always successful.'

And indeed, I have read in another book that Sir Gawain was known to have never failed to achieve whatever adventure he set out upon – save for one only, and that we shall hear of later.

✤ ✤ ✤

WHEN THEY REACHED Carlisle, Sir Menealfe went before the queen and told her all that had occurred and pled his cause. Guinevere, praising Sir Gawain, gave as her judgement that the knight should swear allegiance to Arthur, and join the Round Table Fellowship; and that the girl should become one of her ladies until such time as she was ready to marry, since she had no family to return to.

Meanwhile, Sir Kay spoke to the king. 'My lord, it seems to me that we three have fulfilled our vows, but that we have still to hear from Sir Baldwin. His vow seemed far greater, but it is yet to be proven.'

'I would indeed wish to know if it is even possible for so great a vow to be fulfilled,' said Arthur.

'Then, if you give me leave,' said Sir Kay slyly, 'I will find a way to test at least some part of Baldwin's vow.'

'Very well,' Arthur said. 'But only on the condition that you do him no harm, nor bring shame to him.'

To this Kay gave his promise, then he went and sought out five other knights, all well known to him, and told them that Baldwin had sworn never to turn aside on any road for fear of his life. 'Let us,' said Kay, 'ride together abreast so that he cannot pass. I know well where we shall find him.'

The six knights rode in a body, side by side, upon the road which led to Sir Baldwin's castle. It was raining hard, and they drew their cloaks over their armour to keep it dry and to hide their identity. In this way they rode until they saw Baldwin approaching from the opposite direction, armed and eager like a man ready to do battle.

Kay called out to him. 'Either stay or run, for you must fight us all if you want to pass this way.'

'Though you were twice as many, you would not make me flee,' answered Sir Baldwin. 'Stand aside, for I am on my way to speak to the king, and nothing will deter me.'

'You may take any other route you wish,' answered Kay, 'and no one shall hear of it. But you shall not pass here unless you fight us all together.'

Then the six knights threw back their cloaks and showed themselves armed and ready.

'Very well,' said Baldwin, raising his shield and choosing a spear from those that rested at his saddlebow. 'But don't say I failed to warn you. For I intend to continue on this way despite all you may do!'

Then he charged them and knocked Sir Kay down first and then, just as quickly, swerving and turning this way and that, brought down all five of the others without even breaking his spear. Then he dismounted and stood over Sir Kay, and said: 'Is this enough for you?'

'Go where you want,' answered Kay, groggily.

So Baldwin rode on until he reached Carlisle and stood before Arthur.

'Did you see or hear anything untoward in the forest?' asked the king.

Baldwin looked thoughtful, then shook his head. 'Sire, I heard only the wind in the trees and the song of the birds as I rode.'

King Arthur looked at the knight but said nothing. All went to hear Mass, and by the time they emerged, Kay and his fellows had arrived back at the court. Arthur took the seneschal aside and asked him how he had fared.

'Sire,' said Kay, his face red as sunset. 'Sir Baldwin is indeed a mighty knight. Nothing would make him turn aside. I and five others have the bruises to prove it.'

At this Arthur smiled, but he determined to test Baldwin himself. Calling one of his minstrels, he said: 'Go to the castle of Sir Baldwin and stay there forty days. See whether any man is turned away from his door in this time or if anyone is refused meat who asks for it.'

So, while the knight remained with Arthur, the minstrel made his way as fast as he might to Baldwin's castle and there found ready admittance. There were many guests already at table that evening, and among them the minstrel found that no one was refused anything. He was also free to wander where he might, among both high- and lowborn folk, and to take food or wine from any table. Finally, he went to the high table where Baldwin's lady and her most noble guests sat and was made welcome there also. Saying that he came from the southlands, he entertained everyone with news from distant places, and was rewarded with rich viands, wine, and comfortable lodging – in which he remained for another week, until Baldwin himself returned, bringing King Arthur and Queen Guinevere to dine with him.

Such a royal procession of dishes and fine wines then came from the kitchens that even Arthur was moved to exclaim that he had never feasted so well.

'Well, Sire,' Baldwin replied, 'God has a good plough, and sends enough for us all. Why should we stint ourselves?'

'Your generosity is great,' Arthur said, and declared that he would stay there another day and night. Then he bade Sir Baldwin go and win a fresh deer for the table. But the moment he had set forth Arthur summoned his own huntsman and bade him go out and drive the game away from the place, so that Baldwin would be hard pressed to capture anything and was bound to be away throughout much of the night. When the hunting party had left, the king waited until darkness began to fall, and when there was no sign of Sir Baldwin Arthur called one of his knights to attend him. He went to the door of the chamber where the lady of the house slept with her maids.

The king knocked loudly. 'Open up!' he cried.

'It is late. Why must I do so?' asked the lady, not recognizing Arthur's voice.

'Because I command it. I have come here for some secret sport.'

'Surely you have your own lady here,' replied Baldwin's wife. 'Just as I have my own lord to love me.'

'Open up,' said Arthur again. 'I give you my word that no harm will come to you.'

After a moment one of the lady's maids opened the door, and the king went inside and sat on the edge of the bed where the lady lay, while his knight stood by the door.

'Madame,' said King Arthur, 'this fellow of mine must lie beside you all night. But do not be alarmed,' he added quickly, seeing the lady start and blush, 'for this is no more than a bet to settle an argument.'

To the knight he said brusquely: 'Come, get undressed. Get into bed with this lady – but see that you do not touch her, on pain of death. Don't even stir or turn towards her!'

Hurriedly the knight obeyed, and when he was beneath the covers King Arthur called for lights and a chessboard, and one of the lady's maids to play with him. Thus they sat all night, until the morning dawned, and none slept. Then they heard the sounds of the hunt returning.

Presently Baldwin entered the chamber, where he saw the king sitting by his wife's bedside while the knight lay beside her.

'Come in, sir,' said Arthur. 'How fared you in the hunt?'

'Well, my lord, thank you,' said Baldwin quietly.

'I see you looking at this knight,' said the king. 'I missed him last night and eventually found him here. I decided to await your return to ask you what action you wanted taken against him.'

'Why, none at all,' answered Baldwin, smiling at his wife. 'Unless she wished it, or was so commanded, no man would come into this room. Also, we have been together many winters, and she has never done me harm before. Therefore, I am certain there is no evil intent here.'

'So, you are not angered by this?' demanded Arthur.

'Not at all,' replied Baldwin. He looked calmly at the king. 'May I tell you a story, my lord, so that you may better understand why this causes me no pain?'

'Very well,' said Arthur, and Baldwin sat upon the edge of the bed and began to speak.

'During your father's youth, when his father King Constans still ruled over Britain, the king gathered a host to fight against the Saracens in Spain. I had the honour of fighting in that war as a young knight, and I well remember how we defeated the sultan and his men. I had the fortune to be noticed by the king, whom it pleased to reward me by giving me command over a number of men, and in giving me the lordship of a castle in that land.

'It happened that there were only three serving women to care for our needs, and as is the way of things, one was more lovely than the others, for which reason her companions grew jealous and decided to kill her. This they did and were dragged before me in fear of their lives. I asked them to give me a reason why I should not condemn them to death there and then, and they both fell down and begged for their lives, promising that they would do more work than they or their companion, had done before. 'And,' they said, 'neither you nor your men shall lack for anything, day or night.'

'Well, they kept their promise, fulfilling their duties by day and warming our beds at night, until it befell that one of the two, who was prettier than the other, became jealous of her companion, and one night cut her throat.

'Several of my fellows came to me and asked whether they should not kill the woman at once. But I counselled them to bring her before me and see what she would say. This they did, and as before she promised to do as much work as any one woman could and to satisfy us at night according to our needs.

'So it fell out. By day she worked for us and at night offered us her body. From this I learned that if women of this kind are left to follow their own course, they may well do evil, but that if they are given the opportunity to devote themselves to others, without threats, and with good will, they will follow a better way of life. Therefore, I vowed that I would never be jealous or suspicious of anything that happens because of a beautiful woman, for they are just as full of goodness as they are of evil – as are all men. In my wife, I found this to be so, for she has always been true to me.'

'You speak well,' said King Arthur, 'Therefore I will tell you what happened here.' And he related all that had taken place the night before, and how he had remained there all through the hours of darkness and could vouch for the honour of Baldwin's wife. Then he said: 'Sir, you have truly kept all your vows. But I would know more of your reasoning. Why do you not fear for your life and make all welcome who come to your door? As far as I can tell, your gates are always open.'

'I will gladly tell you,' Baldwin said. 'In the same castle where the adventure I just spoke of took place, it happened that we were besieged. One day we decided to make a sortie and to try to take prisoners for ransom. Only, one of our fellows was so fearful of the death which might come to him that he stayed behind, hiding in a barrel. While we were outside fighting, a projectile from a catapult came like a bolt of lightning and smashed the barrel to pieces. When we returned, we found his head completely severed from his body. From this I learned that death is not something one can avoid – it is better to welcome it when it comes.'

'These are fair words indeed,' said Arthur thoughtfully. 'But tell me why you never turn anyone away from your door that comes asking for food and shelter?'

'That is soon explained,' said Baldwin. 'At the time of the siege that I spoke of just now, our supplies ran very low, and we were fearful that we would starve. Then a messenger came from the enemy and demanded that we give up everything we had and surrender ourselves to his master. I gave thought to this and called the steward to prepare the very best of everything we had left to eat – the best wine, bread, meat and fish that had been preserved against our last days. All this the sultan's messenger watched, and then, as he took his leave, we gave him a splendid flagon of wine and other gifts.

'When the messenger was gone all the men in the castle complained to me that I had given away our last supplies. They were angry and despairing, but I knew what would happen, and I was right. The messenger went back to his master and told him to give up the siege. 'For though we have pressed these infidels for so long, they are as fresh as ever and make merry as though it were a feast-day.' And, because in truth the Saracens had disguised the fact that their own supplies were running low, they took council together and decided to raise the siege. Next day, they were gone.'

Baldwin finished his recital and smiled at the king. 'So you see that I have never ceased to give all that I have, in the knowledge that there will always be sufficient. Nor have I ever been wrong in this belief.'

Then King Arthur embraced the older knight and said: 'Truly, there is no falsehood in you. All that you vowed you have honoured. Let it be recorded that you are foremost in worthiness among all my knights of the Round Table.'

And so it was done. And King Arthur said to Sir Baldwin, turning to his wife: 'If you are wise, as I deem you must be, you will always take this fairest of ladies to your heart. For a deep love lies within her, and in her sight, as well as mine, you have fulfilled all your knightly vows.'

To Sir Kay he said, later, that he should never again use lies to prove another knight false. Only because of the fondness he had for his foster-brother did he allow this to be set aside; but ever after Kay sought to promote his deeds against those of others.

I doubt not that many who read this tale will shake their heads that there could ever be such a man as Sir Baldwin, or that he could behave as he is said to have done. And of his lady, they may raise their hands in disbelief that anyone could be so generous of spirit and so gentle of nature. To these I will say only that I have written the story as it is told, and that in those times men and women did not always think as they do now. And as for the king and his knights, I will say that they strove at all times thereafter to fulfil their vows, and to live their lives with honour and truth. As for King Arthur, as we shall see, he also dreamed of errantry.

EXPLICIT THE STORY OF THE VOWS.
INCIPIT THE STORY OF THE PARROT.

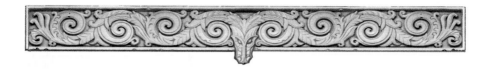

5: THE KNIGHT OF THE PARROT

I HAVE HEARD IT SAID, THOUGH HE FOUGHT BRAVELY AND WELL AGAINST THE KINGS WHO OPPOSED HIS WEARING OF THE CROWN, THAT KING ARTHUR SELDOM UNDERTOOK ADVENTURES OF HIS OWN, DESPITE FOUNDING THE FELLOWSHIP OF THE ROUND TABLE. FOR THIS REASON, SOME HAVE NAMED HIM *ROI FAINÉANT*, A WEAK KING. BUT THIS IS NOT SO, FOR AS YOU HAVE HEARD IN THE STORY OF THE VOWS OF KING ARTHUR AND HIS KNIGHTS, HE WAS EAGER FOR ADVENTURE. ANOTHER TALE THAT MASTER THOMAS DID NOT INCLUDE IN HIS GREAT BOOK SHOWS THE TRUTH OF THIS. HERE WE SHALL SEE HOW KING ARTHUR UNDERTOOK HIS FIRST GREAT ADVENTURE. I BID YOU READ ON AND PUT ASIDE ANY THOUGHTS YOU MAY HARBOUR THAT THE KING WAS WEAK.

✢ ✢ ✢

THE DAY OF King Arthur's crowning took place at Pentecost, and there was much rejoicing and holiday in the city of Camelot the Golden. At the height of the feast a damsel appeared and greeted the young king with these words: 'My lord, my mistress the Lady Ourale sends me to you to ask for help. A terrible, nameless knight comes daily to raid her lands. He has already killed some sixty of her best men. Therefore, I am to ask if there is some brave knight you can send to help her.'

King Arthur answered at once that he would give thought to her request, and that meanwhile she was to be treated as an honoured guest. She was taken to the house of a rich lord and cared for with the utmost respect until the celebrations for King Arthur's crowning were over, at which point the damsel came again before the young king and reminded him of her quest.

'My lady,' said Arthur, 'I have not forgotten your request. Indeed, I intend to undertake this adventure myself, for yours was the first request to be made of me since I am made king, and I would ask no other to undertake it.'

Though his lords protested that one of them should go in his place, King Arthur refused to be moved, and that very day prepared to depart, having made King Lot of Orkney his regent and bade his court to obey him.

Armed with lance and sword but clad in plain armour and carrying a plain shield, the young king set forth with the damsel, whose name was Sibylle, at this side. They had not gone far before they entered the Forest of Cameliarde, and as they rode, chatting as the mood took them, they heard a woman's voice crying for help. Then they saw a well-dressed lady riding full tilt towards them, pursued by a knight with drawn sword. As she drew level with them the lady called out to King Arthur to help her against the knight, who had already slain her companion. Arthur, setting his spear in the rest, called upon the man to stop and face him. 'For you will get no honour from pursuing a woman!'

The knight stopped and stared haughtily at the young Arthur. But though he said nothing, he put away his sword and retreated a suitable distance to couch his own lance. The two charged towards each other and met with a great crash. King Arthur received his opponent's spear on the shield, which broke in half; his own blow struck the man so mightily that he was knocked clean out of the saddle and fell stunned to the earth. As he recovered, he saw King Arthur standing over him with drawn sword, and begged for mercy.

'I shall spare you on one condition,' said the king. 'That you place yourself in the service of this lady whom you lately pursued.'

At this the knight changed colour. 'I would sooner be dead than in her service,' he cried.

'For what reason do you say this?' demanded Arthur.

The knight, sitting up, said: 'You can see how beautiful she is, and in truth her beauty is like a naked sword against my neck. I have loved her this long while, but she loves another, and it was for this reason that I desired to slay her, for if I cannot have her then neither shall he.'

The king was shocked by these words and asked the knight his name.

'I am Sir Alistans, known as the Knight of the Wasteland.'

'Well, sir,' said Arthur. 'You must put yourself at this lady's mercy or I will be forced to kill you.'

'I have no trust in *any* lady's mercy,' said the knight. 'Women are the walls upon which we break ourselves,' he sighed. 'This one most of all! But I will do as you ask, for the sake of chivalry and honour.'

At this the lady herself spoke up, saying that she had no wish to have the man commit himself to her. 'Do what you will with him,' she told King Arthur. 'Kill him or imprison him as you will.'

Arthur made Sir Alistans swear on his honour to return to Camelot the Golden and to place himself under the recognizance of King Lot, and to say that he was sent by the young knight who had but lately departed with the damsel Sybille. When he had left them, the king asked the well-dressed lady, whose name was Laudine, which way she wished to go and whether she needed company on the road.

'Sir,' said she, 'I would rather lead you to a place which lies near at hand. It is the finest court in all the world, and many of the best knights and ladies dwell there. Until recently it was the happiest place, where every year the knights jousted together in friendly sport for the prize of a far-famed parrot which is able to discourse on many matters. But alas, recently a strange knight has proved himself stronger than all the rest, and he has made himself lord of the place through strength of arms alone. Now he forces us to serve him and to pay homage to his lady, who is the most hideous woman you ever saw. Every month we must all assemble at Clausel Field and swear allegiance to this knight and declare that his lady is the most beautiful.'

'This is a terrible thing,' said King Arthur. 'Surely there is something that can be done.'

'There is indeed,' said the lady quickly. 'If you accompany me and become my knight you may claim that I am fairer than his companion. This will cause him to demand your submission and you may contest that with him.'

Arthur turned to the damsel Sibylle, who had brought him thus far. 'Will you permit me to turn aside from the path for a while so that I may help this lady?'

Sibylle shrugged. 'It is not me you serve, but my lady Ourale. If you wish to turn aside, I will certainly not stop you.'

The three turned their mounts towards the lady Laudine's court, which was no great distance away. As they approached, they saw tents set up in the meadows below the castle, and there many knights and ladies disported themselves, singing and dancing and making noise. When they saw the party approaching, they ceased from their games and began instead to call out to Arthur, telling him that he was foolish to come there and would best be served by leaving again at once! Arthur suffered their gibes in silence for a time, then reproved them with all the seriousness of youth.

At this moment the knight of whom Laudine had spoken came in sight. He was fully armed and accompanied by his companion, whose hideous appearance could not be disguised by her fine apparel. Before them came a dwarf, goading on a palfrey on whose back was a golden cage containing the parrot of which you have heard tell. This creature, I am told, had been brought from a far-off land, and had learned to speak miraculously by he who had captured it.

As soon as the knight saw Arthur, he shouted for everyone to clear the way, then without so much as a word of warning, charged straight at the young king with all his might.

The battle was long and furious, and for a while neither man had the upper hand. Then his opponent struck a blow which cut through King Arthur's helm and wounded him in the face so that he bore a scar ever after. The pain and anger this caused was such that Arthur fought back even more fiercely, though half-blinded by blood from his wound. Finally, he struck a blow which all but severed his adversary's sword arm.

The knight fell to the earth, screaming and begging for mercy. King Arthur stood over him and demanded to know his name.

'My name is Armide, but I am known as the Merciless Lion because of all the knights I have overcome.'

'And how have you treated those foes?' demanded the king.

'Those who died, I took their lands and possessions, their women and children. Those who lived I took half their goods and made them come before me every month and swear their allegiance.'

'And for how long have you done these things?'

'For fifteen years I have been supreme. Until today I never met a knight who could overcome me.'

'You have acted against the laws of chivalry,' said Arthur sternly. 'But I will not slay you.' He thought for a moment. 'This is what you must do. First restore everything you have taken from the people you subdued, and right any other wrongs done against them. Then you shall remain here, at this place, and endow a charterhouse to atone for your wrongs. There, every month, until King Arthur of Britain shall summon you to his court, you shall have all those you once forced to pay you homage come and visit you. When King Arthur calls upon you, you must journey to Camelot the Golden in a cart, as knights must who are villains or have no horse. All those who until now served you of their own free will, shall go with you, and shall seek forgiveness of the king. Do you understand all of this?'

Groaning with the pain of his wounds, Armide agreed to everything King Arthur asked. Only then did surgeons rush forward to attend him, and general rejoicing broke out upon every side, save only for the hideous damsel, who stole away quietly, full of hate for the young knight who had felled her lover. As for the lady Laudine, she was overjoyed at the outcome and gave thanks to the king.

At this moment the parrot, who had watched all of this, began to call out to the dwarf to bring it closer. 'Ho! This must be the best knight in the world,' cried the bird. 'I wish to see him who has won me so fairly.'

When the dwarf obeyed, bringing his perch nearer, the wise and astonishing bird looked at King Arthur and uttered these words: 'Now I see that this is the man of whom Merlin spoke when he said that one day a son of a dragon would subdue a lion without mercy!' Then the bird began to speak and sing of the deeds of Merlin, until the king called for silence.

'What are you?' Arthur asked.

'I am what you see,' replied the parrot jovially. Then he added: 'If you take me with you, I shall guide your path and show you many adventures.' Sitting up straight on its perch, the bird began to sing:

Three monstrous beasts on you will make
  affray.
Three times you must forbear, nor make foray.
Within their arms two ladies you'll embrace,
One near your death, the other in love's grace.
Across the bridge of iron must you take your
  quest,
Before you seek your kingdom and your rest.

King Arthur listened in astonishment to this, as did all present, then he took possession of the bird, as was his right as winner of the contest against the Merciless Lion. With it went the dwarf who cared for it and the horse on which its cage rested. Then King Arthur prepared to take his leave of the lady Laudine and her people. Before he departed, they begged to know by what name he was called, and the king, thinking for a moment, answered: 'You may call me the Knight of the Parrot. For such I am now.'

The king and the damsel Sibylle rode on their way, accompanied now by the dwarf leading the horse on which rode the parrot in its cage. As they went, Arthur glanced frequently at the damsel, whose beauty was not lost upon him. The parrot, noticing this, was moved to comment that they would make a fine couple – he so handsome and strong, she so fair and well-born. At this the lady Sibylle looked in wonder at the parrot and said: 'How do you know of my lineage?'

'Lady,' replied the parrot, 'do you not remember when you were a child? I was there, though I did not have so much to say then.'

The damsel was clearly amazed at this, but the parrot addressed King Arthur. 'Sire, would you like to know the lineage of this lady with whom you ride?'

'I would indeed,' replied the king.

'She is named Sibylle, and she is the daughter of the noble Count of Valsin.'

At this the damsel expressed her amazement, while King Arthur was pleased to hear what the wise bird told, for truth be told he was drawn to the damsel and knowing that she was of noble birth recommended her to him all the more. The little company rode on pleasantly together until the time of Vespers, when it began to grow cold. The parrot demanded of the dwarf that his cage be covered and then fell silent as they continued on their way. Soon they sighted a fine castle and sought shelter there for the night, which they were readily granted by its lord.

In the morning King Arthur was woken by the voice of the parrot, which sang that on this day the young knight would receive

great honour. Having dined with the lord of the castle, the company set forth again and had not gone far before they heard a great commotion ahead of them, and saw people running away on every side. A knight came in view, raging and waving his sword, and with a cry Sibylle identified him as the very knight she had hoped King Arthur would fight on behalf of her mistress.

As the knight came thundering towards them, they saw that he was huge beyond mortal size and mounted upon a horse the size of a small elephant. When they saw this the damsel and the dwarf fled, leaving the parrot behind. At which the bird began to cry out to King Arthur to open his cage and set him free. But Arthur merely laughed and reminded the bird of the song it had but lately sung to him concerning honour. Then he prepared to defend himself against the huge knight.

As you may expect, this was a mighty battle, for the giant knight was a terrible foe and King Arthur was still young and untried. But he fought bravely and with skill, and youth was on his side, so that he began to force the

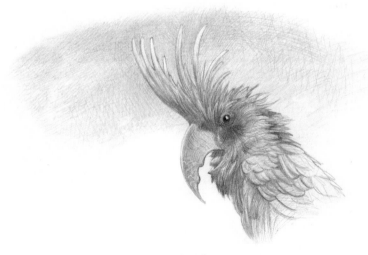

→ *The Parrot* ←

huge creature back before him and to inflict several great wounds upon him. It amazed the king that, whenever he struck the knight on his armour, no matter if it was upon the shield or the helm or the leg, blood gushed forth as if from a far deeper wound. Finally, he struck several blows which brought the huge fellow to his knees and then with all the force in his body King Arthur cut off the man's right arm, which still held his sword.

Then the knight gave forth a great roar and staggered back and forth, crying out and fountaining blood on every side. King Arthur noticed that wherever the blood fell the earth smoked as if it were burning.

Arthur stood in awe at the giant's death throes, during which he felled trees and gouged great trenches in the earth. But at last he lay still, and the king approached to examine the body. There he found a most marvellous and terrible thing. For when he tried to remove the fallen knight's helm, he found it to be all of a piece with the body, and indeed everything, armour, helm, even the weapons he carried, were all of flesh and bone. And the flesh was hot to the touch, though beginning to cool, and it was hard and dry like a snake.

Then Arthur knew that he had fought no mortal man, but some kind of demon, and he marvelled greatly where this frightful creature had come from. He heard the parrot singing close by, praising him for his great deed in defeating the inhuman creature.

After he had rested a while, King Arthur set off to follow the damsel Sibylle and the dwarf. As he rode, he was met by four knights whom she had dispatched to find out if he lived and to offer him any help they might. They were amazed to find him still living and asked to be taken to where the body of the

huge knight lay. They rejoiced exceedingly to see that he was finally slain and praised the Knight of the Parrot greatly for his prowess. Then they set off for the castle where Sibylle awaited them, sending one of their number ahead with the good tidings.

When they were in sight of the city they saw where a great procession came forth to greet them. Everyone wanted to thank the Knight of the Parrot for setting them free. The damsel Sibylle came forth to meet them. She promised that her mistress would join them for supper, and begged forgiveness of King Arthur for fleeing from the attack of the fearsome knight. Then they went inside, and Arthur's wounds were dressed, and fresh clothing put upon him and he was treated as a hero should be.

All this while the parrot complained bitterly about the dwarf, who had left him behind in the forest and fled away. So loudly did the bird cry and squawk that Arthur sought to calm it down and finally brought about a reconciliation between them.

Then they went into supper, where the lady Ourale joined them. Being not unskilled in magic she had already looked upon the face of King Arthur in a secret mirror she possessed, and had evinced a great love for him, though she spoke no word about this at the time. The company supped well among those who could not cease from praising the Knight of the Parrot. Ourale asked if he already had a lady, and upon hearing that he did not expressed great astonishment that so fine a hero should be thus lacking. The parrot, hearing all of this and seeing which way the wind blew, began to sing a romantic song, so that both the king and the lady stopped talking and listened.

After this, wine was brought and then all

retired to bed. A place had been made up in the hall for the Knight of the Parrot, and the bird kept him entertained until he fell asleep by telling him a story about a lady who was wrongly imprisoned.

In the morning, after they had all dined, they went forth to view the body of the dead knight, and like King Arthur himself they marvelled to find that man and armour were all of a piece. Then Ourale ordered her seneschal to skin the creature, which was clearly not human, but must be likened to others of this kind which are mentioned on the *Mappa Mundi*,* which lists many such unlikely creatures that dwell in far-off places in the world.

As the company was returning to the castle a pale maiden appeared, riding hot-foot towards them. She was crying bitterly and wringing her hands and when she was near enough for them to hear they heard that she was calling out for the Knight of the Parrot. Arthur rode forward and asked her what was amiss, but when she saw him, she fell fainting from her horse. Leaping down, Arthur lifted her head and supported her until her senses returned. Then he asked again what he could do for her.

'Sir,' she said, 'my name is Rossignol and I have come from my lady, Flora de Mont, daughter of the late King Belnain of Île Forêt.' She continued: 'He was lately killed in a tournament and his lands given into the care of his marshal, who had served him well in this life. Now this man, whose name is Sir Galardon, has grown greedy. Having won the

barons over to his side he proposes to marry my lady, who has no love for him at all. He has imprisoned both my lady and her mother the queen in a castle, which they are defending as he lays siege to it. Sir, I have ridden far and through great danger to find you. Will you not return with me and set free these noble ladies?'

'I shall do everything in my power to aid you,' replied King Arthur, and prepared to return to the city before departing on this new adventure. Everyone was ready to cheer him on his way, save for Ourale, who was much angered at his willingness to depart with another damsel. Concealing her thoughts, she rode in silence back to the city. Once there however, she announced that there was to be a tournament in eight days' time, the winner of which would win a kiss from her and her promise of friendship for at least a year. She begged the Knight of the Parrot to take part and pressed the damsel from the Île Forêt so hard that she eventually gave her consent, though with great unwillingness. King Arthur himself could not refuse without loss of honour, and so matters stood as preparations went forward to set up the lists and pavilions and send forth messages to all the knights of that land.

✠ ✠ ✠

IN THE DAYS that followed King Arthur – or as we shall henceforth call him, the Knight of the Parrot – and Ourale were much in each other's company. On the evening of the day before which the tournament was to begin, the lady summoned the young knight to a magnificent chamber which he had not seen before. It had in it a great bed over which was set a wonderful carving of a hawk. They

---

* The *Mappa Mundi* is one of the few European maps of the world as it was known then to have survived from the medieval period. Dating from c.1300, it is now on display in Hereford Cathedral.

sat together on the bed and spoke of many things, and all the while the lady looked upon the Knight of the Parrot with great desire, until at last he took her in his arms. It is likely indeed that they would have lain upon the bed and made love had not the lady heard one of her serving women approaching and quickly disengaged herself from the king's embrace. Then she looked upon him and asked him where his heart truly lay.

'I think you know that,' said he. But Ourale was not satisfied with this. Instead, she pointed to the carving of the hawk and asked him to read what was written around the base.

'It says,' the knight answered: 'You who sit here with a lady, give to her whatever she asks.'

'Just so,' said the Lady. 'Will you do what is asked by me?'

'If it is within my power,' replied the knight, the colour rising in his cheeks.

'Then I ask that, if you truly care for me, when you fight in the tournament tomorrow, you will acquit yourself as poorly as possible.'

The knight looked at her in astonishment.

'Surely, you mean as well as possible?'

'That is not what I said,' answered the lady Ourale. 'Will you do as I ask?'

His face now pale, the young king bowed his head. 'Since I have given my word to you, I will keep it. But I had far rather prove myself the best knight rather than the worst in your sight.'

He left the chamber at once and returned to the hall. There he pretended to be light-hearted and content, though within he felt angry and confused. The parrot, noticing this, sang a little song about the lover who turned anger to honour. And when he heard this, the knight smiled and that night slept well, despite all his fears for the outcome of the tournament.

✝ ✝ ✝

NEXT DAY THE games began with a great show of arms and a mighty splintering of spears. Everyone watched the Knight of the Parrot to see how he would perform and were amazed to see him easily overcome again and again – sometimes seeming to fall from his horse without being struck. At the end of the day everyone was speculating how he could possibly have killed the monstrous knight and assumed he must have used magic. But, if he had the power of magic on his side, how could he be so easily defeated?

The overall winner on that first day was one Count Doldays of the Castle of Love, who was heard to boast that he would soon collect the kiss from Ourale. The Knight of the Parrot, overhearing this, exclaimed in the hearing of all that he would prove otherwise on the morrow. At which everyone laughed, thinking him quite the poorest knight they had ever seen.

Meanwhile, Ourale herself, who had overheard this argument, came to join them. She upbraided Count Doldays for speaking so rashly of the hero who had slain the monster knight when he could not. Then she turned to the Knight of the Parrot and asked him who he would serve in the lists tomorrow.

'You, my lady,' he replied with an elegant bow.

At this the parrot, who had been listening to all this, broke out with loud cries, swearing that his knight would do much better at the tournament tomorrow since he would be free to prove himself. Everyone looked in wonder at the bird and asked what it meant.

'Why?' said the bird. 'Since today my knight was in prison, he could hardly do well.'

'What do you mean?' demanded Ourale, staring hard at the bird. 'Surely he was here with us all day.'

'Not so,' said the parrot.

'Then tell us where this prison is.'

'It is here,' answered the bird.

'How can this be?' Ourale said, beginning to lose her patience. 'He has ridden in the field all day.'

'Yet all the time he was in the worst prison ever devised, for it stripped him of his courage and made him seem a fool.'

'Who placed him in this prison you speak of?' asked Ourale, watching the bird carefully.

The parrot stared back, unblinking. 'That I will not say at this time,' he replied.

Returning to the castle, Ourale retired to her room in great agitation. She knew that the Knight of the Parrot had proved himself more than worthy, and that she could never recompense him for the dishonour he had borne in the lists that day at her bidding. Nor could she think of any way to make up for the promise she had forced from him. Finally, she went in search of the knight and with great humility offered herself to him as a reward for all that he had suffered.

The knight, angered by the slights he had been forced to undergo that day, looked at her and wondered how he could have thought her fair. Saying nothing, he turned away and left the room.

The lady now wept bitterly. She imagined what her people would say if the matter ever came out – as well it might – that she had so harshly dealt with the valiant hero who had saved them all from the evil knight!

✠ ✠ ✠

NEXT DAY THE Knight of the Parrot rode everywhere like a whirlwind. Wherever he rode he left heaps of unhorsed and bleeding men, so that soon no one dared face him but did everything they could to avoid him.

The parrot, who had asked to be carried to the lists and placed in his cage near Ourale, spoke to her thus: 'Now that my master is no longer in prison, he shows his true worth.'

Ourale looked on as the Knight of the Parrot proceeded to chase everyone from the field. Finally, only Count Doldays remained, the Knight of the Parrot having made certain to avoid him until this moment. Now they faced each other and everyone else retreated from the lists to give them room. With lances in rest they charged together. Anger consumed the Count because of the loss of honour delivered to his men by the unknown knight. He struck such a blow that it pierced the Knight of the Parrot's side and made a great wound there. He, in turn, struck the Count such a blow that he was unhorsed and sorely wounded. As he lay on the ground the Knight of the Parrot, despite his wounds, came and stood over him with sword at the ready.

The Count begged for mercy and the knight granted it on condition that he place himself forever at the mercy of Ourale, whom he had so recently boasted of conquering. The Count assented at once, glad to avoid a worse fate.

So the tournament ended, with the Knight of the Parrot the undoubted victor. All those who had slighted and mocked him yesterday now praised and honoured him, so that it was as if the previous day's events had never happened. The hero went up to Ourale and there before all the company kissed her and held her to him. And whether it was for the anguish he saw in her eyes, or from courtesy, he forbore to speak of the promise she had forced from him.

The whole company returned in joyous mood to the court, and both Count Doldays and the Knight of the Parrot were taken to be healed of their wounds.

That night, after the feasting held in celebration of the games was over, Ourale and the Knight of the Parrot retired to their separate chambers. But it was not long before the knight, despite his wounds, rose and went in search of the Lady, for regardless of all that she had done to him, he was drawn to her still. Nor was she slow to receive him, for this was her true heart's desire. Her shame fell from her like a cloak, and they spent the night in the pursuit of love and had much joy of each other. And thus it was for several nights after.

✛ ✛ ✛

FOR A WEEK thereafter the disguised king lay abed and waited for his wounds to heal. The Lady Ourale, being skilled in medicines and having some magic of her own, helped him recover more quickly than he might. Nor is there any need to doubt that their loving helped heal the young king. Then the morning dawned when the damsel Rossignol, who served Flora de Mont, came before them and reminded the Knight of the Parrot of his promise to help her lady. Abashed by her reminder, he begged leave of Ourale, and though she was reluctant to see him depart, she saw there was no help for it and gave her blessing.

The knight prepared to leave at once and the Lady Ourale, her damsels, and many of her courtiers rode out with the party. When the time came for them to turn back, Ourale drew the knight to one side and asked him, in a low voice, if she would ever see him again.

'If God grants it, I shall return to you soon,' he replied.

Thus, they parted, and the Knight of the Parrot, accompanied by the dwarf carrying the bird in its golden cage, and the damsel Rossignol, set out upon the next part of their adventure.

✛ ✛ ✛

WHEN THEY HAD ridden for several days, they arrived at a castle of one of the knights in service to the Lady Flora de Mont. This man, whose name was Andois, had remained neutral in the quarrel between the Lady and her marshal, and when the Knight of the Parrot and his companions arrived, he made them welcome. Sitting with him later in a splendid garden, the knight asked why he had failed to serve his lady in her hour of need.

'I will tell you,' said Andois. 'When I was younger, I served the Lady of Flora de Mont's father, King Belnain, in a war against two other lords. They proved to be far stronger than he, and he was losing the war. In the end I gathered a force consisting of my own men and foreign mercenaries. With their help we drove the two lords out of my master's lands and re-established him. In return he gave lands and money to the foreigners, but to myself and my men he gave nothing. When I questioned him about this, he said that I was his vassal already and therefore it was my duty, and that if I had been less rich already, he would have got better service from me far sooner! I confess this angered me beyond speech, and we seldom met or spoke together again. When Belnain died at last and chose to give his daughter into the keeping of the marshal, I swore then that I would never help her, though she remains my lady to whom I owe fealty and therefore neither will I help the marshal against her.'

When he heard this, the Knight of the Parrot called upon him in the name of his honour to help the lady who was rightfully his suzerain. So eloquently did he plead that in the end Andois agreed to offer whatever help he could.

Next morning the Knight of the Parrot and his companions rose early and set out for the castle of the Lady Flora de Mont. The only way there was through a narrow pass which was heavily guarded by the marshal's strongest knights. They had been warned to expect the coming of the Knight of the Parrot, word of whose fame had arrived there well before him. When the disguised king rode up to the entrance to the pass a knight challenged him at once.

'Sir,' said the Knight of the Parrot. 'I have come a long way to this place, and I intend to go further. Either get out of my way or accept my challenge.'

'Who are you?' demanded the guardian of the pass.

'I am called the Knight of the Parrot.'

The guardian looked upon him with pity, thinking him mad, for he did not notice the Parrot in its cage, and did not believe that one so young could possibly be the knight of whose might and courage he had heard so much.

'Laugh if you will,' said the knight. 'But pass I shall.'

Saying which, he set his spear in rest and covered himself with his shield and charged the guardian. The two met in the midst of the way and the Knight of the Parrot easily overcame his opponent. The guardian of the passage rose from the earth where the knight's spear had laid him, and with new-found respect and humility, acknowledged him. Then he offered shelter to the knight and the damsel Rossignol, together with the dwarf and the parrot. The knight accepted gladly, and the companions spent a comfortable night in the lodgings of the defeated guardian.

Next morning, they rose early and continued upon their way. As they drew nearer to the castle where Lady Flora and her mother were imprisoned, Rossignol began to weep. When the knight inquired why, she pointed to a nearby hill from which flew a scarlet pennant. 'There waits the most powerful knight in the world. He is the marshal's champion, and he will surely kill you.'

'Well,' said the knight, 'what will be will be.'

He turned his mount towards the hill and saw coming towards him a tall figure who, having spied him from afar, and realizing his identity, waited no longer but spurred his horse to full gallop against the young king. They met unswervingly, and there ensued a furious combat in which, both men having been unhorsed, continued on the ground with swords.

After they had been fighting for some time the knight drew back and said, panting: 'Sir, never did I encounter a better opponent. Let us continue this fight before the castle of those whom I have come to rescue, so that they may see both defender and aggressor.'

'Agreed,' said the knight. 'For in you also I see a better fighter than any have I encountered.'

So the two adjourned to the meadow below the castle walls, and there, in full sight of the Lady Flora de Mont, they continued their battle, until the Knight of the Parrot finally delivered such a blow to his adversary's helm that it split in twain and the man fell stunned. When he recovered his senses and saw the Knight of the Parrot awaiting him, he at once cried for mercy and this the knight granted him, on condition that he promised to serve the lady of the castle.

At this moment the lady Flora herself, accompanied by her maidens, approached. She gave thanks to the Knight of the Parrot and praised him for his courage and strength. They went up together into the castle, where they were royally entertained. The parrot began to sing songs about his new master, telling of his great deeds. He sang so sweetly that he was soon surrounded by the lady's damsels, who hung upon every word and applauded the parrot for his remarkable skills.

To this scene of rejoicing came the Lady Flora's mother, the Queen of Île Forêt, a sad-faced lady whose presence commanded respect and quiet. She greeted the Knight of the Parrot and asked him from which country he hailed.

'From Britain, my lady,' he replied.

'Then you must be acquainted with King Arthur?'

'Indeed, he is well known to me,' replied the disguised king, smiling.

'Your own fame has flown before you,' said the queen. 'We are eternally grateful to you for your courage.'

'My thanks to you, my lady.' replied the knight. 'Will you tell me where I may find this marshal who has dared to hold you and your daughter prisoner against your wills.'

'It is too soon for that,' said the queen gently. 'First you must rest. I know something of what you have accomplished already.'

'Madame, I did not come here to rest,' said the knight.

'Very well then,' answered the queen with a sigh, remembering other young knights who were as eager as this. 'Stay here tonight and I promise that tomorrow you will be shown the way.'

The disguised king rested there that night, and was well housed and fed. But while it was still the middle of the night, the queen came to the chamber where he was sleeping and woke him. 'Sir,' she said, 'the one who will lead you into even greater danger has arrived.'

The Knight of the Parrot rose and dressed quickly and followed the queen into the meadow before the castle. As he was leaving, the parrot woke up within its cage and called out to him: 'Be careful, Sir King, for there are many dangers ahead of you.' This gladdened the young king's heart, for he still longed for adventure – nor was it lost upon him that the parrot had named him by his true title.

The knight's horse awaited him, freshly groomed and with supplies of food and wine hanging at the saddlebow. When squires had helped arm him, the Lady Flora de Mont handed him his helm herself. On it she had fastened a silken scarf which she had embroidered.

'Wear this for me,' she said softly.

The queen led him to a nearby tree, beneath which stood the strangest creature he had ever seen. It was about the size of a young bull, but with a long slender neck like a dragon and a small head like a deer with two white horns sprouting from it. Its fur was reddish and gleamed in the light of the moon. When it saw the knight, it bowed its head before him. The queen, tears in her eyes, said:

'This beast will lead you to your destiny. Once every three months it appears; but it has not done so in over a year. This tells me that your coming is of great import.' With a sigh, she added: 'Take care, Sir Knight. Come back to us safely.'

The Knight of the Parrot looked at the creature and it gazed back, as if to say it would speak if it might. Then it turned away and he followed without further delay.

They went by a long road through forest and field and valley, until they reached a castle that had once been fair and mighty, but which was now in ruins thanks to the ravages of the marshal. Here the beast made known by gesture that it needed to rest and vanished into the ruins. The Knight of the Parrot tied his horse to a tall and shady tree and sat down beneath it to rest himself. After a while he became aware of a most beautiful perfume, and as he rose to his feet, he saw coming towards him an old man, dressed in white.

'Greetings, King of Britain,' he said.

The knight greeted him in return and asked him how he knew his true identity.

'Fear not,' replied the old man, 'I am he by whose wish you are set upon this greatest of adventures. I am the beast who has led you all this day.'

'How can this be?' asked the knight in astonishment.

'I am,' said the old man, 'that same King Belnain whose wife and daughter you recently met. Though dead, I am permitted to walk the earth for a time in the shape you have seen, until such time as the marshal I trusted with my lands is brought to book for his evil deeds.'

The knight, filled with wonder, asked: 'What place do you inhabit when you are not in either form?'

'I may not speak of that,' said King Belnain, 'save only to say that it is a most beautiful place, and that I shall remain there until a prophecy made by Merlin is fulfilled. After that I shall go to a place of even greater glory, promised by God to all who serve him.'

Then the old king fell silent and looked at the Knight of the Parrot for a long while. Then he said: 'I bid you to remain here this night and to rest beneath this tree. From it you may take a flower and place it within your breast. I shall tell you why. This very night you will see a great company of knights and ladies come to this place, and they will hold a most splendid tournament. Many of the knights will ride up to you and ask: 'Where is the Knight of the Parrot? Will he not join us in our sports?' On no account must you do so, for then you will die as surely as the sun is bound to rise on the morrow. Take care to remain beneath the tree, for as long as the scent of its flowers surrounds you, no harm can come to you.'

The old king bade him farewell and prepared to depart. 'You shall not see me again, I believe, but I wish you well. Do not fail me.'

With that he was gone, melting away like mist. The disguised king prepared for the long night ahead. First, he took care of his horse, then pulled a flower from the tree, breathing in its heady scent. So peaceful and quieting was its effect that he needed neither food nor drink nor sleep. He was alert to every sound however, and soon heard muffled hoofbeats, which announced the arrival of a great company. Varlets and sergeants came first, setting up pavilions and lists in the meadow before the ruined castle. Then came the knights and their ladies, squires and damsels in great numbers, and the tournament commenced just as the old king had said. Many mighty encounters took place, and King Arthur was hard pressed not to join in – especially when men from one side of the general mêlée came and begged him to fight on their side. It was at this point that he wished to forget the old man's warning and even rose and made ready to fight. Before he could do so, he heard a bell ring out somewhere beyond the ruins, and at this the entire company, tents, varlets, squires, knights and damsels, vanished away as though they had never been.

Dawn broke soon after, but there was no sign of the strange beast or the old man. The knight mounted his horse and continued on his way, wondering greatly at the events of the night and wondering how, without guidance, he would find his way. Soon he came to a crossing place, where a great boulder stood. As he drew near, the knight saw there were letters carved on its side. He reined in and read them aloud:

'THREE MISADVENTURES THERE ARE IN THE WORLD

'THE FIRST CONCERNS HE WHO KNOWS THE GOOD BUT CHOOSES TO LEARN NO MORE OF IT

'THE SECOND CONCERNS HE WHO KNOWS WHAT IS GOOD BUT FAILS TO FOLLOW ITS WAY

'THE THIRD CONCERNS HE WHO KNOWS WHAT IS GOOD BUT CHASTISES OTHERS FOR NOT FOLLOWING IT'

Marvelling at this, the knight passed around the boulder and there read another message. It said:

WHOEVER SEEKS A MARVELLOUS ADVENTURE

LET HIM FOLLOW THE PATH TO THE RIGHT

The Knight of the Parrot chose to follow the path to the right as directed. All day he followed it until he heard a voice calling out to him. 'Alas my friend, get away from here, for I cannot save you.'

He looked around and saw a dishevelled lady coming towards him from the top of a hill. Her face was smeared with tears and her clothing was torn. At once the knight asked to know what had happened.

'Alas!' she cried. 'A terrible serpent has carried off my husband, Sir Sador of the Castel Sauvage. I fear for his life – and for yours if you do not flee.'

'Where is this creature?' asked the knight.

The lady pointed silently through the trees at a nearby lake and the disguised king made his way there. There he saw the serpent. Long and scaled in green and yellow, so that its body sparkled in the sun, its fierce eyes regarded the knight, but it did not attack him at once, for it still had Sir Sador in its jaws, only his armour preventing it from crushing him. The Knight of the Parrot spurred his mount towards the evil worm. His lance pierced its breast and heart in one and it dropped the knight and fell thrashing to the ground. So mighty were its death throes that its tail struck the Knight of the Parrot a terrible blow, knocking both him and his horse into the lake. Though sorely wounded and in danger of drowning, it was the water that saved him, washing away some of the poison the encounter with the serpent had inflicted upon him.

Staggering away from the water, the knight

found his horse wandering in a dazed fashion close by. He mounted with difficulty and rode in what he thought was the right direction. He had not gone far before the remaining poison overcame him and he fell senseless to the ground.

Sir Sador, meanwhile, who had been dropped from the jaws of the serpent, recovered his senses, and found his way back to his wife, who was overjoyed to see him. They searched for the Knight of the Parrot and when they could not find him, nor the serpent, which had sunk beneath the water of the lake, concluded that the brave knight must have perished.

They made their way home to the Castel Sauvage and were preparing for bed when they overheard a local fisherman and his wife talking below their window.

'I think he still lives,' the man was heard to say. 'Glory! Look at the armour on him. How it shines!'

'Aye,' replied his wife. 'Thank God we came by when we did!'

Hearing this, Sir Sador leaned out of the window and called down to them. 'Ho! You there! What are you about?'

The man, sounding fearful, called back: 'Nothing, my lord!'

'Villain!' shouted Sador. 'I do not believe you!'

He sent men to investigate and found the fisherman and his wife crouching over a figure who lay in the bottom of their boat. He was barely conscious and seemed paralysed and unable to speak. The men carried him carefully back to the knight's castle and laid him in a bed where his wounds were tended, and warm covers placed over him. When they removed his armour, they found a strange flower caught in his shirt, which gave

off a powerful and pleasing scent. Sir Sador, realizing that this was the very man to whom he owed his life, was happy to see him, and watched over him through the night.

For several hours the Knight of the Parrot neither moved nor spoke, then shortly before midnight he opened his eyes and asked to know where he was. Sador told him and explained how they had found him. They gave him water to drink, and in a while, he asked for food. From there he made rapid progress so that within three days he was as hale and strong as he had been before encountering the serpent.

The knight told the whole story of his adventures to his host and hostess who, on hearing that he was on his way to the castle of the marshal, were able to tell him something of the dangers he would face.

'The place is but three days' ride from here,' said Sir Sador. 'It is called the Perilous Castle, and not without good reason. It is set upon a steep hill, surrounded by water. There is but one way to enter, and that is across a bridge so narrow that only one man may pass it on foot. In the centre of the bridge is a great wheel turned by magic. No one I know who has gone there has ever returned, they have all been crushed by the wheel. However …' He paused and looked at the Knight of the Parrot. 'Though I serve the marshal, you have saved my life I will help you save yours. Know that when you reach the wheel you will see two marble pillars, coloured red as blood, on either side. On each of these is written a message: 'You who seek to cross, come close to me.' On no account take notice of this. If you do you will die. Instead look to the pillar and you will see a small hole there. Inside you will see all manner of wheels and gears turning. Break these with your sword and you will stop the wheel from turning. In this way you will have at least a chance of survival, though I cannot say what further dangers you will have to face.'

With this advice in mind the Knight of the Parrot prepared to set forth. Sir Sador rode part of the way with him, then turned back, wishing him God speed. The road was steep and stony, but the disguised king made good speed that day, and most of the next. This found him in a country of wild heathland, and as he rode through it, he was attacked by a naked wild woman, who leapt out of the bushes and onto the back of his horse behind him. She wrapped her long and powerful arms around him and began to squeeze. Her hands were clawed like a beast, and she threatened to tear the skin from his face and put out his eyes. If he had not been wearing his armour he would certainly have been crushed to death by her embrace. As it was, his horse, startled by the sudden extra weight on its back, reared up, throwing the wild woman to the ground. Drawing his sword swiftly, the Knight of the Parrot clubbed her about the head, then rode on before she could regain her senses.

In the morning he came in sight of the Perilous Castle. It was, if possible, even more forbidding than he had been led to believe. The moat was deep and dark and filled with black, swift-flowing water. The bridge was not only narrow but sharp, being made of fine-honed steel, which trembled whenever anyone set foot upon it. As to the wheel – Sir Sador's words had not prepared him for its most terrible aspect. It too was made of metal, sharpened to the keenness of a sword, and it whirled and thrashed so fast that it could scarcely be seen. Beyond it, on the further side of the bridge, was a tower which

looked as forbidding as did the great pile of the castle itself.

The knight looked at the task before him and his heart quailed. Yet he knew that only by facing this peril would his task be complete. Therefore, he prepared himself as best he might, and tying his horse to a boulder at the edge of the bridge, began to make his way slowly across.

At once the bridge began to tremble so much that the knight was forced to get down on his hands and knees and crawl. The sharpness of the metal was lessened by his mail leggings and gloves, but the trembling of the narrow way was as terrifying as anything he had ever endured.

At last he reached the whirling wheel and saw, just as Sir Sador had told him, both the writing on the pillar and the small hole through which he could see machinery. Drawing his sword and dragging himself into an upright position, he hugged the pillar and pushed his sword point into the hole.

At once there was a loud screeching and the wheel slowed to a stop. Withdrawing his sword, which despite its tempered steel was battered and chipped, the Knight of the Parrot made his way onward across the rest of the bridge, which had now almost completely ceased from shaking.

Entering the tower, he found himself face to face with two powerful knights, who drew their swords and prepared to attack him. Wearily, the Knight of the Parrot raised his own weapon, but spoke to them thus: 'Must every knight who crosses the bridge successfully still die?'

The two men looked at one another, then one of them abruptly lowered his sword and said: 'We have killed a great many brave knights. I for one am sick to my soul of this.

Since you have little chance against the foes who await you within, you shall go without further challenge from us.' The second knight, after a moment's hesitation, put away his sword also and they waved the Knight of the Parrot on.

The disguised king gave them his thanks, and passing on from the tower, entered the Perilous Castle at last. By now the sun had set, and within the castle all was dark. As the Knight of the Parrot entered a great hall, he saw several damsels enter from a side chamber. Every one of them was dressed alike, in purple and red, and each carried a torch, so that by the time as many as fifty of them had come there, the hall was almost as bright as day.

Then the marshal himself came in, clad in red armour. When he saw the Knight of the Parrot, he gave a roar of fury and attacked with all his might. Defending himself, the disguised king began a battle which raged through the castle and lasted until well past midnight, during which time neither man gained ground nor inflicted serious wounds on the other.

Then the marshal became even more enraged and swung his sword with such force that it cut through the knight's helm and into his head. Had not his mail been of the finest steel he would have received his death wound. As it was, when he felt the blood run hot into his eyes, he became so enflamed with anger that he rose up and struck a single blow which split the marshal's head in twain to the jaw, so that he fell dead in a single moment.

For a moment there was silence in the hall, then all the damsels who had stood by and beheld this, placed their torches in silver holders around the hall and came and thanked the Knight of the Parrot profusely, hugging

and kissing him until he felt more dizzy from their thanks than from his wounds.

Four of the damsels went up into the tower and rang a bell that had not been rung since the death of King Belnain, so that all who heard it knew that the marshal was dead and that they were free at last. It is my belief that the ghostly king himself heard its call and was at last allowed to rest. Everywhere bells began to peal out, taking up the carillon of joy, and by the time dawn broke many knights and ladies had assembled before the Perilous Castle to thank the Knight of the Parrot for his courage and chivalry and to do homage to him.

There, the knight addressed them, calling upon them to go with him to the queen and her daughter Lady Flora, and there to rejoice and swear their fealty to she who was still their liege lady. All were glad of this, and once the Knight of the Parrot had rested and bathed his wounds, and been dressed in fair clothes, they all set out, in a mood of great rejoicing, to where the queen and her daughter awaited them. There they met a strong force of knights led by the lord Andois, who had kept his word and brought his men to the service of the queen.

So began a time of celebration and rejoicing for all the people of that land. And no one was gladder to see the Knight of the Parrot than the bird itself. It had waited patiently for the return of its master and had kept the court entertained with songs and tales of honour. When the bird saw him approaching, it fell down into the bottom of its cage, like one dead. The knight rode up to him and said: 'Ho! Sir Parrot! Do not leave me yet!' The bird sat up and began to sing as gaily as ever, to everyone's delight. Then King Arthur revealed to all his true identity, at which they marvelled greatly and with great joy swore to serve him all their days.

King Arthur, who had been the Knight of the Parrot, remained there for a time, recovering his full strength. Then he took ship from a nearby harbour and returned swiftly along the coast to his own lands. On the way he had further adventures, though I will not speak of these here. But at length he landed in the country belonging to Ourale. It was almost Pentecost again, and a full year had passed since he had departed on his great adventure. He sent word to Armide, the Merciless Lion, reminding him that he should go to King Arthur, who would hold court that Pentecost at Carlisle.

He remained for a few days with Ourale, and the story tells that they found as much joy in each other's arms as they had previously. I have heard that the parrot sang sweetly as ever to them, songs of love no doubt, for that was a time of love. At last, King Arthur returned to Camelot the Golden and was made welcome by all his fellows, who had heard nothing of his deeds and had begun to believe him dead. King Lot had proved a good and faithful steward in the king's absence and received his reward as was fitting. And as the time drew near for her to depart, the king and Ourale spoke at length concerning their future. It was, I believe, though the story does not tell it, that the king being but newly crowned and still young, wished for no lasting connection with any lady at this time. And though Ourale wept long and hard she left to return home alone; nor have I found word anywhere that they met again in this life. King Arthur's mind was already busy with thoughts of the realm over which he had but lately become king.

The day of Pentecost dawned and there were celebrations throughout the day. Sir Armide arrived and was received by King Arthur in the great hall. When he discovered that it was the king he had fought, the knight bowed his head in humility, but Arthur raised him up and made him a Knight of the Round Table, where he served loyally to the end of his days. In the evening, during the feasting, the parrot sat in the midst of the hall and sang songs and told of the king's adventures. All were astonished and delighted to learn that the knight was their own lord, and all praised King Arthur for his courage and chivalry.

Last of all the parrot sat up straight in his golden cage and sang these words:

Three monstrous beasts on you made affray,
Three times you did forbear, nor make foray.
Within their arms two ladies took you in
* embrace:*
One towards your death, one to sweet love's
* grace.*
Across the iron bridge you took your quest,
And now have reached your kingdom and
* your rest.*

Hearing this, King Arthur smiled, remembering how the parrot had sung this song at the beginning of his adventures, and how the vision freely offered came to be. And the king raised his cup to the wily bird and drank to its wisdom.

✢ ✚ ✢

THE PARROT REMAINED at the court until its death, at a good age, when it was mourned by everyone, not least King Arthur himself, who remembered when he was the Knight of the Parrot, long years after the adventures told here. As to the history of the parrot, and how it came by such wisdom,

I have heard it said that it was discovered in the forest by Merlin himself, years before, and that it was by his magic that the bird came to speak and sing and challenge all with its wit and wisdom. And in another tale that I have read, it says that when the bird returned with King Arthur to Camelot the Golden, it recognized the king's great counsellor and that they spoke together of many things, including the sorrowful times that were yet still far off in the young king's life, but which were already known to Merlin.

So let it not be said that King Arthur undertook no adventures of his own, for you have seen in this tale how well he stood the tests he encountered, and that the Knight of the Parrot was as brave as any man living in those far-off times. Next, we shall turn to a story of Sir Lancelot, that many say was the greatest knight of all the Round Table Fellowship.

———— ⊹ ————

EXPLICIT THE TALE OF KING ARTHUR'S FIRST ADVENTURE.
INCIPIT THE STORY OF SIR LANCELOT.

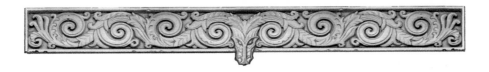

6: HOW SIR LANCELOT EARNED HIS NAME

FEW THERE ARE WHO HAVE NOT HEARD THE NAME OF SIR LANCELOT. MOST KNOW HIM AS THE GREATEST KNIGHT OF THE ROUND TABLE. OTHERS RECALL THE DARKER DAYS WHEN HIS ACCUSERS NAMED HIM LOVER TO QUEEN GUINEVERE AND BROUGHT SHAME UPON HIS HOUSE. BUT FEW SPEAK OF HIS ORIGINS, OR OF HIS COMING TO THE COURT OF ARTHUR. EVEN MASTER THOMAS FAILED TO DO SO. YET IT IS KNOWN THAT LANCELOT HAD TO SEEK FOR HIS TRUE NAME BY ENDURING GREAT HARDSHIP AND TERROR. HOW THIS CAME ABOUT I WILL TELL NOW, TURNING FROM THE ADVENTURES OF OTHER KNIGHTS TOWARDS THE STORY OF THE FIRST AMONG THEM ALL.

✠ ✠ ✠

AT THE TIME when Arthur himself was but a youth, a strong and proud prince named Ban ruled over the kingdom of Benoic, which lay within the borders of Gaul. No longer young, he had fought in many wars and received numerous scars in the process. Possessed of a will of iron, he would brook no opposition from any of his lords, who hated him for his often harsh justice. The people, on the other hand, though they feared him, respected him also, for he treated them exactly as he did any man and meted out justice to both high- and lowborn equally.

This lord had a lady, named Clarine, who was as sweet-natured as her husband was fierce. Whenever and wherever she could she went about doing good to the people of Benoic, and for this was greatly loved. Indeed, it is said that while many of Ban's lords desired his death, they stayed their hands for many years on account of his lady, whom they served with as much faith as they might and spared her husband rather than bring her grief.

As Ban grew older, he went less often to war, and began to look to his home life. So it was that his lady bore him a son, late in both their lives, whom they named Lancelot. Great things were prophesied for him, and his mother nursed him herself rather than putting him out to a wet nurse as was the custom in that time. Many noble women held him upon their laps, and his father was as proud of him as ever a man could be of his son.

The time came when the lords of Benoic could no longer bear the harshness of their lord, and a number banded together against him. They raised a great army and, hearing that Ban was residing in a castle by the sea, laid siege to it, slaughtering the people in the villages around.

So angry was King Ban that he could scarcely be persuaded from going out alone against the besiegers. Only the pleas of his wife prevented it, and instead he took up his place on the walls near to the gate, where the fighting was thickest. And there, in due course, he fell, mortally wounded. Almost too weak to stand he dragged himself to his chamber and begged his wife to help him to a certain spring which rose near to the castle, midway between its walls and a lake of still, dark water. The spring itself was rumoured to be haunted and was said also to possess healing properties. Here the wounded king and his wife made their way – she nursing her child, who was not yet one year old, in her arms.

There, shortly after, the king died, for not even the white water of the spring could save him.

Then the queen, weeping, and much afraid for her life and that of her tiny son, laid the infant down for a moment in the shade of a tree. She fetched water to wash the face and wounds of her dead lord. As she turned away, there came a sudden mist from off the lake, and within it walked a faery woman. When she spied the child lying beneath the tree, she took him without hesitation in her own arms and went with him beneath the waters of the lake.

Finding her child gone, the queen was distraught. Her piteous cries drew her to the attention of the attacking force, and she was taken prisoner.

As to the nature of the being who had stolen the child of Ban and Clarine, I have heard it said that she was of the Undine race, that dwell beneath the waters of either lake or sea, while others report that she was of the faery kind. The story tells that she was a queen in her own right, and that more than a hundred otherworldly women waited upon her. As to the land over which she ruled, it was a fair place indeed, and though it lay hidden

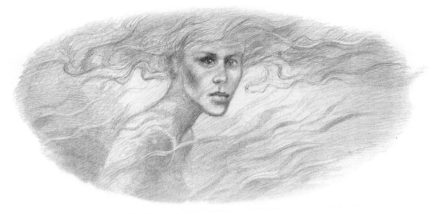

→ *The Faery Queen* ←

beneath the waters, it seemed to those who dwelled there as if it were an open land, lying peacefully beneath the sun. It seemed also as if it was always May-time in that place, with blossom on the apple-trees, and birds singing from every branch. It may be for this reason that in later days Lancelot loved this time of year more than any other.

Around the land was a marvellous enclosure of crystal, and in the centre stood a great crystal mount with slopes as smooth as glass. Atop this sat a castle of great splendour and beauty, with walls of gold adorned with most wondrous carvings. None who lived within that castle aged so much as a single day, nor did they feel envy or anger towards one another, but instead lived together in harmony. Such joy was in that land, that if one were to spend only a few moments within it, he or she would never feel sorrow again, but only perpetual happiness.

In this wondrous place the child of Ban and Clarine grew swiftly to manhood, untouched by fear or sorrow, a stranger to the ways of men. Mostly he was cared for by the women of that place, who found him an apt pupil and taught him manners, the arts of singing and making music, as well as of letters. To many he was a favourite, and there were those among them who were heard to remark that if all humans were like him there might be less problems in the world beyond. (To them our world lay outside, while to us theirs lies within the innermost hidden places.)

⁜ ⁜ ⁜

WHEN THE YOUTH turned twelve, the queen gave him into the care of the men of that place – though there were few of them; only those who served the women day and night. They taught the youth to hunt and shoot with a bow and arrow, to follow the chase on foot with a pack of the strange white-bodied, red-eared hounds that lived in the place. He learned also to fight with sword and buckler, to wrestle and to throw spears. By the time he was fifteen, he could run as fleetly as a deer and walk for long distances without growing tired. Yet he knew little or nothing of riding, nor of the bearing of arms, for none in that company were ever seen to ride a horse or to don mail. Nor did he know his own name, for they were wont to call him 'fair youth' or 'boy'. This irked him greatly, though he spoke not of it. Indeed, as he grew older, rumours of the outside world began to concern him more, and he wondered about his origins, knowing full well that he was not as the other people of that place.

When he turned fifteen, he went before the queen and asked leave to depart.

'Are you not happy here?' she asked.

'I would learn more of the world outside and prove myself there. I do not even know my own name, since none here will tell it to me.'

'Nor shall they,' replied the queen. 'Neither shall I.'

'Who has forbidden you to tell me?' demanded the youth.

'No one,' she replied. 'Nonetheless, I will not speak of it at this time.'

'All the more reason then that I should go forth. Perhaps in the world outside I may learn my true identity and prove myself worthy of your trust.'

'To do that you would have to find and defeat the strongest knight in the world,' answered the queen.

'Tell me his name!' cried the youth. 'Let me seek him out.'

'His name is Iweret of Beforet. His castle lies far to the west, across the sea in the lands of men. He has done me great harm in the past, and if you were to bring vengeance upon him, I should be glad indeed. But I fear that you are no match for him, for I have never seen a mightier fighter in the world of men, and you are as yet untried.'

'Nevertheless, I will try this test, if you will allow it. Give me whatever advice you think best.'

'As to advice,' said the queen, 'I have none to give. But I do have gifts for you.'

Saying which, she rose and went to another chamber and took from a chest a suit of white armour which she showed him how to put on. Then she gave him a mighty sword, with a golden hilt, and a shield on which was emblazoned a golden eagle. And to wear over his armour she gave him a rich surcote sewn with gold thread and hung with small golden bells. Lastly, she led him forth and showed him where a great war-horse stood pawing the earth. This was the greatest marvel of all, for the youth had scarcely ever seen a horse of this kind before. It had a wonderful golden bridle, worked with all kinds of jewels, and a saddle of white leather, tooled with rich decoration.

'These are my gifts to you,' said the queen. 'Take them and go with my blessing.'

The youth (whom we shall call Lancelot even though that name was still hidden from him) took leave of the lady and the folk of the crystal castle, who came forth to see him upon his way. He took ship in one of the wondrous vessels of that place, which soon bore him out of sight of the otherworldly land and in time brought him to the lands of men. There he took leave of the faery woman who had brought him thither, and she in turn bade him treat all whom he met with honour, to be steadfast and true in all things, and ever to do the best he might. Then she left him, and without looking back the youth mounted his new horse and rode east.

Now hear a strange thing. Since he had never properly learned to ride, Lancelot had no notion of how to hold the reins, but simply tucked them around the saddlebow and left the animal to make its own way. At first it wandered in search of grass to eat, but then it came upon a road, and habit – or luck – caused it to canter along as it was used to do.

So the day passed, and the youth was filled with good spirits. He felt no fatigue but looked forward to whatever adventure lay ahead. That night he slept in the open, and in the morning rode on until he came in sight of a castle. The horse turned that way as was its wont, and thus took the youth to where a dwarf sat upon a white horse. Glowering at the youth, the dwarf called upon him to halt. Since the young man had no means to rein in his mount, he continued onward. As he passed, the dwarf swung at him with his whip, inflicting him with a cut on his hand. When this brought no response, the dwarf rode after him and lashed out cruelly at the youth's horse. But this only caused it to run faster still, and in a few moments both the dwarf and the castle lay left behind.

Bewildered, the youth continued upon his way – which was really the way his mount wished to go – until he reached a place where a stream ran through marshy lands. There he met a handsome, richly clad fellow, riding towards him on a fine horse, and carrying a hawk upon his wrist. Seeing how inexpertly he rode, the man called out cheerfully: 'Sir, I would be glad if you would ride more carefully and not knock me down!' As he came alongside, he reached over and caught the reins, bringing the youth's mount to a halt.

'Forgive me for asking,' said the stranger, 'but why do you ride so oddly? Is it some penance that has been placed upon you? Or has some lady demanded that you ride wherever your horse sees fit to take you? Pardon my curiosity, but though you are clad like a warrior you carry yourself like a child. My name, by the way, is Joffrey de Liez. Whom do I have the pleasure of addressing?'

All this was said in so disarming a manner, that the boy could not take offence. Indeed, he was rather glad to have someone to talk to who seemed to know all about horses and did not strike at him with a whip!

Eager to converse, he said: 'Sir, you will understand that I know very little of horses and riding. I have but lately left a land where such things are unknown. It is a land ruled over by women, where knightly deeds and sports have no place, so that I have only read of them in books. But I'm eager to learn of such things, and hence I have set out in search of adventure. Also, I hope to learn something of my name and origin, since both have been kept from me.'

Joffrey de Liez laughed. 'I never heard such a story before. I see that you are well born, but it seems you could use some advice – at least on how to ride! Let me offer you the hospitality of my house, which is not far from here. If you can take more of the company of women, there are many fair ladies at my castle. My mother is there also and is always glad to meet new and worthy people.'

'I shall be glad to,' said the youth. 'And I thank you.'

'Thank me by riding with greater care,' laughed Joffrey. 'Grip the saddle with your knees, hold the reins as I do, and watch where you go.'

The two set forth, and by dint of watching his new-found friend, and copying him faithfully, the youth was soon riding almost as well as if he had done so for far longer than two days!

They soon reached Joffrey's castle, where they were welcomed by his mother and her ladies, who made a great fuss of the handsome young man. The lady herself, being full of curiosity about her son's new friend, asked many questions, and soon elicited from him the story of his life, everything he remembered from his childhood up to the moment. But he spoke nothing of his mission for the Queen of the Lake.

When she had learned all about him, and thinking that he would benefit from some knightly challenges, the lady sent forth messengers to every part of the land, and those that neighboured her own, calling for knights to take part in a *bohourt*, a mock tournament designed to show the abilities of young men who aspired to knighthood. Many came in answer to her summons, and thus Lancelot was treated to a display of horsemanship and weaponry such as he had never dreamed existed.

On the third day, his own mount was brought to him and donning the armour and weapons that the Queen of the Lake had given him, he rode forth – acquitting himself so well that he became the centre of attention among the company. Though his horsemanship still lacked finesse, no one could say that his handling of sword and spear were anything other than miraculous. Everyone called him 'the White Knight', since this was the colour of his armour and shield, and he had no other name.

When the *bohourt* came to an end, the young Lancelot carried off several prizes. He was eager to be on his way, since he felt ready for whatever adventures might befall. He took leave of his hosts and rode on until he reached the dark forest of Moreis. There he journeyed on for much of the day, until he heard the clangour of battle coming from a clearing away from the road. Turning aside, he came upon two knights, who he could see had fought for long hours and were weary, but neither could get the better of the other. When he saw them, Lancelot called out: 'Sirs, cease your battle, or I shall take the side of one of you and fight against the other.'

The two men lowered their swords and expressed relief at the youth's interruption. For in truth neither wanted to fight on, and indeed they admitted they had no just cause to do so; but having once begun, found it hard to stop. Both were young men, and new to knighthood. Their names were Kuraus with the Brave Heart and Orphilet the Fair, and as dusk began to fall it was Kuraus who gave thought to a place where they might find rest and lodging for the night.

'Though I must warn you it is no easy place to be,' he said. 'Its lord is called Gala-gandries, and the castle Moreis. His wife is dead, but he has a beautiful daughter whom he guards as though she were a great prize. It is said that he demands that all who enter his home act with perfect respect – especially to his daughter. Anyone who diverges from this by as much as a hairsbreadth, is liable to meet a terrible end. Galagandries is a proud and quarrelsome man, and few have anything good to say of him. Nevertheless, there is no better place to stay unless we wish to sleep in the open again.'

'This sounds like a good place to me,' Lancelot said. 'Who knows what adventures may await us there.'

The three knights turned toward the castle, where they were met with all honour and a great show of hospitality. Galagandries himself had been gaming and had met with good fortune, and so was in a sunny mood. He greeted the three young men warmly and said that whichever behaved in the courtliest fashion should sit beside him and his daughter at supper.

With one accord the two knights pressed Lancelot forward to accompany their host. And indeed, he proved a good choice; the years spent in the company of the Queen of the Lake had equipped the youth well in the arts of courtly speech and behaviour. He conversed upon all matters with ease, and his pleasant nature endeared him to all who met him. The host's daughter received all three men with smiles and fair words, but soon drew Lancelot aside to sit with her as supper was brought into the hall.

A wondrous feast followed, with so many dishes that it would take days to list all if I were inclined so to do. Suffice it to say that at the end of the day the three knights retired to comfortable beds, praising their host and wondering how he came by so evil a reputation.

Tired out from their day of battle and the distance they had travelled, the three knights were soon asleep. It was then that their host's daughter, accompanied by two maids carrying tall candlesticks, entered the chamber where the young men were sleeping. She was dressed in her finest silks and wore a chaplet of flowers like a bride; for the truth of the matter was that she was inflamed with love for all three knights, and desired to look upon them as they slept. Silently, she gestured to her maids to place the candles either side of the beds in which the knights lay, then dismissed her companions with a nod. Once they were gone, she seated herself on the edge of the bed next to Orphilet, who was nearest, and spoke softly to herself.

'How quickly these warriors are silenced! I had thought all would remain awake talking of love and high deeds, but it seems all they can do is sleep! Perhaps my father is right when he says that love is merely a trap, a burning heat which parches the world like a desert. He's determined I shall never marry, yet I would be as other women are, and if need suffer for the pains of love.'

Orphilet stirred and woke, and seeing the lady bending over him sat up and greeted her courteously. Eagerly the maiden replied: 'I wish to escape from this place, where I am forced to live my days with only women for company.' She took a ring from her finger and offered it to him. 'Accept this as my pledge and take me away from here!'

Orphilet looked over her shoulder towards the door, half expecting Galagandries himself to burst in. To the lady he said, as gallantly as he might: 'If this is your wish, I will do all I can to help you. However, please take back your ring, for I can do nothing at present. I will return here as soon as my present journey is complete. For you I will risk life and limb – but for now I bid you wait and keep silence.'

'That will not do!' cried the girl. 'I have heard about the ways of men, and I know that once you leave here, I shall never see you again. How can you look at me and refuse what I ask? Am I not fair? Do I not delight you? What kind of knight are you that can so refuse the wishes of a lady?'

Orphilet answered: 'I fear more for my knightly honour than anything else. Even if I were to agree to your wishes, I should almost certainly have to kill your father. Would you have me behave so dishonourably?'

'I have heard it said,' the lady replied, 'that no one who wished to achieve true manhood ever did so without some indiscretion with a woman.'

'If that is true – and I do not say it is,' answered Orphilet in a sulky fashion, 'I have no wish to die for the sake of such an act.'

Angrily the lady rose and made her way to where Kuraus with the Brave Heart, the knight whom Orphilet had fought earlier that day, lay slumbering. She had made up her mind that if the first of the three men would have nothing to do with her, she would woo the second so well that he could not refuse. Sitting down beside him as she had with Orphilet, she said: 'Sir, I believe you to be a fair and honourable man, unlike your companion there. I'm sure you will not refuse the wishes of a lady. My father believes he cannot live without me, and that no man is a fit husband for me. This I cannot believe. If you find me at all fair, take me away from here. I would as soon wish for a man of honour than wait for one to be chosen for me.'

Kuraus, who in truth had lain awake listening to the exchange between Orphilet and the lady, answered her. 'Madame, what you ask goes against all the laws of chivalry which I try to uphold. If I did not honour your father, I would be guilty of a great crime. I bid you to forget me as soon as you can, though you can be sure that I shall always be sorry that I had to give you up.'

So saying he pulled the covers over his head and refused even to look upon the lady again.

She, angry and tearful to be twice repulsed, turned now to the bed where Lancelot lay. He, who had heard all that passed between the lady and the two knights, trembled with joy at the thought that she might finally come to him. Indeed, as soon as he heard the rustle of her skirts, he leapt up from the bed and said: 'Lady, you have no need to woo me! I will gladly serve you as long as I live!' Then he took her in his arms and kissed her, and the two of them fell upon the bed and, despite the presence of the two other knights, they knew all the joys of love.

They were awoken at dawn by their host hammering mightily on the door. He burst into the room and saw immediately how things stood. He carried two long knives, one in either hand, as well as two small round shields. 'Never was I treated so evilly by any man!' he cried. 'I gave you every hospitality and see how you betray me! Which one of you has had my daughter, the faithless wretch – or is it that all three have used her!'

Lancelot rose at once and placed himself between the lord and his daughter. Galagandries glared at him furiously and held out the knives. 'So be it. I thought you the best of the three, but it seems I was wrong. I challenge you to defend yourself. Take this shield and knife and stand over by the far wall. I will retire to the other side and we will throw at each other. Whoever wins will keep his honour, whoever loses, let him be cursed!'

To this Lancelot agreed, and taking the shield and one of the knives retreated to the wall. Galagandries took aim and threw. The knife tore through the sleeve of Lancelot's shirt and stuck in the wall, drawing a thin line of blood from his arm.

With only a moment's hesitation, instead of throwing the knife, the youth leapt forward and struck the surprised lord through the heart, killing him outright.

Orphilet and Kuraus were shocked by this, which they saw as unknightly behaviour, though I believe that secretly both thought it a wise action. The lady herself shed no tears for her father, but sought to ensure that neither Lancelot nor his companions were unjustly punished for the killing of Galagandries. Telling them to remain where they were, she went in search of those amongst her father's vassals whom she knew trusted her. To them she told the whole story, praising Lancelot for his bravery in defending her and reminding them of all the knights slain by her father in his jealous rages. They, as one man, elected to follow the lady – who was now mistress of Moreis – and to offer no resistance or punishment to the three knights. They went to the chamber where the deed had taken place and swore fealty to Lancelot, who in turn promised to honour their lady as his own.

Thus did fate deal out a winning hand to the youth, who was soon installed as the new lord of Moreis. Word went forth to all who had served the old lord, and soon a great company gathered. Galagandries was laid to rest in proper fashion, though few mourned him. The people swore fealty to their new lord, and he in turn gave many gifts from riches he found hidden in the vaults below the castle. He chose from amongst the nobles one to be his steward – for he had no intention of remaining there while he had still to find his name and avenge the honour of the Queen of the Lake against Iweret.

Seeing this, and warming daily towards the youth, Orphilet began to talk to him about King Arthur, praising him for his nobility and extolling the virtues of his court at Camelot the Golden.

'No one who is such a strong knight as yourself should fail to go there,' he said. 'The king is the best monarch ever to rule this land, and as for his queen – she would as soon do two good deeds as one bad. Her ladies are fairer than any I have seen. You must go there, for I am sure you'll be honoured and find new adventures.'

Lancelot shook his head. 'I am as yet untried. What could I say when the other knights you speak of tell of their adventures? I must do some deeds of my own before I am fit to go to this court.'

Then Kuraus tried to persuade him to go to his lands in Gaunes, where he promised him fair welcome. But again, the youth declined, saying that he must follow his heart to wherever it was he was destined to be. 'While I am without a name, how can I attend any such noble king or remain in any fine house?'

Thus, the three parted company, for Orphilet and Kuraus wished to return home to their own lands. Lancelot gave them gifts and sent them on their way with many words of friendship. Orphilet returned to Camelot the Golden and spoke of his recent adventures, and of the extraordinary youth who had broken the adventure of Moreis. So it was that Lancelot was first spoken of there, though as yet he was but 'a nameless youth'. But when he heard of their adventures King Arthur said that he hoped the youth would find his way there one day.

✟ ✟ ✟

MEANWHILE, THOUGH LANCE-LOT continued to remain at Moreis, living well and enjoying the favours of the lady for whom he had fought, with every day that passed he longed to continue the quest for his name, and for the evil knight who had dishonoured the Queen of the Lake. One day therefore he donned his armour, saddled his horse and slipped away, telling no one where he was bound. He soon put distance between himself and Moreis, until he came at last to a place where the way divided in three. As many had before him, and doubtless will do again, he chose the middle way and rode swiftly until he came within sight of a castle set amid a thick break of trees.

The story tells that the custom of this place was that any knight who came there must either carry an olive branch signifying peaceful intent or remove his helm and carry it before him as a further sign that he did not seek battle. The youth knew nothing of this as he rode towards the castle. As soon as he was sighted, the alarm sounded, and a veritable torrent of mailed knights poured forth and attacked the unsuspecting youth. First amazed, then angered, he drew his sword and began to lay about him, slaying many men and cutting a swathe through their ranks as he made his way ever closer towards the gates of the castle.

Within this fortress lived a maiden of great beauty and breeding, named Ade of Bingen. When she heard the battle taking place outside the walls, she called for her horse and rode out to view the fighting. Seeing how bravely the young knight defended himself, and how many of her own folk were falling beneath his sword, she rode straight towards him. A path opened before her and her men fell back on all sides. When she reached where Lancelot sat upon his horse, breathing heavily, his sword reddened with fresh blood, she called out to him: 'Sir, I do not know who you are, but I salute your bravery. If you will agree to surrender to me, I promise you will not be harmed.'

Lancelot looked about him at the knights surrounding him, then at the lovely lady who addressed him with kindness. Slowly he put away his sword and bowing his head, accepted her offer.

Thus, he came to the castle of Limors, which was in the holding of the girl's uncle, a proud and violent man named Linier, who gave much of his time to hunting. He it was who had declared that whoever came that way without tokens of peace should be killed outright. As luck, or destiny, would have it, he was away from home that day, allowing Ade to intercede on behalf of the youth, so that he came into the castle unharmed and was welcomed and cared for. But the lady was concerned that when her uncle returned his anger would be such that the brave youth would be condemned to death.

Therefore, when the proud Linier returned next morning, Ade at once fell at his feet and begged for the life of the young hero who had shown himself to be of such prowess that not even a hundred men could subdue him. At first Linier was beside himself with rage, but Ade described how bravely the young man had defended himself, and how he had surrendered to her without hesitation. 'Uncle, you must set him free, for never did I see such a brave and noble youth. To kill him would be to blacken your name for ever. And, if you let him live, who knows what service he may do for you in the future.'

'As to service, I can manage well enough without it,' growled Linier. 'But be assured I shall see to it that he does neither evil nor good to anyone in the future – and be it understood that anyone who calls him friend shall suffer for it.' No one spoke a word, as he glared about him, for they knew how wild

and unbiddable his passions were. He called for the youth to be brought before him and demanded to know who he was and whence he came.

'Until recently I lived in a land ruled over by women,' replied the youth. 'But as yet I do not know my name.'

When he heard this Linier thought the youth was mocking him. He flew into an even greater rage and ordered the prisoner flung into a tower where neither sun nor moon ever shone, and that he be left to languish there. A dish of bread and water was brought to him daily, but otherwise he was left alone. He suffered greatly but never lost hope and was ever cheerful despite his circumstances. In this he was aided by the lady Ade, who often visited his lonely cell in secret and brought him bedding, food and wine – all of which she smuggled in with the connivance of his guards, who in truth thought him ill-treated, so that only fear of their master kept them from setting him free.

One day when Lancelot received a visit from Ade, he asked her to tell him why her uncle had set up such a barbarous custom as that by which he had come to be imprisoned.

The lady looked sadly at the youth. 'My uncle is, as you know too well, a proud and overweening man. Though he cares greatly for his life, he likes to challenge every knight who comes this way. He has made it known throughout the land that adventures await those who come here. This attracts many young errant knights, who know nothing of what awaits them. My uncle has arranged far worse tests – first, they must fight a giant of a fellow, who wields a great club so heavy only two normal men can lift it. Then, if they should succeed – which is seldom the case – they must face two wild lions who are kept in a deep pit. Only then, should good fortune favour them, do the challengers fight with my uncle. Nor is he a poor fighter, and since any who have come through the other trials unscathed are most likely weary and wounded, he has little difficulty in overcoming them. Many have fallen this way.'

'This is an evil custom,' said Lancelot. He was silent for a moment, then asked: 'Lady, you have been more than kind to me. May I ask you one more favour?'

'Whatever you ask I shall try to do,' answered Ade. 'It grieves me greatly to see you in this place.'

'Then, if you can, arrange for me to undertake the tests you have described. I would rather die with my sword in my hand than perish in this filthy place.'

Ade went to her uncle, uncertain what to expect. 'Sir,' she said, 'I would speak to you of the young knight you put in prison recently. I have heard that he greatly honours your strength and courage, and that he longs to attempt the adventures of this place. Uncle, if I have ever done anything to please you, I ask that you give ear to his desire. I will stand surety for him, and if you set him free into my care, I will see to it that in two weeks he will be ready to fight.'

Linier stared at his niece in silence. Then he said: 'It seems this youth has made a great impression on you. Very well, since I am in a mood to favour you today, I shall do as you beg.' He smiled, though without mirth, and added: 'Thus shall I be rid of him for good and have the satisfaction of seeing him humiliated before me.'

'God shall be the judge of that,' replied Ade, and flew to the prison to order the knight's release. At once she had a bath prepared for him and sent for fresh clothing and

good food and drink such as was reserved for the most honoured guests.

Thus, Lancelot swiftly recovered his strength, and as the time appointed for the contest drew near, he began to exercise and practice with sword and spear. Linier, meanwhile, sent word to every noble lord of his acquaintance, telling them there was to be a great festival to celebrate his victory over the nameless knight, who was such a fool that everything he did was but a jest. In his heart he believed that the youth could not possibly succeed in passing the tests prepared for him, and that he, Linier, would soon be boasting of victory over the stranger.

✢ ✠ ✢

ON THE DAY appointed a great crowd gathered at the castle of Limors. The giant warrior arrived, and Linier was to be seen watching the two lions pace back and forth in their pit. He had ordered them to be starved for three days so that they were now quite maddened with hunger.

Soon all was ready, and Lancelot was led out to the ring where he was to face the giant knight. He was permitted no other weapon but his sword, and a shield which the lady Ade herself had commanded to be made for him. Yet he faced his mighty opponent without fear, sizing him up and dancing around him as the huge man lumbered forth with his massive club upraised and an equally large shield held before him. It is certain that, had he succeeded in delivering a blow, that would have been the end of Lancelot, but the youth managed to avoid this and almost immediately, with a single savage blow, cut off the giant's arm, club and all!

Bellowing madly, the huge man tried to fall

upon his opponent, meaning to crush him. But again Lancelot danced away, and delivered a blow to his vital parts which brought the giant crashing to his knees. Another blow severed his head, and Lancelot had the victory without receiving a scratch.

Linier was seen to grind his teeth, and immediately commanded that Lancelot be taken to the lion pit and thrown in with the savage beasts. Maddened by hunger they at once attacked him, one succeeding in opening a deep wound before Lancelot had time to raise his sword. Ignoring the wound, he struck back, splitting the first beast's skull. The second attacked him, driving him back to the wall of the pit. He managed to get in a blow to the creature's foot, which caused it to back away, then he followed up and delivered a death blow to the heart.

Now Linier showed his unworthiness, for he called at once for his armour and had Lancelot pulled forth from the lion-pit and saw to it that he was armed and made ready, without any respite. He appeared on the field looking pale and weak, seeming scarcely able to sit his horse. The onlookers saw where the blood from his wounds ran down from beneath his armour and felt pity for him.

Not so his opponent. Linier was determined to overcome him by any means, fair or foul. He rode his black destrier onto the field and couched his spear. Lancelot steadied himself and urged his own mount forward. They met with a crash and both shattered their spears in pieces. Linier, however, was carried from his horse's back by the force of the blow, and lay grovelling in the dust, cursing his horse like the worthless fellow he was, rather than acknowledging the superiority of his opponent. Lancelot got down from his horse and waited until Linier rose. Then

the two fell to with great fury, striking sparks from each other's steel, and hacking their shields to pieces. Linier fought with care and control, Lancelot responded wildly, knowing that his strength would soon fail, and that he must win swiftly if at all.

Soon enough, the older knight broke through Lancelot's guard, and delivered a blow which wounded him afresh in the place where the lion's claws had already done damage. The youth staggered but recovered quickly. He knew that all was lost unless he could strike back. Summoning all his failing strength, he rushed upon his surprised opponent, who believed him wounded to death, and gave him a blow upon the head which split him to the chin. So great was the force of the blow that blood gushed out of Lancelot's own ears and mouth, and he fell beside the body of his foe.

A great lamentation arose from Linier's folk, and men came forward to carry his body into the castle. No one paid any attention to Lancelot, save for the lady Ade, who came with those knights who were already well-disposed toward him and had him carried inside. Many thought him dead, but the lady detected a slight breath, and ordered a fire lit and the youth's armour removed. Then she tended his terrible wounds, and gave him cordials to bring back his strength, so that he returned from the edge of death and fell into a healing sleep.

When the news became known that the hero still lived, many came to look upon him and to speak to the lady Ade, begging her to save him if she could. For now that Linier was dead and the evil custom of Limors broken, many there became eager that the youth should live, and sought to honour him by offering both the lands and titles of the dead lord, as well as the hand of his niece – which, if truth were known, the lady herself greatly desired.

✠ ✠ ✠

LANCELOT BEGAN SLOWLY to recover, though it was some weeks before he was strong enough to speak. When he did so it was to ask where he was and what had occurred, for he remembered nothing. The lady soon told him everything and praised him greatly for the deeds he had performed. 'For though Linier was my uncle, and a brave and mighty knight, yet he behaved in a cowardly fashion, and deserved to die at your hand.' She smiled, then. 'Let us speak no more of these things until you are healed.'

So the young knight slept, and dreamed, and made a slow recovery, thanks in no small measure to the ministrations of the lady Ade. The fame of his great deeds went out from that place until it reached the ears of King Arthur in his court at Camelot the Golden.

'Who is this brave man?' wondered the king. 'Has no one heard of him?'

'I believe,' said Sir Orphilet, 'that he is the same hero of whom I have spoken before. I hear that he carries a shield with an eagle on it, which I well remember from when I met with him. You may remember, lord King, how he dealt with Galagandries of Moreis, but then declared that he would not come to your court until he had proved himself.'

'That he has certainly done,' said Arthur. 'He should come to us now.'

Queen Guinevere added her own wish to see this brave man, and the king called for someone to go to Limors and fetch the youth. Sir Gawain offered at once and was duly dispatched.

✠ ✠ ✠

MEANWHILE, THE LADY Ade was determined that she should persuade the young knight to go with her to her father's castle, which lay not far from Limors, and, by dint of careful management, so arranged it that they should ride there alone.

It was a bright and cheerful morning when they set out, and Lancelot sang as he rode. He had not a care in the world, save that he wished that another knight might come their way so that he could test his newly recovered strength against him.

It so happened that they did indeed meet such a knight, and that it was none other than Sir Gawain. When Lancelot saw him coming, he set his spear in rest and raised his shield before him. Keen-sighted Gawain saw the shield with the golden eagle upon it and remembered that this was the insignia of the very knight he sought. He stuck his own spear in the earth and propped his shield beside it, then removed his helm and rode open-faced to meet the stranger.

Lancelot privately thought this a great affront, but he greeted Gawain with his customary courtesy.

'What news, sir knight?' asked Lancelot.

'Good news indeed, now that I have found you,' replied Gawain. 'I believe that you are the knight who but lately slew Linier of Limors?'

'I am that man,' said Lancelot guardedly, wondering if Gawain was one of Linier's supporters.

Gawain bowed to the young man. 'I am a knight of the Round Table, and I pray you come with me to King Arthur's court. News of your deeds has outstripped you, and all are eager to make your acquaintance. The queen herself has asked for you, therefore I bid you to come with me.'

'I wonder that you should ask this of me when you know nothing of me save the words of others,' said Lancelot curtly. 'I wish you had not greeted me thus today, for I can go to King Arthur's court whenever I like. I need no messenger to bring me there.'

Gawain, who was ever the most courteous of knights, though at times hot tempered, looked askance at this. 'Sir, I greeted you in good faith, and at the behest of my king. Far be it from me to enforce the invitation. Yet I would ask once again that you accompany me.'

'I ask only that you leave this matter and let my lady and I continue in peace,' Lancelot answered roughly. 'Or else you should collect your weapons and show me how well you can use them.'

At this Gawain's anger began to rise. 'Sir,' he said stiffly, 'I left my weapons behind as a sign that I came in peace. If you would prefer that I went back for them, then I bid you stand ready, for as sure as my name is Sir Gawain of Orkney, I shall not ask another favour of you.'

At this Lancelot brightened. 'I am glad to meet you, Sir Gawain. Your name is well known to me and I have long wished to pit my strength against yours.'

'You shall have your wish,' Sir Gawain cried, and swinging about, rode back to where he had left his spear and shield. Donning his helm and lowering the visor, he rode full tilt at the young knight, who came to meet him eagerly. They met with a resounding crash and both splintered their spears and fell to earth with the strength of their meeting. They fell to fighting on foot with swords, and neither had the advantage.

As they fought, a page bearing the insignia of Camelot the Golden rode up and cried breathlessly to them to stop. 'Sirs, I ask that you leave off this battling, if honour permits it. For I have news of a great tournament this fortnight hence. King Lot of Lothian and Gurnemans de Gohort will lead companies, and both need brave knights to fight alongside them. King Arthur is coming too, with many knights of the Round Table. Be assured that this will be a famous event, and every worthy knight should be there for the sake of his honour.'

Gawain lowered his sword and looked at Lancelot. 'I for one shall be glad to end this needless conflict. It is better that we both attended this tournament than that we waste our blood here for no purpose.' With that he offered his hand.

Lancelot had the grace to look crestfallen, but he too put away his sword and took Gawain's hand. 'I shall be glad to attend the tournament. But first I must complete my journey with this lady. My lord Gawain, I am glad to have met with you, and I hope to continue our sport together again before too long. I bid you greet my lord King Arthur and his queen and tell them that I shall attend upon them as soon as I can.'

With that Sir Gawain took leave of Lancelot and Ade and returned to Camelot the Golden, where he spoke well of the young knight. All marvelled greatly to hear of his skill with sword and spear and at his strange, rough manner.

Meanwhile the young hero continued with the lady Ade until they reached her home, where both were made welcome. The lady's father greeted Lancelot as he might a son, and no comfort was spared him. All talk was of the upcoming tournament and as the date approached the lady Ade made every effort to see that Lancelot was as well prepared as possible, seeing to it that he lacked for nothing in the way of weapons, clothes, and mount. She gave him the best horse in her father's stables and lent him her own brother, Tybalt, as his squire.

The day dawned when they were to set forth. The tournament was to take place in the city of Dyoflê, a setting of great splendour and richness. The lady herself accompanied Lancelot, together with a rich company of her father's household. When they reached the city, they found that Gurnemans had taken the lodging within the walls, while King Lot had pitched his tents outside, as had King Arthur, who occupied a place on a small hill overlooking the city.

Tybalt, a resourceful youth, soon acquired lodgings for his party within the walls and close to the gates. Then, having seen to it that both the lady and the young knight were comfortably installed, he rode forth to gather news of the tournament.

The fields around the city were loud with the clangour of sword on sword and shield against shield. Everywhere knights were practicing for the jousts, breaking spears with each other, fighting with swords and daggers. Lancelot, not wishing to wait a moment, prepared to go at once to the lists. He had ordered a banner of green samite; from which material he had also made a covering for his steed and a surcote to wear above his armour. Then, equipped with a shield of the same green hue, he set forth on his own.

It happened that his way led close to a place where King Arthur and his company had made camp. Sir Kay, proud and boastful as ever, was looking out and saw the green-clad knight approaching. 'Sire,' he said to the king, 'I see a foolish fellow who seeks to challenge us. Give me leave to have some sport with him and, once I have dealt with him,

let me have his fine horse, which is far too spirited a beast for one such as he.'

King Arthur gave his assent, and Kay mounted and rode forth to overtake the knight in green. He, hearing the cries of the pursuing knight, turned and awaited him like a rock. Against this rock proud Kay foundered. He was met by such a buffet that he flew from his horse and landed in a patch of boggy ground, into which he at once sank waist deep in his heavy armour. Those who observed the event, and who knew Kay's boastful demeanour, laughed at his discomfiture.

One of the knights, a popular fellow called Owain, felt sorry for his companion in arms and decided to extract punishment from the stranger. He rode forth as Kay had done, only to meet with the same fate, flying over his horse's crupper and landing in the mud. Tybalt, drawn hither by the noise, took charge of both their mounts by way of forfeit.

King Arthur, who had seen all that passed from the hilltop, remarked that the stranger did well against them. Both the king and his knights marvelled at the skill of the unknown man.

Soon after this, Gawain joined them, and on hearing of the fate of his fellows, declared that this must be the very same warrior whom he had gone in search of. 'For I have not encountered so strong a man as he for many a year.'

✠ ✠ ✠

THE FIRST DAY of the tournament dawned, with bands of knights gathering in companies, some following the leadership of their lords, others seeking out friends and forming their own groups. Then they fell to struggling against each other for the various prizes in the great mêlée.

The knights swirled back and forth in a whirlpool of shifting forces, the sun striking off their weapons and the cries of the knights and their supporters ringing out in the bright air. The knight in green outshone all, so that many spoke of him with wonder. Gawain tried to find him amid the throng, and everywhere he rode he heard only that the green-clad stranger had defeated every knight he encountered.

Gawain told no one of his own suspicions.

Lancelot, meanwhile, returned to his lodging and said to Tybalt: 'Since no one knows who I am, I shall continue to hide my identity.' He commanded the squire to find enough white samite to make a fresh banner and covering for his horse, and that he should bring him a plain white shield.

The next day of the tournament dawned and, on this occasion, just as the knight in green had acquitted himself so well that people looked for his coming, this time the white knight did even better. Wherever the fighting was the thickest, there he appeared, laying into knight after knight, unhorsing and overcoming them with consummate ease. Towards the end of the day he allied himself with a lord named Count Richard, who had fared ill in the mêlée until that moment. With the white knight on his side his fortune soon changed, and that day he captured many brave knights and earned much booty.

Matters fared the same on the third day. This time Lancelot chose red as his colour, and on that day everyone fled from the red knight. Again, he chose to side with Count Richard, and again the nobleman was better off because of it. Finally, the forces of Count Richard and those of King Lot came together and, as before, the red knight carried all before him. At length the stranger and the King of Orkney came face to face, and Lancelot defeated his opponent and captured him with ease.

When King Arthur heard of this, he came to the aid of his ally, who was also Gawain's father. But even the Knights of the Round Table, who as all know numbered among their ranks the bravest and best in the land, could not stand against the stranger. It seemed that, as the day drew to a close and more and more joined in the fray, that his strength increased. So many did he wound or disable, that the tournament was finally halted, though it was supposed to have lasted another seven days.

Everyone now wanted to see the brave hero who had made such a dramatic mark upon the games. Most by now had guessed that he was both the white and the green and red knights, and all wished to know his true identity. He remained in Count Richard's tent, receiving those who sought to do him honour, speaking little and saying nothing of his origins. Here came Sir Gawain, anxious for news of his father, whom Lancelot had sent to Lady Ade to be ransomed, as was the custom in that time. The two knights greeted each other warmly, and once again Sir Gawain asked if the stranger would accompany him to King Arthur, who was close at hand. Again, the young knight declared that his steps lay elsewhere, and that, while in time he would indeed be glad to attend upon the great king, for now he must go elsewhere.

The truth of the matter was that he had learned of a new adventure from Count Richard and was eager to be gone. Gawain parted from him with these words: 'I shall continue to seek news of your deeds and hope that one day we shall meet again. Meanwhile I give you every blessing and wish you well in all your endeavours.'

The two parted on the best of terms, and Lancelot prepared to set forth on his new adventure, accompanied by the Lady Ade and her brother, the faithful Tybalt. Their destination was the Chastel de la Mort, whose master was one Mabuz, an evil and cowardly wretch who possessed a knowledge of magic. A spell was laid upon the castle which ensured that anyone who entered there, even be he the bravest knight in the world, at once became a coward. At the time of which I speak more than a hundred men were imprisoned in the Chastel de la Mort, and it is said that whenever Mabuz became angered, for whatever reason, he ordered one of the prisoners brought forth and summarily killed in front of him. This was the kind of man he was.

But now I must reveal to you certain facts about this cruel and unchivalrous wretch. For as the story tells it, he was none other than the son of the Queen of the Lake herself – she who had stolen Lancelot from his mother's side and brought him up in ignorance of his true lineage. Her reasons for this were subtle. Some hold that she longed for a son who would be faithful and true, for she knew before he was born that her own child would be both a coward and a villain. For this reason she had built for him the Chastel de la Mort and had cast about it the spell I have described, so that her son should never have to face an opponent stronger than himself.

Around the castle lay a rich and beautiful country, which ought by rights to have been enjoyed by Mabuz. But he never went there because of a knight named Iweret, whose lands lay adjacent to his. This Iweret was a proud man who would most certainly have slain the cowardly Mabuz had their paths ever crossed,

for Iweret was given to raiding the lands of his neighbour whenever the fancy took him.

The Queen of the Lake had thus devised a plan – to raise a hero and send him forth to kill Iweret. This was the shameful secret of which she would not speak to Lancelot, and now, as chance or destiny would have it, the young knight found his way to the Chastel, having heard of the evil custom of the place from Sir Richard.

With Ade and Tybalt following a safe distance behind, he rode up to the gates of the castle, and crossed a narrow bridge over a swiftly flowing stream. But the moment he entered the shadow of the gates, all his bravery fell from him and he felt nothing but terror. When he saw Mabuz waiting for him, clad in full armour and mounted upon a fiery steed, he made no attempt to defend himself, but fell grovelling in the dust, where Mabuz several times struck him while he lay defenceless. Then the evil knight pulled off Lancelot's helm, and dragged him by the hair into the castle, where he was carried off to prison.

Ade and her brother, who had seen all that passed, were horrified by the turn events had taken. Tybalt was quick to decry the young knight and name him coward, and though at first the lady Ade defended him, soon she too became convinced that her former hero had lost his courage. 'Alas that I thought him a good and noble man,' she cried. 'I cannot trust him any longer, nor be seen in his company! Such a coward as he would protect neither my honour nor my person.' So distressed was she that she almost swooned, and her brother took the reins of her horse and led her away, whither I know not. Nor shall I speak again of these faithless people.

✠　✠　✠

INSTEAD, LET US speak of Lancelot, who lay in the dungeon of the Chastel de la Mort in great sorrow and travail. So angered was he at his failure to defend himself, and at the fear that was a constant companion to him, that he scarcely ate the food brought by his jailors. The rest of the prisoners, who were not so badly treated, sat down daily to eat at a long table in the dungeon. But Lancelot would not join them, preferring to take a hunk of bread and sit with it against the wall, with his face turned away from his fellows. He grew wasted from lack of food and ceased caring for himself at all, so that he was soon foul and dirty.

It happened at this time that Iweret's men made one of their periodic raids upon Mabuz's lands, burning several villages and pillaging the area. Mabuz himself watched from the walls, sick at heart but too fearful to go forth and defend his property in case Iweret laid an ambush for him.

Then an idea came to the cowardly knight. 'If I send one of my prisoners out to reconnoitre there will be no loss or danger to me,' he thought. 'I will seek out the most cowardly and miserable of the men in my dungeon, for once outside he will become the bravest. And if I never see him again, that will be no loss to me.'

Mabuz went to a secret window that enabled him to observe his prisoners. He saw how Lancelot hid every time anyone entered the dungeon, and how he had ceased to care for his person or to eat the food provided. This marked him out as the ideal subject for the task of facing Iweret. Mabuz therefore had the young knight brought before him, where he stood, cowering and shaking and trying to hide behind his guards. Mabuz told him what was required, but the youth shook his head

and showed the whites of his eyes. 'I could be killed if I go out there,' he cried. 'I beg you not to send me!'

Ignoring his pleas, Mabuz had the terrified knight washed and given fresh clothes, and his armour buckled on him as if he were a child or a sick man. Then he was carried outside, crying and wailing to be set free and left grovelling on the earth with his horse tethered to a nearby tree.

At first Lancelot trembled and hid his face from the world, but in a while the clean air began to clear his clouded mind, and he stood and looked about him in bewilderment – for he remembered nothing that had happened to him since approaching the Chastel de la Mort.

Then Mabuz called down to him from the wall above the gates. 'I remind you that you are a brave and noble man, and that you must undertake a mission for me. If you do not, I shall kill all the prisoners in my dungeon. Do you understand.'

As the circumstances of his imprisonment returned to Lancelot, he looked up fiercely at his recent captor. 'I will do as you ask,' he said. 'But do not try to trick me, for you may be sure I shall find a way to reach you, even behind those coward walls!'

So saying, he rode off towards Iweret's lands. He soon overtook the raiders and dispatched several of them. The rest fled, leaving the young knight master of the field. Now he began to wonder how he might be avenged upon Mabuz and set free those who were kept in confinement. His steps led him to a small monastery which lay close by there. It was called the Sorrowful Abbey, but despite its name Lancelot received a cheerful enough welcome from the abbot, a wise and kindly priest, who informed him that the abbey was in the holding of Iweret. 'Here,' said the monk, 'he offers a tithe of whatever he wins through his knightly skills. If a man is killed by him, he is interred here, and Masses are sung for the repose of his soul. If my lord acquires treasure from taking a knight prisoner, he pays a part of it to us. Thus, we have grown rich, for my lord has slain many brave knights who have come here. If you are wise, unless you wish to join them, you will ride on tomorrow, with God's blessing.'

But Lancelot wished only to hear of the nature of his adversary, and with reluctance, when he knew there was no helping it, the monk told him all.

'Lord Iweret is a mighty prince. He has three kingdoms by inheritance and has acquired more through conquest. He has one daughter, Yblis, who is reckoned to be a great beauty and who is much sought after. Her father has let it be known that any man who wishes to court her must first meet him in combat under a certain linden tree that grows in the Great Wood. It grows beside a fountain that Lord Iweret has had made into a well with a vaulted cover. The spring flows out of a stone lion's mouth into a basin. The tree is green all year round, and on it hangs a bronze bell and a hammer. Whosoever comes to challenge my lord must strike this three times. Before the third blow has ceased echoing, Iweret will be there, fully accoutred, and ready to defend the fountain with his life. I will make no secret of the fact that many men have come there and tried this adventure, and that none have succeeded. Iweret has killed many in the last year alone, and they all lie now beneath the earth in our little graveyard. I counsel you again,' said the abbot, 'avoid this place if you can.'

'That I may not do,' said Lancelot gently. 'Though I thank you for your kindly warning,

my steps must lead me there on the morrow.' For he had remembered that Iweret was the name of his foster mother's greatest foe, for whom he had sought so long – and thus was his determination made all the greater.

'So be it,' answered the abbot. 'Come now and rest and refresh yourself while you may.'

Lancelot stayed that night in the Sorrowful Abbey and next morning set forth for the fountain. As he rode, he became aware that he was entering an enchanted place. The air was still and calm, and on all sides beautiful trees and exotic plants bloomed, many he had never seen the like of before. He remembered that the wood was called Beforet, which means the Beautiful Wood, and now he understood why.

As he went deeper in, he began to wonder if he had not returned to the land beneath the lake. There was much to make this place extraordinary, though Lancelot did not know of it. Not only did a great variety of plants grow there, but many of them had healing properties, known to only a few. It is said that anyone who rode there began at once to feel stronger, and that if he or she were sick they began to recover; while if they were already fit and well, they would become more powerful. This gave Iweret his great strength, and as he came nearer to his adversary's home it affected Lancelot also.

He began to catch glimpses of a rich variety of animal life; bears and deer and foxes, boar and even a lion, and birds of a kind he had never seen, even in the kingdom of the Lake. He began to wonder indeed what paradise this was into which he had come, and if its master could really be so evil. Of Iweret's daughter he wondered also, for the abbot had told him more of her; that she was not only beautiful but wise, and that she lived as a princess, with as many ladies as she wished to attend her.

Of Iweret's castle much has been written that I myself have read, so that it is a wonder to me that Master Thomas did not write of it in his book. It was tall and fair and richly decorated both inside and out. The floors were of marble inlay and the walls and ceilings were decorated with semi-precious stones. Iweret himself slept in a bed with pillars of red gold and a canopy of green samite. The bedding was all of silk and the pillows as soft as down. Iweret was clad in silks and brocades from many distant lands, so that he outshone even King Arthur in his finery.

At length Lancelot came to the linden tree, directed there by the kindly abbot. He tied his horse to a branch and, seizing the hammer which hung upon the tree, beat upon the cymbal so that it was heard throughout the wood and within the castle itself. Then he went to where the fountain gushed forth and, taking off his helm and pushing back his mail coif, he laved his face and hands in the cool water.

Now I will tell something strange and wondrous. On the night just passed, Yblis had dreamed that a strange knight came to the linden tree, and in her dream, she fell in love with him and he with her, and they had joyous sport together. When she awoke, she declared to herself that if he was real, she would marry him. Thus, when she heard the little bell ring forth, she called for her horse to be saddled, and before her father could issue forth to meet the challenge, she reached the tree and saw Lancelot, bare headed, with drops of water from the fountain beading his face and catching the sun, so that he seemed to glow from within.

When she saw that this was indeed the knight from her dream, her heart leapt in her breast, and she got down from her horse and greeted him with gentle words. Struck by her beauty and kindness, though he had never until that moment seen her, he felt as though he had known her for ever, and love entered his heart.

'Never have I seen a lady to whom I felt so deeply drawn,' he said. 'Do not take offence if I tell you that you are the most beautiful creature I ever saw, and that I would do any service that you asked of me, if you will only look with kindness on my suit.'

Yblis smiled and offered her hand to the knight. 'I am of a like mind,' she said, and told him of her dream. 'I ask only one thing – that you do not fight my father today.'

Lancelot's face fell. 'If your father is named Iweret I may not turn aside,' he answered. 'For the sake of my honour and my word to another, ask anything else and I shall do it willingly.'

'You cannot win against my father,' said Yblis. 'For he is well protected. Nor can I bear to see you killed before my eyes. I beg you, do this for me!'

'Alas I cannot,' answered Lancelot resolutely. 'If I am to win, you must let me do so fairly, as is the way of all good knights. Even were I to turn aside now, the time would come when I must meet one as strong or stronger than I. Would you have me behave like a coward, as does Mabuz?' Before Yblis could answer, he struck the cymbal again, angered that Iweret had not yet appeared.

Lady Yblis almost swooned with grief. 'Not even the magic herbs which grow in the valley can cure this sickness,' she thought. 'Nor may I take sides against my own father.'

At this moment, Iweret came in sight,

riding on a huge red horse and clad in the finest armour imaginable. Angered by the repeated beating of the bell his greeting was fierce.

'Where is he who strikes the bell so often?'

'I am here,' answered Lancelot.

'Why are you here?'

'Because I am determined to fight you.'

'That you shall for certain.'

'Nothing would please me better.'

'What do you seek to gain – other than your death?'

'I seek your kingdom and your daughter.'

'Then so be it.'

The two knights set their spears in rest and charged upon one another. Both shafts splintered to matchwood and both riders were bent back against their horse's cruppers. Iweret felt fear, for never before had he encountered an opponent he could not unhorse. And when they drew their swords and fell to hacking and hewing at each other, Lancelot soon delivered a blow which so shook his opponent that he fell to the earth.

Lancelot dismounted and waited for Iweret to get up. As he struggled to his feet the shaken warrior exclaimed: 'Until now, I have fought only children – this knight is a man!' Then they fell to again, and both gave each other a hard time, delivering blow after blow upon their helms and armour, until their blood ran down and watered the earth.

For an hour or more they fought, until Lancelot finally gave his opponent a wound which let out his life. The hero then sat down by the fountain and waited until he could draw breath again. Then he went and raised up the lady Yblis, who had fallen prostrate with grief when her father fell dead. Lancelot bathed her face with water and spoke gently to her.

'How is it with you?' she asked, trembling.

'I am sorry for your father's death,' he said. 'Though it is the way of the world. I hope it does not change your feelings towards me. By all means take out your anger upon me, but do not send me away, I beg you.'

'I shall never do that,' answered Yblis softly. 'I grieve for my father, yet my love for you is greater.' She rose and looked about her. 'We should be gone from here as soon as possible, for I fear that my father's men will not look kindly upon the one who slew him.'

Lancelot hesitated, but he could not gainsay his newfound love, and they both mounted their steeds and rode away through the forest. There they met the abbot of the Sorrowful Abbey, coming to take away the body of the latest challenger. Disbelief marked his face when he saw Lancelot and Yblis, but the lady told him how things stood, and bade him go to her father's castle and bid them take care of her lands and property – for such they now were – until her return.

Lancelot and Yblis rode on through the forest until they came to a sunny glade. There they dismounted and lay beneath the shade of a mighty tree. And there they gave themselves up to the tides of passion and enjoyed each other as well as any man and woman since the time of Adam and Eve. And thus I say that in this instance Master Thomas was mistaken in saying that Lancelot loved only once in his life, though that love was forbidden, and that for Elaine the mother of Galahad he had great love, but for neither that lady nor for Yblis was a love equal to that he felt for Queen Guinevere.

The two stayed happily beneath the trees for a time, until they heard a rider coming towards then, and shortly saw where a maiden came, seated on a white mule. She was dressed in the finest of raiment, and when he saw her the youth recognized her as one of his foster mother's handmaids. He welcomed her by name, and she greeted him from the Queen of the Lake.

'I am glad to have found you,' she said. 'For it is known that you have succeeded in the commission set for you by my Lady. Therefore, I am bidden to tell you your name – that you are called Lancelot, and that you are the son of King Ban of Benoic and of his queen, the Lady Clarine.' Then, while both Lancelot and Yblis marvelled, she went on to tell how Benoic was his rightful home, though it was presently held by others, and how the Queen of the Lake had seen in a vision that he would grow to be the strongest knight in the world, and would kill Iweret, thus setting her true son Mabuz free. Even as they spoke, she told them that the cowardly knight was freeing all his prisoners, just as he had promised to do. 'Thus, all has fallen out as destiny intended,' said the lady. 'Now I bring you a gift from the Queen of the Lake,' and she gave into Lancelot's hands a cunningly carved box.

The young hero was filled with joy, for now he had a name and knew something of his history and the destiny which had brought him there. Gladly he turned to the lady Yblis, who also showed her joy at the news, and together they fell to examining the box.

Within it was a tent of the most remarkable nature that ever was known. When it was folded away it fitted easily into the box or could be carried in the palm of the hand; yet when it was set up, it was as large as its owner wished. You may be sure that Lancelot and Yblis at once erected it and went within. Never was there such an extraordinary object! Each wall was made of a different substance: the first was of samite,

the second of a rare thrice-dipped fabric called *triblat*, the third of a cloth from Arabia called *barracan*, woven from wool and camel's hair, and the fourth from fish skin, sewn by the women of a barbarous land far to the north. But this is not all, for I must tell you that the tent pole was made of emerald, and that around it were written three mottoes. These, as I hear tell, were as follows. The first one read: *Love Dares Anything*. The second: *Love is a Madness that Never Dies*. The third: *Love without Measure*.

The reason these words were set about the tent pole was to ensure that only those who were utterly faithful could enter there. Within the tent was a mirror that showed the true semblance of lovers, each to other. When Lancelot and Yblis entered, they looked within it and the lady saw only her lord, and he no other but her. But I have heard it tell in other books that when Lancelot first set eyes upon the queen, the reflection in the mirror ever after showed only her – but of this no more is told.

✛ ✛ ✛

SO, LANCELOT DISCOVERED his true name and achieved the adventure of the Fountain, bringing about his foster mother's desire by freeing her cowardly son from the shadow of Iweret. And though it is said that Lancelot's love for Yblis was long-lasting, others tell a different tale, as all who have read Master Thomas's book well know. For soon Lancelot went to King Arthur's court as he had promised, and became the greatest of the Round Table knights, and he remained a great friend to Sir Gawain until dark times fell upon them all at Camelot the Golden. But he also fell upon a great love for the queen and broke the hearts of both she and her lord. In time, he won back his own lands, that had been his father's, and brought his aged mother home to die in her own place. But to this day men still speak of Lancelot du Lac, the son of the Lake, rather than Lancelot son of Ban of Benoic. Of his fame we need speak no more here, other than in passing in the stories that follow. Instead, we shall turn to the story of another brave knight, whose name was Palomides, who sought after the strangest creature of all.

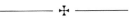

EXPLICIT HOW SIR LANCELOT FOUND HIS NAME.
IMPLICIT THE TALE OF THE QUESTING BEAST.

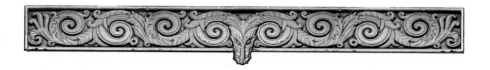

7: THE TALE OF PALOMIDES AND THE QUESTING BEAST

✛

THOSE WHO HAVE READ MASTER THOMAS'S MIGHTY BOOK WILL KNOW THE STORY OF SIR PALOMIDES – HOW HE AND HIS BROTHERS, SIR SAFERE AND SIR SEGWARIDES WERE THE ONLY SARACENS TO SIT AT THE ROUND TABLE, AND HOW ALL THREE DID MIGHTY DEEDS, BOTH TO THEIR OWN HONOUR AND THAT OF THE FELLOWSHIP. IN PARTICULAR, THE STORY THAT MOST WILL REMEMBER IS HOW SIR PALOMIDES CAME TO FOLLOW THE QUESTING BEAST, THAT SOME CALL THE BLATANT BEAST, AND OTHERS THE YELPING BEAST, ON ACCOUNT OF THE SOUND OF TWELVE COUPLES OF HOUNDS THAT ISSUED FROM ITS BELLY.

✛ ✛ ✛

THOUGH I DO so with trepidation – for who dares question the skill of master Thomas? – I have noticed that he does not say how Sir Palomides came to follow the Beast, nor how his quest ended. These omissions are doubtless due to pages lacking in the great books which Sir Thomas studied. Also, it may be that, knowing the story of the Beast's origin, he felt it was too grim a tale to include in his great retelling. I must confess that even I have hesitated whether to put it here – yet my desire to recognize the quality of Sir Palomides, and the strangeness and wonder of the tale, overcame my reluctance. Thus, I have included the beginning and end of the story, since Sir Thomas wrote all else there

was to say concerning the Saracen knight. And if the French books do not mention it, others do, most especially in the language of Italy, where much is told that other lands do not.

✛ ✛ ✛

THE STORY BEGINS in the ancient kingdom of Babylon, and concerns a noble lord named Esclabor, whose wife was out of Ireland. Her name was Etain, a name of one of the ancient faery women of that land, and it happened that one day, when she was no more than fifteen summers, she was playing by the shore of the sea. On that day there came a Saracen ship that raided along the coast of Ireland. Many good people were killed in these attacks, but as word spread, so the men of Ireland rose up and struck at the incomers, slaying many of them, so that they hastened back to their ship and set sail at once. Amongst the booty they had secured was the young maiden Etain, who they designated for the slave market, because of her fair skin and great beauty. But when they returned to Babylon, the Lord Esclabor happened to catch sight of the fair maiden from Ireland, and at once fell in love with her. It was no hard thing for him to purchase her freedom from the raiders, and having done so, he offered to have her returned to her home. But in truth, the maiden had fallen in love with the gentle Saracen, and soon they were married.

In time, the lady gave birth to three sons: Safere, Segwarides, and the youngest and last, Palomides. The family were content with their lives and their three sons grew to be kind and gentle boys in their own right – though Palomides was always of a dreamy nature, and spent long days reading the stories of the great heroes of older times.

At this time the Sultan of Babylon owed fealty to the Emperor Lucius of Rome, and each year he designated a noble lord to carry the offerings of riches to the Eternal City, and to remain there for a year as hostage to Babylon's goodwill towards Rome.

This year the lot fell to Esclabor, who was greatly saddened by this for, as he told the lady Etain, he knew not if he would ever return. Etain, who knew some little magic that was part of her birthright in Ireland, told her husband that he should not go alone, but that she and their children should go with him to Rome. 'For there, perhaps, a greater adventure awaits us.'

So, the family set forth, accompanied by a force of the sultan's soldiers to protect the offering of gold and silver for the emperor.

This time, the emperor had but lately received a visit from Merlin, who had brought to his attention the lady Avenable, whom he made his empress.[*] She and the lady Etain soon became friends and from this time Esclabor also spent time in the emperor's company, and their children played amongst the fountains and gardens of the great city.

☩ ☩ ☩

IT WAS AT this time that word reached Rome of a young king named Arthur – how he attained his heritage by drawing the sword from the stone. Other marvels too were spoken of, and even in the heart of the empire the Round Table of Camelot the Golden was spoken of – such that the emperor began to turn his attention towards Britain, as Sir Thomas has related in his book.

But at this time the war between Britain and the empire was still far off, while the stories of wonder that were told in the emperor's palace made many ponder the worthiness of the far-off land of Britain and its king.

At this time the emperor had a pet lion, which he had raised from a cub and of which he was greatly fond. But as it grew into a mighty beast, many amongst the emperor's courtiers advised him to keep the creature at a distance, or put it away from him entirely, in case it might attack him. This advice the emperor did not take, until the day came when, playing with the beast in the palace garden, the lion turned upon its master and would have rent him in twain, were it not for

---

* See *The Story of Avenable* pp. 12–17

Esclabor, who happened to be walking there. Hearing the emperor's cries for help the Babylonian drew his sword and fell upon the lion, pulling back its head and thrusting his blade into its throat. The emperor thus escaped with little more than a few scratches, and such was his gratitude to Esclabor he at once gave him the favour of high office in the court.

This, not surprisingly, made Esclabor very unpopular amongst the courtiers who constantly sought privilege from the emperor. Several of these men elected to kill the Babylonian, and on a particular day when he was preparing to go into the forest, they went ahead and lay in wait for him. But, at the last moment, the lady Etain, having seen in a vision that those who sought her husband's death were preparing to ambush him, detained him with many subtle questions which delayed his departure. In the meantime, the emperor's nephew Gratian rode alone through the forest and, being mistaken for Esclabor, was killed in his stead.

When he learned of this, the emperor was beside himself, and began to seek out those who were responsible, meaning to execute them. At first, he could find none to confess their plot against Esclabor, and it was then that the lady Etain came forward and told him what she had seen in her vision.

She was able to tell him the names of all those who had plotted against her husband, and the emperor prepared to arrest these men. But before he could do so, the lady Etain spoke again. 'Sire, if you proceed in this way you will have many others set against you, perhaps to the detriment of your rulership. Instead, I would advise that you make peace with these men, and that you should send my lord and I and our family away from Rome, where they can be no threat. Let us go instead to the land of Britain, there to visit with the young King Arthur, of whom so much has been spoken here in recent days. There we may build a new life for ourselves and end this rivalry between my husband and your courtiers.

At first the emperor was disinclined to follow this advice but, knowing the wisdom of the lady Etain, he decided to do as she suggested. Thus it was that Esclabor, his wife and their children went aboard a ship bound for Britain, carrying with them many rich gifts from the emperor, both for themselves and for King Arthur.

✝ ✝ ✝

THE STORY TELLS that the journey was long and perilous, but that at length Esclabor and his family arrived in Britain. Knowing nothing of the land, they followed the advice of the lady Etain, whose knowledge led them to the kingdom of Gales in Northumbria. There, they met and were given shelter by King Pellinore, of whom much is written in Master Thomas's book, and who became one of the first to sit at the Round Table.

It is told that Pellinore had a fate laid upon him, passed down from generation to generation in his family. This tradition was that he must follow a strange Beast, that wandered the world, and this he had done for many years. But fast as he pursued it, it went faster before him, so that he came no closer to it than on the first day his quest began. So old was this tradition that none now remembered its origin, but while he lived none might relieve him of it.

At this time, it happened that the king had returned to his home for a time, and thus

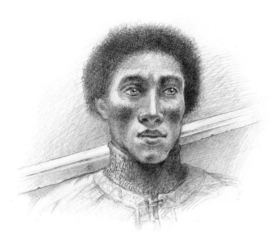

⇢ Palomides ⇠

he was glad to welcome the travellers. He quickly grew to like Esclabor and his family – in particular Palomides, whose eagerness to learn all things brought the king great joy. Most especially did the boy ask about the Beast that Pellinore followed, and the fierce old king described it to him often.

It so happened that ever-wandering Merlin visited Gales at this time, and as the company sat to meat, he joined them. Noticing how King Pellinore looked often towards Palomides, he took him aside. 'Why do you look so often at the boy?' asked Merlin.

'I know not,' answered Pellinore. 'I feel that he should somehow be kin to me, though he comes from a far-off land.'

'He is no kin to you,' answered Merlin. 'But I tell you now, that in time to come he will follow the Beast that you have sought for these long years.'

'How is that possible?' demanded Pellinore. 'You know that it is my fate to follow the Beast while I live.'

'Because you have no sons,' Merlin said. 'When your life ends there will be no one to take up the quest.'

'Then I must succeed in my search,' said King Pellinore.

'That you shall not do,' said Merlin. 'Though you follow the Beast to the last day of your life, you shall not overtake it.'

'That shall be as God wills,' answered Pellinore fiercely. 'For I shall not cease while I draw breath.'

Merlin left the king and went in search of Esclabor, telling him that he should journey to Camelot the Golden, and that his sons would one day sit at the Round Table. He also bade him ask King Pellinore to make Palomides a knight.

This the king was glad to do, and he made no secret that Merlin had foretold that the young man would one day achieve the quest for the Beast. At this, the lady Etain sought out Merlin and spoke with him, asking why her youngest child should be made to follow a creature none could catch, when he might earn honour and fame at King Arthur's court.

'Honour and fame shall be his,' replied Merlin. 'And much more besides. But nevertheless, he will come to follow the Beast when King Pellinore is no longer alive.'

The lady Etain, who knew of the secrets held by Merlin, bowed her head. 'But,' she said, 'will you not at least tell me the nature of this Beast?'

Knowing of her heritage of magic, Merlin said: 'I shall tell you the history of the Beast – though it is a grim tale, and one that few now living could relate.'

Then he told her how, many years before, a king named Ypomens had two children – a son and a daughter – and how the daughter evinced an unnatural love for her brother. When she declared herself to him, the youth turned away in horror, and distraught by

81

this rejection the girl ran away into the forest, intending to take her own life. But there she met a fair young man who persuaded her to lie with him and taught her to hate her brother. So great was her feeling against him whom she had previously loved that she went to her father and gave false witness, saying that it was her brother who had approached her with vile suggestions. The king, sickened by this, ordered his son to be killed and allowed his daughter to decide the manner of her brother's death. Filled with ire against him, she declared that he should be thrown to a pack of dogs that had been kept without food for seven days.

This was done, but before he died this dreadful death, the young prince declared that his sister would give birth to a monster, begotten upon her by the fair-seeming youth in the forest. The book does not say what nature of being this was – some believe him to be a demon out of Hell, others that he was of faery stock; but whatever the truth, when her time came the king's daughter gave birth to the creature that has since been known as Glatisant, the Questing Beast.

Master Thomas described it thus:

'The Questing Beast ... had in shape a head like a serpent's head, and a body like a leopard, buttocks like a lion, and footed like an hart: and in his body there was such a noise as it had been the noise of hounds questing, and such a noise that beast made wheresomever he went...'*

Within moments of its birth, the Beast fled into the forest and when King Ypomens heard of it, and how one of his daughter's

servants had died with the shock of seeing it, he was so sickened that he ordered his daughter to be strangled and her body thrown into the wood to be devoured by the creatures that lived there. 'As for the Beast itself,' Merlin concluded, 'word of its existence began to be spoken of across the land, and knights came in search of it, believing that to catch the creature would bring them honour. But I say this to you, my lady, that none of them shall achieve this quest other than your son, Palomides.'

'Why should he be singled out for this dreadful task?' demanded the lady Etain.

'I do not know why it should be your son and no other,' replied Merlin. 'Only that it is so.'

'This is an evil thing you have prophesied,' said Etain.

'Let me tell you, lady, that all three of your sons will flourish at the Round Table and shall be counted amongst the foremost of the Fellowship.'

Having spoken these words Merlin was suddenly gone, though where he went none knew.

Next day, Lord Esclabor and his lady took their leave of King Pellinore and journeyed to Camelot the Golden. There, having heard word of them, King Arthur welcomed the family, and at once offered Esclabor a place at the Round Table.

'Nay, Sire,' replied the Babylonian. 'You need young knights, not old. But I recommend to you my sons, who shall undoubtedly shine amongst your company.'

King Arthur replied that he would gladly receive them, provided that they agreed to be baptized at the feast of Pentecost. To this Esclabor agreed, for the lady Etain had herself been baptized before she was taken from

---

* Book IX. Chapter xiii

her home, and her sons had been raised with the knowledge of both beliefs.

Next day the festival of Pentecost was celebrated, and there came the Lord Esclabor and his eldest sons to be baptized. But of Palomides there was no sign. King Arthur was displeased by this and sent men to find the youth. At this moment Merlin appeared amongst them and demanded to know why Arthur should delay the ceremony because Palomides was not to be found.

'Where is he?' demanded King Arthur.

'You shall not find him at this time,' replied Merlin. 'He has already begun a quest that will lead him for many years and bring him great honour in turn.'

'What quest is that?' Arthur asked. But Merlin remained silent and therefore were Lord Esclabor and Safere and Segwarides baptized, and the two youths were made Knights of the Round Table. But of Palomides no more was heard for some time thereafter.

Soon after this, King Arthur himself encountered the Questing Beast while out hunting, as Master Thomas has told, and on the same day encountered King Pellinore, who was even then seeking the Beast. Merlin came there in disguise and told the king the nature of the Beast,* which he named Glatisant, after the sound of the hounds yelping within it, or as the French say *glapissant* – and after that Merlin went deeper into the forest and found Palomides sitting beneath a tree.

'Who are you?' asked Merlin.

Palomides looked at him sullenly but refused to give his name or his purpose.

Then Merlin said: 'I know you are the youngest son of the Lord Esclabor, for we have met before.' Then he was in his own

shape again and Palomides remembered him from the castle of King Pellinore. He leapt up angrily and demanded to know why Merlin came looking for him.

'I ask only what you will do, now that you have refused baptism and left your family behind.'

Palomides declared: 'I was taken from my own land without my consent, and now to this kingdom. I have been made a knight though I have yet to prove myself and have not sought it. Now they seek to baptize me so that I am like all the rest! I am no child that I should be so pulled from place to place at the behest of others. Therefore, I have come here to the forest in order to consider what I may do next.'

Then Merlin said: 'Palomides, I will tell you what you must do now. You have a long journey before you. It will begin in your mother's land of Ireland, where you will meet a woman of great beauty whose love you will seek. But she is destined for another and for many years you and he will be both comrades and rivals for her love. And for much of that time you will follow the Beast called Glatisant, that King Pellinore currently seeks. Only time will say whether or not you complete your quest, but while you are engaged upon it you shall earn much honour and encounter many who will seek to destroy you. But you shall more often vanquish them than not, for this is your path.'

When he had heard the words of Merlin, Palomides was somewhat cheered, for although the journey sounded hard, yet he looked to discover more of these things, just as he had done as a child. And those who have read of his adventures in Master Thomas's great book, will know that the woman he came to love was Queen Isolt of Ireland,

---

* *Le Morte D'Arthur* Book 1. Ch. xix.

whose own greatest love was Sir Tristan, he who was second only to Sir Lancelot in strength amongst those who sat at the Round Table. But that story has been told often and therefore I will not write of it here, but go instead to the end of Palomides' quest, which came many years later, towards the time of the breaking of the Round Table and the end of the age of Arthur.

In that time Palomides' fame was as great as any of the Fellowship, which he had joined some time after his brothers because of the mighty deeds he accomplished. Yet there were those who doubted him and stood against him since he refused to accept baptism. Many spoke out against him for his part in the dark webs of love between Tristan and Isolt, and their long and bitter struggle with King Mark of Cornwall. One in particular, Sir Dinadan, mocked Palomides openly, declaring that he had spent too much of his time pursuing the Irish queen, rather than following the Questing Beast, which Merlin had long since predicted he would follow after the death of King Pellinore. Angered by this, Palomides departed the court, determined to devote himself again to the quest for the Beast.

✦ ✠ ✦

KNOWING THAT GLATISANT was most often sighted within the confines of the Great Wood, Palomides went there, penetrating more deeply than ever before into the dark webs of the forest. There, he found himself within a sheltered grove, where a spring bubbled from the ground. Here Palomides rested, giving his horse to drink, and finding respite in the shade of the trees. There, later, he heard a sound that he knew all too well: that of the barking of twelve couples of hounds. At once he concealed himself amid the trees, drawing his mount close to him and quieting it. There he saw the Questing Beast come to drink at the spring, just as had King Arthur many years before. Only while it drank was the sound of barking silenced from within it.

Remembering the times that he had hastened to capture and slay the Beast, and how it had always escaped him, Palomides remained still and watched while it drank. When it had fulfilled its need the barking within it was stilled for a time.

Still Palomides watched.

He saw how the Beast looked always to the West, where the sun was beginning its descent, and how it set off in that direction. Moving quietly Palomides mounted his horse and followed the creature until, as the sun set, Glatisant lay down and slept. Palomides stayed close, but still did not approach the Beast, and very soon the sound of barking began again in the creature's belly, so that it awoke and moved on once again.

All that night and for many days thereafter Palomides followed where the Questing Beast led. He observed that it travelled always towards the sun, and that it rested at sunrise, midday, and sunset, drinking when it could, but seeming neither to eat nor sleep.

Palomides himself began to grow weary, and his horse also, until at last, on a day when he had ridden hard in pursuit of the Beast, his mount fell dead beneath him.

Palomides then knew great despair, for it seemed now that he had little chance of catching the Beast, nor could he think where he might attain a fresh mount. So he left his spear and shield beside the dead horse and followed after the Beast on foot.

Soon the weight of his armour, and the

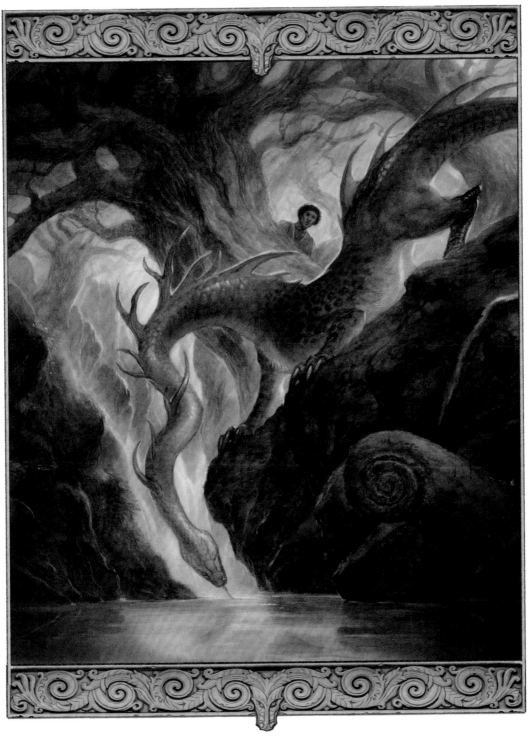

PLATE 3: *'There he saw the Questing Beast come to drink at the spring, just as had King Arthur many years before'*

heat of the day, began to tell on him, but he kept moving despite this. At length, he found himself on a narrow path that led between high banks to a place where a spring bubbled forth amid rocks. There, the Questing Beast had stopped to drink, and when Palomides looked around him he saw that there was no other way out of that place save the path on which he stood.

With a cry he drew his sword and ran towards the Beast which, when it heard him, turned at bay. Rising up on its hind legs, it stretched forth its long neck and snatched the sword from Palomides' hands. Then it advanced upon the knight, hissing and spitting like a serpent, while all the time the dogs bayed within it.

Palomides drew his dagger and leapt towards the Beast, pressing forward into its very shadow. And there he drove the knife deep within its belly and ripped a terrible wound therein. The beast screamed and fell upon its side, and there burst from within it the twelve couples of hounds that had lived within it since its birth.

Palomides feared for his life, believing that he would be torn to pieces, but the hounds were only interested in the water of the spring, and as they fell upon it and drank, so they grew weaker and thinner, until at last, without the body of the Beast to sustain them, the life ebbed from them and they fell dead, one after the other, by its side.

A great weariness now fell upon Palomides, and he desired more than anything to sleep. When he looked at the Questing Beast, he saw that it was dead, yet its eyes were open, and it seemed to him that it looked at him in a way that made him fearful. Therefore, before he slept, he tied a rope around the creature's neck, and the other end to a tree, and so he

settled down and fell into a deep sleep that lasted for three days and nights.

When he woke, he looked where the Questing Beast had lain, but saw it not. Instead, where it had rested, he saw an old woman, her body thin and frail as bracken, her wrists held by the rope that fastened her to a tree. Palomides was filled with wonder at this, and also with fear, for he saw that her eyes were those of the Questing Beast. But the old woman spoke to him: 'Do not be afraid Sir Palomides, for I am she that was once called Glatisant, and for many years I have awaited your coming in the hope that you would set me free. Now I ask but one thing, that you carry me to a place where I may find rest and be baptized at last – for since I have only now taken upon me the form of a mortal, I never had a chance to make my peace with God.'

So Palomides lifted the old woman, who in truth weighed but a little, and put her on his shoulder, and then he made his way back through the forest, his steps now lighter than ever before. There he met with a man who stood leaning upon a staff, and the story tells that this was none other than Blaise, that many have said was Merlin's teacher, and one of the wisest men in the world at that time.

As the knight hesitated, the old man said to him: 'Palomides, I have come to find you and to bring you to the place of rest, and also to help this lady that you carry.'

He led the way through the forest until they came to a hut, hidden amongst the trees, and there the knight laid down the old woman, who was too weak to move, and Blaise baptized her and gave her the last rites – for despite his age and ancient wisdom, he was a priest of the new faith as well as of an older path.

Soon after, the old woman breathed her

last and Palomides and Blaise buried her in a grave in the shade of the ancient trees. Then, since he had been away from court so long, Blaise told Palomides how things stood in the realm of Arthur – how the love of Lancelot for the queen had caused war to break out. He spoke also of the enmity which had grown between Lancelot and Gawain, after the former had accidentally slain Sir Gareth, Gawain's brother.

'I must return at once to Camelot the Golden,' Palomides said. 'For the king shall have need of me.'

'Is there any other thing that I may do for you?' asked Blaise. For he had already found the knight a new steed, but his wisdom told him there was yet another thing the knight needed.

Palomides hesitated. 'There is one thing that I would wish for, if it were possible. I would wish to see my mother and to have her know that I have accomplished my quest at last.'

Blaise nodded his head and spoke some ancient words that called to them the Lady Etain, who because of her faery blood had lived far longer than most and was able to hear the words the old man spoke. She and Palomides rejoiced in their reunion, and Etain heard all the story of the Beast and how it had been resolved at last.

Then Palomides took his leave of Blaise and the Lady Etain, and set off for Camelot the Golden, where he would stand together with King Arthur on the field of Camlann, and there give his life as did so many of the Round Table knights.

Thus is the story ended that is told in full at last. And be it known that Palomides was remembered by those of the Fellowship that lived after those dark times, and that he was ever after known as the Knight of the Questing Beast.

Now we shall turn to the story of the one who was called the Fair Unknown, or as it is written in the Latin tongue, *Libeaus Desconus*.

EXPLICIT THE STORY OF THE QUESTING BEAST.
IMPLICIT LIBEAUS DESCONUS.

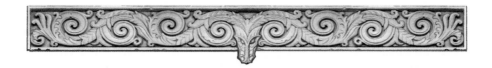

8: THE ADVENTURE OF THE FAIR UNKNOWN

THOSE WHO KNOW MASTER THOMAS'S GREAT BOOK WELL, WILL DOUBTLESS RECALL THE STORY OF SIR GARETH OF ORKNEY, FOURTH SON OF KING LOT AND QUEEN MORGAUSE, WHO CAME TO CAMELOT THE GOLDEN UNKNOWN AND UNDERTOOK ADVENTURES THAT MADE HIM FAMOUS. LATER HE WAS KNIGHTED BY NONE OTHER THAN SIR LANCELOT HIMSELF. YET THERE IS ANOTHER TALE THAT I WOULD TELL HERE – THAT OF ANOTHER WHOSE NAME WAS HIDDEN AT THE BEGINNING OF HIS FIRST GREAT ADVENTURE. IT MAY BE THAT SOME WHO READ THIS WILL SEE A SHADOW OF THAT OTHER STORY HERE. SUCH THINGS HAPPEN MANY TIMES WITHIN THE COLLECTIONS OF TALES THROUGH WHICH I HAVE SEARCHED TO MAKE THIS BOOK. STORIES LIKE THIS CARRY US TO THE HEART OF THE GREAT WOOD, THAT OTHERS TERM 'THE FOREST OF ADVENTURE'. THE TRUE IDENTITY OF THE NAMELESS HERO WILL BE OF GREAT INTEREST TO ALL WHO SEEK TO KNOW THE FULL HISTORY OF THE ROUND TABLE.

✢ ✢ ✢

IN THE MONTH of August King Arthur held court at Caerleon. Most of the great knights were present, too many to list. In the evening they sat down to supper, and you may be sure it was the best meat and drink to be had in all the land! While they were eating a young man rode his horse right into the hall and up to the dais where King Arthur, the queen and several of the knights were sitting.

'Sir. Be welcome,' King Arthur said. 'Dismount and join us.'

'I thank you, noble Lord,' replied the youth. 'But before I do so I crave a boon. Since this is Arthur's court, I know that I will not be refused – whatever it may be and whatever comes of it.'

'So long as it gives offence to no one, I shall grant it,' Arthur replied.

Squires came forward to hold the youth's horse and to help him unarm. His fine armour and weapons were admired, as was the shield he carried, which bore a lion of ermine on an azure field. A place was found for him at table and fresh food and drink set before him and water with which to wash his hands.

When he was seated, King Arthur sent his butler Sir Bedivere to ask the youth's name and parentage. When Bedivere returned, it was to say that the youth had no name that he knew, but that he had always been called 'Fair Son' by his mother, and that of his parents he knew only she. Of his father's name or rank he knew nothing. When Sir Lancelot heard this he looked with kindness on the youth, remembering his own quest for a name and title.*

King Arthur looked to where the youth sat and said: 'Since you have no name and we must call you something, I shall give you a name. Let it be *Libeaus Desconus*.' (Which is to say, in the English tongue 'The Fair Unknown'.)

As they were speaking, there came two more people into the hall. In front came a maiden fair as a summer flower, riding upon a horse the colour of clouds. Behind her, urging on the horse, came a dwarf, who for all his small stature had a face of great nobleness and beauty. Reigning in her mount before the king, the maiden spoke: 'King Arthur, I am here to ask for your help for my mistress, the Lady of Sinadoun. She is held captive against her will in the city of that name, that was once fair but now is desolate. The only way she can be rescued is for a single knight, who must be the best and bravest of all your Fellowship, to endure the adventure of the Fearsome Kiss.'

All this poured forth in a rush of words, and when the maiden fell silent all the court was silent too. King Arthur looked around, seeking a face among the knights whom he might choose to send on this adventure, even though none there knew what its nature was. Before he had time to name anyone, the youth whom he had but now called the Fair Unknown leapt up.

'Sire,' he cried, 'I claim the boon I was promised – that I be allowed to undertake this task.'

King Arthur frowned. 'This is too great a task for one so young and untried.'

'Sire, you gave your word to me that you would grant any boon I asked save that it did no disgrace to anyone. I ask for nothing more than that you honour your word.'

'Very well,' said the king. 'But first, come near, that I may make you a knight of the Round Table, for only thus may you undertake this adventure.'

As the Fair Unknown approached the king, the maiden, who had been silent thus far, cried aloud. 'King Arthur! I asked for the best knight of your Fellowship – not the worst. I see that I came hither in vain, and that I must return to my lady and tell her that there is no help coming from King Arthur!' And before the king could answer, she turned her horse and rode out of the hall, the dwarf trotting at her heels.

'Well,' said King Arthur to the Fair Unknown. 'Do you still wish to pursue this course?'

'I do, Sire,' the youth replied.

'Then I declare before all that you are this day made a knight of the Round Table.'

✢ ✤ ✢

---

* See 'How Sir Lancelot Earned his Name' pp. 55–77

88

S O THE FAIR Unknown was knighted, and before he set forth in pursuit of the maiden, Sir Gawain came forward and offered to arm him, for there was something about the youth that he admired, seeing somewhat of his own high courage in him. Indeed, it seemed almost that he knew the lad, though he could not think how this might be. As well as arms and weapons, Gawain entrusted to him one of his own squires, a clever young lad named Robert.

Armed and accoutred, the Fair Unknown rode swiftly away from Caerleon in search of the maiden and the dwarf. Soon he espied them on the road and hastened to overtake them. The maiden's welcome was far from encouraging.

'Is that you, boy?' she declared. 'Run home before you get hurt. I need a real knight to help my lady, not a beardless boy, only knighted today!'

'My lady,' answered the Fair Unknown. 'The task has been given to me by my lord King Arthur. I must follow you and attempt this adventure.'

To his surprise the dwarf, whose name was Tidogolain, spoke up.

'Lady, I think you should let the boy try his luck. After all, even a newly minted knight is better than none.'

Despite his words the maiden continued to pour scorn on the Fair Unknown, though there was nothing she could do to stop him riding with her. So they journeyed until they came to a place that was known far and wide as the Perilous Ford. It had an evil reputation and most people avoided it. But the maiden's road lay this way, and the Fair Unknown must needs follow her.

As they approached the ford, they saw a rough hut on the far side of the water, outside which leant a shield that was one half gold and the other silver. In the entrance sat a tall knight playing chess with two youths. His name was Blioberis, and he was as proud and evil-hearted as he was strong. When he saw the Fair Unknown approaching with the maiden and the dwarf, he sprang up and the two youths began arming him. The squire Robert brought the arms that Gawain had given to the Fair Unknown, and likewise prepared his master for battle.

Seeing this, the maiden turned to her unwanted companion. 'You had best be going home now,' she said. 'This is a most fierce and terrible knight, and he will certainly kill you.'

But the Fair Unknown ignored her words and rode to the edge of the water. 'Sir,' he called out to the other knight. 'Will you let us pass? I am on a mission for King Arthur on behalf of this maiden's mistress.'

'I have held this ford for seven years,' Blioberis snorted. 'I am not about to give it up to a stripling.'

'Then you are no more than a brigand,' replied the Fair Unknown, and called out to Robert for a spear.

The two men rode together and met with a crash in the midst of the ford. Water splashed high and both were unhorsed, but while the Fair Unknown escaped unhurt, his spear went directly to its target, opening a deep wound in Blioberis's side. The two knights drew their swords and went at it for some while longer, but Blioberis soon grew weak from loss of blood, and finally he fell to his knees and begged for his life.

The Fair Unknown agreed to spare him, but made him promise that as soon as he was fit to ride, he would go directly to Arthur and place himself at the mercy of the king.

To this Blioberis agreed, and as Robert helped unarm his master the dwarf was heard to remark to no one in particular that the young knight had acquitted himself well, and that it was really a very good thing that he was with them.

The maiden merely shrugged her shoulders and again suggested to the young knight that he should return home. And again, just as firmly, he declined.

So they rode on, leaving the wounded Blioberis in the care of his attendants. But, when the Fair Unknown was scarcely out of sight, the proud knight began thinking of how he might be avenged for the disgrace he had suffered. His thoughts turned to three companions with whom he had lately spent time, and who were expected back at the ford any time. These three were Elin the Fair, the Lord of Graie; the Strong Knight of Saie; and William of Salebrant.

That night they returned from journeys of their own, and finding Blioberis lying wounded in his hut asked what had occurred. Blioberis told them the whole story and begged them to pursue the unknown knight and avenge him. 'Kill or capture him, I care not,' he said darkly. 'Only thus may I be freed from the promise I made to him. I have no wish to surrender to King Arthur.'

✞ ✞ ✞

THAT NIGHT THE Fair Unknown, the maiden, the dwarf and their servants camped in a meadow, and there the young knight learned that his proud and unresponsive charge was named Helie. Beyond this they spoke little and soon settled down for the night. Later, when the moon cast its cool light over the land, the Fair Unknown woke suddenly to hear a voice from the depths of the forest crying out for help.

Helie and the others were also awoken, and the young knight asked if they heard the voice. The maiden at once dismissed the cries as something to be ignored. 'If you were thinking of going to answer that call, you would be advised not to. There will be adventures enough on the road ahead.'

The Fair Unknown answered courteously. 'Nonetheless,' he said. 'It is my duty as a knight of the Round Table to answer a cry for help.'

'Go then, if you want,' answered Helie, tossing her head. 'I certainly care nothing for what you do. You have followed me against my wishes, and now you are leaving me against my advice.'

The Fair Unknown called out to Robert to saddle his horse and fetch his armour. Then, once he was properly accoutred, he set off through the forest in the direction from which the cries seemed to come. The maiden, not liking to be left alone in the forest, elected to come too, though she warned the knight that ill would come of his foolhardiness.

Soon they came to a clearing, and there they spied two huge loathsome giants camped beside a fire over which they were cooking a wild pig. One of the two was turning a spit and watching his companion, who was crouched over the body of a woman. They were arguing, in their ugly, barbarous voices, over who should have her first, while the woman herself lay half dead with fear, her cries dwindled to mere whimpers as she watched her terrible captors preparing to rape her.

The maiden Helie whispered to the Fair Unknown to hasten away from that place as quickly as possible. 'I know of these evil creatures,' she said. 'They have laid waste the

90

entire region for many months. Their appetites know no bounds.'

The Fair Unknown was not even listening. Sizing up the situation in a glance, he spurred his mount into the clearing and skewered the giant nearest the woman with a single thrust of his spear, tossing him aside into the fire. The second giant was up and waving a huge club and roaring his defiance, but before he could strike, the young knight thrust again with his spear, then, drawing his sword, split the giant's head in two with a single blow.

The whole thing was over in a moment, and Tidogolain clapped his hands with delight. 'See, my lady!' he cried. 'See how well the young knight performs. I think perhaps you were wrong about him.'

Crestfallen, Helie now craved the young knight's pardon, which he accepted with a silent nod of the head, turning his attention to the woman he had rescued from the giants. Weeping with relief, she thanked him profusely and told them that her name was Clarie and that she was the sister of Sir Sagramore, a redoubtable knight of the Round Table. She had been sitting in her father's garden that morning when the giants had broken in and seized her.

Robert meanwhile had been exploring and had found a cave nearby which had been the giants' den. Within were all the goods and viands they had stolen from the surrounding area, including food and wine and even tablecloths. Helped by Tidogolain, the squire soon had a marvellous feast prepared and you may be sure that all the company dined well that night.

But this was not the end of their adventures for that day. As they were preparing to settle down once more, and as Robert was fetching fresh grass for their mounts, he saw

coming towards them three armed knights who from their bearing seemed anything but friendly. Hastening back to his master, Robert told him of their approach and the Fair Unknown at once sprang up, all unarmed, and drawing his sword prepared to defend the two women and the servants.

He might have fallen to the spears of the three knights right away, for they were indeed the friends of the defeated Blioberis, but Helie herself came forward and called upon them to stop. She reminded them of their knightly vows and begged them to give the Fair Unknown time to arm himself.

All three knights spurned her pleas and insisted they had come to kill the knight who had humbled their brother, Blioberis, and that nothing less would settle their quarrel.

Helie helped Robert to buckle on the Fair Unknown's armour, and as she did so, reminded him again of her own lady, whose life he was pledged to save. The Fair Unknown swore that nothing would prevent him from carrying out his task, then turned to face his new adversaries.

The first to come against him was William of Salebrant, who should have regretted it, since the Fair Unknown's spear passed through shield and hauberk and struck him dead from his horse's back.

With a cry Lord Elin of Graie attacked. The Fair Unknown unhorsed him and left him mangled on the ground, nursing a broken arm.

Third and last came the Lord of Saie, by far the strongest of the three. When he met the Fair Unknown, their shields split, and their lances shivered, and they were both unhorsed. With swords they fought on, until at length the Fair Unknown beat down his opponent and pulling off his helm placed the tip of his sword against the man's neck. The Lord of Saie begged for mercy, and the Fair Unknown granted it, bidding him put himself at Arthur's mercy and tell him all that had taken place.

Thus it was agreed, and next day, after burying the dead knight, the others departed for Camelot the Golden, taking Sir Sagramore's sister in their care.

✛ ✛ ✛

WHEN THE FAIR Unknown was fully rested, he, Helie, Robert and Tidogolain rode on their way towards the city of Sinadoun, where Helie's mistress was held captive. The forest stretched all around them, though the way was wide. The company continued upon their way until their road led them at last to the sea. This was in the month of June, when the fennel hung green in many great halls, and when the summer day was long, and the song of the nightingale was heard. There, at a place which became an island when the tide rose, stood the City of the Golden Isle. It seemed that it must have been constructed with the aid of magic, for its walls were of white marble and its roof of silver bedecked with mosaic, and it had one hundred towers of red marble surrounding it.

The Fair Unknown was about to turn in the direction of the wondrous building when Helie spoke up. 'This is a dreadful place. Within it lives a damsel of great beauty called the Maiden of the White Hands. She is schooled in the seven liberal arts, knows the mystery of the stars, and the ways of enchantment. For five years she has been besieged by a knight named Malgier the Grey. Every suitor who has tried to approach her he has killed.'

'Then let us see if we can achieve this adventure,' mused the Fair Unknown.

Helie shook her head at him angrily. 'Remember – it is my lady of Sinadoun whom you are sent to rescue. It will not help her if you fall to this knight's strength. There is another thing that you should know. Each time one of her suitors is killed, the people of the city command him to hold the bridge for seven more years. Malgier has done so for many years now. This is not achieved without great power and skill.'

But the Fair Unknown would not be dissuaded. He had already turned his horse in the direction of the city and refused to turn back.

As they approached, they saw a causeway that stretched from the entrance to the city over an inlet where the sea rushed in and out with the tide. To one side of the end nearest them stood a tent surrounded by a palisade of sharpened stakes. A dreadful decoration was upon these stakes – human heads, altogether one hundred and forty-three – all that remained of the knights slain by Malgier the Grey. Even as they approached, they could see him, already accoutred, preparing to ride to meet them. His shield bore upon it the emblem of two white hands – his way of showing how secure he felt in his suit to the lady of the Golden Isle.

As the two knights prepared to do battle, the walls of the city were lined with its citizens. Everyone had come to see either Malgier or the Fair Unknown fall. In the tallest of the red towers the Lady of the White Hands watched also.

The combatants hurtled together with such might that when they met both flew from their mounts and lay on the earth stunned. They soon recovered, however, and

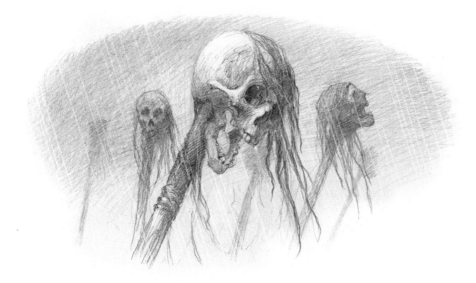

→ *A Dreadful Decoration* ←

with drawn swords fell to with great vigour. This way and that the battle went, until at last the Fair Unknown struck a blow which sent Malgier's helm flying. He followed this up with a blow that split the other knight's head in twain.

A breathless moment of silence followed, then cheers echoed from the walls of the city and as the gates opened the people rushed forth to joyfully lift the young knight upon their shoulders and carry him within. The Lady of the White Hands waited, smiling – for in truth she had hated Malgier and wished fervently for his death. To the Fair Unknown she seemed the most beautiful sight he had ever seen – her beauty took away his breath and left him speechless. She, in turn, liked the look of him, and thanked him profusely, promising him wealth, lands and – herself! She also promised that the custom of the causeway battle would cease henceforward. The Fair Unknown spoke with her politely, more than a little overcome with this turn of events.

He scarcely had time to think, however, as arrangements went forward for a great celebratory feast. Helie and Robert, together with Tidogolain the dwarf, were given quarters in the city, while the Fair Unknown himself was given the fairest chamber and fresh clothing.

In no time at all the feast commenced. The young hero was placed at the head of the table, with the maiden White Hands on one side and Helie on the other. As the evening progressed, Helie managed to speak privately to the Fair Unknown, telling him that White Hands had sent for all her lords, telling them that she intended to take her young rescuer as husband.

'What if I refuse?' he asked, shaken by this turn of events.

'Then doubtless you will either be killed or imprisoned. In which case,' she added, 'you will be ill-equipped to carry out your true task – to help rescue my lady.'

'What should I do?' asked the Fair Unknown.

'There is only one course open to you,' Helie replied in a whisper. 'You must leave secretly. I have lodgings in the city, as you know. Robert will have a horse ready and waiting before daylight dawns. I, together with Tidogolain, will await you near the chapel that lies just beyond the gate. Tell anyone that asks that you go there to give thanks for your victory.'

To this the Fair Unknown agreed, and as the celebration ended, Helie was escorted back to her lodgings, while the Fair Unknown was shown to his chamber, where a bed of great comfort and splendour had been prepared.

There, as he lay abed, thinking over the events of the past few days, and wondering how long before he could leave without being seen, the Fair Unknown became aware that the door to his chamber had opened, and that the Lady White Hands had entered. Through half-closed eyes he saw in the dim light that her hair was unbound and that she had on only a cloak pulled over her shift. He caught a glimpse of her slender white legs and small bare feet.

Softly she approached and stood looking down at him. 'Are you asleep?' she breathed.

'No, lady,' he replied, opening his eyes.

Smiling, White Hands sat upon the edge of the bed. They talked for a while, and she laid her head upon the pillow next to his. Gently, the Fair Unknown reached for her, bending his lips to hers, but at that White Hands drew away quickly. 'There shall be no love-play between us until we are wed!' she cried.

With these words she quickly left the room, leaving the Fair Unknown angry and dismayed. By this time, he was more than a little in love with the lady, and to be this close, only to be turned away, was almost more than he could bear! Now he was thankful that he had decided to flee the place, where before he had been secretly filled with regret.

NEXT MORNING ALL went as planned. The Fair Unknown rose and slipped out of the castle, joining Robert and Helie and the dwarf as arranged. Soon the Isle of Gold was far behind them, and Helie all but sang for joy, for soon they would reach the desolate city of Sinadoun. Only one more obstacle lay before them, and this Helie dreaded already, knowing by now how the Fair Unknown would turn always towards danger.

When less than a day later they sighted the walls of another city, she was already prepared for his question. Yet he surprised her, for after riding in unusual silence for some time he asked if it were a good place to stay.

'It is not,' replied Helie. 'The lord of this city is called Lampart. He fights anyone who comes here and if he wins – which as far as I can tell is always – the loser is driven from the city by the people, who throw rubbish at him in a shameful way.'

For the first time since escaping the Isle of Gold, the Fair Unknown brightened. 'Such an evil custom should not be allowed to continue. Let us go there at once.'

Of course, nothing Helie could say would dissuade him. They rode unchallenged into the city, and once they were within its walls people everywhere began to jeer and point to them – some even began gathering dirt from the streets in readiness for what, to them, was an inevitable outcome.

They found Lampart sitting in the sun outside his great hall. Grey-haired and powerful, he was engaged in a game of chess and, as the companions entered, triumphantly check-mated his opponent.

He rose to meet the Fair Unknown and his party, and greeted them courteously. 'Welcome, sir knight; my lady, welcome to you. If you seek lodging here this night, I shall be pleased to offer it to you. But first you must joust with me. If you win then all shall be well. If you lose you shall depart at once and receive no good escort from this city.'

'I am in accord with that,' said the Fair Unknown, and called to Robert to arm him.

The joust took place inside a great hall where lists had been set up and a magnificent carpet laid upon the floor. The two combatants armed themselves with care – Robert attending his master, while Lampart, seated in a chair which stood upon the image of a grey leopard woven into the carpet, was attired in armour the splendour of which was much at variance with the young knight's battered harness.

Once they were ready, the two mounted and rode towards each other with their spears in rest. In the first course their spears shattered, and though both men were rocked in their saddles neither had the advantage. The second course was the same – but on the third encounter the Fair Unknown unhorsed his opponent fairly, landing him on the earth with a crash. Lampart rose and, putting off his helm, courteously offered lodging to the party.

To the surprise of the Fair Unknown, Helie now came forward and greeted him warmly. To the young knight she said: 'Sir, this knight is my lady's seneschal, the finest knight in our land. By defeating him you have indeed proved – if proof were necessary – that you are well able to attempt her rescue.' Then she turned again to Lampart and told him of

their adventures, admitting that at first she had spoken harshly to the Fair Unknown. 'Since then, he has proven himself over and again to be a strong and worthy champion. One whom, I daresay, has the blood of nobility in him, for all that he chooses to hide his true name and rank.'

✠ ✠ ✠

THAT NIGHT THE company were royally entertained, and in the morning prepared to depart for Sinadoun. Lampart insisted on giving the Fair Unknown fresh arms, and in riding with the companions to within sight of the walls. As they rode, he spoke quietly with Helie, while the Fair Unknown rode in silence, secretly fearful of his ability to overcome the danger which lay before him. Until now he had felt no such fear, but as the end of his journey approached, he began to doubt his own strength, and only with difficulty hid his desire to turn aside.

Nor was this helped by the appearance of the city, for when they came at length to a place which overlooked it, it appeared ruinous, with broken towers and fractured walls, half hidden amongst the twining branches of the forest. Here, Helie and Lampart prepared to turn aside to take shelter until the battle was done. First, they helped arm the Fair Unknown in his new armour, and all the while Helie wept openly, and even the seneschal had tears in his eyes.

'You must go on alone,' said Helie. 'In the heart of the city you will find a hall still standing. It is made from white marble, of ancient design. It has many windows. In each one you will see a *jongleur*, every one with a different instrument. Greet them all with these words: 'May God curse you!' How they respond will determine what happens next. If you survive thus far you may enter the hall. Await whatever comes then. But be warned, do not enter any of the side chambers.'

If he wondered at Helie's knowledge of these things, the Fair Unknown said nothing. He promised to follow her instructions and having bade farewell to his companions rode on alone. As he approached the city, he saw where two rivers ran past its fractured walls. Over one of these a bridge stood intact, though it led only to a broken gate. The whole place seemed empty and desolate, rightly earning its name, though once it must have been splendid beyond dream.

Reining in before the broken gates of Sinadoun, the Fair Unknown crossed himself and went forward through tumbled walls and shattered pavements. In a while he saw what he knew must be the hall, its white walls sparkling in the sun. There, just as Helie had told him, were dozens of jongleurs, dressed in a mad assortment of patchwork clothing, each one carrying a different instrument. Among those he saw were harp, rota, bagpipe, hurdy-gurdy, fiddle, shawm, lute, horn, tambourine and tambor, cornemuse, psaltern, pipes and trumpets.

As the Fair Unknown approached, the singers began to proclaim: 'God bless King Arthur's knight, sent hither to help the lady of this place!'

This made the knight at once puzzled and wary. But he remembered the instructions which Helie had given him and drawing his sword he cried: 'God's curse upon you!' and rode swiftly into the hall.

One of the jongleurs leapt down at once and slammed the door behind him. Within, the hall was brightly lit by many candles, and in the centre stood a seven-legged table. The Fair Unknown reined in his mount and sat waiting. Then a knight with a green shield appeared from a side chamber and attacked him. Two or three blows with his sword proved enough to drive the fellow off, and in his eagerness the Fair Unknown pursued him to the very door of the chamber from which he had emerged. At the last moment the young knight paused, remembering Helie's words to him, and as he did so he saw two great axe-blades descending towards him in a rush of cold steel. He backed quickly away, and the chamber door banged shut. Retreating into the hall again, he called upon God to protect him as the lights were extinguished by a breath of stale wind, and the place became as dark as night.

After a moment some of the candles lit again, seemingly of their own volition, and as the Fair Unknown prepared himself, a second knight appeared from a further door. This one was dressed entirely in black armour and rode on a horse which sprouted a horn from its brow. Smoke and flames issued from its nostrils as if it were a dragon!

The two champions came together with a mighty crash and both were unhorsed. Drawing their swords, they fought on – never was there such a battle since Tristan fought the Morhault. But at last, the Fair Unknown, wounded and exhausted by his long fight, gained the upper hand – he struck a blow with all the force of his arm and the black knight's head, still helmed, went spinning across the floor, striking sparks as it went. As the body fell to the floor a plume of black and sulphurous smoke arose from it, and the body became putrid at once.

At this the jongleurs reappeared and doused all the candles, then departed, slamming shut both doors and windows, so that the hall became dark, and the very walls seemed to shake.

In terror, the Fair Unknown stumbled across the hall until he felt the edge of the table beneath his hands. He clung to it as if it were a piece of spindrift on a merciless sea. He found himself thinking of the Lady White Hands and regretting his precipitous departure.

Slowly his senses adjusted to the dimness. He found that he could see – though only a little. He made out the shape of a huge cupboard set against the wall behind the table and, as he looked, the door to this began slowly to crack open.

A strange red light shone through, and by its glow he saw a most terrible thing. A serpent, its body as thick as a cask of wine, emerged and advanced towards him. Its fearsome and terrible head towered over him, its tongue darting forth, dripping with venom. But worst of all its face was that of a beauteous woman.

Never had the Fair Unknown felt such fear. Surely this was a monster from Hell itself! But despite his horror the young knight grasped his sword and prepared to face it, but as he raised his shield the serpent stopped and bowed its head almost to the floor. The Fair Unknown hesitated and as he did so once again the serpent slithered nearer. Again, he raised his sword, and again it stopped and bowed low.

Bewildered, the Fair Unknown stared at the creature, and as he did so met its eyes. They were fierce and mesmeric, but, set in a face fair as morning, seemed also human. As he stood irresolute, the creature drew suddenly closer and, before he could do anything to prevent it, shot forth its head and touched his mouth with its lips.

The Fair Unknown drew back in horror, the slick, vile taste of the serpent on his lips. The creature was already withdrawing. The door of the cupboard closed upon it and a silence fell, even deeper than before. Bewildered and fearful the Fair Unknown waited in the darkness.

Then, into the silence, a voice spoke clearly. 'Son of my lord Sir Gawain, no other knight could have done what you have done. No one but you could have endured the Terrible Kiss – save perhaps your father himself. Only you could deliver the lady from the danger which beset her. King Arthur named you the Fair Unknown – I tell you now that your true name is Guinglain. You are the son of Gawain and Blanchemal the Faery. She it was who armed you and sent you to King Arthur, and she who placed upon you a spell which caused you to forget who you were. You have done well! Rest now.'

The voice ceased, and the Fair Unknown, Guinglain in truth, sank into one of the chairs by the table and fell into a deep sleep, his head resting on his folded arms.

✛ ✛ ✛

WHEN THE YOUNG knight awoke, the day was well advanced and there, sitting at the table beside him, was a lady more beautiful than any he had ever seen – save perhaps for White Hands. She wore a dress of the faery colour and her hair where it tumbled around her shoulders and breast was as bright as the brightest gold. At once Guinglain recognized her face, which had but recently adorned the body of the vile serpent. He started back, reaching for his sword.

'Do not fear me, Sir Guinglain. I am no longer enspelled, no longer half-serpent.

Indeed, I am she whom you were sent to rescue. My name is Esmerée the Blonde, daughter to King Guingras and lady of Sinadoun.'

'I am glad to see you so well,' said Guinglain, shaking off the last trails of sleep and feeling his fear abate.

'That is thanks to you. I have waited long for your coming. Only three months after my father died a powerful enchanter named Mabonagrain entered this land. He made the people run mad and destroy the city before they fled into the forest. Then when I would not marry him, the enchanter laid upon me the shape of the serpent you saw last night. Only one brave enough to endure its kiss could save me. Not only did you succeed but you also slew the enchanter himself, the black knight whom you fought in this very hall.' Smiling, she added: 'You have won me also. I am yours to marry.'

Guinglain stared at her in wonder. In his memory was the cold and sickening touch of the serpent's lips. Those of the Lady Esmerée were red and ripe as any he had seen.

At last, he forced himself to look away. 'Let us return to King Arthur. Only he may say whom I marry, for he is my cousin.' But in truth, as he spoke, he was thinking of the Lady White Hands, and in that moment the effect of the long battle against the demonic knights overcame him so that he fell to the ground.

Helie, followed by Lampart and the others, arrived soon after, and at first all were filled with joy, Helie and Esmerée to see each other, Lampart to see she whom he served restored, and both Robert and Tidogolain to see their master and mistress happy. But when they saw how Guinglain lay as one dead their delight turned to sorrow. Gently they removed the young knight's armour and

saw at once that he was sorely wounded in many places. The two women sent for water and herbs to wash and cleanse his wounds, then they called upon others to carry him to a chamber where he was laid in a great bed and where he fell into a deep sleep.

✣ ✣ ✣

THANKS TO THE care of Esmerée and Helie, Guinglain slowly regained his strength, and in that time the work of the enchanter was gradually undone. First the people, who no longer wandered madly in the wild forest around the city, returned; then came the bishops and clergy, who blessed the walls with holy water so that the illusion that had been cast upon them vanished and it was seen that they were in truth not broken at all. Then the celebrations began for the restoration both of Esmerée the Blonde and the city of Sinadoun.

All this while Guinglain lay resting, recuperating from his many wounds, reflecting on his adventures, and remembering the life he had known before ever he set out for Arthur's court. And there at length came Lampart, with other nobles, and a bishop of the place, to request formally that he take their lady to wife.

Just as formally Guinglain replied that he could wed no lady without the permission of King Arthur and suggested that Esmerée herself should travel to the king to thank him for sending his knight to rescue her. This was agreed, and in a matter of days the lady set out with a fine entourage, leaving Guinglain still resting, placed in the tender care of her doctors.

As he lay in bed in the great palace, Guinglain had thoughts for no one but White

Hands, and at night he dreamed of her entering his chamber with hair unbound, clad only in her shift, just as she had in truth done in her own castle. He determined then to return to the Golden Isle, and to ask her forgiveness for his sudden departure, and to give his reasons for it.

Rising from his bed despite the protests of the doctors, Guinglain set out and soon overtook Esmerée and her party. There he excused himself from riding with them by saying that he had other urgent business to conclude. And if Esmerée was saddened by this, or puzzled by it, she said nothing, but gave him her leave to go.

✜ ✜ ✜

GUINGLAIN RODE FULL tilt for the Golden Isle. As he neared the city, he encountered a hunting party and his heart leapt when he saw that White Hands was among the riders. Greatly daring he rode up to her and haltingly confessed his love for her. White Hands looked coldly upon him and demanded to know who he was.

Guinglain gasped: 'I am Guinglain, that was known as the Fair Unknown! Do you not remember me?'

White Hands' expression did not change. 'Yes, I remember you! You are the one who crept away when no one was looking – doubtless to the arms of some other lady. Be sure of one thing, I shall never allow you to have such a hold over my heart again.'

'Then I shall die in your land,' Guinglain said. 'No other place is as holy to me as this over which you rule.'

He watched as the bright-clad hunting party rode on, leaving him in their dust. With sorrow weighing heavily upon him he made his way to the city and sought lodging in an inn in the town that gave him a good view of the castle where he knew White Hands would be.

✜ ✜ ✜

WEEKS PASSED, AND gradually Guinglain gave away all his goods to pay for his room. Finally, even his fine arms and armour were gone, after which he took to his bed – too weak and sorrowful to get up.

Soon after this, a maiden arrived at the inn with fresh clothing and an invitation to visit White Hands. Trembling with joy, Guinglain washed and dressed and hurried after the maiden. She took him to a beautiful garden filled with the song of birds, where White Hands awaited him. She bade him sit beside her and took his hands in hers.

'Sir, how are you?'

'I have not fared well,' answered Guinglain truthfully. 'These last weeks have been unkind to me. But I am better for the sight of you.'

'What proof have I that if I were to let you reassume that place you once held in my affections you would not run off again?'

Guinglain hung his head in shame. 'Lady, the truth of the matter is that I had to leave to honour the promise I made both to my king and the lady who had begged for aid. I feared you would not allow me to go. I know now that this was wrong, and I beg your forgiveness.'

White Hands looked at him and, in her heart, knew that she loved him as much as he loved her. Only memories of his secret departure kept her from holding him close. Instead, she spoke sternly: 'Sir Guinglain, I must think upon these things. Meanwhile you may stay in my castle.'

Guinglain's heart leapt at these words, but he kept his eyes lowered and merely thanked White Hands for her generosity.

Soon after, they went in to dinner, and when they had eaten the splendid repast laid out for them, Guinglain was shown to the same richly decorated room as before. There, White Hands bade him good night with these words: 'My chamber is just across the way from yours, Sir Knight, and I shall sleep with the door open to see that you do not run off again! See that you do not enter unless you are invited!'

Guinglain lay down in a turmoil of confusion. Over and again he repeated the words White Hands had uttered. What did they mean? Her look had seemed to say to him that he should come to her that night, yet her words belied this. Several times he got up and went to the door of his own chamber, looking across to where he knew White Hands lay. Each time he returned to his own room and tossed and turned some more.

At last, the desire to find out how the lady truly felt towards him grew too great, and he left his chamber and started towards hers. At once it seemed to him that he stood upon a narrow bridge over a roaring stream of black water. As he stood in bewilderment and fear the bridge began to shake, and next moment he found himself clinging to the edge above the churning water. At that he cried out – waking both himself and others and found himself clinging to a hawk's perch in the hall of the castle!

Shamed, he made his way back to his chamber and once more tried to sleep. Again, he could not, and in a while rose again and made his way towards White Hands' room. This time, as he stepped across the threshold it seemed that the walls began shaking and were about to fall upon him. He leapt back, crying out – and woke in his bed with a pillow over his head!

Thoroughly miserable, Guinglain lay down again, still inwardly debating. Then a sound alerted him to where a maiden entered his room with a candle. She approached his bed and smilingly beckoned him to follow her. At first, he thought her another dream, but she urged him to rise, and when he did so led him to White Hands' chamber. Right up to the bed she led him and then retired, leaving the two alone. Softly White Hands placed her hand in his and drew him beneath the covers. There the two made merry and were fulfilled of the love each felt for the other.

Later, as they lay side by side, Guinglain laughed aloud at the thought of his two earlier forays, and when White Hands asked to know why he laughed, told her of his dreams. Now it was her turn to smile. She told him that these were not dreams, but her own working of magic, in which, along with many other arts, her father had bid her be educated. Then she confessed that she had always known that Guinglain would come, that he would leave her and return. Indeed, the whole of his great adventure had been her doing. She it was who had sent Helie to Arthur's court to ask him for help. It was her voice that announced his true name after he had braved the serpent's kiss. 'You see, my love, I have been waiting for you this long time.'

'Now I am here, I shall never leave again,' said Guinglain.

'See that you remember those words,' said White Hands seriously. 'For if you forget me, you shall just as surely lose me.'

'That could never happen,' Guinglain replied, and the two turned again to loving.

Next day, White Hands summoned all her

lords and barons and declared her happiness to them all. Even as she did so, Esmerée the Blonde and her followers were getting closer to Camelot the Golden. On the road they encountered four knights: Blioberis, the Lord of Saie, the Proud Knight of the Glade and William of Salebrant – all of whom had been defeated by Guinglain. Esmerée declared that she was betrothed to the Fair Unknown.

Soon after they reached the court, where Arthur received them all graciously and heard of the adventures of the Fair Unknown. There Esmerée formally asked for Guinglain's hand in marriage, and Arthur promised to consider the request, while wondering aloud how they were to locate the young knight. One of the Round Table Fellowship suggested a great tournament, which was sure to attract knights from all over the land, including, surely, the Fair Unknown. To this Arthur agreed, and a date was set one month hence on the plain below the Castle of Maidens. Tristan was to lead one side in the lists, and the King of Montesclaire the other.

✢ ✤ ✢

THE MONTH SOON passed, and far off on the Isle of Gold, Guinglain heard of the great tournament. He longed to go, to tell Arthur of all that had occurred. Yet when he spoke of this to White Hands, and begged leave to go, she would not hear of it. 'I have seen in the stars that if you leave this place, you will never return to me.'

'I swear that could never happen!' cried Guinglain with passion.

'Nevertheless, you shall not go by my leave, since you evidently do not love me enough to forgo this one small pleasure! The decision is yours alone to make.'

Hotly denying these accusations, Guinglain declared his intention of going to the tournament, and of returning soon. That night he fell asleep beside White Hands – but in the morning he awoke in the forest, horse and arms at his side and Robert the squire sleeping nearby. Angered by what he saw as his lady's doubt of his faithfulness, Guinglain set forth at once for the Castle of Maidens, arriving there three days later. But as the distance between him and the Golden Isle grew greater, so the memory of White Hands faded, so that by the time he reached the tournament lands, he had quite forgotten her.

A great company of knights was already gathered there, including those whom Guinglain had defeated during his first adventures. He chose to fight with Tristan on the side of the Cornish knights and, though he kept his identity secret, he carried the same shield that he had borne on first arriving at Arthur's court – an ermine lion on an azure field.

The day the tournament began Guinglain distinguished himself with such might that by the end everyone was talking of his prowess and the King of Ireland invited him to dine in his tent. Next day he did even better, defeating knight after knight, until it was clear to all that he was the outright winner of the tournament.

Arthur summoned him to join the royal party on the road to Camelot the Golden. On the way Guinglain revealed his true identity and Arthur welcomed him as the son of Sir Gawain.

Arriving in Camelot, they found Esmerée the Blonde awaiting them. She greeted Guinglain with delight and Arthur proposed they be married as soon as matters could be arranged, and to this Guinglain gave his assent, having quite forgotten White Hands.

Next morning a great and splendid party set off for Esmerée's lands. Arthur himself agreed to attend the wedding, and he rode with them. Sir Gawain had at this time returned from an adventure of his own and was greeted by the knowledge that he had a son. Now he understood why the youth had seemed to him so familiar. Guinglain and he spoke together at length, and though he could no longer remember how he came to know this, Guinglain told him that he was a child of the faery Blanchemal.

Gawain had the grace to look askance at this, for he had met several faery women in his adventures and got more than one child as a result. But more important to him was the glory and honour his son had gained in his adventure – not to mention his most beautiful spouse. Of these matters he said nothing but embraced his son warmly.

The wedding was celebrated in great splendour and Guinglain was later crowned king of Sinadoun. It is told that he lived a long and happy life with Esmerée and was well remembered as both a good lord and a true knight of the Round Table. Yet he never returned to the Isle of Gold, nor did he ever see White Hands again. As she had predicted, he forgot her utterly. If there was magic at work in this, I know it not, and therefore will not speak of it. Instead let us hear next the Tale of Sir Lanval, whose adventures are most wonderful and pleasing to the ear.

———— ✛ ————

EXPLICIT THE TALE OF GUINGLAIN.
INCIPIT THE STORY OF SIR LANVAL.

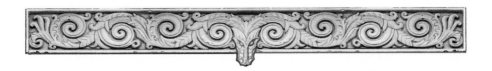

9: THE TALE OF SIR LANVAL

THERE WAS A TIME WHEN THE LANDS OF BRITAIN WERE BEING RAIDED BY THE PICTS AND SCOTS. KING ARTHUR MADE CARLISLE HIS HEADQUARTERS, FROM WHERE HE LED AN ARMY TO DRIVE OUT THESE ATTACKERS. SUCH WAS THE SUCCESS OF THESE ACTIONS THAT AT PENTECOST ARTHUR REWARDED ALL THOSE WHO HAD AIDED HIM WITH LANDS AND RICH WIVES. BUT ONE KNIGHT WAS OVERLOOKED, DESPITE HIS COURAGE AND COURTESY. THIS KNIGHT, WHOSE NAME WAS LANVAL, WAS NOT WELL LIKED. MANY WERE JEALOUS OF HIS QUIET GENTLENESS, AND FOR THIS REASON SPOKE NO GOOD WORDS TO ARTHUR ON HIS BEHALF. ARTHUR ALSO FORGOT HIM UNTIL, DESPITE THE FACT THAT HE WAS PART OF THE KING'S HOUSEHOLD, SIR LANVAL SOON POSSESSED ALMOST NOTHING SAVE HIS HORSE AND ARMS.

✛ ✛ ✛

THEN ON A day at the height of summer, when the sky shone blue and the air was like wine, Lanval went for a ride – hoping to meet adventure along the way. His course took him through the woods below Carlisle, following the bank of a bright stream, until he came to a broad meadow. There he stopped, and as the day was warm, took off his horse's saddle and allowed the beast to roll in the grass and drink from the stream. Then, having folded his cloak and placed it beneath his head, he lay down in the sun and gave thought to his troubles.

He was so disconsolate that he was scarcely aware when two girls came along the riverbank towards him. Lanval jumped up and greeted them politely. One, he saw, carried a golden bowl, and the other had a towel draped over her arm.

'Sir Lanval,' one of the maidens said. 'Our mistress, who is nearby, sends us to fetch you to her. You may see that her tent is very near.'

Looking across the meadow, Lanval could indeed see a magnificent tent set up in the shade of the trees – something he had not noticed earlier. He allowed the two maidens to escort him thither. They ushered him into the cool interior of the tent and retired discreetly.

103

Within was a great bed, the cover of which alone was worth more than the price of a castle. On it lay a lady of such surpassing beauty that it almost caused Lanval's heart to cease beating. Stretched out under a mantle of white ermine, trimmed with Alexandrian purple, her face and neck, one arm and part of one white flank were uncovered. As Lanval entered, she stirred and sat up.

'Sir Lanval, I have come on a long journey from my own lands in search of you. I have watched you from afar and in this time have come to feel only love for you. I have seen, also, how your king neglects you, and this I would change. But most of all I wish to give you all the joy you could desire.'

Lanval gazed upon the lady and the spark of love woke within him. 'Madame,' he replied. 'If it gives you pleasure to love me, be assured that my own pleasure is all the greater for knowing this!' Then, even more wildly, he said: 'From this moment I shall forsake all others for the sake of the love I have for you!'

At this the lady held out her arms to him, and he went to her in deep delight. Later, as they lay together on the great bed, the lady said to him: 'Beloved, I must ask that you do not reveal our passion to anyone. Let it be our secret, and all will be well. If you ever forget this, and speak openly of our love, you will lose me.'

To this Lanval gave his word, and the two remained there disporting merrily throughout the day. When it was time for supper they rose, and the two maidens brought Lanval fresh clothing – far superior to the old clothes he had worn before. They also gave him a purse of gold, and told him that his horse, which had been well cared for, had a new saddle and fresh harness. Then they brought wine in golden goblets and food on golden plates.

When they had eaten, the lady turned to Lanval and said: 'My love, the time has come for us to part. This must be our understanding. Whenever you have need of me, I shall come to you, no matter where it may be. Meanwhile, you shall have all that you need by way of goods, money and other riches – all you need to proclaim you a wealthy man. No man save you will see me or hear my voice. Our secret is for no other to share.'

And though this seemed a passing strange thing, Lanval agreed. In his heart he knew well that the lady was of the faery race and that her ways should not be questioned. He returned to Carlisle a happy man, and there found that his servants were clad in fresh attire, and that all his goods were renewed, and his fortunes completely restored.

Thereafter Lanval's life changed. He gave gifts. He clothed and fed poor folk. He ransomed prisoners. There was no one, friend or stranger, who did not owe something to his generosity. And, whenever he wished it, there was his lady by his side, ready to comfort and love him.

✠ ✠ ✠

THAT SAME YEAR, close to St John's Day, several of the Round Table knights had gathered in the garden which lay beneath the windows of the queen's lodging. Sir Gawain was there, and his cousin Yvain, as well as maybe twenty others. Gawain said: 'My friends, we do ill by our companion Lanval. Is there anyone here who has not benefited from his generosity – yet we have not included him in our company today. Let us go and fetch him.'

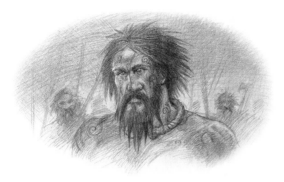

→ *The Picts* ←

The other knights agreed and dispatched several of their number to find Lanval and bring him back. Now it happened that Queen Guinevere was sitting in the window chatting with two of her ladies, and seeing the company gathered below, summoned more of her women to accompany her to the garden, where they might spend time with the knights and make merry. The knights were delighted and made the women welcome – all save Lanval, who had joined them willingly enough, but at the sight of the knights walking arm in arm with the ladies of their choice, felt nothing but a desire to see his own love.

The queen, seeing where Lanval had drawn to one side and was standing alone, went to him and begged him to sit with her. Once they were settled, she leaned close to him and said: 'I am so happy to be with you, Sir Lanval, and to have this opportunity to speak with you. I have been watching you for a long time, and to be honest I have never seen a more handsome, charming man.' As Lanval stammered his thanks, the queen moved closer to him. 'If you wish, we could spend more time together, alone that is. I will give you all my love if it pleases you.'

Hearing these words, Lanval drew away in alarm. 'Madame,' he said. 'Though I am aware of the honour done me by your words, I must say that this does not please me at all. I have served the king faithfully for years. I will not break that faith now.'

At this Queen Guinevere became angry. 'I swear you must love boys more than women!' she cried. 'Now that I think of it, I have never seen you with a lady of your own.'

Lanval rose angrily. 'I assure you that you are wrong. Furthermore, I love and am loved by a lady whose poorest serving-wench is worth more than you, in beauty, wisdom and honesty!'

At this the queen fled to her chamber in tears. She took to her bed and swore that she would not get up until the king heard her complaint and saw that justice was done.

The king, meanwhile, returned from a pleasant day hunting in the woods. He entered the queen's chamber and when she saw him Guinevere fell at his feet, weeping and demanding justice for the insult done her by Lanval. 'I saw him in the garden, and thought he appeared lonely when all the other knights had ladies with them. But when I approached him, he demanded my love. When I refused, he said that he already had a love who was so much more beautiful than I that even her chambermaid was worth more than me!'

This angered the king and he declared that he would have Lanval brought before him at once, and that if he were unable to answer for his words he should either be hanged or put to the flame.

Lanval meanwhile had returned home and was in great distress. He knew that he had almost certainly lost the attentions of his lady by speaking of her to the queen. He sat in his chamber and called to her repeatedly, but to no avail. When the king's men arrived to take him into custody, he made no attempt

105

to resist them, and would indeed have been quite happy if they had slain him.

He came before the king in a sad state, subdued and unspeaking. Arthur demanded to know the reasons for the dishonourable approach he had made to the queen. 'You have been my good vassal for many years. Now you return my favour in this way. Answer me! Why do you do this!'

Lanval said little, merely swearing that he had not asked the queen to betray her lord, and that in speaking of his own love he had lost her forever. Arthur, frowning, heard him in silence. Then he said that he would take no action then, but rather await the return of the whole court in a few weeks, then ask them all for a judgement that would be unbiased. Meanwhile he asked for sureties that Lanval would not flee, under which condition he could remain at liberty.

At first no one would come forward to stand surety for him, but at length Gawain offered to make good his bail, and several of the knights followed suit, for in truth, though they did not love Lanval, many had benefited from his recent largesse and were more than a little ashamed of their earlier treatment of him. The king accepted their guarantee against all the lands and fiefs they held from him. Lanval then returned to his lodging, where he stayed, very miserably, awaiting the day appointed for his judgement. Gawain and the rest came daily to visit him, afraid that he might do himself harm, but to them he hardly spoke at all.

The weeks passed, and the lords arrived at Carlisle, where Arthur demanded that they sit in judgement upon Lanval. Many were reluctant to do so, knowing him for a good and faithful man, but Arthur insisted and pressed them hard for a verdict. At length, after much deliberation, it was decided that since only

the queen was witness to the things that Lanval had said, that he should at least be given the chance to prove his innocence. 'Let him produce this lady that he spoke of so boldly. If she comes then we shall make our judgement accordingly. If not, then we shall order him banished.'

Lanval shook his head and said that no help would come from that quarter. The lords therefore prepared to make their judgement. At that moment, there appeared two maidens of surpassing beauty, richly clad, riding on twin white mares.

'Is one of these your love?' demanded King Arthur, but Lanval shook his head. The two maidens rode right up to the dais on which the king sat and dismounted. 'My lord,' said one of them, 'we beg that you prepare the best room you have for our mistress, for she wishes to stay here this night.'

'Do I know your mistress?' asked Arthur, but the maidens said nothing but only bowed their heads. Wondering at this, Arthur nonetheless called two of his knights to show them to the best chambers in the castle. Then he turned again to the lords and angrily demanded that they reach a verdict. As they again spoke together two more maidens, even fairer than the first had been, were seen approaching, richly dressed and riding two white mules. They approached the king and again requested lodging for their lady, who would appear shortly.

Sir Yvain, seeing their beauty and richness, spoke to Lanval and said: 'Surely you are saved. One of these must be your love!'

Wearily Lanval looked to where the two newly arrived maidens were standing together with downcast eyes. He shook his head and answered that he neither knew nor loved either of them.

Hearing this, Arthur demanded that his lords reach a verdict at once, for the queen had waited all day and like him was becoming angry. But just as they were about to comply, a woman came riding through the streets on a white palfrey. On her wrist sat a fierce and splendid sparrowhawk, and behind her mount trotted the finest hunting dog anyone had ever seen. It was as though the sun shone out of a darkened sky. There was not a person there who thought her less than the most beautiful woman they had ever seen. Her skin was white as the whitest clouds, her lips red, her hair tawny gold. Her figure and deportment made her the envy of every woman there, but the brightness of her eyes and the gentleness of her looks won everyone's heart.

Several of the knights hurried to Lanval and said: 'Surely, the woman who will rescue you is even now approaching. Her hair is gold, her lips are red, and she is by far the most beautiful creature we have ever seen.'

When he heard this, Lanval turned first white, then red. He rushed to a window from which he could see the street, and when he caught sight of the lady a cry escaped him. 'It is my beloved! So my fate is sealed. For she will not forgive me for breaking my promise to her, and I am as good as dead.'

The lady rode right into the hall as had her maidens and came to the place where King Arthur sat. She addressed him thus: 'Sire. I have loved and been loved by one of your vassals. Lanval is his name, and he is a worthy knight. Because I wish him to come to no harm, I have come to defend him. You should

know that your queen is wrong, and that he never demanded her love. Though none but she can show this to be true or not, I at least will stand by my love and hope that my presence will help prove him innocent.'

The lords looked at one another and with one accord declared that Lanval was innocent. All agreed that there could be no other woman as fair in all the land, and if Lanval's honesty was proved in this, it was as well to believe all that he said. The queen flushed red as a rose at this, for thus her shame was revealed. King Arthur turned away from her and left her to return to her chamber alone.

When she had heard the verdict, the Lady turned about and rode away from the hall without another word – nor would she turn back even though King Arthur called out to her to stay. But as she came close to the gates of the city, she passed a mounting block. And there Lanval was waiting and sprang onto the back of her horse and kissed her lips. All who saw this marvelled greatly, for thus he sat behind the lady on a palfrey rather than on a mighty steed such as befitted a knight.

The white horse bore them both away, and since that time no one has seen Lanval or his lady again. Some say they went to the island of Avalon, which was the lady's true home, and all agree that she was of Faery. As for Queen Guinevere, King Arthur forgave her in time, for he knew she was lonely for all that she was greatly loved. More than this I cannot say, for I have heard no more. Other tales of rivalry and adventure there are and such a one shall I tell next.

EXPLICIT THE TALE OF SIR LANVAL.
INCIPIT THE STORY OF THE PRINCE OF CAMBRIA.

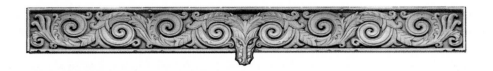

10: THE ADVENTURES OF
MERIADOC, PRINCE OF CAMBRIA

—— ✛ ——

IT IS SAID THAT, BEFORE THE TIME OF KING ARTHUR, BRITAIN WAS DIVIDED INTO THREE PARTS: CAMBRIA, WHICH NOW WE CALL WALES, ALBANY, OR SCOTLAND, AND LOGRES, THE TRUE NAME OF ARTHUR'S KINGDOM. DURING THE REIGN OF UTHER PENDRAGON, ARTHUR'S FATHER, CAMBRIA CAME TO BE RULED OVER BY TWO BROTHERS. THE ELDER WAS CALLED CARADOC, AND HE RULED OVER THE MOST PART OF THE LAND; THE YOUNGER, WHO WAS NAMED GRIFFIN, HAD A SMALLER PORTION, BUT SERVED HIS BROTHER WELL AND FAITHFULLY.

✛ ✛ ✛

ONE DAY KING Caradoc set his mind to conquer Ireland, which he achieved through strength of arms and a powerful army. Thereafter he took the daughter of the Irish king in marriage, and in due time she bore him twin children, a son and a daughter. But all was not well with the king, for as time passed, he began to grow weak and lose the vigour of his body. Though still a young man, he began to age, and within the space of a few years was forced to hand over the governance of his kingdom to his younger brother, while he himself ruled in name only.

For several years Griffin served faithfully, but gradually his mind began to turn to thoughts of ruling alone. Evil men, concerned only with their own overweening ambition, approached him, and whispered in his ear that his brother was old and senile and ought to be put away. Surely, they said, it is a shame that this great kingdom should be ruled over by a weak and foolish old man when you are strong and in your prime. You already rule in all but name. Why not make this a reality? Be rid of your brother forever.

Though Griffin tried not to listen, when he learned that Caradoc was seeking to wed his son to a princess of Albany, his resolve was further weakened, for this would have placed him further from the crown. Then those who had spoken to him before approached him again, reminding him that the king's son was already growing towards manhood and showing great skill and strength. Surely Griffin must realize that in time he would be stripped of everything, either through the marriage of his niece to a foreign king, or through the succession of Caradoc's son to the throne. Then they put forward a scheme to murder the old king as he rode hunting. They sought only Griffin's approval to act; they flattered him and spoke of possible internecine strife which could only tear the kingdom apart, and at last Griffin gave way, agreeing to the evil deed they had suggested and promising the assassins high rank once they had fulfilled his command.

It happened that on the very night before the king was due to ride to the hunt, he dreamed a dream in which he saw Griffin lying in wait in the forest, sharpening two arrows, which he then gave to two men. They, in turn, waited until the king was riding by and shot at him without warning.

Caradoc woke with a cry, hands pressed to his chest where the arrows had struck. The queen, waking by his side, first reassured him, then spoke of her own fears. 'I am certain,' she said, 'that your brother is plotting to kill you. Please don't go hunting today.'

But King Caradoc refused to believe his brother capable of plotting against him and dismissed his dream as of no import. With the first light he set out with a party of nobles to the hunt. There, sure enough, just as Griffin had planned, the aged king became separated from the rest of the hunt, being unable to keep up; and there the two men who had been bribed to carry out the evil deed fell upon him and carried him deeper into the forest, where they ran him through with a hunting spear, leaving it in his body so that it would look like a hunting accident.

It was not long before the king's absence was noticed, and still less time before his body was discovered. Amid much weeping and sorrow the body was conveyed to the castle and there, with great mourning, interred in the earth. An attempt was made to discover how the king's death had occurred, but there was no evidence to indicate who had perpetrated the deed. Griffin, who had absented himself on administrative business so that there was no possibility of his being suspected, was informed, and wept bitterly for the death of his beloved brother. Caradoc's queen, sick at heart and knowing full well that he was the victim of murder, fell ill and died within a month of her lord's passing.

Griffin now set about seizing power utterly, and his first act was to set up an investigation into his brother's death. Alarmed, the two killers approached him, reminding him of his promise to pay them well and to raise them to high office. Griffin's answer was to order them hanged forthwith without trial or appeal – having first had their tongues torn out so that they could not speak of his own part in the affair.

All of Cambria was shocked by this savage act, and many began to suspect Griffin's part in the crime. Several of the most notable lords of the kingdom came together to discuss the matter and decided that they must secure the protection of King Caradoc's children, since Griffin might well decide to remove them from the succession. Two lords in particular, Sadoc and Dunewall, who were both highly respected, spoke out against Griffin, and suggested that the royal children be taken to Cornwall and the princess betrothed to Moroveus, the duke of that land, who had no wife and was loyal to Caradoc's family.

To this end the two lords went to Griffin and demanded custody of the royal children, under the pretext of preventing any possibility of unscrupulous lords seizing them and setting them up as rival claimants. Griffin, though inwardly raging, concealed his anger and requested time to consider the request. Then, when the lords had departed, he sent a messenger to the man who had been given the task of caring for the orphaned children, ordering them to be brought before him at once.

Now, this man was named Ivor and he was the master of the royal hunt. The royal children, whose names were Meriadoc and Orwen, had been entrusted to him by the old king himself, and Ivor's wife Morwen had suckled them from the day of their birth due to the queen's ill-health. Neither of these honourable folk suspected anything was amiss and at once escorted the twins to Griffin. He, foreseeing the intention of the nobles, had already planned to have them killed, sending his most loyal men to do the task.

The intent of these assassins was to take the children deep into the forest of Arglud and there hang them on a certain ancient tree which had long since been used for this purpose. But when the time came, they were so moved to pity by the sweetness and gentleness of the twins that they found it was not in their hearts to kill them after all. Therefore, they contrived matters so that the rope by which they were to be hanged was so thin that it would break almost at once, letting the children fall to the earth unhurt. Thus, the men could swear to Griffin that they had done their work, while the royal children remained alive.

Ivor, meanwhile, had learned of the fate intended for his fosterlings from a servant who had overheard Griffin's instructions to his men. Tears running down his face, he told his wife what was to occur. 'We must find a way to save them!' she cried, and the couple

at once set out for the forest, taking with them Ivor's bow and hunting horn, his sword and his faithful dog, Dolfin.

Having reached the forest ahead of the murderers and knowing that he was no match for them armed with only a bow, Ivor devised a plan. He shot and killed a large buck and, having slaughtered it, scattered the pieces of raw flesh all around the tree where Griffin's men were bound to come. Soon, as he had known would happen, many wolves began to assemble there, drawn hither by the smell of the meat. When the murderers at last arrived, they were briefly frightened off, but as Ivor and his wife watched from the shelter of some bushes, they began to return.

The forester was ready to rush out and sell his life dearly, but he heard the men discussing how they would arrange matters so that the children were not killed, and so held his hand. The wolves were coming thickly now, and their howling alerted the men, who now looked fearfully around them. One drew the attention of the others to the tree on which they had intended to hang the children. Its vast trunk had a hole on one side, and within was a hollowed-out place big enough for several men to get into. They quickly crawled inside, taking the frightened children with them, and prepared to defend themselves against the wolves.

Ivor, drawing his bow, shot several of the creatures from his hiding place, and the rest fell on the carcasses of their fellows and began to rend them. Under cover of this, Ivor crept closer to the tree and began heaping dry brushwood against its bole. Then he struck flint and tinder and started a blaze. As the men within began to cry out in terror, Ivor blew a long blast on his horn, which sent the wolves scattering in panic for fear of a hunt.

Then the wily huntsman called out to the men in the tree to come out, or else he would burn them all to ashes.

The would-be murderers cried out for mercy, and Ivor ordered them to send the children forth first. This done, he snatched up a sword which had been left outside and, as the men emerged one by one through the narrow opening, he killed them, leaving them there to be consumed by the wild beasts. Then, together with his wife, he fled deeper into the forest.

Here there was a secret place discovered by Ivor long ago. It was a marvellous cave, deep in the rock known as the 'Cliff of the Eagles' from the fact that four of these great birds perpetually nested there. Indeed, a series of caverns were there, carved like rooms from the living rock. It was believed to have once belonged to a terrible Cyclops, and it had lain undiscovered until the huntsman had chanced across it. There, for the next five years, Ivor and his wife and the two children remained in hiding. Ivor hunted daily for their needs, while Morwen cared for the children. Thus, they wanted for nothing and remained hidden from the spite of Griffin, who believed them dead, and the murderers fled away.

✢ ✢ ✢

THE TWO CHILDREN grew swiftly in the wild, learning all they needed from their wise and skilful foster-parents. In time they forgot all that had passed in the forest, how they had almost died and how Ivor and Morwen had saved them. To their young minds these were their true parents. Nor did they think it strange to live in caves within the forest, for to them this was as it had always been.

Then a day came when they were out in the forest seeking game and kindling, and there they met two knights. These were Sir Kay, King Arthur's seneschal, and Sir Urien, who besides being a knight of the Round Table, was also king of Scotland. It was because of his desire to return home that he passed that way, Kay going with him part of the way as an escort. Ivor's wife, together with the girl Orwen, had become separated from Ivor and Meriadoc as they foraged for dry wood, and it was these that the two knights chanced upon. They passed by with a greeting, and soon after Sir Kay took his leave of Urien to return to King Arthur's court. Urien rode on alone but found that he could not forget the face of the young girl he had seen in the forest.

So greatly was he haunted by this chance encounter, that he turned around and rode back to where he had first seen her. It chanced that she was still there, having travelled only a short way, and without warning Urien swooped down upon her and lifting her up into the saddle rode off with her, taking no heed of her cries or those of her foster mother, who collapsed by the roadside.

Sir Kay meanwhile encountered Ivor and Meriadoc, who were laden down with spoils of the hunt. Kay, seeing the tall, handsome youth dressed in ragged clothes, evinced a malicious plan to carry him off. He needed a new squire, and in his arrogance felt he was permitted to take whoever it pleased him to. He therefore charged straight at Ivor, with spear at rest, shouting furious battle-cries at the top of his voice. The huntsman, terrified by the sight of the mail-clad, bellowing knight, dropped his catch and ran away into the trees, leaving Meriadoc to be snatched up and knocked unconscious by Sir Kay, who rode back towards Camelot the Golden in high glee with the boy draped across his saddle.

✚ ✚ ✚

DEEPLY SADDENED, IVOR returned to the cave alone, where he met Morwen, likewise in a state of shock and misery. They comforted each other, bemoaning their loss and wondering what they could do to recover their lost children, for after so long together they now regarded Orwen and Meriadoc as their own.

'I will not rest until I have found our daughter,' said Morwen. 'I remember that the man who carried her off was called Urien by his companion, who spoke of coming to see him in Scotland. I propose to set out to look for her in that land.'

'You are very brave, my love,' said Ivor. 'Then I will search for Meriadoc. I am sure the knight who chased me away was Sir Kay the Seneschal. I have been to King Arthur's court and have seen him there on several occasions. I will go to the royal court and seek news of our lost son.'

With many tears and blessings, the couple parted company, and each set out upon the road in different directions. Morwen took the road to Scotland and after a long and difficult journey arrived at the home of King Urien – only to find that he had that very day taken Orwen for his wife – who truth to tell had fallen as deeply in love with her captor as had he with her. Morwen stood amongst the crowd begging alms outside the great cathedral where the couple had been married and saw Orwen come forth, clad in a splendid gown and wearing a circlet of gold in her hair.

With tears in her eyes Morwen watched her foster-daughter walking amid the nobles of Urien's court, until it chanced that the girl caught sight of her. At once her eyes widened and she grew pale with shock. She fainted into the arms of the nobleman standing behind her.

Urien rushed forward in some alarm, and as soon as Orwen recovered enquired what was amiss. 'I saw a face in the crowd that I knew,' replied Orwen, sitting up. 'The face of one whose life is as dear to me as my own. It was my own dear foster-mother, who saved me from death and brought me up as her own.' Looking everywhere, she called out to Morwen, and when the older woman stood forth from the crowd she fell into her arms. 'Now, my lord,' she said to Urien, 'if you love me you will take care of this woman and honour her as you would myself.' This the king did, ordering Morwen to be clothed in the finest silks and to be given everything she needed for her comfort.

✚ ✚ ✚

IVOR, MEANWHILE, HAD arrived at King Arthur's court, walking boldly into the hall as the king was at supper. Many there were amazed at his appearance and even recalled the arrival of the fearsome Green Knight – for the huntsman was above average height, tall and powerful and with a thick and bushy beard. He was clad in a suit of clothes made from woven reeds, giving him an outlandish appearance. A long sword was belted at his side, and a bow and arrows were at his back. Over his shoulders he carried a large deer which he had shot on the way. This he now flung down at the feet of Sir Kay, having singled him out from among the entire throng. Then, before anyone could speak, a figure detached itself from the crowd of knights at the table and flung himself at Ivor. It was Meriadoc, whom the huntsman had not even recognized, so finely dressed was he, and with freshly barbered hair. For despite his being carried off in such a brutal fashion, he had grown quickly to enjoy the luxury of the court after his years living in the Cliff of Eagles.

The two greeted each other with tears and embraces, then the whole story came out. Kay was censured by the king for his rash act in taking Meriadoc away from his foster parents, and in recompense the seneschal offered to take Ivor into his own service as a huntsman. All was thus agreed, and Ivor's only thought now was for his wife: how she had fared and what success had greeted her quest for Orwen.

Within a month, Sir Kay remembered his promise to visit Urien, and himself set forth for Scotland, taking with him a retinue of servants, among them the favoured huntsman, Ivor. Meriadoc also went with them, having now been virtually adopted by Sir Kay, while still serving him as squire. Upon their arrival at Urien's court a great reunion took place between Ivor and Morwen, Meriadoc and Orwen. Amid great rejoicing, all elected to remain at Urien's court together.

✠ ✠ ✠

NOW MERIADOC AND his sister, having learned at last the circumstances of their early lives and their true parentage, began to debate how they might be avenged upon King Griffin, both for his part in the death of their father, and for his usurpation of their rightful inheritance. Knowing full well that he was one of the kings who held their lands in trust for King Arthur, they knew that to attack Griffin openly they required the support of the king. Therefore, they journeyed to Camelot the Golden and laid before Arthur the whole tale of Caradoc's death and of the subsequent behaviour of their uncle. Arthur, angered by the story, summoned Griffin to appear before him, and told him to be prepared to defend himself against accusations of fratricide and other wrongdoings.

Griffin's answer was to prepare for war. Having heard rumours of his niece and nephew's escape, and of their new status, he had already fortified several of his castles, and now he himself retired to the mountain fastness of Snowdon, where once the evil King Vortigern had hidden until the coming of Merlin.* Blocking every pathway and road until there was only a narrow passage between high cliffs which would admit a single column of men, Griffin then sent back a defiant answer to Arthur. This so angered the king that he allied himself with Urien and marched forthwith against Griffin.

Finding every path blocked or heavily defended, Arthur led an attack upon the narrow path, which was held by Griffin himself with a handful of men. For a week Arthur attempted to break through but was always repulsed. Many were reminded of the pass of Thermopylae, which in the time of the Greek Heroes was held in similar fashion with a handful of warriors. In the meantime, Sadoc and Dunewall, the two lords who had helped to save Caradoc's children, knowing the lie of the land as well as any men, raised a small force of knights to attack Griffin from behind. He, learning of this, was forced to abandon the narrow pass and retreat to the mountain fastness he had prepared against this very contingency.

---

* See 'Merlin and the Dragons', pp. 18–23

Thither King Arthur pursued him, and laid siege to the castle, which was so deeply entrenched in a bastion of rock that within a week the king realized that no simple assault would overcome it. He thus began to build entrenchments and brought up powerful siege engines with which to batter the walls.

Griffin, who was no coward, saw how things lay, and determined to give in to nothing. Week after week, month after month, he sent sorties out against the encampment of King Arthur, often leading the assaults himself, and earning the grudging respect of his enemies. But in the end, it was hunger that brought him low, as gradually the supplies within the fortress dwindled away.

Finally, Griffin gave himself up and threw himself on the mercy of King Arthur, who convened a court and laid the matter before not only his own judges but before that of the council who had once served King Caradoc. Here Griffin found no mercy, and in due course he was executed for his crimes.

✛ ✛ ✛

THE KINGDOM OF Cambria now fell to the lordship of Meriadoc. He, being as yet young and untried, declared his intention of proving himself by undertaking a knightly quest for adventure. He therefore entrusted the kingdom to his sister's husband, King Urien of Scotland, and returned with King Arthur to his court at Carlisle.

There, as the king rested from the long and arduous siege against Griffin, a certain knight, known as the Black Knight of the Black Forest, appeared and demanded that his right to ownership of the said forest be recognized. Arthur's reply was that his father, Uther Pendragon, had stocked the forest with black boars, the descendants of which roved there at will to this day, and that this gave him full entitlement. To this the Black Knight replied that his very name spoke for his own rights in the matter, but declared that, so long as his tenure was recognized, he would be glad to allow free hunting rights of the black boars at any time to King Arthur. To this the king replied that the rights were his to begin with and that he saw no need to ask permission of anyone to hunt in his own forest.

Thus, the matter stood, with first one side and then the other stating a contrary case. At length King Arthur placed the whole question in the hands of the judiciary and awaited their verdict. The Black Knight, believing that the council were bound to find in the king's favour, broke in upon their deliberations and demanded that the matter be settled by strength of arm and body – his own person against forty of Arthur's knights. 'Send but one man every day for forty days,' said the powerful man. 'If I survive, let the Black Forest be recognized as mine forthwith.'

Despite himself, King Arthur liked this bold speech, and so he agreed. But in the days that followed he began to regret his decision as, one by one, his knights returned battered and bleeding from their encounter with the Black Knight. At last, the king sent for Sir Kay and spoke to him thus:

'I am ashamed by this defeat of my best men at the hands of this upstart knight. There are but three days left before the forty are up and we must do all that we can to save our honour. Today therefore I would have you go and undertake the adventure. I know you to be both clever and resourceful, and it is my hope that you succeed where others have failed. Should you not succeed, then tomorrow it shall be my nephew Sir Gawain's turn;

and following that, on the last day, I shall myself go forth and do what I can to redeem my honour and that of the Fellowship of the Round Table.'

To this Kay agreed, delighted to be singled out for such a task. He began to prepare himself for the combat, assuring everyone that he could not fail to overcome the Black Knight. Meriadoc, who had been knighted by Sir Kay the year before, took him to one side and begged to be allowed to take his place. 'Surely,' he said, 'this matter can do little or nothing to increase your renown – and should you fail, which of course I do not believe you would – your shame would be great indeed!'

At first Kay refused, but as he considered the wisdom of Meriadoc's words his resolve weakened. Finally, he agreed, making much of the matter, as was his wont, and impressing upon the younger man his willingness to step aside for no other reason than to give him a chance to prove himself.

Meriadoc thus set out at once for the Black Forest, and on arriving at the ford which divided the lands of Arthur from those claimed by the Black Knight, blew a blast on his horn. Immediately the Black Knight appeared and without waiting charged full tilt at Meriadoc, catching him as he was crossing the water. Meriadoc, levelling his spear, caught his opponent's blow squarely on his own shield and drove the tip of his lance towards the Black Knight's throat. He in turn parried and received the blow in the centre of his shield. Swiftly Meriadoc released the spear and drawing his sword reached over and grasped his opponent's helm, dragging him sideways bodily from the saddle and preparing to cut deep into his neck. The Black Knight cried out and begged for mercy, which Meriadoc granted.

'Tell me who you are,' begged the Black Knight. 'Never have I felt such strength as you possess, and surely this must come of a great lineage.'

'I see no reason to discuss my ancestry,' said Meriadoc. 'It is enough that I represent King Arthur, and that I have won against you. Therefore, I ask if you submit to the stewardship of my lord over the Black Forest?'

The Black Knight drew his sword and holding it by the blade presented the hilt to Meriadoc. 'Sir,' he said. 'I fully renounce any claim to this place, and I honour you for your courage and strength. Will you not tell me now whose son you are and of what lineage you come?'

With only a moment's hesitation, Meriadoc told all that you have heard here, from his birth and upbringing and the treachery of Griffin to this very adventure. At the end the Black Knight bowed his head and declared that such a story was no less than he had expected. Then he swore undying allegiance to Meriadoc, promising that he would accompany him wherever he wished, and remain at his side as a loyal companion for as long as he was permitted. Meriadoc gravely accepted this, and the two knights returned side by side to King Arthur's camp.

There, Meriadoc was received with astonishment, for it seemed amazing to them that an inexperienced knight could overcome one who had defeated no less than thirty-seven of their kin. Arthur greeted the youth warmly and offered him any reward he cared to name.

Then Meriadoc astonished everyone by asking that the Black Knight's lands, on which the whole dispute was based, be returned to him, and despite King Arthur's evident displeasure, he would accept nothing other than this. In time, Arthur assented, and the Black Knight received full reparation of his lands.

Listen now to what happened next. Once word of Meriadoc's adventure spread, a second knight, calling himself the Red Knight of the Red Forest, appeared and made a similar demand of the king. Meriadoc defeated him, just as he had the Black Knight, and received his fealty. Shortly after, he performed the same set of deeds in response to a challenge by the White Knight of the White Forest. In each instance the knights bowed before him and swore undying allegiance. With the three sworn vassals at his side, Meriadoc set out in earnest in search of adventure.

THEIR FIRST GOAL was the land of the Emperor of the Alemanni, in the place that is called Gaul today. At that time the emperor was at war with Gundebald, King of the Land of No Return, who had stolen away his daughter. The emperor had sent word everywhere, inviting knights and heroes who would fight against his enemy, and it was in answer to this summons that Meriadoc, together with the Black, Red and White Knights, came to Alemanni. In a very short time Meriadoc proved his worth to such a degree that he was promoted to a place of high authority, commanding the mercenaries and errant knights who, like he, had responded to the emperor's call, while his companions also received important roles within the army.

Soon there came a messenger with news of a fresh attack by Gundebald, who had landed with a large army on the coast of the emperor's lands. Meriadoc, at the head of a strong force, led the counterattack. Skilfully

deploying his forces under the leadership of his three companions, Meriadoc routed the enemy so thoroughly that only a handful escaped, while all of the plunder they had taken was recovered.

Pursuing the remnant of Gundebald's army, which was under the command of a general named Saguntius, Meriadoc found himself in the depths of a wild forest which, his men were quick to tell him, was believed to be haunted. Despite this, Meriadoc and his men rode on amid the trees, pushing on until the evening began to deepen, when Meriadoc called a halt. He posted guards and settled down in the shadow of an oak tree. The guards were instructed to awaken the camp at first light, but it seemed they had hardly begun their watch when the day began to dawn. Rubbing their eyes blearily, they awoke Meriadoc, who was astonished that so little time seemed to have passed since he had composed himself for sleep. Nevertheless, he roused the rest of the camp and the company set out again on the road, soon reaching an open plain where Meriadoc remembered hunting with the emperor. To his astonishment however, a great castle now stood where, three weeks earlier, he had ridden to the hunt through forest paths.

'Let us try to find out more about this place,' Meriadoc said.

As they approached, a company of servants emerged from the castle and came to meet them, inviting them to enter and rest for a time. After a moment's hesitation Meriadoc decided to accept the invitation, and he and his men entered the great building, which was richly decorated with the finest marble and porphyry, its walls hung with silken banners and elaborate tapestries.

They were led, by way of a mighty stair, to a chamber decorated with great taste and richness. There, on a marble throne, sat a lady of extraordinary beauty and nobility. When she caught sight of Meriadoc she rose to her feet and called to all her retainers to do like-wise. 'Welcome, Meriadoc,' she said. 'I have waited a very long time for this moment.'

Astonished, Meriadoc replied: 'I am amazed that you even know my name. But even more a cause of wonder is this palace, for I swear it was not here when I rode this way but a few weeks past.'

'Do not be surprised,' said the lady. 'I have known of you for a long time, though you may not realize it. As to this place, it is not what it seems. It has existed since ancient times. Nor is this where you think it to be, for that is merely an illusion.'

More than this she would not say but bade Meriadoc and his men be comfortable and dine with her. Servants brought many dishes, rich and rare, and wines and sweetmeats as fine as any they had ever seen. but no one spoke at all during the meal, servants and guests alike being utterly silent.

After a time, Meriadoc could stand this no longer, and beckoning to the seneschal who had been overseeing the feast, asked him what the name of the place, and its lady, might be. By way of answer the man simply pulled a face at him. Meriadoc, puzzled, repeated his question, and this time the man stared wild-eyed at him, and putting his hands to his head, waggled his fingers and opened his mouth so wide that he seemed like a demon about to devour his prey. Meriadoc started back, and half rose from his seat. At this the lady spoke angrily to her servant, reproving him and demanding that he cease his foolish behaviour. But by now both Meriadoc and his men were so disturbed by the unnatural behaviour of their hosts that they rose as a body and hastened from the hall, hearing the calls of their hostess fade into the distance.

They found their horses still waiting where they had left them and rode hurriedly from the place. It seemed to be only just past mid-day as they departed, but almost at once the darkness of night overtook them, and with it their horses seemed possessed of an even greater fear than they had felt themselves, so that they became unmanageable.

Rearing and plunging, their mounts charged through the forest, crashing into one another, screaming, and striking out at their fellows. Completely maddened, they ran throughout the rest of the night until they were at last exhausted and either fell or stood trembling in every limb.

When the sun finally rose, Meriadoc and his men found themselves by a rushing stream. More than half their number were lost, carried who knew where by their mad-dened horses. Mourning their lost compan-ions, they prepared to ride on. 'I believe we have spent some time in the Otherworld,' Meriadoc told his companions. 'Even now we cannot be sure that we are safely out of this strange place. Let us proceed with caution.'

With little notion of where they were going, the little company rode on. At noon a terrible storm blew up from nowhere, with sheets of rain and fierce bolts of jagged light-ning and mighty crashes of thunder. Battered and driven half mad from the noise and the icy water which lashed at them from the heav-ens, they sought shelter beneath the trees and Meriadoc enquired if anyone among them recognized the country and knew if there was a place to rest until the storm passed.

One man spoke of a castle he knew of, and which he believed, from the look of the land-scape, was close by. 'But it is a deadly place,' he added. 'For I have heard that no one who enters there comes away without shame. In my view we should pass it by.'

More than this he would not say until another man, Waldomer, the emperor's brother-in-law, pressed him hard to show them the way. Finally, the man shrugged and said that he would take them there. 'But I myself will not enter that place,' he said. 'If you do so, you may be sure you will regret it before you leave.'

They followed the knight through the lashing rain, until the walls of a castle rose up before them through the murk. Waldomer, seeking Meriadoc's permission, led a party of men to investigate the place, since Meriadoc would not risk all of their party in another strange place until he was certain it was safe.

Waldomer and his men rode through the gates of the castle, which gaped wide, and went within. They found the place entirely deserted, though in the great hall a fire burned brightly, and there were warm carpets on the floor. The stables also contained fodder for their mounts, and when he saw this Waldomer ordered his men to look to their horses and then to repair to the hall.

'Everything is laid out ready for us,' he said. 'And since it seems as though we were expected, it would be foolish to turn down such excellent hospitality.'

So the knights stabled and fed their horses and then gathered about the fire in the great hall. But when they had been there only a short while a sudden, inexplicable fear overcame them. They sat staring at the floor, afraid even to move a hand or eye, as though Death himself was stalking them and might strike at any moment.

✠ ✠ ✠

MERIADOC, MEANWHILE, WAITED under the dripping trees. The storm grew ever more intense, and the men who had stayed with him began to grumble. Finally, when no word came from the castle, Meriadoc decided they should follow their comrades. But the knight who had originally led them there refused to come, retreating alone into the darkness of the wood.

Meriadoc led the remainder of his troop into the castle, where they found Waldomer and his men sitting, still as statues, staring at the floor.

'What is amiss here?' demanded Meriadoc.

Waldomer started visibly. 'Lord,' he said, 'we are too afraid to look one another in the face.'

'Then I command you all to get up,' answered Meriadoc sternly. 'Only your fear holds you thus. Rise now and set the tables. I will search for food and drink.'

As though released from their fear, the men began sheepishly to obey. Meriadoc set off alone through the empty echoing halls in search of victuals. Passing through several rooms, he entered a chamber where he saw a young woman sitting alone. The table before her was laden with bread and wine, and at the sight of it Meriadoc became so overcome with hunger and thirst that he snatched up an armful of bread and several skins of wine and left the room without even speaking. As he did so he encountered a tall figure who, seeing the food and drink in his arms, demanded angrily to know who he was and what he meant by robbing the maiden's table. When Meriadoc did not answer, but rather pushed forward to pass him, the tall man struck him a blow to the temple which felled him where he stood and sent the sword which he had been holding skittering across the floor.

Staggering to his feet, still clutching most of the bread and wine, Meriadoc fled from his adversary, only stopping when his breath failed him.

Now he found himself in a strange part of the castle, with no idea of how to get back to the hall where his men awaited him. Also, his sword was gone, and he had no means of defending himself. At this moment the tall servant appeared, carrying the knight's own sword. Berating him for taking the food and drink, and for running away from an unarmed man, he tossed the sword at Meriadoc's feet and withdrew.

Meriadoc, shamefaced, picked up the sword, but still intent upon the acquisition of food, followed his nose until he reached the kitchen. There he saw a huge shaven-headed man with a grossly fat body asleep before a fire over which was stretched a roasting spit on which a number of cranes were skewered. As soon as Meriadoc entered, he awoke and with a cry of rage, seized the spit and attacked him, striking him about the head and shoulders until Meriadoc fell groaning to the earth.

Angry as well as hurt by this unprovoked attack, Meriadoc sprang up and seizing his opponent around the waist flung him down. Then, seeing where a well opened in the floor close by, he dragged the huge man to it and with a great heave flung him down into the watery depth.

This done, Meriadoc gathered up as much food as he could carry and found his way back, not without some difficulty, to where his men still waited, gathered into a tight knot, looking all the while over their shoulders.

The sight of the food and drink revived them considerably, and they fell to with a will. But hardly had they eaten above a few mouthfuls when an enormous man, carrying what looked like a whole roof beam, came crashing into the hall, roaring out that they had stolen his master's food. Before anyone could react, he had felled more than a dozen of Meriadoc's men. He, furious at the continuing attacks, drew his sword, and shouting his battle-cry chased the huge creature from the hall and through the maze of tunnels and passageways, which seemed to lead everywhere and nowhere in that strange place.

At length he emerged into a large chamber which was full of armed men. At once they turned upon him and attacked him. Against so many he had little chance and was quickly driven back against the wall. But such was the strength and courage he exhibited that in a while the attackers withdrew to within a few feet and granted him the right to surrender and depart as he willed.

Exhausted, Meriadoc made his way slowly back through the maze of passages until he once again reached the great hall. There he found no one except those of his company who had been felled by the giant. The rest had fled or been carried off.

Sick at heart, Meriadoc went in search of his horse and those of his companions. The stables were empty, however, and no longer sure what to do, Meriadoc wandered out of the castle alone and on foot and took the road back towards the forest. In his heart he knew that these events were part of a journey that had taken him into the Otherworld, and that the beautiful woman who had seemed so well disposed to him was almost certainly of faery blood. By no other way could he account for the shifts in time, or the strange stupor that had gripped his men. But to these things he gave no further thought, for he knew that his life lay outside the world of such dangerous illusions.

FOR THE REST of the day Meriadoc pursued his way wearily, then, just as the sun was setting, he encountered the man from his own company who had refused to enter the castle and had warned them all against doing so. Meriadoc was glad to see him and begged forgiveness for ignoring his sound advice. The two then rode on together until they saw a large party of armed men on the road ahead. Overtaking them with caution, Meriadoc recognized Waldomer among the group, and realized with delight that they were his own men! The greetings which then ensued were great indeed, the knights glad to see their commander and he equally glad to see them.

Thus reunited, the company continued through the forest until they were halted by the sounds of battle: cries and the clashing of armour and swords. Quickly, Meriadoc dispatched scouts to discover what was happening. Pressing forward under cover of the trees these men found themselves looking upon the great and terrible battle. Such was the carnage that rivers of blood seemed to flow across the plain that stretched before them, and the dead lay heaped in piles. Seeing a boy crouched in the bushes, watching, one of the scouts demanded to know who the combatants were.

'That is the army of the emperor,' said the boy, pointing. 'The other belongs to King Gundebald's brother, Guntrannus.'

'How is this possible?' asked the scout.

'When last we heard, that battle was taking place many leagues from here.'

Wide eyed, the boy told them: 'I have heard that the leader of the emperor's forces vanished into this very forest, and when the rest of the soldiers went in search of him, they met with the army of their enemy. Now it seems they are losing. Only those three mighty knights hold back the enemy.'

Looking where the boy pointed, and where the fighting was thickest, the scout saw three men, one in red armour, the other in white and the third in black.

They knew at once that these were Meriadoc's companions and, returning swiftly to where their leader waited, the scouts told him everything they had seen. Meriadoc almost wept when he heard how their forces were faring. Then he rallied and gathering the remnant of his own small contingent around him, gave them words of encouragement, reminding them of their honour and strength and the needs of their beleaguered fellows. Then, dividing his force in two, one under his own command and the other under that of Waldomer, he led a charge against the enemy from two sides.

They, thinking a far greater force had come against them, turned at bay, and at this point the emperor's tired army, along with others who had fled to the forest in fear of their lives, turned and fought with renewed vigour. Within a few moments, the tide of the battle turned and Meriadoc, reunited with his three friends, drove the enemy from the field, killing most, including King Guntrannus himself.

In the weeks that followed, the victorious army of the emperor, led by Meriadoc, passed through and over the lands of the enemy with fire and sword. City after city fell to them, either by force or willing submission. At the end of this time Meriadoc was able to send word to the emperor that the greater part of King Gundebald's lands was won over and that he, Meriadoc, now sought only one final glory to prove his worth.

The emperor's reply was swift. If Meriadoc could but rescue his daughter from the clutches of Gundebald, then Meriadoc would inherit the emperor's own kingdom and the hand of his daughter in marriage.

⊹ ⊹ ⊹

UNKNOWN TO THE emperor, his daughter had already heard of Meriadoc's extraordinary prowess and had contrived to send him a message of her own, in which she promised him every aid in her power, and a warm welcome if he should succeed in rescuing her. However, she counselled him to come with only a few supporters, for thus she believed he would fare much better. With this advice in mind Meriadoc selected only his three friends, the Black, Red and White knights, to accompany him, and accordingly they set out together for the very heart of Gundebald's kingdom, where lay his most powerful city.

As fortune would have it, being unfamiliar with the roads, they became lost in a forest, and wandered there for five days without seeing any sign of human habitation. They began to grow hungry, having consumed their victuals, and were thus more than glad to meet a herd of home-coming cows upon the road. Meriadoc at once dispatched the Black Knight to search ahead, for where there were cows there must also be a village or farmstead.

The Black Knight soon returned with news that they had in fact found their way to a city, strongly fortified and heavily defended. It did not take long to discover that this was in fact Gundebald's citadel; all that remained was to find a way to gain entry.

Meriadoc decided upon a bold approach, and the four knights followed the herd of cows through a narrow gate and right up to the main gates to the citadel, where they were challenged by the porter, who opened the postern gate a crack and asked them to identify themselves.

'We are knights from Britain,' said Meriadoc. 'We have been in service to King Arthur and just recently learned of the need of your king for soldiers in his fight against the emperor. We are here to offer our services.'

'Then you are welcome,' replied the porter. 'The king has given orders that no one else is to be admitted. He himself has but lately ridden forth to encounter the knights sent daily to rescue the emperor's daughter. Go and find lodging in the city and await the king's return.'

'First,' said Meriadoc, 'since the king is not here, I would speak to the seneschal of this castle. Go and tell him that four knights stand before his gate awaiting entry.'

'That I shall not do,' answered the porter, beginning to be suspicious. As he spoke, he began to close the postern gate. Meriadoc, realizing the porter was alone, kicked the gate open. The blow was so hard that it felled the man, and Meriadoc seized him and threw him into the river which ran past the gate. Then he opened the door and admitted his companions.

It so happened that the emperor's daughter was housed in a tower which abutted the wall next to the very gate where Meriadoc and his men gained entrance. And, as fortune would have it, she was at that moment standing by one of the windows with her two

121

ladies-in-waiting, looking out sorrowfully at the world beyond her prison. Seeing what took place at the gate, she guessed that only Meriadoc could be daring enough to attempt such an entry, and at once sent one of her trusted handmaids to bring the four knights to her.

When they stood before her, all four were overwhelmed by her beauty. She smiled at them all, but her fondest look was for Meriadoc. 'You are most welcome,' she said. 'Now I may perhaps be quit of this place.' She began to tell them how best they might arrange her escape, pointing out that King Gundebald had treated her with honour, more as a daughter than a prisoner, and that, within the confines of the castle, she was free to come and go at will. Thus she was able to find rooms for all four of her would-be rescuers, and then proceeded to instruct Meriadoc how he might best secure her release.

'Gundebald is hated by all his people,' she told Meriadoc. 'For this reason, you will find many here who will support you when the time comes. Here is what you should do. First, make yourself known to the king on his return and tell him that you have come to offer your service to him. It is his custom that he will only accept a new knight into his ranks after he has tested their prowess in single combat. He is exceptionally strong, and very proud, and will expect to beat you easily, after which he will admit you to his company.'

'I am confident that I can beat him in a fair fight,' said Meriadoc.

'That may well be,' replied the emperor's daughter. 'But there are conditions to this combat which make it less than fair – unless you are prepared.'

'Tell me everything you can,' said Meriadoc.

'Listen well then,' said the emperor's daughter, and proceeded to tell him that Gundebald would choose to fight on a stretch of country called 'The Land of No Return'. This was a strange and terrible waste, an island in the midst of the land, on which nothing grew, and where the very ground consisted of shifting mud-banks. Anyone who walked there unprepared was swallowed up at once. At the very centre of this evil place was a great tar pit, surrounding the only patch of solid ground. Gundebald had caused two causeways to be built which connected the solid earth to the surrounding countryside from four directions. Great timbers sunk in the shifting ooze supported these, enabling a single rider to cross the mud-banks and the pits of tar to reach solid ground at the centre. There Gundebald had built himself a splendid palace. Four towers protected the approaches to this place, each one well-guarded.

'This is how Gundebald has managed to defeat so many brave knights,' said the emperor's daughter. 'Only those lucky enough to be felled by him on the road itself have survived, providing they are not killed outright. The rest fell into the pit of tar and were consumed. The other thing you should know is that Gundebald possesses a remarkable horse of exceptional strength. You will be certainly overcome without my help, for I have in my possession a steed of equal prowess – in fact Gundebald gave it to me himself as a gift to make me like him better!' She shuddered and went on: 'I will give you this horse, and fresh arms and armour. You are my only hope. If you fail, I am destined to remain here for ever.'

'I shall do all within my power,' said Meriadoc.

✠ ✠ ✠

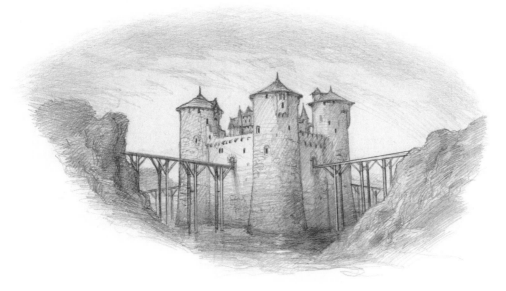

→ *The Castle in the Pit* ←

THUS IT WAS that Meriadoc came to encounter Gundebald on one of the causeways which crossed the sea of shifting mud, armed in fresh and brilliant armour, and riding the magnificent Arabian horse which the emperor's daughter provided for him. For on Gundebald's return he had, as the emperor's daughter had promised, been glad to welcome four of King Arthur's knights to his camp, but also, as was his custom, challenged them all to single combat. If the king suspected anything, he gave no sign of it, and agreed to fight Meriadoc first. He also, such was his confidence in his own strength and the setting of the challenge, and more in jest than earnest, promised that if Meriadoc could defeat him then not only was the sanctity of his person assured but, as challenger, in the event of Gundebald's death, he would become heir to the king's lands and titles.

It was only when the day appointed for their battle dawned, and he saw the steed ridden by Meriadoc, that King Gundebald realized he had been tricked. He grew pale when he saw this, for it had been prophesied to him long since that he would be overcome by a man riding such a horse. Then his colour went from white to red and he screamed in rage that he had been betrayed and spurred his mount to meet Meriadoc in the midst of the causeway.

Now see how fate may change things in a matter of moments, for as the goddess turns her wheel, so do men rise and fall. The battle was quickly over when Meriadoc gave Gundebald such a buffet with his spear that both king and horse spun away and fell from the causeway. Both were swallowed in a matter of moments by the stinking tar and perished utterly. Then Meriadoc continued on to the palace on the island, where he was made welcome and, under the terms of Gundebald's own agreement, received the submission of the dead king's followers.

Word went forth swiftly that Gundebald was dead, and it was not long before the identity of his slayer was also known. This was a cause for great rejoicing, since, just as the emperor's daughter had said, Gundebald had been much hated in his own land, and many rejoiced at the thought of gaining so famous and honourable a lord.

Meriadoc called a council of all the lords who owed allegiance to the dead king and explained to them that he acted in the name of the emperor, and that they should prepare themselves to submit to him as their new lord. Many responded by saying that they would take no one but Meriadoc himself as their liege, and it says much for the worthiness of the hero that he sought to dissuade them, until at length they swore that, so long as the emperor kept his word and married his daughter to Meriadoc, they would accept his rule over them.

✚ ✚ ✚

DURING MERIADOC'S ABSENCE, matters had altered radically in the emperor's domain. War had broken out on another front, against the King of Gaul, and so hard had this powerful ruler pressed the emperor that he was forced to concede, not only many of his lands, but also the hand of his daughter – the same maiden whom Meriadoc had but lately set free and to whom he was pledged.

Now, the emperor was careful to prevent this news escaping, and Meriadoc remained in ignorance of how matters stood. He returned to a hero's welcome, bringing with him a huge force of knights formally in the service of King Gundebald and now sworn to serve Meriadoc to the death. The emperor

immediately appointed him regent over the empire; yet, while he smiled and heaped rewards upon the hero of so many battles, in secret the emperor plotted his death so that he could fulfil his bargain with the King of Gaul.

To aid this plan he first placed his daughter in a tower, where apartments suited to her station had been prepared. Then he set a watch over her, and having given Meriadoc free access to her, soon received reports of them whispering and kissing, embracing, and making merry together.

At this the emperor smiled and began to plot against his loyal vassal. First, he summoned all the nobles of his own land, together with those who had journeyed with Meriadoc from the lands of King Gundebald. Then, with the hero himself seated among them, he addressed them thus:

'My lords, I have called you here to discuss a serious matter which concerns you all. I refer to the question of this Meriadoc, whom you all know well. Just who is this mercenary knight whom I took to my service? Just what has he achieved? Little, I would say. For was not everything provided by me? Was not the gold to provision the army from my own war chest? And did he not succeed only with my soldiers at his back? As to my daughter, even in this case he was only able to rescue her with her own connivance and support.'

A murmur ran through the crowd, as man looked at man and questioned all they heard. Meriadoc himself sat as though stunned. The emperor continued:

'Despite these things, I was ready and willing to reward this man with all the riches and lands at my disposal – had it not been for word of a grave matter which reached my ears just in time. Not content to await the promised betrothal of my daughter to him, he has forced her and, I believe, from the swelling of her belly, left her with child. I put it to you, my lords, is this the proper behaviour of a faithful vassal to his lord? I submit that it is not. What, then, must I do? I ask you all to consider this matter and answer me from your wisdom.'

At this Meriadoc could contain himself no longer. He leapt to his feet and stormed into the centre of the room, ready to challenge the emperor. At this, pandemonium broke loose. Armed guards, set there for this purpose by the emperor himself, entered and took Meriadoc prisoner. At the same time, in other parts of the city, Meriadoc's loyal followers were rounded up and either killed or confined. The gathering broke up in confusion, no one being certain whether Meriadoc should be deemed innocent or guilty.

When news of this reached the ears of the emperor's daughter, she was beside herself with anguish, and had to be restrained by her women from doing herself harm. Gradually, as she became calmer, she began to think that Meriadoc would be certain to find a means of rectifying matters. But within a few days of Meriadoc's arrest, the King of Gaul arrived with a huge train of wagons and men, expecting to marry the emperor's daughter himself.

When he discovered that she was indeed with child, and at that by Meriadoc, he repudiated the treaty he had lately signed with the emperor and swore that he would not rest until the slur to his honour was satisfied. He then withdrew and began once again to ravage the empire.

His plot having gone awry, the emperor was forced now to call all the soldiers and knights remaining in his service and to prepare again for war. This time he would lead the army himself – though he already

regretted making Meriadoc his enemy and placing him under arrest.

Meriadoc himself heard of the new war and prepared to make his escape. He was only lightly guarded, now that every available man was required to fight at the emperor's side, and with this in mind he laid his plans with care. Waiting until the imperial army had departed, leaving the city strangely quiet, Meriadoc cut his clothes into strips and, making a rope from them, climbed down from the window of the tower where he was imprisoned and made his way to the house of a knight whom he knew was sympathetic to him. There he was warmly received, and before his escape was detected he had been supplied with food and drink, equipped with armour, weapons and a horse, and had set forth from the city.

Once clear of its walls, Meriadoc rode swiftly after the army. Soon he reached the place where the two forces, of the emperor and the King of Gaul, were drawn up. There he secretly joined the king's troops. Now battle was joined, and riding and fighting like twenty men, Meriadoc cut a swath through the emperor's men. In quick succession he felled the leader of the imperial troops, and then the emperor's nephew, who was named as his heir.

When he saw this the emperor rose in his stirrups and screamed that he would be avenged on this knight who slew the best of his fellows before his eyes. Seizing a spear, he rushed madly towards Meriadoc, who turned to face his adversary, and letting go of his reins grasped his own spear with both hands and rode with all his might at the emperor. Such a blow he struck that the spear passed though shield and armour alike and pierced the body of the emperor through and through. As he fell dying Meriadoc called out: 'Thus do I repay the wages you offered me!'

Then he rode swiftly back and joined with the King of Gaul's men, doing his best to lose himself among them. But the king, who had observed everything that occurred, quickly sent for the knight who had performed such astonishing feats of strength and courage, and who had singlehandedly rid him of his bitterest foe.

When Meriadoc stood before him, the king recognized him from the descriptions that were upon every man's lips. He smiled and said: 'Surely you are the worthiest man I ever met. Well have you served the emperor for the unjust treatment he gave to you. I know your story, and I swear this, that I shall restore not only your intended bride, but as many of the lands of the former emperor as you will promise to rule over in my name.'

Meriadoc gave his grateful thanks to this and soon he and the dead emperor's daughter were married, and thereafter lived out their lives in great harmony. Vast estates were given to Meriadoc by the King of Gaul, who became the new emperor. In time a son was born to Meriadoc and his wife, and of him came many other brave knights and kings. In time Meriadoc himself returned to Britain and there, as one of the greatest of King Arthur's vassals, ruled long and wisely over his father's kingdom of Cambria.

Thus ends this tale, and now we turn to the story of Guingamor and Guerrehes, who met with many strange adventures in that land that many call Faery.

———— ✠ ————

EXPLICIT THE STORY OF MERIADOC.
INCIPIT THE STORY OF GUINGAMOR AND GUERREHES.

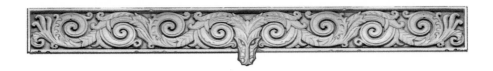

11: THE TALE OF GUINGAMOR AND GUERREHES

I

MANY TALES ARE TOLD OF THE FAERY RACE THAT LIVED IN THESE LANDS IN THE TIME OF KING ARTHUR. MYSTERIOUS AND POWERFUL, IT IS SAID THAT AT ONE TIME AN ACCORD EXISTED BETWEEN THE TWO RACES, BUT THAT A DEED WAS DONE WHICH ENDED THAT AGREEMENT FOR MANY YEARS AFTER.* THIS STORY SHALL BE TOLD LATER, BUT THERE IS ANOTHER WHICH MASTER THOMAS DID NOT INCLUDE IN HIS GREAT BOOK, AND THIS I WOULD TELL NOW. AT ITS HEART LIES A GREAT MYSTERY, WHICH MUST CAUSE ANY WHO READ IT TO PONDER ITS MEANING. FOR MYSELF I SHALL SAY NO MORE, BUT TELL IT AS IT WAS TOLD TO ME LONG AGO BY ONE WHO KNEW MORE OF THESE MATTERS THAN I.

✢ ✢ ✢

IN BRITTANY, MANY years before the time of King Arthur, there was a powerful king named Höel, who ruled over wide lands. He had a nephew named Guingamor whom he loved deeply and who was most popular among the people of that land. Since it happened that the king himself could not have children, he decided to make the youth his heir.

One day the king went to the woods to amuse himself hunting. Guingamor remained behind since he had just been bled and was still feeling weak, and once the king had departed, he retired to his lodgings to rest. Later, he returned to the castle, where he met the king's seneschal and the two men decided to play draughts.

Now it chanced that the queen passed that

---

* 'The Elucidation of the Grail and the Story of Sir Perceval' p. 309

way on her way to the chapel. She paused for a while to watch the men playing, and a beam of sunlight fell across Guingamor's face, causing the queen to view him with new eyes. At that moment she began to feel love for him and returning at once to her chamber sent one of her serving maids to ask Guingamor to come to her. Excusing himself from the chessboard, he accompanied the maid at once.

When he arrived in her rooms the queen made him sit down with her. Then she said, with great weight: 'Guingamor, you are young, valiant and handsome. It is scarcely surprising that someone should fall in love with you. I have heard that someone has done just that. She is courtly and beautiful, and I know of no other who is so worthy in all this realm. She loves you greatly and would, I am certain, become your mistress.'

'Lady,' answered Guingamor in puzzlement, 'I know of no such person, and I believe I would find it hard to love someone whom I had neither seen nor spoken to. Besides,' he added, 'I do not wish to begin an affair at this time.'

Disturbed by this response, the queen answered: 'My love, do not refuse me. I love you from the bottom of my heart and will always do so!'

Guingamor, startled, answered: 'Lady, I know that I ought to love you – but as the wife of my liege lord and uncle, nothing more.'

'I do not speak of that kind of love,' the queen replied; 'I would be your mistress if you will. You are handsome and I am still young. We could be happy together.'

At that Guingamor blushed and felt deeply ashamed. 'Madame, that can never be,' he answered, and made to leave the room. Desperately the queen caught him in her

arms and attempted to kiss him. Then, as Guingamor pulled away, the queen snatched at the edge of his cloak, so that he was forced to pull away from her. The clasps which held it broke, and Guingamor left the garment in the queen's hands.

Hurriedly, he returned to where the seneschal still sat at the game-board, where he tried to hide his distracted feelings and continue the game. The queen, meanwhile, grew fearful, having revealed her innermost feelings. Realizing that she still had Guingamor's cloak, she bade her maidservant carry it to him. So intent was he in keeping his thoughts in order that he scarcely noticed when the girl stood by him and draped it about his shoulders.

Not long after this, the king returned, full of the day's sport. All through dinner the knights who had been with him talked and boasted of their success in the hunt, and all the while the queen shot covert glances at Guingamor. Then, during a lull in conversation, she began to talk about the great white boar that haunted the woods nearby. 'What a pity,' she said, 'that none of you here – though you boast so much about your prowess in the field – has the courage to hunt that dreadful beast.' As she spoke, she looked straight at Guingamor.

The king frowned. 'My dear, you know that I do not like any mention of that creature to be made in my hearing. I have lost too many knights to that terrible beast.'

After this the party soon broke up, and everyone retired to bed. But Guingamor could not forget what the queen had said. Instead of retiring he knocked on the door of the king's chamber. On being invited to enter, he knelt at his uncle's feet and begged to be granted a favour.

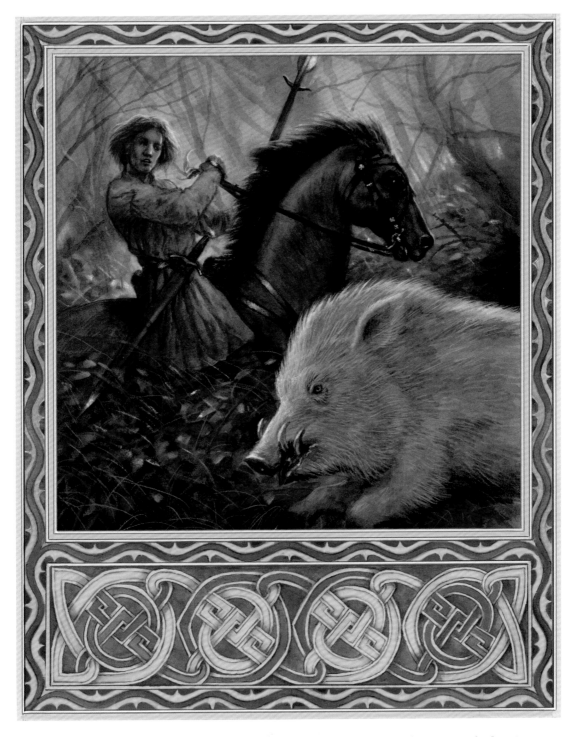

PLATE 4: *'Guingamor wheeled his horse and the boar rushed by, hurtling on into the forest'*

'You know there is nothing I would not give you,' the king said, smiling.

'Then, Uncle, I ask that you give me a bloodhound, a bratchet and your own best horse, and give me leave to hunt the white boar.'

Dismayed and saddened, the king wished profoundly that Guingamor had not asked this thing. He begged his nephew to reconsider.

'You are my heir. If anything should happen to you, the kingdom could be left without a lord.'

'Sire, nothing will change my mind,' said Guingamor. 'If you will not lend me what I have asked for I shall go anyway.'

At this moment the queen entered the room, and when she heard what Guingamor had requested, she added her own words to his, pleading with the king to grant his wish for the sake of his honour. In this way she hoped to be rid of the youth, and thus of her fears for what he might let fall concerning her protestations of love.

Reluctantly, the king gave his consent, and Guingamor hurried away to spend a sleepless night in his lodgings. In the morning he rose with the dawn and sent for the king's hunting horse, his bloodhound and bratchet, which were duly brought to him. A group of huntsmen with two packs of hounds were gathered. The king himself, and all his knights and their ladies, as well as most of the population of the city, turned out to see him depart. Many wept openly, for they expected never to see him again.

It was easy enough to trail the boar to its lair, and Guingamor sent the bloodhound in to drive the beast his way. It came thundering out of the undergrowth and charged straight for him, its eyes gleaming red and foam flying from its clashing tusks. Guingamor wheeled his horse and the boar rushed by, hurtling on into the forest. Guingamor sounded his horn and let loose one of the packs, bringing the others on but not yet giving them the signal to pursue the beast.

The pursuit was long and wearisome, and soon the rest of the hunt fell behind. But Guingamor kept on. The first pack of hounds grew exhausted and began to fall back, whereupon Guingamor released the second pack, and then the bratchet, and set himself to blowing the horn as best he might to guide and encourage the hounds.

After a time, they entered a denser part of the forest, and for a while Guingamor could no longer hear the barking of the dogs. He feared that he had lost them and began to think what the king would say when he returned empty-handed. Then he came to a high hill and rode to the summit, from where he could see across several leagues.

It was a clear day and the sun shone down on the trees, turning them green and golden. On all sides birds sang, though Guingamor had no ear for them. However, as he sat his horse and strained to catch a glimpse of movement in the forest, he heard the yelping of the bratchet and then saw the boar itself, closely pursued by the dog, appear and pass him on the way to higher ground.

Eagerly Guingamor spurred his horse down from the hill and went full tilt after his quarry. He rejoiced that he might succeed where no other had done and imagined what the king – and the queen – would say when he returned with the boar's head on his spear.

Fast though he rode, he could not seem to overtake the two beasts. The ground rose steadily, and he found himself leaving the woodland behind and entering a part of the country he did not recognize. Then, before him, he saw a most beautiful castle, rising from a meadow starred with flowers. Its walls were of green marble and its towers seemed all of silver, flashing in the sun. A wide gateway opened in the wall and reigning in his mount Guingamor sat and gazed in wonder, for the gates were of ivory inlaid with gold and seemed to have no clasp or fastening of any kind.

Since there was no sign either of the bratchet or the white boar, Guingamor determined to enter the place, certain that he would find a guardian of some kind within who might have seen them. Besides which, he was curious to know more of this place, of which he had never heard mention, despite its beauty and richness.

He rode boldly into the castle and looked about him, but could see no one moving anywhere. He dismounted and entered the most beautiful palace he had ever seen. Tables were laid with plates and goblets of solid gold as if for a feast, but not a living being was there.

Wondering greatly at this, Guingamor left the hall and mounted his horse again. In the meadow, he listened but could hear no sound of either the bratchet or the boar. He began to regret his impulse to enter the castle, and without a backward look rode on until he entered the forest again. There he thought he heard the barking of the bratchet, and spurred his mount in that direction, blowing his horn the while as strongly as he might.

The way led again into more open ground, and there he found a fountain that rose beneath a single great tree, feeding into a nearby river. The fountain was most beautifully and elegantly carved, and the gravel surrounding it seemed to be made of silver and gold. But nothing was more beautiful to his eyes than the maiden who was bathing

herself in the fountain. Her limbs were long and smooth, her breasts slight, and her hair a cloud of gold.

As he checked his horse, openly staring at her naked beauty, Guingamor saw that her clothes were laid out to one side. On an impulse he gathered them up and placed them high up in the fork of the tree, thinking that he might still capture the boar and return in time to find the Lady of the Fountain still there – for he was sure she would not leave without her clothes.

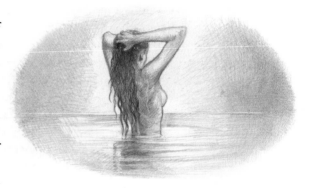

→ *The Lady of the Fountain* ←

But the maiden had seen him and now she called out, addressing him by name.

'Guingamor, leave my clothes. You would surely not wish it to be said that you had stolen a maiden's clothing in the depths of the wood. Come here and talk to me. You have ridden far today without success. Stay with me a while and all will be well, I promise.'

Shamefaced, Guingamor gave the lady back her clothing. Then he excused himself, saying that he must continue his search for the boar and the bratchet. The maiden smiled and offered him her hand. 'I promise you will search for ever and not find either of them without my help. I am called Brangepart. If you stay with me for three days, you shall have both the boar and your dog at the end of that time. Then you may go home. This I promise.'

Uncertain, but believing that the Lady of the Fountain spoke the truth, Guingamor dismounted and stood by while she dressed herself. Then he helped her to mount his horse, so that she sat before him, and set off as she instructed.

Guingamor soon realized that they were approaching the castle which he had recently visited. As they went, with the maiden Brangepart held close in his arms, his heart began to pound, and his palms to sweat. Finally, he could keep silent no longer.

'My lady,' he said. 'You should know that I feel great love for you. Is there a chance you might feel the same towards me? If so, I promise I will never so much as look at another woman.'

The Lady of the Fountain smiled at Guingamor and replied that she did indeed have such feelings for him. There and then they kissed and embraced with passion.

Soon they entered the castle, which was no longer silent and empty. Now it was all a-bustle with servants running hither and thither, preparing food and drink for the couple, while minstrels tuned their instruments in the galleries, knights and squires welcomed them and pages hurried to stable Guingamor's horse and to offer him water to wash in and fresh clothing of the finest kind.

They dined well, and Guingamor was put to rest in a great bed where, later, Brangepart joined him. For three days and three nights they were together thus, enjoying the sports of love. On the third day, Guingamor declared reluctantly that he must return to his uncle. 'I ask that I be given the bratchet and the head of the white boar, as you promised, my lady. As soon as I have returned home and shown my prize I shall come back here.'

The maiden looked at him oddly. 'I will give you the things as I promised. But there is something you must know. Though only three days have passed here, in the world from which you came a hundred years have gone by. All those whom you knew are long since dead, and I dare say you will not even find anyone who remembers your name.'

'My lady and my love, I cannot believe that what you say is true!' cried Guingamor in the greatest distress.

'Nevertheless, it is so,' said she.

'I must go forth and see the truth of this for myself. Do you give me leave to depart if I promise to return at once when I have satisfied myself that what you say is true?'

'Very well,' said the lady. 'But I warn you: once you leave the borders of this land – by the fountain where we first met – you must neither eat nor drink anything, no matter how hungry or thirsty you are. If you do so, you will never be able to return here.'

Guingamor gave his word on this, and the lady had his mount, ready saddled, brought out. With it came the dog, which he took, holding it by the leash, and the carcass of the boar, the head of which he took and placed on the end of his spear. Then he set out, Brangepart riding by his side until they reached the riverside, where a boat awaited him. There he took leave of the lady and crossed the swift water to the other side.

He found the forest much deeper and more entangled than he remembered it, and many other things seemed changed also. Where before there had been but a rough track, now a well-set road crossed the land. Guingamor wandered for most of the morning until he came upon a clearing where a charcoal-burner was at work. Guingamor asked for news of the king, and after some thought the man replied that he had heard tell 'in old stories' of such a monarch, but that he was long dead, close on a hundred years ago. Guingamor asked if he had heard any-thing of a nephew of this old king, and the charcoal-burner, thinking deeper, said that he had heard something about a nephew, but he had gone into the forest to hunt one day, and had never returned.

'I am that nephew,' said Guingamor, pale and trembling. He told the man the whole story and showed him the boar's head. 'I bid you take this trophy of mine, and show it to anyone you meet, and tell them my story. For I must return now whence I came.'

Guingamor turned his horse about and rode back through the forest the way he had come. It was well past midday and as the after-noon sun rose higher in the sky, he began to experience terrible thirst and hunger, until he believed he would go mad. Then beside the road he saw an apple tree laden down with fruit and forgetting the Lady of the Foun-tain's warning, took three of the apples and ate them hungrily.

As soon as he had done so, he began to feel the weight of his years. His body and limbs grew wasted and he no longer had the strength to sit on his horse. He fell there by the roadside and could not lift so much as a finger to help himself.

There the charcoal-burner found him, having followed him there out of curiosity for his strange story. He found Guingamor so aged and frail that he seemed unlikely to live out the day. Then he saw two damsels riding towards him who, when they came abreast, dismounted, and began to reproach the knight

for failing to obey his lady's commands. Yet it was with tenderness and care that they helped him once again to mount his horse, and supporting him on either side, made their way towards the river. The charcoal-burner saw them cross in the boat which had brought the knight there earlier and after that he saw them no more.

The peasant returned home and showed the boar's head to everyone and told them of the knight's story, at which all marvelled greatly. At last, the head was taken to the court of King Arthur, and hearing the strange story of Guingamor, he insisted that the boar's head should be preserved for as long as might be, and that the story should be set down in writing, so that it was not forgotten.

But this is not the end of the story that I would tell here.

II

ON A HOT night years after this, King Arthur lay sleepless in his bed. The sky was overcast, and thunder rolled along the horizon and lightning split the sky. The king summoned two of his chamberlains and asked them to bring him a silken cloak and light boots and breeches. Then he called for torches and went into a lodge overlooking the sea, from where he was wont to watch the play of the wind and the waves, and from where, at need, he could descend through a gateway, and thence by a path, to the edge of the sea.

The king sat for a time watching the storm, and in a while saw it pass, leaving the hori-zon clear. And there he observed, towards the horizon, a light like a star that seemed to grow larger as he watched.

'What do you see there?' he demanded of one of his servants.

'My lord, it seems like a strange light.'

As they looked the light grew brighter, till it cast a glow over the surface of the sea, and they could see a barge, freshly painted, draped with a rich dark pall of silk. There seemed to be no one alive on it, but most astonishing of all was a great swan, its neck enclosed in a golden collar to which chains were attached, which drew the craft.

As the barge came level with the place from which the king and his servants watched, the swan stopped, and then began to cry and beat the water with its wings. Astonished, Arthur went out through the little gate and took the path down to the shore where the barge had come to rest. There he stepped aboard, finding the craft curtained with rich hangings, and with two great candles burning, one at each end of the deck. It was these that gave forth a light brighter than any lantern. In the midst of the boat was a shelter, which the king entered. There he found the body of a knight lying under a cloth of richest brocaded silk, trimmed with ermine. From the breast of the dead man protruded the haft of a great spear.

Gently the king drew back the coverlet and inspected the body. Never had he seen so strong and handsome a person! His clothing was richer than the king's own, and at his belt was a purse richly embroidered with gold thread. This the king opened, and inside found a letter, which he read:

'Sir King. The corpse which lies here requests, before death comes upon him, that you allow it to lie undisturbed in your hall until such time as one may come who can draw forth the spearhead from this flesh.

May he who draws it forth successfully take revenge upon the one who struck the blow – or may he have as evil a fate as Guerrehes had in the orchard. Let him strike the villain in the same place with this same spearhead. If this is done, you shall know all there is to know concerning this corpse. If the spear is not withdrawn before the year be out, then have the body interred with such honour as you think fit. Meanwhile know that the corpse is well embalmed and will be preserved for as long as needed.'

When Arthur had read this, he replaced the letter in the purse and drew the coverlet up as before. Then he called to his servants to take the body and lay it in the midst of the castle, in a side chapel. 'Let it be known,' he said, 'what has taken place this night.'

While his commands were carried out the king returned to the window and once again looked out on the sea. There he saw the swan trumpet with joy and once more beat the water with its wings. Then it turned about and drew the barge away, and the two candles, which had not ceased from burning, were suddenly extinguished, and with them the light went from the sea and darkness returned. As the king stood there marvelling greatly, he heard the voice of the swan raised, this time in lament, until it faded at last from his ears. Then the king returned to his bed and lay for a long while thinking upon all that he had seen, until he slept at last.

In the morning the first to rise was Sir Gawain. He roused several of his brothers-in-arms and they set out to celebrate Mass in the chapel. When they entered, they were astonished to see the body of the knight lying there before the altar. At first, they thought he was asleep, then they spied the spearhead in his breast and marvelled even more.

'Who is this?' demanded Gawain. 'Does anyone here know him?'

The knights looked closely at the dead knight's face, but none could recognize him.

Word soon spread throughout the city, and people began to crowd into the hall to see the dead knight. Gawain meanwhile went to rouse the king, but he said nothing of the body in the hall, and Arthur himself chose to hold his council on the matter. In the hall he drew back the mantle and exclaimed over the strange beauty of the corpse and the fineness of its apparel. Then he drew forth the letter. Everyone crowded near to hear what it might say.

'My lords,' said King Arthur. 'This man who lies before us had great faith that he would be avenged by one of the Knights of the Round Table.' He then read the letter out loud for all to hear.

Tor, the son of Ares, said: 'This is a great mystery. How can we know who killed him, or how, when nothing of this is told in the letter?'

'Aye,' said Gawain. 'Where indeed should we even begin to look?'

'As to that,' said King Arthur, 'we must wait and see.'

'And how is it that the writer knows of my brother, Guerrehes?' demanded Gawain. 'And of some shameful thing that happened to him?'

'That is for him to tell us,' said King Arthur, and he ordered a fine coffin to be made to contain the body, which was thereafter to rest in state before the altar for all to see, until such time as one came forward to attempt the adventure.

Gawain, meanwhile, sought out Guerrehes, who had not been present in the great hall, and knew nothing of the coming of the barge with the dead knight.

When Gawain spoke to him of the letter and its contents, Guerrehes was at first reluctant to speak, though he turned pale. In the end, he gave in to his brother's urgings and told how, some weeks before this, he had set out in search of adventure, and how he had ridden for three days without meeting anyone, until he came to an area of rich grassland, through which a broad river flowed. Following this for a time, he came in sight of a city of great beauty, its walls of green marble and white limestone, carved all over with the shapes of beasts.

He was very hungry by this time and hastened to enter the city, where he believed he would find shelter. But the streets were strangely deserted, and Guerrehes was able to ride right up to the castle that dominated the heart of the city without seeing a soul. He went into the splendid building, through gates of ivory, and found this too to be deserted. Advancing further, he passed through a great and elegant hall, beyond which he found a chamber in which were four beds, richly adorned with gold and ivory and covered in costly bedspreads. He sat down on one of these to remove his helm, since the heat of the day was irksome.

Next, he found himself in an even larger chamber, in which were two beds, even more richly apparelled than the first. Beyond this lay still another room, decorated with gold, in which a single bed of unparalleled richness stood. This room had a window, and on looking out he saw an orchard filled with apple trees, each one bearing a rich load of fruit. In the centre was a green lawn where two silken pavilions had been set up, and as Guerrehes looked, he saw a hideously ugly dwarf pass from one to the other, bearing a silver bowl and a towel.

Wondering what kind of place this was, and why were there no people except for the dwarf and whoever lay within the tents, Guerrehes climbed out of the window and made his way across the lawn to the larger of the two pavilions. Peering in through the entrance, he saw a beautiful woman sitting in a silver chair. She was dipping bread into a silver bowl, held by the ugly dwarf, which also contained milk and almonds. With this she was attempting to feed a man who lay on a bed with a blood-stained bandage bound around him.

Guerrehes bade them God's greeting, startling the wounded man, who glared at him and cried: 'Get out of here!' He struggled to sit up and knocked the bowl of milk from the dwarf's hands so that it spilled upon the floor. The effort of moving caused his wound to break open again, and he fell back with a groan.

Guerrehes begged forgiveness, having no notion why his presence should cause such distress, but this seemed only to anger the man even more, though he could do little but groan and clasp both hands to his open wound. Then it was that the hideous dwarf spoke up. 'Fear not my master. This insult will be quickly avenged once the Little Knight comes.'

All this time the damsel had spoken no word at all, but simply stared at Guerrehes as though she knew him. Then there entered the tent a small knight on a small horse. He was no more than two feet high, yet he was no dwarf, being perfectly proportioned and wearing a suit of armour to match his size. Without speaking a word, he drew his sword and struck Guerrehes hard across the thighs, crying out that he would have his head for this 'insult' to his master.

The wounded knight now found his tongue and declared that Guerrehes should not be allowed to depart unpunished, since he had shown great arrogance by entering where he was not wanted.

Retreating outside, Guerrehes found his horse and shield and helm placed in readiness. Once mounted, as he towered over the Little Knight, he declared his intention of leaving at once, and peaceably, but the small man would not have it. 'Not until you have jousted with me, arrogant fool!' he shouted.

Astonished at his ferocity, Guerrehes set his spear in rest and charged at his opponent. When his lance struck home on the centre of the Little Knight's saddlebow it shattered, while he was knocked from his horse's back by what seemed the merest tap of the other's spear.

As he lay half stunned, the Little Knight dismounted and came and set his foot on Guerrehes' neck. The weight of his small foot felt as though it were crushing the life from him, and when the small one demanded his submission, he extended his hands and gasped out the words of surrender.

'Now learn the custom of this place,' the small knight said, with his hands on his hips. 'All whom I overcome – and they are many – are given three choices. The first is to become a weaver, to make and sew costly linens and draperies, to learn to make brocade curtains for my master's beds. The second is to fight me again – and, if you are victorious, leave here without further trouble. The third choice is to lose your head. You have a year to think about this. At the end of which time, you must return here to me and give your answer. Fail in this and your honour is lost for ever. Do you understand?'

Guerrehes could only nod his head.

'Good,' said Little Knight in satisfaction. 'You were too bold entering this orchard the way you did – now you can leave the same way as you came, through the window!'

Guerrehes climbed back the way he had come and was astonished to find the room beyond filled with maidens making lace and ribbons and purses of leather, their hands flying like birds between weft and woof. With one accord they began to laugh at him and to call out insults. Quickly he made his way into the next room – the one with the two beds – and this he found to be full of squires and damsels who were all busy at making things. They too mocked him, crying: 'Craven! Coward! The Little Knight beat you soundly! So much for your size and strength!'

Face crimson, Guerrehes hurried into the third room, where he found several knights playing chess and backgammon. These too hurled insults at him, comparing his great size to that of the Little Knight and mocking him for being so easily overthrown.

Pausing in his telling of these events, Guerrehes admitted to his brother that he had never felt such shame. But this was as nothing compared to what still awaited him, for in the hall of the castle, now filled with knights and ladies and their retainers, he was noticed at once, and everyone there cried out that this was the miserable fellow who could not even defend himself against the least of men.

Hiding his grief as best he might, Guerrehes escaped to the courtyard, where he found his horse waiting. Mounting swiftly, he trotted out through the gates, meeting no one. Thus, he thought to have escaped further

vilification, but the streets of the town were now filled with people, and even they seemed to have heard of his misfortune. They pelted him with stones and offal and fish guts, crying all the while 'Behold the craven knight!' until Guerrehes thought he could bear no more.

Finally, he was beyond the walls of the city and set himself to put as much distance between himself and it as he might. All the while he marvelled at the strength of the Little Knight and at the beauty of the city and the castle that seemed so fair while its inhabitants were yet evil natured. He rode by way of fields and woods, avoiding roads or trackways where he might encounter people who might know of his shame. For two more days he rode, scarcely pausing to rest and not at all to eat. Then, as the country grew more familiar, he chanced to meet a group of knights from Arthur's court. All greeted him in friendly fashion, and thus reassured, Guerrehes rode on until he reached Camelot the Golden.

'Now you know of my shame, brother,' he said to Gawain.

Having heard the whole sad tale, Gawain said: 'I believe we should go together and look at the body that came here last night. Since the letter that was found in the barge mentioned you, I believe these two things to be connected. This is a mystery which is best attempted at once, lest it fester and grow within you, brother.'

Protesting that he could think of no such connection, Guerrehes accompanied Gawain to the hall, and there, along with several other knights who were present, he looked upon the corpse. After a while he said, 'I do not know this man!' Then he added, angrily: 'May this spearhead never come out!' But as he spoke his hand brushed against the broken shaft of the spear, and at once it leapt clear of the body and fell to the floor with a clash.

The knights stared in wonder and Sir Gawain was heard to say: 'Brother, it seems you were over-hasty in this matter. It seems there is indeed some link between these things.'

All marvelled greatly and examined the spearhead, which was as fine and bright as the day it had been cast and bore neither stain nor darkening from the blood of the dead knight. Finally, they gave it to Guerrehes, who said grimly that he would honour the words of the letter, which bound him to avenge the death of the knight whether he wished or not. 'Though how I shall find the one who killed him since I know nothing more of him, I cannot say.' Then he returned to his chambers and, having called for one of his own best spears to be brought before him, had the weapon from the dead knight's body affixed to its shaft. But in his heart, he could not help but think of the other oath he had sworn – to face again the Little Knight. For it was plain to him that there was a deep enchantment in this adventure, and he could not think how he would succeed against such supernatural power with naught but his strength to call upon.

A few days after this, King Arthur held a great feast to celebrate Easter, and on this occasion asked that Guerrehes sit near him. Throughout the evening the knight spoke little and never once laughed. Observing this, Kay the Seneschal asked the king if he would grant him a boon. When Arthur gave his assent, the seneschal said that he wanted to hear why Guerrehes was so solemn and sad, and that the king should bid him tell the reason to the whole court. At first Arthur refused, but Kay reminded him of his custom

to always grant a boon asked before a feast. Reluctantly, and not without stern words to his foster-brother, the king turned to Guerrehes and commanded him to tell the reason for his sorrowful mien. Guerrehes, flushed and angry, obeyed and told again the whole story as he had told it to Gawain. Then he said: 'Now that you know of my shame, and since I am bound for the sake of my honour to carry out the request of the dead knight to avenge him, I shall remain here no longer.'

King Arthur gave him leave to depart, and without more ado Guerrehes left the hall, and calling for his horse and weapons set forth from the court.

✠ ✠ ✠

HIS JOURNEY WAS a long one, and took him far from home, and though he asked far and wide concerning the dead knight and the barge drawn by a swan, no one could tell him anything. So the year turned, until at length the day appointed for his return to the mysterious city drew near. Guerrehes turned towards the place, and as he neared it, met the hated Little Knight on the road. 'Well,' sneered the small man, 'I was on my way to King Arthur's court to remind you of your promise.'

'I need no such reminder,' answered Guerrehes grimly.

Thereafter the two rode in silence until they reached the meadowlands and the city of green marble. There, in redemption of his promise, Guerrehes chose to fight the Little Knight again. And this time, whether by skill or luck or magic none can say, he was the victor, and killed the small man without compunction and in fair combat.

The lord of the castle, whom Guerrehes

137

had last seen lying wounded in the silken pavilion, was so angered by the death of his diminutive champion, that he declared that he himself would fight Guerrehes, and accordingly called for his arms and weapons.

When the two met, Guerrehes chose the lance that bore the spearhead drawn from the body of the dead knight, and with his first blow, though he was himself unhorsed, he ran the spear deep into his opponent's breast. Dismounting, Guerrehes drew his sword and went to finish the work he had begun. But the lord was already cold, his spirit fled. And in that moment, all the people of the castle began to depart, seeming to melt away into the very air.

As Guerrehes stood looking down at the body of his opponent, a maiden appeared, clad in a robe of silk embroidered with silver flowers. She it was who he had last seen in the pavilion, caring for the wounded man, who now lay dead before her. Guerrehes expected her to begin weeping when she looked upon the corpse, but instead she was silent. When she looked where the spearhead was lodged in his heart, she said to Guerrehes: 'Sir, tell me the truth. Where did you get this spearhead?'

Guerrehes told her everything concerning the dead knight in the barge.

With a sigh, the maiden placed her hand upon his arm. 'You have done more than you can ever understand this day. That knight was my true love, a most worthy and hon-ourable man, and a king in his own right. This evil lord whom you have slain was the cause of his death. Now you have truly avenged him.'

Guerrehes looked down at the dead man more closely and saw that the spearhead had entered his body in the exact same place as the dead knight from the barge, and he marvelled greatly. He made to draw out the spearhead, but the maiden prevented him. 'Let it stay where it is! So long as it remains where it is, there will be no more vengeance.'

'So be it,' agreed Guerrehes. He consented to escort the maiden back to King Arthur's court, that she might see the body of her dead lover and see to his interment. They left the evil castle behind, and in all the town they saw not one person.

All that day they rode together, and when evening came they found themselves by the shore of the sea. There, but a short distance across the water, lay an island on which a fair castle stood, with many lighted windows.

'Here we are certain of a good welcome,' said the maiden, and called out to a boatman who came to ferry them across to the island. There they were well met and ushered into a great hall. Never had Guerrehes seen such a splendid gathering. There were more knights and ladies and squires there than he had ever seen – even in King Arthur's court. Nor had he ever received such a generous welcome. Everyone there treated him with the utmost honour, providing him with fresh clothing, water in which to wash and finally sitting him at a table on which the choicest foods and wines were laid.

Guerrehes was by this time exhausted from all that he had endured that day. He scarcely heard the talk of the people around him, save that afterwards he remembered them speaking of the sorrow they felt for their lord, King Brangamor, and of the joy of their lady, Queen Brangepart, who rejoiced for the avenging of her son.

At some point Guerrehes fell asleep. He slept deeply and dreamlessly and awoke refreshed to find himself lying in a great bed that swayed gently from side to side. He discovered that the reason for this was the motion of the barge in which the bed was set and, rising quickly, he found that it was being pulled by a swan. He knew this must be the very same barge that had brought the dead knight to Camelot the Golden. In vain he looked for the maiden who had brought him to the island castle, but it seemed to him that he was alone. Exhaustion overcame him again and lying down on the bed he quickly fell into a deep sleep.

Soon the barge came in sight of the cliffs where the king's lodge was set. Word spread of the coming of the strange craft, pulled by a swan, and this being the Eve of All Saints, King Arthur went at once to see what new manner of wonder it might bear. With several knights and lords he descended by way of the path to the shore, and there went aboard the barge. On the deck he met with a maiden, whose cloak was sewn with silver roses. She greeted the king and said: 'My lord, beneath the curtains of that bed sleeps a noble knight. I pray you let him sleep a little longer.'

For answer the king looked beneath the curtain. Then he said: 'He will have as much time as he needs to sleep later. For now, I would speak with him.'

Then King Arthur woke the sleeping man, whom he had at once recognized as Sir Guerrehes, and welcomed and embraced him, and they all repaired to the great hall of Camelot the Golden, where the body of the dead knight still lay as though asleep in the side chapel. When the maiden looked upon him, she sighed and then wept. 'Ah, fair love!' she cried. 'You were ever the best of men, and I have mourned you this long while. But I am glad that you are avenged.'

Then she turned to King Arthur and said:

'Sire, I may not remain here for long, but let me tell you the history of this noble lord. Here lies King Brangamor, the son of the knight Guingamor and the Lady Brangepart, whom he loved. I am sure you have heard the story of how he hunted the white boar and how afterwards he vanished from this world? Know then that he went to the land over which the Lady of the Fountain ruled, and that they lived out their time together there until the time of his death. Because the child the Lady bore him was part-mortal and therefore must die in this world, it was needful that he return here. Thus he arrived in the boat drawn by the swan, with the letter that began these mysteries. He might not rest until his death was avenged. Now that has been achieved by this brave knight, that part which is not of this earth may return to the place where he was born, to his queen, and to his mother, who lives yet in that place and mourns him, as do all his people. It is right that he should return to them and to the island over which he ruled, which is one where no mortal man may dwell.'

When he heard this Guerrehes felt a coldness in his blood, for he knew that he had walked in a faery realm and had eaten of their food, that many said meant death to those who did so. But as though she knew his thoughts, the maiden laid a hand upon his arm and told him to fear not. 'The food and drink you had were of this world and will do you no harm, for we were glad that you were able to avenge our king.'

King Arthur said: 'Let all be as you wish, lady.' He gave instructions for the body and all its fine wrappings to be carried down to the barge. There the damsel took her leave of Guerrehes and thanked him again. The swan beat its wings and made its way towards the place where it had first appeared. The last the people heard were the notes of its triumphant song.

King Arthur ordered these events to be set down and added to the story of Guingamor and the Lady of the Fountain, so that all might be read over and pondered upon at leisure, as I hope it may be here. And whether King Brangamor returned to life in that other place, or was buried in the sweet earth, none may say, for these are matters beyond the knowledge of men.

———— ✠ ————

EXPLICIT THE STORY OF GUINGAMOR AND GUERREHES.
IMPLICIT THE ADVENTURE OF THE EAGLE-BOY.

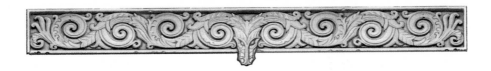

12: THE ADVENTURES OF EAGLE-BOY

IN THE DAYS FOLLOWING KING ARTHUR'S ASSUMPTION OF HIS FATHER'S THRONE, A NOBLE KING NAMED RICHARD RULED OVER THE COASTLANDS OF THE BRIGHT AND SHINING KINGDOM OF SORCHA. THIS KING HAD A CHILD WHOM HE NAMED RICHARD THE YOUNGER, AND WHO GREW TO BE EVERY BIT AS FAIR AND KIND AND NOBLE AS HIS FATHER. THE BEST EDUCATION POSSIBLE WAS GIVEN TO HIM, AND EVERYTHING CONCERNING THE LAND OVER WHICH HE WOULD ONE DAY RULE WAS TAUGHT TO HIM. BUT OF ALL THE THINGS HE LEARNED, THE ONE THAT HE MOST LOVED WAS TO HUNT. WHENEVER HE COULD HE TOOK HIMSELF OFF TO THE BORDERS OF THE FOREST, THERE TO SPEND THE DAY HAPPILY IN PURSUIT OF GAME OR IN CONVERSATION WITH THE HERMITS HE ENCOUNTERED THERE. BECAUSE OF THIS, THE NAME BY WHICH MOST PEOPLE IN THAT LAND KNEW HIM WAS 'THE KNIGHT OF THE CHASE'.

✠ ✠ ✠

THEN IT FELL out that the Queen of Sorcha conceived a second son, who was named John. Like his older brother every kind of good teaching and wisdom was given him – but he loved the arts of war above all things and became so proficient with weapons that he was nicknamed 'The Knight of Prowess'.

Richard the Younger grew quickly towards manhood, until his father declared that it was time for him to marry and asked him if there was any noble woman he could love.

'There is only one,' replied Richard. 'The daughter of the King of Scythia, whom I met while travelling there in search of adventure. She is fair above all others, and wise also.'

So the King of Sorcha wrote to the King of Scythia and asked that his son be permitted to woo the princess – making it clear in the writing that if the request was refused he would make war on Scythia and destroy it utterly.

When the King of Scythia heard this, he called his advisors to him and asked them for their verdict. When they had considered for a while, they responded that it seemed reasonable for the prince to woo the princess, for if they refused, they would be at war, and Sorcha's army was far more powerful than their own.

The King of Scythia sent word of his consent and Richard the Younger journeyed to Scythia to woo the princess. Happily, she responded to his attentions with delight, and soon after a great wedding feast was prepared, and the nuptials of the two young people was celebrated by both countries.

For a time, all was well, until King Richard of Sorcha fell sick and died. Then at the behest of all the nobles of the land, Richard the Younger was crowned with much rejoicing. When he called together his first council, he declared that the land lacked but one thing – and that was the presence of its champion and most powerful defence, John; his brother was, as ever, away in distant lands in search of adventure.

Messengers went forth to seek him and having found him and told the tale of his father's death and his brother's crowning, begged the Knight of Prowess to return to his own land. This he did willingly and was warmly welcomed. The new king enquired of his brother if there was anything he required, and he lamented the fact that he had no wife.

'Is there one woman in the world whom you would wed?' asked King Richard the Younger, echoing his father.

'I have heard,' replied Prince John, 'that the King of Persia has a beautiful and marriageable daughter. Marriage to her would be a great thing for our land and would make me happy.'

So King Richard the Younger sent forth messengers and ambassadors to seek a marriage for his brother with the King of Persia's daughter. But they met with stony refusal,

and when he heard this King Richard was angered and sent word to his commanders to ready the army of Sorcha for war.

When they arrived on the shores of Persia, they proceeded to make red warfare upon the land, burning and pillaging where they would, meeting little resistance. Meanwhile the nobles of Persia assembled and made known their anger to the king that he had refused the suit of the King of Sorcha's brother.

'The reason is simple,' answered the king. 'My daughter has obtained from me a promise that I may not break – that she shall have the choosing of her own husband.'

'Then let us call her before us to answer to this unreasonable demand,' said the nobles.

When the princess stood before them, she said: 'Long since, I had a dream in which I was told that I should have the choosing of my own husband, and that if this was not permitted me then great trouble would come upon our kingdom because of it. Now that I hear what has befallen us, I believe the time has come for me to choose. I will choose the Prince of Sorcha and so end this strife forever.'

So it was agreed, and the nobles of Persia went to the King of Sorcha and informed him that they were prepared to agree to the match. With great rejoicing the war was over, and the young couple wed, and neither disliked the look nor the manner of the other.

But evil thoughts now came into the mind of Prince John, and he began plotting to overthrow his brother and take the kingdom for himself. It befell that when he came upon the king in his private garden, the prince drew his sword and stabbed his brother three times in the back so that he fell dead. Then the prince called his own followers to him and prepared to overthrow any who opposed him.

It transpired that several courtiers and noblewomen had seen the terrible deed, and word of it soon spread, so that many were opposed to the prince. But he, in a height of anger and pride, summoned the lords to him and told them that if they stood against him, they would all be slain without hesitation, along with their families, and their bodies cast out to rot in the sun.

When they heard this, the courtiers were greatly fearful and agreed to crown the prince King of Sorcha – though at heart they were reluctant. Only when this was done were they permitted to bury King Richard, who was laid to rest with great pomp and much sorrow.

Meanwhile a certain knight, who was famed for his counsel, came to the new king with praise and flattery and spoke to him thus. 'Sire, great is your noble prowess and strength, and long and noble shall be your reign. But one thing may cloud it. The queen – wife to your late lamented brother – is with child. If she bears a son, he will surely grow up to hate you and wish to take revenge for his father's death. Therefore, I suggest that you imprison the queen until she gives birth. Then, if she has a son, he should be killed. And if by chance she bears a daughter, let both she and her mother be banished for ever from Sorcha.'

'These are wise words,' said King John, and gave orders for the queen to be seized and imprisoned in a tower with but a single window overlooking the sea.

So the queen lay in wait for the birth, fearful of her life and that of her unborn child. Every other day the evil counsellor came and brought food and drink for her and enquired after her health. When it finally came time for her to give birth and she endured the pains of delivery, the child she bore was beautiful indeed, and it was, as she had feared, a boy.

Then the queen gave vent to many cries and moans, beseeching heaven that her child be spared. As she thus wept, an eagle flew down – and before she could do anything to prevent it, seized the child in its claws and flew away.

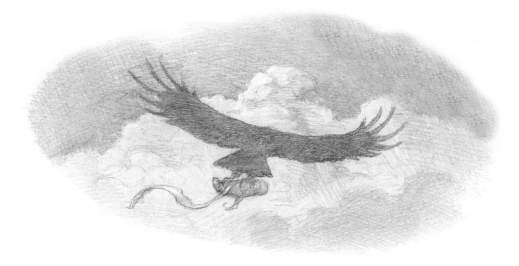

→ *The Eagle and the Child* ←

Then the queen wept even louder and rent her clothes and was for a time inconsolable. But after a time, she realized that it was better to lose her child thus than to see it killed before her eyes. Therefore, she dried her tears and dressed herself in her best robes and prepared for the visit of the king's counsellor.

✝ ✝ ✝

MEANWHILE KING JOHN began to wonder that he had heard nothing from the counsellor regarding the birth of a child to the queen. His mind was so clouded with hatred that he began to wonder whether the man had not been deluding him all along, and that he was secretly still loyal to the old king. Perhaps he had taken the child and fostered it safely. Therefore, he went to the counsellor's house and insisted that he accompany him to the tower where the queen was kept.

When they arrived, they found the queen peacefully working at her embroidery, with no sign of the terrors that had overcome her. Then King John's suspicions grew, and he insisted that women be brought to assure him that the queen was indeed no longer with child. This they assured him was the case, and at that the anger of the king we even more inflamed. He ordered the evil counsellor to be bound and put to the question, and when he got no further information in this way regarding the birth, commanded him to be hanged forthwith.

Thus did the evil man receive his just desserts. But now the king turned his attention to the queen and had her closely questioned concerning the birth of her child. Since she would say nothing, the king determined that she too should die. Only the intervention

of his chief advisors prevented this. 'Do not do this thing, which will but prey upon your mind and cause your people to hate you,' they said. 'Rather send the queen away to a place where you will never see her again.'

So this was decreed, and King John also let it be known that if anyone helped the queen, or provided food for her for at least five days following, he would seize their lands.

Then the queen took thought and decided to buy poor clothes and to disguise herself by dirtying her face and hands so as to pass as a poor woman. This done, she set out on the long road back to her father's country, and so for a while passed from the knowledge of the people of Sorcha and their king.

✝ ✝ ✝

IT HAPPENED THAT on the same day that the eagle carried off the queen's child King Arthur held a great assembly. It was widely known that it was the king's custom that he should not sit down to meat until he had seen a wonder, and on this occasion, it fell to the Black Knight, son of the King of France, to go forth in search of such a wonder. When much of the day was gone without his return, King Arthur himself went forth in search of his knight. Arriving at the Pillar of Virtue, which stands in the centre of the Plain of Wonders, the king found the Black Knight lingering there, waiting for an adventure to begin. The king sat down beside him, with his back against the stone, and together they looked in all four directions.

But it was from above that the adventure began. Both saw a great eagle which dipped low over the stone and dropped something that fell upon the edge of the king's robe. Both King Arthur and the Black Knight were astonished to see that it was a child, one evidently but lately born, and still living despite being carried by the eagle.

King Arthur looked upon the child and commanded the Black Knight to carry him home and to find a noble mother to foster him, and to see that he lacked for nothing. 'Tell everyone that he is to be treated as though he was my own son, and that he shall be called Macaoimh-an-Iolair, which the story tells means 'Eagle-Boy' in the language of Erin.

King Arthur and the Black Knight returned home, and the latter sought out the daughter of Carraig-an-Scuir of Lochlann, who had but lately given birth to a still-born infant and bade her foster and care for the king's child. This she did right willingly and cared for Eagle-Boy until he grew to twelve summers. During this time, he became adept at arms and skilled in horsemanship and sports. And everyone loved him for his fair, open face and gentle ways. And all of this time he believed he was King Arthur's son.

One day the son of the Black Knight and the son of the White Knight were playing the ancient game of hurling on the lawns beyond the walls of Camelot the Golden. Eagle-Boy happened to be sleeping nearby in the shade of a tree, and the noise of the match woke him. At once he went to help his foster-brother, the son of the Black Knight, and together they won the match, but the son of the White Knight complained bitterly that he would have won but for the unfair aid his opponent received from Eagle-Boy.

'It ill befits the son of a knight and the grandson of a king to complain thus,' said Eagle-Boy. 'But even if you and all your fellows stood against me, I would still win the match against you.'

The game began at once, and just as he had boasted, Eagle-Boy won, which caused a black anger to rise in the heart of the son of the White Knight. He cried aloud that it was an evil thing to be beaten by the son of a bird, a thing of feathers, whose parents were unknown.

'I am King Arthur's son,' cried Eagle-Boy, angrily.

'That you are not,' was the answer. 'Nothing is known of either your mother or your father.'

Eagle-Boy blushed fiery red and trembled greatly, for until that moment he had known nothing of his true origin. Such was the anger and despair he felt then that he attacked the son of the White Knight, and in a while the youth lay almost dead upon the earth.

At this the son of the Black Knight seized Eagle-Boy and forced him to go before King Arthur. There the youth fell on his knees and begged the king to tell him the truth about his origins.

With a heavy heart, King Arthur did so. Before he had finished, Eagle-Boy sprang up and cried that he would not rest a single day or night until he had discovered his true parentage. Then he begged the king to give him arms and the order of knighthood, so that he might better succeed in his undertaking.

Against his desire King Arthur did as he was asked, though Eagle-Boy was still by rights too young to bear arms, and in the morning the youth departed, much to the sorrow of everyone who knew and loved him.

ALL THAT DAY Eagle-Boy rode until he came to a valley, where he made camp and lit a fire. Next day he set forth again, and as night fell met a rider coming toward him. He saw that it was a girl, young and fair indeed, who rode a grey palfrey. They greeted each other and Eagle-Boy asked her name and whither she was bound. The girl replied that she called herself the Maiden of the Grey Palfrey, for she was in flight from a husband who had treated her evilly and did not wish to reveal her true name. 'Indeed, I am seeking the court of King Arthur, for I have heard tell that he offers succour to all women who have been badly treated.'

'It so happens that I am a knight of King Arthur's court,' said Eagle-Boy.

'Then I beg you to escort me thither,' cried the girl.

'That is not so easily done,' answered he. 'I have come far already on this horse, and I fear it will not carry me back to Camelot the Golden without some rest.'

'We can take turns to ride your horse and mine,' said the girl. 'That way we shall be there this very day.'

Somewhat against his will, Eagle-Boy gave his assent, and they rode back along the way to Camelot the Golden, where they were warmly welcomed. The girl told how she was in flight from her knavish husband, whom she would never have married had it not been that he carried with him a magical flute which had the power to cast a sleep upon whoever heard it. In this way she had been bespelled and forced to marry the villain, who was known as the Knight of the Music.

'It is my belief that he will come here and take me away, whatever you or any of your men may do.'

Nonetheless King Arthur took the girl and conveyed her to a chamber deep within the castle and commanded that she should be well guarded. The rest of his company he set to guard the walls and gates of Camelot the Golden, and he further ordered that the windows and doors be shut tight so that no one could enter without being seen and captured.

But that night, while everyone kept guard over the Maiden of the Grey Palfrey, the Knight of the Music came, and drawing out his silver flute, played such music as placed everyone in the castle into a deep sleep. And while they slept, he entered and took away the girl.

When they awoke in the morning, great anger and consternation was felt by all, none more so than Eagle-Boy, who declared his intention of seeking out the Knight of the Music and releasing the girl from him for good. Nor would he take anyone with him, for as he said: 'If I fail in this undertaking, you may send the host of your warriors after me, but otherwise this is my quest.'

'Very well,' said King Arthur. 'But it seems to me that the girl spoke of crossing the sea to this shore on her journey. Therefore, I bid you take the magical ship which was given to me as a gift by the Queen of Land-Under-Wave, for it has the ability to take you wherever you wish to go. Step into it and say that you wish to be taken to the home of the Knight of the Music and it shall be done.'

Eagle-Boy gave thanks to the king and went aboard the magical craft, which lay at anchor below the walls of Camelot the Golden. He asked that he be taken to the country of the Knight of the Music, and at once the craft set sail of its own accord and flew across the seas until it reached an island. There it grounded on the shore and Eagle-Boy hid it from sight. Then he set out to explore the island and soon found himself outside the walls of a castle.

At first, he could find no way in, but then he took one of his hunting spears and used it to vault over the high wall. Inside he found a garden and sitting in the garden a girl of such beauty that his heart melted within him. He found that she was called Niamh Fair-Hair and that her father was a king in his own right. She had been stolen away by the Pirates of the White Plain, whose names are Grug, Grag and Gragan.

'They are terrible people,' said Niamh. 'Almost giants, and very evil natured. When they brought me here, they fell to quarrelling over who should have me for his own. They fought so furiously that I believed they would kill each other. But in the end, none could get the upper hand. Therefore, I laid upon them a *geis** that they should none of them have me until they had found two other women who looked like me in every way, so that there should be one for each of them. This has kept them occupied for almost a year. Every day they set out to seek women who resemble me; they return at night having always failed. But I fear greatly that one day they will succeed in their search, and I will be forced to stay with one of them.'

'Then I shall wait their coming,' said Eagle-Boy. 'For I would set you free and end their reign of terror.' And despite the protestations of Niamh Fair-Hair, who believed only his death could follow, he sat down to await nightfall.

At the end of that time the three huge men arrived. Ugly they were to look upon. When they saw Eagle-Boy they laughed aloud and began to speak of consuming his flesh.

'You will find that hard to do,' said Eagle-Boy, and drew his sword.

Then there ensued a mighty and terrible

---

* An Irish word signifying a sacred undertaking or prohibition.

battle, that went from the night into the day. But in the end Eagle-Boy slew all three of the evil brothers, and despite being wounded himself, was prepared to depart again in search of the Maiden of the Grey Palfrey. But Niamh of the Fair-Hair spoke gently to him and gave him a drink that strengthened him and made good his wounds. Then she begged him to remain with her for a while and to tell her his own story.

As night fell around them Eagle-Boy told her everything and she in return told her own life story, and as they spoke, their feelings for each other deepened, until in the end they pledged eternal love each to other. And it fell out that Niamh knew of the Knight of the Music, who was indeed a friend of the three dead pirates.

'He is a formidable opponent,' she said. 'Strong in both magic and cunning.'

'Nevertheless, I shall defeat him,' answered Eagle-Boy.

Next day he and Niamh Fair-Hair set forth again in the magical ship. It took them to other islands and on each one there was adventure and danger. But Eagle-Boy overcame each challenge as would the hardiest of knights. On the way he fell in with a knight known as the Champion of the Island, who after Eagle-Boy defeated him, decided to throw in his lot and help the youth in his attempt to overthrow the Knight of the Music. Taking ship again and leaving Niamh in the care of the Champion's wife, they arrived at last at a desolate island where stood the Fortress of the Black Rock – home to the evil knight.

'This will not be easy,' said the Champion of the Island. 'There is but one narrow path to the top of the island, and there the walls of the castle meet the earth seamlessly. There is only a single entrance-way and that lies so far above that one may only get there by being winched up. The Knight of the Music has a way in, but only through his magic.'

'We shall see,' said Eagle-Boy, and he went upon the narrow path secretly and walked around the castle until he was satisfied that all was as the Champion of the Island had said. Then he ran back as far as he could from the walls and, taking his best spear, used it to vault upwards until he reached the door to the castle.

So confident was the Knight of the Music, the door was not even barred, and Eagle-Boy crept in unseen. It did not take him long to find where the evil knight lay, sleeping with his head in the bosom of the Maiden of the Grey Palfrey. Beside him lay the silver flute, and this Eagle-Boy seized and hid before he drew his sword.

The eyes of the girl opened, and she saw him, but she said nothing as Eagle-Boy advanced. With a single blow he severed the Knight of the Music's head, and carried it to the door, from where he tossed it down to the Champion of the Island. Then he assisted the Champion to climb up to the door and the three of them celebrated the death of the Knight of the Music together.

Next day they departed that dark place and set out once more for Camelot the Golden, where, as you may surmise, they became the centre of great rejoicing. Eagle-Boy told all his adventures and gave the Maiden of the Grey Palfrey into the keeping of King Arthur.

✠ ✠ ✠

EAGLE-BOY COULD NOT rest, however, since he had still discovered nothing concerning his parentage. So, accompanied by the Champion of the Island, with whom he had become fast friends, and leaving the women in the care of the court, they set forth again. Many adventures they had together, but of these the story does not tell. It says rather that after a long time of wandering they found themselves in a country that seemed overrun by enemies and was most desolate.

Here a most wondrous thing occurred. As they followed the road, they came upon a woman sitting by the way weeping bitterly over the body of a dead knight.

'What has happened here?' asked Eagle-Boy.

'Sad and terrible things,' replied the woman. 'An evil man who was brother to my kingly husband contrived to murder him and had me imprisoned, and that any child I bore should be killed if it were a boy or exiled if a girl. In truth I bore a sweet boy, but before he could be killed, he was stolen away by an eagle, and I know nothing of his fate. The evil king had me exiled and I made my way home to my father's lands in disguise. But evil King John somehow heard that I had given birth to a son and believed that I had smuggled him away. Now a dreadful war has broken out and every day more good men fall in battle. This knight that lies dead at my feet is my brother. He fell today in the fight against King John.'

Eagle-Boy heard all this in silence, then he said: 'I and my companion are knights wandering in search of adventure. We would gladly pledge our swords to your cause.'

'No help is too little or too great for us,' answered the lady, and gave directions for them to join the Scythian army. There they were welcomed, for many warriors had fallen and the king was grateful for all who would fight on his side.

Secretly, Eagle-Boy spoke to the Champion

of the Island. 'Now I thank all the gods that I have discovered my origin. For I am certain I am that child the eagle carried off, which delivered me to the keeping of King Arthur. Tell no one of this for the moment but let us see what we can do to right the great wrongs that have been done to my family.'

Next day the armies of Scythia and Sorcha met again, and wherever the fighting was thickest there were Eagle-Boy and the Champion of the Island. At last, they came into the thick of the press where King John fought, and there, seeing a gap in the warriors that surrounded him, Eagle-Boy took his spear and threw it so that it struck King John and pierced him through the heart. Then the tide of battle turned, and in a matter of hours the field was won by the Scythians.

Amidst great rejoicing Eagle-Boy was declared a hero and the King of Scythia asked him to tell the story of his origins. There and then Eagle-Boy told them of his life to that day, and how he was indeed the son of the king's daughter and good King Richard the Younger who had been so foully slain. And if the rejoicing had been great before, now it was redoubled, and the queen especially, after all her hardships, was overjoyed to be reunited with her son. And he who had been hitherto known only as Eagle-Boy took the name Richard after his father and grandfather. He thus became the third prince with that name to rule over Sorcha.

So it was that Eagle-Boy returned home in triumph and assumed his rightful place as king. Afterwards he sent for Niamh Fair-Hair and married her and made her his queen, and they reigned long and happily after that, as the story tells. As to the Maiden of the Grey Palfrey, whose true name was Gráinne, she married a brave knight of the Round Table and King Arthur gave them lands and a castle in which to live.

Thus I have told this strange tale and now I will move onward to relate another – this is the story of Caradoc of the Strong Arm, who underwent a terrible ordeal in the name of love, but who came to a good end.

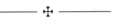

EXPLICIT THE TALE OF EAGLE-BOY.
INCIPIT THE STORY OF CARADOC.

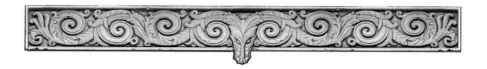

13: THE STORY OF CARADOC
OF THE STRONG ARM

✛

ONE DAY WHEN KING ARTHUR WAS HOLDING COURT AT CAMELOT THE GOLDEN, THERE CAME TO HIM A STRONG YOUNG KNIGHT NAMED CARADOC, WHO WAS A KING IN HIS OWN RIGHT. IT IS SAID THAT HE WAS RELATED TO KING ARTHUR, BUT I HAVE BEEN UNABLE TO DISCOVER HOW THIS WAS. THE YOUNG LORD WAS IN SEARCH OF A WIFE, AND AS WAS THE CUSTOM IN THESE TIMES, HE WANTED HIS BROTHER MONARCH TO FIND ONE FOR HIM. SOON AFTER, ARTHUR DID JUST THAT, MATCHING HIM WITH THE BEAUTIFUL YSAVE OF CARAHES. THE WEDDING WAS A VERY SPLENDID AFFAIR, AND NOBLE MEN AND WOMEN CAME FROM ALL OVER THE COUNTRY TO ATTEND. AMONG THEM WAS A MAN DEEPLY SKILLED IN MAGIC, WHOSE NAME WAS ELIAVRES. WHEN HE SAW YSAVE, HE FELL DEEPLY IN LOVE WITH HER AND DESIRED HER SO MUCH THAT HE DEVISED A DARK SCHEME TO OBTAIN HIS WISH.

✛ ✛ ✛

ON THEIR WEDDING night the couple thought they lay together, but in fact Eliavres cast about them both such spells and confusion that they had no idea of the truth – which was that King Caradoc lay with a greyhound bitch, while the enchanter enjoyed the delights of love with Ysave, who believed that she was with Caradoc. The same thing occurred on the second night, when Caradoc thought he enjoyed his wife, but in fact lay all night with a pig. And, on the third night,

it was a mare that he encircled with his arms and whose favours he enjoyed! Eliavres, meanwhile, spent the nights with Ysave, and on the third engendered a child upon her.

Soon after this, the court disbanded, and Caradoc and his new queen returned to their own lands where, in due course, Ysave gave birth to a beautiful son. King Caradoc was well pleased and gave the child his own name.

The child grew tall and strong and handsome, and soon began to outstrip his tutors

150

in all things. When he was only twelve, he asked his father if he might go and visit King Arthur's court and learn what he could of the ways of chivalry. King Caradoc was glad to agree, for his pride in his son knew no bounds. So the young Caradoc set forth, accompanied by a party of his father's knights, and several of his own young friends, Together they took ship, arriving in Britain and making their way to Carduil, where King Arthur was holding court at that time.

The king was very glad to see the noble youth, and made a great fuss of him, taking him hunting and instructing him personally in the arts of coursing and hawking, as well as telling him much concerning the arts of war and chivalry, the proper way to behave around ladies, and such noble pursuits as the games of chess and checkers.

Thus, Caradoc remained at the royal court and learned everything that he could. He was often in the company of the king and queen and became firm friends with Sir Gawain and Sir Yvain, as well as many other knights and ladies who were resident at the court. By the time he was fifteen he was as strong and well favoured as any of the older knights and though yet untried, in his heart he felt prepared for his first adventure, whenever it came his way.

Now King Arthur was much enamoured of hunting and, since the land was at peace, he remained at Carduil for some time, enjoying the plentiful game to be found in the woods and meadows around the city. Then the day dawned when he decided that it was too long since he had worn his crown and held a great court. So he commanded that arrangements be made to celebrate the feast of Pentecost, and at the same time declared that he wished to make the young Caradoc a knight. All

agreed that this was an excellent idea, and plans were set in motion for the great celebration, with a tournament, feasting, and general rejoicing.

This was a court to remember for long years. Knights and nobles came from all over the lands to celebrate with King Arthur and his knights. Not only Caradoc, but fifty other young men were destined for knighthood, and the king saw to it that they were royally clad. Queen Guinevere herself sent embroidered shirts to all the novice-knights, and when the day came the king himself gave his nephew the accolade, while Sir Gawain fastened on his right spur and Sir Yvain his left.

When the ceremony was over, they all went to the cathedral to hear Mass, and after that to the great hall, where the feast was prepared. But just as Sir Kay the Seneschal was about to have the trumpet sounded to summon everyone to dine, King Arthur reminded him that it was his custom, on such occasions, that no one should eat until they had seen or heard of a wonder.

At this moment, a stranger knight came riding towards the court and entered there in great haste. Tall and well-muscled he was, with a great mane of red hair. He fell to his knee before the king and asked him for a boon. 'If I may, I shall grant it to you,' replied Arthur. 'Tell me what you desire.'

'Sire,' replied the knight. 'I ask but one thing, and that is a blow on the neck in exchange for another.'

'That is a strange request,' replied Arthur.

'Sire, all I ask is that I should give my sword to one of your knights. If he can strike off my head, then so be it; but, if I survive, I shall have the right to return the blow one year from now in your sight.'

'By St John!' exclaimed Sir Kay the

Seneschal. 'A man would have to be simple to accept such an offer.'

'I have asked for this gift,' said the red-haired knight. 'If you refuse me it will soon be known everywhere that King Arthur's word is worth nothing.' And he drew his sword and held it up by the blade for all to see.

At that Caradoc, who was standing near, rushed forwards and made to seize the weapon.

'Are you the best of these knights?' demanded the challenger.

'No, only the greatest fool,' answered Caradoc. Then he took the sword, and the knight laid his head on the table, stretching his neck for the blow.

After a moment's hesitation Caradoc delivered his stroke. The blow was so hard that it cut through the knight's neck and buried the blade in the table. The challenger's head flew from his body, but to everyone's horror he followed it and, picking it up, set it once more on his shoulders. Then he spoke, calmly, as if nothing had happened.

'Now that I have received a blow, I am satisfied. But remember, I shall be back in a year to return the favour.' He looked at Caradoc: 'Do not forget!' Then he departed from the hall before anyone could stop him.

Everyone looked sorrowfully at Caradoc, who was quite cheerful, if a little pale. 'Do not fear, Uncle,' he said to Arthur. 'My fate is in God's hands now.'

King Arthur commanded everyone who was present to attend the court exactly one year from then, and all promised to do so. Then they went to dine, though few were in any mood to feast or celebrate that day.

✠ ✠ ✠

THE YEAR TURNED, and Caradoc went forth in search of adventure as any newly made knight should. Great were the deeds he performed, and his name was spoken of in many places. But as the time drew near for the dawning of Pentecost, when the court would assemble again, everyone began to think of the terrible fate that awaited the young hero, and people came from all over the land to witness it, not only those who had been present the year before, but others, whose curiosity to see what would happen brought them to Carduil. Having heard, along with everyone else, what had occurred the year before, King Caradoc and Queen Ysave did not come, being too afraid to witness what they believed would be the death of their son.

Pentecost came, and all was ready for the feast. Mass was heard, and all went into the hall to dine. Then came the one who had survived Caradoc's blow and he called to the young knight to come forth. Caradoc leapt forward without hesitating, but the king himself spoke up.

'Wait, Sir Knight. If you spare my nephew's head, I will give you a great ransom.'

'What do you offer?' demanded the challenger thoughtfully, leaning on his sword.

'All the gold and silver plate you see in this court,' answered the king.

'Not enough,' said the knight, and raised his sword.

'Wait! All the treasure that is in my coffers shall be yours if you spare him.'

'Not enough. I would rather have his head,' said the other.

Then Queen Guinevere came forward with all her ladies.

'Sir,' she said. 'I beg you for this boy's life. I offer you the choice of these ladies, the most beautiful in all the land, if you will agree.'

'They are fair indeed,' replied the knight politely. 'But I have no need of them.' Then, when he saw that the queen and many of the other ladies were distressed, he added: 'If you do not want to watch I suggest you return to your quarters.' Then he turned again to Caradoc, who cried aloud: 'Do what you must, Sir Knight. Let us delay no longer.' And he laid his head on the table just as the other had done a year before.

The knight raised his sword and brought it down – but he only struck Caradoc's neck with the flat of the blade. Then, as the youth leapt up, he said: 'Come, it would be a great shame if I were to kill you.' Then he looked to the king: 'With your leave my lord I wish to speak to the young man privately.'

In astonishment the king nodded, and the two men went to one side. There the knight spoke quietly to Caradoc. 'I will tell you why I spared you. I am your father, and you are my son.'

'That is not possible,' answered Caradoc fiercely. 'I will defend my mother's honour with my last breath. She is not and never was your lover.'

But the knight – who was, of course, Eliavres – bade him be silent. Then he recounted everything that had occurred all those years before, how he had deceived King Caradoc and had lain with Ysave and begotten the young man upon her.

Caradoc listened with mounting anger and disbelief. When the knight fell silent at last, he cried: 'I do not believe any of this. It never happened! If you repeat this to anyone else, I will seek you out and kill you!'

The knight said nothing more, but simply turned on his heel and left the court as swiftly and mysteriously as he had come.

Then there was great rejoicing, and many came forward to praise Caradoc's bravery, and to give thanks that his life had been spared. None noticed how withdrawn and silent he had become, and as soon as he could he excused himself and, for the first time in many years, went home to Vannes.

There, in the city of Nantes, he found King Caradoc and Queen Ysave. When he heard that the young man was there, the king went forth to welcome him and embraced him warmly. 'Welcome home, my son,' he said.

'Yet I have heard that I am not your son,' answered Caradoc.

'Not my son!' cried the king. 'What foolishness is this?'

Then Caradoc took him to one side and repeated everything that Eliavres had told him. 'I tell you these things not to hurt you,' he added. 'For of all men I honour you as my father – whatever the truth.'

At this moment the queen arrived and came forward to embrace her son. But Caradoc thrust her away, saying coldly: 'I can no longer bear to see you. You have done too much to hurt my lord the king.'

'What can you mean?' cried Ysave.

Then the king turned upon her and ordered her to go from his sight. 'You have done great evil to me – such that I no longer wish to see you either.' So saying, both men turned away from her and waited, unspeaking, until she had left the room.

You may be sure that the queen was distraught, for she knew nothing of what Caradoc had told her husband, any more than she knew what had happened at the time of her wedding.

When she was gone, the king brokenly asked Caradoc what he should do with her. 'For you are just as much harmed by these terrible deeds as I.'

'I wish her no harm,' said Caradoc. 'Since she is, in truth, my mother, and perhaps knew nothing of what occurred. If you will be guided by me, you will build a strong tower and shut her away with only women for company. That way Eliavres can never see her again, and no one may boast that he had what was rightly yours.'

This the king did, and the tower was soon built and Ysave enclosed within it. She had only her women for company, just as Caradoc had suggested, and no one spoke to her or saw her save those who attended her. And if the people of Vannes wondered at this strange act of their king, they were none the wiser, for he remained silent and withdrawn, while the young Caradoc, as soon as the tower was complete and his mother shut away, left at once for Arthur's court.

✛ ✛ ✛

CARADOC ARRIVED AT Camelot the Golden in the month of May, when the roses were all in bloom. It was nearing the time for the royal court to assemble again, and Caradoc remained there as lords and ladies came from every part of the land.

Among the nobles who set out at that time was a young lord from Cornwall named Cador, who brought with him his sister Guinier, a very beautiful maiden as gentle and loyal as she was fair. Their father, the King of Cornwall, had died that summer, and his son came to swear fealty to King Arthur. However, on the way, an adventure befell them which was to have far-reaching consequences.

Now you must know that before the old king died, a knight named Allardin du Lac had sought the hand of Guinier in marriage. She however had spurned him, and both her father and brother had defended her right to choose a man she liked! So matters stood, and the king died, and Cador and his sister set out for Arthur's court. But, as they rode, Allardin came after them and overtook them.

Cador was only lightly armed, but when he saw the other knight coming, he turned to face him and to defend Guinier. Alas for them both, Allardin knocked Cador from his horse with the first blow of his spear, and the young lord lay upon the earth with a broken leg. Allardin stood over him and said: 'If only you and your father had granted my suit when you could. Now I shall take what I asked for, but not for myself! I want you to know that I shall give your sister to my men for their sport. Think of that as you lie there!' Then he seized the reins of Guinier's horse and rode away with her.

You may imagine how the maiden cried out against the cruel blow that fate had dealt her! But even as Allardin spurred his mount to carry her away, there came in sight another rider. It was Caradoc, on his way to Arthur's court after carrying out an errand. When he saw the wounded man lying in the road and heard the piteous cries of the maiden, he swiftly gave pursuit, crying upon Allardin to stop.

He, when he saw a fully armed knight approaching, turned and drew his sword. 'Leave us, Sir,' he shouted. 'This is none of your business!'

'I think it is, when I hear a lady call out in such distress. Let her go or prove yourself against me.'

Cursing, Allardin swung his sword, cutting off Caradoc's lance near where he held it. Caradoc responded by striking him over the head with the butt of the spear, felling him from his horse. Then Caradoc dismounted and battle commenced.

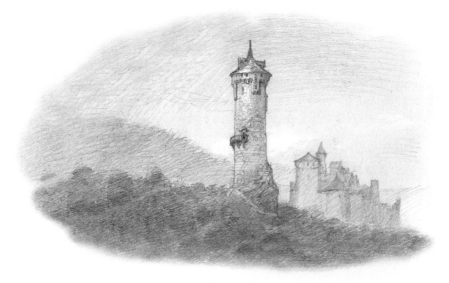

→ *The Prison Tower* ←

That was a mighty battle indeed! The two knights were well matched and for a long while neither could gain the advantage. There is no telling how long they might have continued, if Allardin's sword had not broken. At this he gave ground and surrendered, placing himself at the mercy of Caradoc. He, breathing hard from his long fight, ordered the knight to surrender to the lady he had tried to carry off. This Allardin did, but Guinier refused him. 'I can no more accept your surrender than I can find it in my heart to forgive you. I must know how my brother fares. If he is dead from the wounds you gave him, you shall pay for it!'

'My lady,' replied Allardin. 'I am more than willing to do as you ask. Let us return to where we fought.'

All three rode to where Cador had fallen. He lay still upon the way, scarcely breathing. The two knights, who were themselves weak and weary from their battle, lifted him together onto Caradoc's horse, then the young knight mounted and supported the wounded man on the saddle before him.

'We must find shelter,' said Caradoc. 'And soon – or I fear this good man may not see the light of day again.'

They rode on slowly, until they saw, off to one side of the road, a large and splendid tent. Within they could all hear the voices of several lords and ladies raised in song. Caradoc and Guinier stared in astonishment and wondered aloud who the owner of this remarkable tent could be. Then Allardin confessed that it was his, and that those within were his own people.

Then he said, 'Do you see that in front of the entrance to the tent are two golden statues? Let me tell you about them. They are automata, which move and do many marvellous things. The one on the right opens the door to the tent; the one on the left closes it again. But this is not all they do. The right-hand statue plays the harp most beautifully and, if a woman enters there who claims to be a virgin when she is not, then the harp will go out of tune, and a string break. The left-hand statue holds a spear and, if any false or churlish fellow enters there, he will find that the spear is thrown at him!'

Then Allardin dismounted painfully from his horse and called out to those within. When they came out, they gathered around and helped the wounded Cador down and carried him inside. Then came forward a most beautiful maiden, whom Allardin introduced as his sister. He asked that she care for the badly wounded knight, and for Caradoc and himself! Guinier, he bade her protect as if she were her own sister.

To all this the Maiden of the Pavilion (this is the only name I have heard her called) agreed readily. You may be sure that all four people were cared for as well as ever they could be. And so they all began to mend their hurts, and in the weeks that followed the three knights became firm friends, and Allardin begged forgiveness of Guinier and it was given. And she, Cador's beautiful sister, began to fall in love with Caradoc, while the Maiden of the Pavilion looked with longing at Cador.

The weeks passed, until the three knights were well enough to ride again, and Caradoc declared his intention of returning to King Arthur's court, for he was sure to have been missed by now and longed to be at the place he thought of as home. Cador also wished to continue his journey, and Allardin declared that he would accompany them. The whole party set forth in merry mood on the road to Camelot the Golden, where the court was newly assembled.

As they neared the city, they began to meet others on the road, and learned from them of a great tournament which was to be held there. Organized by two kings, Cadoalant of

Ireland and Ris of Valen, it was rumoured to have been arranged to impress a certain lady. All three knights wished to take part, and by chance it fell to Allardin to go first. He put on his finest armour and, mounted upon his favourite steed, rode in the direction of the lists. On the way he passed a tower from which a maiden looked out upon the passing throng. When she saw the bold knight, she leaned out and called to him. Allardin reined in and greeted her gently.

'Sir,' she said. 'Forgive me for speaking to you so boldly, but my heart tells me you are the best of all those I have seen pass this way! My name is Guigenor, and I am the daughter of Sir Guiromelant and the Lady Clarrisant, Sir Gawain's sister. I am pursued by both King Cadoalant and King Ris, and this tournament to which you are doubtless headed is intended to prove to me which of the two is the better man – and therefore the one I should take as husband. Sir – I hate them both, and never will I marry either. If you will be so good as to look with kindness upon my plight, I shall evermore think of you as my own knight.'

When Allardin heard these words, and looked upon the Lady Guigenor, his heart was moved both by her plight and by her beauty. Forthwith he swore to uphold her honour in the tournament. Whereupon the lady tossed down her sleeve to him, to wear as a favour in the fighting to come. Then Allardin rode on, his heart high with expectation.

✝ ✝ ✝

NOT MUCH TIME is needed to tell of the tournament and all the great deeds that were done there. Suffice it that there were many brave and bold knights present, including some of the finest of King Arthur's

Round Table Fellowship. The knights who fought for the two kings were particularly outstanding in their prowess, none more so than Allardin and Cador, who soon joined with his companion and fought as bravely as any man could. You may be sure that the maiden of the tower, Guigenor, watched every move that Allardin made, and when she saw what an excellent fighter he was, her heart warmed to him even more. He was brave as well as comely! Another maiden, Ydain, who was the niece of Sir Yvain and a cousin of Caradoc's, could not help but notice the brave display made by Cador, and she sought among her companions to know who he was. When she heard that he was the son of the King of Cornwall she was glad indeed and sent him a favour to wear in her honour.

Extraordinary feats of courage were achieved that day! Knights were unhorsed, spears and swords broken, armour dinted, and shields shattered. Many a brave man sent prisoners to the lady of his choice, and among them Cador sent the champion Guigambresil to the lady Ydain, whose favour he now wore, and whose bright eyes and fair form had charmed him utterly.

Soon after, Caradoc himself joined in the fray, displaying all his great skill and power and overcoming everyone who stood in his way. On that day both Sir Gawain and Sir Yvain chose to fight, and both encountered Caradoc. Both were defeated by him! Never had such a mighty fighter appeared in that land. Everywhere people spoke of him with wonder! He was truly the most outstanding knight to enter the lists. Because of him, King Ris and his men, on whose side Caradoc fought, began to win the day – despite the efforts of Cador and Allardin, who fought against him for King Cadoalant.

In the end the three heroes won the day and attained the greatest honours in the tournament. When the time came for them to reveal their names – for as was the custom they had fought in disguise, or under a plain shield – there was much rejoicing. Gawain, especially, was glad to greet his cousin Caradoc. Even the two kings agreed to shake hands and pledge friendship to each other, the more so once they saw that the lady Guigenor, over whom they had fought, had given her heart to Allardin.

At the end, amid general rejoicing, Guigenor married her knight, while the beautiful Ydain chose to marry Cador, to whom he had utterly lost his heart. As for Caradoc, he was well pleased, for he had his own love, Guinier, by his side. Even the Maiden of the Pavilion, Allardin's sister, was made happy. For though she had felt drawn to Cador while nursing him back to health, her eye had been caught by another young knight, Sir Perceval of Wales, who would one day seek out the Grail, and who had deported himself so well in the tournament that everyone said that he would soon be as great a knight as any at the Round Table. Thus, three weddings were celebrated, and the tournament broke up amid great rejoicing. Caradoc, Cador and Allardin all returned home with King Arthur, who demanded that they remain at court for the time being and grace his table with their presence.

✛ ✛ ✛

NOW WE MUST return to Caradoc's mother, Lady Ysave, who all this time had remained enclosed in the tower built for her by King Caradoc. There the enchanter, Eliavres, who had caused all the trouble in the first place, found her. He took to visiting her often, using his knowledge of magic to penetrate the locked doors and high windows of the tower. At first, I believe, the lady was far from happy to see him, for it was through his magic that she came to be imprisoned in so ignominious a way, and his dark plan that had cost her the love of both her husband and child. But in time he won her round, reminding her of the way her husband and son had behaved towards her, and pledging his own love to her in terms she could no longer refuse.

Things might have continued thus for a great deal longer, had it not been for a mistake which the enchanter made. In order to please the lady he loved so much, he brought ghostly musicians into the tower to play for her. But they could be heard outside as well, and soon the king's followers could no longer keep silent. They sent messengers to King Caradoc, who seldom came to Nantes these days, telling him of the sounds of revelry which issued nightly from the tower.

The king sighed deeply and sent men to search for Eliavres, for the king knew that no other was likely to be the cause of such enchanted music. In vain did King Caradoc's soldiers search, for with his magic Eliavres was able to move invisibly, and to enter the tower unseen. In the end, the king despaired, and sent for his son.

When Caradoc received the news, he was greatly troubled. He begged leave of King Arthur and set out at once for Vannes, having entrusted Guinier to the care of her brother Cador. He was afraid that if he took her with him, she would learn the secret of his mother's disgrace and turn against him. As it happened, he was not to see his love for a long time, and much hardship was to encompass them before they were reunited.

Arrived in Vannes, Caradoc went at once to the king, who told him all that had occurred. Caradoc was angry beyond measure at this and set out to take revenge on Eliavres. He journeyed to the enchanter's home and pretended he had forgiven him – and that in time he might do the same for his mother. Each night he sat at table with the enchanter, watching him all the while in order to find a way of trapping him. At last, Caradoc caught him abed with the lady Ysave and before the evil man could defend himself, bound him fast with ropes which had been dipped in holy water and were thus impervious to his spells. Within days Caradoc handed over Eliavres to the king, since he forbore to take revenge on his own father. King Caradoc however, had no such compunction and devised a terrible punishment. He forced the enchanter to do just what he had tricked he and his wife into doing years before. Eliavres was forced to lie with a greyhound bitch, a sow and a mare.

☩ ☩ ☩

NOW HEAR WHAT happened, though it grieves me to speak of it. From this carnality, though it may seem an impossible thing, emerged three offspring: a mighty greyhound which was named Guinloc, a boar called Tortain, and a stallion which they named Loriagort. These were Caradoc's 'brothers' in their way. As to the enchanter himself, once this dreadful deed was accomplished, he was set free, though Caradoc longed to see him dead and would have flayed him alive if Eliavres had not been his father.

As for Eliavres himself, he suffered greatly. At the earliest opportunity he stole back to the tower and there visited the queen, who had now so completely transferred her feeling to him that she wept and bemoaned his fate with as much vehemence as if he had been her lover from the start. Then her sorrow turned to cold anger, and she urged him to be avenged on Caradoc.

'I cannot kill him. He is my son, after all,' said the enchanter.

'Waste no pity on him, for he wasted none upon you,' cried Ysave.

'I may not kill him,' declared Eliavres. 'But I can cause him to live only half a life, if you will help me.'

'Gladly,' replied the queen, who seemed to have forgotten that Caradoc was her son.

The enchanter went away and returned with a terrible poisonous serpent, which he hid in a closet in the queen's room. Then he instructed her what she needed to do and departed.

Soon Caradoc came, wanting to see how his mother fared. To him she seemed nothing but kindness, and even begged his forgiveness for the betrayal of the king. Caradoc, though inwardly sorrowful, felt some measure of peace at this. He stayed with his mother for much of the day until, as dusk began to fall, she complained of a headache and declared that she must let down her hair and comb it out. 'Fetch me the comb from within that cupboard,' she asked, and Caradoc went willingly to do so. Alas! when he reached inside, the serpent sank its fangs into his flesh and curled itself around his arm.

Then Caradoc knew such pain as no man may stand for long and strove to free himself from the serpent's bite. But the harder he struggled to free himself the tighter grew its hold, until he almost fainted. The queen, meanwhile, made a great show of horror and anguish, screaming for help for her poor son. The king and his servants came running, to find Caradoc lying on the ground while his

mother sobbed over him. The king was so enraged that he was ready to kill Ysave at once, for he believed her responsible despite her protestations of innocence. Her women took her into another room before he could do her harm, and the king turned his attention to helping his son.

Caradoc was carried forth and laid in a great bed in another part of the castle. There he lay, scarcely conscious, while the king sent far and wide for doctors and anyone with knowledge of healing to save his son. Many came, but none of them could effect a change in the young man, who grew paler and thinner with each day that passed. He could scarcely sleep from the pain and ate but little. The doctors gave him two years to live at best, some even less than that. King Caradoc despaired.

The queen, meanwhile, was triumphant that the plot she had hatched with Eliavres had succeeded so well. She gloated over her son's sickness, the terrible pains he felt, for these she saw as a fitting punishment for all the suffering she had experienced since his discovery of the trick played upon her and King Caradoc.

When King Arthur received the news, he was struck with the deepest sorrow. He declared that he would not rest until he found a cure for the young man's suffering and set out to visit him, on a ship bound for Brittany. Delayed by storms and finally blown off course, he arrived in Normandy instead and proceeded by road towards Nantes.

Word of these events soon reached Cornwall, where Cador groaned aloud at the news. As for Guinier, she almost fainted from the shock and cursed heaven for inflicting such torment upon her lover and forcing her own heart to break. 'Alas!' she cried to Cador. 'Fair sweet brother, I implore you to take me at once to where he lies. If I may see him but once more before he dies then I, too, shall die happy!'

Word soon reached Caradoc that King Arthur was coming to see him, and that Cador had left Cornwall and was on his way by sea with his beloved Guinier. But instead of comforting him this only made him feel worse, for he could not bear them to see him so wasted from the deadly bite of the serpent, which still clung to his arm, feeding from his blood and stealing his strength.

So it was that Caradoc devised a desperate plan. A messenger had come from Britain with word of King Arthur, and that night Caradoc begged the man to stay with him, pleading that he wanted no one present who had known him as he was before. When they were alone, he spoke of a certain holy hermit who lived close by in the forest. 'I am certain this good man can bring me relief,' he said. 'If you would but help me to go to him you would earn my undying gratitude.'

The messenger willingly agreed, once Caradoc assured him that it was for the best and that he sought to save his family from any further sorrow. As darkness fell and the castle grew silent, the two men stole outside, escaping unseen through a narrow postern gate. Then they set off on foot through the forest, the messenger supporting Caradoc, who was almost too enfeebled to walk.

They soon reached the hermit's cell and there Caradoc made his confession, telling the wise man everything that had happened and bemoaning his own guilt concerning both his mother and his true father. 'I see now that I was unjust to blame the queen for the sorrow that has come upon us all; even Eliavres acted out of love, albeit misguided. I have behaved wrongly to them and now

I suffer the consequences. I pray that God will have mercy on me and upon them.'

The hermit felt nothing but pity for the young man who suffered so greatly both in body and soul, and he saw that he was genuinely contrite. Therefore, he gave him absolution and invited him to remain for as long as he wanted. Caradoc gladly accepted and asked the hermit not to reveal his presence no matter who came looking for him. He swore the messenger to secrecy also, then sent him away.

Now Caradoc led a simple life in the forest, eating only one day a week and fasting for the rest. And in this way, he found solace, and even a measure of healing, for though the serpent was still fastened just as tightly around his arm, yet the pain seemed to abate a little, so that Caradoc was able to live in peace for a time.

Meanwhile King Arthur had arrived in Brittany with all his followers, and shortly after that came Cador and Guinier. They were met with news from King Caradoc that his son was fled, none knew where. Then was there great sorrow amongst all those who had come to see the young man. Guinier was, above all, heartbroken. She knew why Caradoc had run off, and she longed to be with him – even though it might mean her own death! A great search was mounted, though in truth Caradoc was close at hand, just a short distance from the city in the hermit's cell. But when the seekers came there, they saw only the old monk himself, and a young neophyte clad in a simple robe with a hood that concealed his face. So gaunt and marked by suffering was Caradoc that it was doubtful if anyone would have known him, save perhaps Guinier, who after long months of waiting, had also set out upon the road in search of her beloved. She and Cador together journeyed through the lands of Arthur until, having failed in their quest, they returned at last to Cornwall, and there Guinier remained, praying daily for the safe return of her beloved, while Cador went on alone, always searching for his friend.

✛ ✛ ✛

TWO YEARS PASSED, and at the end of that time Cador returned to Brittany, worn out with fruitless searching. Caradoc, meanwhile, left the hermitage, driven by a terrible longing to find a new place to live out his days. He found his way to a sheltered valley where stood a lonely chapel seldom visited by anyone. There he took up residence in a deep thicket of trees, living on roots and berries and water from a stream that ran close by. Every week he went to the little chapel to pray and hear Mass, and the good brothers who lived there treated him and gave him what little food they could spare.

Here at last, by chance, came Cador.

He sought shelter with the brothers and asked, as he did in every place that he found people living, if they had seen a tall, dark-haired man who had a terrible snake fastened to his right arm.

'Indeed, we have,' answered the monks. 'He comes here often, and we treat him as best we might. You will see him tomorrow if you remain here.'

Overjoyed to hear this, Cador lay down on the rough bed provided, though in truth he slept but little that night, and in the morning was up early awaiting the coming of the one he had sought for so long. In case Caradoc should take flight when he saw him, Cador stood at the back of the chapel with his cloak pulled around him, and there he saw the emaciated figure of his friend enter and kneel

and begin to pray. Bearded and unkempt, wrapped in an assortment of ragged garments, Cador would not have recognized him until he heard his voice. Then he ran forward and gently embraced his friend.

'Before God, how long have I searched for you!' he cried. 'And all the while you were here. Why did you run off like that? You knew that I would care for you, and as for Guinier, had you no thought for her?'

When he heard the name of his love, Caradoc began to weep. He found no words to answer Cador, but instead fell down upon the earth and lay there unspeaking. Cador, much moved by the terrible suffering of his friend, tried to raise him, all the while pleading to him to return to Nantes and place himself in the hands of those best able to care for him.

But no matter how he begged, Caradoc only shook his head and pulled away from Cador's touch. Then the Cornish knight knew that he wasted his breath and, turning to the brothers, begged them to care for his friend for a while longer, promising them great reward. Then he rode in haste to Nantes and sought out Caradoc's mother, who lived now in almost total seclusion.

'Madame,' he said. 'I am come to tell you that your son still lives. I have thought about the matter all the time I have been searching for him, and I truly believe that you are the only person who can offer a cure for him, if you will. Many, including myself, have thought ill of you for betraying your son to such a terrible fate, but I know that if you can help him now, you will regain favour in the eyes of all people.'

The queen turned pale. 'Is my son truly living?' she asked.

'He is indeed,' replied Cador. 'Will you help him?'

'Return to me on the morrow,' said Ysave. 'I will see what I can accomplish.'

That night the enchanter Eliavres came to visit the queen, as he still did with remarkable faithfulness. Unseen as ever by any of the guards, he entered her bed and together they knew great joy. But Queen Ysave was uneasy and could find no rest until she had unburdened herself.

'Though it was at my behest that you found the means to cause our son suffering,' she said. 'Yet now I regret what we did! I fear for my immortal soul if what was done is not undone. My love, I have learned that Caradoc still lives. Is there anything that can be done to free him?'

'If this is your true desire,' said the enchanter grimly, 'I will tell you.'

Then Ysave wept and begged him to tell her, and Eliavres answered that there was indeed a way in which Caradoc might be cured. 'If a maiden can be found who is his match in goodness of heart and spirit, she might save him. If two barrels are brought, one filled with milk and the other with vinegar, and if they are placed no more than three feet apart, on the full moon; and if the maiden gets into the one of milk and Caradoc into the one of vinegar, and if the maiden places her right breast on the rim of her barrel and calls out to the snake, it will leave Caradoc's wasted body in search of richer fare. While it passes between them, if a man is ready with a sword, he could cut the creature in twain. This is the only way that I know of to save our son.'

Ysave wept and thanked him, and on the morrow, she sent for Cador and told him all that Eliavres had said. Thus was a spark of hope ignited in Cador's heart, and he thought deeply upon all that had been said. He knew at once that there was but one being in all the

world who might do what was needed, and that was his sister. Therefore, he departed for Cornwall, taking the next available ship, and soon after he was with Guinier. You may imagine her joy when she heard that Caradoc was found! Then Cador told her everything that Queen Ysave had said to him, and Guinier declared that nothing on earth would prevent her from going to him and offering her body to the snake.

They took ship and returned to Brittany, where they made their way to the little chapel. When Caradoc laid eyes upon his love, he tried to hide himself, so great was the shame he felt at his appearance, wasted and with shrunken flesh and beard and hair all tangled and unwashed. But Guinier took him gently in her arms and kissed him with such joy that all who saw it could not help but weep. Then Cador told his old friend how he might indeed be cured.

Caradoc, his face streaked with tears, spoke more forcibly than he had in a long while.

'This may not be. I will not suffer my love to risk so much.'

'You shall not deny me,' Guinier said with equal firmness. 'This much I may do for you, for I have no wish to live without you.'

At first Caradoc refused to be persuaded, but both Cador and the maiden would not be denied. They sent for two tubs to be brought and filled, one with vinegar and the other with milk, just as the queen had told them. Then Caradoc climbed into the tub filled with vinegar and immersed himself to the neck, while Guinier climbed naked into the tub of milk and laid her soft white breast upon the edge. Then she called out to the snake, reminding it that there was little sustenance left in Caradoc any longer, but in her there was much goodness and plenty! And the snake, which hated the vinegar as much as it longed for a tastier meal, leapt from Caradoc's arm and arced across the distance between the two tubs. Cador, who had hidden behind a curtain, leapt forth and cut off its head with a single blow. In doing so he also sliced off Guinier's left nipple, which she bore with silence and good grace. Then he fell upon the evil beast and cut it into many parts so that it was quite dead.

There followed great rejoicing, and Guinier and Caradoc, helped from their tubs, embraced and wept and consoled each other for their wounds, and laughing as well as weeping, were taken into the care of the brothers. The hermit with whom Caradoc had long stayed was summoned and took over the care of the young man, who began to recover with remarkable speed. Guinier too was treated, her breast bound up and salves applied to the wound caused by her brother's sword. In a surprisingly short time Caradoc was restored to his former strength, though it was to be some time before he felt able to undertake adventures such as he had once lived for. The arm which had born the snake curled around it for so long, as it recovered its former strength, was ever after larger than its fellow, from which afterwards Caradoc received the epithet *Briebras*, meaning 'strong arm'.

Soon after, word of his recovery reached the ears of King Caradoc, who rushed to the little chapel and there greeted his son with great joy. Caradoc too was glad to see the man whom he still called father, and they embraced and wept and were filled with joy for the youth's recovery.

Thereafter they returned to Nantes, where Caradoc spoke at length with his mother. Though the story does not say what passed between them, there at last their old enmity towards one another was laid to rest and they made their peace. Caradoc intervened with the king to have his mother set free of her long imprisonment, and it is said that in time the king and queen remembered the great love they had once felt for one another and were reconciled – though whether this is true or not I cannot say.

As for the young Caradoc, he journeyed to King Arthur's court and there was well received. Many honours were heaped upon him, and in due course, with the blessing of King Arthur and her brother Cador, himself now crowned King of Cornwall, Caradoc married his dear Guinier. After this he lived a long life and had many adventures – too many to tell here. It is said that Guinier was the most faithful wife of any man living in those times, and that in time Caradoc's old friend Allardin du Lac – who also made a splendid marriage – made for her a miraculous golden nipple, to replace that which Cador had cut off, and that because of this she was known far and wide as 'Gold Breast'. Whether this is true or not I cannot say, but of one thing I am certain: Caradoc and Guinier lived a long and happy life together, and when in time the old king died, Caradoc became King of Vannes and reigned well and happily for many years thereafter.

EXPLICIT THE TALE OF CARADOC AND THE SERPENT.

INCIPIT THE TALE OF ORLANDO AND THE
DAUGHTER OF KING ARTHUR.

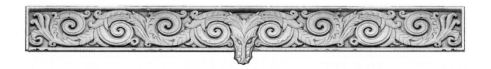

14: THE ADVENTURES OF MELORA
AND ORLANDO

✠

THE TALE THAT I SHALL TELL HERE MAY SURPRISE MANY WHO
HAVE NOT HEARD IT BEFORE. IT IS RARE THAT WE HEAR
STORIES OF KING ARTHUR'S CHILDREN, PERHAPS BECAUSE
NOT ALL OF THEM WERE LEGITIMATE, OR MAYHAP THAT THE
SHADOW OF THE DARK CHILD MORDRED HAS FALLEN OVER THE
MIGHTY SAGA OF THE KING AND HIS KNIGHTS. I DO NOT KNOW
IF MASTER THOMAS KNEW THIS TALE, AND IF SO, WHAT DECIDED
HIM TO OMIT IT. IT MAY BE THAT IT CAME FROM A FAR-OFF LAND
AND DEALT WITH MATTERS THAT SEEMED TO HIM TO HAVE NO
PART IN THE TALE OF THE ONCE AND FUTURE KING. YET I BELIEVE
IT TO BE BOTH WORTHY OF INCLUSION AND TO SPEAK OF THINGS
OF A WONDROUS KIND; THEREFORE, I MAKE NO EXCUSE FOR
INCLUDING IT IN THIS GATHERING OF ANCIENT TALES. ABOVE
ALL, THIS IS A TALE OF DREAMS, WHEREIN MAY LIE BOTH WISDOM
AND WONDER.

✠ ✠ ✠

MUCH IS WRITTEN of King Arthur's children, but few ever speak of his daughters. These, I have found after much searching, were Emaré, Archfedd, and one other, the result of a night of love when Arthur visited the house of one of his barons and was drawn to the beauty and gentleness of the man's daughter. Though I have sought far, I have not been able to discover the name of this lady, nor that of her father, but the name of the child is recorded as Melora.

The story tells how one night, this girl, who lived at the time within the walls of Camelot the Golden, had a dark and disturbing dream. It seemed to her that the sun rose in the south and that a great beam of light struck her directly on the breast. She was full of delight and joy in that light, until a horseman on a black steed came and stood between her and the sun. Following that, a lion appeared and gave a palm-frond into her hand. With this she struck the rider a blow which caused him to fall dead. Then the sunbeam shone again so that it seemed to her that the upper part of her body was made of light.

When she awoke, Melora went in search of Merlin, who still visited Camelot the Golden at that time, and told him her dream. Merlin was silent a while, his sight turned inward, then he said: 'A king's son is coming here from the south of the world, and he will seem like the sun to you, and you shall love him. But others will make trouble for you, and things will go badly for you before they go better.'

Though she questioned him further, Merlin would say no more, and with these few words Melora had to be satisfied; but in the days that followed she wondered much about the king's son who was to come.

At this time King Gustavus ruled over the land of Thessaly. He had a proud and spirited son named Orlando, famed for his strength of arms and his skill in hunting and other manly accomplishments. And it happened that the fame of King Arthur's great Fellowship of knights reached the young man's ears, and at once he was seized with a great desire to visit Britain. Asking his father's permission, he received it and prepared to set out at once. But on the night before he was due to depart, he too had a dream.

It seemed to him that he was in a vineyard where there grew the tallest and most beautiful trees he had ever seen, hung with every kind of fruit, including apples. Orlando loved apples, and in his dream he stretched forth his hand to pluck the largest and ripest that grew there. But a poisonous serpent came toward him and wrapped its coils around his body. He remained held fast, struggling to breathe, until the apple for which he had been reaching fell down and struck the creature such a blow that it fell dead.

When he awoke, he consulted his father's wisest advisor about the meaning of the dream. After some thought, the wise man said: 'You will give your love to a most powerful and lovely woman who is not of this land. She will return your love, but this happiness will soon be followed by great danger that will threaten your life. However, the woman you love will save you in the end, and you will gain great happiness.'

When he heard this Orlando could not wait to depart, for in his heart he believed that the woman with whom he was destined to fall in love would be found in Arthur's land. He set forth next day, and after a long and tempestuous voyage, reached the shores of Britain, where he was greeted by a company of the noblest knights of the king's household. When they heard that he was the son of King Gustavus, they bade him welcome in Arthur's name and conducted him to Camelot the Golden.

When he stood at last before the king, Orlando knelt before him in homage. King Arthur welcomed him most warmly and bade him take his place at the Round Table with the other kings' sons who were present. All were in awe of the beauty and nobleness displayed by the prince and felt that he excelled them all in every virtue.

Melora also saw him and was dazzled by his brilliance. In a moment she began to fall in love with him, feeling his presence like the sun's warmth, just as in her dream. From that moment onward she was unable to sleep or rest at all but thought of nothing and no one save Orlando.

For his part the prince felt the same love toward the king's daughter, whose beauty and sweetness he had seen on the day of his arrival in Camelot the Golden. But he had not the courage to mention it yet, for he had no idea how his suit would be received, nor indeed who among all the courtiers were destined to be his friends or enemies.

Soon it was obvious that the prince outshone all but a few at the court. He was best at jousting, best at hunting, best at weapons-play. King Arthur thought so highly of him that he sent meat and drink from his own table to the young man. Soon enough Orlando and Melora declared their feelings for each other, though they kept them secret from the king and his courtiers.

At that time there was amongst the Fellowship of the Round Table a knight named Sir Mador, the son of the King of the Hesperides. He too fell deeply in love with Melora, though he kept it secret out of fear of her refusal. It was not long before he saw, by subtle glances between the two, that Orlando and Melora had grown close. This so enflamed his anger that he began to spread lying tales about the prince in the hope that Arthur would banish him from the court. It made no difference; rather Orlando's fame seemed actually to grow despite Mador's efforts to discredit him.

So it was that the knight devised another plot. He went to see Merlin and asked for his help, telling him how, if he could be aided in a secret task, he would be able to consolidate control over his own lands, which had lately been in disarray and rebellion against him. He told Merlin how he loved King Arthur's daughter, and wished to marry her, thus forging a great alliance. 'But I see that the Prince of Thessaly has won her love, as indeed he has won the hearts of so many here. Yet I feel that he is an evil influence over us all, and indeed may be using magic against us. If it were possible to turn King Arthur and his

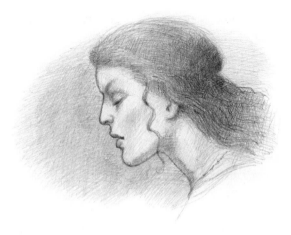

⤙ *Melora* ⤚

daughter against him, I would stand a chance of forming an alliance.'

Now it happened that at this time the kingdom was much threatened by forces from without, and as Master Thomas tells, Arthur found himself threatened by Rome herself. So persuasive and mild was Mador that Merlin, thinking of these things, began to think how Orlando could be tested.

✛ ✛ ✛

AS YOU WILL have heard often in these tales, it was King Arthur's custom never to sit down to dine until he had seen or heard of a wonder. For this reason, every day, one or other of the Fellowship would go into the Great Wood in search of adventure. Nor were they disappointed, for it was the quality of this place that whoever went there always found what they sought.

The day came when it was Orlando's turn to go forth. He put on his armour and went into the forest. Scarcely had he entered the shadow of the trees before he saw two disembodied arms, each holding a sword, engaged in combat. Like thunder the blows they struck echoed among the trees.

Orlando watched this for a while, then murmured: 'It seems to me that King Arthur would be happy to eat when he hears of this wonder. Yet I will search for something more, in case he does not deem this a worthy thing.'

So, he continued onwards, and in a while heard the sound of singing from above him. Looking up he saw a wondrous ship, seemingly made of crystal, sailing above the tops of the trees. He could see there was no one on board except for several swans, that sang sweetly from the deck.

'This is a wonder indeed,' said Orlando. 'Yet I will seek still another thing before I return to King Arthur.'

He continued on his way, and in a while saw a young warrior walking before him. But this was no ordinary man, for he carried his severed head before him, and blood was streaming from his neck even while he combed the hair of his head with an ivory comb.

'That is surely enough wonders for this day,' Orlando said, and turned for home. But before he had gone far, he met the strangest figure he had encountered so far. A creature it was, shaped like a tall and powerful man – but having only one leg, one arm and a single eye in the centre of its head. In its single arm it cradled a harp, and on it played such music that no one could hear it without feeling soothed and restored.

Orlando at once fell under the spell of the music and followed the strange creature deeper into the Great Wood. When night fell, they came to a beautiful castle amid the trees. Entering there, Orlando found himself in a most elegantly furnished hall.

Of the one-armed, one-eyed, one-legged being he saw nothing, but in the centre of the hall was a table set out with a chessboard and intricately carved pieces. A hand and arm, seeming attached to no one, was playing both sides of the game.

Orlando watched in wonder until one side outmatched the other. Then the arm put away the board and pieces and laid the table for a meal. A chair was placed there for Orlando and rich food and wine set out on the table. While he ate, music played that once again lulled him into a stupor.

When he had eaten, he saw coming towards him a hideously ugly, shrunken hag, whose skin was as black as the coals from a smith's forge.

'King of Thessaly's son, you should not have come hither,' she said.

'Why is that?' asked Orlando.

'Because you will never leave here. You shall be forever without companionship, without the light of the sun or the moon.'

'How can that be?' demanded Orlando, turning pale.

'You have fallen in love with King Arthur's daughter,' answered the hag. 'But she is loved by another, in secret, and he has obtained the help of Merlin to work against you. Merlin it was who took the form of the one-legged, one-armed, one-eyed harper that led you here. It is his intent that you should be imprisoned here for the rest of your life, and that I should be your guardian. Furthermore, he has required that I should take from you the power of speech, so that you may not cry out.'

'Who are you?' demanded Orlando, beginning to feel more fearful than ever before.

'I am called the Destroyer,' answered the hag. 'And now I shall take the power of speech from you.'

'Wait!' cried Orlando. 'Before you do so, is there anything I can do to escape from this place?'

'Nothing,' replied the hag. Then she hesitated. 'Unless you were somehow able to obtain three treasures that are hidden far away from here. Namely the lance with which the centurion Longinus pierced the side of Jesus Christ – for only can that spear shatter the walls that surround us here. The second treasure is a precious green stone which is in the possession of the King of Narsinga, far to the east. Only by means of the light contained by that stone can the darkness that will shortly surround you be pierced. And lastly you would have to obtain oil from the Pig of Tuís that belongs to the King of Asia, for only by touching a drop of that oil would your speech be restored. But since no warrior at present alive could do this, it is clear that you will never escape.'

Then she placed both her hands to either side of Orlando's face and took from him the power of speech. After which she departed, and the lights were put out and the music ceased, so that the prince was left alone in the darkness and silence of that dreadful place.

✠ ✠ ✠

IN KING ARTHUR'S court meanwhile, Orlando was missed. Because no one showed him a wonder the king went without food that night, and in the morning sent men in search of the missing prince. But though they encountered many wonders in the forest they found not a word of Orlando. When Melora learned what had happened she was stricken with grief. She thought often of her dream, and the rider on the black horse who kept the sunbeam from shining upon her. In her heart, she knew that the sunbeam represented Orlando, and she began to guess that the dark rider was none other than Sir Mador.

So it was that Melora began to speak more kindly to Mador, and even to encourage him to believe she might care for him. She did this in the hope that he might let slip knowledge of Orlando.

One day Mador came to her chamber. She made him welcome and bade him sit beside her. After a while she said: 'You come here far too seldom, Sir. You must know that there is no one else here at the court who is dearer to me.'

'Had I known that sooner,' replied Sir Mador smiling, 'I would have come more often.'

'Had I not been concerned that Prince Orlando, whom my father set to watch over me, might bring ill-report to the king's ears, I would have sent for you more often.'

'You may be sure of one thing,' said Mador, 'Orlando will not bother you ever again – nor anyone else for that matter.'

'If I thought that were true,' said Melora, 'I would make it possible for us to be together whenever we wished.'

'Dear Lady,' said Mador. 'If you really feel this way about me – and if you promise to keep it secret – I will tell you what has happened to Prince Orlando.'

'There is no need to bind me to secrecy,' answered Melora with a smile. 'It seems to me that making known my feelings for you should be enough. I have never told anyone of this before.'

'That is true,' said Mador, smiling with delight. 'Hear then, what fate I have decreed for my rival.'

He told Melora everything that had occurred and described to her the dreadful prison in which Merlin had placed him and how only by obtaining the three treasures could he be set free. 'And Merlin told me,' he added, 'that no man born of woman may obtain these things.'

When she heard this Melora was silent for a long while, then she smiled upon Mador and said: 'I have a plan that will enable us to be together always. It is certain that my father would not grant you permission to pay court to me unless he is convinced that you are the best of all his knights. Here is how we can prove it to him. I shall leave here tonight and remain hidden for a time. Soon the king will send forth knights to search for me. They will find none. Then I shall return in disguise and for the information I shall give I shall ask permission to choose any man I wish from Arthur's knights. I shall then choose you.'

This, of course, delighted Mador, who agreed to Melora's plan, and promised to remain at court until such time as she returned.

Melora now prepared herself for the journey. First, she put off her rich clothing and donned instead the arms and weapons of a knight, and over all she placed a plain blue surcote. Then she chose the fastest and strongest horse from her father's stable and so set forth.

Of course, she had no intention of hiding out in the forest in order to help Sir Mador, but rather she had set her mind on seeking the three treasures which would gain the release of her beloved Orlando. She set off first of all for the Eastern lands where she had heard tell the Lance of Longinus was kept.

For weeks she journeyed until she found herself in a land that was burned and desolate. There she met a young warrior wandering in a wasted land and asked him what had turned it into a wilderness.

'You must have come from very far away if you do not know the cause of this,' he replied. 'What country are you from?'

'I am from the Court of Britain, far to the west,' answered Melora. 'I am called the Knight of the Blue Surcote, and I am travelling in search of adventure.'

'There is need for such as you,' said the lone warrior. 'This land is called Babylon, and it has been at war with the kingdom of Africa these long years. The king of that land has destroyed all our country and captured our king's son. Now he lays siege to the last of our cities that has not fallen. If you are in search of adventure, you need look no further.'

So Melora set off for the besieged city and managed to gain entrance. There she was at once surrounded and taken before the king who, thinking Melora might be a spy, demanded to know who she was and whence she came.

Melora gave her story as she had given it to the young warrior and added that she had come to give help to the beleaguered king.

'I am surprised,' said he, 'since our enemies are so much stronger than we and able to offer far greater rewards. Are you certain that you have not come to betray us?'

'It is a true knight's task to give aid and succour to those who are weaker and in greater need,' answered Melora. 'If you doubt my honesty, send me out alone against your enemies. Then you will know whether I am your friend or not.'

'Very well,' said the king thoughtfully, and he gave instructions that a room be set aside for Melora and fresh clothes and what little food could be spared brought to her.

Next day she sought out the king and said to him: 'Remaining here behind your walls is the least good means of defeating your enemy. Every day you grow weaker and he stronger. You should rather send out your battalions every day to attack him. That way he will think you are as strong as ever.'

'That is a wise thought,' said the king. 'Spoken like a true champion. I had intended to watch how you fared today from the walls, but instead I shall come forth with my best knights and accompany you.' Then he sent for his captains and commanded them to prepare a sortie.

So it was that Melora, in her guise as the Knight of the Blue Surcote, went forth at the head of the Army of Babylon. The King of Africa, seeing them emerge, mustered his own forces, which far outnumbered the warriors of his adversary. But when battle was joined it was the Babylonians who slowly turned the tide, for wherever the enemy was thickest there was the Knight of the Blue Surcote, and so great was her skill with weapons, her strength and speed, that she laid waste a vast number of the enemy.

It happened that the King of Babylon himself was surrounded and unhorsed, so that it seemed he must soon die or be captured, but the Knight of the Blue Surcote came to his aid and carved a swathe through the enemy on every side until she reached the king. There, she rehorsed him, and fought on against her foes. Amid the slain lay the son of the King of Africa, whom Melora slew with a single blow. When they saw this, the forces of the African king were thrown into disarray and began to retreat. As night fell, the warriors of Babylon held the field triumphantly through the courage and strength of the Knight of the Blue Surcote.

Next morning a messenger came from the King of Africa demanding that the King of Babylon either come forth and fight in single combat or send a champion to fight in his stead. If Babylon were victorious then Africa would offer restitution for all the ills they had caused and furthermore set free the king's son.

At once Melora offered to fight on behalf of the Babylonians, asking only that if she had the victory, she might have the choice of anything she might honourably ask, for in thus wise she believed that she could win the Lance of Longinus, which she knew was in the king's keeping. The king agreed, though reluctantly because of her youth, and next morning the Knight of the Blue Surcote went forth alone to meet the King of Africa.

The combat that ensued is still spoken of in that land. The king was angry and filled with hatred for his adversary because of the death of his son, but Melora, though by far the weaker, was strengthened by her love for Orlando and her determination to win him back. Thus she fought as never before and in the end had the victory, inflicting terrible wounds on the King of Africa and bringing him bound before the King of Babylon.

Thus were the Africans defeated, through the strength and courage of Melora, and as he had promised, the King of Africa released the King of Babylon's son and made full restitution for all the damage he had done to the kingdom.

Now Melora went before the King of Babylon and asked if she might have her reward.

'Ask anything, and if it is in my power to give it shall be yours,' was the reply.

Then Melora asked if she might speak with the king in private, and when they were alone, she told him her story and who she really was and the reason for her needing the lance.

The king was astonished. 'Dear child,' he said. 'Your story is both pitiful and amazing, as are the deeds you have performed. We owe you greatly for your strength and honour. As regards the spear, you shall of course have it to use as you will. But the other treasures of which you speak will be even harder to obtain. Therefore, I propose that my son, Levander, who owes his freedom to your efforts, shall accompany you. You shall have my fastest ship and an honour guard of my best warriors to accompany you.'

For this Melora gave due thanks, but bade the king keep her secret until such time as she returned or was reported dead. Then she made ready to start, and the king's son, whose gratitude knew no bounds, decided to wear a surcote of green, so that he should be known only as the Knight of the Green Surcote – companion of the Knight of the Blue Surcote.

Next morning, they sailed with the early tide and the wind filled their sails so that they made good speed to the shores of Asia, where the king of that land happened to be holding an assembly close by the place where they came ashore.

Melora and Levander went before the King of Asia, who demanded to know who they were and whence they came. But when he heard that they were knights of King Arthur (for so they had decided to call themselves) he flew into a rage and ordered them to be imprisoned. 'There is no king in the world I hate more than this Arthur,' he cried. 'For his audacity in claiming to be the greatest king alive I distrust him. I am sure you came here as spies and that he will afterwards invade us.'

Despite their protestations Melora and Levander were seized and thrown roughly into a dark cell. There they might have remained had it not been that the captain of the guard who was on duty that night was himself from Britain. His father having performed a great deed in battle between the King of Asia and the Emperor of Rome, had been promoted to high office, and his son, who was named Uranus, was likewise trusted by the king.

Once the city slept, he went alone to the cell where the young knights had been thrown and spoke with them, asking their names and history. Melora assured him that they were both of royal blood and closely related to King Arthur, who would certainly take revenge for their ill-treatment.

'If only because of the blood that links us I shall help preserve your lives,' said Uranus. 'But since you are not spying for King Arthur, what is your real reason for coming here?'

After swearing him to secrecy, Melora told him of her search for the oil of the Pig of Túis.

'That is an impossible task,' said Uranus in dismay. 'The oil never leaves the person of the king.'

'Yet we must try,' answered Melora.

Uranus thought deeply. 'I will tell you of a way it might be accomplished,' he said at last. 'Tomorrow the king will go hunting, and when he returns, I am sure he will order your execution. But tonight, I will bring you clothing of the Asian style and help you to escape. In the morning you must find a way to accompany the king to the hunt. Then, when he takes his rest, go to him. Pretend that one of you is dumb and have the other ask for a drop of the oil. He will give this freely, believing you to be his own people. That will be your only chance to get what you seek.'

So it was agreed. Uranus released their fetters and guided them by secret ways from the prison and out into a remote part of the city. There he brought them suitable clothing and led them to get what rest they could.

In the morning they were able to join the large group that accompanied the king to the hunt. All day they remained in sight of the king, shadowing his every move. It happened that the rest of the hunt drew ahead somewhat, so that the king was alone. Soon he decided to rest in the shade of some trees and at this moment Melora and Levander went up to him and bowed very low. Melora pretended to be dumb and Levander spoke to the king, declaring that his companion was the son of one of his own earls, and that he had been struck dumb. 'We have heard that you possess a miraculous thing that gives speech to those bereft of it.'

The king questioned them closely, but Uranus had schooled them beforehand and Levander was able to answer everything correctly. Then the king drew out the vial in which was the magical oil and made to touch the girl's lips with it. At that moment Levander snatched it away. Then they both flung the king to the earth and bound him fast and gagged him so that he could neither move nor speak. Then they hurried away to where Uranus awaited them and all three hastened to return to the ship. Thus they escaped with the second of the three things that Merlin had declared that no man born of woman could achieve.

✢ ✠ ✢

A FEW DAYS' SAILING brought them to the shores of the kingdom of Narsinga. There Levander, who was well versed in the nature of the kingdom, declared that they should leave their weapons and armour on the ship and take instead musical instruments and put on the garb of minstrels. This they did, and when they arrived at the court of the King of Narsinga they were warmly received. When he heard that they were minstrels from the court of King Arthur, the king showed every sign of delight, even declaring his intention of sending a shipload of pearls home with them as a gesture of fellowship with Britain's king. When he heard them play, the king was so pleased with the unfamiliar sounds they made and the beauty of their singing, that he sent Levander to play for his daughter, while Melora was summoned to the king's own chamber to play for him in the evening.

There she learned that the king always carried the sacred pearl with him during the day. Only at night did he set it upon a table, from where it lit the whole room. The king never allowed anyone else to touch it.

Every night thereafter the king requested the two musicians of Britain to play for himself and his daughter. Then one day he began to ask them about the customs of their land and especially what music King Arthur liked to hear. Melora described the richness and strength of Camelot the Golden and the might of the Round Table knights. The king responded by asking what musical signals, trumpet calls or such like means King Arthur used to direct his warriors in battle.

Melora replied that they had many such, and that if the king wished to know more, he had but to accompany them to their ship where they could show him the instruments of war and instruct him in their use. So fascinated was the king that he agreed to accompany them, and next day, together with his daughter, he went with Melora and Levander to the harbour. There they went aboard their ship and while Levander went below with the princess, Melora began to demonstrate the many ways in which music could be used to call warriors to battle and to direct them in the field.

So fascinated was the king that he never even noticed when Uranus weighed anchor and set sail. Not until they were already far from land and a particularly large wave struck the ship's side, did he become aware of what had happened.

The king was furious and demanded at once to be put ashore. But Melora refused and requesting that he sit down, told him the whole story. 'We need the pearl which you carry around your neck to release Prince Orlando from the darkness in which he is imprisoned. But I promise, by sun and moon and stars, that it shall be returned to you once we have used it.' And she added that she wished to take the king to Britain, there to meet with and agree friendship between his country and Arthur's.

'If that is true, then I am glad to be with you,' the King of Narsinga answered. Then he placed his hand inside his shirt and drew forth the mystic stone, placing it in the hands of Melora. 'Use it well,' he said. 'No other man, or woman, has touched it this many a year.'

✚ ✚ ✚

THE VOYAGE HOME to Britain was without incident. Before they went ashore Melora said to the king and the princess: 'I bid you allow me to speak first on your behalf, while you are in my country, for the ways of Arthur's court are better known to me than to either of you.'

To this they agreed. Then Melora said: 'Until the release of Orlando is achieved it would be better not to reveal our true identities. Therefore, I shall continue to dress as the Knight of the Blue Surcote, and I ask that you also dress as knights and pretend to be warriors from your own lands. Even you, Uranus, should not reveal that you are of British origin.' To the King of Narsinga she said, 'Let your daughter be clad in the finest raiment possible. Then we shall proceed.'

All this was done, and the company set forth for Camelot the Golden.

While Melora had been absent from the court much had happened. On discovering that not only his daughter but also the Prince of Thessaly had vanished, King Arthur had sent forth search parties throughout his kingdom to look for the couple – believing indeed that they had fled together. Great was his sadness when no single word could be learned of their whereabouts. He even sent messages to the King of Thessaly, asking after his son, so that this monarch also was filled with sorrow for the loss of the prince, as was King Arthur over the loss of his daughter.

When Melora and her party arrived, they were greeted by one of King Arthur's best knights, Sir Brandamor, who welcomed them and brought them before the king. There Melora spoke up, and though it saddened her to keep her true identity concealed from her father, she maintained her disguise as the Knight of the Blue Surcote and announced her companions as knights from the lands of Babylon, India and Asia, and the princess as a noble woman who travelled under their protection, declaring that they had all come thither to visit the court of the greatest king in the world and to complete an adventure on which they were all engaged.

Arthur made them welcome and bade them sit down with him. He said: 'I am most glad to see you all, but there is one thing I would ask of you, and that is whether you have any news of the Prince Orlando of Thessaly, or of my only daughter, Melora, who vanished from this court and have not been seen since. I have made it known that anyone who brings word of them shall be rewarded with anything they ask that I can worthily provide.'

As he spoke tears filled the king's eyes, and Melora was forced to look away lest she break down and tell him who she really was.

'Noble king,' she said at last. 'The adventure upon which I and my companions are engaged may well bring answers that you seek. But first I ask that you send warriors of your household to accompany us to a certain place that I shall make known to you shortly. Thus we may help each other.'

When he heard this the light came back into King Arthur's face and he commanded his knights to be ready and to follow where the Knight of the Blue Surcote led.

A great party set out from Camelot the Golden and made its way to the edge of the Forest of Wonders. Melora led the way to where a great rock stuck up out of the earth amid the trees, and there she took the Lance of Longinus and struck the rock with it three times. With the third blow the rock split in twain with a great roar and out of it rushed the terrible hag who was known as the Destroyer. All drew back in fear of her coming, save Melora herself, for as soon as the hag encountered the open air she turned into a ball of fire and was drawn up into the firmament. Behind her gaped a great dark hole in the earth. Drawing forth the stone from the King of India, Melora held it up. At once

a brilliant light was ignited within it and the darkness fled upon all sides.

There was revealed a pitiful sight. Orlando, Prince of Thessaly, lay within. Scarcely alive was he, all skin and bone and his hair grown thick and rank all over his wasted body.

Melora took him in her arms and raised him up and carried him forth into the daylight, where King Arthur and the whole company were shocked and astonished by the sight of him. Then Melora drew forth the vial containing the oil of the Pig of Túis and said: 'Son of the King of Thessaly, drink this remedy, that you may be restored to us all.'

With a trembling hand the prince took the vial and drank three draughts from it. With the first his speech was restored, with the second he began to grow stronger, and with the third the thick hair fell from his body, and he was restored to his old strength and vigour.

King Arthur and the whole company were astonished and asked how the prince had come to be in this situation. Orlando told them all that had happened, how Mador had received help from Merlin and how he was imprisoned in that dreadful place without light or speech, and from which only the three treasures could release him. 'Yet I was told that no son of Adam could recover these things, and I am astonished beyond belief that it was accomplished at all.'

'It seems that this knight and his companions have worked a miracle on your behalf,' said King Arthur, indicating Melora and her companions. 'Are they known to you?'

'I believe I have never seen them before,' answered Orlando.

'Then this is indeed a mystery,' said the king.

At this Melora fell on her knees before him and cried aloud: 'Great and noble king, I shall no longer hide myself from you!' Then she drew off her helm and allowed her long hair to fall free. 'Beloved father,' she said. 'Here is your daughter.'

King Arthur was overjoyed and took her in his arms, while all those present cried aloud in wonder and astonishment, and Orlando looked on in even greater delight.

'How is this possible?' asked the king at last. So Melora told the whole story of her adventures and revealed the true identities of her companions. And King Arthur thanked them all and welcomed the King of Narsinga and his daughter, and the son of the King of Babylon. And he thanked Uranus and bade him doubly welcome home to his own land. But if Arthur himself was astonished, the wonder of Melora's companions was even greater, for now they knew that it was a girl who had accomplished the great deeds that she had undertaken on her journey and now all understood how it was no son of Adam but a daughter of Eve who had achieved the adventure.

Then King Arthur gave orders that Sir Mador should be brought before him. And, when he saw Melora and Orlando, the knight fell on his knees and begged for his life, claiming that everything that had happened was due to Merlin.

(I have heard it said that some who have heard this tale think that Merlin acted unwisely, seeming ignorant of the truth, but I believe that, as the story implies, he saw what was to come and permitted what followed in the knowledge that good would come of it.)

As it was, Arthur summoned his old friend and counsellor and demanded to know the truth. Merlin looked at Melora and Orlando and smiled. 'How else could this have been brought about. I am sorry that you had to

suffer, Prince Orlando, but the king's daughter has proved her worth and brought new strength to the kingdom of Britain. As to this man,' he added, turning to where Mador stood shivering before them. 'Do what you will with him.'

At this, King Arthur commanded that Mador be taken to a place of execution. But Melora spoke up: 'Sire, since you gave us your word that whoever brought news of your daughter and of the Prince of Thessaly should receive anything they wished, let me ask now that as my reward the sentence be commuted to banishment. For the son of the King of the Hesperides did this out of mistaken love for me. Therefore, let him be sent away but granted his life, and let the King of Britain show his wisdom and compassion.'

'Very well,' said King Arthur. 'Since you ask it, so shall it be.'

'There is a second thing I would ask, if it pleases you,' said Melora.

King Arthur smiled indulgently and asked her what it was she required.

'That the son of the King of Thessaly and the daughter of the King of Britain be married.'

'That too shall be as you wish,' answered King Arthur, with great joy.

So it was done, and when Melora and Orlando were married, so too were Levander and the Princess of Narsinga, who had found time and inclination to fall in love during their adventures.

Thus, the story of Orlando and Melora is brought to a good end. And as she had promised, King Arthur's daughter sent word to each of the kings who had owned the sacred relics that she would send them back. All of them, without exception, declined to take them back, such was their admiration for

Melora and for King Arthur. So these mighty treasures were given into the keeping of the wisemen of Britain, where they remained, and the kings and princes of Asia and Babylon and Narsinga went home, taking many gifts from King Arthur, and accompanied by some knights of the Round Table, who remained in their lands learning their languages and seeking out new adventures. And of the Lance of Longinus more shall be told in the Book of the Grail, but for this time I shall end this tale of King Arthur's daughter.

━━━━ ✛ ━━━━

EXPLICIT THE TALE OF KING ARTHUR'S DAUGHTER.
INCIPIT THE STORY OF THE GREY-HAMMED LADY.

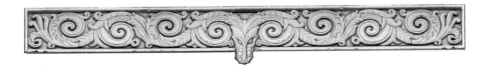

15: THE VISIT OF THE GREY-HAMMED LADY

— ✠ —

MANY TALES THAT ARE TOLD OF KING ARTHUR AND THE FELLOWSHIP OF THE ROUND TABLE SEEM LIKE DREAMS TO US IN THIS TIME – MOST OF ALL THOSE WHICH CONCERN THE UNEASY ACCORD BETWEEN THE KINGDOM OF ARTHUR AND THAT OF THE FAERY RACE.* MANY OF THESE HAVE I HEARD, BUT NONE ARE STRANGER THAN THE ONE I WILL TELL NOW. MUCH THAT IS IN IT SEEMS IMPOSSIBLE TO ME, DESPITE THE MAGICS THAT WERE EVERYWHERE IN THE LANDS AT THAT TIME. YET I TELL IT NOW BECAUSE IT SEEMS TO ME THAT IT SPEAKS OF MANY THINGS THAT SHOULD BE REMEMBERED IN FUTURE TIMES. AS TO THE ONE WHO TOLD THIS TALE, THEY ARE AS MYSTERIOUS AS IS THE STORY, AS THEIR LAST WORDS CLEARLY SHOW.

✠ ✠ ✠

THERE WAS ONCE a noble king who ruled over the lands of Gascony. For a long time it seemed that he was to be childless, so after the custom of the time he commanded a great feast to which all the nobles of the land were invited. The purpose of this feast was that everyone there should offer prayers that the queen might bear a son. And so it fell out, for little more than nine months after, the queen gave birth to a large and healthy boy.

The child grew apace, and everyone thought him the most handsome and wonderful boy. Lords from the four corners of the land sought to foster him, but this the king refused, asking instead that the nobles send their children to him to be brought up. So the king's son, who everyone called the Gascon Lad of Great Deeds, grew up surrounded by other noble youths, and learned the tongues of all their countries, and performed feats of arms such as few could equal in that time.

---

* See 'The Elucidation of the Grail & The Story of Perceval' pp. 309–25

177

Finally, the youths who studied the skills of the warrior with him formed themselves into a band, which was known far and wide as the Gascon Boy-Company.

Such was the strength and heroic nature of the king's son and his fellows that soon everyone began to ask where he might find a suitable wife. Attention fell upon the daughter of King Buille Bradanaighe, the King of the Salmon Pool. The Gascon Lad decided to go and see her, and took a hundred of his best companions with him. So impressed was the King of the Salmon Pool, both by the Gascon Lad and his company, that he offered his daughter in marriage, and the lad was glad of that, for he loved her as soon as he saw her.

The dowry that came with the king's daughter was twofold: a wondrous, beautifully fashioned horn, which whenever it was sounded brought every wild beast in the area to the one who carried it. Besides this the Gascon Lad received several hounds from which no beast could escape.

When the Gascon Lad and his new bride returned home, a feast was prepared to receive them. Much alcohol flowed, and when all were pleasantly intoxicated, a visiting noble arose and stood up straight in the hall. 'Never have I seen a fairer or richer court than this in all the world,' he said. At that another man sprang up and declared that he had indeed seen a greater and more wondrous court – that of King Arthur of Britain, the son of Uther Pendragon.

He continued: 'That is truly the greatest court in all the world, where wisdom and great feats of arms are to be found. Anyone who undergoes training there can go anywhere in the world and find welcome, for in truth none can compare with that king and that court. I tell you that on no day does King Arthur sit down with less than one hundred and fifty knights and several kings at his table!'

When he heard this, the Gascon Lad leapt up and cried that he would go at once to the lands of King Arthur. 'I will not use my own name,' he declared, 'for I do not seek to be honoured for my lineage. Instead, I will call myself 'The Hunting Knight', and prove myself worthy of a place at that court.'

So it was done. A ship was prepared and the Gascon Lad and his new bride, who elected to go with him, along with several of his favourite companions – and of course the fearsome pack of hounds – set sail for the shores of Britain. When they arrived, they made their way to King Arthur's court, where they found an assembly in progress. The king made them welcome and spoke kindly to them, asking them for news.

The Gascon Lad answered: 'I am a knight who has come here to learn feats of arms and to see for myself this court, which is said to be the finest anywhere in the world. I am called the Hunting Knight, for all creatures fall prey to my dogs and to the sound of my horn. If I remain here for a year, in all that time I promise to supply everyone in this court with game for their tables.'

'That is a great boast,' said King Arthur. 'May you be successful!'

Then he gave orders for rooms to be prepared for the Hunting Knight and his wife and declared that on the morrow the whole court would go hunting.

So it fell out. A great day of sport they had of it, and before all the Hunting Knight displayed his prowess and skill, as well as the uncanny abilities of his hounds. So great was his enthusiasm for the sport that when the day drew towards evening and King Arthur and his followers turned for home, the Hunting

Knight elected to remain behind in the forest. Scarcely had the court vanished from sight with a great jingling of harness and the thunder of hoofs, when the Hunting Knight spied a most beautiful deer that seemed to glow with unearthly light.

He grew pale when he saw the deer. 'What shall I do?' he wondered. 'If I release my hounds, they will certainly kill the deer, and that I could not bear, for it is so beautiful that it should not die. Yet I long to show it to others at the court, who would surely not believe me if I simply told them of it.'

Though torn, in the end he decided to let his hounds pursue the deer, which they did, all through the forest, until they reached a certain mound. There, the deer simply vanished – leaving the knight sad and sorrowful, for never had any prey escaped him before, and he was anxious to share the mystery of this with others.

Next morning King Arthur and the court returned with the Hunting Knight to the mound where he had lost sight of the wondrous deer. So began another day of sport, with many beasts brought down by spear or arrow – but never a sight of the strange deer. At the end of the day the Hunting Knight again remained behind in the forest, and there, sure enough, the wondrous deer came again, and once again the knight released his hounds. But, as before, they soon lost the scent and returned to him with their tails between their legs.

That night the Hunting Knight vowed to search the length and breadth of the land until he found the deer and caught it. Next day he returned to the forest and almost at once he saw the deer coming toward him. He loosed the hounds upon it, and followed them at full pelt through the forest until he

found himself at the gates of a most beautiful garden hidden among the trees. There the hounds awaited him, crying loudly.

Approaching cautiously, the Hunting Knight saw that a most splendid mansion stood in the midst of the garden, its windows a bright blue that flashed in the sunlight. And there he saw a delightful yellow-haired girl dressed in a gown of green silk and a cloak of brilliant red. She welcomed the hunter gently and said to him:

'I must tell you that I was that deer you have hunted these past three days. So greatly did I admire your abilities in the hunt, the way you led the troop through the woods, and the skill and daring in the way you rode and threw your spears, I took upon myself the form of the deer, the better to play the game we have played. Now I say that you are welcome to my house, and that so long as you stay here with me you will lack for nothing.'

Greatly moved, the young man remained there for the rest of the day, passing the time in conversation with the girl, and sadly taking his leave of her that night to return home to his lodging, where his wife awaited him. But the next day and the next he returned there, remaining all day long in the house amid the trees, only returning home to his lodging in King Arthur's court at night.

A week passed in this way, during which time the Hunting Knight went out in the morning, as if to the hunt, but returned home having caught nothing, and looking pale and withdrawn. It came to his wife that he had been visiting another woman, and when he set out that day, she followed him to the house in the woods. There she was met by the Deer-Woman.

'You are welcome indeed,' said she. 'Have you come to ask for your husband?'

'I scarcely think I should ask any such thing of you, since you can have no knowledge of him.'

'Indeed, I know him well,' said the Deer-Woman. 'But I give you my word that your husband has not betrayed you in any way with me. I belong to no man of this world, and no man shall possess me.' And she smiled so warmly at the Hunting Knight's wife that her heart melted at once and the two became friends.

Later, when it was time for the Hunting Knight and his wife to return to Camelot the Golden, the Deer-Woman asked if she might go with them.

'That would be our pleasure,' answered the knight, and they set out for the court. When they arrived there the Hunting Knight told the king everything that had occurred, and the king made the Deer-Woman welcome, seating her at his own right hand. Then, as was his custom, he asked what news she brought.

'I bring no news,' said she. 'Rather, I came to see the greatest court in all the world, to meet with your women and witness the feats of your warriors.'

The Deer-Woman was thus made welcome and remained at the royal court for a year. During this time, she became a great favourite among the noble warriors, who perceived not only the beauty, but also the magic and wisdom of the girl. She, in turn, brought many wondrous gifts of gold, and to the Hunting Knight she made an even greater gift – a shirt that would protect him from harm of any kind – for neither weapons, nor fire, nor water, nor any of the elements could hurt him while he wore it.

Meanwhile the knight's wife and the Deer-Woman spent much time together – and after a time, despite their friendship, the knight's wife was in no small degree jealous of her. One day as they were conversing, the Deer-Woman said that there was no one else in all the world to whom she would rather trust her greatest secret.

'What secret is that?' asked the knight's wife.

'There is a nickname I have – 'Grey-Ham' – and the reason for it is this: a tuft of grey hair sprouts from the hollow behind my right knee. No edge of a weapon can cut even the smallest hair of that tuft – and if anyone were to see it, they would surely no longer wish to share my company.'

'That is a terrible thing,' said the knight's wife, with tears in her eyes.

'Let us speak of it no more,' said the Deer-Woman. 'And never mention it to anyone in the court – for if it became known, I would be forced to leave at once and never return.'

The knight's wife swore that she would keep her friend's secret, but later that day, when she was visiting with the other women of the court, one of them said to her: 'This is a rare visit. Since you came here a year ago you have almost never visited us.' King Arthur's daughter said: 'The woman who shares your house has brought no blessing upon us. Since she came, our menfolk speak only of her and stare at her all the time like love-sick calves.'

The knight's wife smiled at that, and said: 'What would you say if I could bring an end to this situation?'

'Whatever we had we would give you,' said the women.

'Then listen, for I know her secret.' And the knight's wife told them what the Deer-Woman had told her.

And one amongst them, who was wife to Sir Gawain, said: 'Let us call her by that evil

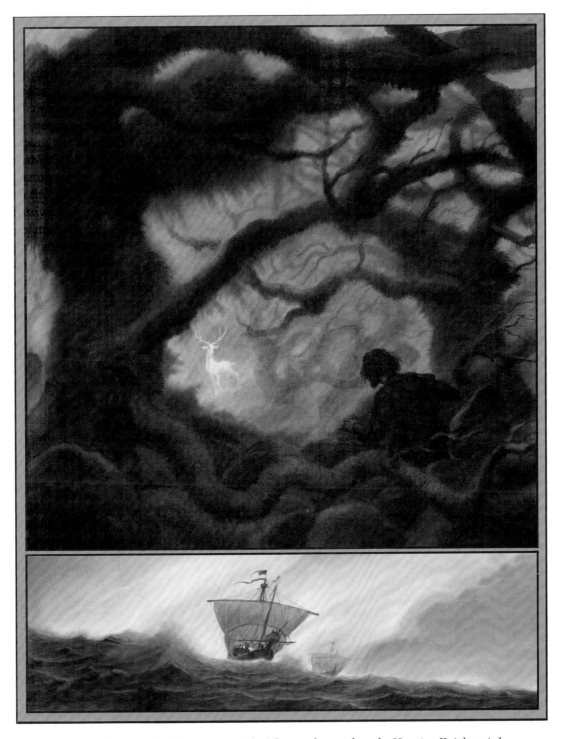

PLATE 5: 'Scarcely had the court vanished from sight … when the Hunting Knight spied a most beautiful deer that seemed to glow with unearthly light'

nickname before all of the court. Then surely she will leave here for good.'

It was thus agreed between the women, and that evening Sir Gawain's wife stood up in the court and asked to be heard. When everyone was silent, she said: 'A woman came here, and has been here for a year, during which time our husbands have ceased to pay us any attention at all. I say this is not a good thing for the Fellowship of the Round Table, or for this court. But it seems to me that if you all knew her secret you would pay her less attention – for I have heard tell that she has a tuft of thick grey hair in the hollow of her knee, and that for this reason she is known far and wide as 'Grey-Ham'.'

The other women nodded their assent to this, and one said: 'Evil is the visit of Grey-Ham to this court.'

At this the Deer-Woman blushed scarlet from head to toe and leaned swiftly across the king and struck Sir Gawain's wife in the face. Then she looked at the king with great calm and great anger and said:

'King Arthur, this court has shamed me greatly, and for that shame I shall have answer. If it were your men that had done this to me, I would have taken their wives from them; but since it is the women of the court who have caused me hurt, it is they who shall be punished. But first I would show you the blemish that was said to be upon me.'

She lifted her skirts above the knee so that all there could see that her legs were beautiful and straight, and that there was no sign of any blemish. Then the Deer-Woman said: 'Now let all your women be brought hither and let each one of them bare their legs before the court.'

And, because in his heart King Arthur knew that she was right to feel such great anger, he commanded that this be done, and shortly all of the women, young and old, were forced to parade before the assembly and to raise their skirts above the knee. Then it was seen that every single woman there possessed a tuft of thick grey hair behind one of their knees, and most wept for shame at this.

Then the Deer-Woman said: 'I have suffered great humiliation at your hands, lord King, but I tell you this. My name is not that which has been told to you in this place. And because of the hurt I have felt, I lay this wish upon you all – that this story shall be told whenever the company is gathered together, and all shall wish to hear it because of the protection they receive from it – for they shall be saved from hurt or harm for a year after they have heard it. Thus, shall my story be told for all to hear.'

Then she spoke this poem:

'Famous my visit
To the Round Table
When I gave great love
To the Hunting Knight.

In the form of a deer
I ran in the forest
Seeking him out
As my true companion.

For one year after
I shared a room with his wife;
I fashioned a wonderful shirt
In a beautiful, mysterious place.

Because of her envy, a story
His wife told of me –
That behind my knee
A tuft of grey hair sprouted.

Though honoured my name
Throughout the West
My name was not 'Grey-Ham'
To the People of the Sidhe.

Whoever hears my story
Will be safe for a year,
If they tell the story
Of 'Grey-Ham's visit'.'

When they heard this many there grew pale, for they knew that of all the races of Faery the Sidhe were the most powerful, and the fiercest.

Then the girl turned to the women of the court and said: 'Though you have humiliated me greatly, greater still shall be the suffering that comes to you because of this. I predict that a year from now not one among you will possess a husband or a man that loves you, for I declare you to be women without luck, without fortune, without honour.'

As she spoke, and as all the women recoiled before her terrible words, news came of a golden chariot with a canopy of gold over it and three powerful steeds with golden bridles pulling it that approached the court. In the chariot stood a handsome, powerful champion.

When she saw him, the girl said: 'If this champion should hear of the great disgrace I have had at the hands of this court he will certainly avenge it. Then I promise you that this court and the walls of your house would be cast down and scattered entirely. For now, King Arthur, I ask that you come with me and talk with the one who comes.'

All the court arose and followed the king and the girl outside. And they saw that the champion had upon his head a helm of gold adorned with a shining, precious stone, and

that his jerkin was sewn with gold thread, and that his face was radiant and royal as any king. The girl twined her two arms around his neck and kissed him gently.

'Well, foster-child,' said the champion, 'are you pleased with your visit to this place?'

'Pleased and not pleased, dissatisfied and not dissatisfied.'

'How may that be?'

'I am pleased by the men of this court, but displeased by its women,' the Deer-Woman answered. 'They shamed me without good cause and for that they shall be punished. However, dear foster father, I ask that you refrain from harming the men of the court. They cannot help their ways or their manners.'

At this, King Arthur said calmly, but with a glint in his eye: 'We bid you welcome, Sir. Will you enter our court?'

Before the champion could answer, the girl spoke up again. 'My foster-father is not used to entering any court that is not decorated with gold. Wait here while I see to it.'

The Deer-Woman went into the hall, and when she emerged again moments later every wall was hung with gold, and every chair had golden ornaments about it, and the doors themselves were covered in gold from hinge to bolt. Only one area in the hall remained ungilded, and to this the girl led the women of the court and bade them be seated. Then she led the king and all the rest within and seated the champion in Arthur's own seat and the king in the seat of one of the noble lords' places. All this she did, and because of the power she wielded none there dared raise a hand to prevent her.

Then she spoke loudly and clearly for all to hear: 'My lords, I came to visit to see what a great court this was. But your foolish weak-willed women humiliated me beyond measure. I have given my word that none of them shall ever get a husband or a lover while they yet live. Now I promise that all the noble warriors of this court shall not lack for women, for among my own handmaids there are more than enough for you all, as you shall see. Every one of them is more nobly born and of better disposition than any of the women of this court.'

Then she uttered the following poem:

'Evil is the disposition of the women
In the household of King Arthur;
Though mighty your courage
Your spouses are unworthy.

To these impetuous women
I told an untrue secret,
Afterwards the hollow behind my knee
Was shown to be without grey hair.

Every woman who hears of my visit
And fails to curse the women of this court
May their substance fail
And may they never find a mate.

I, Aileann Bright-Complexion,
Daughter of Dáire of the Brown Shield,
Speak these words; no better place
Than my father's house have I yet seen.

A woman from me for every man
Who has a woman in this house:
Payment in kind for my coming
Unannounced to the Round Table.'

All there looked on in wonder and many shifted in their places, feeling the discomfort of what had taken place and no small degree of fear at the curse laid upon them all. And the warrior from the chariot sat still and proud in the king's place – but spoke to no one.

Then the Deer-Woman, whose true name all now knew, spoke again: 'I shall tell my story here, so that you are better able to understand what has occurred. Aileann am I, the daughter of Dáire of the Brown Shield, King of the Picts. The reason he is given that name is because of a rare shield he possesses, covered in red-brown gold from Arabia. No wounds can ever be inflicted upon the one who carries it. Enemies break before it in battle and no less than a thousand shields in the hands of warriors are raised when it is raised.

'The wife of this king, my mother, is Rathleann, daughter of the King of Iceland. She bore my father two twin children, myself, and my brother. And when she was about to give birth, the great king of Salabearna, he who now sits beside you, King Arthur, asked that he should foster us. And so it was done. His other name is the Champion of the Mound, and there is no one in the world stronger than he, for if he so wished he could upend the world. One child has he, Bé Thuinne, the Woman of the Wave, who is one of my own handmaids. A fitting bride she would be for one of your own kin. But I promise you that I have many more women in my company, each as beautiful as the sun and moon, and that they are more than worthy to be wife to any man here. If you and your men will come with me to the House of the Dead, better spouses than you had before will be found for you all. So shall you be happy. But as for these women...' and she turned to where the women of Arthur's court stood huddled together in great misery, 'you shall never know another night of joy in your lives, nor shall you remain in this house another night.'

183

Such was the strength of the spell that the daughter of Dáire had over King Arthur and his court that no one gainsaid her, and in the morning the knights prepared to go with the girl and her foster-father to the House of the Dead – and many a woman wept that night, believing they would never see their men again. Indeed it seemed as though they slept, though they could see and hear and speak as readily as anyone.

In the morning the great company entered into swift ships and set sail upon the ocean, and soon sighted a wooded land in which all of the trees had scarlet tops that shone in the sunlight like rubies.

'What land is this?' demanded King Arthur.

'It is known as the Plain of the Purple Hazel,' said the girl. 'Another name for it is the Plain of Fruits. Three kinds of wood grow there: the purple hazels themselves, on every branch of which grow nuts as long as the arm of a warrior. Beside them grow grapewoods with fruits upon them as large as the head of a man. And over all these grow the great flame-headed trees that you see which protect the others from storm or tempest.'

The ships came to land and they disembarked. King Arthur and his men feasted upon the hazel nuts and the purple berries, which tasted like honey and sustained them well. The hazels also made them merry and amorous, for such was the power they had.

When they had feasted, they left the wood and journeyed across the plain until they came to a great mound, and there they prepared to make camp. Then they saw coming towards them a wondrous stag with golden antlers of more than a hundred tines. When King Arthur's men saw this, they released their dogs upon it. But the stag merely stood by until the dogs were close to it, then caught them up on its great antlers and shook them until they were dead. Then the knights cast their spears at the stag, but it merely deflected

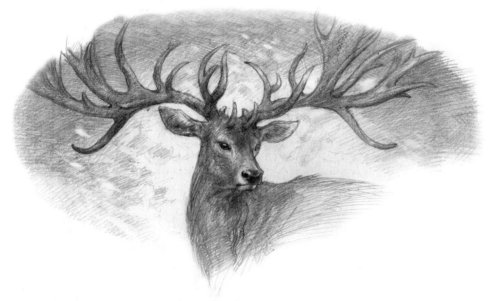

❖ *The Wondrous Stag* ❖

them and then broke them under its feet. After which it vanished away.

Then King Arthur said: 'Our hounds are killed, and our weapons broken. This is not a good day for us.'

'Though you may consider it bad, it is no worse than the shame I felt when the women of the Round Table gave away my secret,' said Aileann Bright-Complexion. 'Now let us go into the House of the Dead.'

King Arthur and his knights followed her onto the plain, and there ahead of them they saw a great tree, on which sat many hundreds of birds. As the host approached, they began to sing, and everyone there forgot their former life when they heard them and seemed like people who dreamed. Then the Champion of the Mound called forth the women who lived in the House of the Dead and gave one each to Arthur's knights. And to Arthur himself he gave Dathchaoimh, whose name means Pleasing Colour, with whom he fell instantly in love. And to Sir Gawain he gave his own daughter, Bé Thuinne, the Woman of the Wave. Nor did any one of the knights refuse the offer of the beautiful women – for these were of the Sidhe and none could deny them anything they asked – for truth to tell they had forgotten their wives and sweethearts at home in Britain.

Time passed, while the knights listened to the singing of the birds and spent time in dalliance with the women. Then on a bright morning she who had been known as the Deer-Woman said: 'Let us depart now.' And at once the music of the birds was stilled, and the warriors were released from their dreams – though they remained entranced by the women from the House of the Dead.

The great company set forth again, crossing the Plain of Purple Hazels, and there

they saw the mouth of a huge cave gaping in a hillside. And as they approached, there came out of it five hundred ugly cats, each one as big as a three-year-old boar. A drop of blood gleamed on the end of each hair on their bodies, and they were both fierce and hungry.

'What things are those?' asked King Arthur.

'These are the cats who will destroy you all if you do not kill them first,' answered Aileann.

So there began a great battle between the men and the cats. But it seemed that whenever one of the knights struck one of the cats it was not hurt, but that whenever one of the cats struck one of the knights, he was terribly wounded. And each time, the cats dragged off the bodies of these men into the cave.

'Do you regret the death of your men?' asked Aileann Bright-Complexion.

'I do indeed,' answered Arthur.

'Just as I regret the humiliation I received at your table,' said the girl.

As she spoke, out of the cave mouth came six hundred magnificent mares. Each one had a great black mane upon it, but other than that they were hairless.

'What are these?' demanded Arthur, wearily.

'These are wild mares that have come to kill you and your men,' replied the girl.

Once again battle was joined, and once again the efforts of the knights proved fruitless. For though they struck out at the mares, their swords were turned aside, and the mares caught the men by the nape of the neck with their great teeth and carried them off into the darkness of the cave.

'Do you regret this also, King Arthur?' asked the girl.

'Indeed, I do,' answered the king heavily.

'Just as I regret the humiliation I received in your court,' said Aileann.

Then they saw a huge man coming toward them from the cave. Before him came a great white hound with red tipped ears, straining at the golden chain that bound it. The man came to the place where Arthur and his remaining knights huddled together, and suddenly there were dozens of hounds everywhere, that began to attack them from all sides.

Once again battle was joined, and once again the greatest efforts of Arthur's men proved fruitless. The king watched in despair as more of his men were dragged off into the cave by the hounds.

Then Sir Gawain, who was standing nearby, said: 'See how the great hound tugs at the chain that binds it. It is clear to me that this beast is challenging me to battle. Give me leave to go against it.'

Arthur gave his leave and Sir Gawain drew his sword and rushed towards the hound, and the giant let fall the chain that held it.

Just as with every one of the warriors, Gawain's sword could make no impression on the creature. But when he saw this, he put aside his weapon and threw both his arms around the neck of the hound and bore it to the earth and began to choke the life from it.

When she saw that, Aileann Bright-Complexion begged Gawain to stop. 'That is your own woman you are killing!' she cried. And to King Arthur she said: 'Call off your champion and you shall have all your men restored to you, unharmed.' As she spoke, the hound changed into the form of a beautiful woman, and Gawain recognized her as Bé Thuinne, the Woman of the Wave.

Then Arthur saw all his men coming out of the cave, each one with a woman at his side, followed by all the hounds they had thought killed by the great stag. And none of them, men and dogs, were hurt at all.

'You see,' said the girl. 'Your men are safe, as are their hounds. It was the women from the House of the Dead who fought with them, to test them.'

Then, much chastened, Arthur and his knights returned to the House of the Dead and celebrated a great feast. Then it was that Aileann Bright-Complexion said:

> 'Good was your visit to this place,
> Great Arthur, son of Uther.
> Whether good or bad my coming
> Only time will tell.
>
> Treasure and wealth of women
> You will have during your life.
> All I got, from my visit,
> Was shame and a red face.
>
> Take the fair brown shield of Dáire
> Before which armies break.
> I will remember, without anger,
> What is said concerning my visit.
>
> The Sword of King Salabearna,
> Take also, and increase your courage.
> My story will last forever –
> Many will seek to hear it.'

Good as her word, the girl gave these treasures to King Arthur. Then she said: 'Rejoice! Tomorrow you shall return to your court, O great Arthur. And let this be a warning to all who would bring grief to any one of the Sidhe. For if your women had not spoken ill of me, none of this would have happened. Only now will I release you from the spells I placed upon you.'

Then it was as though King Arthur and his knights woke from a long dream, and they stared about them at the great hall within the House of the Dead in bewilderment. And the champion of that place looked upon them all and smiled, for he knew all too well the weaknesses of humankind.

Arthur and his knights returned home to Britain, where they found their wives waiting to greet them. As to the women of the Sidhe, nothing more was seen or heard of them in that time, but neither the knights nor the ladies of Arthur's court ever forgot the visit of Aileann, the Grey-Hammed Lady. Only the Gascon Lad found a new wife, who was truly fitting for him, but throughout his life thereafter whenever he spoke of his journey to Arthur's court and all that came of it, he spoke little of the Deer-Woman whom he had caught, and how they had journeyed to the Otherworld, and how the whole of Arthur's court had been enspelled for a time.

This I know, since I am one who is, who will be, and who was.

———— ✠ ————

EXPLICIT THE STORY OF GREY-HAM.
INCIPIT TYOLET'S TALE.

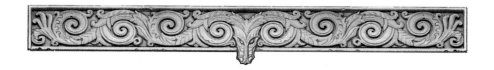

16: THE STORY OF TYOLET

--- ✛ ---

THERE WERE LESS PEOPLE IN BRITAIN IN THE TIME OF KING ARTHUR THAN NOW, BUT DESPITE THIS THE GREAT KING ASSEMBLED A FELLOWSHIP OF KNIGHTS THE EQUAL OF WHICH HAS NOT BEEN SEEN BEFORE OR SINCE. THOUGH IT IS TRUE THAT THERE ARE BRAVE KNIGHTS IN THIS LAND STILL, THEY ARE NOT AS THEY WERE IN THOSE OLDER TIMES. THEN, THE BEST AND BRAVEST KNIGHTS WERE WONT TO WANDER THROUGH THE LAND IN SEARCH OF FRESH ADVENTURE, OFTEN FINDING NONE AND BEING FORCED TO SLEEP OUT UNDER THE STARS WITH ONLY THEIR HORSES FOR COMPANY. WHEN THEY DID FIND ADVENTURES, THEY PURSUED THEM, AND AFTERWARDS RETURNED TO THE COURT TO TELL WHAT HAD OCCURRED, SO THAT THEY COULD BE WRITTEN DOWN BY CLERKS AND RETOLD IN LATER TIMES, WHENEVER FOLK MIGHT LIKE TO LISTEN.

✛ ✛ ✛

MANY OF THESE I have sought out for this book, and one such tale I am about to tell: of a brave knight named Tyolet, who was fair, proud, skilful and valiant. This youth had a particular ability, which was that he could whistle and call up any creature of the woodland that he liked. It is said that a faery woman taught him this skill, and he used it well, for he lived in a distant and lonely tract of the Great Wood, all alone with his mother, and whenever they needed meat Tyolet would go out and summon a beast and slaughter it for the table. But he never slew more than they needed, and indeed he loved the creatures of the wood as if they were his kin.

Tyolet's father, who was a great knight, had died when he was but a child, leaving his mother alone. She brought up her son in the Great Wood and kept him from the world outside, though he was allowed to wander wherever he wished in the woodland. Thus, he saw few other people, and grew towards manhood in ignorance of the world.

One day his mother asked Tyolet to go forth and kill a stag for the table. Straightway

188

he set forth and wandered the woodland until noontide without sight of a single beast. Then he was sorely vexed and thought to return home, when under a sheltering tree he saw a great white stag with a mighty spread of antlers. Tyolet drew his knife and whistled to call the proud beast to him.

Hearing his whistle, the stag looked toward him, but made no move to approach. Rather, it turned away, and went at a slow and stately pace among the trees. Tyolet, in astonishment, followed it to a riverbank and watched as it swam easily across. He himself dared not follow, for it was a wide and swiftly flowing stream, and beyond it lay open country where he had never been before. Then, as he looked across at the stag, which stood as though waiting for him on the further bank, he saw a fat roebuck approach along the bank where he stood. At once he called it to him and dispatched it with a swift blow. Then, as he looked up, he saw that the stag had vanished, but that in its place stood a figure, fully armed, mounted upon a gallant war-horse.

Tyolet stared at the apparition with jaw a-gape. He had never seen anything like this in his whole life and wondered what manner of creature it was. The knight called out to him across the water, asking who he was and what he was doing there.

'I am the son of the widow who lives in this forest. I am called Tyolet. What do they call you? And, please, what are you?'

'I am called a knight,' said the figure.

'What manner of beast is a knight?' asked Tyolet. 'Where do you live and what are you for? And how do you come to speak as I do?'

'I am a beast that is much feared,' said the knight, slowly. 'Sometimes I live in the forest and sometimes in the open lands. Sometimes I take other beasts and consume them.'

'You are a wonder indeed,' said Tyolet. 'In all the time I have spent in these woods I never saw a creature like you. I have seen lions and bears, and every kind of deer, and never one of them that I could not call to me. Tell me, knight-beast, what is that thing on your head and what hangs around your neck all shining and bright?'

'The thing on my head is called a helm, and it is made of steel to protect me. That which hangs about my neck is called a shield. It shines brightly because it is painted and banded with gold.'

'And that stuff in which you are clad, that seems full of little holes, what is that?'

'It is called a hauberk, and it is made of rings of iron, wrought to form what is called chain-mail.'

'And those things on your feet. What are they?'

'Those are called greaves. They cover my legs and feet and protect them from harm.'

'And that long thing at your side. What is that?' demanded Tyolet eagerly.

'Why, that is my sword,' replied the knight patiently. 'It is long and sharp and fair to look upon.'

'And that long wooden thing you hold in your hand. Tell me what that is?'

'That is my lance,' was the answer. 'Now I have told you all that I may and must be upon my way.'

'I thank you, Knight-Beast,' said Tyolet. 'But before you depart, I pray you tell me one more thing. Are there any more of you in the world. For I would dearly love to see them.'

'Indeed, there are many,' replied the knight, and it seemed that he laughed quietly behind the metal of his helm. 'If you wait here but a moment longer you shall see more than a hundred.'

As he spoke there came a great jingling of harness and a thunder of hoofs, and a great company of knights came into view. They were of King Arthur's court, and had but lately attacked and destroyed a fortress of evil intent and were returning home.

When Tyolet saw them, he cried aloud in amazement. 'How can I be like them?' he demanded. 'For never in my life did I wish for anything half so much as I do this.'

The knight asked: 'Are you brave and valiant?'

'I think so,' answered Tyolet. 'Certainly, I would like to be.'

'Then you should come to King Arthur's court, which lies to the west of here beyond the borders of the Great Wood. If you get there tell whoever you meet that you want to be a knight.'

'Thank you,' answered Tyolet, and watched in wonder as the cavalcade of knights, their harness jingling and their armour and weapons reflecting the sun, rode way out of sight.

Then Tyolet sped home as fast as he could and gave his mother the roebuck he had killed and told her of his adventures. Tyolet's mother expressed her grief at what he had seen. 'These beasts devour others, indeed,' she said. 'How may that be a good thing?'

'I do not know, mother, but I would go and be one among them, for if I do not, I shall never be happy again.'

Then Tyolet's mother went to the chest in which she kept her dead lord's armour and weapons, and she brought them and put them upon her son until he seemed in very truth a knight-beast. Then she said: 'Son, when you reach King Arthur's court, remember to keep company only with men and women of good breeding. For you are of noble birth and should be with your own kind. Also, be sure

to learn the ways of chivalry and follow its dictates as you would my own words.'

And though Tyolet did not understand her words he kissed his mother and set forth over hill and through valley until he came to Camelot the Golden. He stared in wonder at the great walls of the city, and the many banners which flew from the towers, and saw how knight-beasts came and went through the gates, to the accompaniment of the music of trumpets and drums. Then he passed through the open gates himself and went within into the great hall where the king was seated at high table for the evening meal. Tyolet walked right up to the dais, clad in his armour, and there he sat down in an empty place, speaking not a word.

King Arthur looked at him kindly and said: 'I think you have a tale to tell. Let us hear it.'

'Sire, my name is Knight-Beast, but once I was called Tyolet and I am the son of the widow who lives in the forest. I can catch any beast you like and am skilled in hunting; but now I would learn the ways of the court and this thing that I have heard of called chivalry.'

'You are most welcome,' said the king, smiling. 'Come now and eat.'

Squires came forward to unarm Tyolet and put upon him a fine mantle and brought him water with which to wash his hands. Then he sat down to eat, staring all the while at the wonders of the court.

As they sat at table, there came into the hall a very fair damsel indeed, riding upon a white palfrey and holding in her arms a white bratchet with a small bell of gold around its neck. Right up to the dais she came and greeted the king.

'What service may I or my knights do for you?' asked Arthur.

'Sire, I am the daughter of the King of

Guittonia, who died but recently,' said the maiden. 'I have come here to see if there is one among your company who will pursue and bring me the right foot of a certain white stag, the hair of which shines like gold and which is guarded by seven lions. Only he who is brave enough to do this may win my hand, for I will take no other but he for my lord. And he that wins me shall be Lord of Guittonia also.'

'This is just such an adventure as is proper to my knights,' said King Arthur. 'Do you give your word that the one who succeeds in this task shall be your husband and ruler of your lands?'

'I do,' replied the maiden.

So it was agreed. King Arthur looked about him to see who would undertake this adventure. You may be sure there was not a man there who did not leap up from his place and cry that the adventure be given to him. But one among them, Sir Lodoer, made the greatest plea, and to him King Arthur awarded the task.

'How shall I know where to find this white stag?' asked the knight, and the maiden gave him the white bratchet and told him that he should follow where it led. Thus, he set forth and followed the dog, which led him through a wild land to the bank of a wide, fierce, greatly swollen river. The dog leapt in and swam strongly, but Lodoer sat upon his horse and looked with dismay upon the flood and dared not venture into it, for there was nowhere to cross.

Shortly the dog returned and swam across the river again. The knight took it up on his saddlebow and rode back the way he had come to the court. There King Arthur asked how he had fared, and if he had the foot of the white stag. But Lodoer only shook

his head and said that if another wanted to risk his life the adventure still waited. Then the other knights mocked him, but Lodoer merely said that they should go and try for themselves before they decried his efforts.

So it was that many of King Arthur's knights set forth in quest of the white stag, but each one returned home empty-handed and were forced to admit that Lodoer was right. Then Tyolet, whom everyone had taken to calling 'Knight-Beast', came forward and begged the adventure for himself. 'Be sure that I shall not return until I have succeeded, or die in the attempt,' he said.

Though in truth he thought the youth would not get far, the king gave him leave to go, and Tyolet took the bratchet and departed as soon as ever he might. He followed the little dog to the side of the great flood and, when it plunged in, he followed, urging his steed into the racing waters. These proved to be less fierce than they seemed, and both dog and youth soon reached the further bank. There the bratchet ran ever before him until it came to a broad meadow, where Tyolet saw the white stag grazing in the shade of some trees.

At that moment there was no sign of the lions which guarded the prize, and Tyolet made good advantage of this, riding as close as he could and then whistling as he had been taught to draw the beast to him. When he had whistled seven times the stag came and stood submissively by, and without thought Tyolet took his sword and smote off its right foot and hid it in his shirt. Then the stag cried out in pain, and the lions, who were near at hand, came in haste to defend it.

The first leapt at Tyolet's horse and wounded it terribly, tearing the flesh from its shoulder. Tyolet struck it such a blow in

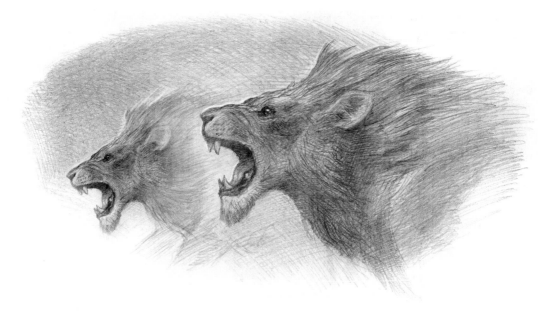

→ *The Lions Attack* ←

return that it fell dead, but his mount fell to the earth, and he was thrown clear into the path of the rest of the pack, which attacked him from every side.

A dreadful battle now ensued, in which Tyolet received terrible wounds on his back and ribs and shoulders. But in the end, he slew all of the lions before falling unconscious from loss of blood. Thus he failed to see how the white stag was restored, its missing foot replaced by the magic of that place.

As Tyolet lay thus, there came a knight named Forêt, who was not known to him, who looked upon his wounded body and deemed him almost dead. Tyolet roused himself enough to draw forth the stag's foot and proffer it to the stranger, bidding him take it to King Arthur and tell him all that had befallen.

Forêt took it with secret delight, for he had heard the story of the quest for the white

stag and had longed to succeed in it. Now the chance had come that would enable him to seem successful. Therefore, he took the foot and made to ride off, without even a thought for the wounded Tyolet. Then he bethought that if the youth should survive, he might return to claim his right, so he turned back and drawing his sword plunged it into the youth's body. Then he rode on and found his way back to the court, where he showed the foot to King Arthur and claimed the hand of the maiden.

But he failed to bring back the bratchet, for in truth he knew naught of it and indeed it had returned alone some days earlier. King Arthur, deeming this a sign that Tyolet had perished, had sent the good knight Sir Gawain in search of his body. Thus, being wise in the ways of men, and wondering at the success of Forêt, the king sought to delay matters for a further nine days, giving as his reason that he

192

must summon his court to witness the wedding of the knight and the maiden.

Gawain meanwhile followed the bratchet, which led him to where Tyolet lay as though dead. Gawain saw the bodies of the lions and the dead horse and the dreadful wounds that were upon the youth, and he mourned greatly. But as he knelt by the body, Tyolet opened his eyes and, in the merest thread of a voice, told what had happened. Then as Gawain thought to use his great skill as a healer to aid the wounded knight, there came in sight a damsel mounted upon a white mule, and Gawain recognized her as a messenger of the Lady of the Lake, whom he had encountered on other occasions. He called out to her to help the wounded man, and she greeted him well and they embraced. Then the damsel and Gawain took counsel together and decided to take the wounded man to the leech of the Black Mountain, who lived nearby. 'If anyone can help this good knight to recover his health it is he,' said the damsel.

They lifted Tyolet onto Gawain's horse and took him to the healer, who washed and cleaned his wounds and searched them and declared that he would live and be as strong as ever within a month. Very gladly indeed Gawain made his way back to the court, where the false knight Forêt was about to wed the maiden. But Gawain burst in and cried that the knight was false, and that he had stolen the right of Tyolet to be acknowledged the successful contender in the matter of the white stag.

Angrily the traitor protested his innocence and sought for reparation at the hands of his accuser. So a day was set when he and Sir Gawain should meet on the field of battle to decide the matter. But before that day could dawn Tyolet himself returned to the court, pale and drawn from his ordeal, but hale enough to ride a borrowed mount. When he saw him, Forêt turned first red and then white in turn and began to bluster and cry out that his was the right to wed the King of Guittonia's daughter. But Tyolet turned from greeting the king and all the knights who had rushed forward to embrace him, and asked, mildly enough, on what grounds he made this claim.

'Why, because it was I who took the stag's foot!' cried the false knight.

'And who slew the lions that were its guardians?' asked Tyolet.

Forêt grew red, and waxed wrathful, but he had no words to answer.

'Then tell me who was the one smitten with the sword and who the smiter?' Tyolet said. 'For in truth I believe the last was you and the first myself.'

The knight looked away in shame, and Tyolet demanded to know if he would deny the charges. 'For if so then I offer my glove to you in King Arthur's name, and promise to prove the truth of this before all.'

The knight began to fear for his life, and there before all he fell down on his knees and confessed his crimes and begged for mercy. At which Tyolet, looking upon him with gentleness, pardoned him, so that the knight fell down and kissed his feet. Tyolet raised him up, and kissed him on the cheek, and from that day they spoke no more of the matter. But Tyolet took back the stag's foot and gave it to the maiden, who blushed with all the beauty of a new-blown rose. There and then did King Arthur marry them, and afterwards they returned home to the maiden's own land, where they reigned long and wisely together. And it is said that the White Stag, which in truth was the very same that

Tyolet had seen and followed, and which had led him to the start of his adventure, was a faery creature, and that Tyolet had been tested by it, as were many of King Arthur's men, and had proved himself both wise and noble.

So ends this story and now we turn to the knight named Jaufre.

———— ⴲ ————

EXPLICIT THE STORY OF TYOLET.
IMPLICIT THE TALE OF JAUFRE.

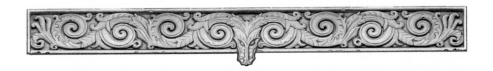

17: THE STORY OF JAUFRE AND THE GREAT LAMENTATION

✢

IT HAPPENED AT PENTECOST ONE YEAR THAT THE GREATEST OF THE KNIGHTS OF THE ROUND TABLE WERE GATHERED AT CAMELOT THE GOLDEN. LANCELOT WAS THERE, AS WAS TRISTAN. GAWAIN WAS PRESENT, TOGETHER WITH YVAIN, CALOGRENANT, PERCEVAL AND CARADOC, AND MANY MORE BESIDE. IN THE MANNER CUSTOMARY AT THAT FESTIVAL, WHEN THEY HAD HEARD MASS, THEY ALL ASSEMBLED IN THE COURT TO TELL TALES OF THEIR ADVENTURES, TO DISCUSS MATTERS OF CHIVALRY, LOVE, AND HONOUR. THERE CAME SIR KAY ALSO, SARDONIC AS EVER, WHO ENTERED THE HALL WAVING A BATON MADE FROM AN APPLE BOUGH.

✢ ✢ ✢

SURELY IT IS time to eat,' he cried.
King Arthur frowned. 'How often must I remind you,' he said, 'that I will not sit down to eat until we have seen or heard of some adventure.'

Kay shook his head and went to listen to the conversations of the knights and to interrupt them with caustic comments of his own. But as the day drew on, until it was well past noon, King Arthur called to Sir Gawain and ordered him to have horses saddled and armour prepared. 'It seems we shall wait forever for something to happen. Let us go forth in search of adventure for ourselves.'

Gawain did as he was bid, and soon the whole company were setting forth, following the ancient track deep into the mighty forest of Broceliande, where everyone knew that all kinds of adventures were to be found.

After a while, the king reined in and listened. 'I hear a voice raised in a cry for help,' he said. 'I shall try this adventure alone.'

'Let me come with you,' begged Gawain. But the king shook his head and rode off alone amid the trees, following a narrow pathway until he reached a riverbank. There he saw a fine mill, at the door of which stood a woman tearing her hair and screaming for help as loudly as she might.

'What troubles you,' demanded the king.

'Ah, sir,' she cried. 'A terrible beast has come down from the mountain and is eating all the grain in the mill!'

'Stand aside,' said King Arthur, and he dismounted and looked into the mill. There he saw the strangest creature he had ever seen. Large as a bull it was, or larger, with not two horns, but five! Its eyes were huge and glowing, and its feet were the size of flat irons. It was covered all over in coarse red hair and had long yellow teeth, with which it was eating its way through mounds of grain.

King Arthur stared at the creature in amazement, but he drew his sword and, putting his shield before him, advanced upon the beast. It completely ignored him however and continued eating. Then the king decided it looked fiercer than it truly was and gave it a hefty whack across the rump with the flat of his sword.

The beast continued to ignore him, so the king circled around it and gave it a prod in the shoulder with his sword. Still it did not move or even raise its head. So, King Arthur sheathed his sword and laid down his shield and grabbed it by the largest of its great horns and tried to wrestle it away from the grain.

Despite his considerable strength the king could not move the beast a fraction. But when he went to let go of its horns in order to give it a blow with his fist between the eyes, he found, to his dismay, that his hands were stuck fast, and that no amount of pulling and wrenching could move them at all!

As soon as it felt the king straining to get free, the beast raised its head and departed from the mill, carrying the helpless Arthur dangling from its horns. It proceeded at a gentle pace through the forest, passing close

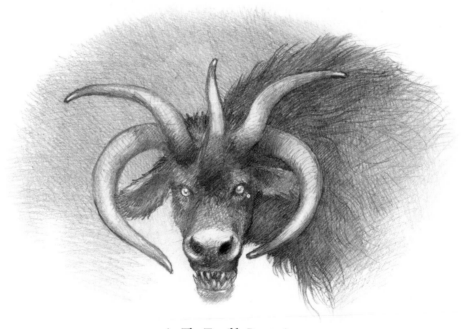

→ *The Terrible Beast* ←

196

by Sir Gawain, who had remained there in case the king needed help.

When he saw King Arthur being carried thus by the monster he cried out in alarm, and gave chase, drawing his sword. But the king called out to him to hold his hand. 'I think I may die if you kill this creature,' he said. 'But if I spare it, I believe it may spare me!'

At that moment Tristan and Yvain came riding full tilt, having been alerted by Gawain's cries and the noise of the beast moving through the wood. Gawain called out to them both not to attack, but to keep the beast in sight until they could discover what its intentions were.

The beast meanwhile simply cantered along the forest paths, seeming unaware of the knights or any of the clamour around it. It chose a path that rose steadily, and then with a burst of speed ran ahead of the pursuing knights and leapt swiftly up a steep escarpment. At the top it stopped, then turned and stuck its head out over the edge, leaving King Arthur dangling from its horns above the drop.

You may imagine that this caused the knights to become desperate, seeing their monarch in such dire straits. As for the king, now he clutched even tighter at the beast's horns, rather than trying to get free.

Then one of the younger knights suggested that if they all took off their clothes and piled them up at the foot of the cliff, so that if it chanced the king should fall, he would at least have something soft to land on! Gawain thought this was an excellent notion and urged the others to follow suit. About fifty of the knights began to tear off their garments, flinging them in a heap beneath the luckless king.

When it saw this the beast shook its head a little from side to side, causing King Arthur

much dismay and all those watching to moan aloud. Then, seeming as though it would turn away from the cliff edge, the monster took a sudden leap outward and down. It landed in among the naked knights, and King Arthur found himself suddenly free. At the same instant the beast was itself transformed into a handsome man, who stood there laughing.

'Have your men get dressed, my lord,' the man-beast said. 'Now you have found a marvel, you can all go and eat.'

The king was astonished, for he recognized the man as a clever and audacious fellow who had come to the court some weeks before and had begged as a promise from the king that, if he was able to change his appearance enough to fool everyone, he should receive a golden cup, the best horse in the royal stable, and the right to kiss whichever maiden he deemed the most beautiful. (Others have said that it was none other than Merlin, playing a trick upon the Fellowship, but of this I cannot say.)

Now it was King Arthur's turn to laugh, for he loved a jest as well as any man, and the sight of his knights clustering around naked, scrabbling for their clothes, struck him as a test of their quality. 'Let us return to the court and eat,' he said. 'I believe we shall all be warmer inside.'

Laughing and joking, the knights regained their garments and set out for the court, soon arriving there and settling down to a fine feast. They had everything to eat that so noble a company might expect: cranes, bustards, peacocks, swans, geese, partridges, refined bread and good wine. And there the handsome wizard received his reward – though which lady he chose to beg for a kiss the book does not say. The court had not been eating long before there came a fresh disturbance. A young man, very handsome and well dressed, rode into the court and dismounting, approached the king's chair and fell to his knees before it.

'God bless the lord of this host,' he said.

'And His blessing upon you,' replied King Arthur. 'What do you wish of us?'

'Sire, I have come here because I have heard that you are the finest king that ever lived, and I pray that you make me a knight.'

'It shall be our pleasure,' said the king. 'Though we would know more of you first, since knighthood is not granted without reason. Be seated and join with us in our celebrations.'

'By your leave, not until I have been promised a boon,' said the youth.

'You shall have what you ask, so long as it does not harm anyone here,' said the king. With that the youth seemed satisfied, but as he went to wash his hands there came yet another disturbance. A fully armed knight galloped into the hall and before the horrified eyes of all present, ran a knight sitting at the table though with his lance. Then he wheeled his horse and cried out: 'My greetings to you, King Arthur! I have done this to bring dishonour to your house. If you or any of your brave Fellowship wants to pursue me, my name is Taulat de Rogimon. It is my intent to return here every year on this day until I am stopped!'

King Arthur, both angry and abashed, leapt to his feet. But the young stranger was quicker. 'My lord,' he cried, 'let this be the boon I have requested and which you have promised to grant. Let me follow this evil knight and bring him to justice.'

'Keep silent, fellow,' snapped Sir Kay. 'You may speak thus when you are drunk. For now, sit down and I will tell you later how to go about being brave.'

The young knight said nothing to this,

though his fair skin coloured. But the king rounded upon Sir Kay and bade him be silent and keep his tongue to himself. To the youth, he said: 'Young man, I shall gladly make you a knight, as I promised, and give you arms and a horse to ride. But I bid you not to fight this Taulat until you are stronger. There are few of my best knights whom I would expect to vanquish him.'

'Sire, how shall I know my strength until it is tested?' answered the youth. 'Let this be the test, and the boon I asked for.'

'Very well,' said Arthur. 'But if I am to knight you, I must first know your name.'

'In my own country I am known as Jaufre, the son of Dozon.'

'Ah,' sighed King Arthur. 'I knew your father well. A braver knight never bestrode horse than he. He died fighting at my side in Normandy. I was there when the arrow pierced his breast. Now I see where you get your courage and strength.'

Thus Jaufre was made a knight, and almost at once a squire came with a proud, high-stepping war-horse, and Jaufre vaulted onto its back with a single bound. Then he took up the shield and lance that were proffered to him and saluting the king with a ringing shout, spurred his mount from the hall.

✠ ✠ ✠

WITHIN DAYS OF leaving the court Jaufre had defeated his first opponent, a powerful knight named Estout of Verfueil, whom he sent back to surrender himself to King Arthur. After this he encountered an evil fellow who used a beautiful lance, left propped against a tree, to lure knights to their death. But Jaufre defeated him and hung him where he had hung others before him and sent back the man's dwarf to tell King Arthur that one less evil custom obtained in his lands. Then, still following the road in search of Taulat, Jaufre encountered a soldier guarding a narrow pass, whose practice was to capture and torture any knight who came that way. Him Jaufre dealt with summarily, cutting off both his feet and leaving him to die. Then he released twenty-five knights whom the soldier had held prisoner and sent them all back to King Arthur. Then he rode on, not wanting to halt, or even to eat, so determined was he to overtake the knight who had challenged the honour of the Round Table.

He came at last to a place where the road ran between open fields, and there he saw a leper stumbling along holding a baby in his arms, while behind him ran a woman crying out for her child. When she saw Jaufre she ran and clung to his stirrup, begging him to help her, saying that the leper had stolen her child without reason.

Jaufre at once gave chase, and saw the leper run into the lazar house, where such poor unfortunates were wont to live. Dismounting, Jaufre hesitated for a moment at the door, then drew his sword and went in.

The room where he found himself was dark and mired, but there was sufficient light for him to see where another leper lay in bed, holding a lovely woman who had no sign of the disease. She was weeping quietly to herself, and Jaufre could see that her clothes were torn and disarrayed from her struggles with the evil man.

When he saw the knight, the leper jumped up and hefted a huge club in one hand. He was hideous to see, with misshapen features and red eyes. His gums were blue and swollen, his breath stank of venom and his face was as red as a burning coal. His breathing was laboured and his voice a rough croak as he demanded to know what Jaufre wanted.

'I am looking for the leper who stole a woman's child. I saw him come in here.'

'It was a bad day when you did,' croaked the misshapen man, and without warning swung his club at Jaufre. The knight raised his shield just in time and took the full force of the blow there. Staggering from the force of the attack, for though diseased the leper was immensely strong, Jaufre struck back with his sword, catching the leper on the arm and almost severing it.

Bellowing with pain, the leper renewed his attack and caught Jaufre a glancing blow on the helm which almost felled him. Drawing his breath, the knight struck with all his force at the leper's head. The blow split his skull, but with his dying breath the leper kicked out so viciously that Jaufre was lifted from his feet and flung against the wall, where he lay, stunned from the blow and with blood pouring from nose and mouth.

The maiden, who had been on the point of ravishment by the leper, came forward cautiously and unlaced the knight's helm. When she saw the blood, she cried out and ran to fetch some water which she flung in his face. Jaufre, still dazed and momentarily blinded by the blood in his eyes, struck out, still thinking that he held his sword. He knocked the maiden to her knees and then tried to stand, staggering around the room until he struck the wall. There he rested, gulping air, until his senses slowly cleared.

The maiden, approaching him with caution, asked how he did.

'I am well enough, lady,' answered the knight. 'But I seem to have lost my sword.'

'You dropped it when you were hurt. See, it is here on the floor by the man you killed.'

199

Jaufre looked at where the leper lay dead upon the ground and quickly retrieved his sword. Then he looked around. 'Where is the other that I pursued? Did you see aught of him?'

The maiden only shook her head. She had been too fearful for her own life and safety to notice anything.

'Then I shall look outside,' said Jaufre, and made for the door. To his astonishment, he found that he could not cross the threshold. Try as he might he was stopped each time as though by an invisible wall.

'What enchantment is this?' he cried, and ran at the door, only to fall back again. Panting, he slumped down dejectedly on the bed. Then, just as he was bemoaning his evil luck, he heard loud cries coming from another room in the lazar house. Jumping to his feet, he ran down a corridor until he came to a door that was shut fast and barred. The cries came from within.

Furiously, Jaufre beat upon the door with the hilt of his sword, and when it remained firmly shut, raised a foot and kicked it open.

A terrible sight met his eyes within. The first leper, the one he had been pursuing, was there, as were a number of children of all ages. The leper had already killed four of them with a large knife and was threatening the rest, who cried out piteously. As Jaufre entered the man turned and threatened him with the knife, screaming out that his master would soon be there and that Jaufre would regret it if he did not flee.

'If that was your master I saw in the other room, he is dead,' replied the young knight. 'And you shall soon follow him.'

The leper threw down his knife at once and fell on his knees, begging for mercy. It was his master who had forced him to steal

children and then kill them, wishing to bathe in their blood to cure his disease.

'Is this the truth?' demanded Jaufre.

'I swear it on my immortal soul,' cried the leper.

'Then tell me why I cannot leave here,' said Jaufre.

'My master had great knowledge of magic,' answered the leper. 'He made it so that no one who entered here with intent to harm him could escape unless he personally took them out again – usually to kill or torture them. But there is a way for you to escape. In the other room there is the head of a boy, enclosed in a glass box. If you smash it, my master's spells will be undone. But beware, there is very strong magic here. The whole house may fall upon you.'

Jaufre took the leper back into the main room and bound him fast. Then he gave instructions to the maiden to take him and the remaining children outside, for the magic did not bind them as it did him. 'If I fail,' he said, 'be sure this wretch meets with his just deserts.'

The maiden did as she was bid, and once he was alone Jaufre went to look at the cavity in the wall where the glass box was, enclosing the strange head. He took it down with caution and not a little revulsion, and saw that it was an artificial thing, but made extremely lifelike. Carefully he placed it on the floor and then took his sword and struck it with all his strength.

At once the head cried out and rose into the air. It flew around the room several times, belching fire and clouds of dense black smoke. The very earth quaked then, and huge hailstones lashed down out of the sky outside the lazar house. Lightning flashed and rain began to fall, striking the walls of the building, which began to crumble. Every timber and beam and brick seemed to dance and waver before his eyes, and Jaufre raised his shield above his ahead to protect himself as the roof collapsed with a great roar. Winds screamed through the ruins, lifting them and scattering them. Rocks and earth rose into the air and a great whirlwind caught up everything and took it away. At last, all that was left was Jaufre, and as the dust settled it was as though the house had never been, walls and foundations were all gone and not a trace remained of the evil magics.

Then Jaufre fell to the earth and lay like a dead man for a while. When his senses returned, he found the maiden and the woman whose child he had saved bending over him anxiously, tending him with water and gentle words. In a while he was able to stand again and bade the two women take the leper and go to King Arthur and tell him all that had happened that day. 'Greet the king from his knight, Jaufre son of Dozon, and tell him that I search still for Taulat, and will continue until I find him or die in the attempt.'

Then he mounted his horse and, taking up lance and shield, set forth once again.

☩ ☩ ☩

JAUFRE WAS VERY tired, both from his journey and the many adventures and hardships he had experienced since leaving King Arthur's court. So it was that he rode almost blindly, letting his horse choose its own path, while he almost slept in the saddle, several times being close to falling off. Thus wandering, he came to a castle, the gate to which stood open. Entering, it seemed to him deserted, so he began to search it until he found himself at the entrance to a garden enclosed by high walls. It was the most beautiful place he had ever seen, with so many fair and sweet-scented plants that he deemed he must be in paradise. Birds sang in the trees, and lush grass grew underfoot.

Jaufre was so exhausted that almost without thought, he unsaddled his horse and turned it loose to graze. Then he placed his shield beneath his head and lay down in the shade of the trees. In moments he was asleep.

Now I must tell you that this castle and garden belonged to a most beautiful maiden named Brunnisend. There was none more fair in all the land, nor one so filled with sorrow. For both her parents were dead, and having no brother she ruled the castle, which was called Monbrun, alone. Now, hear what a strange custom there was in that land: for both its lady and all her people must make great mourning four times every day and again three times in the night; and if anyone asked the reason for this terrible lamentation they were at once put to death. Thus, the lady slept but little, and was given to frequenting a room overlooking the garden, where the singing of the birds lulled her to sleep.

That night she retired early but was disturbed to find that the birds were silent. 'Who has entered my garden?' she demanded. 'Nothing else would cause my birds to stop singing.' She summoned her seneschal and sent him into the garden. There he found Jaufre so soundly asleep that it took several minutes to wake him.

'For the love of God, let me sleep,' begged the young knight. But the seneschal only prodded him harder and demanded that he attend upon his mistress.

'You will have to make me,' said Jaufre, and promptly fell asleep again.

The seneschal went to fetch armour and weapons, and when he returned, kicked

Jaufre awake. 'Fight with me or become my prisoner,' he cried. Jaufre stumbled to his feet, angry at being woken again. He took up his sword and shield and defended himself against the seneschal. In a few blows he had defeated him and sent him scurrying back into the castle. There the Lady Brunnisend waited to see how he had fared.

'Where is the intruder?' she demanded.

'Lady, he has defeated me. I had great difficulty in waking him and even now I think he sleeps again.'

'Then let us wake him up indeed!' cried the lady furiously. 'Summon the guard at once.'

In a matter of moments, a dozen knights were assembled in the hall, and one of them, a man named Simon the Red, offered to go and bring the stranger inside as his prisoner.

'You may find it less easy than you expect,' said the seneschal.

Nevertheless, Simon went forth and found the knight sleeping just as before. It took several prods with his spear to awaken Jaufre, who rose up so furiously that he disarmed the knight in moments.

Simon returned despondent and battered, and it was the turn of another knight, who fared exactly the same. Indeed, so filled with sleep was Jaufre that he thought it was Simon returning to disturb his rest once more, and accordingly he dealt with the second challenger even more summarily. This displeased the Lady Brunnisend greatly, and she ordered her seneschal to take a dozen knights and to bring the intruder so that she could see for herself what kind of monster defeated her knights so easily and without even being fully awake!

The next thing Jaufre knew was when he was seized by a dozen pairs of hands, some holding his legs, another his arms, the rest his shoulders, body and head. He was carried from his place in the garden into the castle, all the while struggling mightily, and this time fully awake, demanding to be put down and to be told the meaning of this un-knightly behaviour. But the men ignored his pleas and dumped him, unceremoniously, in front of the Lady Brunnisend.

Looking with curiosity as much as with anger at the tall young knight, she at once saw that not only was he handsome, but also, clearly, of noble birth and armed in the finest armour.

'Are you the fellow who has caused me so much trouble?' she demanded haughtily.

Jaufre turned to her and saw the loveliest woman he had ever beheld.

'I was not aware I had done anything to cause you displeasure, my lady,' he said.

'By all the saints!' stormed Brunnisend. 'You shall be punished nonetheless. I think you will make a fine corpse as you swing in the wind when we have hung you!'

'My lady,' said Jaufre, staring even more intently at her fair form. 'You may do with me whatever you will, since you have defeated me with no other weapon than your beauty. If I have unwittingly done you any harm then you must punish me, I see that. But I beg that you grant me one favour before you have me killed.'

'You speak boldly for one about to die,' said Brunnisend. Yet even as she spoke, she changed colour and her anger began to abate. 'What is this favour you would ask?'

'Why, madame, only a good night's sleep,' replied Jaufre.

Brunnisend hesitated, and as she did so one of her knights spoke up, reminding her that it was only right to allow the condemned man one last wish.

'Well, it seems to me that you will soon

have all the time you wish to sleep,' she said. 'But, if my knights undertake to guard you, you shall have your wish.'

'My lady,' answered the seneschal. 'No one shall be better guarded.' And he gave orders for a bed to be made up in the midst of the hall and dispatched a dozen soldiers to keep watch until morning to see that Jaufre did not escape.

With that the Lady Brunnisend retired to bed, lulled once more by the song of the birds from her garden. Despite this, and despite the manner of her life and the traditions of the castle, she lay awake, thinking of the handsome young knight who lay asleep in the hall below. She wondered greatly who he might be, why he had come there, and if he might, just possibly, find her worthy of love.

Jaufre, meanwhile, despite the threat to his life, fell asleep surrounded by mail-clad soldiers.

So the night passed, until the watchman called the hour of midnight. At this moment everyone in the castle woke and began to mourn loudly, crying and wailing and making such a complaint that even Jaufre was awakened from his profound sleep. He lay there unmoving, wondering what caused the lamentations, and thinking too that he should try to make his escape from this strange castle – even if it meant leaving the beautiful maiden behind.

If he had known that the same beautiful lady was at that moment lying awake thinking of him, he would certainly have remained where he was. As it was, he saw that his guards, worn out from their lamenting, which had at last ceased, had themselves fallen asleep, and he hastened to exit the hall as quietly as he could. Good fortune attended him in that he found his horse, armour and weapons with ease, and in a short time he had

left the castle and was once again on the road, wondering still about the strange castle and its sorrowful inhabitants.

Brunnisend, meanwhile, lay awake until morning, then rose and joined again in the lamentations with which the people of that place greeted every day. When all was still again, she hastened to call the seneschal to her and demanded news of the prisoner.

The seneschal had already discovered the absence of Jaufre and feared greatly to admit that he had failed in his duty, and so he told his mistress that the knight was dead.

'How did this happen?' cried Brunnisend in dismay.

'My lady, last night after you had retired, the stranger woke during the time of the first lamentation. He asked the question which must not be asked, and paid the penalty for it. As many as a hundred blows fell upon him, cutting him to pieces like a butchered stag. We have already buried him, since we did not wish to grieve you further.'

'Alas, you have grieved me more than you know!' cried Brunnisend. Then she said to the seneschal: 'I must know all there is to know about this knight. I bid you go and seek out his name and rank and history.'

'But where shall I look?' demanded the seneschal, regretting his lies.

'Where all good knights are found – at the court of King Arthur. Go there and find out all that you can. It may be that he has family who will wish to know how his life ended.'

With that the seneschal departed, albeit reluctantly, knowing that in truth Jaufre was not dead, and dreading to meet him on the road.

As for Jaufre himself, he made his way as best he might, putting as much distance between himself and the castle of Monbrun as he could. He was soon regretting that he had not eaten either the night before or that morning, and when he came upon a friendly herdsman, preparing his morning repast by the roadside, he hesitated scarcely at all before accepting the man's invitation to join him.

The herdsman was cheery enough and shared his food with a will. The two men chatted of this and that, and among other things Jaufre learned the name of the lady of Monbrun. Soon he prepared to continue upon his way, but as he was preparing to mount and ride off, he turned back to the herdsman and asked him if he could tell him the reason for the strange lamentations which took place at the castle. The herdsman's response was immediate; he turned in the blink of an eye from a friendly, garrulous fellow into a raging madman, attacking Jaufre with a club and screaming abuse at him.

Feeling nothing but bewilderment, the knight defended himself as best he might while taking care not to hurt the herdsman. Finally, the wild man was laid unconscious on the earth, and Jaufre rode on as quickly as he could. All that day he continued on his way without meeting anyone, though twice more he heard the terrible sound of lamentation seeming to come from the earth itself. Then, as the day was drawing in, he fell in with two young men who were out hunting. They quickly offered him the hospitality of their father's house, which was nearby, and Jaufre accepted it willingly. His host was named Augier d'Eixart, and he made the young knight welcome. When he heard Jaufre's name and parentage, he wept and embraced the youth. 'Your father and I fought side by side in many a skirmish,' the kindly lord explained. 'You are welcome in my house for as long as you desire.'

'I am glad indeed to accept your hospitality,' said Jaufre, 'though I regret that I may not stay for more than a night.'

They went in and sat down to dine, and there Jaufre made the acquaintance of the lord's daughter, a very fair maiden indeed, who won the knight's heart with her gentle ways and lovely face.

When they had dined Jaufre was shown into a clean and comfortable bed and went to sleep for what seemed the first time in weeks without fear or discomfort. So deeply did he sleep that he failed even to hear the lamentations which took place in the night, and in which both the lord of the castle and his family took part. In the morning Jaufre prepared to depart, and his host came to bid him a reluctant farewell. 'I wish there was something I could do for you in honour of your father's friendship,' he said.

Jaufre hesitated. 'My lord, there is one thing that you might be able to do – to settle a matter which has been troubling me these past days.'

'And what is that?' asked Augier kindly.

'Everywhere I have ridden in these lands I have heard a terrible lamentation on every side, three times a day, and I know not how many times at night. Can you tell me the reason for it?'

Almost before the words were out of his mouth, the old lord had drawn his sword and sprung at him like a tiger, screaming abuse and threatening to kill him. Jaufre defended himself as best he might, turning aside the blows with his shield and retreating until he could leap onto his horse and ride pell-mell for the gate. He could hear the old lord shouting to his sons and calling out for their mounts to be fetched, and soon enough he heard the sound of hoofs on the road behind him.

Just as he was thinking of turning at bay

and defending himself in earnest, Jaufre again heard the morning lamentation, and sped on even faster, hearing the voices of the three knights behind him cry out with all the rest. Then the noise ceased, and after a moment Jaufre heard the voice of Augier d'Eixart calling upon him to stop and begging his forgiveness for his unchivalrous behaviour.

Cautiously Jaufre reined in, loosening his sword in its sheath. But the lord and his two sons were no longer mad with fury or sorrow. They rode up to him and the old lord fell in the dust at his feet, begging Jaufre to forgive him in the name of God and of the young knight's own father.

Sheathing his sword, Jaufre answered that there was nothing to forgive since no harm had been done to him. Augier gave thanks and got back on his own horse. Facing Jaufre he said: 'My friend, I cannot speak of that which you asked me, but I will do anything else I can to further your way. Is there any deed I may do to serve you?'

'There is but one,' replied Jaufre with caution. 'I seek a knight by the name of Taulat de Rogimon, who has done ill to my lord King Arthur. Have you by chance heard anything of him?'

The old lord sighed heavily. 'I do indeed know of this knight,' he said. 'You would be well advised to avoid him if possible, for he is both evil hearted and strong. Yet if you truly must seek him, and I see in your face that you will not turn aside, then here is what you must do. Ride a few leagues onward until you see a great castle with many banners flying from its walls. Outside the walls will be many tents and pavilions filled with rich lords and brave knights. Do not speak to any of them but make your way into the castle itself. No one will stop you as long as you keep silent. In the hall you will see a sad sight – a noble knight lying on a bed, all wounded and close to death. At the foot of the bed will be a young maiden, at its head an older lady. It is she with whom you must speak. Tell her I sent you and ask about the cry. When she has told you all there is to tell, you will know the whereabouts of the one you seek. Now I bid you be gone, for I have said too much, and my head is near to bursting with sorrow!'

With this the old lord turned away, and calling his sons to him, rode off, leaving Jaufre to follow the way indicated – though in truth he did not know whether to be elated by the possibility of finding Taulat at last, or puzzled by the mysterious words concerning the wounded knight.

✠ ✠ ✠

JAUFRE RODE ON until he came to the castle, which was just as the old lord had described. He continued as swiftly as he could through the assembled encampment. On every side he saw knights come out of their tents to watch him pass, but no one tried to stop him, either there or at the gates to the castle, which stood wide. Hastening onward, Jaufre made his way through several rooms, each one more splendidly furnished than the one before, until he saw a small door that was standing half open and, looking within, he saw a knight lying on the bed, his upper body bound up, his face pale and drawn with suffering. Beside the bed sat two women, just as Augier had described, and Jaufre went in softly and spoke to the older of the two asking her if he might talk with her for a moment. The lady rose and guided him outside the chamber. Then she asked him, in low tones, what he was doing there.

'Lady, I have come from the castle of Augier d'Eixart. I am seeking one Taulat de Rogimon, who has done much harm to my lord King Arthur.' He went on to describe the events at the court, and while he spoke the lady listened sadly. Then she said: 'Sir, I am not surprised to hear what you say, for there was never a more evil and black-hearted villain than he whom you seek. He has brought suffering more than I can scarce speak of to this house.'

'Tell me if you will,' said Jaufre. 'And where I may find Taulat.'

'I will tell you everything,' said the lady. 'The knight who lies within this room is a victim of Taulat's evil ways. His father was killed by that devil, and he himself received a fearful wound in the breast. Now hear what Taulat does. Every month, when this brave knight's wounds are almost healed, the evil one returns and forces him to climb the hill beyond the castle in full armour. This causes his wounds to open again and his fever to return. For more than seven years this has occurred, and I fear greatly for the knight, who grows weaker each time he is forced to undergo this ordeal.'

'That is indeed a terrible story,' said Jaufre. 'This Taulat has much to answer for.'

'Indeed so. But I fear there is no knight now living – save perhaps Sir Gawain or Sir Lancelot – who can overcome him.'

'Sir Gawain will follow me, if indeed I fail,' said Jaufre. 'But tell me, who are all these knights encamped around the castle?'

'They are all brave lords who have sought to defeat Taulat. None have succeeded, and all are his prisoners. Expect no help from them, for they are sore afraid of this dread knight.'

'Will Taulat return here soon?' Jaufre asked.

'In one week,' answered the lady. 'If you will be guided by me you will leave here and return only when that much time has passed. But in truth you should go far away and never return, for I fear you will find only death at the hands of Taulat.'

'That I may not do,' said Jaufre. 'But I shall return in one week and do all that I can to relieve your suffering.' He hesitated. 'I would ask one more thing of you, and that concerns the dreadful lamentation which I hear everywhere in this land. Lord Augier told me that you would speak of this, though no other I have asked has yet done so but has instead become maddened.'

The lady sighed. 'I will tell you indeed, though it grieves me to do so. This knight who lies here so desperately wounded is the noblest of men, and much beloved of all his people. It is they who cry out every day and night for the sake of the suffering he must endure. So deeply do they feel his pain, that it is as though it was their own. They cry out whenever his suffering is at its worst and are driven half mad by the anguish and fear that all who encounter Taulat come to feel sooner or later. Because of this we have all sworn not to speak of this thing, and those strangers who come here ask at their peril. Only I, as a woman, may speak of this to you – but I warn you again that only death or pain await you here.'

Jaufre thanked the lady and departed from the castle and rode away into the forest to await the passing of the week before Taulat was due to arrive. He felt nothing but sorrow for the fate of the wounded man, and anger on behalf of all who suffered because of the evil knight.

✠ ✠ ✠

S O THE DAYS passed, until it was time for Jaufre to return to the castle. But he had not gone so much as a mile when he came upon an old woman by the roadside. As he approached, he saw that she was the strangest and most hideous female he had ever seen. She had long green teeth, straggly hair, thin shanks and a bloated belly. Her eyes were huge and long tusks poked out of her slobbery lips. Her skin was blackened and withered, and she drooled over her fine velvet gown like an infant.

When she saw Jaufre she called out to him: 'Where are you going, foolish man? Turn back at once!'

'Not until I know of a good reason to do so,' answered Jaufre.

'If you follow this way, you will regret it,' said the hag.

'Why should I believe you,' said Jaufre. 'Who are you?'

At this the old woman stood up suddenly, and she was as tall and straight as a spear. Suddenly she did no look so old, though her appearance was still terrifying.

Jaufre crossed himself at once, but the hag only laughed. 'I see you will not turn aside,' she said. 'So be it. You will see far worse than me before long.'

She refused to say more and Jaufre hurried on, glad to put space between himself and the strange creature. He continued until he saw a small hermit's cell. Thinking that perhaps he might rest there, he approached the humble dwelling. But just as he drew near, a knight in black armour appeared as if from nowhere and rode full tilt at him. Caught by surprise, Jaufre was knocked from his horse. Angrily, he scrambled up and drew his sword. But as he looked about him the black knight was nowhere to be seen. Bewildered, Jaufre

got back on his horse, and at once there was the same knight, or one just like him, riding furiously toward him. This time Jaufre was more prepared and managed to lower his spear. The black knight ran upon it so fast and hard that it pierced right through his body. Yet the force of his attack again unhorsed Jaufre and when he got up and prepared to finish off the wounded man, there was no sign of him.

Again, Jaufre re-mounted, and there at once was the black knight, seemingly unhurt. Again, they charged against each other, and again Jaufre was unhorsed. On the ground, he turned at bay, but again the knight had vanished.

So it continued, throughout that afternoon. As long as he was on horseback Jaufre could see the black knight clearly. When he was on the ground he could not. In the end he grew so tired of this game that he remained on the earth and leading his mount made his way towards the chapel.

Then the black knight reappeared, this time himself on foot, and attacked Jaufre with sword and shield. As dusk was beginning to fall, it became increasingly difficult to see his attacker. But Jaufre defended himself as best he might and succeeded in cutting off the black knight's arm. In a blink however it grew back, and when, a moment later, the young knight struck a blow that split his opponent's skull to the teeth, the wound healed so quickly that he scarcely had time to withdraw his sword.

They continued fighting for another hour. The black knight could not succeed in wounding Jaufre, but the youth began to tire as he was struck with punishing blow after punishing blow, while he himself seemed unable to kill his terrible opponent. Matters might have gone on in this wise until Jaufre was worn down, had not the hermit himself intervened. Tired of being kept awake by the incessant noise of battle, he rose from his bed and issued forth with his stole around his shoulders and a vessel of holy water in his hands. When he saw this, the black knight fled, and the hermit helped Jaufre to stumble into the shelter of his hut, where he removed his armour and fell into a deep sleep of exhaustion.

In the morning he awoke to find that the hermit had fed and stabled his horse and laid out fresh garments for him. The good man then came to say Mass, and afterwards offered Jaufre bread and water before asking him who he was and what brought him to this place.

'I am of King Arthur's court, and I am seeking an evil knight named Taulat.'

'This is not the place to look for him,' said the hermit. 'This is a borderland. Beyond it is an evil region, through which no man may pass.'

'How can this be?' asked Jaufre. 'Who was that knight with whom I fought?'

'That was no knight, but a demon of hell, called here by an evil old woman who lives near here. She is the mother of a creature that has terrorised these lands for more than thirty years.'

'Indeed, if she is hideous to look upon, I met with this woman,' said Jaufre.

'Then you know of what I speak,' said the hermit. 'I will tell you the story of how they came here. Years ago, the old woman had a husband, a monstrous fellow like herself. But after he had led a cruel life for many years he was at last slain, and his wife, fearing for her two sons, summoned the demon who now guards the path. Her sons are grown now, and they are as evil as their father. One was cursed with leprosy and his mother made a house for

him to the east of here. I have heard it said that a knight came here recently and ended his miserable existence. Now his brother has gone to seek confirmation of this, and to take revenge on the one who slew his sibling.'

'It was I who slew the leper,' Jaufre said. 'No doubt his brother will soon return to find me.' With that he told the hermit the whole story of his quest and his fight with the lepers. At the end he said: 'I must leave this place and find somewhere else to wait, for I fear that the creature may do you harm if he finds you have sheltered me.'

'He cannot harm me,' replied the hermit calmly. 'Yet it may indeed be wise for you to depart, for I do not think you would be able to stand up to the creature when it returns.'

'Be sure I shall do my best,' said Jaufre grimly. 'For now, I shall go elsewhere and await the return of Taulat.'

'Truly, you must wish for death,' said the hermit. 'That you should look to encounter two such devils is surely a sign of madness.'

'If so then it is a good madness,' replied Jaufre. 'It is the duty I owe to my king and to those who have been made to suffer that brings me here.'

With this he departed, taking the blessings of the hermit with him. But he had not ridden more than a mile when he saw the leper approaching. Under one arm he carried a maiden who was crying out in terror and distress. At once Jaufre lowered his lance and charged. He struck the misshapen creature in the middle of his breast and pierced him right through. Still, it was able to grab the spear and pull Jaufre from his horse, striking him so hard in the process that the young knight was almost knocked unconscious.

With spinning head, he staggered to his feet and drew his sword as the maiden cried out a warning. He struck the leper such a blow that it cut away part of his left arm and flank. As blood poured from the wound the creature bellowed in madness and Jaufre, rushing in quickly, cut off its head with a single blow. Then he fell down in an exhausted heap, until the maiden came and helped to revive him. He looked up at her and recognized her as the daughter of Augier d'Eixart, though it was a moment before she in turn knew him. Then she fell at his feet weeping with relief.

Rising with difficulty, Jaufre placed the maiden on the saddle before him, rode on towards the castle of the wounded knight, where he was destined to meet with Taulat de Rogimon.

⊹ ✠ ⊹

H E SOON CAME in sight of its walls, and there he saw Taulat's men dragging the wounded man forth with bound hands and preparing to force him to climb the hill. Jaufre rode up in haste and begged them to stop. At that moment Taulat himself, who had seen the young knight arrive, emerged from his hall, and haughtily demanded that he get down and surrender himself and the maiden into his power.

'I shall not do that,' responded Jaufre, 'since I have come here with no other intent than to fight with you. Therefore, I ask that you release this noble knight whom you have tortured for so long and return with me to King Arthur, for you have done him great ill, and he requires an apology.'

Taulat looked at him in disbelief. Then he laughed. 'Are you aware that I have defeated a hundred men better and stronger than you? I will give you a moment to surrender, or else I promise to kill you.'

'That is for God to decide,' said Jaufre. 'I shall wait here until you are armed and ready.'

'I do not even need any armour to defeat you,' said Taulat scornfully. 'My spear and shield will be enough.' Then he called out to his squire to fetch only these things.

The two men came face to face at last and set their spears in rest and charged upon each other. Taulat's spear struck Jaufre's shield in the centre and lifted him out of the saddle. But Jaufre's spear passed clean through his opponent's shield and pierced his side and opened a great wound there. Taulat fell to the earth and lay there moaning. Jaufre came and stood over him with drawn sword.

'Sir,' cried Taulat in anguish and disbelief. 'You have beaten me. Alas for my folly that has brought me to this. Spare me I beg you and anything in my power shall be yours.'

'As to that,' said Jaufre sternly, 'I shall give you mercy, but only if you promise to set free all your prisoners, including the wounded knight, and go as soon as you are able to King Arthur. I can forgive the pains you have caused me, but the king must decide the rest for himself.'

To this Taulat swore, and Jaufre allowed a surgeon to come and search his wounds and dress them. Then the knight who had been Taulat's plaything for so long came forward, walking stiffly and still weak from his long ill-treatment. 'Sir,' he said, 'I owe you my life and more. If there is anything I can do to repay you, you need only name it.'

'I ask for nothing,' replied the hero, 'save that you go to King Arthur and tell him what has taken place here.' Then he added: 'If you see a knight named Sir Kay, tell him he had been better advised to hold his tongue when he last spoke to me.'

Then Jaufre requested a mount for Augier's

daughter, and set off at once to take her home to her father. As for the wounded knight, he set out as soon as he might, accompanied by the slowly recovering Taulat, and on arriving at Arthur's court he told the king all that had happened and praised Jaufre for his courage and bravery in the face of so many dangers. The king turned his attention to Taulat, who went upon his knees and begged for mercy.

At first Arthur was reluctant to pardon the knight, but he begged so greatly and in such evident anguish, that at last Arthur did forgive him. But the knight whom Taulat had held prisoner and treated so vilely for seven years, could not so easily forgive. So a trial was decreed and the knight gave witness to Taulat's cruelty. The judgement of the court was this: that Taulat be placed in the custody of his own former prisoner, who was instructed to whip him up the hill every week just as he had formerly whipped the knight, until he was deemed sufficiently punished. Thus it was agreed.

Jaufre, meanwhile, returned to the castle of Augier d'Eixart, where you can imagine he was warmly welcomed, both for his overcoming of Taulat, and more especially for the return of the old lord's daughter. But Jaufre found himself thinking more and more of the fair Brunnisend. Even while he thought thus, her own seneschal arrived, who had been looking for Jaufre ever since he had escaped the castle where he was imprisoned. When he saw Jaufre he was both glad and fearful – glad that he had found the knight and fearful at

what his mistress might do when she discovered how he had lied to her. Nevertheless, he begged Jaufre to return home with him, and this the young knight agreed to do, though he asked that the seneschal protect him from the wrath of his lady, for the youth had no knowledge of Brunnisend's feelings for him and feared that she would still be angry. The seneschal reassured him that she was not likely to do this – for had Jaufre not overcome Taulat and restored her overlord to freedom.

So Jaufre returned to Monbrun with the seneschal, and the Lady Brunnisend came out to meet him and was both glad and amazed to see him alive. When she heard all that had occurred, and that the lord of that land was set free because of Jaufre, she was glad indeed, as were all her people, for now they need lament no more. And you can be sure that she soon forgave the seneschal for his lie, for in truth she loved Jaufre, and in a while she was able to tell him her true feelings. Then the young knight declared his own love, and they were of one accord and set out for Arthur's court to declare their wish to marry. You may imagine the rejoicing which took place when Jaufre finally returned home, bringing with him as fair a lady as anyone had ever seen.

In due time Jaufre married his Brunnisend, and the two of them lived happily together for the rest of their days. And Jaufre had many more adventures, which perchance I shall be enabled to tell on another occasion, if I am spared.

⊹

EXPLICIT THE TALE OF JAUFRE.
IMPLICIT THE STORY OF SIR MARROK AND THE WOLF.

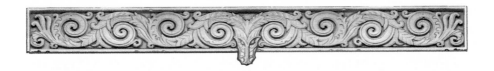

18: THE TALE OF SIR MARROK
AND THE WOLF

✛

OF ALL THE TALES TOLD BY MASTER THOMAS, ONE HAS GIVEN ME PAUSE FOR REFLECTION THIS MANY A LONG YEAR. FOR IT IS A TALE THAT HE MENTIONS BUT DOES NOT TELL,* AND ON THIS I HAVE WONDERED UNTIL RECENTLY, WHEN I FOUND IT IN AN OLD BOOK. SO, I SHALL TELL IT HERE, THAT THE STORY MAY BE BETTER KNOWN AND NOT FORGOTTEN.

✛ ✛ ✛

NOT LONG AFTER King Arthur founded the Round Table Fellowship, there lived in Brittany a strong and handsome knight named Sir Marrok. No one in the lands over which he ruled had a bad word for him, and he was known far and wide as a pillar of justice and honour, such as few others possessed.

Sir Marrok was married to a lady as fair as a summer's day, whose kindness was the stuff of legends. Her name was Alys, and she and Sir Marrok were happy together, and were but seldom heard to offer harsh words either to other. One matter only came between them. Three nights out of every week Sir Marrok vanished into the Great Wood. He went alone and none knew where he went or why.

For a long time Marrok's lady wondered about these mysterious absences. In her heart she knew that her husband was a faithful man, so she was certain he did not run off to meet with another love. But still the question nagged at her, until at last she could no longer remain silent.

One day, when Marrok returned from one of his journeys into the forest, his lady brought him wine to drink and sat by him by the fire until a flush of warmth covered his cheeks. Then she laid a hand upon his arm and begged him to tell her where it was that he went three days a week.

---

* See *Le Morte D'Arthur*, Book XIX Ch. ii.

At once Sir Marrok grew pale.

'Do not ask me, my lady. If I were to tell you, I should bring great evil upon us both.'

So for a time the lady Alys said no more, but always the question of Sir Marrok's absences ate at her – until at length she could no longer keep silent, and again begged her lord to tell her whither he went and why.

Once again Marrok, with even greater concern, refused to tell her what she asked, saying again that no good would come of her knowing. But the lady could not keep silent, and after this, daily she asked Marrok the same question.

In the end he could bear it no longer, for in truth he loved the Lady Alys greatly, and longed to put her mind at rest. So it was that he sat her down beside him before the great fireplace in the hall of their castle and told her the truth.

'My dear lady, I must tell you that many years ago I encountered a faery being in the Great Wood, and though I did no harm to him, yet he cursed me with a dreadful curse. That three days out of every week I must take on the form of a wolf. In which guise I go into the forest to live off what I can catch until it is time to return home.'

At this the Lady Alys grew pale and hugged Sir Marrok tightly.

'Surely, something can be done?' she said. 'There are those who dwell in this land who have knowledge of such things. No spell can remain unbroken for ever.'

Marrok shook his head. 'At first, when I felt the power of my curse, I did all that I could to break it. I travelled far and wide in search of an answer, asking every wise man or woman that I met. But all said that a faery curse is the hardest of all to remove, and that in all likelihood only he who set the curse, or one of his kind, could undo it. Yet never again since that time have I met one of the faery kind in the Great Wood. Thus it was when you and I first met, my love, and ever since I have left the castle and gone into the forest so that you should never witness my change.'

For a long time, the lady Alys said nothing. Then she asked a question: 'What happens to your clothes while you are in the shape of a wolf?'

Marrok smiled, for this seemed a practical question such as his wife so often asked. 'I set them aside in the forest, for if they were ever found while I am in wolf form, I would have to remain thus for ever, or until I turned to dust.'

To this the Lady Alice did not respond, but in her heart at this moment a terrible thought was born. For as she listened to the story of Marrok's transformation, the love she had known for him began to turn to hate. Once, whenever she looked at her lord she would smile and feel her heart leap for joy; now she thought only of his transformation, of fur and claws and teeth sprouting from his flesh, until he no longer resembled the man she called husband, but something other, terrifying.

So great became her fear that she began to dread Marrok's return from the Great Wood, and even sought to avoid him, until their marriage bed grew cold, and the joy they had once shared ebbed away entirely.

With this anguish tearing at her, the Lady Alys began to consider how she could rid herself of the man she no longer loved. Again, she begged him, until he told her where he hid his clothing in the forest – beneath a stone with a hollowed-out heart, under an ancient tree near a certain path through the wood. This she got him to tell her by promising that if anything happened, or if the clothes were stolen, she could replace them. Thus, with honeyed words she wove her lies around Sir Marrok, but at the same time sought out a knight whose lands were adjacent to those of Marrok. This man she had long known as a friend, and he in turn had loved her from the time before she had become wife to Marrok. The Lady Alys summoned this man, whose name was Jocelyn, and after binding him with the strongest oaths of secrecy, she told him the story of Marrok's curse.

'Surely this is an evil thing,' said Sir Jocelyn. 'But I believe I can see an answer to it … If it is my lady's will to be rid of this half-man forever?'

The Lady Alys swore that she no longer loved Marrok and sought to be rid of him, for to her he was but a monster.

So, on a night when Marrok was a wolf in the forest, Sir Jocelyn crept forth, and following the Lady Alys' directions, found his way to where the knight had hidden his clothes. These Jocelyn carried back to the castle where Lady Alys hid them in a box bound with hoops of iron and sealed with many keys.

Thus was Marrok condemned to a terrible fate, for without the clothing he had entered the forest wearing, he could not resume human shape. For long days, months, and finally years he lived alone in the Great Wood, hunting for his supper, drinking from streams and living the life of a wolf. Yet his mind and heart remained human, and every day he mourned for his old life, and wept salt tears for the lady he had loved, but who he knew must have betrayed him.

She, meanwhile, after a year had passed, during which time there had been no sight of the wolf, believed that Marrok must have perished, and so she married Sir Jocelyn and

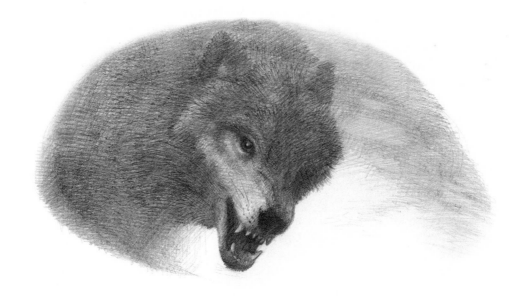

→ *Marrok the Wolf* ←

213

they lived together in the castle once owned by Marrok and united their lands together to form a wide country.

✠ ✠ ✠

IT HAPPENED THAT the king who ruled over that land, who was brother to King Ban of Benoic, and uncle to Sir Lancelot, used to hunt in that part of the forest where the man-wolf lived. On a particular day he sought sport there and gave chase to a mighty boar. It happened that this beast was brought to bay, and having slain several of the king's hounds, attacked the monarch himself. While the king's horse reared in fear, suddenly there came out of the trees a great grey wolf that attacked the boar, causing it to flee. Then, as the king and his huntsmen looked on in amazement, the wolf came close and laid its head against the king's foot.

All were amazed and many noted that the king's horse showed none of the fear it had displayed when the boar attacked them. So struck was the king with this that he ordered the hounds driven off. 'See here, my lords,' he declared. 'This is no ordinary behaviour, but a miracle. I will not have this beast injured. Let us leave it in peace.'

But when the hunting party set off back to the king's castle, they saw how the wolf followed them. Nor did cries and shaken spears, or the barking of the hounds, deter the beast, which followed the company all the way back to the royal castle, and entered it behind them, and went with them right into the Great Hall. When the king saw this, he approached the savage creature and to his amazement it bowed before him and licked his hand with its great red tongue. Seeing this, the king commanded his followers to offer no harm to the

wolf, but to allow it free rein of the castle, so long as it offered no harm to anyone. Thus the wolf stayed within the castle, accompanying the king wherever he went and even sleeping across the door to his chamber at night. Soon he was so much a part of the court that none feared him or thought to do him harm.

So the time passed until it chanced that the king decided to hold a solemn court, and summoned all his nobles to attend. Amongst these was Sir Jocelyn, the knight who had betrayed Sir Marrok, and made Lady Alys his own. When it caught sight of this man the normally gentle wolf became as savage as all of his kind and would have attacked the knight. Three times it leapt towards him, baring its teeth and howling most piteously. Each time the king called the beast off, and the wolf obeyed, though it continued to snarl and show its hatred of the knight. Many there began to wonder if the man had done some evil deed, since the wolf was normally so friendly, and all were glad when he departed the court earlier than the rest of the nobles.

After this the wolf was as gentle and friendly to all as he had been before, and the king and his knights soon forgot the incident, until the king decided to make a progress through his lands, coming again to the part of the Great Wood where he had first encountered the wolf.

When she heard of the king's coming, the Lady Alys thought to herself that this was an opportunity to win favour for herself and her lord, so she petitioned the monarch to visit her home and prepared a rich feast in his honour.

Soon the king arrived, and with him came the wolf as was now the custom. The moment the beast set eyes upon her, it flew at

Lady Alys and before anyone could prevent it, bit off most of her nose. As the lady screamed and blood gushed from her ruined face, the knights drew their swords and would have slain the beast, but the king stopped them, and called for healers to attend the lady and summoned her husband to come before him

The wolf made no move to attack Sir Jocelyn this time but growled low in its throat when the knight appeared.

'I am mindful of the last time we met,' said the king. 'And how this beast, which is normally playful, sought to do you harm. There must be some reason for this.'

When neither the knight nor his lady offered any reason, the king had them taken to separate rooms and questioned. Very quickly the Lady Alys gave way – and weeping bitterly told the story of Sir Marrok's curse and how she had come to hate him and had stolen away his clothes so that he must remain in wolf form for ever.

When he heard this the king demanded that the lady bring the clothes from where she had hidden them. Then he had the wolf brought to the same place and saw how it howled and yammered.

'Why does it not transform?' asked one of the courtiers, who like the king was amazed by what he saw.

An elder knight spoke up. 'Sire,' he said.

'It is my belief that this change may be long and painful, since the man has so long been the wolf. Would it not be better if we leave it alone with the man's clothing?'

To this the king agreed, and they closed the door of the chamber on the wolf and departed from it.

When a certain time had passed, the king returned to the chamber with two of his men and opened the door. There they saw the body of Sir Marrok, returned to his human shape, lying asleep on a bed. They left him to sleep, and in the morning great rejoicing took place as Marrok emerged and was welcomed back into the world of men.

After this the king gave back all his lands to Marrok, along with those of Sir Jocelyn, and he and the Lady Alys were banished from the kingdom. It is said, in the story that I have found, that they had several children together, but that all were girls, and that each one was born without a nose.

In all Sir Marrok spent seven years in the form of a wolf, and I have heard that in time he was rid of the curse that had bound him. Soon after he met and married a sweet-natured lady who cared for him throughout his days. And in that time, he joined the Fellowship of the Round Table, and is listed amongst the knights in Master Thomas's book.

And thus is his story told at last.

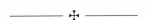

EXPLICIT THE TALE OF MARROK.
IMPLICIT THE STORY OF THE GOLDEN CIRCLET.

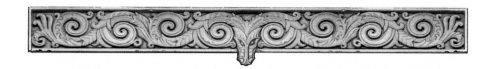

19: THE TALE OF SIR TOREC
AND THE CIRCLET OF GOLD

AMONGST THE ROLL CALL OF THE GREAT KNIGHTS OF THE ROUND TABLE, MASTER THOMAS WROTE OF MANY WHOSE NAMES ARE WELL REMEMBERED. THERE IS ONE, HOWEVER, WHOSE NAME ONCE RANG OUT AS THE VERY EPITOME OF KNIGHTLY SKILLS. YET IN RECENT TIMES THE NAME OF SIR TOREC HAS FADED FROM THE KNOWLEDGE OF MOST WHO LOVE THESE TALES. WHY THIS SHOULD BE, I CANNOT SAY, FOR HE WAS TRULY A DOUGHTY KNIGHT. I SHALL TELL IT HERE, THEREFORE, AMONGST THOSE WHOSE TALES I HAVE RECOVERED FROM THE DARKNESS OF IGNORANCE.

✠ ✠ ✠

IN A TIME before the coming of King Arthur there was a land that was not marked on any map. Only those who braved the dark forest of Broceliande, which cloaked a great deal of the land, could discover the adventures that lay within. One such man was a king named Briant des Isles. One day he felt the pull of the forest, and being thus made restless, took his horse and rode alone between the trees. I do not know how long he journeyed, since the tale does not tell it, but as he rode he heard a voice, singing sweetly, and as he came into a small clearing, looked with amazement at where a beautiful woman sat in the high branches of a tree heavy with fruit, combing her golden hair and delighting the birds and beasts of the forest with her song.

Briant called out to her. 'Is all well with you, my lady?'

The woman in the tree ceased her song and smiled at the king, whose heart melted in that moment.

'I am well, Sir King. I have awaited you since dawn.'

Astonished, Briant asked how she could know he would come that way.

'Because it was foretold,' the lady answered. 'On this day the man I am to marry would appear to me here.'

The king was full of wonder when he heard this, for he had fallen in love with

216

the woman the moment he saw her in the tree.

'Since you know my name and status, will you tell me who you are?' he asked.

The maiden looked down at him merrily. 'I am called Mariole. My mother is the queen of this land. If you marry me, I will promise you a gift that will bring both honour and wealth.'

Saying which, she climbed down from the tree and the king helped her to sit before him on his mount. Without another word he turned, and they rode back together to the king's castle.

Against the advice of his courtiers, who thought the lady one of the *longaevi* – the long-lived ones – the king married Mariole, for despite her promise of the gift of wealth and honour he needed no such urging, so great was his passion for the mysterious woman.

From her he learned that she was the guardian of a certain Circlet of Gold. This, being forged in Faery, brought good fortune to whoever owned it. I have heard tell that Merlin knew of this magic thing, though neither he nor the Knights of the Round Table were able to discover it in times to come. But the Lady Mariole, being herself – so I believe – of faery blood: a *longaevi* indeed – was able to offer it to Briant. There was but one rider to this agreement. 'There is,' said Mariole, 'one called the Knight of the Red Lion, of whom it is prophesied that he will try to steal it. You must make sure that this does not happen, or all will be lost.'

The king gave his word that this would never happen while he lived, and for a time they were happy together, all kinds of riches accruing to them through the power of the circlet. But in another place in that time, far from the realm of King Briant, lived three sisters – cousins to Mariole through her father's blood – who longed to possess the golden thing.

As it happened, the sisters received a great legacy at the same time that King Briant married Mariole. They had fifty castles between them and met to see how these would be divided. The eldest of the siblings, who was named Miraude, surprised them all by saying that her sisters could have half the castles between them – but that she longed for something else – the Circlet of Gold, which she claimed through her family's descent. In return for gifting her share of the lands and castles of the inheritance, she demanded that her middle sister's husband, whose name was Bruant, get it for her.

This Bruant was a cunning man. Nor should it surprise us that his title was Bruant of the Red Lion – the very one that Mariole's mother had prophesied would steal the golden circlet. He waited and watched for many months until a day came when the king was away, and the Lady Mariole sat alone in her hall. Then he broke into the castle and by the strength of arms entered, took the circlet from her and carried it off to his sister-in-law. When Briant returned he found his wife weeping for the loss of this great prize. Though he comforted her and reminded her that they had all that they might desire, she remained inconsolable. And soon enough her prophecy proved true, as the riches they possessed began to dwindle, and shortly thereafter King Briant himself caught a sickness and died.

At this time Queen Mariole was expecting the birth of a child, and a daughter was born soon after. So full of sorrow was the lady that, instead of rejoicing, she placed the infant into a small boat, with money, rich clothes and a letter which told the circumstances of her birth. Then at midnight she set the boat adrift on the sea, committing her daughter to the mercy of the waves, watching it dwindle to a shadow on the horizon and calling upon the fates themselves to see to the future of her daughter. Then she returned home, weeping for her sad state.

The small craft was caught by the waves and carried first out to sea then back towards the land, until it came ashore in the neighbouring kingdom of the Lower River, ruled over by a young king named Yder. When the king's men found the ship and within it the tiny child, together with its rich goods, they carried all these things to the royal court, and there King Yder read the letter.

Knowing little of his neighbour's life, he felt great sadness at the story and chose to adopt the girl. She was given to a wet nurse and the king ordered her baptized with the name Tristoise, which means 'Born in Sorrow'. Nor was this the end of her story, for when she grew to womanhood, being judged of great beauty, King Yder asked her to marry him. Though his years were greater than hers, she had grown to love him and so was happy to give her assent.

In time she gave birth to a son, who was named Torec. And it is said that in all her life the lady laughed only three times: this was the first time, when she learned that she had given birth to a son. He grew quickly to a strong and much-loved youth. His father saw to it that he was trained to ride, to fight and to read – at all of which things he proved an apt pupil – and by the time he was fully grown there was not a single man at his father's court that he could not defeat in arms.

Then one day Tristoise took him aside in the privacy of her chamber and told him the story of his birth, showing him the letter written by his grandmother, Mariole. When he had read this, Torec stood up at once. 'I shall not rest until I have regained the circlet,' he cried. 'And if it is within my power, I shall avenge myself upon the Knight of the Red Lion, if he is yet living.'

He went to his father and begged leave to set out on this quest. At first King Yder refused him, but Torec declared that nothing would prevent him from seeking the golden circlet, and though it troubled the king, he gave way to Torec's demand and blessed his son's endeavour and knighted him there and then.

Thus, Torec set forth upon his first adventure, knowing little of his family's history or the whereabouts of the Circlet of Gold. Strength and wisdom led him; his courage made him formidable.

✢ ✢ ✢

MOUNTED ON HIS splendid horse, Moreel, Sir Torec rode deep into the Great Wood. Everywhere trees stood sentinel and shadows deepened wherever he looked. At last, he came to a sheltered glade, where a knight lay asleep with his head in the lap of a beautiful maiden. When they heard Torec approaching, the knight woke and leapt to his feet, reaching his sword. 'How dare you disturb my rest!' he bellowed. 'Prepare to lose your life!'

Torec waited calmly while the knight donned his helm and took up shield and spear and mounted his horse. Then the two rode against each other, meeting with a clangour that sent birds whirling from the trees.

I cannot say how long the fight continued, only that blood was spilt on both sides, and that finally Torec defeated his opponent, leaving him in the dust. At this the knight's lady pled for his life and Sir Torec granted it. The two men sat beneath the trees while their wounds were tended by the damsel. The defeated knight told Torec that he was called Sir Melions the Proud. Torec told him his own name and the two men fell to talking. Torec told Sir Melions of his quest, and to his astonishment the knight said that not only did he know something of Torec's history but that he also knew the whereabouts of the golden circlet.

'Sir Bruant, the Knight of the Red Lion, the man who stole the circlet from your grandmother, lives close by. His reputation is one of great evil and his name spreads terror wherever it is mentioned. He has lived beyond the normal span of a man and has made his castle impregnable. I'm told it is guarded by two lions, which Bruant keeps close to starving so that they are more savage than ever.'

'Can you tell me the way to this place?' asked Torec, feeling the blood waken in his veins at the mention of the knight he had promised to revenge himself upon.

Sir Melions shook his head in dismay. 'Even if you got into the castle you would still have to face Bruant himself. I know of no man who has beaten him in combat. If you take my advice you will not even attempt to go. I have heard of many brave knights who ventured there, but none ever returned.'

'Nevertheless, it is my quest to reclaim the circlet,' said Torec. 'And I have promised my mother to take revenge on the Knight of the Red Lion.'

When he saw that the young knight would not be swayed, Sir Melions offered him hospitality for that night, so that he might be rested and ready for the battle to come. The two

men were fast becoming friends and returned together, along with the maiden, to Melions' castle. That night Torec dined well at his host's table and slept in a comfortable bed.

In the morning they arose early and set forth for the castle of Bruant. It was indeed but a few miles distant, in a deeper part of the Great Wood. The air grew colder the closer they got to Bruant's home, and shadows deepened beneath the trees. In the end Sir Melions' nerve failed him, and he sought to turn back, wishing Torec good fortune and hoping that he would still be alive at the day's end.

Soon the grim walls of the castle came in sight. They seemed darker than normal, despite the fact that the sun shone from a clear sky, and Torec felt a strong reluctance to go further. But he remembered his purpose and rode on.

Thankful for Sir Melions' warning, Torec was watchful for attack, and when he neared the gates of the castle, he saw the two lions bounding towards him, great roars issuing from their wide-open jaws. Torec's horse reared at the sight and smell of these beasts, but Torec calmed him and set his lance in readiness. He caught the first lion with his spear and ran it through the heart, and as the second leapt upon him he drew his sword and buried it deep in the beast's brain.

The fight was over in moments and both lions lay dead. Breathing hard, Torec headed onwards until he sat his horse beneath the shadow of the gatehouse. The air was even colder here and Torec felt the ill-will of the place. But the gates stood wide and Torec rode onwards, his sword at the ready.

Within, darkness seemed to hang over all. The courtyard lay empty before him, and he dismounted, tethering his mount, which seemed as fearful as he was himself. Ahead loomed the walls of a stone hall, and once again the doors stood open. Torec entered and saw where a table was set out with a chess-board. Sitting there was a grim man, who studied the game before him. Hearing Torec's approach he looked up and anger darkened his face.

'Who are you that comes to disturb my play?' he demanded. 'Whoever you are, you should leave now, before I kill you.'

'Perhaps it is you who should run,' answered Torec. 'Or maybe you would prefer to prove your boasts against me.'

The dark man stared at him more closely, though he made no move to draw his sword or attack.

'Who are you?' he said again.

'I am Sir Torec, son of King Yder and Queen Tristoise, daughter of King Briant and Queen Mariole, my grandmother, from whom you stole something of great value.'

The man, who was indeed Bruant, showed no surprise but measured Torec with a glance. Still he made no move to attack but showed his hands empty of weapons. Then he stood up and bowed to Torec. 'Rest assured that you shall have your chance to fight me. But it grows late, and the light is fading. I offer you my hospitality this night. Stay here and we shall fight in the morning.'

Surprised by the dark knight's courteous behaviour, Torec hesitated only for a moment before he agreed. Sheathing his sword, he grasped Bruant's hand, which felt cold and dry to the touch.

Bruant's servants, who moved silently, set up tables and brought supper – a fine repast, the story tells us. Others took care of the proud steed, Moreel. Bruant spoke no word to his guest beyond what was deemed polite,

though Torec felt his eyes upon him more than once. The two men soon retired and despite the chill aspect of the place, Torec slept well.

The morning dawned bright and Torec and Bruant faced off against each other. Well matched, they felled each other from their horses and at once began to fight with swords. Neither could gain an advantage of the other. Then Torec delivered such a blow to Bruant that his sword fell from his hand. Quickly Torec retrieved the weapon and offered it back to Bruant, who seemed surprised by this honourable gesture.

They fought on through the morning, until at last Bruant delivered a blow to Torec which left him wounded. Inflamed by this, Torec swung his sword so swiftly and might-ily that it severed Bruant's sword-hand. The knight fell to the earth, screaming in pain as Torec wrenched off his helm and prepared to deliver the death blow.

'Wait, I beg you,' cried Bruant. 'Do not kill me.' Then he added: 'It will be to your advantage – for the wound I gave you was made with a poisoned blade and only I know how it may be healed.'

Torec fell back, already feeling the effects of the poison.

Bruant, nursing his bloody stump, spoke grimly. 'I am well punished for the deed of stealing the Circlet of Gold, since you have cut off the hand with which I did so. If you allow me to live, I will heal your wounds. Also, I will swear allegiance to you as your vassal.'

To this Torec agreed and the two men embraced – and thus was Torec able to avenge the despite done to his mother and grandmother. Now he helped his foe into the castle where both could receive healing. Bru-ant gave Torec a drug that cooled the poison in his blood. 'But,' he said, 'be aware that it will work within you again, and that only my brother Druant's wife can wholly heal you.'

Torec was dismayed, for he thought the circlet still in Bruant's possession, but the knight explained to him that he had stolen the circlet on behalf of the Lady Miraude, elder sister to his own wife and she who was wife to his brother Druant, and that she held it still, drawing on its power for herself.

'I must go to her at once,' said Torec. 'Where shall I find her?'

'Miraude lives some way from here,' answered Bruant. 'But I must warn you this lady is the fairest you will ever meet, and you will doubtless fall in love with her.'

Torec gave some thought to this, but in the end he said: 'It shall be as fate, or God, decides. My quest for the Circlet of Gold is all that matters to me.'

'Then I advise you to travel first to Druant's castle, for only his wife can heal you of the poison in your blood.'

Torec stayed with Bruant until his wounds were healed, and though it was still a dark place, with each day that passed it seemed to him less so, and his host too lost something of his grimness.

The day finally came when Torec was well enough to set out again, and went forth, determined to reach the castle of Druant and the healing that awaited him.

Not far on the road, he encountered a knight clad in red. They fought, and Torec, with difficulty, overcame his opponent – only to have him vanish as though he were not really there. Torec deemed him of elvish stock but knew nothing more of him.

But this part of the tale does not end here, for soon after this Torec arrived at the Ford of Adventure, of which we hear tell in many tales from this time, and though he longed to continue to Druant's castle, he could not forbear turning aside to test his strength against any knight he might encounter there.

Sure enough, when he came to the ford, he found a knight in black armour waiting, and they fought. Again, to Torec's bewilderment, no sooner had he overcome his opponent, than the man vanished away, just as the Red Knight had previously. There was nothing for it but to continue on his way, and after a night beneath the stars, Torec arrived at Druant's castle.

Though it was his intention to issue a challenge to those within, he was turned aside by the welcome he received. The lady of the castle, whom Torec knew must be the second of the three sisters, and the one who alone could heal Bruant's poisoned blade, rode out to meet him, inviting him to take supper with them. Disarmed by her charms and generous words, Torec accepted the offer and rather than doing battle against his host, he sat instead between the lord and his lady while a rich and bounteous feast was served.

Though there was a likeness between the brothers, Druant seemed a very different kind of man, quieter and less grim than his sibling – though no less powerful for that. Nor did the castle share the darkness of Bruant's home.

At length Druant asked to know the name of his guest, and Torec told him. At once the lord rose from his chair and sad: 'Had I known this sooner, Torec son of Yder, you would not be sitting here now, but lying dead in the dust outside my castle walls!'

Torec also stood up. 'If it is your wish, I will fight you now.'

The lord hesitated, then his expression relaxed. He sat down and waved Torec to do the same. 'You are my guest, and by the laws of hospitality I cannot ask you to fight me now. Stay the night with us and we shall meet in the morning.'

To this Torec agreed, and the feasting continued. Druant looked at Torec and said: 'Why have you sought me out, and why do you wish to fight with me?'

Torec told him all – how he was in search of the Circlet of Gold and how he had met and fought with Bruant. When she heard the part where the young knight had been wounded by the poisoned blade, Druant's lady looked hard at Torec, and said: 'By no means will I heal you, for you are my sister's enemy, and as such you are my enemy also.'

With that Torec had to be content, though you may be sure he tossed and turned that night. But morning came as mornings will, and he arose and he and Druant went out into the meadow below the walls of the castle and there did battle.

As had been the case with the lord's brother, the two knights were evenly matched, though Torec was still weakened by the poison in his blood. Druant inflicted a wound to his opponent's head which caused blood to flow and he made a jest that now Torec had a different kind of circlet, red rather than gold; but Torec ignored this and attacked again even more strongly.

Driving home his advantage, he delivered three terrible blows to Druant's body, so that the lord fell to the ground and lay as if dead. Torec approached and dragged off the fallen man's helm and waited until he recovered his senses.

Knowing himself beaten, Druant begged for mercy. Torec hesitated and then said: 'If your wife heals me of your brother's poison, I will spare you.'

At once the lady was summoned and the case explained. Though she looked with sorrow on her fallen lord, she shook her head: 'I have sworn that I will not do this. My mind is not changed.'

Druant looked at her and groaned. 'My lady, for the sake of the love that is between us these many years, I ask you to do this for me. If you do not, then you love your sister more than me.'

At this the lady showed her nobility. She agreed to heal Torec, and with that he granted Druant mercy. The two men embraced as well as they could for their wounds, and the lady, who was indeed skilled in herb lore and other healing arts, set about making them both well again. In less than a week they were hale once more, and Druant swore allegiance to Torec, as had his brother.

Then Torec asked again for directions to the castle of the Lady Miraude and was given them. He set forth on a fair morning – but he had not gone far before he met a knight dressed in white armour. As was the custom in those times they fought, and Torec, strength given him by the healing he had received from Druant's wife, beat the white knight easily. But when he drew his sword to continue the fight, he found that the man had vanished away.

'By God,' swore Torec. 'This is the third time this has happened. Surely I am plagued by demons.'

Since there was nothing further to do, Torec continued on his way, until he encountered a lady who rode weeping through the forest.

'My lady, what causes you such pain?' asked Torec.

At first the lady, whose name was Edein, could not answer for weeping, but at last, when Torec continued to speak gently to her, she told him her story. Recently she had inherited lands and castles belonging to her grandfather, but these were held in fiefdom to King Arthur. Three times she had been summoned to attend the court to proclaim her right to the inheritance, but each time she had been prevented by matters over which she had no control. This last time she had arrived two days late and found that the king had given her lands to another.

'This is no fair judgement,' said Torec. 'I am surprised that so noble a king would make this choice.' Then he was silent for a while, and finally spoke up. 'If it is your wish, I will help you contest this.'

The lady almost fainted with joy at this. 'Sir, if you do so, I will be your friend for ever. King Arthur holds court at Tintagel this month. It is not far from here.'

So Torec fell in with the lady Edein, and they took the road together to the mighty fortress of Tintagel. There Torec sought out King Arthur and presented the lady's case to him. 'I am sorry for this,' the king answered. 'But the verdict was approved by all here, and by their ruling I will abide.'

Sir Gawain, who stood near, rose and spoke courteously, saying that he had not been present and that therefore he did not stand by the verdict. At once shouts and arguments began, and several knights offered to fight with Torec to prove the matter in combat.

To each of these Torec agreed, but King Arthur himself spoke up and declared that only one knight should represent him in the matter. That knight was to be Yvain, King Uriens' son, who was amongst the greatest knights of the Fellowship.

Gawain came forward again and invited Torec and the lady to accept his courtesy that

night, and later he offered Torec all that he might need in terms of weapons, armour, and care for his steed. The two men became fast friends from this moment on.

Next morning the two knights met on the field and fought a mighty battle. Evenly matched, they rained blows upon each other so that the walls of the castle rang loud with the clangour. In the end both men were exhausted and Torec called for a halt so that they might rest. Yvain agreed and his squire and the lady defended by Torec bound their wounds. Torec meanwhile began to feel again the effects of the poison in his blood and knew that he must win soon or fail utterly.

When the battle was rejoined Torec flung himself with renewed strength on his opponent, and soon Yvain lay bruised and bleeding on the ground, at which point both King Arthur and Sir Gawain approached and required Torec to call a halt to the fight. He did this willingly and the king declared the battle in his favour and that thus the lady had recovered the rights to her lands.

Never was a lady so grateful to any man as was Edein to Torec. She saw to the binding and treatment of his wounds and together she and Sir Gawain nursed him day and night until he was fit to ride again.

At this time, the lady Edein proclaimed her love for Torec. He, kind and gentle as ever, told her that his quest must come before all other things, and that his heart was not ready to be given in love. Though greatly saddened, the lady's gratitude to Sir Torec was not lessened, and she bade him fare well and safely on his quest.

Torec prepared to leave, and both the lady and Sir Gawain came to see him on his way. Torec's road led him along the shore of the sea for a time, and he rested each night for several days beneath the stars, his mind as ever focussed upon the quest for the Circlet of Gold.

⊹ ✚ ⊹

ONE MORNING TOREC woke to a marvellous sight. Lying close to the shore was a ship, everything about it white as bone. From hull to deck, masts and sails – all were bleached. No one moved on board that Torec could see.

At this moment a wise-looking man came by and Torec asked if he knew aught of the ship, whither it came and whence it went. The man looked at Torec as if he were deranged. 'How is it you have not heard of this vessel? This is the Ship of Adventure. It appears here but one day each year, no one knows where from. Many brave knights have ventured on board, but none have ever returned.'

Torec stared at the vessel and decided at once that he would go aboard. Perhaps he believed it would lead him to the Circlet of Gold, but the tale does not say. As Torec looked, a small boat came across the water. No mariners were aboard to operate it, yet it floated to the shore and lay waiting. Torec gave his horse into the keeping of the wise man, and told him that if he did not return, he could keep it as payment. Then he waded into the water and climbed aboard the small craft, which at once began to cross the water between shore and ship.

Torec climbed aboard the silent vessel, finding it empty of life. At once, just as the smaller craft had done, the ship began to move. Its sails filled – though Torec noted that there was only the smallest breath of wind – and sped across the ocean.

How long the ship sped onward, the story does not tell, but in time it came to the shores of an island and drifted into a small and sheltered harbour. Torec disembarked and saw before him the most beautiful castle he had ever seen. Like the ship, it was all white and shone like ice beneath a blue sky. As he came nearer, Torec saw that it was made all of marble, and that many carvings decorated its walls. Its gate stood open wide and Torec walked through into a hall the like of which he had never seen.

On all sides the walls were painted with scenes depicting men and women at play: feasting, playing chess, backgammon and other sports, or hunting with dogs and birds, while still others danced together, some singly, others in circles. Every one of them was as finely dressed and as handsome as any Torec had encountered.

There, in the midst of the splendid hall, sat a tall knight. He watched Torec for a time and noted his wonder. Then he arose and said: 'None who enter this place may do so without facing me, and none to this day have beaten me in combat.'

Torec bowed. 'I am ready to face you at any time.'

When he heard the eagerness in Torec's voice, the knight looked at him more closely and said: 'As to that, we shall see. Certainly, we shall not fight this day. For now, you are welcome as my guest.'

The two men shook hands, and at once squires appeared who led Torec to a chamber where the light entered through crystal windows so that everything shone. They helped Torec to remove his armour and gave him fresh clothes to wear. Then they led him into dinner, where his host, who sat alone at a wide table, made him welcome. Several

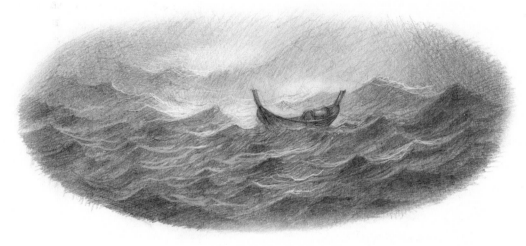

→ *The Ship of Adventure* ←

times Torec thought to ask to know more of the strange castle and the Ship of Adventure, but instead he held his tongue. Soon he was led away to a splendid chamber in which was a great bed, carven from white wood and draped with fine hangings. Stories of knightly adventure were painted on the walls, as they were in the great hall.

Torec fell asleep gazing upon the woven story of Sir Tristan and the Lady Isolt and woke next morning refreshed. Torec's host was waiting for him in the great hall. But instead of armour and weapons, he wore a splendid gown.

'There is something you must see,' he said. 'Depending on what you learn in this place, will decide if we fight or not.'

'Let fate and God decide,' answered Torec, and followed his host to the entrance to a chamber, hidden deep within the castle.

'Here is the Chamber of Wisdom. Let me tell you that few have entered this room save myself,' the host told him. He opened the door and the two men passed within.

Never had Torec seen such a place. The walls were made entirely of marble, with great windows of blue-tinted glass, framed in copper. Costly spices burned in basins of silver, filling the air with healing scents. But most amazing of all was a great long table, made of ivory, at which were seated a number of aged men, whose white beards fell to their knees, and women, still young, who sat like flowers amidst the white-haired elders. So deeply were they in conversation that they seemed unaware of the knights. Torec's host laid a finger to his lips and showed where two chairs were set to one side. Together they sat and heard all that the people at the table were saying.

It seemed to Torec that this conversation had been going on for a long time – perhaps for many years. One of the elders was speaking: 'I know of no joy greater than listening to fine words. Thus is the greatest wisdom conveyed to others and all who hear them grow daily more enlightened.'

'Indeed,' said another. 'But many do not listen, for their wits are dull and they think only of riches and war and of getting.'

225

'So are the ways of all men and women brought into disrepute,' added a third.

Then they fell to talking of the evil that men do, and the many lords and ladies who thought only of their own power and cared nothing for the needs of others. Some spoke of King Arthur and the Knights of the Round Table, who though they were drawn from the finest in the lands, yet were not without cruelty and greed.

Thus, Torec and his host sat silent, listening to the wise men and women talk of many things, as it seemed they had done for a long while. Often, they bemoaned the fate of men and women, and the dangers of lust and false belief, and of those who sought to destroy all that was good and replace it with darkness and evil. 'Once, wisdom was all powerful; now it is money that rules all.' (From which it seems to me that things have changed not at all since the time of which we speak.)

They spoke also of bravery and chivalry within the kingdoms and throughout the world, and of prudence and temperance and honour. Lastly, they spoke of love, which some declared to be dangerous for the way it inflamed the heart and mind and caused men and women to act without rationality. One of the ancients responded that all virtue came of love, and that acts of kindness and wisdom were a true part of it, but that it seemed to him that the world was made up of false deeds.

A woman spoke up then, reminding all of the faithlessness of lovers and the ways in which they brought love itself into ill repute. This caused a further discussion, at times heated, that followed day into night. Yet Torec felt no fatigue, such was the wisdom and power radiating from the speakers.

Time itself fell away in that place, and all too soon it was day again.

For three days Torec stayed in the chamber, listening to the discussions of the aged men and fair women, who spoke and argued on so many matters. Truths he learned, and wisdom also, though I cannot say here what they were since the story does not tell of it – but you may be sure that Torec was greatly changed by what he heard.

On the third night Torec fell asleep at last, and in the morning found that he was no longer in the white castle but back on the shore where he had first boarded the Ship of Adventure.

So amazed was he at this that he could scarcely think. Then he remembered his quest for the Circlet of Gold and went in search of the man to whose care he had entrusted his mount. The fellow was astonished to see Torec alive and asked him to give an account of his adventures. But Torec would say nothing at that time, for the wonders of the White Castle were still fresh in his mind and it would be many days before he could consider all he had learned.

Torec continued his quest that same day, riding hard in the direction he had been told to go, for it seemed to him that he had been delayed too much.

So, at last, Torec came in sight of the castle where the Lady Miraude dwelled, which was named Blancemont, the White Mound. As he was nearing it a damsel appeared, who hailed him by name. 'Sir,' she said. 'My lady has sent me to bring you comfort. Just a short way from here she has ordered that a pavilion be set up for you, and food and drink provided. Here you may rest and replenish yourself before the coming trials you will face when you challenge the knights who guard and protect her.'

Torec was amazed by this. Not only was

his coming expected but had been prepared for. He followed the damsel and there, indeed, was a most fair tent set up in a meadow below the walls of Blancemont, and squires brought food and wine for him and took care of Moreel.

When he had eaten and drunk his fill, Torec took a walk towards the castle, and there on the walls he saw a woman watching. And with the last glint of sunlight, he saw the reflection of the Circlet of Gold on her head. From this he knew that this was Miraude herself, elder sister to the wives of Bruant and Druant. When he saw her, he fell in love with her at once, just as Bruant had predicted. What he did not know was that she already loved him greatly, having watched him for many days in a magic mirror in her possession. Seeing him in the meadow below her castle she near-fainted and almost called out to him to enter. But the pride that filled her heart, placed there, I believe, by the Circlet of Gold that she wore, would not allow this. Instead, she sent four of her strongest knights with a message: that she would only grant him the gift of the circlet, and of herself in marriage, if he could defeat all the Knights of the Round Table in single combat.

When he heard this Torec bowed his head and agreed that he would undertake this task. The four knights returned with his answer to the Lady Miraude who commanded that word be sent to Camelot the Golden – knowing well that King Arthur and his knights would not refuse such a presumptuous challenge.

So began many days of waiting. Torec practiced daily in the meadow where his tent was pitched, and every now and then he would catch sight of Miraude on the walls. Each time his heart leapt in his breast, and he

longed more than anything to be with her. The quest for the Circlet of Gold seemed far less important now, as love blossomed in him.

One day, as he rode Moreel through the woods to the north of the castle, he met a knight on the way. At once Torec called out to him if he would wish to break a spear in combat. To his surprise, the knight refused and, as he came level, raised his visor, showing a face that Torec recognized as his host from the White Castle.

'Do not be amazed,' said the knight. 'I have followed your adventures for many days. I was the black knight you fought with and that vanished, and I was also the red knight and the white, who you also defeated. Lastly, I brought you to the White Castle and showed you the Chamber of Wisdom, where the wise come together to discuss the ways of the world – and shall continue to do until the world ends.'

Seeing Torec's look of astonishment, the knight added: 'My name is Ydras, and I am brother to your grandmother, Lady Mariole, who once possessed the Circlet of Gold. Three times I made passage of arms against you, seeking to test your strength. In truth I found you the strongest man I have encountered for long ages.'

When he heard this, Torec dismounted, as did Ydras, and the two men embraced. Together they made their way back to the pavilion and there enjoyed a splendid supper. There Ydras told the history of the Circlet of Gold, and Torec learned that both his grandmother and her brother – who indeed seemed no more than a mature man, despite the years that had passed since the circlet was stolen away, were of the hidden people – and that therefore he also was possessed of faery blood.

Yet all of this seemed as nothing before the love he felt for the lady Miraude, and seeing this, Ydras took his leave, declaring, before he left, that Torec would see him again, when he had won the Circlet of Gold.

✠ ✠ ✠

A WEEK LATER the first of the Round Table knights began to arrive at Castle Blancemont, followed soon after by King Arthur himself and his circle of courtiers. Only fifty of the knights were present, since none believed that Torec could beat any of them, and certainly not every one of the Fellowship. Many, too, remembered his battle against Sir Yvain, and some were given pause by this.

Meanwhile Torec composed a letter to the Lady Miraude, in which he poured out all the love he felt in his heart, his passion for her, and his determination to defeat all-comers until he could rightfully claim her.

When she received this, Miraude's heart was ready to burst. She regretted her declaration that she would marry only the one who could defeat the Knights of the Round Table. She decided, therefore, to send Torec a token of her love: a ring set with a stone that would render him invincible. He wore it at all times thereafter, and as you shall see, his prowess was indeed wondrous to behold.

However, it must be said that Torec was unaware of the power of the ring, deeming it a love token which made him fight even more mightily for his lady. It is therefore not certain whether it was the ring itself or the power of love that sustained him. Just as Sir Gawain wore the green sash given him by Lady Bercilak, which she promised would protect him from the Green Knight's axe, none knows if this was truly so, or if it was Gawain's courage alone that saved him.[*]

Amongst the knights sent by Arthur to answer Lady Miraude's summons, were Gawain himself, and the grim Sir Kay. Gawain, whose friendship had not diminished since they had met at Tintagel, was already inclined to aid their would-be adversary. When they arrived at the home of Lady Miraude, who welcomed them splendidly, and heard the story of her rash proposal, Gawain addressed the knights who were gathered there privately and said: 'It seems to me this is a most unfair and unknightly thing. Many here know Sir Torec to be a gentle and honest man. I am thinking we should all cut through half of our saddle girths so that he may easily unhorse us. What say you?'

At once Sir Kay spoke up: 'Why should we consider this boastful fellow who thinks he can defeat us all! I for one shall do my best to punish him for his pride!'

Half the knights agreed with Kay and prepared to do battle with Torec. The rest sided with Gawain and secretly cut their girths.

Even with this, Kay was not satisfied. 'I shall go forth myself against this churl this very day,' he said.

'Very well,' agreed Sir Gawain, though he smiled inwardly, knowing all too well how boastful Kay was.

Together with the knights who had sided with him, Kay rode to the meadow where Torec's fine tent was pitched.

'You there!' shouted Kay. 'You think you can beat us all! It will be my great pleasure to knock you into the dust.'

---

[*] As told in the story of *Gawain and the Green Knight*.

Saying which he fewtered his spear and ran at Torec, scarcely giving him time to prepare. A moment later Sir Kay lay on the ground groaning and crying out that his back was broken.

This greatly angered Grevoen, Kay's son, who was among the party from Camelot the Golden. 'You shall pay for unhorsing my father!' he raged.

'It would be as well if you were to throw yourself on the ground now, and save me the trouble,' answered Torec calmly. And sure enough, when Grevoen charged furiously upon him, he went flying over his horse's tail and landed hard on the earth, where he lay groaning next to his father.

At this the remaining knights, grim visaged, lined up to attack Sir Torec.

Not one of them was able to stand against him, and soon lay broken and bloodied on the ground. Torec, despite several wounds, remained unhorsed, though his shield was split asunder, and his armour bore many dints.

Thus ended that first day of jousts. Kay and his fellows were taken back to the castle to be restored of their wounds, and all dined together, with Torec seated next to the Lady Miraude, which pleased them both. Next morning, Gawain was the first to ride against Torec, who unhorsed him easily. The same happened with each of the knights who came after. I shall not name them for the sake of their honour, but each one had nobly cut part-way through their girths, so that these broke in the fray and they were all unseated. If Torec wondered at this I cannot say, but as the day closed Gawain came forward and declared him the victor.

'Let us go to your lady and tell her you have succeeded in your promise,' he said.

Miraude, who had watched all that day, and the one previously, from the walls of the castle, came to meet them.

She had eyes only for Torec.

Gawain addressed her. 'My lady. This knight has performed all that you asked of him. You should be glad to take him for your husband, for not only is he a mighty fighter, he is a good and noble man also.'

'If Sir Torec will have me, I will be most pleased,' answered Miraude with lowered gaze.

At this moment Sir Kay spoke up loudly. 'Did you not ask that the man you would marry must defeat *all* the Knights of the Round Table? This is but fifty. A hundred more await him!'

'He has done enough and more,' said Miraude.

'It seems to me,' Kay said, 'that this is now a matter of honour. If this churl is permitted to defeat only us, then the Fellowship is forever tarnished.'

'Sirs,' said Torec. 'I am more than willing to accept this challenge.'

At this Miraude began to weep, believing that even with her ring to protect him, he could not possibly fight so many and win.

Torec comforted her, and Gawain, who was preparing to ride ahead to Camelot the Golden to inform King Arthur what had happened, spoke to her also, promising that all would be well.

Then Gawain departed with those who favoured Torec. On reaching the court he told the king all that had transpired. Arthur was astonished at Torec's bravery and skill. 'It seems to me that we must have him as a member of our Fellowship,' he said.

Gawain agreed, then he and King Arthur, and others of the court, rode out to meet

Torec – an honour granted to very few in that time.

That night the whole court dined as well as ever anyone could. Torec was seated near to King Arthur, who praised both his courage and the honour he gained for undertaking the task before him when he might have avoided it. All the time Sir Kay glowered and nursed his bruises and plotted with his friends to bring shame to Torec on the morrow. Gawain, meanwhile, once again spoke with others of the Fellowship, including the great Sir Lancelot, Sir Tristan and Sir Palomides, urging them to cut their girths as he had done to allow Torec to win. Though at first several were doubtful of this, Gawain won them over by telling them what he knew of Torec's life and deeds to date. 'Surely,' Gawain said, 'this man will make a great addition to our Table. Let us give him a chance to do so. Let him win his lady as he has striven so hard to do.'

So it was that when the morning dawned, and Torec sat mounted alone on Moreel, facing as many as a hundred knights, more than two thirds of them had done as Gawain urged and cut through most of their girths.

Spears were put in rest, horses spurred forward. Lances shattered, shields splintered, armour dinted. Cries of triumph which turned quickly to moans of sorrow echoed around the lists, as knight after knight fell victim to Torec's strength. And once again I cannot say whether it was love, or fate, or Gawain's work, or the power of the magic ring, but at day's end not one knight of the Round Table had been able to stand against Sir Torec. And who knows if this is the reason that this tale is so little told, though in my view the knights were, with the exception of Sir Kay and his fellows, as noble and generous as ever.

King Arthur watched as one by one his knights fell to Torec's spear. And when all were fallen, he stood and walked into the lists and called for his grey mount, Llamrai, to be brought forth and his armour to be put upon him. Then he too faced Sir Torec.

'My lord. I have no quarrel with you – nor with any of your knights,' Torec declared. 'Nor does my lady's test require that I fight you.'

'Let it be for the honour of the Round Table,' King Arthur replied.

Then the two men fewtered their spears and charged together, and this time both fell to the earth. Silence fell over the lists as first King Arthur, then Sir Torec, rose and drew their swords. But before either could strike a blow, Arthur threw aside his sword and shield and ran forward, seizing Torec in a mighty grip. Torec was unable to break free, and in a moment the king threw him to the ground and placed a foot upon his breast.

'Do you yield, Sir Knight?' the king asked.

'Willingly, my lord,' answered Torec.

Then Arthur helped the young knight to stand and smiled upon him.

'Then I declare this matter settled,' he said. 'Let no man fail to hold his head high, for today you fought a great knight.'

Everywhere cheering broke out, and the ladies who were crowded into the stands looked with envy at Miraude, each in their hearts wishing that Torec had fought for them that day.

✢ ✢ ✢

LITTLE MORE REMAINS to tell. Torec returned to the pavilion where Miraude awaited him and the two embraced and swore their oaths to each other. Messengers went forth from Camelot the Golden to King Yder and Queen Tristoise, announcing the wedding of their son to the lady Miraude. When Tristoise heard of this, and that Torec had exacted revenge upon the Knight of the Red Lion, she laughed aloud for the second time.

So great was the event that it seemed as though no one in all the lands of Britain was absent. Druant and Bruant came also, with Miraude's sisters who, though they felt no joy to see her wearing the circlet, yet spoke no harsh words to her. Then it was that Torec's mother laughed for the third time, as had been predicted, when she witnessed the joy of her son, wedded at last to she who possessed the circlet.

Many that Torec had met on his quest came also, and the lords of Miraude's land, who all swore allegiance to him. Last of all came Ydras, Torec's mysterious uncle. Before all he said: 'Now is the Circlet of Gold returned to one of our blood, and now is the quest

of Torec ended.' At the ceremony Miraude wore the golden circlet, which sparkled like a sun on her brows, and many came to hear the story of Torec's quest.

King Arthur begged Torec to stay at the court and become one of the Round Table Fellowship, but though he declared himself honoured, Torec declined. His own new lands, acquired through marriage, awaited his coming, and indeed in times to come he would be called king. And when Yder died, his son inherited the kingdom and brought the two lands together, and it is said that Torec's descendants have the blood of the *longaevi* within them to this day. Nor may I end without saying that, in times to come, when darkness threatened Arthur's kingdom, Torec was among the first to stand at the king's side in the last dread battle of Camlann. Thus should the name of this great knight never be forgotten, and so have I placed it here, where I am certain Master Thomas would have wished it so to be.

---------- ✠ ----------

EXPLICIT LIBER SECUNDUS.
INCIPIT LIBER TERTIUS.

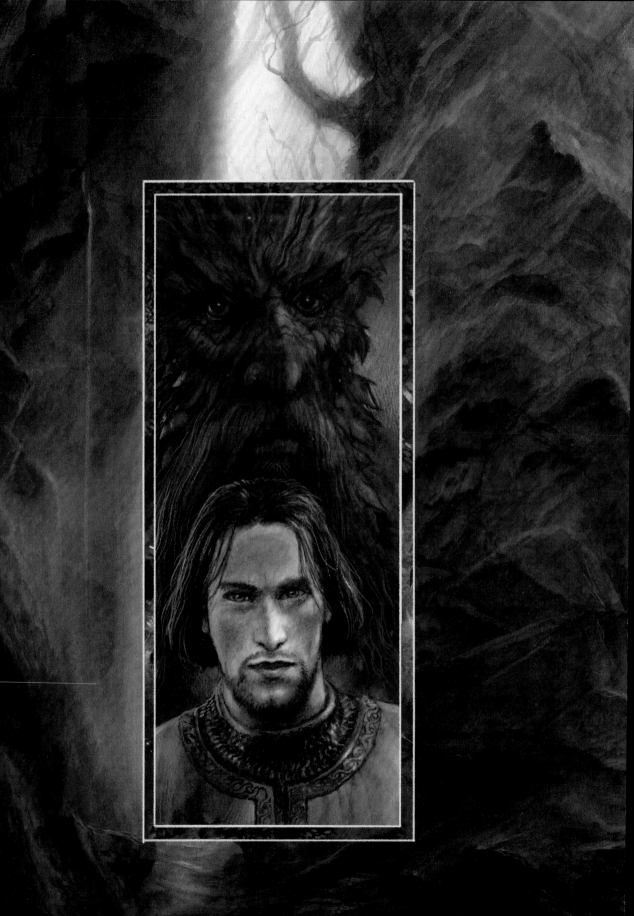

BOOK THREE

❦

THE BOOK OF
SIR GAWAIN

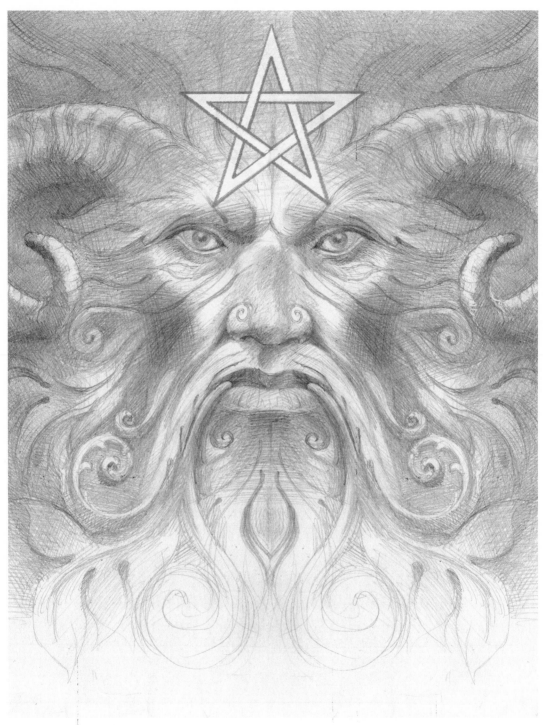

↦ *The Green Knight* ↤

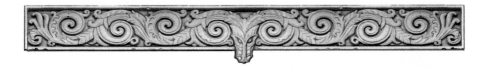

20: THE RISE OF SIR GAWAIN

✠

MANY TALES HAVE BEEN TOLD OF THE GREAT KNIGHT SIR
GAWAIN, NEPHEW TO KING ARTHUR, OF WHOM IT IS SAID
THAT HE NEVER FAILED TO RETURN VICTORIOUS FROM
ANY QUEST OR ADVENTURE HE UNDERTOOK. MASTER THOMAS
HIMSELF TELLS HOW QUEEN MORGAUSE OF ORKNEY CAME TO
CAMELOT THE GOLDEN WITH HER THREE SONS: AGRAVAIN,
GAWAIN AND GUERREHES, AND HOW LATER A FOURTH BROTHER,
GARETH, JOINED THEM. HE TELLS ALSO OF THE COMING OF
ANOTHER SON – MORDRED – AND OF HIS HATRED FOR HIS FATHER
KING ARTHUR AND ALL THAT FOLLOWED IN THAT DARK TIME.
BUT THERE IS ANOTHER TALE, WHICH TELLS A DIFFERENT STORY
OF GAWAIN'S RISE, ADDING MUCH TO THE STORY. IT IS MY BELIEF
THAT THIS IS A GREAT TALE, AND ONE THAT EXPLAINS MUCH
THAT WAS NOT RECORDED BY MASTER THOMAS. OTHERS THAT
TELL OF SIR GAWAIN'S GREAT DEEDS, WHICH I HAVE FOUND IN MY
SEARCH AMONG THESE ANCIENT TALES, WILL FOLLOW HEREAFTER,
SHOWING THAT ONCE, BEFORE THE COMING OF LANCELOT – AND
AT TIMES SINCE THEN – SIR GAWAIN WAS RANKED FIRST AMONG
THE FELLOWSHIP OF THE ROUND TABLE. IT MAY PERHAPS BE SAID
THAT THERE IS BUT ONE STORY OF SIR GAWAIN, AND THAT IN ALL
ITS VARIATIONS HE IS THE NOBLEST KNIGHT OF ALL.

✠ ✠ ✠

IN THE TIME of King Arthur's father, Uther Pendragon, a number of royal children lived at the British court. Uther had them there as hostages for the good behaviour of the neighbouring kings over whom he held sway. One of them, Lot of Orkney, nephew of King Sichelm of Norway, was a youth of such outstanding qualities that he became familiar with Uther and his family and was often to be found in their private quarters.

235

Uther also had a daughter named Morgause, who was still very young and lived with her mother. She and Lot were often together, laughing and joking, and no one thought more of it. But the truth of the matter was that they had fallen in love with each other, and that after a period of shyness, they both gave way to their impulses, with the result that Morgause became pregnant.

Fearing her father's anger, by means known only to her she concealed the fact of her condition to everyone save her most trusted lady-in-waiting, and when the time came for her to give birth, she feigned illness and retired to her chamber with only her lady as companion. There, in due time, she gave birth to a male child of surpassing beauty.

With the help of her lady-in-waiting, she had previously made contact with certain wealthy merchants, whom she had bribed with gold to take care of her child and bring it up in secret in a foreign land. When she entrusted the child to them, she also gave them, in keeping for her son, a rich cloth of gold, an emerald ring which had belonged to her father, and a scroll sealed with the royal seal which offered proof that the child, to whom she gave the name Gawain, was the son of herself and Prince Lot.

The merchants received charge of the infant and took ship for Gaul, where they had business. Landing near the city of Narbonne they travelled inland, leaving the ship to ride at anchor with only a boy to watch over their merchandise and the child who had been placed in their care. And here by chance came a merchant named Viamundus, a man of noble birth who had fallen on hard times. When he saw the apparently deserted ship anchored close to the shore, he went aboard, finding only the sleeping servant and the child,

along with many riches. Struck by this piece of good fortune, Viamundus decided that the fates were smiling upon him, and he took as much gold and other riches as he could carry – and also the child, along with the chest containing all the things pertaining to its birth and station. Then he went home laden to his wife and gave her the infant to nurse.

In a while the merchants returned to their ship and were horrified by the loss of the child and their goods. They sent messengers throughout the land around Narbonne to search for any news of the theft. But these returned in a few days with no word, and sadly the merchants were forced to continue on their way, not daring to tell anyone the true nature of their loss.

Viamundus, meanwhile, hid his stolen wealth with as much care as he hid the child. He dared do nothing while questions were being asked about the crime, for which, if the truth be known, he felt considerable guilt. Indeed, he pretended that nothing had happened, spending only a little of the money he had acquired, and that with great circumspection. Thus seven years passed, during which time both Viamundus and his wife became very fond of their unlawful child, coming indeed to think of him as their own offspring, which all who knew them believed as well.

At the end of this period, Viamundus decided to pack up everything he possessed and make the journey to Rome. In part this was because he wished to expiate himself for the theft of the child and the gold – though a shrewder part of him knew that he could improve the fate both of himself and his family with the money he had kept hidden for so long.

So, accompanied by his wife and the child whom everyone believed was theirs, he set out and soon arrived in Rome, which in this time had been repeatedly sacked by barbarians, and was looking as poor as it ever had in several centuries. However, a new emperor had recently been crowned there, and was exerting himself to restore the city to its former glory. When he heard this, Viamundus hit upon a scheme whereby he might establish himself in the emperor's favour. To this end he retired outside the city and acquired a number of slaves and much fine raiment. Then, dressed like a prince, he entered the city and sought an audience with the emperor. Claiming to be a former military governor from Gaul, he offered whatever aid he might in terms of money and men. Delighted and impressed by the dignity of Viamundus, the emperor made him welcome and offered him great estates both in and around the city.

From this moment onward, the career of Viamundus was that of a noble and popular man. Swiftly elevated to the rank of senator, he conducted himself with such kindness and nobility that soon he came to be regarded as one of the most important men in Rome. He was often consulted by the emperor on matters of state, and personally endowed many new buildings in the gradually restored city.

At the same time, the youth whom everyone believed was Viamundus' son grew towards manhood and was as well liked and popular as his adoptive father. He spent much of his time in and around the emperor's palace and became fast friends with several of the noble youths who dwelt there.

Then, when the boy was in his twelfth year, Viamundus was stricken with a fatal illness. Realizing that the end of his life was near, he begged the emperor and the pope (Sulpicius was pontiff in these days) to attend upon his deathbed and hear what he had to say. Because of the great love and respect they bore him, both the great men agreed to come.

When they were present, Viamundus told them everything about his past: how he had come by his wealth, and, most importantly, that the youth whom everyone called his son was in fact stolen away by him as an infant.

'My lords,' said the dying man, 'I have delayed too long in telling you these things – though I have often longed to do so. Now that my time on this earth is almost over, I ask this of you. That you, my emperor, care for the future of the youth, and see to it that he receives an education in chivalry and the ways of knighthood. For I will tell you now, and I ask you, the Pope of all Christendom, to bear witness, that this boy is indeed the nephew of the renowned King Arthur, of whom so much praise is spoken in this time. I am sure that in time he will be recognized and reclaimed by his true parents, though I do not know how this will happen. Meanwhile I ask that you speak to no one of his true identity, least of all to the child himself, but to keep these things that I have told you secret until the right time. When he reaches full manhood, let the boy be sent home, with the proofs which I will show you, and a letter explaining all that has occurred.'

Having heard this in some wonder, the emperor gave his word, the pontiff witnessing it. Then the boy was sent for and heard his dying father give him into the care of the master of Rome. He wept to see his father so close to death, until the old man reassured him that he was dying happy in the knowledge that his son should enter the household of the emperor. Then, having received the last rites, and with the emperor at his bedside, Viamundus died.

Thereafter the youth became part of the emperor's court and was treated much as were his own sons. And when, three years having passed, he attained the age of fifteen, the emperor himself invested him with his arms. At that time there were a number of other noble youths due to receive the accolade of knighthood. All were tested in the Circus, where once chariot races had been held, but which now served as lists to the knights of Rome. In the trials which followed, the youth outmatched all his peers and shone so greatly in the field that everyone agreed that he was the finest young knight they had ever seen.

At the end of the trials the emperor awarded the first place to the young man and gave him as tokens a circlet of gold oak-leaves, and a surcote of crimson silk, which the bold youth declared he would wear with pride for all his days. Then he asked, by way of a boon, that he be permitted to undertake the first single combat required by the emperor against any enemy that came forward. To this the emperor agreed, and the youth was much praised. In the days that followed, he became known by a new title: 'the Knight of the Surcote', because of the splendid garment the emperor had given to him. And this name replaced his own for a time, so that the name Gawain was seldom if ever heard in the halls of the imperial palace.

✠ ✠ ✠

A T THIS TIME war broke out between the Persians and the Christians remaining in Jerusalem. Each side was eager to join in battle, but their leaders were wiser and sought to end the affair through single combat. A truce was arranged while the Christians sent word to Rome asking for a champion.

Hearing of this, the emperor called a council to discuss the matter, and it was here that the Knight of the Surcote came bursting in, begging the emperor to forgive him for the interruption, and reminding him of his promise to allot the first single combat to him.

At first the emperor was reluctant to give the task to so young and untried a knight, but he could not forswear his promise, and his counsellors reminded him of the prowess displayed by the youth in the lists. So the emperor gave his consent, and the Knight of the Surcote set forth, accompanied by an escort of one hundred knights.

They took ship as soon as was possible and set sail for the Holy Land. For twenty-five days they were tossed on the backs of great waves, then a storm blew up and drove them off course, bringing them to shore at last on the edge of an island ruled over by a cruel and powerful lord named Milocrates. This same man had recently abducted the emperor's niece, who had been betrothed to the King of Illyricum. It had proved impossible to rescue her, due to the heavy fortifications with which the island was guarded, and the overwhelming fierceness of Milocrates' followers.

The Romans came ashore on the far side of the island from its strong forts, in a part heavily forested. Wild animals were to be found here but were carefully protected because of their scarceness. In fact, they were intended for Milocrates' table alone, and fearsome punishments were meted out to anyone who hunted there without leave. The Romans of course knew none of this, and since they required food they went ashore and began hunting. Under the leadership of the Knight of the Surcote they soon took six stags. They were in pursuit of a seventh when they were met by the guardian of the forest, along with fourteen knights, who demanded by what right the strangers hunted the royal preserve.

'We have taken only what we needed to preserve our lives,' said the Knight of the Surcote.

'That is not good enough!' cried the forest warden, and he demanded that they lay down their arms and place themselves in his custody.

'That we shall never do,' replied the young knight, and flung his spear at the warden, who received it in his shoulder. Crying out in agony, he nonetheless pulled out the spear and flung it back at the youth. It narrowly missed him and stuck in a tree. This was the signal for general fighting to commence, and even though the Romans were without armour, while their adversaries were fully armed, under the leadership of the Knight of the Surcote the islanders were soon killed or put to flight.

Of those who escaped, one went straight to Milocrates, who was staying in a nearby city, and told him of the strangers. Word of the Roman champion and his followers had already spread throughout the lands around the Aegean Sea, and all who sided with the King of Persia had been warned to look out for their coming and to do all in their power to prevent them from reaching the Holy Land. Thus, when he learned of the strangers who had raided his hunting lands and defeated his men, Milocrates at once guessed who they were and immediately summoned his knights and soldiers.

The Romans, meanwhile, returned to their ships, where the Knight of the Surcote was much praised for his courage in leading the foraging party. They now prepared to up anchor and depart, but contrary winds made it apparent that they were not destined to leave just yet. The centurion in charge of the Roman knights expressed his concern that their enemies would, by now, know of their presence and were probably even then assembling a force to attack them.

'We must,' he said, 'send spies inland at once to get some idea of their numbers and disposition.'

Two men were chosen for this: the Knight of the Surcote and an officer named Odabel, a blood-relative of the centurion. While they were still preparing to depart, an outcry announced the discovery of scouts sent out by Milocrates. These were soon brought before the centurion, and through a mixture of threats and bribes, the Romans acquired much information, including the knowledge of whom they were soon to face in battle.

Now the two spies set out together and journeyed inland to the city where Milocrates was assembling a huge force to attack the Romans. Due largely to the number of soldiers and knights who were gathering there from all corners of the island, the two Romans were able to mingle with their enemies and enter the city itself. There they learned that reports of the Roman force had been so exaggerated that Milocrates believed a much larger army was arrayed against him. He therefore elected to hold off the attack until his brother, Buzafarnan, could arrive from a nearby land, bringing an even larger number of men. All of this the Knight of the Surcote heard and committed to memory.

But spying out the strength of the enemy was not all that was in the young man's thoughts. He had in mind a daring plan to rescue the emperor's niece, news of whom had been obtained from the captured spies. Thus, the Knight of the Surcote slipped into the palace, mingling easily with the enemy, and sought the way to the king's own suite of rooms, where the captive princess was held.

As he made his way through the corridors, the Knight of the Surcote espied a man he recognized, a knight named Naboar, whom he had known at the emperor's palace in Rome. This man, he remembered, had been captured along with the princess, and was now likewise held in captivity. With great daring the Knight of the Surcote attracted Naboar's attention, and when the two men had embraced and exchanged news of each other, they spoke of the princess.

'She is indeed in this very palace,' said Naboar. 'And what is more she had heard of you.'

'How is that possible?' asked the youth.

'Your fame has gone before you more than you realize.'

'Do you think she would be willing to be aided by me?'

'Indeed, I believe you would find her most willing. For though it is true that Milocrates has honoured her greatly, she cannot forget that she was abducted by force.'

With the help of Naboar, who was a familiar figure about the palace, the Knight of the Surcote made his way to the chambers occupied by the emperor's niece. As Naboar had suggested, when the youth revealed his identity, he found her eager both to escape but also to help the Romans in any way that she could. The three of them set about devising a plan, for it had quickly become clear that the force which Milocrates was assembling was far superior to their own, and that they had little chance of victory without considerable luck. With all the preparations for battle going on everywhere, they deemed it

safe for a small party of Romans to lie hidden just outside the city walls. Then, when the army of Milocrates set forth to overwhelm their enemies, the princess would open the gates and admit the hidden contingent, who would capture the city itself and set it ablaze, thus distracting Milocrates and convincing him that another large force was behind him.

To this the Princess most willingly agreed, and to further aid the Knight of the Surcote, she gave him a sword and armour belonging to Milocrates, of which it was said that if another wore it then its real owner would soon perish. With these gifts, and strengthened by the help of both the princess and Naboar, the young knight slipped out of the palace and, having rejoined Odabel, who had been spying out the size of the enemy force, the two left the city and returned to their own camp.

The centurion heard their news with elation. He quickly dispatched Odabel with a small force, to await the signal to enter and possess the city. Then he gathered the rest of the Roman force and went forth to meet Milocrates.

The latter had divided his army into two parts. One, under the command of his brother, was to attack from the sea; the rest, under his own leadership, marched towards the Roman camp.

As for Milocrates himself, he was filled with fear and had little expectation of victory, despite his superior numbers. For that morning he had gone in search of the armour which gave him superior strength, only to find it missing. So filled with despair was he at this, that even though he did not know that the enemy had somehow succeeded in stealing it, he became fearful of the prophecy against himself. When he reached the field of battle and saw the Knight of the Surcote – whose prowess rumour had already exaggerated – and saw that he wore the armour and carried the sword, Milocrates wished to turn and flee. However, it was too late to stop what he had begun, and so battle was joined.

At first there seemed no movement on either side. The Romans, though outnumbered nearly twelve to one, fought with such heroism that they held the enemy at bay. Then, as the plan devised by the Knight of the Surcote began to be put into operation, smoke was seen to arise from the city. At once panic ensued among Milocrates' men. So great was their sense of doom that his entire force turned tail and fled. They found the city gates closed against them and thus, caught between their own walls and the attacking Romans, they were cut to pieces.

When he saw the slaughter, Milocrates rallied his forces and, in a brave attempt to reverse his fortunes, attacked the centre where the Knight of the Surcote was fighting. Inevitably the two came face to face, and at their first encounter the knight unhorsed the king and sent him stunned to the ground. The battle raged on around them, as Milocrates regained his feet and struck out at the young knight. A lucky blow opened a wound on the youth's brow, and as he felt the blood flowing down into his eyes, he struck out furiously, severing the king's head from his shoulders.

When they saw that, the last resistance among Milocrates' men failed and they threw down their weapons and surrendered on every side. The prophecy that the king should die at the hands of the man who wore his armour was fulfilled. The Romans took possession of the city and were welcomed by the emperor's niece, who gave orders for the dead to be buried and the wounded cared for.

So it seemed that the battle was over. The centurion secured the island and placed a governor loyal to Rome over its people. Then he dispatched a company to escort the emperor's niece to her rightful lord, the King of Illyricum. With an additional levy of soldiers from Milocrates' own guard, the fleet prepared to set sail to their original destination.

However, they had reckoned without the dead king's brother, who had been sailing up and down the coast all this time, blown hither and thither by the winds which had kept the Romans from sailing. Now as he saw the Roman fleet approaching, he at once attacked.

A pitched battle ensued, with ships ramming each other with their iron prows, smashing great holes in the sides of their adversaries and causing great loss of life. The Knight of the Surcote himself was in charge of one of the most powerful of the ships and wreaked great havoc wherever he went. Grappling irons were flung against the sides of the enemy ships and the knight himself led the way aboard more than a dozen of them. At one point the enemy surrounded him and flung Greek Fire onto the deck of his craft. This evil weapon, which clung to everything it touched and consumed it upon contact, seemed as though it would overwhelm the Romans. But thanks to the Knight of the Surcote, the tables were turned. Singlehandedly he took the assault to the enemy ship, leading his own men aboard, where they swiftly overcame their adversaries and took possession of the craft. While their own ship sank burning beneath the waves, the knight turned the enemy's weapons against them. In less time than it takes to tell, the enemy were routed, with more than twenty ships captured and dozens more sunk. Milocrates' brother was

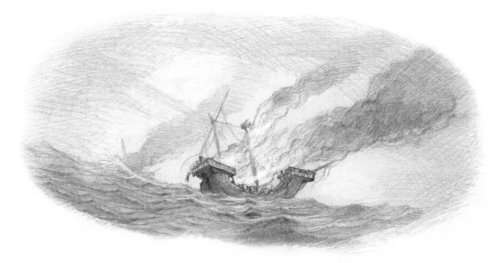

→ *The Burning Ship* ←

himself captured, and the centurion sent him in chains to Rome before turning once again for the Holy Land and the completion of their original mission.

✠ ✠ ✠

WITH PREVAILING WINDS, they reached Jerusalem in a matter of days, and were received with joy and expectation. The Christian forces had placed all their hopes of a peaceful outcome in the person of their champion, and if some were concerned by his youth, all were impressed by his bearing and by word of his battle against Milocrates.

On the day appointed, the two armies began to assemble on the plain outside the walls of the city. The Knight of the Surcote now learned for the first time something of the adversary he would soon be fighting. The Persian champion was named Gormundus, a huge man, almost a giant, with tree-like limbs and immense strength. So large was he, indeed, that no horse could be found to carry him; therefore, the combat was destined to take place on foot, a fact which many deemed a disadvantage to the Knight of the Surcote.

Having prepared themselves, the two champions advanced together and met with a fearsome clash in the midst of the field. Blows were exchanged, blood was shed, taunts were exchanged, but neither had the advantage. Like two great boars they rushed together, hammering at each other's mail-clad bodies with all their strength like blacksmiths in the smithy. The Knight of the Surcote, the lighter of the two by no small measure, danced around his opponent, causing him to work harder at his task. Gormundus, for his turn, delivered slow and ponderous strokes which slowed down the Christian champion considerably. Thus, the two fought on wearily throughout the long hours of the day, and when sunset fell neither had succeeded in inflicting any serious wounds upon the other.

The day ended in uncertainty for both sides, for no one could say how the battle would go on the morrow.

The next day the combat recommenced, with both champions striving ever more greatly to find an advantage. Sparks were struck from their swords and it was a wonder to all that their armour did not crack from the blows they rained down upon each other. Yet as the day advanced neither could be said to have gained an advantage. Then the Knight of the Surcote, plunging in past his enemy's guard, struck him in the mouth, knocking out two teeth and breaking half his jaw. It was not a serious wound, but it stung Gormundus to rage. He pressed his attack with even greater force and delivered a blow which caused the young knight's sword to break off near the hilt. The knight himself was now at a disadvantage and gave ground swiftly. A great roar went up from the Persians. Gormundus pressed home his advantage, but as things looked black for the Knight of the Surcote the sun dipped below the horizon and the combat was at an end for that day.

Next morning there was some argument over whether or not the young knight should be permitted to use a new sword, but in time agreement was reached and the combat began again. By this time the two men had gained a measure of each other, and as they renewed their attacks they struck ever more cunningly, inflicting countless minor wounds. But slowly the Persian champion began to weaken, driven back by the sheer force of the younger knight's attack. His people cried out in alarm at this, encouraging him and taunting him at the same time until, driven half mad with pain and shame, he struck such as blow that he brought the knight to his knees.

Then the young champion sprang up, and with great fury and passion renewed his attack. Lifting his sword high he cried: 'Here is the blow that ends it all!' Then he struck such a blow that it penetrated the helm and brainpan of Gormundus and felled him to the earth stone dead. A great moan went up from the Persians, quickly drowned by the cheers of the Christians.

Thus war was averted, both sides abiding by their agreement and proceeding to exchange prisoners, pay dues and agree the reparation of goods. The Knight of the Surcote, needless to say, received praise and gifts from all sides, and returned to Rome in triumph. There, the emperor himself welcomed him and awarded him with the highest rank and titles.

The Knight of the Surcote soon became restless for further acts of adventure and began actively to seek about for word of conflict in which he might engage. Word came to him of the renowned King Arthur (his own uncle, though he knew it not), whose knights were said to be the best in all the world, and whose court offered more adventures than any other. It was said that in this time the kingdom of Britannia was under attack by many hostile forces, and that its king was much in need of knights. At once the young hero desired to go there and, believing that this might in time bring the old province of Britain, long separated from the empire, back into a relationship with Rome, the emperor agreed.

Before the knight departed, the emperor summoned him and gave him certain gifts. He also handed to him the chest which Viamundus had given into his keeping, instructing him not to look within it but to present it to King Arthur himself and none other. Then the Knight of the Surcote took his leave of the emperor and set out upon the long journey across the Alps, through Gaul, and across the Narrow Sea to Britannia. There he enquired after the whereabouts of King Arthur and was told that he was at present in the city of Caerleon.

The hero set out at once in the direction of the river Usk, but when he was still several miles from his destination a sudden violent storm struck, driving him from the road to seek the shelter of a nearby grove of trees.

It happened that King Arthur and Queen Guinevere were abed at this time, discussing matters of note to do with the kingdom. The queen was not only one of the most beautiful women in the kingdom, she was also possessed of great wisdom, so that the king consulted her regarding many things. On certain occasions she had even been known to foresee events that were yet to come, this strengthening the belief, which I have mentioned before, that she was possessed of faery blood. To these visions King Arthur listened always, since they were so often true. On this occasion, after they had talked long into the night, the queen suddenly said: 'Arthur, you are often said to be one of the best knights in Britain, every bit as strong as your own followers. Do you believe it to be true?'

'Of course,' replied the king. 'Do you not feel this in your own heart?'

'Indeed, I do,' said Guinevere. 'But my dreams tell me that even now there is approaching the town of Usk a knight who is of boundless strength. By mid-morning tomorrow he will send to me a gold ring and two horses. I do not say that he is stronger than you, but he is certainly a very powerful champion.'

The king said nothing to this, but as soon as the queen was asleep, he rose from his bed and went quietly outside, calling his squire

and servants to him and instructing them to bring his armour and weapons and to prepare his horse. Then he summoned his seneschal and foster brother Sir Kay to accompany him, and shortly after the two rode forth secretly, telling no one in the castle.

Soon they arrived at a tributary of the river Usk which was swollen by the storm, and there they found the Knight of the Surcote, casting about to find a crossing place.

'Who are you, that wanders the country in the dead of night?' cried the king. 'Are you a spy or a fugitive?'

'I am neither,' called back the knight. 'I wander because I do not know the way.'

'You are quick to defend yourself with your tongue,' replied Arthur. 'Let us see if you are as good with a lance and sword.'

'As you wish,' said the young knight, and there beneath the moon's rays he lowered his lance and charged to meet the king.

They met in the middle of the stream and King Arthur flew from his horse's back and landed in the water. The knight at once secured the king's mount and returned with it to his side of the stream.

When he saw this, Sir Kay issued his own challenge and rode to meet the stranger. The Knight of the Surcote dealt with him as easily as he had the king, and Kay quickly joined his master in the river. As before, the knight scooped up the reins of the riderless horse and secured that too. Then he took the path away from there, leaving the king and his seneschal to walk home, wet and chastened by their humiliation at the hands of the young knight.

When he arrived back at the castle King Arthur hastened to bed to get warm. The queen, stirring at his arrival, asked why he was so wet and cold. 'I heard a noise in

244

the courtyard,' said Arthur hastily. 'I thought it might be some of my men fighting and went out in the rain to see.'

'Well,' said the queen sleepily, 'we shall see what news my messenger brings in the morning.'

The Knight of the Surcote, meanwhile, continued on his way with the two captured horses and found lodging nearby for the night. When day dawned, he rode on towards Caerleon, and on the way he met a boy wearing the royal arms.

'What is your duty?' asked the knight.

'Sir, I am the queen's messenger.'

'Then if you will, I bid you take a message to the queen from me.' He gave the two horses into the care of the boy, along with his ring and a gold coin for his trouble.

Queen Guinevere, meanwhile, knowing what was to occur, watched the road leading to the castle, and when she saw her messenger approach, leading two horses, she went down to meet him. The boy explained that he had met a knight on the road and gave the queen the ring. When she heard the name of the knight, she smiled and then went at once to where King Arthur lay still abed and woke him.

'My lord,' she said. 'Lest you doubt my words to you last night, here is the ring which I was promised, and outside are the two horses which I foretold. They are all sent by the knight whom I described. It seems that he overthrew two knights last night at the ford.'

Shamefacedly, the king rose and looked out of the window. Of course, the horses were his own and Sir Kay's, as anyone could see. Then Arthur laughed and ruefully confessed all to the queen.

Later that morning the king held an assembly of his nobles which, due to the fine weather, took place under a certain ash tree in the gardens of the castle. Here, as they sat in conference, the Knight of the Surcote arrived and rode right up to where the lords of Britannia were gathered.

Arthur, not knowing who he was, addressed him sternly for interrupting. The youth held his own however and declared that he was a knight of Rome who had learned of the problems facing the king of Britannia and had come to offer help. He announced that he brought mandates from the emperor himself and handed over the sealed casket.

Then he called the Knight of the Surcote before him and said that, while he appreciated his coming and the letters from the emperor, at that time he had no need of more men. 'I have such a great fellowship of knights around me – most of whom serve me without stipend – that I must be careful of whom I admit to their ranks. As an untried youth, I can hardly invite you to be part of the Fellowship.'

When he heard this the Knight of the Surcote blushed furiously. 'I came in good faith to serve one of whom I had heard only good things. I see now that I was mistaken. Nevertheless, I shall not depart from Britannia until I have found service with someone, for to do so would be to imply cowardice on my part. Let me remain in this land, and if there is any task which you or your knights are reluctant to undertake, I beg you to give it to me.'

Liking this answer, King Arthur agreed. Less than twelve days later he received news that a certain lady, who was bound to him by deep ties of loyalty, was besieged by wild Picts at the Castle of Maidens in Scotland. She begged the king to come to her aid.

Arthur had encountered the leader of the Picts, named Coil, before, and each time he had met defeat. Nonetheless, he hastily assembled an army and marched north. He was still a good way from the Castle of Maidens when he met a second messenger, who brought news that the castle had fallen, and that its lady had been carried off. At once King Arthur gave chase to the Picts, but their wily leader had news of his coming and lay in wait with his strongest warriors to intercept them.

At the first encounter the forces of King Arthur were scattered and cast into confusion by the unexpected fury of the assault. They quickly regrouped, and the king himself led them in a rousing attack. However, the British were considerably outnumbered, and despite their heroic efforts, were gradually pressed back. King Arthur, judging the situation with the skill of a seasoned warrior, decided to withdraw and regroup. As they were doing so, they suddenly met with the Knight of the Surcote, who had followed the army at a distance.

'Are they deer or rabbits that you hunt, my lord?' he demanded. And Arthur, angry at this taunt, shouted back that he saw no proof of the knight's reported prowess, since he chose to hide from the battle. At this the young knight grew angry also, and spurring his horse past the retreating Britons, flew straight towards the Picts.

So astonished were they at the suddenness and fury of his attack that they gave way, parting like a sea before him. For his part he rode directly to where the enemy banners fluttered and drove in straight for King Coil. Before anyone could do more than stare, he had dealt the enemy lord a fatal blow, snatched up the reins of the captive lady and galloped back towards the British lines.

The Picts, recovering from their surprise

and howling now with fury, surrounded him, attacking from every side. It was nothing short of a miracle that the knight survived death. He struck about him furiously, dealing out death to all who came against him. But he was hampered by the presence of the lady and looked around desperately for a way to escape. So it was that he spotted a bank and ditch crossed by a narrow bridge – all that remained of a once-proud fort. Spurring his mount towards this place he succeeded in gaining sufficient space between himself and the Picts to allow the lady to cross before him. Then, grim-faced, he turned at bay and for the next half-hour defended the bridge against all-comers. Such was the ferocity and strength of his defence, that at the end of this time the Picts began to withdraw, dismayed at the death-toll which mounted around the hero.

At this point King Arthur, who had been regrouping his own forces, returned and attacked with renewed force, driving the Picts before him. After this the battle was soon over, and the Britons gathered around the Knight of the Surcote and the lady whom he had rescued, filled with praise and gratitude for his heroic effort. King Arthur himself publicly thanked him, admitting that such a one as he ought indeed to belong to the Fellowship of the Round Table. 'I was wrong to doubt you, Sir Knight. I gladly welcome you among us. But first, I would know more of your lineage and birth.'

'I can tell you that easily,' replied the youth. 'I was born in Gaul, the son of a Roman senator named Viamundus. My true name is Gawain, but I have been known as the Knight of the Surcote for a long time.'

'It is my task to tell you that you are wrong about much of this,' said the king, smiling.

'How is it,' demanded the knight in some astonishment, 'that you know more of my origin than I?'

'You shall learn all once we are returned to Caerleon,' replied the king.

It thus befell that when the tired army was safely returned to the court, King Arthur called before him King Lot of Orkney and his queen, Morgause, and announced before all the court that the Knight of the Surcote was truly their son. 'And thus,' he added, embracing the astonished youth, 'you are my nephew. And I am glad to acknowledge you before all this company.'

Then there was great rejoicing, as you may imagine, with the son restored to his parents, and the brave hero discovered to be the king's own nephew. And though this story differs from that told by Master Thomas, yet I feel it tells more truthfully the origins of Sir Gawain. And, as you shall see, many more adventures befell him thereafter, some that are omitted from the great book of King Arthur.

EXPLICIT THE STORY OF GAWAIN'S RISE.
INCIPIT THE CROP-EARED DOG.

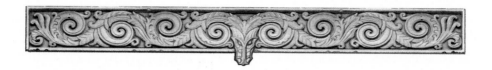

21: SIR GAWAIN AND THE CROP-EARED DOG

KING ARTHUR, THE SON OF UTHER, THE SON OF AMBROSIUS, THE SON OF CONSTANTINE, CONVENED A GREAT HUNT IN THE GREAT WOOD ACROSS THE PLAIN OF WONDER. NEVER IN ALL THE WORLD WAS SUCH A GATHERING BROUGHT TOGETHER. MORE WARRIORS AND WOMEN, SINGERS AND POETS, MUSICIANS AND SERVANTS WERE THERE THAN THERE ARE JOINTS IN THE HUMAN BODY, OR DAYS IN THE YEAR, OR PLANTS ON THE EARTH. BY MY ACCOUNT THERE WERE TWELVE SENIOR KNIGHTS OF THE ROUND TABLE, TWELVE KNIGHTS OF COUNSEL, TWELVE KNIGHTS OF ACTIVITY, TWO HUNDRED AND TWO SCORE OTHER KNIGHTS OF THE TABLE, AND SEVEN HUNDRED KNIGHTS OF THE ROYAL HOUSEHOLD.

✣ ✤ ✣

AS WAS THE custom of the time, a hunt was convened, and the great company spread out through the Great Wood and across the Plain of Wonder, following the hunt through glen and valley and thicket. But on that first day the king sat in his own tent and listened to the voices and whistles of the huntsmen, the barking of the dogs, the shouts of the nobles and the songs of the bards and said nothing. At the end of the day the hunt returned with word that they had seen not so much as a hare all day long, and so, as they all foregathered for the evening feast, they petitioned the great king to ask

what they should do. King Arthur replied in a loud clear voice:

'My people, there are many *gaesa* upon me (by which he meant that a command was laid upon him that he could not refuse) and one of them is that I must convene this great hunt once every seventeen years, and if the first day is unsuccessful, then I must remain for the second, and the third, and so on until the hunt has brought back sufficient spoils.'

When he had said this the king looked around upon every side and saw coming toward him a young knight dressed in a tunic of fine silk and armour of the utmost

248

splendour, and with a mantle of gold around him. At his side he had a beautiful sword with a hilt of gold, and about his brows a thin diadem of gold, and in his right hand two white ash spears, and in the other he carried a brightly glowing lantern. He was as handsome as the dawn, with fair, white skin and clear grey eyes, and shapely mouth. There was not a single thing about him with which you could have found fault.

The stranger came right up and stood before King Arthur, who asked who he was and what he wanted there.

'I have come to seek combat with three of your best knights, for I have heard that there is not a king in all the world with a better or more glorious band of heroes, and I would find out for myself if this is true.'

When they heard this the entire court changed in a moment from a mood of welcome to one of hostility, and they rose up against the knight with the lantern as though he was their bitterest foe. He, on seeing this, thrust the edge of his shield into the earth, and his two spears beside it, and drew his gold-hilted sword, and stood ready for combat. King Arthur looked about him and asked whom among his household would accept this challenge.

The White Knight, the son of the King of France, stepped forward, and the two of them drew apart and engaged in combat. The very ground quaked at their meeting, and both fought with all their strength. But the White Knight was no match for the stranger, and in a little while he stood beaten and bound as a prisoner to he whom everyone there was beginning to call the Knight of the Lantern.

Then the Black Knight, who was the son of the King of Caolachs, came forward in his turn, and engaged in mighty battle against the stranger. But the Knight of the Lantern defeated him just as easily as he had the first challenger and bound him. Then he took on several more of Arthur's knights, and none might stand against him save Sir Gawain, who was but lately come to the court, and who, despite his youth, held his own until the Knight of the Lantern gave a great cry and departed suddenly, wrapping a dark druid mist around him so that none might see where he went. After he was gone, all of Arthur's men, and the king himself, could in no wise leave that place, but stood still and frozen, able only to speak and move their eyes – all except for Sir Gawain who, because he had come so close to defeating the Knight of the Lantern, was still able to move freely.

Then Arthur looked around at his knights and said: 'Evil betide this day! If word of this gets out, we shall be mocked until we enter the grave! We must find someone to help us defeat the Knight of the Lantern.'

'Sire, may I not go and find a way?' asked Sir Gawain. But King Arthur answered that his nephew was too untried, despite him holding his own against the knight.

So the whole court waited, held fast by the knight's spell, some within the king's tent and others outside, until the sun rode high in the sky and all began to feel a great thirst. Then King Arthur spoke to Sir Gawain: 'I wish you would fetch us some water.'

'Sire,' replied the young knight. 'If you will lend me your arms and tell me where I may find a well, I shall gladly go.'

'Alas,' said Arthur. 'The only spring near here, which is the Fountain of Virtues, lies in a valley full of monsters and evil creatures. I would not order anyone to go there, even if I was dying of thirst.'

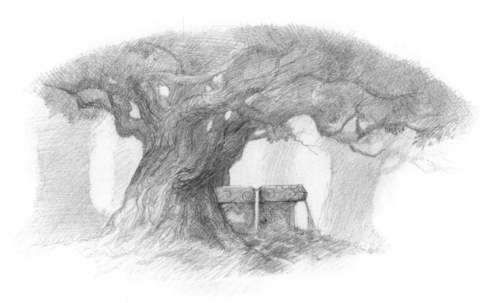

→ *The Fountain of Virtues* ←

'Say not so!' cried Gawain. 'I shall go at once, for it would be improper for anyone less than a knight to go on your behalf.'

'My thanks to you, Sir Gawain,' said the king. 'Be sure to take the Quartered Cup, which holds enough for fifty men, and go west of here across the Plain of Wonders until you come to the fountain.'

Sir Gawain set out at once, wearing the king's own armour, and took the best route that he knew to the Fountain of Virtues, which was a very fair and marvellous place, and beside which grew a mighty tree. Gawain filled the great cup to the brim, and as he did so he heard a roaring noise coming from the roots of the tree. As he looked, he saw a strange grey dog come forth. It had neither ears nor tail, and so thick and shaggy was its pelt that one could have stuck apples on the spikes of it, and around its neck it wore a heavy iron collar.

The Crop-Eared Dog came bounding up to Gawain, and to his astonishment it spoke to him in a low and growling voice, asking him why he came there.

'I did not come here to tell stories,' answered the knight. 'I am more used to giving gold and silver to *listen* to tales rather than tell them to others.'

'I ask in the hope that you will tell me your news willingly,' said the dog. 'If you do, I shall be your friend. If not, I will destroy you.'

'Perhaps you could indeed,' answered Gawain. 'But I tell you I am come in search of water for King Arthur, whom I serve. My name is Gawain of Orkney. Now you have all my news.'

When he heard this the dog welcomed the knight most heartily and asked him why the great King Arthur should send one so young across the Plain of Wonders.

Gawain told him all about the Knight of the Lantern and how he had defeated Arthur's knights, before vanishing utterly.

'Now I perceive,' said the Crop-Eared Dog, 'that the Knight of the Lantern has laid a binding spell upon your king and his men. Believe me that there is no one else in all this land who can release them except me. Therefore, take me back with you, and I will help. For I fear that the Knight of the Lantern will return tonight to cut off the heads of all those whom he has bespelled. And I assure you that there is not a man in all the kingdom who could beat him in a fight unaided.'

Gawain, accompanied by the Crop-Eared Dog, returned to the Great Wood. He gave the king and his knights a drink from the great cup, but scarcely had they done so when they saw the Knight of the Lantern approaching with his drawn sword in one hand and his lantern held high in the other.

When the Crop-Eared Dog saw the knight approaching, he ran full tilt at him. And when the Knight of the Lantern saw him coming, he turned around and departed as swiftly as he had come, leaving such a dark mist of druidry behind him that no one could follow him even if they tried. Then Gawain and the dog returned to King Arthur, and the dog said that Sir Gawain and he should go to the top of a certain hill in the morning and there they would be sure to pick up the track of the knight. Then he released the spell which had bound the king and his men, and there was much rejoicing because of this, as well as much wonder at the Crop-Eared Dog.

Early next morning Gawain and the dog arose and prepared to depart; and King Arthur and his knights and the women of the court all wished them well, for though there were those who would have prevented the youth from setting forth, he would not be gainsaid. They went to the hill that the dog had indicated and there the beast cast about until it caught the scent of the Knight of the Lantern. The dog declared that he had gone over the sea, where they must follow if they wished to capture him.

Gawain returned to King Arthur and asked for a ship, and the king granted it gladly and sent word to the harbour that a craft should be prepared, and that it should be well victualed. Then Sir Gawain and the Crop-Eared Dog set out and went aboard the ship, and the knight raised the great sails and they sailed out of the harbour and onto the tumultuous sea.

✤ ✤ ✤

THEY WERE ON the ocean for five days and five nights, and at the end of that time they sighted an island.

'Steer for that place,' said the Crop-Eared Dog.

Sir Gawain brought the ship safely to shore and dropped anchor. Then they went ashore and wandered about the island, finding it the fairest place, filled with lush vegetation, tall trees and streams of pure water that fed the green earth. And they came at last to a beautiful house and went within. There was a great fire burning on the hearth, and tables spread with cloths of pure flax, and golden plates thereon, laden with fine food. But there was not a soul to be seen except for one old man, of whom Gawain asked to know who the owner of the house was and what was the name of the island.

The old man stared at him rudely and said: 'Were you brought up in a cave that you have not heard of this place?'

This made Gawain so angry that he drew his sword and would have struck the old man, had he not cried peace and praised the young knight's strength. Then he told them that the name of the place was the Dark Island, and that a great champion lived there. Gawain asked about the Knight of the Lantern, and the old man replied that he had been there lately but that now he was gone.

'Tell me where he has gone if you know,' demanded Gawain.

'That is no hard thing,' said the old man. 'He has gone to a place of his in a land not far from here. On the shore of that land there is a great cave, and beside it a tower which is called the Tower of the Dark Cave. The Knight of the Lantern always stays there when he comes to that land. It has two doors, one issuing on the land, the other on the sea, and at the sea-door he keeps a ship always ready. But let me tell you now that he is most likely to flee before you to the Island of Warrior Women. For there is his greatest friend and ally: the Druidess Abhlach. You will never encounter anyone stronger in magic than she, and she guards certain treasures which belong to the Knight of the Lantern, for as long as these are protected, he cannot be hurt, much less killed.'

'Tell me more of this,' demanded Gawain.

'I will tell you everything I know, for I have no love for the Knight of the Lantern,' said the old man. 'Regarding these treasures I can tell you that there are three: the cup of the King of Iorruaidh, which the king's daughter, Deilbhghrein, which means 'Shape of the Sun', gave him as a wooing gift. While he has this the knight's strength will not abate even though he fights for a day and a night. The second treasure is the cauldron of the King of France, which the Knight of the Lantern took after he slew that king. While he has this, if he washes himself in it once every year, no age will fall upon him. The third treasure is

the ring which belonged to the King of India, who is in truth the knight's father. Its virtue is that whoever looks at the jewel which is set therein then any wound he has will at once be healed. Now I have told you everything I know.'

Throughout this, the dog began to growl, and when the old man had finished, he let forth a great howl. Then he fell silent and lay down upon the earth and spoke not at all. Gawain thanked the old man, who made them welcome and invited them to share his master's table. This they did, with pleasure, and afterwards slept that night in the house. But on the morrow they rose early, and Sir Gawain asked how they might find their way to the cave and the tower that was the Knight of the Lantern's stronghold. The old man gave them directions willingly, and they went aboard the ship and set sail as they were directed. When they came close to the land where the knight lived the Crop-Eared Dog said: 'Let us devise a scheme to defeat our enemy. Take the collar and chain that is about my neck and go onto the land. Then, when you are close to the tower, shake the chain so that the knight will think it is I who am coming. Then he will flee from the seaward door into his ship; but I shall be hidden there and will fight with him. If by chance he ventures forth from the other door, you will be there to stop him.'

'That is well said,' answered Gawain.

But while the two comrades were laying their trap, Abhlach the Druidess, was aware of them and all they planned to do. And she put upon her a magical green cloak and made a great leap which took her from the Island of the Warrior Women to the Tower of the Dark Cave. There she found the Knight of the Lantern and told him what was afoot. At this he grew fearful, until Abhlach said to him that she had brought a magical curragh with her, and that in this they could escape without being seen, even by the Crop-Eared Dog.

And so it was. The druidess and the knight got into the magical boat and sped across the surface of the sea unseen. Only when they were almost out of sight did the dog, who was hidden aboard the ship, know that they were there, by which time it was too late to capture them. The dog swam to the shore and found Sir Gawain and told him what had happened. 'Be not downcast,' said the dog. 'I promise you we shall discover the knight if we have to search the whole world.'

✠ ✠ ✠

SIR GAWAIN AND the Crop-Eared Dog set forth again on the ship and did not stop until they reached the Island of the Warrior Women and went ashore there. But Abhlach and the Knight of the Lantern were already gone, and there waiting to meet them were the Queen of the Island and all her women, armed to the teeth and ready to defend themselves against all-comers.

So there began a long and furious battle there on the shore of the island, and the outcome of it was that Sir Gawain, with the help of the Crop-Eared Dog, won a great victory, and when they left the island, they had with them the three treasures belonging to the Knight of the Lantern, which had been left behind in the speed of his flight. And when they sailed away in pursuit of their enemies, they left Abhlach's hall in flames.

✠ ✠ ✠

THEY WERE THREE days and three nights on the sea, until Sir Gawain saw land to the west and told of it to the dog.

'Let us go there,' said the dog. 'It is the home of the King of the Little Isle, who is father-in-law to the Knight of the Lantern. I am certain our quarry is close by.'

They sailed in close to the shore and dropped anchor, and the dog gave Gawain a silver whistle and told him to go ahead to the king's hall and to pretend to be a bard. 'If you play the whistle, it will be as though you were the best musician in the world. And if you see the Knight of the Lantern, blow it once, sharply, and I shall hear it and come swiftly. Meanwhile, I shall remain outside and wrap myself in a druid mist so that no one can see me.'

Gawain did as he was bidden and went straight to the house and knocked. He said that he brought a poem for the king, at which he was admitted, and went inside. There he saw the Knight of the Lantern, and at once he blew the whistle sharply. The Crop-Eared Dog burst into the hall and began battling with the warriors who were gathered there. But the Knight of the Lantern recognized the whistle, and once again fled swiftly from that place.

Then Gawain and the Crop-Eared Dog fought side by side until they had defeated all the warriors of the place and killed the King of the Little Isle. Then the dog said they should wait for nine days and nine nights, for at the end of that time the knight would be sure to return, thinking them long gone and wishing to know his father-in-law's fate.

This they did. And at the end of that time the Knight of the Lantern did indeed return. When he saw the corpses that lay about in the hall as they had fallen, and became aware of Gawain and his companion, he gave a great cry and an even greater leap which took him into the clouds above the hall and none might know where he had gone. Greatly disappointed, the knight and the dog departed that place, having first set fire to the hall. Then they went forth again upon the sea.

✠ ✠ ✠

THE STORY DOES not tell how long they sailed or where they went, or what adventures overtook them. But when next we hear of them they were off the coast of Egypt, and when Gawain asked about that land the Crop-Eared Dog told him it was ruled over by a king who was also father-in-law to the Knight of the Lantern – for he had married this king's daughter before that of the King of the Little Isle. 'Furthermore,' said the dog, 'the champion of this land, who is called Inneireadh, is the foster-brother and friend to the Knight of the Lantern, for both were brought up by the daughter of the King of the Land of the Living, who is therefore their foster-mother.'

Then Gawain looked at the dog in silence for a time. Then he asked: 'I do not know how you come to know so much of the knight and his family. Nor do I know aught of you. I would ask you, since we have been comrades this long time and have journeyed far together until I am quite worn out with it – tell me who you really are, and who put you in the form you now wear – for as surely as I know my own name I cannot believe that you were always in this form.'

'I do not like these questions,' growled the dog. 'But since we are comrades indeed, I shall answer them. I am called Alastrann, and I am the son of the King of India and Niamh,

the daughter of the King of the Caolachs. Four sons she bore to my father, as well as I, but then she died and the king my father took another wife, who was called Libearn Lanfolar, daughter of the King of Greece. So you see that the Knight of the Lantern is her son, and thus also my half-brother.'

Gawain was amazed to hear this; but the dog had yet more to tell.

'It came about one day that Queen Libearn was praising her son and telling him that he was heir to vast lands and riches, when a passing youth answered that the king had other heirs indeed, five sons in all. This made the queen angry, for she had known nothing of myself and my brothers. When the king returned that evening from the hunt, she demanded to know the truth, and why it was that she had never seen these sons. The king told her that it was indeed true and that the reason why she had not seen his other sons was because they were all leading armies in different lands and would not return unless he summoned them.

'The queen pretended to be satisfied with his, but secretly she longed to destroy the king's other sons, so that her own child might rule India after him. So she sent word to her father the King of Greece, asking him to come and visit her, and to bring an army with him. And just as she had hoped, when the king her husband heard of the army approaching, he sent for his own sons, and their armies, to return home at once.

'So it was that all were gathered to meet the King of Greece, and when the gathering was complete there was no one who spoke more highly of myself and my brothers than the queen. But secretly she spoke to her father and told him that unless we were killed her own son would not inherit the kingdom. The king her father thought on this and deemed it right. Therefore, he pretended that a great war had broken out in his own lands between himself and the King of France, and he asked our father to accompany him with his army and fight at his side. And he advised that we should be left at home with the queen to care for the land.

'To this our father agreed, and set forth with the King of Greece, as he thought, to war. As soon as he was safely gone, Queen Libearn ordered a great feast in our honour. But in truth she drugged us all and made us drunk. Then, while we slept, she used her magic to put upon us the shapes of dogs.

'When we awoke, it was a desperate case! We ran away from that place and began to wreak great damage upon the lands around there. But in a while, we realized that our enemies were the King of Greece and Queen Libearn, and so we went there and began ravaging the lands until news of us spread far and wide and the king's counsellors advised him to gather as many dogs as he could and to set them upon us, to hunt us down and kill us before we destroyed all the wealth of Greece.

'At this time, we were living in a valley which had become known as the Valley of the Rough Dogs because of us. There the hosts of our enemies came and found us, and there was a great battle between them and our-selves, and all my brothers perished. I myself almost lost my life for, having retreated to a certain cave, I was surrounded, and the host was set to burn me out. But I grew angry and desperate, and drawing upon all my strength I ran forth and attacked my enemies. I can tell you that I did great damage to them in that place, and in the end I escaped and ran straight to the King of Greece and threw myself down before him. He in his wisdom

decided to spare me when he heard me speak, and knowing nothing of the queen's dark druidry, took me home with him to the city of Athens and put this great chain around my neck.'

Sir Gawain marvelled greatly at this strange and terrible tale. And when the dog fell silent, he asked him how he came to lose his ears and tail.

'I will tell you,' said the dog. 'Though it is the saddest story of my life.' After a moment he continued: 'The King of Greece soon saw that I had human senses, and I think divined that I was under an enchantment, though a part of the queen's magic forbade me to speak of the spell that she had laid upon me. But one day, as I knew he would, the Knight of the Lantern came to court, and when he learned of my existence, quickly realized that I was one of his half-brothers, and so wished to kill me. But the king had seen to it that I was well protected, and so my evil foe set about another scheme. He spoke to the king's daughter, who was his own mother's child, and persuaded her, with great cunning, to have me killed. One day, when I lay doz-ing in the garden, she came and laid a spell of sleep upon me. Then she took a sharp knife, meaning to wound me, but found that because of the enchantment laid upon me, all she could do was cut off my ears and tail. At that I awoke with a great howl and struck her down dead upon the ground.

'You may imagine there was a great outcry, and soldiers and warriors came at me from every side, but I defeated them all, and in the end I fought with my former protector, the king, who was wild with grief at the death of his daughter. Well, I slew him also, and countless numbers of his guard, and drove the Knight of the Lantern from that place.

I have been pursuing him ever since until we met. And now you have all my story,' said the Crop-Eared Dog.

'Never did I hear a stranger or sadder tale,' said Sir Gawain. Then the two companions went ashore into Egypt, and the king of that land, when he heard that Sir Gawain and the Crop-Eared Dog had come into his lands, sent messengers to welcome them and bring them before him. He greeted them both with kindness, for as he said, the Knight of the Lantern was no friend to him since he had divorced his daughter and married another – namely the daughter of the King of the Little Isle, whom Gawain and the dog had slain. But when they asked for news of their quarry, the king could tell them nothing.

'However,' he said, 'It may be that my daughter, who was once his wife, may know more. She lives now in seclusion in a distant part of the land, in a place called the Fortress of Obscurity. Go to her and it may well be that she can help you.'

✠ ✠ ✠

EARLY NEXT DAY Sir Gawain and the Crop-Eared Dog set out once more and soon arrived at the Fortress of Obscurity, where they were made welcome, for the King of the Little Isle's daughter had no love for the Knight of the Lantern since he had used her badly, so that she wished him nought but ill fortune. When she heard how they were pursuing him she said: 'I believe the wretch is in a place called the Tower of the Three Gables, far to the west of here. There is only one way into it and that is through a dark cavern that has a most sinister reputation. He is there now, I am sure, with my brother, the champion, Inneireadh.'

So they set off at once, and when they reached the tower the Crop-Eared Dog saw the Knight of the Lantern playing chess with Inneireadh; and when the knight saw who was watching them, he turned himself and his companion into two gnats and flew out of the window. But in his haste, he left behind his lantern, and the Crop-Eared Dog took it with him and returned with it to Gawain. 'Now we have a great part of the knight's power,' said the dog. And Gawain looked at the lantern and asked how the knight came by it and therefore by his name.

'I will tell you,' said the dog. 'Though you ask too many questions. The King of Scythia had two daughters, Beibheann and Beadhchrotha were their names, and both of them very fair indeed, so that many kings and princes fought over them. But Beibheann declared that she would only marry the man who could bring the lantern of Bobh of Benburb from the lands of Cruithneach. And the property of this lantern was that if he who possessed it should be wounded, he had only to look upon it and he would be healed.

'Well, you may be sure that the knight set out at once to get the lantern. He went straight to the land of Bobh and demanded to borrow it. 'For if I do not have it, I shall take it by force of arms.' Bobh's porter laughed at this but went and fetched his master. Bobh came forth in his battle array and they fought a great battle. Suffering many wounds at the hands of his opponent, Bobh turned his back to return to his house and look upon the lantern, and at that the knight leapt after him and cut off his head. Then he went within and took the lantern, for no one gainsaid him. He returned to Scythia with the lantern, but when he arrived there he heard a strange and terrible tale. For the two sisters had both desired him so greatly that the elder had taken a knife and murdered the younger. For that crime she had been burned at the stake. And since both of them were dead the Knight of the Lantern left there and returned home with his prize. So you see,' concluded the dog, 'no good comes of anything to which he sets his mind.'

'That is a terrible tale indeed,' said Sir Gawain.

Having taken counsel of each other, they returned to their ship and left Egypt, sailing on until they reached an island called the Island of Light.

'We will get no word of our quarry there,' said the dog, and so they sailed on until they reached another island, and the name of that one was the Black Island. The dog explained that, once, its name had been the Island of the Sun, because the sun rose above it every morning. Now it was called the Black Island, because the Knight of the Lantern came here and fought with the champion of the place and slew him. Thereafter the sun rose no longer and so it gained a new name. Then the dog told Gawain: 'I know that there is a place along the shoreline called the Red Cave, and when he is here the Knight of the Lantern lives within it. I believe he is there now, with the champion Inneireadh. If you go there alone while I conceal myself nearby, they may be lured to come forth. Then I shall fall upon them also, and together we may defeat them.'

To this the two companions agreed. But they did not know that the Knight of the Lantern had overheard their plot through his druid-magic, and that he had at once devised a way to defeat them. He had four rods of magic power stolen from the champion of the island. They had the power to put anyone

to sleep for a day and a night if they were set around him. This is what the Knight of the Lantern did: he waited until the dog was hidden near the mouth of the cave and then he crept up close and set up the four rods so that the dog fell at once into a deep sleep. Then the knight rejoined the champion Inneireadh and together they went out and confronted Sir Gawain. So began a terrible battle with the two of them against the one of him, while the Crop-Eared Dog slept on. But we shall say no more of these events at this time but turn instead to King Arthur and his people.

✠ ✠ ✠

A WHOLE YEAR HAD passed since Sir Gawain departed, and in that time King Arthur and his court bemoaned his absence. They had no news of the knight, and wondered often where he was or if he still lived. So, at the end of the year the king dispatched ten ships to search for his nephew. The expedition included many of the greatest knights of the Round Table, including Sir Lancelot, Sir Galfas, Sir Lionel, Sir Bors, the White Knight and the Black Knight and many more.

The story does not tell of their adventures, but they followed the path of Gawain and the Crop-Eared Dog throughout all the lands where their adventures had taken them. And fate decreed that they arrived on the Black Island the very same day and the very same moment when the dog lay in enchanted sleep and Sir Gawain himself was being hard pressed by the Knight of the Lantern and his ally.

When he saw King Arthur's knights approaching, the Knight of the Lantern leapt up high into the air and vanished into the clouds, leaving the champion Inneireadh to fight on alone. When he saw this, Gawain's spirits rose in him and he renewed his attack and slew the champion in a moment. Then he greeted Arthur's knights with extreme gladness, and together they went in search of the Crop-Eared Dog and released him from his enchanted sleep.

'Now is the last of the knight's druidry taken from him,' said the dog when he saw the silver rods. 'If we can catch him now, we can easily overpower him.' And, though Arthur's warriors were eager for them all to return home together, neither Gawain nor the Crop-Eared Dog would hear of it, but desired to pursue their quarry once again. In the end, after much discussion, they bade farewell to their fellows and set forth once again upon the ocean.

✛ ✛ ✛

NINE MORE DAYS and nights they were sailing, until they sighted a fair and bountiful land that was called Sorcha. 'The king of this land is friendly to me,' said the dog. 'Let us go there and ask for news of the Knight of the Lantern.'

The King of Sorcha greeted them warmly and with great hospitality, for word of their great quest had gone throughout all the lands and he knew of their might and prowess. Indeed, he was somewhat fearful of them, and that night he made certain that both were given as much to drink as they could, until they both fell into a stupor. Then he ordered that the Crop-Eared Dog be taken away during the night, so that when Sir Gawain awoke with a headache in the morning no one could tell him anything of its whereabouts. This angered Gawain so much that he hastened into the court, and making a sudden leap at

the king, held him powerless and in fear of his life.

The king cried out for mercy then and offered Sir Gawain all the gold he could carry. Then Gawain knew that he must be cunning, so he pretended to agree and to forget all about the Crop-Eared Dog. But in truth he sought to discover by secret means what fate had befallen his comrade.

And it befell that soon after, as Sir Gawain was walking in the garden of the king's palace, he saw the Crop-Eared Dog himself coming towards him, and with him was the Knight of the Lantern, bound and fettered as a prisoner. Astonished, Gawain demanded to know what had happened.

'That is a long tale,' said the Crop-Eared Dog. 'But though I still say that you ask too many questions, I will tell it briefly. It was the druidess Abhlach who took me away while you and I were both too drunk to notice. She laid a spell of sleep upon me and, when I awoke, we were already at sea. I rose up in a rage and struck the druidess with a single blow that laid her dead upon the deck. Then I jumped overboard and swam until I came to the Island of the Speckled Mountain, for there I judged I might find the Knight of the Lantern, since the champion of that island was a great ally of his. But I found only the champion, and so I fought him and slew him and then jumped in the sea again.

'This time I swam for seven days until I arrived at the Island of the Black Valley. But the knight was not there either, so I killed that champion also, and swam on. Nor did I stop until I came to the Island of the Naked Monks, for it was there that the Knight of the Lantern first learned his druidry. But he was not there, and the monks fell upon me, so that I was forced to defend myself and kill them all. Then, when I had rested a while, I set myself to swim on once more.

'Again, I did not stop until I reached the Isle of the Dead, which is so called because any man or women who comes ashore there, and falls asleep, is found dead in the morning. But those who live there already – who, by the way, are all women – are not affected by any of this.

'Well, to tell it shortly, I came there and went to the cave where the women of the island were wont to sleep, and there at last I found the Knight of the Lantern, and he took the form of a lion and fled from me. But I chased him and caught and bound him. The knight then regained his own form, and pleaded with me, and spoke of our kinship, and begged me not to kill him. For, he said, if I spared him he would restore me to my rightful shape and do whatever else I wanted until the end of my life or his. So I made him swear an oath to this, by sun, moon and stars, and by every creature in the world that would bear witness. And now I am here, and here is the Knight of the Lantern, who will do no more evil, and soon I shall be restored to my own shape.'

With much joy and delight Gawain and the Crop-Eared Dog went before the King of Sorcha and told him everything and showed him the Knight of the Lantern, who was much cowed. That night they dined royally, and in the morning took their leave of the king. They set sail at once and went to the island that is called the Isle of Shaping, for there everyone receives their rightful form. There the Knight of the Lantern gave back to the Crop-Eared Dog his own shape, which was truly the finest that might be seen upon any man from the rising of the sun to the setting of the moon. Thus Alastrann, who was no longer the Crop-Eared Dog, forgave the Knight of the Lantern, who swore to serve him from that day forth.

Then the two heroes returned to Camelot the Golden, where King Arthur and his Fellowship came forth to greet them. All their long story was told by Sir Gawain, since the dog (who was a dog no longer) still disliked the telling of tales, and a great celebration was held in which even the Knight of the Lantern took part, serving his newly restored brother as a squire might have done. And afterwards, it is said, he mended his ways, and became the first lieutenant of Alastrann when he inherited the crown of India. As for Sir Gawain, he sorely missed his old friend and went often in later times to visit him. And in due time Alastrann, who had been the Crop-Eared Dog, inherited his father's lands and became a famous champion. But of this the story tells no more.

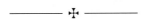

EXPLICIT THE TALE OF THE CROP-EARED DOG.
IMPLICIT THE ADVENTURES AT TARN WATHELYN.

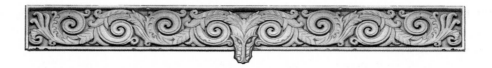

22: THE ADVENTURES AT TARN WATHELYN

✛

I

ONE DAY, AT THE EDGE OF WINTER, KING ARTHUR AND QUEEN GUINEVERE RODE HUNTING IN THE DARK FOREST OF INGLEWOOD, NOT FAR FROM THE CITY OF CARLISLE, WHERE THE KING HELD COURT AT THAT TIME. WITH THE ROYAL COUPLE WENT SIR GAWAIN, SIR CADOR OF CORNWALL AND SIR KAY THE SENESCHAL. ALL WERE DRESSED IN THE FINEST CLOTHING IMAGINABLE. SIR GAWAIN, AS WAS HIS CUSTOM, WORE GREEN, TRIMMED WITH RIBBONS AND GEMS; QUEEN GUINEVERE HAD ON A BLUE CLOAK, TRIMMED WITH FUR AND SPRINKLED WITH PRECIOUS JEWELS; KING ARTHUR, MOST SPLENDID OF ALL, WAS DRESSED IN SCARLET TRIMMED WITH ERMINE.

✛ ✛ ✛

THE BELLING OF the hounds and the cries of the huntsmen sent shivers through the air, ringing out across the cold lands. All that morning they chased a herd of deer through woodland and across open moors, slaying many, until finally the king blew his horn to summon back men and hounds to rest. Only Gawain, who rode with the queen, failed to answer. They had gone far ahead through vales and valleys and by woods and glens unknown to them and did not hear the call. They grew tired and sought a sheltered spot in a green grove, shaded by

laurel trees and bordered on one side by a dark and solitary tarn.

There they witnessed a strange and terrible vision. The sky, which had been fair until that moment, turned suddenly dark as midnight. Rain began to fall heavily, turning swiftly to sleet and then, in moments, to snow. The queen and Sir Gawain hurried to take what shelter they could beneath the trees, and from there they saw something frightful arise from the waters of the tarn.

Human in shape, though bony and wasted, shreds of clothing, clods of earth and what might have been rotten flesh, clung to it. It rose into the air and advanced across the water, shrieking and yammering like one in torment, all the while wringing its hands.

'A curse! A curse!' the vile thing screeched. 'A curse upon the body that bore me! Because of my life, my suffering consumes me!'

It made straight for Gawain and the queen, who backed away from it in fear. Guinevere cried aloud and raised her hands in horror.

'This must be caused by an eclipse of the sun,' Sir Gawain said, hoping to calm the queen's fears. 'I have heard that strange things may happen at such times. I will speak with this creature and try to find out what it wants. Perhaps I may calm it.'

Inwardly quaking, Gawain approached the edge of the tarn where the creature now hung stationary. It seemed confused. staring madly before it. Its eyes were like hollow pits, red and glowing, and as he approached Gawain saw with revulsion that a toad crouched in the hollow of its throat, and that snakes crawled around its wasted body.

Gawain drew his sword – though he doubted it would be of any use against such a thing – and demanded to know what business the spectre had with them. The ghost's jaw and all its body began to shake as though it would fall apart. Gawain called upon God to protect him and again demanded to know what the fell being wanted and who or what it was.

Gradually the shaking and shivering ceased. The red eyes turned upon the face of Gawain. 'Once I was the fairest of women,' it said, in a low, grating voice. 'Kings were among my ancestors. Now I am come to this. And so I have come to speak to your queen, for once I was a queen myself, more fair than Isolt or even Mariole the bride of Torec. Treasure

and beauty were mine, and I had power over vast lands. But now I am lost, exiled in eternal cold. Pain entraps me, and I lie at night in a bed of coldest clay. See then, what death has done to me, sir knight, and bring your lady hither, that I may speak with her.'

Moved to pity by this fearful account, Gawain returned to where the queen stood, shivering with cold and fear.

'Lady,' he said. 'The spirit would speak with you. Though it is a fearful thing I believe it means us no harm.'

Drawing her cloak closely about her, Guinevere advanced at Gawain's side to the edge of the tarn and looked with horror upon the spirit.

'Welcome, Queen Guinevere,' the apparition said in its low and earthy voice. 'Look what death has done to me. Once I had roses in my cheeks, and skin soft as the lily. How easily I laughed. Now I am brought down to this, tied to this spot with invisible chains. And for all the youth and loveliness and power you now possess – in time you shall become as I am. As shall every king and queen now living. Death will bring you to this, have no doubt.'

Then the spirit, trembling and rattling, edged nearer. Its red eyes glared at the queen. 'Do you not know me?' it hissed.

Guinevere forced herself to look more closely at the apparition.

'Truly,' she said, 'I do not believe so.'

For a moment the spirit hung still, then it rose up high into the air and flew across the tarn and back, shrieking all the while. Coming to rest close to Sir Gawain and the queen, so that they could smell the odour of the grave, it spoke again.

'Guinevere, once I was your mother.'

The queen turned pale and raised her hands to her cheeks. Tears coursed down her face and her breath came almost as raggedly as the vision's. Scarcely able to stand, so that Gawain moved closer to catch her if she fell, the queen answered: 'Are you truly my mother?' To which the spirit replied, grimly: 'Aye. I am she that bore you. And by this shall you know it. Once I broke a vow, which only you and I know of.'

'This chills my blood,' said the queen at last. 'What can I do to ease your pain? Are there Masses to be said, or prayers to be offered that will help you find rest?'

'Prayers melt in the air like dew, and all the wealth in the world goes away at last,' intoned the spirit dolefully. 'Perhaps if enough Masses are said I shall indeed find rest. But more important than this are the deeds you can do while you are yet living. Offer mercy to all who need it, give food to the needy. These things alone will help me – as they will help you in time to come. Remember, life is brief.'

Gawain, silent all this while, now spoke up. 'May I ask,' said he, 'what destiny awaits those who, like myself, must fight in battles and warfare, who invade lands not rightfully theirs, and may massacre those who deserve to live?'

The apparition turned its red eyes upon him. 'Your king is greedy, as are all kings. All the lands he reaches out towards fall to his hand. King Ban and King Arawn are dead, and many others with them. In time to come even Rome itself shall bow the knee to Arthur. Yet his end shall come sooner than he would wish. At the height of his powers, he shall be laid low on the shore of the sea. The Goddess of Fortune shall turn her Wheel against him.'

The creature paused and seemed to be seeking new strength to continue. Gawain had grown pale at the words it spoke. Now it addressed him further.

'I tell you this, Sir Gawain. You should leave here now. One is coming who shall challenge you at Carlisle. Who knows if you will survive his coming?'

At this Sir Gawain stood back; fear rose within him for all his courage. The spirit rose high into the air again and declared: 'Soon others will come who will bring sorrow and strife to Britain. You, Sir Gawain, shall die in a steep valley at the hand of one you now call friend. Arthur himself shall fall in Cornwall, slain by one who carries a shield of sable with a saltire engrailed in silver upon it. Now this one is but a child, playing at ball, but he shall grow to manhood and shall conquer all. On that day the Fellowship of the Round Table shall perish, and the dream of Camelot the Golden shall end. This is all that I can say. Remember me. Hold these things in your hearts.'

The spirit's voice trailed away mournfully, and a most terrible silence fell.

As Guinevere and Gawain watched, the ghost began to withdraw, floating away across the lake and dissolving amid the trees like smoke. At once the sky began to clear, the rain and wind ceased, and the sun shone again. The winding of the king's hunting horn came to their ears and they realized that they were but a short distance from the rest of the hunt.

Thither they returned and told all that had occurred, and many were the grim looks shared by the company that day. Guinevere especially looked upon her lord with new eyes and thought perhaps what might come of her love for Sir Lancelot, while Arthur wondered at his end at the hands of a knight with a sable shield, remembering perhaps the killing of innocents who had died at his command for fear of one that would come to do

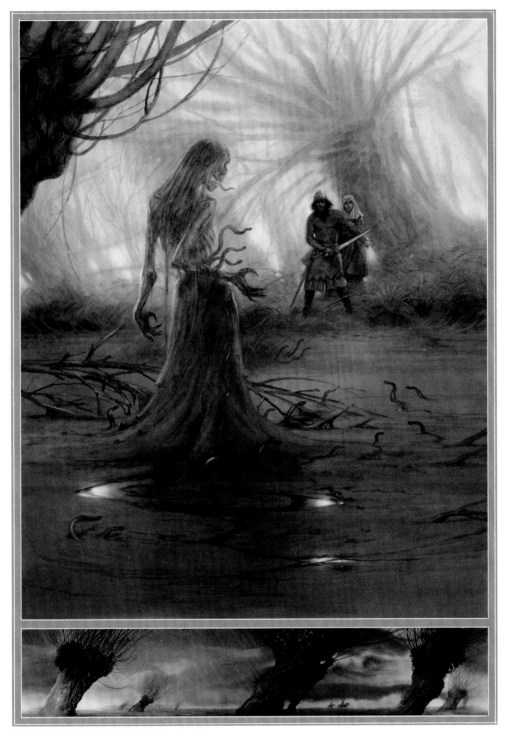

PLATE 6: 'Human in shape, though bony and wasted, shreds of clothing, clods of earth
and what might have been rotten flesh, clung to it'

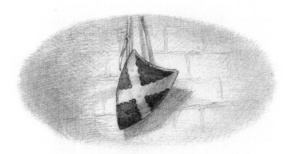

↠ Mordred's Shield ↞

him harm.* Gawain, in turn, contemplated his death-day in a steep valley by one he named friend. But none spoke of these things aloud.

For myself I can only marvel at this tale. For it seems that the spirit who had once been the queen's mother saw much that was to come, and which Master Thomas wrote of in his great book.

II

BUT THIS IS not the end of the tale, for that night, as the company were seated at supper in the hall of Randalholme, home to one of the king's great knights, where they had withdrawn to rest from the exertions of the day, there came a commotion at the entrance to the hall, and into the presence of the king and queen and the knights came a strange procession. First came two musicians, playing on cittern and cymbal; next came a lady mounted upon a palfrey leading a knight in full armour with visor lowered.

---

* This is the tale told by Master Thomas, that King Arthur on a black day ordered the killing of firstborn children to destroy Mordred, the child of his incest with his half-sister, Morgause. But of that story I shall make no further mention here.

All eyes were upon the lady, for they thought her the most beautiful creature they had ever seen. Her gown was of grass green silk, her white cloak embroidered with colourful birds, her hair caught up in a net of precious stones, over which she wore a coronet of brightest gold. The knight too was magnificently clad, in mail so polished that the torchlight illuminating the hall was reflected back from it. The knight's shield was of silver, with the arms of three black boars' heads, fierce and challenging, painted upon it.

Up to the dais on which the royal party were seated rode these two, and all the while the musicians continued to play. Then they fell silent, and the lady addressed the king thus: 'My lord, here is a wandering knight in search of reparation. Will you receive him as befits your reputation?'

'My lady,' answered the king with his customary courtesy. 'I bid you both a warm welcome. Tell me whence you come and what your purpose is here?'

Then the knight lifted his visor and spoke haughtily. 'I am Sir Galeron of Galloway and I come in search of recompense for the hurts you have done me, King Arthur!'

'What hurts are these?' asked Arthur. 'Do I know you?'

'As to that,' answered Sir Galeron, 'I neither know nor care. Once I held lands in Cumnock, in Cunninghame and Kyle, in Lomond and Lennox and the burnished hills of Lothian. All these lands are now given over to Sir Gawain – by you, lord King. Thus am I come to challenge any knight here to stand against me for the right of this matter. For never shall Sir Gawain hold my lands while I live unless he or his champion stand against me in single combat!'

'This matter is one that concerns me

greatly,' said the king. 'I know not how it came about that Sir Gawain received your lands while you yet live. Did you offend me in some manner that this occurred?'

Sir Galeron explained that he had been away many months on an adventure, and that in this time it had been decided that he must have died. So, Gawain was gifted with his lands. 'Thus I am come to reclaim them,' said Galeron. 'Let Sir Gawain or some other of your knights face me in combat, and if I win, I shall have my lands again.'

The king was thoughtful. 'This is not the way that I wish justice to be served in my land, but I see that you have been wronged, so I will grant you the right to single combat. Rest here tonight, and on the morrow we shall be glad to find someone to fight you.'

Sir Gawain, who had heard all that passed and was only restrained from breaking into the exchange by his courtesy, came forward to lead Sir Galeron and his lady and their retinue to rest in a splendid pavilion which had been set up outside the hall. Tables were placed within and rich food and drink in fine glasses brought and set before the couple. Then Gawain withdrew. Never once were words spoken between the two knights, save only courtesies, politely uttered, and if they exchanged looks of anger the story does not tell of it.

Having seen to the needs of their guests, Gawain returned to the hall, where Arthur addressed all the knights who were present.

'You have heard Sir Galeron's story and we have granted him the right to combat. Who will accept this challenge?'

'None should do so but I,' Sir Gawain said, before anyone else could speak. 'The matter is between him and me.'

'So be it,' Arthur said. 'But do not take the matter too lightly. Remember that my honour as well as yours is at stake.'

'I shall not forget, sire,' answered Sir Gawain. 'God shall be my guide and my guard in this matter. If this arrogant knight escapes without scathe it shall be no fault of mine.' But in his heart, he remembered the words of the spirit, that one would come to challenge him, and that winning was by no means certain.

Next morning the two champions prepared to do battle. They heard Mass and ate breakfast and made their way to the lists which had been set up overnight.

Both were clad in shining mail, decorated with gold. They saluted King Arthur and, setting spurs to their eager mounts, charged together and broke their spears upon each other's shields. Then, drawing their long-swords, they fell to hacking and hewing at each other with all their strength.

In one pass Gawain missed his stroke, and quick as light Sir Galeron struck, cutting through shield and mail and biting deep into Gawain's collarbone. Gawain groaned aloud and staggered. Sir Galeron's lady cheered him on, while Arthur and Guinevere looked askance.

Angry, hurt, and dazed, Gawain regathered his strength and struck back. Such was the power of his blow that he broke his opponent's sword, while his own blade pierced Sir Galeron's side. Maddened by the pain Galeron swung wildly. The blow missed its mark and cleft the head of Gawain's steed half off. The beast fell dead, and Gawain was thrown from its back.

Gawain wept. 'Brave Grisselle! You were the strongest and best steed ever to carry me. As God is my witness, I will have vengeance for this!'

Like wild beasts the two knights came together again. Their shields were dented and their armour shiny with blood. Gawain lunged beneath his opponent's guard and the blade cut through the mail and opened a wound in Galeron's belly.

The shock of the hurt made the knight stagger, and for a moment he stood as still as a stone; then, summoning up his remaining strength, he aimed a blow at Gawain's head which cut away part of his helm.

For a while longer the two knights continued to swing at each other, missing more often now as they grew weaker. Finally, they clung to each other, unable to lift their heavy swords.

Then Sir Galeron's lady cried out to the queen: 'Lady. I beg you to have mercy on this brave knight who has suffered so greatly.'

Guinevere turned to the king and asked him to make peace between the two men.

Meanwhile, Sir Galeron spoke to his opponent. 'Sir, I never believed there could be a knight as strong, or as brave, as you. I willingly give up all rights to my lands and I will freely do homage to your king.'

King Arthur arose and commanded them to leave off fighting. Others came forward to support them and to help them stand before him.

To Gawain, Arthur said: 'As a reward for your bravery I give you lands in Ireland and Burgundy. In return I ask you to relinquish all claims upon this knight's lands, which I gave you unknowing of his existence.'

To this Gawain readily agreed, and to his opponent he said: 'So brave a knight as you should sit at the Round Table. If my lord agrees, stay here awhile and learn to know us better.'

Sir Galeron gave thanks to the king and to Sir Gawain and promised to give his finest Friesian steed to recompense his opponent for the death of his own mount. King Arthur invited the knight to join the Fellowship, which he gladly accepted. Thus they were all accorded, and the knights taken to the surgeons to have their wounds searched and dressed.

The whole company now returned to Carlisle, where Sir Gawain and Sir Galeron rested from their battle. There, in a while, the latter married his lady, and Queen Guinevere, mindful of her encounter at Tarn Wathelyn, ordered Masses to be said for the repose of her mother's soul.

Thus ends the adventure of Tarn Wathelyn and the Forest of Inglewood, which were ever after known as places where adventures were certain to be found. And in time, as is known by all who have read the great book by Master Thomas, the prophecies of the ghost fell out as she had told them.

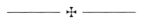

EXPLICIT THE ADVENTURES AT THE TARN.
IMPLICIT THE TALE OF GORLAGROS.

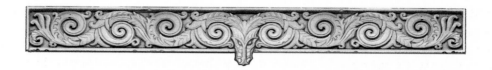

23: THE TALE OF GORLAGROS AND GAWAIN

✠

A TIME CAME, AS IT MUST TO ALL CHRISTIAN KINGS, WHEN KING ARTHUR AND CERTAIN OF HIS NOBLES AND KNIGHTS DECIDED TO MAKE A PILGRIMAGE TO JERUSALEM, THERE TO MAKE OFFERING AT THE BIRTHPLACE OF THE SAVIOUR. ON THE WAY THEY PASSED THROUGH A LAND OF EXCEEDING RICHNESS; YET NEVER IN THAT COUNTRY HAD SUCH A MAGNIFICENT SIGHT BEEN SEEN AS THAT BRAVE COMPANY WHO RODE, BANNERS FLUTTERING, ARMOUR GLEAMING IN THE SUN, SPEARS AT THE SLOPE, SWORDS ON HIP – A RIVER OF STEEL FLOWING ACROSS THE GREEN LAND.

✠ ✠ ✠

BUT WHEN THEY had been travelling for some time the weather turned evil; rain fell steadily from grey skies, the earth turned liquid, and gleaming mail began to rust. Food, too, was scarce, for such a large company required a great repast every day, and soon the wagons of provisions began to fall behind as they grew ever emptier.

So, all were glad to crest a hill and see a city spread out below them. Huge walls surrounded it, and a mighty fortress guarded its gates. Only the birds that flew over its walls could enter there without permission.

'Let us send a messenger to that city,' Arthur said, 'to ask for food and permission to lodge outside these walls.' For he knew

that to bring so large a company to that place unannounced might be seen as a threat.

'Let me go, lord,' cried Sir Kay the Seneschal eagerly.

'Very well,' said the king. 'But see that you offer to pay for all that we require. And Kay – speak gently, for these people do not know us, nor we them.' He knew that Kay's hot temper had a habit of bringing trouble in its wake.

Kay rode swiftly down to the city. He found its gates standing wide and its streets strangely deserted. Tethering his horse, he went into the first hall he came to.

A very great place it was. The walls were hung with tapestries depicting the deeds of the greatest heroes of that land, and letters of gold were woven into a pattern that told of their names and adventures.

But Kay saw no living person. He went from room to room, calling out, seeking sign of anyone to answer his request. At last, in a wide chamber with a bright fire laid, he saw a dwarf scuttling about, turning a spit on which several birds were roasting, setting the room to rights for a private feast. Kay was so hungry by this time that he went straight up to the fire and snatched one of the birds, which he began to consume with greedy bites.

At once the dwarf cried out, his voice echoing in the lofty room. In answer to his yells a large, fierce knight strode in. When he saw Kay standing there with the juice of the meat running down his chin, he spoke angrily:

'Sir, where are your manners? I do not know you, yet you seem to have made yourself at home as if you lived here. By what right do you steal our food? Your armour may be bright, but your manners are as dull as any peasant's!'

At once Kay's hot temper flared. 'I apologize for nothing!' he cried. 'Your judgement means nought to me!'

Without a word the knight swung a huge fist at Kay, knocking him to the floor where he lay like a stone, his wits scattered like leaves. When he regained consciousness, the huge knight had vanished, and without pausing to think Sir Kay hurried back to his horse and rode full pelt back to the king.

'Sire!' he cried. 'We shall get no good greeting in that place. Its lord has only scorn for your name!'

Sir Gawain, overhearing, spoke up: 'My lord, you know that good Sir Kay is often sharper of tongue than he means to be. May I ask that you send another in his place who will speak in less crabbed tones? Our people

are weakened with hunger, and we need the provisions they can provide.'

King Arthur mused for a moment, looking at the sad and sodden troop of knights and lords. 'Very well,' he said at last. 'Sir Gawain, prepare yourself to go, for no one is fairer spoken than you.'

Gawain followed where Kay had been. The gates of the city were open as before, the streets empty. The hall was as richly appointed as ever, but now it was filled with stately people; the lord of the place sat on the high dais, surrounded by richly clad nobles and ladies. Gawain went and stood before him with bowed head and spoke as gently as a knight should.

'Sir, I bring you greeting from my lord King Arthur of Britain. He asks that he may quarter his followers outside your walls, and that he may buy food and drink for his knights and their steeds. He will pay whatever price is asked.'

The lord of the castle looked down at Gawain, unsmiling. 'I will sell nothing to your lord,' he said.

'As you wish, sire,' Gawain replied, and made to leave. But the lord raised a hand and beckoned him back. 'I would be no kind of noble if I were to sell goods to your master. Everything I have is at his disposal freely for as long as he wishes to remain.' Then he smiled. 'A rough, boorish fellow came here lately. He was dressed like a knight, but his manners were those of a fool. I do not know who he was, but if he has any connection with your lord or his men, he had better stay out of my sight.'

Gawain bowed again and departed swiftly, returning to King Arthur with the good news. Then he led the way back to the castle where its lord greeted King Arthur warmly.

'Sire," said he, 'I am more than glad to welcome you here, for I have long heard of your goodness and the bravery of your knights. Let me say now that everything in my land is yours to command. If you ask it, I have thirty thousand men who will answer to you, every one of them armed and mounted.'

'I give you thanks indeed,' said King Arthur. 'Such friendship as this I hold dear and will reward in any way that I may.'

Then he and the noble lord, along with all their knights, dukes and ladies, went into the hall and dined in most splendid fashion, eating from golden dishes and drinking from golden cups. Sir Kay, unhappily, remained in the shadows, fearful of his actions earlier. Never had there been such a feast in all the history of that land, and never again did such great and noble folk sit down together – except in King Arthur's own great hall in Camelot the Golden.

✠ ✠ ✠

THUS PASSED FOUR days and nights. Then King Arthur and his followers took their leave of the noble lord who had been such a generous host and continued upon their way.

Soon they were far from that place of hospitality, travelling over mountain and hill, through valley and forest, crossing rivers and open moorland, until they came at length to the sea. There they saw where a rocky bluff pushed its way out of the earth beside a river that curved around its sides and flowed into the ocean. Atop this outcrop stood a fine castle. Beneath its protecting walls lay a great harbour filled with ships which plied their way without hindrance, such was the strength of that place.

'Now by my faith,' said King Arthur, 'I would dearly like to know who rules this land, so fruitful and pleasant is it, and so filled with good things.'

'I have heard,' said one of the Round Table knights, whose name was Sir Spinagros, 'that the lord who holds these lands owes no allegiance to any man.'

'How can that be?' demanded Arthur. 'All men, unless they are kings in their own right, owe allegiance to someone higher than themselves. Witness the lord whose hospitality we shared just now. Can it be that the man you speak of has broken the bonds between himself and his sovereign?'

'There is more to it than that, sire,' Spinagros answered. 'I will tell you the tale as it was told to me.

'First of all, you must know that this man, who is named Gorlagros, is very stubborn, possessed by a will of iron and as great a sense of power as any I have heard of in all the lands of the west. In truth he behaves as a king, yet in all his life has neither given to nor received homage from any man. He is immensely rich and keeps a great army which he unleashes upon an unsuspecting world whenever he thinks fit. I have heard that he has a wayward temper as well, and that he answers to any act he sees as threatening with violence. In short, my lord, you should pass this place without pause – no good will come of any encounter with this proud man.'

King Arthur frowned. 'All that you have told me only makes me more determined to bring this powerful lord to heel. I am determined upon this, so let no one deny me! Once we have accomplished our task and reached the Holy City, we shall return this way and speak further of this matter.'

When the king spoke thus, no one would

gainsay him. So it was that, as the year turned, the king and his party reached Jerusalem, and there made appropriate offerings at the shrine of Our Lord. Then, without further ado, they turned back and made all haste until they were once again near the fortress of Gorlagros. At this point King Arthur made camp near to the valley of the Rhone, and when his royal pavilion had been erected, he called a council of war to hear how best they might overcome the proud lord Gorlagros.

Spinagros spoke up once more. 'Sire, it seems to me that we should first of all dispatch messengers to speak with this lord. Even though I have heard nothing to make me believe he will listen and bend the knee to you, it may be that when he learns with whom he must deal he will bow his proud head.'

'You speak wisely,' King Arthur answered. 'Sir Gawain! Sir Bors! Sir Uwain! I charge you with this task. See that you convey my commands to this Gorlagros – that he submit to my lordship and give homage as is his due.'

'My lord,' said Spinagros. 'If I may advise further...?'

The king nodded.

'Sirs,' said Spinagros, addressing the three great knights. 'I know this lord, and I would advise you to be careful how you speak to him. His manner is mild, and he is as handsome and kindly in appearance as a bridegroom. Yet beneath all he wears a warrior's countenance and bends his knee to no one. I counsel you to speak gently to him, and not to threaten him in any way. For though I know you to be powerful men in your own right, yet I believe he is stronger than any one of you – maybe even more than all three together.'

'We thank you,' replied the three knights.

'Your words are wise, and we will keep them in mind in our dealing with Gorlagros.'

Though they spoke thus, none believed that Gorlagros could defeat even one of them. They set forth at once and rode to the gates of the city, where they were welcomed and, once they had stated that they were emissaries of King Arthur, received with utmost courtesy. Led through the outer wards of the castle, they reached the great hall, where Gorlagros sat on a high dais surrounded by fair ladies and noble knights. A handsome man he was indeed, just as Spinagros had said. He bowed his head in greeting and called them forward.

Gawain, ever the noblest and most well-spoken of all Arthur's knights, spoke first.

'We bring you greetings from our lord King Arthur. He is the noblest and mightiest king alive in this time. Hundreds of castles he possesses, and many houses, towns and cities. No less than twelve kings owe him allegiance and his deeds are known far and wide. In his hall at Camelot the Golden stands the Round Table, at which one hundred and fifty knights sit at one time. We three are honoured to be part of that Fellowship.'

Sir Gawain paused to judge the effect of his words. Gorlagros nodded politely. 'We have heard of your lord and send him our greetings. What message do you bring from him?'

'Merely that word of your deeds and your great nobility have reached his ears, and that he wishes to extend his friendship to you. He asks that you name yourself his friend from this day forward.'

Gorlagros nodded again, then spoke at length and with great courtesy. 'I thank you for your words, good sirs, and I am glad that your lord offers me friendship. Were I able, nothing would please me more than that

I should align myself with the noble King Arthur. Yet I fear I may not do so, for neither I, nor my family, have sworn fealty to anyone, or bound ourselves to another in any way, either by word or deed. Such a gesture of friendship would be seen as an act of submission. Anything I may do for your king by way of gifts or honour I shall gladly do, so long as it is not seen as a token of my submission. I will bow my head to the sovereignty of any noble man, though never to threats of any kind. I know that King Arthur comes at the head of a great army, and he is welcome, as is any man who comes in friendship, and as do you yourselves. However, I will not bend my neck to any show of force, which I shall surely meet with equal show of arms. Take these words to your king, with my greeting from one lord to another.'

With this the emissaries had to be content – and taking their leave of Gorlagros returned to King Arthur. He, when he heard what they had to report, was angry and determined at once to lay siege to the city. 'For,' said he, 'no man may speak thus to an anointed king unless he is ready to back his words with feats of arms and a show of strength.'

✛ ✛ ✛

SO KING ARTHUR and his men prepared to lay siege to Gorlagros' castle and the city beyond. The siege began in earnest. Great bows, mighty cannon and huge catapults were set up; trees were cut down to build palisades and battering rams. Trumpets blew at all hours – King Arthur's to signify challenge, those of Gorlagros to signal his defiance. Every morning there were new shields arranged on the walls, gleaming in the sunlight – many were known to the heroes of

the Round Table, for their fame had spread beyond the confines of Gorlagros' lands. King Arthur, looking upon them, said: 'Never have I seen such a strong city, nor one so well defended. Yet I shall give them enough to think of before much time has passed.' Grimly, he continued: 'If need be, I shall remain here nine years, until I have brought this proud prince to his knees!'

'Sire,' said Sir Spinagros. 'I fear you will remain here longer even than that before you see any sign of yielding on the part of this lord or his men. I believe they are a match for any of us, even Sir Lancelot or Sir Gawain.'

Even as he spoke, they heard a loud trumpet call from one of the towers of the city, and a figure in armour rode forth from the gates.

'What does this mean?' murmured King Arthur.

'I believe it may be a challenge,' said Gawain.

'You are right,' said Sir Spinagros. 'I know this youth from his arms. His name is Galiot, a knight of great prowess. It seems to me that he desires to test this while defending the honour of his lord.'

'Then we shall give him the opportunity to do so,' said King Arthur. He called forth Sir Gaudifer, a strong knight who held many estates in Britain and had but lately joined the Fellowship of the Round Table. 'Undertake this task for me, sir knight, and you shall be well rewarded.'

To this Sir Gaudifer was glad to agree. He sent his squire to prepare his war-horse and armour, and before the sun climbed to mid-heaven, the two knights were prepared, and rode out onto the level plain before the walls of the castle. The walls were crowded with defenders, who longed to see King Arthur's man defeated, while the Britons watched from behind their palisades.

Like two swords heated in the smith's fire, the two knights seemed as they rode at each other with spears in rest and swords at the ready. After their first resounding clash, where neither gained the upper hand, they fought on through the afternoon, neither winning over the other. Their horses tired quickly, and they fell to fighting on foot, hacking and hewing until the blood ran down their bright armour and soaked into the earth. It seemed as though both were mad, as though some demon had overtaken them both and would not let them rest.

But at the last Sir Gaudifer gained the victory by sheer refusal to submit, and Sir Galiot was carried back into the castle on a stretcher. While King Arthur's men cheered, Gorlagros glowered in fury. He called to one of his strongest knights, a man named Sir Rigel of Rhone, and bade him go forth and uphold the honour of his lord. 'I shall not rest until this defeat has been avenged!' cried the proud lord. 'For my sake make this day a costly one for our adversaries.'

With the customary horn-call to battle Sir Rigel prepared to go forth. And King Arthur, hearing that call, knew well what was to occur and had already turned to another of his younger knights, Sir Rannald, and bade him prepare himself for battle. This the good knight did, and soon enough the two fresh combatants faced each other on the field of war.

This time the fighters were even better matched. Back and forth they went, but as the sun declined towards the west neither got the advantage, and both were sorely wounded and lost so much blood that they grew steadily weaker. At last Sir Rannald summoned his failing strength and attacked Sir Rigel with renewed fury. He, in turn, responded with his best. But once again neither could overcome the other, and for both this final effort proved too much. Both fell

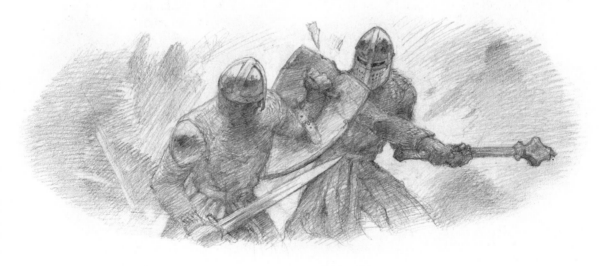

✦ *The Knights Battle* ✦

upon the earth and lay still, while their life-blood drained from them.

At once their squires rushed forward to help, but it was too late. Both men lay dead upon the field, neither having won honour for their lords. With great mourning and sorrow their bodies were carried back to castle and camp, and soon after were buried with pomp and ceremony. The deeds of both men recorded, that they might be remembered in days to come.

Thus the day ended, and on the morrow the contest began again. This time Gorlagros sent forth four knights. These were Sir Louys, a noble man by birth and a true fighter; with him went Sir Edmond, known to be a lover of women, and Sir Bantelles, a captain who was called a wise leader of men. Lastly was Sir Sanguel, who was accounted both handsome and savage. These four were matched against four of Arthur's greatest knights: Sir Lional, who was Lancelot's cousin, against Sir Louys; Sir Yvain against Sir Edmond; Sir Bedivere against Sir Bantelles, and Sir Grimolance against Sir Sanguel.

These eight strong men set to against each other, with all the fierceness of warriors from an earlier time; their mounts, held in check until the last moment as they charged together, leapt forward like sparks struck from flint. Thick and fast fell the blows of sword on shield. Armour was dinted and flesh torn. Helms were broken and dreadful damage done to the skulls within. Swords broke in their owner's hands and horses fell dead upon the earth. No one could tell which way the mêlée went, so fast and furious was the onslaught.

King Arthur was fearful for his men, so hardy were their opponents, but at length the battle resolved itself and the outcome

could be seen by all. Sir Lional was captured by Sir Louys; as was Sir Bedivere by Sir Bantelles; Sir Sanguel was taken prisoner by Sir Grimolance; Sir Edmond fell dead to the swift sword of Sir Yvain, who in return was terribly wounded. As the day ended, Bedivere and Lional were taken back to the castle, along with the body of Sir Edmond, while Yvain was helped back to King Arthur's camp and the victorious Grimolance brought his prisoner before Arthur.

⁜ ⁜ ⁜

WHAT NEED IS there to tell more of this battling? Suffice it that five more knights rode forth from each side on the day following, and that at the end each side had captured two of their opponents while the others had shown themselves worthy champions. Gorlagros, when he saw how things stood, and how well both he and King Arthur were matched for the power and skill of their fighting men, elected to go forth himself on the morrow, and to this end let ring forth two bells from a tower within the castle.

When he heard this, Sir Spinagros spoke to King Arthur. 'My noble lord, this means that Gorlagros himself will come forth to give battle on the morrow. I have seen him fight and believe me when I say that I scarcely saw a better man bestride a horse or wield a sword and spear. It will take a mighty warrior to defeat him.'

When Sir Gawain overheard these words, he begged to be allowed to face Gorlagros. To this Arthur assented, and prayed to God that his nephew might be victorious. Sir Spinagros however, said nothing, for in his heart he already believed Gawain as good as dead. Thus, as the good knight prepared himself for battle, Spinagros sought him out and did his best to dissuade him from undertaking the fight. But Gawain responded as indeed he would until the end of his days. 'If I die, I ask only that it be valiantly, for I would rather lose my life than my honour.'

Sir Spinagros sighed and bowed his head. 'If you must fight, listen well to this advice. When you charge Gorlagros, make certain to aim for the centre of his shield, for that is his weakest point. And, if and when you fight him on foot, remember that when he is surprised, he is given to shouting loudly and becomes as fierce as a wild boar. But do not let that distract or anger you, for then you will surely lose your life and the king's honour. Remember that if you can tire him you will have a better chance of beating him. Let him rage as he will; if you remain cool you have a chance of overcoming him.'

Sir Gawain nodded. 'I thank you for your words, Sir Spinagros. If I win this day we shall raise a cup together in celebration.'

While Sir Gawain continued to ready himself for battle, testing his weapons and every last strap of his armour, we must turn to Sir Kay, who was jealous of Gawain and thought that he should have been chosen to fight Gorlagros. Therefore, he swiftly put his own armour on and went out towards the city. As he rode, he saw an armed knight coming toward him. When the knight saw Sir Kay, he cried his battle-cry and rode full tilt toward him. And though he could see from his opponent's shield that this was not Gorlagros, Kay responded, setting his own lance in rest, and spurred his horse to the gallop.

The two met and splintered both their spears, then fell to fighting with swords, at first on horse, then on foot. Finally, the stranger conceded defeat and Kay returned

with him to the camp of King Arthur, glad to have achieved this much of a victory, but far too bruised and battered to think of encountering Gorlagros as he had intended.

Meanwhile Gorlagros, accompanied by a magnificent entourage, had entered the field. A silken pavilion was set up and no less than sixty knights, clad in the most magnificent armour, attended upon their lord. Gorlagros himself rode on a white horse and was clad in armour that shone like the sun and gave back glints of light from the gems that covered it liberally. Even King Arthur's knights were in awe of such splendour, as they were impressed by the bearing of the lord himself. Gorlagros was over six feet in height and both handsome and strong. His proud bearing and haughty demeanour were shown off to good effect as he rode his prancing steed past the ranks of his own men and saluted the company who had accompanied Sir Gawain onto the field.

With both armies looking on, the two combatants faced each other and made two exploratory passes with their lances before joining battle seriously. When they met it was as though thunder rolled across the place of battle. Both their shields were shattered, as were their spears, and both men rocked backwards in the saddle by the power of the blow. Their horses were winded, and both took time to recover. Then they came together again, this time with swords raised, and proceeded to hack and hew at one another with all their strength. Yet neither could find an advantage, for they were so well matched in strength and skill that every feint and parry seemed to come from a single mind.

As the combat continued, so Gorlagros' anger increased, and he swung harder and harder at his foe. Gawain, remembering the advice of Sir Spinagros, remained cool, and hacked so hard that he sheared right through Gorlagros' shield and left a dint in his breastplate from which blood oozed. Enraged, Gorlagros fought back harder, driving Gawain before him with a series of furious blows which broke his shield and sent pieces of armour flying. Both men were panting heavily, a red mist swimming before their eyes.

As they fought on grimly, the onlookers shouted loudly, each for his own champion, and King Arthur offered up a prayer for the safety of his nephew.

The end came swiftly. Both men were sorely wounded in a dozen places, their once-bright armour reddened with blood. Then, after delivering a particularly powerful blow, Gorlagros' legs gave way beneath him and he fell where the stamping of their feet had turned the earth to mud. Gawain drew his dagger and leapt upon his opponent, pinning him down and demanding his submission.

'I would as soon die as be disgraced,' snarled Gorlagros. 'Never have I been defeated, nor has any man ever called himself my master in battle or elsewhere. I rule myself as I rule my kingdom – owing allegiance to none. Do what you will, for you will get nothing more of me this day.'

When he heard this Gawain felt nothing but sorrow. 'Sir,' he said. 'You know you are vanquished. Nothing will be changed by being thus obdurate. If you give up now and swear fealty to my king, you shall have nothing but honour. You will have all that you have now and more, for you will be under the protection of my liege lord King Arthur.'

'To profit thus at the expense of my honour would be a foolish thing,' Gorlagros replied heavily. 'All I would gain would be shame – which would follow me to my death.

Nothing will make me do anything which will cause me to hide from my own people. Believe me, no one disparages the fate of a man who gives his life honourably. I am not afraid to die.'

Hearing these words, Sir Gawain felt only pity for this brave man. 'Sir,' he said. 'Is there nothing I can do to help you?'

Gorlagros was silent for a moment. Then he said: 'There is but one way that I know of to resolve this without loss of honour. Let it seem as though I have beaten you this day, then come to my castle later and you shall be well rewarded.'

'That is a hard thing you ask,' said Gawain. 'I know nothing of you save that you are proud and strong and that your courage is beyond question. Yet if I do as you ask, I am placing many noble knights in jeopardy and perhaps allowing this war to continue for longer than it needs to. With one blow I could end all of this, yet you would have me give back your life and freedom for a promise of reward.'

'It is that, or strike me down,' answered Gorlagros. 'You have my word.'

'Then,' said Gawain, 'I put my trust in your honour for the sake of all that depends upon it, for such a noble man I cannot slay in cold blood.'

Then to the amazement of all those who had watched the encounter, Gawain stood back and leaned upon his sword as though weary. Then Gorlagros regained his feet and drawing a short sword rejoined the combat. Only they knew that they no longer fought in earnest, but rather feinted so that no further blood was drawn from either. After a time, Gawain made it seem that this strength failed him, and he surrendered his sword. Then both returned to Gorlagros' castle, to a stunned silence from the Round Table knights and thunderous cheers from the followers of Gorlagros.

'Alas,' said King Arthur, 'now is the flower of my knighthood taken prisoner, and our honour is in the dust.' And he wept long and bitterly at this loss and defeat.

✠ ✠ ✠

MEANWHILE, WITHIN GORLA-GROS' castle, all was joyful celebration. A great feast was prepared and Gawain, together with the knights who had been defeated and taken prisoner, were seated at the high table where only Gorlagros, his wife and daughter normally sat. But Gorlagros seemed ill at ease and restless, far from one who had won the day. Finally, he struck the table with an ivory rod and called for silence.

'My lords,' he began. 'I have a heavy task before me, and I require your agreement and advice before I can undertake it. You are the greatest lords in my kingdom, and you must decide whether you will have me for your king, or whether I should give up my life and let you be ruled by another.'

There was great consternation among those gathered in the hall, and some began to suspect that their lord had not won the day after all. 'Let us have no sham favours,' said one old lord at last. 'You have been our noble lord for too long to give up everything so easily. We would have you for our governor in war and peace – as long as we may do so with honour.'

Then Gorlagros told them what had really occurred that day, and how Sir Gawain had nobly agreed to the deception rather than take his life. 'No man may do more for another,' he said. 'This knight has earned praise beyond any that I can give. I make no secret that my life is his to do with as he wills, and to him I give all rights in this matter.'

Then he turned to where Sir Gawain sat, and said: 'Sir, my life and properties are yours to do with as you will. When Fortune turns her back upon us, we can do nothing to gainsay it. You had my life in your hands, and out of nobility chose to spare me. For that I am in your debt for ever, and to you, and to all these brave knights, I give back your freedom and place myself in your hands.'

'Then I bid you go now to my lord King Arthur,' answered Gawain. 'For his justice is greater by far than any I could mete out to you.'

✠ ✠ ✠

SO IT WAS that the watchmen of Arthur's camp saw a torch-lit procession approaching from the city. In the forefront rode Gorlagros himself, with Sir Gawain at his side, and behind them came a great gathering of nobles, among whom were to be seen the knights of the Round Table that had been taken prisoner.

'Now I believe we may have Sir Gawain to thank for this,' said King Arthur, and Sir Spinagros, who was standing nearby, agreed. 'I see many glances of friendship between the lord Gorlagros and Sir Gawain, and surely this bodes well for peace between us.'

As the cavalcade approached, Gorlagros raised a hand so that all halted. Then he came forward alone and greeted King Arthur, and the two monarchs embraced. Gorlagros told all that had taken place on the field of battle that day, and how Sir Gawain had graciously agreed to all that he asked and had placed his own honour in the hands of his rightfully defeated foe. 'Never have I encountered such bravery, or such high honour. It is to this that I bow, for surely only a king of the greatest and noblest ideals could command such a man.'

Then Gorlagros formally made his allegiance to King Arthur and promised to serve him as his liege lord from that day forward. 'All my lands and properties, from the sea to the hills, are yours to command, and all those who offer allegiance to me from henceforward will call you lord as they have done to myself since I became ruler of this country.'

King Arthur received the word of the noble lord, and then, along with his foremost lords and knights, returned to the city, where an even greater feast than before was prepared, and the warriors sat down together in friendship. For many days that followed, the feasting and celebrations continued, until finally, on the day that King Arthur prepared to return home, he called Gorlagros before him and said: 'Sir, for the sake of the honour you have shown toward me and my followers, I hereby grant you your freedom from the oath of allegiance you made to myself. Receive back all your lands and titles as they were before. In return, I ask only that you retain the friendship towards me that you have already shown, and that I may call upon you in time of need.'

With tears in his eyes Gorlagros gave thanks to King Arthur and promised him any help he might wish for in future time. Then the Britons took their leave, and especially warm was the parting of Gawain and Gorlagros, who had become firm friends in their time together. Thereafter they remained true companions through the days of their lives, and Gorlagros ever praised the honour of King Arthur and of his brave and noble knights. Nor should this act of Sir Gawain ever be forgotten, for it is my belief that not even the greatest of knights, Lancelot, or Gareth, or even Sir Galahad himself, would have excelled as did the king's nephew on that day in the field before Gorlagros' city.

---- ✠ ----

EXPLICIT THE TALE OF GAWAIN AND GORLAGROS.
INCIPIT GAWAIN AND THE CARLE OF CARLISLE.

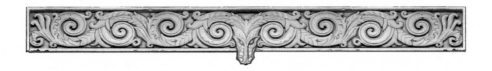

24: SIR GAWAIN AND THE CARLE OF CARLISLE

MANY TIMES HAVE I HEARD THE STORY OF THE GREEN KNIGHT WHO CAME TO CAMELOT THE GOLDEN TO PLAY THE BEHEADING GAME, WHERE KING ARTHUR'S KNIGHTS WERE CHALLENGED TO EXCHANGE BLOWS WITH THIS FEARSOME FOE. SOME HAVE TOLD THAT IT WAS SIR GAWAIN WHO UNDERTOOK THIS DREADFUL TASK, AND SUCH – AS YOU SHALL SEE – IS THE CASE IN THE TALE I SHALL TELL. SOME SAY THAT IT WAS SIR CARADOC WHO UNDERTOOK THE CHALLENGE,* AND THIS STORY I HAVE ALREADY TOLD. SO, TOO, THERE ARE TALES WHICH SPEAK OF GAWAIN'S WEDDING TO THE FAIREST LADIES OF THIS OLD EARTH, BUT I DO NOT KNOW THE TRUTH OF THESE – THOUGH I HAVE HEARD IT SAID THAT IN ALL HIS DAYS GAWAIN'S ONLY LOVE WAS THE LADY RAGNALL, WHOSE STORY I SHALL ALSO TELL IN GOOD TIME.† PERHAPS IT MAY BE UNDERSTOOD THAT THESE FAIR LADIES WERE ONE AND THE SAME, AND THAT THEY WERE OF OTHERWORLDLY ORIGIN? BUT OF THIS I CANNOT BE CERTAIN.

✝ ✝ ✝

BE IT KNOWN, then, that one day King Arthur held court at the city of Carlisle, preparing for a hunt that would take him into the heart of the Great Wood which lapped its walls. The story tells that among those present were Sir Gawain, and with him Sir Lancelot of the Lake, Sir Lanval, Sir Owein of the White Hands, Sir Perceval, Sir Gaudifer and Sir Galeron; Sir Constantine and Sir Raynabrown of the Green Shield, Sir Petypase of Winchelsea, Sir Grandoynes and Sir Ironside.

This last named was a noble man indeed. Ever he sought adventure, summer and winter alike. His armour was the best; his horse,

---

* See 'The Story of Caradoc of the Strong Arm' pp. 150–63
† See 'The Wedding of Sir Gawain and the Lady Ragnall' pp. 299–305

Sorrel-Hand, was the strongest and fastest of any; he bore a shield of azure, blazoned with a griffin and a fleur-de-lys; his crest was a lion of gold. Giants he fought, and dragons, and he loved hunting as much as King Arthur himself.

This day it was Sir Gawain's turn to gather the huntsmen and steward the pack. When Mass was ended, they set forth, and those I have named were among the first. King Arthur followed after with as many as a hundred more, but it was Gawain, along with Sir Kay and that great bishop, Baldwin of Britain, who led the way. From morning to midday, they followed a huge stag, and when the mist began to rise they found themselves alone on the edge of the forest.

'We'll find no more game today,' Sir Gawain said. 'Let us dismount and take our rest for a while. We can shelter beneath these trees.'

'I say, let us go on,' said Sir Kay, who was ever wont to take the opposite view of any man. 'Doubtless we shall find lodging near at hand.'

'True enough,' said Bishop Baldwin. 'I know of a castle nearby. Its guardian is a fierce wild Carle, from Carlisle I believe, who may give us a rougher welcome than we like. I hear no one has ever gone there who failed to get a sound beating. Indeed, those who do so are lucky to escape with their lives.'

'Then let us go there,' said Sir Kay at once. 'I'm not afraid of this Carle, whoever he is. In fact, I'll beat him black and blue if he tries to stop me from entering. He'll wish he'd never seen us!'

'Enough of your boasting,' Gawain said. 'I'll not be any man's guest against his will. Let us go there by all means, but we shall ask politely for lodging.'

The three companions rode on until they sighted a fine large castle, where they knocked at the door. A surly porter answered and asked what they wanted. Sir Gawain replied with courtesy, asking for food and shelter for the night.

'I'll take your message to my master,' the porter said. 'But you may not like the answer you get. My lord knows nothing of courtesy and will soon send you about your business.'

'Go, oaf!' shouted Sir Kay. 'Or I'll have your keys from you and open the gate myself.'

Without another word the porter vanished from sight and went in search of his master. When the Carle heard there were two knights and a bishop at the gate, he was glad. 'Let them come in,' he said. 'I shall be glad to welcome them.'

The knights were ushered into a huge hall where a fire burned fiercely in the centre. There stood the Carle of Carlisle, and a fiercer fellow was never seen. Twice the height of a normal man, with arms and legs like tree-trunks and massive hands and feet, he had a harsh face, broad and heavy, with a hooked nose and a wide mouth. A grey beard as broad as a battle-flag covered his chest and he was roughly dressed. But it was not the Carle that they noticed first, but the four beasts who lay untethered at the edges of the fire: a huge wild bull that snorted and pawed the earth; a lion fierce as a hot coal; a boar that glared and whet its tusks; and a bear that rose on its hind legs and roared at them.

At once the knights prepared to draw their swords, but the Carle ordered his beasts back with a single word, and they obeyed him at once, cringing at the sound of his voice.

Then Sir Gawain bowed his knee before the Carle, as guest to host, but the Carle commanded him to stand up at once. 'I'm not about to knight you, fellow,' he bellowed. 'No man kneels to me. I'm no lord, but a simple Carle who offers only a Carle's hospitality. Be welcome all.' Then he called for cups of wine to be brought, and when they came they were in vessels of gold that shone like the sun and held at least a gallon of wine each. But this failed to satisfy the Carle, who called for his own cup, a massive vessel which held at least two gallons. 'Now let's really drink!' he roared.

The knights began to feel happier and joined with their host in drinking the sweet wine he offered them. Then, as the time for supper approached, they went out to see that their horses were being properly cared for.

The bishop went first and found that all had been well supplied with fodder, but he noticed that a little foal was eating from the same trough as their own mounts. At once he pulled the small beast away, exclaiming that it should not 'eat from my horse's trough while I'm bishop here'.

At that moment the Carle himself came out. When he saw that the foal had been pushed to one side a dark look came onto his face and he demanded to know who had done this thing.

'I did,' the bishop said.

'Then you deserve the blow I'm going to give you,' the Carle said.

'Let me remind you that I'm in Holy Orders,' blustered the bishop.

'That may be, but it means nothing to me,' said the Carle. 'All I know is that you lack courtesy.' And with one blow he felled the bishop to the ground, where he lay unconscious.

Now Sir Kay came out to look to his own steed. He failed to notice the bishop, lying where he had fallen, nor indeed the Carle, who stood to one side in the shadows; but he did notice the foal, which had moved back

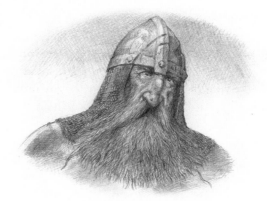

→ *The Carle of Carlisle* ←

to feed again at the trough. With his usual brusqueness Kay slapped the beast across the rump and drove it off. When he saw this, the Carle stepped forward, and before Sir Kay could even raise a hand to defend himself, gave him such a buffet that he fell down senseless.

'You evil-hearted dogs,' the Carle rumbled. 'I'll teach you manners yet.'

✝ ✠ ✝

IN A WHILE Kay and the bishop regained their senses and hobbled back into the hall, where they found Sir Gawain toasting his toes by the fire and drinking the Carle's wine. He kept a wary eye on the four beasts, who had crept under a table and lay watching him with less than friendly gazes.

'Where have you been, friends?' asked Gawain, eyeing his companions, and noting their dishevelled appearance.

'Seeing to our horses,' said Kay. 'But we got sore heads doing it.'

'Well,' said Sir Gawain, thoughtfully, 'then I had better see to mine.'

Outside a terrific storm had begun and rain lashed the earth. As he drew near to the stable

Gawain saw the little foal standing outside, shivering in the cold. At once he led the beast inside and covered it with his own green mantle. 'Eat well, little one,' he said, then turned to his own mount. The Carle, who was hidden nearby, saw all this and smiled to himself.

✚ ✚ ✚

As the time for supper drew near, tables were spread with food and the Carle's servants showed the bishop to the head of the table and Sir Kay to a place opposite the Carle's wife, who now came to join them. She was the fairest lady the knights had seen since leaving the court; as fair, indeed, as the Carle seemed foul, as richly dressed as he was garbed in rough clothes, as delicate and bright as a butterfly, as he was rough and solid as a tree. Kay, staring across the table at her, could not help thinking what a pity it was that such a lovely creature should be wasted upon a man like the Carle.

Their host, who entered at that moment, closely followed by Sir Gawain, stopped by Sir Kay's chair and leaned over him. 'Be careful what you think, my friend,' he growled. 'Or be prepared to speak your thoughts aloud!' Then he turned to Sir Gawain, who had been left standing in the centre of the hall with nowhere to sit.

'Sir knight – do as I bid you,' he said urgently. 'Do you see that axe resting by the door to the buttery? Well, I want you to take it and cut off my head with it. Do as I say, and all shall be well. Do not fear, for you cannot harm me!'

Gawain, startled, nonetheless bowed his head and took up the axe, which was a magnificent weapon sharpened to the keenness of the wind. The Carle bowed down to the earth and with a single blow Gawain cut off his head. But the Carle did not fall dead as might have been expected. Instead his form wavered like smoke, and there, in place of the ugly, powerful fellow, stood a handsome man dressed in fine clothes. And from that moment no sign was there of the four wild breasts that had shared the Carle's home. Smiling, their host embraced Sir Gawain and thanked him.

'You have set me free from a spell of more than twenty years' duration. In all that time I have done only evil to everyone who came here – for it was said that until I could find a man who would do everything that I asked of him, and behave with perfect courtesy, I should never be free. By your gentleness to my foal, and by your obedience in striking me down, I am released. My thanks to you, and my blessing!'

As the other knights looked on in astonishment, the Carle escorted Gawain to the table and seated him next to his wife. When Sir Gawain saw her, he was so enamoured of her beauty that his thoughts betrayed him. But the Carle, who despite being released from his spell which had bound him, still seemed able to read the minds of his guests, merely said, mildly enough: 'Be comforted, my friend. I know how lovely the lady is, but she is mine remember. Drink up and eat heartily and put your thoughts to other things!'

Gawain blushed at what had been in his mind and applied himself to his food and wine. Then there came into the hall a lady who was it seemed even fairer than the Carle's wife. She sat down near the fire and proceeded to play the sweetest music on a harp of finest maple, the pins of which, I dare say, were of solid gold. Now it was towards she that all three knights looked with equal longing – even the bishop! And the Carle smiled, and said: 'Sirs, this is my daughter. Never was there a fairer or gentler girl in all the world, as I am sure you can see.'

✠ ✠ ✠

WHEN SUPPER WAS ended, the Carle's servants came to escort the knights to their beds. The Carle himself, together with his wife, went with Gawain, and showed the knight into his chamber, in which was a magnificent bed covered with a golden cloth. There a squire came quietly in and helped Gawain undress himself. Then the Carle turned to his wife and ordered her to get into the bed. To Sir Gawain he said: 'Now I command you to kiss my lady in my presence!'

Gawain turned a little pale, but steadily he said: 'Sir, out of courtesy I will do as you ask – even though you strike me down for it.'

Then he took the lady in his arms and kissed her long and lingeringly on the lips.

The Carle stood by with an unreadable look upon his face. Then he said: 'Enough, Sir Gawain. More than this you shall not do. But since you have done all that I asked of you without question I shall reward you.' Then he beckoned to his daughter, who had entered the room unseen, and bade her get into bed with Gawain. 'I give you both my blessing,' said the Carle. 'I am sure you shall have joy of each other!' Then he left the room and the two were alone together. They looked upon each other, and each liked what they saw and were well pleased. But as to what took place thereafter, I shall not speak, for it is not too hard to guess!

✠ ✠ ✠

IN THE MORNING, Sir Kay and the bishop were up early. Sir Kay was all for fetching his horse and setting forth at once, but the bishop said they must wait for Sir Gawain.

Soon the bell rang for Mass, and Gawain came to join them, stretching and yawning, for he had slept little that night. When the service was ended, the three knights prepared to depart, giving thanks to the Carle for his hospitality.

He, however, was not quite ready to let them go. 'First you must eat and then go on your way with my blessing,' he said. Then he took Gawain to one side and requested that he follow him. They went to a hut in the woods and there the Carle showed Gawain a great pit full of bones. 'Here is what remains of the men who came here asking for shelter. While I was under the spell from which you released me, I could not help myself from acting as I did. The four beasts you saw, which were not of this earth, made sport of them and in due course killed them all. Now I am free, I take God and you Sir Gawain as my witness, that I shall make what amends I may for these evil deeds. From now on, everyone who comes this way shall be greeted and entertained as warmly as I know how, and here I shall erect a chantry for the souls of those I killed, and a priest shall be brought hither and instructed to sing Masses for them for as long as I live.'

Gawain and the Carle returned to the castle and sat down to a hearty breakfast, during which Kay and Bishop Baldwin looked often from their host to Gawain and exchanged meaningful looks. The Carle asked the bishop to give them all his blessing, which that good man did. And in return the Carle gave him a golden ring, a splendid mitre, and cloth of gold. And to Sir Kay he gave a splendid blood-red steed, more fleet of foot than any that knight had ever possessed. But to Gawain he gave his daughter, as well as a white palfrey and a packhorse loaded down with gold – for she had expressed her love for Gawain and a fear that she might never see him again when once he had left that place. Gawain was glad indeed, for he too was struck by her beauty and gentleness, and desired greatly not to leave her behind.

'Now depart with my blessing,' said the Carle. 'And greet me to your lord King Arthur and bid him come hither to feast if it pleases him.'

The knights took their horse and their rich gifts and rode away singing through the Great Wood until they reached the place where King Arthur was encamped. There they relayed to him the Carle's invitation to feast with him.

'I am glad to see that you escaped without harm,' said the king to Gawain. Hearing which, Kay said, wryly: 'I too am glad to be safe! In fact, I was never so glad of anything in my life.' Then Arthur welcomed him also, and the bishop too, and listened to them relate the whole story of their adventures.

✛ ✛ ✛

NEXT DAY THEY rode to the Carle's castle, where they were greeted with music from silver trumpets, harps, fiddles, lutes, gitterns and psalteries. The Carle himself knelt before Arthur and made him welcome. Then the whole party went into the great hall, where a magnificent feast was laid ready. Nothing was lacking, you can be sure! The tableware was of gold, the wines of the finest, and the food such as one may only dream of. Swans there were, and pheasants, partridges, plovers, and curlews enough for all. Wine flowed in rivers into golden bowls and cups of finest glass. Not a single person was there who did not eat and drink to their fill.

So pleased was King Arthur with all of this, that at the end of the feast he summoned the Carle before him and made him a knight and gave him all the lands about Carlisle to hold for the rest of his days. Then they feasted and made merry for the rest of the day and prepared for bed that night. On the morrow Gawain married the Carle's daughter, Bishop Baldwin himself conducting the ceremony.

Then the Carle was happy indeed and called for a further week of feasting and games. In time he built a fine palace and a rich abbey in the fair town of Carlisle, where Franciscan monks sang Masses for the souls of those slain by the Carle and the wild beasts while he was under enchantment. As for Sir Gawain, it is said that he enjoyed the love of the Carle's daughter until the pains of birth took her from this world. He mourned for her long thereafter, it is said, and of their son, who was named Guinglain, more may yet be told, if I am spared.

——— ✛ ———

EXPLICIT THE TALE OF GAWAIN AND THE CARLE.
INCIPIT THE TALE OF THE ENCHANTED SWORD.

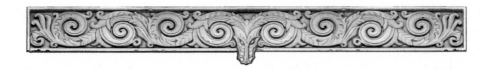

25: THE KNIGHT WITH THE ENCHANTED SWORD

✛

FOR ALL HIS GREATNESS AND MIGHT, SIR GAWAIN IS NOT SO WELL REMEMBERED IN MASTER THOMAS'S GREAT BOOK. YET WHEREVER TALES ARE TOLD OF THE FELLOWSHIP OF THE ROUND TABLE THE NAME OF THE ELDEST SON OF ORKNEY IS SURE TO BE MENTIONED, AND PRAISE DULY GIVEN HIM. FOR OF ALL THE KNIGHTS OF ARTHUR, SOME SAY HE WAS THE BEST – JUSTLY FAMED FOR HIS COURTESY TO ALL, AND FOR HIS GENTLENESS TOWARDS ALL WOMEN. NEVER HAVE I HEARD A STORY WHERE A MAN WAS SO GREATLY TESTED AS THIS, BUT YOU SHALL SEE IF IT FALLS OUT WELL OR ILL.

✛ ✛ ✛

THIS TALE TELLS of a time, one summer, when King Arthur was at Cardueil. Many of the knights were away on adventures of their own, but Gawain, Kay and Yvain were all present, as was Queen Guinevere. Sir Gawain, as was his wont, became bored with life at court, and began to hanker after a new adventure. To this end he dressed himself in his finest clothes, saddled his great steed, Gringolet, and rode out alone, following the way which led into the great forest of Inglewood, where so many adventures began in that time. As he rode, he fell to thinking of another adventure that had happened some time before, which still puzzled him. So engrossed in this was he that he let his mount choose the way forward, and it was not until much later that he awoke to the fact that dusk was falling, and that he had no idea where he was. Deciding to turn back, Gawain followed a narrow track which led in what he hoped was the direction of Cardueil.

He had not gone far when he saw the glow of a fire off to one side of the track and made his way there in the hope of finding a woodcutter or charcoal burner who would put him on the right road. When he came within sight of the fire, he saw a charger tethered to a tree and a knight seated there enjoying his supper. Sir Gawain greeted him courteously, and the knight replied in kind, asking where he was going at that time of day. Gawain replied that he had lost his way and asked how best he might find his way back to Cardueil.

'You are far from there,' answered the knight cheerfully. 'But I can put you on the right road tomorrow – on condition you stay and keep me company this night.'

'That I will be glad to do,' replied Sir Gawain, and the two men settled down by the fire, to share food and conversation. The knight, whose name was Sir Galidor, asked Gawain to tell him of his adventures, which the great hero did without hesitation. But I will tell you now that the other was not so truthful, and that he invented much of what he told his new-found companion. As to the reason for this – well, you shall discover if you read on!

Next morning Sir Gawain awoke first, followed shortly after by Sir Galidor, who smilingly told him that since his own house was closer than Cardueil, Gawain might like to accompany him there, where he could be sure of the finest hospitality. To this Gawain agreed, and the two men rode on in companionable fashion until they left the forest behind and came into open land. There Galidor excused himself, declaring that he must ride ahead and make sure that all was prepared as befitted an honoured guest. He rode off in haste, leaving Gawain to follow more slowly and enjoy the bright splendour of the day.

Not far along the road Gawain passed a group of shepherds. He greeted them courteously and rode on, but as he did so, he heard one of them say to the others: 'What a shame that so fine and gentle a knight will soon be dead.'

When he heard this Gawain was puzzled. He turned back and spoke to the shepherds, asking them what they meant by this remark.

'It is simple enough, my lord,' answered the one who had spoken before. 'We have seen many men follow that knight on the grey horse who passed this way a little while ago – but we have never seen a single one of them return.'

'Why do you think that would be?' asked Gawain. 'Have you heard anything of what happened to these men?'

'They do say,' answered the shepherd, 'that if anyone contradicts him the knight kills them at once. Such is the story we have heard. But since no one has ever seen anyone return from there we cannot say if it is true or not.'

'Well, I thank you for your words,' said Gawain. 'Though I fear I cannot turn aside for a mere child's tale.'

'Then fare well, Sir Knight,' said the shepherd. 'We trust you will come to no harm.'

Gawain rode on until he sighted the castle. It lay in a sheltered valley and seemed like the finest he had ever seen except those belonging to a king or a prince. The moat was wide and deep, crossed by a stone bridge, and within the walls were many fine outbuildings. The keep itself was richly decorated with carvings and its roof shone as though made of gold. Gawain rode right up to the gates, which stood open in welcome, and entered without fear. Crossing the courtyard, he was met by Sir Galidor himself and three squires who took his horse to the stable and his armour and weapons to where he was to sleep. Then his host led him inside.

The hall was as fine as anything Gawain had ever seen. A huge fire burned in the hearth, and couches covered with purple silk were arranged before it.

'You are most welcome, fair sir,' said Sir Galidor. 'Even now, your dinner is being prepared. Meanwhile I bid you relax and be at ease. If there is anything at all which causes you displeasure be sure to tell me at once.' He smiled. 'Now I must go in search of my daughter, for I wish very much for you to meet her, and I am sure she will be delighted to converse with so great and courteous a knight.'

The lord returned in a matter of moments, bringing with him by the hand the girl of whom he had spoken. When Gawain saw her, he jumped up and bowed low to her. He could not ever remember seeing a more beautiful creature: her eyes, her lips, her hair and above all her lovely form, were graceful and fine as that of any woman living. She, in turn, saw in Gawain the finest and most handsome knight ever to cross her path, and she blushed at the mere thought of being in his presence.

Her father, smiling, led her to the couch on which Gawain had been sitting and bade her be seated at his side. 'Sir,' he said, 'I present my daughter, Eliade. It is my hope that she will provide you with pleasant company for as long as you are in my house. Be sure to tell me if she displeases you in any way.'

'I am sure that so fair a maiden could never cause displeasure,' replied Sir Gawain. His host smiled even more widely at this and took himself off to enquire after the meal.

Gawain seated himself next to the girl and engaged her in polite conversation. Despite his dismissal of the shepherd's warning, he could not silence some measure of disquiet, for there was something about his host's demeanour which did not seem to him natural. Therefore, he was careful to say nothing that might be understood as too forward or uncivil, though at the same time he made it clear – by look and gesture only – that he was greatly attracted to the maiden. His naturally courteous nature stood him in good stead here, and it was not long before the maiden read his intent and answered him directly.

'Sir,' she said. 'You honour me greatly by your attentions, and your courtesy is such as any woman would wish to respond to at once. Yet I must warn you that my father is a dangerous man and would have you killed for less than you have said to me this day. At all costs be careful what you say in his presence and be sure not to gainsay him in anything he may ask of you, for to do so would bring only disaster.'

Before Sir Gawain could answer, his host returned and announced that the meal was ready. Tables were brought and set up before them, with knives and plates and cups of gold and silver, and water with towels of the finest linen to wash their hands. A splendid range of dishes were then brought in and placed before them. All the while the host urged Gawain to engage his daughter in conversation, and subtly implied that if he were to fall in love with her, he would raise no objection.

When they had dined, the lord declared his intention of going out to inspect the woodlands around the castle. Gawain he instructed to remain where he was, and to his daughter he gave instructions to do everything she could to make their guest comfortable.

Once the knight had departed, Gawain and the maiden Eliade began to discuss the matter of her father's strange behaviour.

'Had I known what he was planning I would have tried to warn you,' she said. 'As it is, I do not know how best to help you escape unharmed. I am sure that my father has instructed his servants to keep watch and to see that you do not leave here before he returns.'

'Do not fear, madame,' said Sir Gawain. 'In truth, your father has shown me nothing but kindness and courtesy, and I can scarcely blame him for that. I would be churlish if I thought ill of him for any reason that I have been shown. Who can blame him for wishing to protect his daughter from unwanted attentions?'

'I hope you are right,' said Eliade. 'There is a saying I have heard, which is: 'Never praise the day until it is over, and never thank your host until morning.' God grant that you may leave here tomorrow with nothing but good words for your host of this night.'

Shortly after, Sir Galidor returned. He seemed glad to see Gawain, and that he was apparently getting along so well with his daughter. He asked if Gawain was hungry again, and required anything for supper, but the hero declined with polite words, asking only for fruit and a little wine before bed. His host seemed well pleased with this and called to his servants to make up a bed. 'Tonight, Sir Gawain, I wish you to lie in my own bed,' he declared. 'It is the most comfortable in this house and I seek only the best for you.' He smiled. 'Indeed, nothing pleases me more than that any guest of mine should have everything he wants. The only thing that distresses me is to offer hospitality to those who fail to ask for anything that gives them joy.'

Sir Gawain assured him that he was well pleased, and that there was nothing more that he required. The host nodded sagely and clapped his hands. At once servants appeared with tapers to light them to bed. The knight himself ushered Gawain into his room. And very fine it was too, decorated with rich hangings and illuminated with tall candles in golden sconces. The bed itself was large and bedecked with silk and samite and with the softest pillows imaginable.

'Rest well, Sir Knight,' said the host, 'and be sure to leave the candles burning. That would please me greatly.' With these words he withdrew. But as the door to the chamber closed Gawain saw that the knight's daughter had entered and was standing quietly by the bed. Before he could say anything, she removed her shift and slipped naked between the sheets. Then she laid a finger to her lips and whispered: 'Sir, it is my father's wish.'

Full of wonder, Gawain undressed and got into bed. He lay beside the maiden for a time, then took her in his arms. For a while they lay thus, until Gawain's ardour began to get the better of him and he clasped her closer and began to kiss her face and breasts. When he would have gone further, she said: 'Forbear, sir. I am not unguarded.'

Gawain looked around. By the light of the candles, he could see nothing untoward in the room.

'Tell me the truth,' he said. 'Is someone present that I cannot see?'

The maiden shook her head. 'Do you see that sword that hangs on the wall?' she asked. Sir Gawain looked and saw where a great weapon hung in a richly embroidered sheath on the wall opposite the bed.

'It is an enchanted sword,' the maiden told him. 'If anyone does anything in this room which is not honest and true to the highest moral code, it leaps forth of its own volition and runs him through. If you do what you want with me, you will die. Many have tried in the past,' she added sadly. 'I have seen many dead men lie beside me in the morning, their blood rather than mine staining the sheets.'

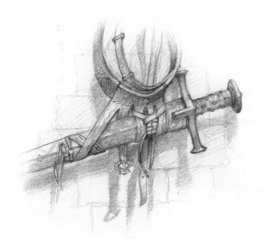

→ *The Enchanted Sword* ←

Sir Gawain was aghast. Never had he heard of such a thing. He began to wonder if the girl was not simply saying this in order to save herself, and he reflected that if ever it came out that he had lain all night next to a woman, and the two of them naked, but had done nothing, he would never be able to hold his head up again.

'I do not fear this enchantment,' he said boldly, 'half as much as I long to hold you and love you!' He clasped the maiden so tightly that she cried out. At once the sword leapt out of its sheath and drove point down into the bed. It shaved a piece of skin from Gawain's flank and stuck through the sheets and covers into the frame of the bed itself. Then just as swiftly it withdrew and returned to its scabbard.

Gawain lay stunned, all desire quite gone from him. Gently Eliade staunched the trickle of blood from his side. 'Now lie still, my lord,' she said. 'I do believe that you thought my words nothing more than an excuse! Yet I promise you I have never warned any other man as I have you. My father is most strict

about this and, believe me, you are lucky to escape with no more than a scratch! Be still now and forbear to touch me in that way again and you may survive the night.'

Now Sir Gawain felt both anger and shame. Anger that he had been brought to this place, and shame that his prowess as a lover was frustrated. He looked at the sword and then at the maiden, wishing that the candles did not burn so bright, for they showed all the beauty of the maiden, and awoke in him again all his former desire. Despite himself he could not help reaching out to caress her.

At once the sword flashed forth again, this time causing a slight wound in Gawain's neck. It sliced through the sheet by his ear and returned to its sheath. Then Gawain realized there was nothing he could do, and he lay still and silent. After a moment the maiden asked him if he were still alive.

'Aye,' he said. 'But you will get no more trouble from me this night.'

Thus they both lay until the morning, neither speaking nor sleeping. With the dawn the host came knocking at the door of the chamber. When he entered and saw Gawain, and his daughter lying next to him, he could not conceal his wonder. 'What! Are you still living?'

'That I am, my lord,' replied Gawain. 'Though no thanks to you.'

Coming closer the knight saw the blood on the sheets. 'So,' he cried, 'you did try to dishonour my daughter! How is it you are not dead?'

Then Sir Gawain saw that there was no point in trying to hide the events of the night. 'That sword did the damage to me that you see. Yet I am not much hurt. I assure you that your daughter is just the same now as she was last night.'

The host stared at Gawain in astonishment. 'So, it has happened at last,' he said. 'I have waited long for this moment, Sir Knight. That sword has great and powerful spells set round it, that it should kill every unworthy man who lay beside my daughter. Only when one came who was able to resist would it spare him. I see that it has chosen you. I am glad that this long enchantment is finally over. Sir, you may have my daughter if you wish. Besides which, everything else in my castle is yours to do with as you will.'

'Sir,' said Gawain. 'This maiden is enough of a reward for any man. I have no need of anything else.'

Then came a time of rejoicing. For word soon spread that a knight had come who had lain beside the maiden and not been killed by the evil sword. The lord's people began to arrive from every part of his lands, and a feast was prepared at which everyone had enough to eat and more. Entertainers sang and played, and merry sports were enjoyed by all. At the end of the day the knight himself married his daughter to Sir Gawain, and then led them back to the room where the enchanted sword hung. Then he left them alone, and this time there was no barrier between them. You may be sure it was no sword that was unsheathed that night! For Gawain and the maiden desired each other greatly and passed the night in joyful disports.

Thus Gawain remained at the knight's castle for several weeks, until he thought that he had set out from Cardueil in search of a day's adventure and stayed away far longer than that. Also, it was borne in upon him that he was married and that this had never been his intention when he left the court. It seemed also as though he lived a dream that, though pleasant indeed, was all too real. His thoughts turned towards the court and his friends and his king. He spoke to the host, asking leave to return home and to take the maiden with him. To this the host gladly gave his assent, for he knew that his child would be honoured at Arthur's court. Next day Sir Gawain and Eliade set forth, but they had not gone far before the maiden wanted to turn back, speaking of how she missed her greyhounds, which she had raised from a litter and had spent long months training. Willingly Gawain returned to the castle and fetched them for her, then they rode on companionably together until they espied a fully armed knight riding towards them. Without a word of greeting or challenge, he galloped up, and seizing hold of the reins of the maiden's horse, made to ride off with her.

Now Gawain had no armour or weapons on him save for his sword, having deemed that he would simply return to the court with his lady. Yet he spurred his mount fiercely and came abreast with the stranger.

'Sir,' he cried. 'You can see that I am not armed. Yet you have behaved churlishly by attempting to take my lady from me in this fashion. I bid you unarm and then let us fight on equal terms. Or if you will not, then wait here while I return to the castle which lies close by and I will bring armour of my own. Then we shall have a proper contest, and perhaps you may win this lady fairly.'

The knight glared back at Sir Gawain haughtily. 'You are in no position to command me to do anything,' he said. 'But since you are unarmed, let us have a contest of another kind. You say this lady is your love and expect me to believe that, simply because she rides with you. I say let us place the maiden in the road here and you and I shall withdraw to either side. Then she can choose between us. If she wants to go with you, I will not contest it; if she chooses me you will allow it.'

'Very well,' said Gawain, for in his heart he was certain that the maiden loved him so well that she would choose him without hesitation. Thus the two knights withdrew a little and both called out to the maiden to choose between them.

Now hear what the maiden did. She sat on her horse and looked from one to the other. She was thinking that Gawain would indeed protect her if she went to him, but she also wondered if he were truly strong enough to overcome the stranger. Gawain wondered only why she was taking so long to come to him. Then he saw with astonishment that she turned her horse and rode towards the stranger. You may be sure that Gawain felt only grief at this, and that this grief turned swiftly to anger. Yet he said nothing, for his courtly training would not permit him to speak unkindly to any lady.

'Now sir,' said the knight. 'Are you in agreement that the lady has chosen to ride with me?'

'You will get no trouble from me,' answered Sir Gawain grimly. 'I will not fight over anyone who does not care for me!'

So the stranger knight and the maiden rode off together, but when they had gone only a little way the maiden began to cry piteously for her greyhounds, which were left behind with Gawain.

'Weep not, maiden,' said the knight. 'You shall have your dogs.' He rode back the way they had come until he overtook Sir Gawain and called upon him to stop.

'Those dogs belong to my lady!' he cried. 'Give them up at once.'

Gawain looked at him scornfully. 'Shall we make the same arrangement as before?' he said. 'Let the dogs decide.'

He untethered the greyhounds and went apart a little way. Then both knights called and whistled. The greyhounds went to Gawain, whom they knew from the maiden's home. 'It seems they have chosen,' he said.

Then Eliade, who had ridden up, cried that she would not go another step until the dogs were returned to her. Gawain shook his head. 'You shall not have them,' he said. 'They chose to remain with me, just as you chose to go with this knight. They at least are faithful,' he added, with a touch of bitterness.

'Sir, will you give up the dogs?' cried the knight.

Gawain shook his head.

'Then we must fight after all.'

'As you wish,' said Sir Gawain, and drew his sword.

Thus they fell to hacking and hewing, and even though Gawain wore no body armour he soon defeated the stranger and dispatched him with a single blow.

Then Eliade, weeping, threw herself at his feet. 'Ah, sir,' she said, 'I am glad you are the victor, and if I behaved foolishly towards you, I beg for your forgiveness. I was afraid that you would be hurt since you had no armour. I only wanted to save you from harm.'

'It seems to me that you care for me less than for your dogs,' said Sir Gawain bluntly. 'Indeed, I see that this is so, and that you never really loved me at all. It is well said that women are faithless, and this I have found to be the case.'

Then Gawain recovered his horse and rode away, ignoring the cries of the maiden. Nor did he ever see her again after that, and nor can I say what happened to her. As for

289

Gawain he returned to Cardueil a sadder and wiser man and told his adventure to King Arthur and the knights, how at the beginning all was fine and dangerous, but how it ended badly because of a faithless woman.

More of this I cannot say, nor if the maiden returned home and what her father said, or did, in answer to her tale. Yet, it is certain that Sir Gawain had more than one wife, and many more lovers, as the stories tell.

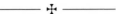

EXPLICIT THE TALE OF THE ENCHANTED SWORD.
INCIPIT THE STORY OF THE MULE WITHOUT A BRIDLE.

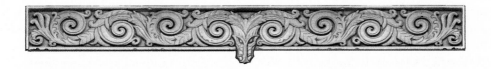

26: THE MULE WITHOUT A BRIDLE

✟

ONE PENTECOST, KING ARTHUR HELD COURT AT CARLISLE. KNIGHTS AND THEIR LADIES CAME FROM ALL OVER THE COUNTRY AND THE QUEEN WAS THERE WITH HER COURT, CONSISTING CHIEFLY OF BEAUTIFUL MAIDENS. AFTER SUPPER THE KNIGHTS RETIRED TO ROOMS ABOVE THE DINING HALL, WHERE THEY SAT TALKING AND LAUGHING. THEN ONE OF THEIR NUMBER, WHO HAPPENED TO BE LOOKING OUT OF A WINDOW, CALLED THE OTHERS TO JOIN HIM. THEY SAW A YOUNG AND PRETTY GIRL RIDING A WHITE MULE WHICH CAME AT A FAST PACE ACROSS THE MEADOW BELOW THE CASTLE. AS IT APPROACHED, THEY SAW THAT THE MULE HAD NO BRIDLE, ONLY A HALTER OF ROPE, WHICH MADE IT VERY HARD FOR THE GIRL TO STEER IT PROPERLY, AND WHICH SEEMED TO BE CAUSING HER SOME DISTRESS.

✟ ✟ ✟

THE KNIGHTS WONDERED much at this and Sir Gawain, who thought the girl especially pleasing, said to Sir Kay: 'Go and welcome her, and ask the king to find out what she wants.'

Kay hurried off to where Arthur and Guinevere were sitting and told them what they had seen and what Sir Gawain had said.

'Bring the girl here,' said Arthur.

Several of the knights, including Gawain, had already gone outside, and having helped her to bring the mule to a halt, spoke kindly to the girl and made her welcome. She, however, made it clear that she had no time to exchange pleasantries, and asked to be taken to the king immediately.

When she stood before Arthur and Guinevere she said: 'Sire, do you see how distracted I am? I shall be like this until I get back the bridle belonging to my mule. It has been wrongfully taken from me, and until I have it again, I cannot inherit the lands which should be rightfully mine. If there is any knight here who will do all that he can to get it back for me, I promise that I shall give him everything he could possibly desire. I shall be entirely his to love and cherish once he has succeeded.'

291

Arthur smiled and answered: 'I am certain there is more than one here who will do as you ask. Tell us how the bridle came to be lost, and where it might be found.'

'Sire, all I can tell you now is that it was taken, and that it means far more than you might believe. As to how and where it can be found: my mule knows the way. All that is required is to climb upon its back and it will take you right to my castle. But I warn you, the winning of the prize will not be easy.'

When they heard this, many there looked with renewed interest at the girl and her mule, for they knew at once that this adventure had more to it than the search for a simple bridle – even were it to be made of purest gold.

'It may be hard to find a knight bold enough to ride on such a lowly beast as a mule,' replied Arthur, looking around at the knights. 'Who will undertake this?'

All this while Kay had been looking at the girl with hunger in his eyes. Now he said: 'I will undertake this task. But first, I would like a kiss.'

'That you shall not have, until you find my bridle,' the girl answered quickly. 'Then you will have as many kisses as you want, and my castle to boot.'

'Very well then,' said Sir Kay. 'I will leave at once.'

'Be sure and let the mule have its head, since it knows the way,' the girl told him.

Kay strode off and mounted the beast. He did not even stop to call for his armour and weapons but took only the sword he was already wearing. When she saw this the girl began to weep. 'He will never succeed!' she cried, 'I shall never have my bridle again!'

✠ ✠ ✠

ALL THAT DAY Sir Kay rode along the road on the mule's back, giving it its head. Soon after midday they entered a part of the Great Wood, and as they plunged deeper in, Kay heard the sounds of wild beasts all around him. He began to feel anxious about this, and when he saw several lions, tigers and even a leopard draw near, his discomfort turned to terror, and he called out to them as though they could understand his speech – that he had only come that way because the mule had brought him. But when the animals saw the mule, they stopped snarling and growling and bowed low before it, out of deference to the lady who had but lately ridden upon it, and who allowed them all to live there in the forest in peace.

Sweating a little, Sir Kay rode on, and soon came to a narrow, unfrequented path that led out of the forest and into a deep valley with sheer sides over which hung a pall of darkness. Such a breath of cold came from every side that it seemed like winter there. Then, as the mule picked its way onwards, Kay became aware of a terrible smell, the worst he had ever known or was to know. When he saw from whence it came his terror knew no bounds, for on every side of the valley were snakes, scorpions, and serpents, larger than any he had ever seen. They all breathed fire and smoke from their mouths, and it was this that created the terrible reek.

Holding his hand over his mouth, Kay managed to stay on the mule's back until it passed through the dreadful valley and came out on a flat plain. In the distance he saw where a spring of very pure water bubbled out of the earth. It was surrounded with flowers, and bushes gave shelter and shade. Kay dismounted and took off the mule's saddle, then he allowed it to drink and splashed the cool

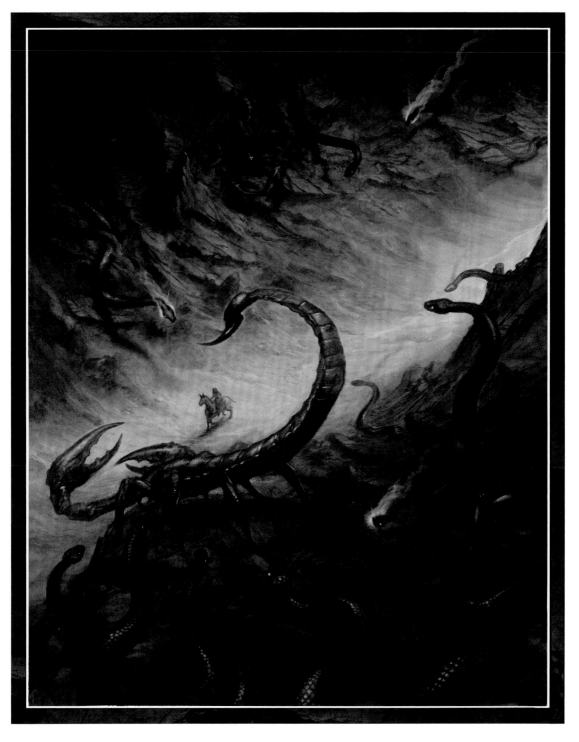

PLATE 7: 'on every side of the valley were snakes, scorpions, and serpents,
larger than any he had ever seen'

water on his face and drank his fill also. Much refreshed, he saddled the mule again and rode on once more, wondering how much further he must go to obtain the bridle.

Soon, he reached a wide stretch of water, which ran in spate between steep banks. Kay looked at it in dismay, seeing neither barge nor crossing place nor bridge in either direction. Turning the mule to the left he began searching for somewhere to cross, and finally found a place where a narrow iron plank stretched across to the other bank. It looked strong enough to bear him, but certainly not the mule. It was certainly a perilous place, and as he looked at it, he began to grow angry.

'All the way through that forest and that hideous valley and now this! I'll be damned if I go any further. All just for a stupid bridle!'

So saying, he turned the mule around and set its head in the direction of Carlisle. At first the animal resisted, trying to turn back the way it had come, but Kay kept it firmly on the path back through the poisonous valley and the Great Wood, as fast as he could make the mule go. Very glad he was when he saw the walls of Carlisle in the distance.

As he rode across the meadow Sir Gawain, Sir Gareth and Sir Griflet came out to meet him, while others went to find the girl. 'Come,' they cried, 'Sir Kay is returned already. You will soon have your bridle.'

'I shall not,' said she. 'If he has returned this soon, he cannot possibly have got it!' And she began to weep loudly.

It was soon clear that she spoke the truth, as Sir Kay admitted that the way the mule had taken him was evil and dangerous, and seemed unending.

When he heard this, Sir Gawain spoke cheerfully: 'Lady, will you grant me a boon?'

'What do you wish?' the girl asked warily.

'That you will cease weeping and go inside to supper. I will undertake to retrieve your bridle.'

'How can I be sure you will succeed any better than your companion?'

'I promise I shall not rest until I have succeeded, or die in the attempt,' said Gawain solemnly. At this the girl dried her tears and looked happier than she had been from the start, for she knew of Sir Gawain's fame and prowess, and had far greater faith in him than Sir Kay.

Then, while Kay himself retired to his lodgings, shamed by his failure and reluctant to speak of it, Gawain requested of the king that he be allowed to ride in quest of the lady's bridle. To this Arthur and Guinevere both assented willingly, and gave Gawain their blessing.

Without wasting any time Gawain prepared to depart at once. Before he did so the girl came forward and flinging her arms around his neck gave him a kiss. Thus encouraged, Gawain set forth. He soon came to the forest, where the wild animals came racing towards him. Then, when they saw the mule, they stopped and bowed low. Gawain continued on his way, until he came at length to the dark and dismal valley, through which he passed, not without a shudder, and emerged safely in the meadows beyond.

There, as Kay had done, he rested the mule and drank some of the pure water that flowed from the spring. After that he rode on until, like Kay, he was stopped by the rough and furious river. Following its banks, he arrived at the iron platform, and after hesitating and studying it for a time, dismounted and led the mule onto it. The plank quivered and shook, and for much of the time one or other of the mule's hoofs were off the edge, but Gawain pressed onward and at length came to the further bank. There, he looked across a wide meadow to where a fair and well-appointed castle stood gleaming in the sun.

All around the walls stretched a wide moat, while around that, forming another ring of defence, was a palisade of sharpened stakes. As he drew nearer, Gawain saw that each of them bore a human head upon it – a grisly indication of the fate of those who had ventured here before. To make matters worse, the outer walls of the castle revolved continuously, like a giant spinning top, so that as he watched the gate passed by again and again.

Undaunted, Sir Gawain pressed forward until he found a level spot outside the walls. There he waited until he saw the gate coming towards him. Then, at the moment it came level, he spurred the mule forward. The poor beast jumped like a hare, and they passed through the gate in a flash, leaving several hairs from the mule's tail behind! Gawain praised his steed as he looked around him, seeing to his consternation that the place seemed deserted.

Slowly he rode through the streets, until he drew near to the castle keep. There, suddenly, he espied a dwarf hurrying to meet him. As the small man came abreast Gawain called a greeting, which the dwarf answered, but did not stop, hurrying on as though on urgent business.

Puzzled, Gawain got down from the mule's back and advanced towards the keep. He saw a wide archway set in the side, which opened onto a vast deep cellar, going down into darkness. Gawain hesitated, thinking to himself that this place might be worth exploring. At that moment a figure emerged from the shadows: a huge churl, very hairy and wide as a corn-stook, with a great sharp-looking axe resting on one shoulder.

'I give you greeting and hope you have good luck,' the churl said.

'Why, thank you,' answered Gawain. 'Do I have need of it?'

'That you do,' said the churl. 'So does anyone that comes here. Anyway, you have wasted your time. The bridle you seek is in a safe place, and very well guarded. You would need to be a hero indeed to overcome the tests you would face.'

'That is why I am here,' answered Gawain. 'I shall certainly try.'

The churl shrugged and beckoned him to follow. He led the way away from the keep to a house where lodgings had already been prepared. Setting aside his axe the churl brought clean towels and a bowl of water in which Gawain could wash. Then he served the knight from the plentiful viands already set out on the table. Then, when he had eaten, the churl led him to a room with a fine bed and a bright fire made up in the grate.

Gawain prepared to lie down, but before he could do so, the churl spoke again. 'Sir Gawain, I know you for a man of courage and honour. Before you go to your rest – and I promise you shall lie in comfort and with no threat to your safety tonight – I ask that you undertake a test that I shall set for you.'

'I will gladly do so,' said Gawain steadily. He felt no fear of the man, for all his ill-looks and rough way of speaking. 'What is this test? Am I to know?'

'That you shall,' said the churl. 'It's this. Cut my head off tonight with my axe, and in the morrow let me cut off yours.'

Now Sir Gawain remembered how twice before another test of this kind had been offered to him – and that he had succeeded

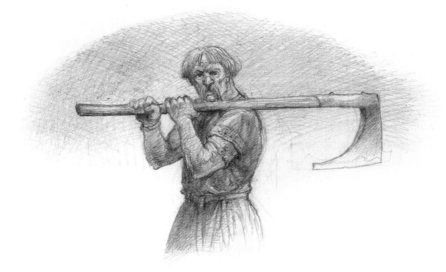

→ *The Churl* ←

on both occasions.* He did not hesitate. 'Very well. Though I'd be a fool if I didn't realize there was more to this than you are telling me.'

The churl made no answer but handed his axe to Sir Gawain and then stretched his neck on a block close at hand. The knight took the fearsome weapon, and hefting it high above his head, delivered a blow which sent the churl's head flying. No blood came out of him, however, and in a moment his body stood up and went to retrieve its head. Carrying the grisly object, the churl left the room. Gawain went to bed – and slept without trouble.

Next day, at first light, Gawain arose. He saw the churl coming, with his head back on his shoulders as though it had never been off. 'Sir Gawain,' he said. 'I hope you haven't forgotten our bargain?'

---

* See 'The Story of Caradoc of the Strong Arm' pp. 150–63, and 'Sir Gawain and the Carle of Carlisle' pp. 277–82.

'Not at all,' replied the king's nephew. 'I am ready.' And he lowered himself down until his neck was stretched on the block where the churl himself had knelt the night before. 'I wish I could be as certain as you that the blow would do me no harm,' he said. 'But strike anyway.'

The churl raised the axe on high and brought it down – but the blade thudded harmlessly into the wood by Gawain's ear, and the churl praised him for his courage.

Gawain got up – a little shakily – and asked if he could now take the bridle.

The churl laughed and said: 'There will be enough time for that soon, and enough fighting for you, Sir Gawain. For you must fight two fierce and terrible lions who are set to guard the bridle. For now, you should eat, for you will need all your strength to overcome them.'

'I need nothing,' Gawain said, 'but it would be helpful to have some armour and weapons, for as you see I have only my sword.'

'Come then,' said the churl. 'There is plenty of gear in this castle, and a good horse which no one has ridden for months. But first let me show you the lions, so that you have an idea what awaits you.'

'There is no need for that,' Gawain said. 'But I should be glad if you would arm me right away.'

The churl led him into a room in the castle where many suits of armour lay about – doubtless having belonged to those whose heads now decorated the stakes outside the castle – and there he armed Gawain well, and then took him to where a fine horse was stabled. Gawain mounted and went outside.

At once the churl let out the first lion, a huge and fearsome creature with a shaggy mane and tough hide. Clearly it had been starved, for it sprang at once with a roar at the knight and knocked aside his shield. Sir Gawain struck back and only succeeded in blunting his sword, for the lion's hide was hard and tough. The churl threw him a second shield, but he soon lost that, and two more like it, in the flurry of blows he exchanged with the lion.

'You're slow,' commented the churl.

Gawain gritted his teeth and with a huge effort drove his sword between the beast's jaws and pierced its heart. He stood panting for a moment, then cried: 'Let the next beast loose.'

The churl obeyed and the second lion sprang forth. Already angry, it became savage when it saw that its fellow lay dead. Hurling itself at Sir Gawain, it tore his mail down to the ventail with a single blow of its great clawed forefoot. The knight struck back with all his might and split the beast's head in twain. He stood there breathing heavily, with blood running down from a dozen slashes in his flesh.

'Now fetch me the bridle,' he said, through gritted teeth.

'Not quite yet,' the churl answered. 'You need food and rest. This is not over yet.'

He led Gawain into the keep and through a maze of corridors and passages to a room where there was a bed. On it lay a huge knight whose bloody condition spoke of many wounds. Yet, when he saw Gawain, he cried: 'Welcome, sir knight. Your bravery has healed me. Now let us fight! For everyone who comes in search of the bridle must do so, and if you lose, your head will join those that already adorn my house.'

Wearily, Gawain drew his sword and prepared to do battle. But the churl drew him outside and showed him the place where they would fight. He explained that Gawain must beware, because even if he won, the only prize he would get would be to have his head on one of the spikes – unless he could slay the knight of the castle outright.

The two men mounted their horses and prepared to fight. In their first course they both broke their spears and were almost unseated. They descended to the earth and drawing their swords fell to with a will, neither giving an inch of ground. Like blacksmiths they struck sparks from each other, until at last Sir Gawain struck a blow which cut through his adversary's helm and left him stunned. Gawain raised his sword to finish the fight once and for all, but before he could strike the knight begged for mercy. 'I was wrong to fight you, Sir Gawain. Until now I thought there was not another man in the world who could best me. Now I see the foolishness of such a thing, and I beg you not to kill me!'

Disgusted, Gawain turned and strode away. The churl followed him, and Gawain said, bitterly: 'Now may I get the bridle?'

The churl shook his head. 'Shall I tell you what you have still to do?'

Wearily, Gawain nodded.

'There are two dragons, very fierce and terrible, that void hot blood and breathe fire. You must defeat both to win the bridle. No one has ever succeeded. If you do, there are no more trials.'

'Go and fetch them,' Gawain said grimly.

'First let me get you water and a fresh harness,' said the churl. 'The one you wear now will not avail you against these creatures.'

As good as his word, he found a fresh hauberk and bright mail to put over it. He also brought a new shield which was especially large. Then Gawain said: 'Go then. Bring out these creatures.'

THE DRAGONS WERE terrible indeed. Black and red scales covered their bodies, and noisome smoke and flame belched out of their mouths. Hot black blood spurted from their nostrils, and where it fell the ground smoked. Sir Gawain was glad of the wide shield, which protected him somewhat from their fiery breath, but it was soon afire, and he was forced to drop it. Gathering all his strength, he dodged in beneath the jaws of one of the beasts and with a great blow cut off its head. The other dragon roared and attacked with even greater ferocity, beating the knight back almost against the walls of the castle. There he turned at bay and leaping high in the air slashed the beast's neck half through. As it roared in agony he leapt upon its head and stabbed into its brain with his sword. The beast fell dead, and Gawain slumped to the earth, spattered with blood and filth.

With surprising gentleness, the churl came forward and helped Gawain unarm, and washed his wounds. As he finished, the dwarf whom Gawain had first seen as he entered the castle, appeared, and greeted him politely. 'Sir, on behalf of my lady I greet you and ask that you come with me and eat at her table. After that you shall have, without further hindrance, the thing which you seek.'

Gawain looked down at the small man. 'I will only go if this churl accompanies me,' he said. 'I have greater trust in him than in any other man here.'

The churl led him once again through a maze of passages to a room in which the lady of the castle lay abed. As Gawain entered, she sat up and smilingly beckoned him forward. 'Welcome, Sir Gawain. Though it is a cause of grief to me that you have slain my pets, yet I acknowledge that you are the greatest knight ever to enter this castle. Let us eat together and talk for a while, then you shall have the bridle.'

So saying she bade Gawain sit on the bed beside her, and the churl served them with food and fine wine. When they had dined the lady turned to Sir Gawain.

'You have done well, and now you will be rewarded. I will tell you that she whom you have helped in this way is my sister, and that by coming here you have done both of us great service. If you are willing, I will take you for my lord and give over not only this castle but five more as well.'

Gawain bowed politely. 'Lady,' he said. 'I thank you, but I must refuse. I am already late for my return to King Arthur, and besides the lady your sister must be worried that I have failed in my task.' He looked directly at the lady and said again: 'May I now have the bridle?'

The lady sighed loudly. 'Very well. Take it, Sir Gawain. You surely deserve it.' And she pointed to where the bridle, a rich thing encrusted with many jewels, hung from a silver nail on the wall, though Gawain had not noticed it there before. He took it in his hands, and giving thanks to the lady, went outside, where the churl had brought the mule. There he put the bridle on the beast and saddled it. Then he prepared to depart.

The lady had given instructions that no one was to hinder his departure and ordered the churl to stop the walls of the castle turning. At the gate Gawain paused to take his leave of the churl, and as he looked back saw that the streets around the castle were suddenly filled with people, who made a great babble of noise, and danced and made merry as though they had been released from some terrible imprisonment.

'What is the meaning of all this?' he asked the churl.

'These are the people of the castle,' said he. 'They were forced to take refuge in the cellars while the creatures whom you slew were at large. Now they are free, and they are all thanking you in their own language for what you have done for them.'

Gawain left the castle, looking back once at the rotting heads on their spikes, and in a while crossed the narrow bridge and passed through the valley and into the woods beyond. There, the beasts came as before, but now they accompanied him, pressing right up to him, rubbing themselves against his legs and feet and the sides of the mule. Only at the edge of the Great Wood did they leave him, after which he made swift passage to Carlisle.

There King Arthur and Queen Guinevere and all the knights came out to greet him, and of course the girl who had come in search of help was there also. She rushed right up to Gawain, and when she saw the bridle on the mule, she embraced the knight and kissed him a hundred times. 'Sir,' she said. 'You have done more than you can ever know for me and my people. No other knight out of more than a hundred who came to the castle succeeded where you have triumphed. I give you my thanks and promise that anything I can ever do for you I shall.'

Then all went inside, and Sir Gawain told the whole story of his adventures. At the end of his recital Queen Guinevere turned to the girl and asked if she would now stay there at the court. But she only shook her head. 'Would that I might, but I am not free to do so. Now that I have the bridle, I must return from whence I came.'

No persuasion would change her mind, and next morning she set off, alone as she had come, riding the mule with its bridle glittering in the sun. The court watched her go from sight, and after that they saw her no more. Nor does it require any great knowledge or wisdom to understand that this was no ordinary test, but another that showed the ill-will of the faery kind towards King Arthur. And you shall hear more tales yet that show this to be true.

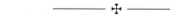

EXPLICIT THE MULE SANS BRIDLE.

INCIPIT THE STORY OF GAWAIN AND RAGNALL –
WHO WAS HIS WIFE FOR MANY YEARS.

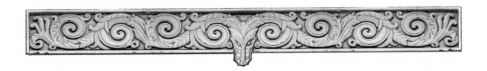

27: THE WEDDING OF SIR GAWAIN AND THE LADY RAGNALL

—— ✛ ——

IT IS SAID THAT SIR GAWAIN WAS THE GREATEST LOVER OF WOMEN IN ALL THE ROUND TABLE FELLOWSHIP, AND CERTAIN IT IS THAT HE KNEW MANY A FAIR LADY AND WAS MARRIED MORE THAN ONCE. BUT ONE ABOVE ALL HE LOVED THE BEST, AND THUS THE STORY OF THEIR MEETING IS TOLD HERE.

✛ ✛ ✛

ONE DAY IT happened that King Arthur went hunting in Inglewood Forest – a part of the Great Wood which many say is a place of darkness and danger. The prey was a mighty hart – and having reached the part of the forest where the beast had been last sighted, the king and his company stayed very still in the underbrush, bows at the ready, waiting for it to appear. But the hart was aware of them and stayed hidden.

'I will see what I can achieve alone,' declared the king. 'The rest of you remain here and keep still!' He advanced, stalking the deer like a woodsman, following it from thicket to thicket for nearly a mile. At last, he had a clear shot, and let fly an arrow, which transfixed the buck and brought it low. The king drew out his hunting knife and began to butcher the meat as was the custom. He was so intent upon his work that he did not hear the figure who came up behind him until it spoke.

'Well met, King Arthur.'

The king turned quickly and saw an extraordinary man, very tall and powerful and with a strange, unchancy look about him. He wore a helmet from which sprang curving horn, for all the world like antlers, and his face was hidden behind a plate of steel. His sword was drawn and his stance far from kindly.

'You have done me a great wrong, Sir King. I shall repay you by taking your life.'

'At least tell me what this wrong is that I have done to you,' said Arthur calmly. 'You might begin by telling me your name.'

'My name is Gromer Somer Jour,' replied the stranger. 'As to the wrong you have done me – you gave my lands to Sir Gawain. What do you have to say about that, Sir King, since we are alone here?'

'First, if you are planning to kill me, I would advise you to think again,' said Arthur. 'My

299

friends are close by, and if you kill me without honour you will get nothing good from it. I think you are a knight – then surely you must remember your vows. Give up this foolishness and let us talk. If I have really done you harm, I shall make amends.'

'Fine words,' answered Gromer Somer Jour. 'But I am not so easily gulled. Now I have you at my mercy. If I let you go, you will escape my punishment.' He raised his sword.

'Listen to me,' said King Arthur. 'Killing me will avail you nothing. I have given you my word that I will make reparation for any hurt I may have caused. You will only defame yourself if you slay me while you are fully armed and I only in forest green.'

'Such words cost nothing,' said Gromer. He hesitated. 'Do you give me your word to meet with me again at this spot one year from now?'

'Willingly,' King Arthur replied. 'If that is your wish. Here is my hand upon it.'

'Wait. You have not heard my provision. In that year you must find the answer to a question. Swear upon my bright sword that you will discover what thing it is that women love best. And by that, I mean both country girls and fine ladies. All women. One year from now you must be here, at this spot, unarmed and alone. Do you swear?'

'Very well,' said King Arthur. 'Though I must tell you that I find this distasteful, I give you my word as a king that I shall return here with an answer one year from now.'

'Good!' said Gromer. 'You can go. But king or not, see that you don't try to trick me. Remember, your life is at stake.' He turned away and vanished amid the trees.

With that King Arthur called his companions to him. They found him with the slain deer, but he was silent and spoke little on the journey home, despite the praise they heaped upon him for his successful kill.

At that time the court was at fair Carlisle. For several weeks the king remained sunk in gloom, until at length Gawain went to his uncle and asked him why he was so withdrawn. At first Arthur would not speak of the matter, but when Gawain pressed him, at length he told the whole story of his meeting

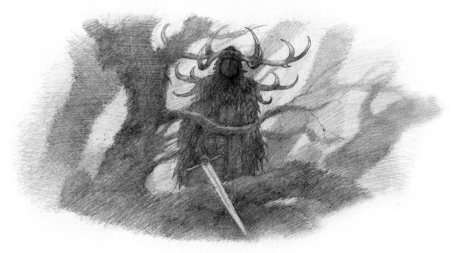

→ *Gromer Somer Jour* ←

with Gromer Somer Jour, and of the promise he had made.

When he was done, Gawain said: 'Sire, do not be downcast. Let us send for our horses and go together into far-off lands. There we shall ask everyone we meet, be they man or woman, the answer to this question. We shall take a book with us, and every answer shall be written down. One at least is bound to be the right one.'

Arthur brightened. 'This is good advice, Nephew,' he said. 'Let us set out at once.'

Having made all arrangements for the king's absence from court, the two men departed, each riding in a different direction – the king disguised so none could know him. Everywhere they went they stopped people they met on the way and asked them Gromer's question. They received some curious answers you may be sure. Some said that women love to be flattered, others that their best joy is to have a lusty man in their arms. Still others said a new gown, or a sparrow-hawk, or a bratchet. In short, they gathered as many different answers as those they asked, and hardly any were the same. They wrote everything in their books and in a short time had hundreds of answers. Both arrived back in Carlisle within days of each other and sat down to compare what they had learned.

'Surely we cannot fail with all these words,' Gawain said.

'I am not so sure,' Arthur replied. 'I am going to go into Inglewood Forest again. There is still some time before the date appointed for my meeting with Gromer. I may yet find more answers.'

'As you wish, sire,' said Gawain, and added: 'Have no fear, my lord, you will succeed.'

King Arthur set forth again, this time undisguised, and rode throughout the forest wherever the paths led him. There he met more people and added their answers to his book, though most looked askance at the sight of their king riding alone through the dark woodland. But it was as he set out to return to Carlisle that Arthur met a strange woman upon the way. She was sitting beside the road on a low hillock from which grew a thorn tree. As he drew near the king saw that she was the most hideously ugly creature he had ever seen. Her back was crooked, her nose snotty, her mouth wide, her teeth yellow, her eyes rheumy. Her neck was as thick as a tree, her hair long and matted. As she peered at him Arthur saw that both her hands and feet were webbed and that the nails grew out like claws.

'Well met, Sir King,' she said. Her voice was low and mellow. 'I am glad we have met like this, for I have the means to save you.'

'How so?' demanded Arthur, in bewilderment.

'There is a question for which you have been seeking the answer. And let me tell you now that all the answers you and Sir Gawain have collected will avail you nothing. Gromer will have your head.'

'How do you know all this?' asked King Arthur.

'Never mind,' said the hag. 'But I am something more than dung! Now, make me a promise and I will tell you the answer that will save your life.'

'It seems to me,' said Arthur, 'that when I make promises it always gets me in trouble! What would you have of me, lady?'

The hag peered at him again. 'I want a handsome knight for my husband. Not just any knight either. Sir Gawain is the name of the man I want. Promise me he shall marry me, and I will give you the answer you seek.'

'I cannot speak for Sir Gawain in such a matter,' said Arthur, aghast.

'Then you will lose your life,' said the hag.

'If what you say is true, and you possess the only answer that will suffice, all I can promise is that I will do all in my power to persuade my nephew to agree to your request.'

'Well then, that will do,' she said. 'Go home and speak persuasively to Sir Gawain. I may be ugly, but I have plenty of life in me. Even an owl can choose a mate. Remember, too, that I can save your life.'

'Lady,' asked King Arthur. 'May I know your name?'

'Kind of you to call me lady,' said the hag, baring her long, yellow teeth at him. 'For I see that you do not think it ... My name is Ragnall.'

'God speed, Lady Ragnall,' said Arthur.

'God speed, King Arthur,' said Ragnall. 'I will be waiting here.'

Heavy of heart, the king returned to Carlisle. The first person he met was Sir Gawain, who asked him how he had fared.

'Not so well,' replied the king. 'Today in Inglewood I met the ugliest woman I ever saw. She said that she knew the answer to my question, but that she would only give it if she could have you for a husband. Since this is clearly impossible, I am in fear for my life.'

'There's no need to fear, my lord,' answered Gawain, cheerfully. 'I will marry this hag, even if she is as ugly as Beelzebub. How could you think otherwise? I am your man and you have honoured me in a hundred battles and jousts. Just say the word and I will comply.'

'Sir Gawain, I thank you,' said Arthur humbly. 'And I dare say you are the best knight in all my lands. My honour and my life are yours to command forever.'

Thus it was agreed between them, and within five days King Arthur set out for his meeting with Gromer Somer Jour. Sir Gawain rode a little of the way with him, until at length Arthur declared that he must ride on alone as he had promised. He had not long left Gawain's company when he saw Ragnall sitting by the roadside as though she had never moved.

'Welcome, Sir King. Do you bring Sir Gawain's promise with you?'

Arthur nodded curtly. 'It shall be as you wish. Now tell me the answer that will save my life!'

'Very well,' said Ragnall. 'I shall tell you what it is that women want above all things, no matter their age or estate or appearance. Our desire is to have sovereignty over men, for thus are we acknowledged and recognized in all things. Now, go your way, Sir King, and tell Gromer what I have said. He will be angry when you do so, for he will know whence you came by the information. But that matters not. Your life is safe now, of that you may be sure. Go now, I will await your return.'

The king rode in a whirlwind of scattered thoughts from that place to the place appointed for his meeting with Gromer. There the fearsome knight waited, a grim look on his face.

'So,' said he, 'let me see what answers you have gathered.'

The king pulled out the two books of answers which he and Gawain had collected and gave them to Gromer. The tall knight scarcely looked at them before tossing them aside. 'Not one of these is the right answer,' he growled. 'Prepare to die, Sir King!' and he drew his sword.

'Wait!' cried Arthur. 'There is one more answer that is not written there.'

'What, then?' demanded Gromer impatiently.

'It is this,' said the king. 'Above all else women desire sovereignty over men, the power to be free – just as this answer gives me my freedom!'

'I know who gave you that answer!' shouted Gromer Somer Jour furiously. 'And I hope she burns for ever for giving it to you. For that was my sister, Lady Ragnall, that you met upon the way, and she has brought me low through her spite. Alas that ever I saw this day, for now is my plan brought to nothing, and that is a sad song for me!' He stared gloomily at the king. 'I suppose you will be my enemy for ever.'

'Of that you may be sure,' Arthur said. 'For I hope never to see you again.'

'Then I give you good day,' said Gromer.

'Good day indeed,' answered King Arthur, and turning his horse rode back to where Ragnall awaited him.

'Well, Sir King,' the hag greeted him. 'I see that you still have your head! I am glad you were successful – this is no more than I promised. I trust you will keep your word now that all is well?'

'Lady,' said King Arthur stiffly. 'Be sure that I shall keep my word.'

'Then I shall accompany you back to Carlisle,' said Ragnall. 'For I long to meet my husband-to-be.'

Thus King Arthur returned home with Ragnall riding at his side. His discomfort was great to be seen with so hideous a creature, but there was no help for it.

As soon as they entered the great hall Ragnall called out that Sir Gawain should be brought to her, so that they might plight their troth in front of all the court. Gawain came forth and took the hag's hand in his and swore to honour her for the rest of his life. Then Ragnall was happy and clapped her bony hands in delight and asked that the wedding be as soon as might be. Queen Guinevere, who felt only sorrow for Sir Gawain, as did all the ladies of the court, did her best to persuade the hag to settle for a quiet wedding, some time early in the day and as secretly as possible. But Ragnall would have none of it.

'Not so, gracious lady,' she said. 'The agreement made between your husband and myself was that I should marry Sir Gawain openly, before all. So I shall. I want there to be announcements made in every part of the land and as many guests as may be entertained here. Indeed,' she added, casting down her eyes, 'I am sorry that I am not more beautiful for the great knight I am to marry, but I am as I am, and I will have my wedding be an honourable feast.'

Shuddering, Queen Guinevere agreed, and let post the banns that day. All across the land women wept when they heard of the wedding of Sir Gawain, for he was ever a most welcome knight among ladies.

The day for the wedding soon dawned, and many turned out to see the great knight wed the monstrous hag. All were agreed that her wedding dress was the finest they had ever seen, and that her jewellery was the richest, but as to the woman herself – to make short the story – they thought her ugly as a sow.

After the wedding there was a great banquet, to which all the guests were invited. It was one of the finest anyone could remember, though Gawain spoke little to his new bride, beyond such pleasantries that honour required of him. All were aghast at Ragnall's table manners. She tore her food apart with her long nails and stuffed her big mouth with it as fast as it could be served. She ate more

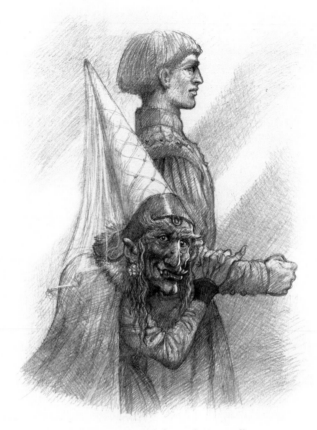

✧ *Sir Gawain and the Lady Ragnall* ✧

than anyone else – at least three capons, three curlews, several huge baked dishes and who knows what else beside. She finished every scrap of food on the table and went on eating until the servants took away the tablecloth and brought water for everyone to wash their hands. Then, the banquet over, Gawain and Ragnall retired to their chamber.

'Now, my lord and husband,' said Ragnall. 'Now that we are wed, I dare say you will show me every kindness, both in bed and without.'

When Gawain did not at once answer, she said: 'At least give me a kiss.'

Gawain, who had been staring into the fire,

turned to her. 'I shall do more than kiss you,' he said. Then he stopped in wonderment, for there before him stood the fairest woman he had ever seen in his life.

'What is your will?' she asked, softly.

'Who are you, and where is my wife?' demanded Gawain.

'I am she,' replied the lady.

'Forgive me,' said Gawain, tears in his eyes. 'A moment ago, you seemed the most hideous creature I had ever seen, and now ... how can this be?'

'First, you must kiss me,' laughed Ragnall, and Gawain complied with her wish most willingly. Then he asked again the meaning

304

of the mystery. Ragnall looked at him heavily. 'My beauty is not constant,' she said. 'You may see me thus fair by day, so that all may admire your wife, but ugly by night to your despite. Or you may have me fair by night for your own pleasure, but hideous by day, so that all will pity you. You must choose.'

Gawain wrung his hands. 'Alas, fair love,' he said at last. 'The choice is hard. To have you fair by night alone would grieve me, since my honour would be hurt by this in the day. Yet to have you ugly at night would bring me less than pleasure. I confess that I cannot decide. But it is, in any case, yours to do as you wish, my lady and my love. I put the choice in your hands. Whatever you decide I shall abide by it. All that I have, body and goods, are yours to command.'

Then Ragnall clapped her hands and cried: 'O you good and courteous knight! Because of this you shall have me fair both day and night! I was enchanted into that hideous form by the one known as Morgan le Fay, that some call Morgan the Goddess, until such time as the best man in all Britain would marry me and give me sovereignty over him. And you, fair and courteous Gawain, have done just that! Now come and kiss me and let us have all the joy we may, as is our right.'

There they came together and spent many a joyful hour until the morning. Then King Arthur, fearing for the life of his nephew at the hands of his hideous bride, came in person to call them to dine. Gawain rose and opened the door to his chamber and invited the king to enter. And there Arthur saw the fairest of women standing by the fire in her shift, her red-gold hair falling below her knees and the light of the morning sun in her eyes.

'Welcome, sire,' said Gawain. 'Here is the lady who saved your life, and who has made mine happier than I thought possible.' And he told all that had occurred, and Ragnall spoke of the spell that was upon her and how Gawain had set her free with his love and the gift of sovereignty.

King Arthur frowned to hear the name of his half-sister invoked as the cause of these events, but he spoke no more of it at that time.

Then Gawain reminded the king of his promise to Sir Gromer Somer Jour, and asked that he should have his lands restored, which he lost because he had been missing for several years and therefore forfeited his claim upon them. This was done and in time King Arthur received Gromer at his court with no ill feeling.

Gawain and Ragnall were joyful together thereafter and in due time the lady bore a son whom they named Guinglain, who was himself a great knight and brought much honour to his father and to the Fellowship of the Round Table. But after only five years Ragnall died, and Gawain mourned her greatly. Indeed, it is said that though he loved often, and was married several times, he never loved another as he did the Lady Ragnall.

Here ends the adventure of King Arthur in Inglewood Forest, and the marriage of Sir Gawain and the Lady Ragnall, as it is told in the old books of this land.

---- ✠ ----

EXPLICIT LIBER TERTIUS.
INCIPIT LIBER QUARTUOR.

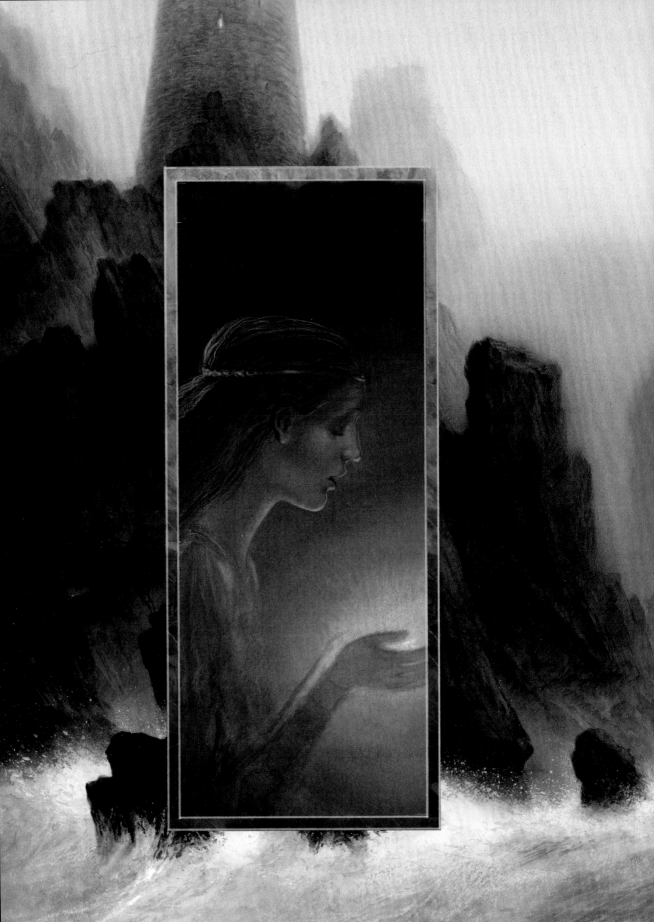

BOOK FOUR

THE BOOK
OF THE GRAIL

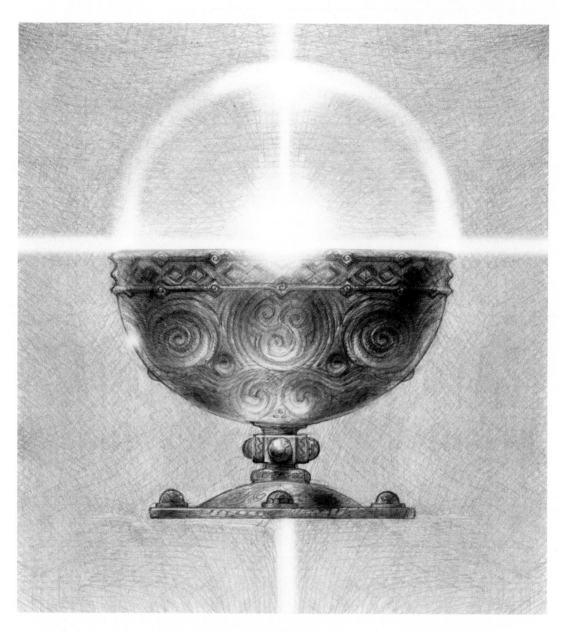

→ The Holy Grail ←

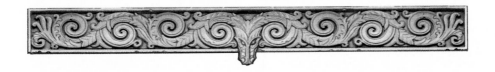

28: THE ELUCIDATION OF THE GRAIL AND THE STORY OF SIR PERCEVAL

⊹

THIS STORY IS TAKEN FROM ONE WHO CALLED HIS WORK *L'ELUCIDATION*, IN THE BELIEF, IT SEEMS, THAT HE COULD EXPLAIN THE MYSTERY OF THE GRAIL TO ALL. SUCH A TASK I BELIEVE TO BE FAR REMOVED FROM THE SKILL OF ANY MAN, MYSELF MOST CERTAINLY, BUT I WILL SET IT DOWN HERE IN MY OWN WORDS, THAT IT MAY PERHAPS PROVE OF INTEREST TO THOSE WISER THAN I. THOUGH I HAVE ALWAYS SOUGHT TO INCLUDE THE STORIES THAT MASTER THOMAS OMITTED FROM HIS GREAT BOOK, YET I HAVE NEVER INCLUDED ONE THAT OFFERED SO DIFFERENT A VERSION OF ONE OF THE TALES HE TOLD. HERE, I HAVE MADE A TALE THAT SPEAKS OF AN OLDER TIME, BEFORE THE COMING OF SIR GALAHAD, IN WHICH SIR PERCEVAL IS THE SEEKER OF THE GRAIL.

⊹ ⊹ ⊹

IN A TIME long before the coming of King Arthur, when ancient magic flourished everywhere, hidden in the depths of the Great Wood was a sacred well – one of many that once existed in these lands. Few came there, but those who did always found welcome, for the well was watched over by women of Faery, who offered sustenance to any who travelled that way. No one was turned away, and it is said that those who drank from the waters of the well, offered to them in cups of gold, never suffered sickness from that day forward, and were forever strengthened.

Also, it was said that if anyone who came to the well desired knowledge, or the answer to some trial in their life, so too the wise women would give them aid. For this reason, they were called 'the Voices of the Well'.

In time, word of this miraculous and mysterious place became known to a cruel and greedy king named Amangons. Hearing of the secret well, and especially of the golden cups and dishes from which the women served their guests, Amangons assembled a party of his men and went into the forest to seek out the place.

When, after long days of searching, they came to where the well was, they were met by the faery women, who made to offer them hospitality. But Amangons, in his greed, ordered his men to attack the women, raping them and stealing their golden cups. He himself sought out she who was the leader of the guardians, and having had his way with her, took her cup to serve as his own drinking vessel.

So it was that the faery women were ravished and wounded and as a result they vanished away into the depths of the Great Wood, while the place where the well lay became silent and desolate. Those who knew of it said that they had lost the voices of that well, and that a light had been extinguished in the land. Indeed, nothing grew there any longer, and darkness spread out on all sides, so that the land turned to waste, and the trees in that part of the forest were no longer leafy. Thus far and wide it became known as the Wasteland, and as a place where no one ventured unless they sought despair and death.

You may be sure that no good came of this, for scarcely a year passed before Amangons was killed and many of his men with him. The memory of the well passed out of mind, and the land which had flourished for so long remained waste and dead. It is also told that for many ages before this time there had existed an accord between the races of men and of Faery, but because the women attacked by Amangons were of the faery kind, there was afterwards enmity between the two races – even to the time of King Arthur, when he and his knights were so often challenged by creatures of magic – in memory of the attack by Amangons. Whether this is true or not I cannot say, but to this day the breaking of the Faery Accord

is spoken of by those who know the hidden ways between the worlds.

✛ ✛ ✛

SO PASSED MANY years, until the time of King Arthur, when it happened that one of his knights entered the Wasteland. There he met the folk who dwell there in great sorrow, and from them learned of the evil deed of King Amangons and his men. Greatly troubled, the knight carried word of this to King Arthur, and when the Fellowship of the Round Table heard of it, they swore to seek out those who had done this dreadful thing, and to punish them with sword and fire.

But though they looked long and hard, venturing into the heart of the Great Wood, not one of Amangon's men did they find. Instead, they encountered a company of most beautiful women, who wandered amongst the trees and were protected by a body of knights, all fair and tall, who took swift vengeance against anyone who approached the maidens with ill-intent. Not even King Arthur's knights could defeat these guardians – though at last Sir Gawain was strong enough to capture one of the forest knights and to return with him to Camelot the Golden. This man, whose name was Bleheris, was soon known to be a good man and a great teller of tales, and once he had learned that the Fellowship were in search of Amangons and his men, he told the knights to look no further: 'For both the Maidens of the Wood and we who are their protectors, are the living descendants of those who guarded the well and of the evil men who ravaged them. Ever since that time we have been doomed to wander the land and have hidden from all others in the Great Wood. Thus, if you seek to kill us, you will be doing so to innocent men, for the means of our coming into this world was none of our doing, nor should we be punished for the actions of the evil king and his men.'

'Have you lived so long?' said King Arthur in wonder, for when they heard this, the Knights of the Round Table knew that their task was fruitless. But Gawain thought to ask Bleheris about the cause of the Wasteland and what could be done to heal it.

'That is a hard task indeed,' answered Bleheris. Then he told them of a secret that had long been forgotten in the lands over which King Arthur ruled: that the wells and the women who guarded them were part of the kingdom of one called the Rich Fisher, which had been made desolate by the actions of Amangons and his men, and which could not be healed until a knight came who was seeking the cause of these things. Many there were who sought out the Rich Fisher's court, but few ever found their way there, and those who did were seldom seen again in the world of the living, or else wandered still in search of answers to the causes of the Wasteland. It is of one of these, Sir Perceval, whose name is well known, that I shall write now, concerning his coming to Camelot the Golden and what followed thereafter.

✣ ✚ ✣

NOT LONG AFTER King Arthur won the test of the Sword in the Stone, and had been crowned, Merlin the Wise came to him and said: 'Sire, I cannot stay here any longer, for I am bidden to depart for another place from where I may observe what passes within the world. But before I depart there are certain things that you must know.' Then, as King Arthur listened, Merlin spoke to him of the

Holy Grail, which had been used by Our Lord to celebrate the Last Supper and had been given into the care of Joseph of Arimathea, Christ's uncle, and, later still, placed in the Court of the Rich Fisher, that many sought. 'The good man who goes by this name cannot die until a knight from this court comes to that hidden place in search of the Grail. If he succeeds in achieving it, the Rich Fisher will be able to die, and the enchantment which has lain upon the Wasteland since before the time of your father, because of the actions of the evil king, Amangons, will be lifted. All these things I tell you so that you may be prepared for what is to happen when I am no longer here to advise you.

'And this also will I tell you. When the Holy Grail was given into his keeping, Joseph of Arimathea made a table in the likeness of that at which the Last Supper was celebrated. Twelve places there were at this table, and one that was always empty, in token of the betrayer Judas. In our own time I have had a table made in memory of the one made by Joseph. It is the Round Table, at which you and your knights will sit. There will be a place empty there also, until a destined one comes to fill it. When that knight comes you will know that the mysteries of the Grail are beginning.'

When he had said these things, which greatly puzzled the young king, Merlin departed, and none might stay him. He went into Northumberland, to his old master, Blaise, to whom he told all that had happened since the beginning of time, and all that was to come in the time of King Arthur. And though other tales tell how he was imprisoned by the wiles of the Lady Nimue, I would say that not all that is written about Merlin is true.

✣ ✚ ✣

THE STORY TELLS that King Arthur ruled well and justly for many years, and knights came from far and wide to fill the seats at the great Round Table. It was said, and justly so, that no knight was worthy of praise until he had served at least a year at Arthur's court.

Word of this reached a great knight of Wales named Alain le Gros, who declared that when his son, who was called Perceval, came of age, he should go to King Arthur. Many times he spoke of this openly to the youth, but each time the boy's mother spoke against it. Perceval, however, heard only his father's words, and when the time came for Alain to die, his son waited only until he was buried before he set out for Camelot the Golden. He went so quietly that no one knew he was gone until the end of the day. Then his mother wept and prayed that he should not be eaten by wild animals, or slain by evil men, and when no word came from her son in the weeks that followed, she became sick with sorrow, and in a little while she died.

Perceval knew nothing of this but continued on his way until he reached the court of King Arthur, where he found a good greeting and soon proved himself both gentle in manners and skilled in the use of arms. For though he knew next to nothing of such matters when he arrived at the court, yet he learned quickly, and was soon accepted among the other knights until finally he came to sit at the Round Table itself, along with Lancelot of the Lake, Sir Gawain of Orkney and his brothers, and many more.

Thus all was well within the land of Britain, until King Arthur determined to hold a court that should be the greatest in all the world, and that every good knight and all their ladies should attend. And in the great hall of Camelot the Golden would the peers of the Round Table be at his side, for he wished to exalt the order that he had founded, and the work of Merlin who had made the Table in the time of his father.

When the time came for this gathering to take place it was indeed the greatest that had ever been seen in that land. Men said that King Arthur was the most splendid and regal lord ever to wear a crown, and that never in all the history of the world had such a noble gathering been assembled. Over a hundred knights and their ladies sat together in the great hall to celebrate the festival of Pentecost and that was the most joyful and splendid affair that anyone living could remember. Afterwards they repaired to the lists and there held a great tournament at which King Arthur himself entered the field to see that there was peace and accord between the combatants.

With him rode the young knight, Perceval, who had taken the title Le Galles, which is to say, 'of Wales', and who desired greatly to prove himself. He was much troubled that he could not fight in the tournament because of a wound to his hand which made it difficult to hold a spear or sword. But even though he made no brave show of arms, he caught the attention of Elaine of Orkney, sister to Sir Gawain and daughter of King Lot, and who was reckoned the fairest maiden in all the land at that time.

When she saw Sir Perceval riding pale and proud beside the king, she fell deeply in love with him, and that night, when everyone was turning towards their beds, she sent word that she wished him to joust in her name the next day. To this end she sent a messenger bearing a suit of red armour and asking that he accept it as a gift from one who admired him deeply.

Perceval was much flattered that so lovely

and noble a lady should show him favour and sent word that he would indeed fight for her on the morrow. And you may be sure that he slept but little that night but fell to exercising his hand that it might better serve him in the jousts.

Next day the king and all his court heard Mass in the cathedral, and then the peers of the Round Table assembled and ate together. The king honoured them greatly and spoke highly of their courage and bravery, and of their goodness. Then once again they repaired to the jousting.

Sir Perceval, clad in the scarlet mail sent to him by Elaine, and bearing a plain shield so that no one should know who he was, performed such feats of arms that day that no one might withstand him – not even Sir Lancelot or Sir Gawain. And many people who saw these feats began to say aloud that the knight in red should be asked to sit at the Round Table. Thus, at the end of the day King Arthur called the knight to come before him and asked him his name.

Then Perceval removed his helm, and all were astonished. Perceval explained that the armour was a gift from one who loved him, at which everyone smiled, and Lancelot remarked that such deeds as he had performed that day, when done in the name of love, were less astonishing, though they ought still to be praised. To this King Arthur agreed, and said to Perceval that, if he desired it, as soon as a place became vacant at the Round Table, he should have it. But Perceval looked and saw that there was already an empty seat, and he asked who might sit there.

'That seat is a great wonder,' replied the king, and told him what Merlin had said: that this was an empty place in token of the betrayer. 'And he told me also,' said Arthur,

'that once a disciple of Joseph of Arimathea attempted to sit in that place and was swallowed up. Only the best knight in the world may sit there.'

Then Perceval looked at the seat and, in his heart, longed to take his place in it. But when he spoke of this to Arthur, the king shook his head. 'By no means,' he said. 'You are a good knight indeed, too good to be lost to us – but I doubt that you are the best in the world.'

When they heard this, many of the knights, including Sir Gawain and Sir Lancelot, spoke up and begged the king to let Perceval at least try the test of the Perilous Seat. At first Arthur would not agree, but in a while, with a sigh, he said that if Perceval was of a mind to try it, then he might. And Perceval said that he would do this in humility, and because his heart bade him, not because he deemed himself the best knight in the world. Then he crossed himself and uttered a prayer and seated himself in the chair.

At once there was a terrible cry, as though the earth itself groaned aloud, and the chair split, emitting a cloud of black smoke such that no one present could see more than a small space around them. Then a voice spoke out of the smoke, which said: 'King Arthur, know that you have allowed a deed that will cause suffering to many. And know further that this knight, Sir Perceval, shall suffer great pains because of his rashness, and that only because of the goodness of his father Alain le Gros and his grandfather the Rich Fisher, is his life spared. And know too that the Grail is in this land; and only when one of the knights of this Fellowship has done great deeds and achieved many perilous adventures will he come at last to the place where it is kept. And if he is able to achieve its mysteries, then shall the land be healed and the stone that

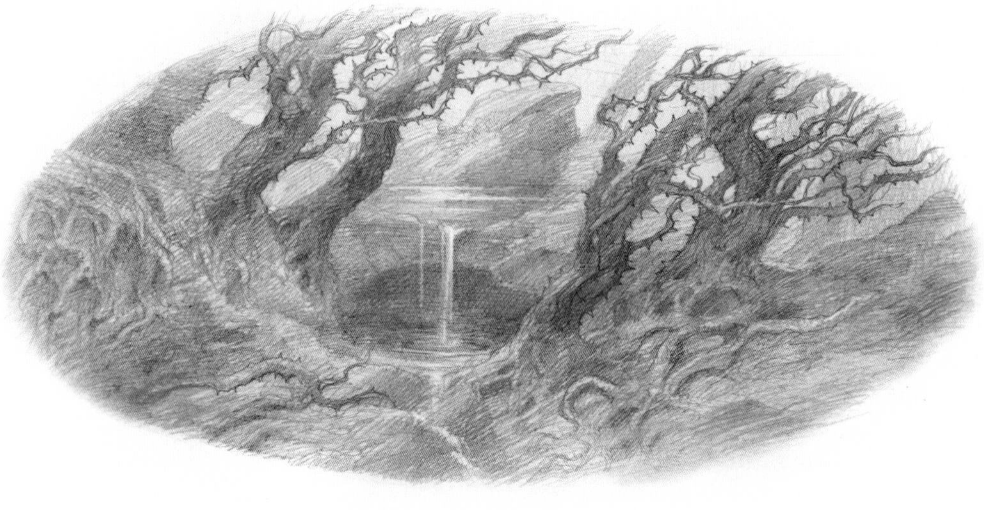

The Fountain in the Wasteland

has broken this day re-united. Then and only then, will the enchantments be lifted from the Wasteland.'

The voice fell silent, and all marvelled greatly. Then as one man all the knights swore that they would go forth in search of the Grail; and Perceval, who was greatly ashamed by his rash act and the sorrow which it would bring, swore that he would not remain in any place for longer than one night until he found the Court of the Rich Fisher and undid the enchantments.

King Arthur was sorrowful when he heard this for, as Master Thomas has told, he believed in his heart that never would his great Fellowship meet all together again. And though he could not fail to give them leave to depart, he did so with a heavy heart.

Next day the Fellowship set forth and rode for a time together until they reached a place where several roads met at a stone cross. Then Perceval said: 'We shall meet with no adventure while we ride together. Let us go our own ways, and hope that God will bring us together again one day.' And to this they all assented, and each one chose a path to follow and went forth upon it. Many adventures they had, as Sir Thomas has told, but I will not speak of these but turn instead to the deeds of Sir Perceval, which are different from those described in 'The Book of the Sankgreal'.*

✠ ✠ ✠

IN THE DAYS that followed, the young knight met with many adventures, and in each one he conducted himself with grace and nobility, always dealing with his adversaries as a knight should, and causing more than one fair lady to weep for longing when he continued upon his way. For Perceval would stop in no place more than a night, just as he had sworn, but rode upon the quest of the Grail with single-minded intent.

Thus he came one day to a castle in the

* Malory's name for the Grail, meaning the 'Sacred Grail'.

depths of the Great Wood, and saw that the drawbridge was down and the gates open, and he entered with caution and saw no one. Dismounting at the horseblock, he tethered his steed and went inside. The castle seemed empty on every side, despite the fact that fresh rushes were strewn on the floors. And Perceval wondered greatly at this, and where the people of the castle might be.

When he had looked around, he returned to the great hall and there espied a chessboard set up before the window as though in readiness for play. And the chessboard was of silver and the pieces of black and white ivory. Perceval stood in contemplation for a time, looking at the fine chess set. Then he moved one of the pieces, and to his astonishment an opposing piece moved of its own volition against him. In wonder Perceval moved a second piece and lo! another piece moved against him. Then the knight sat down at the table and began to play. He played three games, and each time he was beaten. Then he was angry, and said aloud: 'I am no beginner at this game, yet I am beaten every time. This is an evil magic I think, and no one else should have to suffer it.'

Then he took up the pieces and went to the window. But as he was about to throw them into the moat a voice came to him. 'If you throw the chess pieces away you will bring great harm upon you!'

Perceval looked up and saw a damsel standing at a window high above the one where he was.

'I will forbear if you will come down and speak with me.'

'I do not care to do so,' she replied.

'Then I shall cast them away,' said Perceval.

'Do not do so!' exclaimed the lady. 'I would rather come down.'

So Perceval took the pieces back to the silver board and placed them upon it, where they arranged themselves as they had been before play.

Then the damsel entered, with five other ladies and servants, who welcomed the knight and hastened to unarm him and to care for his horse. Despite her earlier reluctance to talk with him, the damsel welcomed the knight sweetly and bade him sit with her. Perceval was soon filled with love for her, and there and then he asked if she could return his passion. The maiden, whose name was Honorée and who was indeed very fair, smiled at him and answered: 'Sir, I believe I could love you, even though I know nothing of you at all. But I need assurance that you are as valiant in deeds as you are ardent in your wooing.'

'My Lady,' said Sir Perceval. 'You may ask anything of me, so long as it be not against my knightly vows.'

'Very well,' said the damsel Honorée, 'I shall tell you what I most desire. In the wood near here is a white stag. I bid you capture it and bring me its head. To help you in this I will give you a bratchet that is most skilful in the chase.'

To this Perceval agreed. Then, as dusk was already falling, they ate a fine supper, and all retired to bed. But Perceval lay awake for much of the night, thinking of Honorée and how greatly he loved her. In the morning he prepared to set forth in search of the stag. The maiden brought her dog to him and commanded that he should care for it with his life. To this he gave his word, and with the dog perched on the saddle before him, went forth into the wood.

Soon the dog gave tongue and Perceval set it down on the road, where it hastened to lead him to where the stag hid in a thicket.

Perceval gave chase to the beast, which was as white as snow and heavily antlered. In a while, he caught up with it and slew it and took its head. But as he was hanging it by his saddlebow there came an old woman riding on a palfrey, and she snatched up the little bratchet and rode off at full speed.

Then Perceval angrily mounted his steed and gave chase. When he overtook the woman, he seized the bridle of her steed and cried out to her to stop and to give back the dog. But she only looked at him evilly and said: 'A curse be upon you if you say this dog is yours. I know that you have stolen it, and I will take it back to she who owns it.'

'That is untrue,' said Perceval. 'The dog belongs to my lady, and you shall not have it.'

'You may use force against me if you wish, though you know it is false to do so,' said the old woman. 'But if you will do but one service for me, I shall deliver the dog to you willingly.'

'What service is that?' asked Perceval.

'A little further along this road you will see a stone tomb, and on it is painted a picture of a knight. If you will go there and say aloud that he who painted the image is false, then I promise you shall have back this bratchet without further delay.'

Perceval said that he would do as she asked and rode on his way until he saw the tomb with the painting upon it. Then he looked all around him and said, out loud as he was bidden: 'False was the one who painted this image.' Then he turned to go back the way he came, but at once heard a great noise behind him. When he looked over his shoulder, he saw a huge knight coming toward him at a great pace. He was clad from head to foot in black armour, and his horse was of the same hue, and when he saw him Perceval was sore

afraid, for there was something uncanny about the knight. Then he remembered that he was a knight of the Round Table, and he crossed himself and set his spear in rest and charged toward the black knight.

They met with a fearsome crash and both fell from their horses and lay stunned on the earth for a time. Then they recovered and fell to battling against each other with tremendous force – until Perceval struck his opponent such a blow on the helm that it felled him. But at once the knight jumped up and continued his assault. And thus it ever was, that as fast as Perceval struck down his adversary, the other arose again with renewed strength.

As they fought there came another knight, who rode right up to where the two men were battling and took up the stag's head from where it hung at Perceval's saddle, and snatched the bratchet from the old woman and rode off. When he saw this, Perceval was so angered that he redoubled his efforts and gave the Black Knight such a buffet that he fell back. Perceval followed up with such a rain of blows that his opponent retreated before him and then, to Perceval's astonishment, ran to the tomb and opened it and jumped inside, pulling the lid upon himself.

Perceval, wondering greatly, cried out three times to him to come out, but the tomb remained firmly closed. Then the knight knew that he would get no answer there and returned to where the old woman sat upon her palfrey.

'Who was that knight who took the stag's head and my lady's bratchet?' he demanded, but the old woman merely shrugged and said: 'Evil curse the one who asks me about that, since I know nothing of it. As you have lost the dog, you should look for it.'

Hearing this, Perceval knew that he wasted

his breath and turned away and mounted his steed and rode in the direction which the knight had taken as fast as he might. But though he searched for a long while, and always asked after the knight with the bratchet and the stag's head, he found no trace of him.

Perceval rode for many days until he came at length into a part of the forest that seemed dead. Great entanglements of undergrowth fouled the way, yet the knight pressed on until he came at length to a great castle. As he came near to the walls a damsel with hair the colour of night came forth and greeted him and told him that he was welcome to stay there. This Perceval willingly accepted, for he was tired from struggling with the forest. The dark-haired damsel led him inside and helped him to unarm, and other women came forward and took away his horse to feed it. Then they all went inside, and the damsel directed Perceval to a chair and sat down opposite him. She looked upon him for a long while and then suddenly began to weep, until Perceval asked what it was that grieved her.

'Sir,' answered the damsel. 'I have a brother and we are both the children of a brave knight and his lady. When we were still young our father died, and soon after that my brother departed for King Arthur's court, whence he had always longed to go. After he departed our mother took sick and died, since when I have heard no word from my brother. It seemed for a moment that you reminded me of him.'

Perceval looked at the damsel with the night-dark hair and he stared around him at the hall. It was as if scales fell from his eyes, and he rose and took the maiden in his arms and said: 'Sister, I am Perceval, your brother.' And the two fell to weeping and kissing each other.

Then the damsel's people entered and were amazed, until she broke away from her brother's embrace long enough to tell them who he was. At which there was great rejoicing, and food and wine were brought, and brother and sister sat for long hours talking of the events that had passed. And the damsel asked if he had yet found the Court of the Rich Fisher. 'Not yet,' replied Perceval. 'But I will not rest until I have done so.'

'Surely you should give up this search,' said his sister. 'For you have laboured long and found nothing. Remain here I beg you, for you are still young, and I fear for your life if you continue through this dangerous land.'

'Nothing would please me greater, if I had completed my quest,' said Perceval. 'But until I have done so, I cannot stay.'

Then Perceval's sister wept, and when she could speak again, she begged him to do one thing for her before he set forth again, and that was to visit a certain wise hermit who lived close by in the forest. 'He is our uncle and brother to our father, Alain le Gros. He has told me much of our grandfather, who has the Grail in his keeping, and that it shall pass to you, if you can only find it and set him free.'

Perceval said that he would willingly go and see the hermit, and next day they set forth to his house. When they arrived. the hermit himself came forth to meet them, leaning upon a crutch, for he was very old. And when he saw that it was his niece who was come there, he wondered aloud whom the knight was that accompanied her.

'Dear uncle, this is my own brother, Perceval, your nephew, who left to go to King Arthur's court. Now he is a great knight and is engaged upon the quest for the Grail.'

The old hermit greeted Perceval warmly

and embraced him. Then he asked if he had yet been to the Court of the Rich Fisher, that was his own brother and the young knight's grandfather. Perceval shook his head and answered that he sought it, but in vain. The hermit responded: 'Let me tell you that my brother and I were both present when the Holy Spirit commanded your grandfather to carry the Grail to this land. And also, it was said that an heir would be born to Alain le Gros that would one day become the keeper of the Grail himself, and that the Rich Fisher would be unable to die until that heir should come to his castle and achieve the mystery of the Grail. I believe that heir is you, Perceval. You must take care to follow the path of the Grail faithfully, for you are of a lineage that God has greatly honoured, and if you pursue the path of honour you will find a great destiny awaits you.'

'Sir,' said Perceval, much moved. 'I shall do all that I may to honour this great trust.'

With that the hermit blessed him, and wept for his coming, and that night all three remained a long while in prayer before retiring. Then, when the sun rose, Perceval begged leave of the hermit and of his sister to follow the Grail, and the wise man blessed him again and said that he would continue to pray for him. Then Perceval and his sister departed together for her castle.

They had not gone far when a fully armed knight came galloping towards them at great speed, crying out to Perceval to defend himself or give up the maiden who rode with him. Perceval was so deeply sunk in thought for his task and, if the truth be known, of the lady of the bratchet to whom he had failed to return with the stag's head, that he failed even to notice the knight until his sister cried out loud to him. Then he saw the knight

coming and without even thinking he set his spear in rest and met the other head on. The stranger's lance shattered, but Perceval's drove right through shield and hauberk into his breast, killing him outright.

Then Perceval mourned the death of his opponent. 'I wish that I had defeated you rather than killed you. I do not even know your name.'

Perceval dragged the dead knight across his horse's saddle, and they rode on to the castle, where they were received by his sister's people and made comfortable. Next morning, Perceval called for his horse and armour. When she saw that, his sister grew sorrowful.

'Must you leave so soon?'

'I must follow the path of the Grail as my uncle told me,' replied the knight. 'But you may be sure I shall return as soon as I can, so long as my life is spared.'

Then despite all his sister's pleading Perceval set forth again on his road, to follow it wherever fate might lead. The way was long and led the knight through lands both rich and barren, sleeping by turns upon the earth or in castles where hospitality was readily granted. Then one day he came to a place where there was a very fair meadow, and a stream running beside it, and a fording place. Beside the ford was a tent, and a knight awaited all who came there and forbade them passage unless they jousted with him. This Perceval did, and quickly overthrew the fellow. Then he demanded why he prevented travellers from passing that way or from getting water.

'Sir, I will tell you,' said the knight, whose name was Urban of the Black Pine. 'I am a knight of King Arthur's court, and after I received the accolade of knighthood I set forth in search of adventure. And, if I may say so, I found few who could withstand me. One night I was on the road, and a storm overtook me. Lightning flashed from the sky, and by its light I saw a maiden riding swiftly ahead of me. I followed her and soon arrived at the fairest castle in the world. The gates stood open, and I followed the maiden within. She greeted me warmly and made me welcome. Within a few days I had fallen in love with her and made bold to woo her. She said that she would be my love so long as I never went beyond sight of the castle. I answered that I would do so willingly, but that I would be sad to give up errantry. Then the maiden said that I should wait beside this tent and offer battle to all who came this way. That way I could be with her and still enjoy the life of a knight. Since then, I have been here almost a year, and have not been beaten until now. And so this place has become known as the Perilous Ford.'

Perceval looked around him. 'Where is this castle of which you speak?'

'It is close, but only I can see it,' replied Urban. Then he looked at Perceval and said: 'Now that you have defeated me you must remain here for a year and defend the Perilous Ford.'

'Not for anything will I remain here,' answered Perceval. 'I am on a quest that will not wait. But I bid you cease lying in wait for those who come here and return to King Arthur.'

To this the knight agreed, but scarcely had he spoken when a great noise broke out on all sides, from an unseen source, that sounded like the crumbling and crashing of stones, and a black cloud enveloped them both. Then a great voice spoke, that said: 'Perceval le Galles, you have done a terrible deed this day, and you are cursed for it!' To the knight it said: 'Urban, you too have failed me. Hurry now or you will lose me.'

When the knight of the ford heard this, he fell on his knees before Perceval. 'Sir, you have beaten me fairly and I owe you my life. But I beg you not to send me away from this place! Let me go to my lady.'

'By no means!' cried Perceval. 'You shall go to King Arthur!'

At this Urban tried to run away, but Perceval seized him and held him back. As they struggled the voice came again, urging Urban to make haste. When he heard this the knight drew his sword and would have attacked Perceval again, though he had given his word when he was overcome.

Angrily Perceval fought back, but as they were engaged a cloud of great black birds appeared and began to attack Perceval furiously. He was so angered by this that he struck the knight to the earth with a single blow and then, turning upon the birds, ran one of them through with his sword. As it fell to the earth, its form shivered, and it became the body of a maiden of surpassing beauty. Perceval stared in wonder as the rest of the birds broke off the attack, and seizing the fallen body, carried it into the air and away from sight.

Urban, meanwhile, lay groaning where he had fallen. As Perceval stood over him, the knight opened his eyes and begged for mercy. 'I will spare you,' said Perceval. 'But first you must tell me the meaning of what took place just now.'

'I will do so gladly,' replied Urban. 'The great noise which you heard was the breaking of the walls of my lady's castle. For when I was overcome and promised to return to King Arthur, her magic failed her. Then it was her voice that you heard, cursing both of us. Lastly it was my lady herself and her women who became birds and attacked you. She whom you wounded was my lady's sister.

But she is not harmed at all, for even now she is in the sacred isle of Avalon, where my lady and her women can go in an instant by ways known only to them.'

Then Perceval marvelled greatly, and Urban begged him again to release him, so that he might return to his love. Perceval bent his head and gave him permission, and Urban was so glad that he ran off up the road, forgetting his horse and all his equipment. Perceval watched him go and saw a damsel appear on a black horse and carry him up before her. In moments they were gone from sight, far more swiftly than mortal riders could go. Perceval shook his head and rode upon his way, for he knew it would be folly to pursue them.

⊹ ✝ ⊹

NOW PERCEVAL ENTERED a part of the land which seemed deserted. Night after night he was forced to sleep on the ground, and it became harder each day to find anything to eat. All the time he turned his mind to the nature of his quest and of whether he was worthy to achieve the Grail. And by and by he came to a meeting of four ways, and there the most beautiful tree he had ever seen grew by the roadside. Next to it stood an intricately carved cross. As Perceval reined in his mount, he heard a sound in the tree, and looking up saw two children, a boy and a girl, as it seemed about six years of age, clambering from branch to branch. Perceval called out to them and asked them to speak to him.

'Perceval le Galles,' said one of the children. 'We are come to help you, if you will let us. Yonder lies your road. Follow it and you will see things that will aid you in the completion of your quest – if it is right for you to do

so.' So saying, both children pointed towards the right-hand path.

Then Perceval was filled with wonder and looked to where they pointed. But when he looked again towards the tree it was no longer there, and the children also could no longer be seen. Thus he deemed this to have been a true vision – if the children were indeed not demons. But as he wondered whether he should take the road indicated, there came a shadow that passed before him, causing his horse to snort and rear. And a voice came to him, that said: 'Perceval, you have heard of Merlin. He wishes you to know that the two children were indeed messengers, and that if you follow this path, if you are worthy of it, you shall succeed in your quest.' Then the voice was silent, and though Perceval called out three times to it, it answered him not.

The knight set forth on the way that was indicated, and he liked it not for it was open country, and he could not rid himself of a feeling that he was being watched. He rode until he came to a rich land through which a broad river coursed. There, in the midst of the water, he saw a small boat, and in the boat lay an old man, richly clad, that fished from the side. Two servants were with him, and he called out to Perceval, inviting him to stay that night in his castle, which lay upstream a short way. Perceval was glad of that, for it seemed a long while since he had slept in a bed. So he took his way, but as he rode on he saw no sign of a castle, and began to doubt the words of the old man in the boat.

He wandered for a while until dusk began to fall. Then he became aware of a castle that lay in a sheltered valley. Never had he seen so fine and splendid a place, and his spirits lifted at once. He rode up to the gate and was admitted by the porter, who took his mount

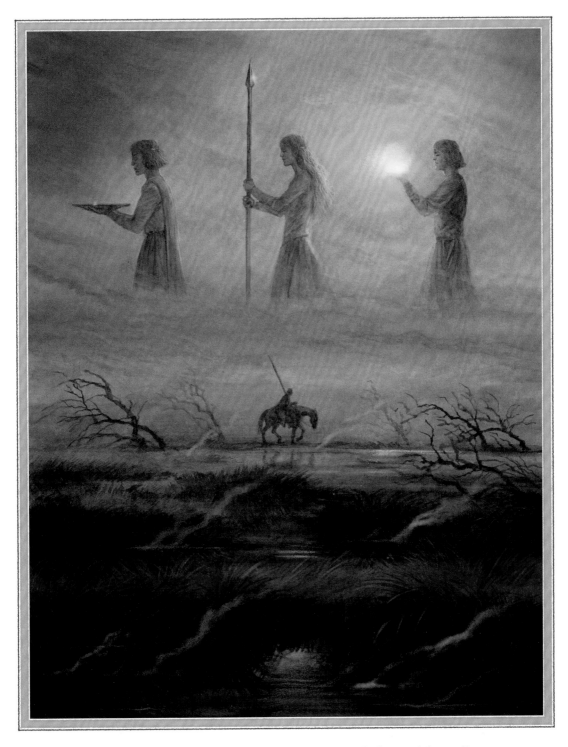

PLATE 8: *'Now Perceval entered part of the land which seemed deserted'*

and gave him into the care of several squires who escorted him into the hall and made him comfortable. When he had been there a short time, there came in four servants, who between them carried an old man in a litter. Perceval saw that it was the same man that he had seen fishing earlier that day, and that he was so frail that he could not stand unaided but must be borne about by his servants.

When he saw the old man, who seemed to him like a king, Perceval jumped to his feet and said: 'Sir, you should not have troubled yourself to greet me.'

The old man smiled and said: 'I wish to honour you, sir knight.' Then he called to his servants and bade them bring food and drink for his guest. They brought tables swiftly and set them up and laid them with white cloths and set dishes of gold and silver upon them. Then, as Perceval and the old man were about to begin eating, there came into the hall the most curious procession the young knight had ever seen.

First came a damsel, very richly dressed, who bore in her hands a silver platter. After her came a youth, carrying a lance – and three drops of blood came from its head and fell to the floor. And last of all there came another youth, who bore between his hands the vessel that is called the Grail. And when they saw it the king and all his people bowed their heads in prayer, while Perceval looked upon it and wondered greatly at its beauty and richness. But though he was much moved to ask concerning the procession, he remembered how his mother had told him not to ask too many questions, and therefore he kept silent while the procession passed before him and went out of the hall by another door.

Perceval was so tired from the nights spent in the open, where he had slept little, that he almost fell asleep at the table. Then the old king grew very sad indeed, for he was indeed the Rich Fisher whom Perceval sought, his own grandfather, who had brought the Grail to the land of Britain. It had been prophesied that when a knight came to the castle where he lived and asked concerning the mysteries of the place, then and only then would the old king be permitted to die. And he had been alive these many hundred years and longed greatly to depart. But he could not, for Perceval failed to ask the question he should.

Then the old king begged leave to be excused and went to bed, and Perceval followed soon after, being put to bed in a splendid room with a soft mattress and pillows. He still wondered about the procession and thought that he would ask of the youths who carried the spear and the cup in the morning.

Next day Perceval rose and went in search of his host. But though he walked all through the castle he could find no one, and when he went outside it was the same. Then he saw that his harness was cleaned and laid ready for him, and in the stable he found his horse all saddled and bridled and well fed. He mounted and rode forth, expecting at any moment to see someone from the castle, whom he believed must have gone forth to gather fresh rushes or herbs for the old fisherman.

All morning Perceval rode through the forest and saw no one. Then he spied a maiden wandering in the wood, weeping bitterly. When he came up to her, she said: 'Ah, Perceval, what a wretch you are! Last night you lay in the Court of the Rich Fisher, and you saw the procession of the Grail, and yet you said nothing. Know that if you had asked concerning the wonders you saw, your grandfather would have been healed and the enchantments which lie upon the Wasteland would have been lifted. But you are too foolish, and you have not done sufficient deeds to warrant such a reward. But for this, you might indeed have become the new guardian of the most holy Grail!'

When he heard these words Perceval himself began to weep. He cried aloud that he would never rest until he had undone the evil of that day and promised to return at once to his grandfather's house and ask the question which he should have asked. And though the damsel shook her head, Perceval commended her to God and turned back the way he had come.

NOW PERCEVAL FOUND that, although he tried to retrace his steps, the way went differently, and though he rode for the next two days without stopping for sleep and scarcely to rest, he could in no wise find the Court of the Rich Fisher. At the end of that time, he saw ahead of him a damsel with golden hair, sitting by the side of the road, and on a tree by her side hung the white stag's head which Perceval himself had cut off days before. When he saw it, he was very glad and rode right up to the tree and snatched it down without a word to the damsel. Angered by his impetuous act, she cried out for him to put back the head. But Perceval merely laughed and said that he would not do so, for it belonged to another and to her he would return it.

While they spoke, Perceval heard a noise of barking, and there came first a doe, running, and in pursuit of it the very bratchet which he had lost previously. When it saw Perceval, it leapt up into his arms and was very glad. But again, the golden-haired maiden cried

out in anger, and at that moment there came in sight the knight who had taken the dog. He too called out to Perceval to give back the bratchet, but Perceval said: 'By no means, sir. You must be mad to ask this, since you stole this dog from me less than a moon ago.'

'Then defend yourself!' shouted the knight, and the two rode at each other with great fury.

Perceval was quickly the victor, and soon the knight grovelled in the earth before him. 'I will spare you on one condition, that you tell me why you stole the bratchet, and if you know the identity of the knight of the tomb and the old woman who cursed me so roundly.'

'That I will, and willingly,' replied the knight. 'Though I am ashamed to tell you what you ask. For you must know that the knight of the tomb was my brother, and he was at one time the finest knight in the world – until he met a faery woman who claimed his love and enchanted him. She rode with him to a fair meadow, where they stopped to eat and there my brother fell asleep. When he awoke, he found himself in the finest castle he had ever seen, and the faery woman told him that here he would be able to prove himself against anyone who came that way. She showed him a tomb, that stood by the castle – though none could see it save those whom she allowed – and bade him remain there and challenge all-comers. As to the old woman whom you saw there, she is in truth the very same faery, who can seem like the most beautiful maiden when she chooses.'

Perceval wondered at this, then asked the beaten man if he knew anything about the damsel of the Chessboard Castle who had given him the bratchet and asked for the stag's head.

'She is also an Otherworldly woman, the sister of the one who enchanted my brother. I am sure that she sent you on the quest of the White Stag because she knew that it would lead you to the tomb and thus to a battle with my brother. She hoped that you would free him, I believe, for she is in deadly rivalry with her sister for his love, and I believe she seeks his death so that her sister may have him.'

At this Perceval began to feel anger at the deception to which he had been submitted. He asked if he were far from the Chessboard Castle, for by now he was wholly lost. The knight replied that he need only follow the road he was on and that he should arrive there before nightfall. Then Perceval made the knight promise to surrender himself to King Arthur and set off as quickly as he might for the Chessboard Castle.

He soon reached his destination and was met by the damsel Honorée who, when she saw him coming, opened the gates and came forth herself to greet him. She told him how much she had wondered at his long absence and that she was displeased with him because of it.

Perceval told her all that had occurred from the moment he had departed in quest of the White Stag, and how he had learned at last the identity of the knight of the tomb and the reason for the theft of the bratchet and the stag's head. When she heard all of this the damsel was silent for a while. Then she praised him greatly and said that she hoped he would remain with her and be her lover. But to this Perceval could only shake his head. 'For though in truth I did love you, I have learned that you have played more than one trick upon me, and upon others.'

At this the maiden turned her face away and Perceval felt her anger. But in the end, she turned back to him with lowered gaze and told him that she had sought only to test him, for she had heard of his quest, and wished to see if he was worthy. Then she told him that she was herself related to the women of the well and that she longed to see the enchantments of the Wasteland lifted. 'Only thus will you see the sacred thing you seek,' she said. 'For it is indeed in the house of the Rich Fisher.'

Then the maiden said that he must do what he must and wished him well upon his journey. Then he set forth again at once, for he would not remain there even one more night, having already slept under that roof before.

✛ ✛ ✛

PERCEVAL CONTINUED UPON his way, and many adventures he had; but never once did he find his way back to the Court of the Rich Fisher. Thus, seven years passed, and he continued to wander through the world. So long was he upon the way, and in such bleak conditions, that in the end his wits left him, and he forgot who he was and even the reason for his quest.

It befell that upon the morning of Easter he came upon a group of pilgrims making their way to church to hear Mass. They wondered greatly how he rode in full armour and with weapons at the ready on such a holy day. At first Perceval only looked at them madly, but then his mind cleared, and he remembered his quest and all that had happened to him since he left King Arthur's court. He fell from his horse and knelt in the roadside and prayed aloud for forgiveness. The pilgrims helped him to stand and took him with them to the chapel where they were to hear Mass. And lo! it was the very same chapel at which

Perceval's uncle, the hermit, lived out his holy life. When he saw the old hermit, Perceval was overjoyed and fell at his uncle's feet and begged absolution and confessed to him all that had happened since he left there.

The hermit blessed and forgave him, so that his soul was eased, and thereafter Perceval remained with him in the hermitage for three months, absolved for that time of his vow while he recovered his strength. But when he would have gone to visit his sister, he learned that she had died a year past, and that she was buried close by. Then he wept most bitterly, and asked to see her grave, and when he saw it, he wept again and offered prayers for her soul.

Then nothing would prevent him from going forth again in quest of his grandfather's house. 'For he has waited overlong already, and nothing must prevent me from the testing of my true path.'

Then the hermit blessed him and gave him leave to go, for he saw that nothing else would do for him. Perceval set forth again and rode day and night in search of the Rich Fisher's house. His way led him through many more adventures, and with each one his fame increased, but still he did not find what he sought.

Then on a day he saw coming toward him an old man carrying a scythe as though he were a reaper. And when he saw Perceval, he went up to him and seized his bridle. 'Why are you idling here when you should be at the place where lies the Grail?' he demanded. Perceval was astonished at this and asked the old man how he knew so much about him.

'I knew your name even before you were born,' replied the reaper.

'How may this be?' asked Perceval in wonder.

'I am Merlin,' answered the old man. 'I have been in Northumberland for many days and now I am called to help you.'

'Sir,' said Perceval in wonder. 'I have heard much of you and of your wisdom from my lord King Arthur. If you can tell me how to reach my grandfather's house I shall be forever in your debt.'

'I know that you seek the house of the Rich Fisher,' said Merlin. 'If you follow the path I indicate, you will be there within the year.'

'Is there no quicker way?' asked Perceval.

'You are overly impatient. Go where I send you and trust that all shall be well. Once you find your goal, do not forget to ask about what you see.'

'I will,' said Perceval. And with that Merlin showed him the way that he should follow, and then vanished away he wist not where.

Perceval followed the road as he had been shown, and within that same day he saw his grandfather's court – from which he knew that Merlin had been testing his patience. Then his heart was high, and he rode to the gates and was well received. Servants took his horse and arms and clad him in fine raiment and then led him into the hall where his grandfather sat. The old king was much cheered to see him again and rose as well as he might to greet him. He seemed little changed, save that he was perhaps more weak and hollow than before. He and Perceval sat and talked of many things, until it was time for supper. Then tables were brought in and set before the old king and the knight.

Then, just as it had been before, so it was again.

There came the procession through the hall of the bleeding lance, the Grail and the platter. And when he looked upon them Perceval asked concerning them. At this there was a great noise and a bright light, so that Perceval could not see, but when his sight returned, he saw that the Rich Fisher was as strong as he had ever been, and he leapt up like a young man and knelt before Perceval, who raised him up and said: 'Sire, know that I am the son of Alain le Gros, and your grandson.'

The Rich Fisher was very glad and embraced Perceval and led him before the Grail. Then the old king knelt before the holy thing and begged that he should be released from his long service. And there came forth a music from the Grail that some say was like the voices of the Well, and a scent as of Paradise, and a voice spoke telling the Rich Fisher that he should teach the mystery of the Grail to his grandson, who should be the new guardian of the vessel. 'Do this, and in three days you shall walk free of this service,' said the voice.

So it was that the Rich Fisher taught the secrets of the Grail to Perceval, and much more beside. And on the third day the old king died as the voice had foretold. And on that same day, where King Arthur was in his court, there came a noise from the heavens of such great magnitude that all were sore afraid, and the stone which had split when Perceval sat upon it was re-united, at which all were astonished.

Soon after this Merlin came, who had not been seen at the court for many a year, and he told King Arthur all that had occurred. 'Know this,' he said. 'The greatest miracle that could occur in this time has happened, for the Rich Fisher is healed and Perceval, your knight, is now lord of the Grail. Thus, the enchantments are lifted from the Wasteland, and all shall be well.'

Then Merlin vanished away and returned to his master Blaise and told him all that had taken place so that he might write it down in a great book. And I have heard it said that afterwards Blaise went to the castle of the Grail to be with Perceval, while Merlin went into his *esplumoir*,* where no living soul might see him again.

Thus was the Quest for the Grail achieved by Sir Perceval, and the enchantments that were upon the Wasteland lifted for that time. The land flowered and grew green, and the trees were leafy again, and the Damsels and Knights of the Wood rejoiced, for thus the evil work of Amangons was undone and the mysteries of the Grail achieved, and they were no longer forced to wander. And it is said that on that day a new light shone out of the west, that was neither of sun, nor moon, nor star.

---- ✠ ----

EXPLICIT THE ELUCIDATION OF THE GRAIL AND
THE QUEST OF SIR PERCIVAL.

IMPLICIT THE TALE OF MORIEN.

---

* A mysterious word that refers to the place to which Merlin retired to observe the events of King Arthur's life. An *esplumoir* or 'moulting cage' for hawks, was used as a complement to Merlin's French name.

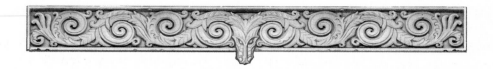

29: THE TALE OF MORIEN

✛

OF LATE, MANY THAT HAVE HEARD OF MY LABOURS IN COMPILING THIS WORK, HAVE COME TO ME AND SAID: WILL YOU WRITE THE STORY OF MORIEN, WHO WAS A GREAT KNIGHT OF THE ROUND TABLE? TO THESE I HAVE REPLIED THAT I MUST LOOK INTO CERTAIN MATTERS, FOR I HAVE READ OF THIS KNIGHT THAT HE WAS THE SON OF SIR PERCEVAL, BUT SINCE IT IS WIDELY KNOWN THAT PERCEVAL DIED A VIRGIN, LIKE HIS BROTHER KNIGHT SIR GALAHAD, THIS SEEMS NOT LIKELY. NOW, AFTER MUCH SEARCHING IN THE OLDEST BOOKS THAT SPEAK OF KING ARTHUR, I HAVE FOUND IT WRITTEN THAT MORIEN WAS IN FACT THE SON OF SIR PERCEVAL'S BROTHER, SIR AGLOVALE DE GALLES, WHO AT THE TIME WHEN SIR LANCELOT RAN MAD FOR LOVE OF THE QUEEN (AS MASTER THOMAS HAS TOLD)* JOINED WITH MANY OF THE FELLOWSHIP OF THE ROUND TABLE AS THEY TRAVELLED IN SEARCH OF THEIR COMRADE.

ON HIS TRAVELS, SIR AGLOVALE REACHED THE LAND OF THE MOORS, AND THERE MET AND FELL IN LOVE WITH A HIGH-BORN LADY. FROM THIS LIAISON CAME A CHILD, WHOSE MOTHER NAMED HIM MORIEN. BECAUSE HIS SKIN WAS DARK, MANY TOOK HIM TO BE OF PURE MOORISH BLOOD, AND WHEN LATER HE CAME TO BRITAIN, AS YOU SHALL HEAR, HE FARED POORLY AMONG THOSE WHO REGARDED HIM AS A DEMON. BUT MOST REGARDED HIM AS A NOBLE KNIGHT, THE COLOUR OF WHOSE SKIN MADE NO DIFFERENCE TO THEM OR TO THE NATURE OF HIS GENEROUS HEART. SO I WILL TELL HIS STORY NOW, RESTORING SIR MORIEN TO HIS RIGHTFUL PLACE AMONGST THE FELLOWSHIP OF ARTHUR.

✛ ✛ ✛

---

* *Le Morte D'Arthur*, Book XI, Ch. ix.

DURING THE TIME when most of the Knights of the Round Table were seeking the Grail, King Arthur held a great court at Camelot the Golden, to which all were invited that were not lost upon the road in quest of the holiest relic. It was widely known that no suppliant should ever be turned away from this gathering, and on the day when the court came together to feast, a tall horse entered the gates of the citadel and made its way to the doors of the Great Hall. On its back sat a sorely wounded knight, his armour and the trappings all stained with blood – as if he were a Red Knight indeed. So weak was he that he could not even dismount. When Sir Gawain, who happened to be present, saw this, he hastened to help the man, but when he had descended from his horse, his wounds were such that he fell to the ground. Gawain was much saddened by this, and lifting the wounded man, carried him within and laid him on a couch near the dais where King Arthur sat with Queen Guinevere at his side. Though the man tried to speak, his voice was so quiet that none might hear him, and at that Gawain called for servants to help remove the bloodied harness and to wash the wounds beneath. Then he himself, who was greatly skilled in the healing arts – learned from one of the faery women with whom he was wont to spend time – searched the wounds and dressed them. Lastly, he called for a cordial to strengthen the knight.

At length, the wounded man was strong enough to speak, though he could still not stand. 'King Arthur, my lords, forgive my addressing you thus, but I am surely like to die, despite the kindness of this brave knight, and I wish to tell you my story while I am able to do so.'

'Speak, Sir Knight,' the king said. 'We are sorry to see you so gravely hurt. How did you come by these dire wounds?'

'My lord, once I was a proud knight who fought in tournaments and rode in search of adventure. Always I was eager to give of my bounty to strangers, whether they be servants, pages or squires. Whoever was in need I willingly gave them largesse. But in time I fell upon hard times, having lost or given away all that I inherited from my father. And so, although it shames me to say it, I fell to robbery, stealing from any that I met upon the road. Thus, I am in breach of my knightly vows, and may ask nothing but your forgiveness, great lord.'

The wounded man fell silent, and all in the court, from king to lowest servant, felt only sorrow for his fall from grace. Yet it seemed to them that the knight was truly contrite, and therefore all felt that he had suffered for his crimes.

'Tell us how you came to be so sorely hurt,' asked King Arthur.

'On this very day I met two knights on the road, one of whom rode a mighty horse. When I saw it, I desired it greatly to replace the one I had ridden for many weeks, so I challenged the knight to battle. At first, he would not, seeing that my armour and weapons were greatly dinted and broken. But I insisted, and so at last we rode together. Alas not a single stroke did I lay upon him, while he struck me over and over, inflicting the wounds you see upon me now. Then he gave me such a blow to my helm that for a time I forgot everything.

'When I awoke, I found that the knights had laid me in a sheltered place beneath some trees and had tethered my horse to a branch. But of them there was no sign and I was alone. I managed to climb onto my mount's back and turned for this great citadel, of which all men say is the most noble court in all of Britain.'

'What can you tell us of the two knights?' asked Sir Gawain. 'How did they look, and what device was upon their shields?'

'Of the second knight I can say nothing, but of the one I fought, he was a very powerful man it seemed to me, with great strength of arm. His accent I believe was Welsh and his shield bore many golden crosses.'[*]

When he heard this, King Arthur sprang up. 'Before God!' he cried. 'This can be no other than Sir Perceval. Since he rode in search of the Grail, we have heard almost nothing of him, though he has sent more than one defeated knight to our court.'

Several men called out that if Perceval was close by, he should be sought out. First to speak, as ever, was Sir Kay the Seneschal, who swore that he would bring back Sir Perceval at whatever cost. But King Arthur laughed at this and reminded him of a time before when he had sought out Sir Perceval, not long after he first arrived at court. 'You may have forgotten how thoroughly he beat you then. Do you really wish to suffer such a defeat again?'[†]

At this, Sir Kay hung his head, and both Sir Gawain and Sir Lancelot declared that with the king's approval they would go forth at once in search of their brother knight. To this the king consented – though many lords and ladies bemoaned the sending forth of their two greatest knights at this time.

Before they departed, Sir Gawain took upon himself the task of healing the wounded

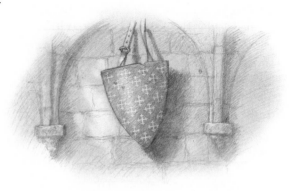

→ *Sir Perceval's Shield* ←

man whose name, they discovered, was Sir Gladoains. Such was the skill of the king's nephew that he was soon restored to health and, forgiven for his earlier transgressions, joined the Fellowship.

So it was that the two greatest Knights of the Round Table set forth together from Camelot the Golden in search of Sir Perceval. None had heard from him since he set forth in search of the Grail – surely the greatest quest ever undertaken by that Fellowship. Lancelot's own search had ended sadly when he was turned away from the Chapel of the Grail, as Master Thomas has told; Sir Gawain's own quest was yet to lead him into darker waters, as may be told another time.

✢ ✢ ✢

SOON AFTER LEAVING the court, the two men met with a knight who rode alone. He was clad from head to foot in night-black armour and sat like a thundercloud upon a steed of the same colour. On his shield was a black raven upon a ground of blood red. When Sir Gawain and Sir Lancelot advanced and greeted him, the stranger

---

[*] Perceval's arms were: Purpure, semy of plain crosslets Or.

[†] This episode appears in *The Story of the Grail* by Chrétien de Troyes.

only stared at them from between the bars of his helm and then cried out, in a voice that seemed to them as dark as his armour and weapons: 'I have sworn an oath that I will ask a question of any knight that I encounter. If they do not answer I will fight with them. If they refuse me, I will fight with them. What say you?'

Lancelot looked askance at the Black Knight. 'You ask too abruptly,' he said. 'It is neither wise nor honourable to demand an answer so roughly.'

At this the Black Knight, without another word, pulled back and laid his spear in rest. Lancelot did the same and the two rode together at full tilt. Both shattered their spears, but though rocked in their saddles neither fell to the earth. Sir Gawain, who had drawn aside, watched grimly as the two men drew their swords and struck at each other. Always before he had seen Lancelot beat every opponent save one – and that was his own son, Galahad – but here he seemed well matched.

The two knights fought on until even their strength began to wane. When their horses could no longer bear them, they dismounted and fought on, on foot. Such blows they struck each other, that if it had been midnight, one could still have seen from the sparks that flew from their clashing blades.

At length Sir Gawain could no longer stand by impassively. As the two men briefly paused to draw breath, he stood between them, and begged them both, for the love of God and King Arthur, to cease.

'Sirs, you fight for no reason. It is clear neither of you will cease until one is dead. Such no man would wish. I beg you, therefore, put aside your pride and valour and speak to one another as simple men.'

At this, the Black Knight rested his sword point on the earth and for the first time raised his visor. Bold and handsome as well as grim was his face, and his skin was as dark as the armour that clad him. Only his eyes and teeth flashed in his dark visage. Despite his strength, they saw that he was still but a youth.

'I pray you in the names of the two greatest men I have heard tell of, namely Sir Gawain and Sir Lancelot, that you answer my question.'

Astonished, Gawain stood silent and Lancelot, despite the tide of his warrior blood, lowered his sword and raised his own visor. Gawain said: 'In the names of those you invoke, tell us what it is you seek?'

'I have sought long and hard this past year,' began the Black Knight. 'Many adventures I have faced, and many strong men fought, but never could I find any word of the one I seek. Tell me if you will, what do you know of Sir Aglovale de Galles?'

Now Gawain laughed aloud. 'Sir, tell me what it is that you seek of Sir Aglovale, and we will tell you what we know of him.'

Hope shone briefly in the eyes of the Black Knight.

'I seek him because he is my father, though I have yet to set eyes upon him. My mother has told me how Sir Aglovale came to the court of Moraine, where she was a princess in her own right. He came there because he was in search of the great Sir Lancelot, who had run mad they say, so that he and his fellows, all of whom were from the good King Arthur's court, had sworn they would not cease from seeking until they found him. Such was the nobility and gentleness of Sir Aglovale that my mother declared her love for him and consented to all that he wished of her.'

The Black Knight fell silent for a moment, head bowed, and thus did not see how Gawain and Lancelot stood amazed – the latter even more so, remembering the dark days of his madness.

Then the knight continued: 'I am the result of their love. Because of his great oath to continue his search, my father was not able to stay, but before he left he plighted his troth with her and promised, on pain of death, that he would return when he had found Sir Lancelot.

'No good came of this, for both my mother and I are outcast and have lost all our goods. My mother's family have cast her aside and she lives now a poor life where before it was rich. Thus, I became a knight in order that I might seek my father. I swore that I would let no other knight I met upon the way pass until they had told me of what I sought, or else fall by my hand. Now tell me, sirs, if you have heard aught of Sir Aglovale.'

Gawain spoke up at once. 'This is indeed a marvellous thing. For we too are seeking Sir Aglovale and his brother Sir Perceval whom, we have heard, travel together on their own great quest. Your father is known to us well – for like us he is a Knight of the Round Table.'

Then the Black Knight wept openly and let fall his sword to the earth.

'Never did I believe that I would find as much as one who knew of my father. Yet here are two such knights. Sirs, I beg of you – tell me your names.'

Gawain smiled upon him. 'I am Sir Gawain of Orkney and this is my friend and brother in chivalry, Sir Lancelot du Lac.'

The Black Knight was so astonished that he had no words, and all three men came together and embraced each other where they had but recently fought. Sir Lancelot praised the strength and fortitude of his opponent and told him that he should go to King Arthur and tell him his story. 'But first of all, tell us your name.'

'I am Morien. I am, as you see, a Moor, as is my mother. But the blood of Sir Aglovale runs in my veins, and I am proud to unite both bloods within me.' Then he said: 'I will be more than glad to go from here to the court of the great King Arthur, yet it seems to me that we three should go together first, for if you are successful in finding Sir Perceval, so also will you find my father. Will you let me ride with you?'

'Provided you promise not to seek combat with every knight we meet upon the way,' said Lancelot with a smile. 'Unless it be in answer to a challenge. If that is agreeable to you, let us take the road together.'

The three were thus agreed and together followed the way ahead, speaking much of each other's lives and deeds, as men will.

+ + +

SOON THEY CAME to a place where the path divided in three and there was a sign with words written upon it in blood. Gawain, who was learned in the art of letters, told his companions that the sign said this was the border of King Arthur's lands, and that any knight who came there should know that they would encounter nothing but peril and most likely death should they go ahead.

For a while the three spoke together of the best way forward. Then Gawain pointed to where a small building lay close by. 'I believe this to be a hermitage,' he said. 'Let us go there and enquire of the good man if he knows what dangers lie before us, should we choose to go ahead.'

'I, for one,' said Morien eagerly, 'desire only to see what adventures there may be ahead of us. Surely such a place would be where my father and uncle would go?'

'We shall soon discover if this is so,' Sir Gawain said.

The three knights rode to the building, which was indeed a hermitage. The good and saintly man who dwelled there came forth to greet them, inviting them to partake of such plain fare as he could offer. When they had eaten and drunk, Sir Gawain asked if the hermit had seen two knights, one of whom wore red armour, pass that way. The hermit nodded: 'I did see two such as you describe,' he said. 'I thought they were brothers from the likeness I saw in their faces. They came this way but a week ago and stopped to pray at the cross that stands nearby. Both, I believe, were upon some sacred quest, for they spoke little and had about them the look of men who have seen the face of God.'

At this Morien grew excited, for it was clear to him that these knights must be his own father, and his uncle Sir Perceval. But when he enquired as to which road the knights had taken the hermit shook his head.

'Alas, I did not see which way they went, though I believe it to be one of the three roads that lead from the sign that stands close by.'

The three knights spoke together, and all agreed that they should each take a road in the hope they might find those they sought. Sir Gawain turned again to the hermit and asked what might lie in wait for them according to which path they followed.

'I have heard it said that the road which lies directly ahead leads to a wasteland where only sickness and sorrow are to be found and where cruel knights lie in wait for all who come there. As to the other two: the

road which lies to the right goes to a land terrorized by a dreadful creature that men say comes from Hell itself. None who approach it have ever survived, for it spits a frightful poison that kills any it strikes within three days.

'The road to the left leads to the sea, I am told, though what lies there or beyond I cannot say.'

When he heard this, Lancelot at once spoke of following the road which led to the dreaded beast. 'For such I have heard spoken of before, and it has long been my wish to pit myself against such a creature.'

'Then I shall go to the wasteland,' said Sir Gawain. 'For I believe that may test me the most.'

Morien heard these words and frowned. 'Do you think so little of me that you apportion the road that offers the least challenge, while you test yourselves against greater odds?'

'By no means,' said Gawain. 'All that determines our paths are the finding of your father and his brother. What lies between here and the sea is unknown and is certain to offer challenges to whoever follows it. Will you deny yourself this task?'

'I will not,' said Morien, with reluctance.

'Then I bid you remember the words we spoke before – that you will behave courteously to all that you meet and ask of them with honour the question you asked of us.'

Morien bowed his head. 'I will do as you ask,' he said.

The hermit, who had heard all of this, looked upon the three knights with sorrow in his face. 'I fear that I shall not see any of you again,' he said. 'Where you go is only darkness and doom.'

'Do not sorrow for us,' answered Sir Gawain. To the others he said: 'Let us agree to meet here again when we can – and if any one of us reaches this spot before the others, let him leave word of himself and if he has succeeded in finding our brothers. In time we shall meet again in Camelot the Golden.'

Then the hermit gave them his blessing, and the three rode together to the place where the road branched out. There they took leave of each other and went their ways.

✙ ✙ ✙

MORIEN FOLLOWED THE road towards the sea. The way was deserted, and he met no one to ask if they had seen two knights, one in red and the other with the badge of Arthur's men. For more than a week he continued on his way, sleeping at night beneath the stars, with only his mount for company. At length he reached the shore of the sea, where a sheltered bay sat between cliffs. At first, he saw no living soul, then he espied where several small ships lay at anchor a little way from the shore. Pulling off his helm he called out to them, asking if any of them had taken two knights across the water to whatever lands lay beyond. But when they saw his dark face and black harness, they were fearful, deeming him a demon of Hell, so that they turned away from him and did not answer his cries.

Morien grew angry and threatened to punish the seamen if they did not help him, but none replied and some even cast off and sailed further away from the shore. So, at last, Morien turned away and rode back with heavy heart the way he had come. Again, though he journeyed for more than a week, he saw no one. The land seemed without habitation, so that he was forced to sleep under the stars once more.

Then, as he drew near to the place where the road divided, where he and Sir Lancelot and Sir Gawain had set forth, he saw a strange sight. Along the road and in the fields on either side lay many fallen knights, some with fearsome wounds, others hurt but still able to stand. One group were working to make a great wheel with the intention of breaking a prisoner upon it. The man whose fate would end in this dreadful death, sat upon the ground, naked and covered in blood. Yet he held his head high and when he saw Morien he called out a greeting.

Morien recognized him at once. It was none other than Sir Gawain. At that, Morien drew his sword and fell upon the company who had captured his friend. Many he slew outright, and others caused such wounds as they were unlikely to recover from. At last there were no more to fight, and Morien turned to where Sir Gawain sat and set him free. The two embraced and Morien brought water and a cloak to cover his brother knight's nakedness. And he saw then how many wounds Gawain had received – though none were fatal it seemed.

It happened that they found Gawain's steed, the brave Gringolet, close by, having been taken by one of the dead knights and then abandoned on the field of battle. How mightily had the horse fought alongside his master, breaking many heads and limbs with his hoofs. Unhurt, though bespattered with blood, he greeted his master gently and such was the reunion of these two that Morien wept for joy. Then he asked how Gawain had fared and how he came to be so vilely treated.

Sir Gawain told how he had entered the wasteland and there met with a brutal knight beating a woman with sword and fist. Gawain had challenged the man and after a long battle had slain him. Then had come a company who sought the lady, but who fled when the followers of the evil knight came seeking him. Gawain had defended himself well against this band, and afterwards continued onwards until he reached a castle, where he was made welcome by its host. Soon after, men had arrived bearing the dead body of the brutal knight, who was the son of the castle's Lord. When the body was laid in the hall its wounds broke out afresh, from which all knew that the man's slayer was somewhere present. Gawain was quickly identified, and the company sought to kill him. However, the Lord of the Castle, despite his sorrow at the loss of his son, respected the laws of hospitality and showed himself to be a paragon of chivalry. For he did his best to spare Gawain's life, and thus was he allowed to depart. But those of the dead knight's kin who sought revenge followed him, and though he fought bravely and slew many who came after him, yet he had fallen at last and had not Morien arrived in that moment, his life would surely have ended there at the meeting of the ways.

✝ ✝ ✝

WHEN GAWAIN WAS sufficiently recovered to enable him to ride, Morien and he made their way back to the hermitage from where they and Sir Lancelot had set forth but weeks before. Once again, the hermit greeted them warmly and gave Sir Gawain a place to rest and recover from his wounds.

They remained at the hermitage for several days, until there came a knight riding swiftly. When Sir Gawain saw him, he was glad indeed, for it was his own brother, Sir

Guerrehes, sent by King Arthur in search of the two knights. So, too, he brought news of Sir Perceval and Sir Aglovale. When he heard this Morien was most glad, even though Guerrehes told how Aglovale had been wounded in a tournament. Sir Perceval had saved him, and the two had sought refuge on an island just a little way off the coast. There they had journeyed but a few days before Morien. Sir Perceval was filled with despair that he had not found his way to the Grail and sought to spend his time praying and seeking to know how he might achieve his quest. He and Aglovale found rest on the island, where holy men would care for both body and spirit, as each in turn required.

When he heard this, Morien desired to set forth at once to find his way there and fell to railing against the seamen who had refused to carry him to the island or tell him of the knights who had but recently passed that way. Guerrehes and Gawain both sought to calm him, and the former promised to go with him so that he might find his father and uncle. Sir Gawain meanwhile declared that he would go in search of Lancelot, of whom there had been no word since they had departed each on their separate ways. Gawain was fearful for his brother knight, who had demanded to encounter the fell beast.

For several days more they remained with the hermit, while Sir Gawain recovered his strength, and Guerrehes and Morien foraged for food and drink where they could find it.

At last, Morien could no longer hold from setting out, and so he and Sir Guerrehes parted from Sir Gawain, who set forth to follow the road taken by Lancelot, while Guerrehes and Morien secured places aboard a ship which agreed to carry them to the island. At first, when they saw the Moorish knight, the seamen sought to flee, deeming him a devil, but Guerrehes assured them that he was a man like them and a noble knight.

Thus they took ship together and soon crossed the water to the small island. Guerrehes enquired of the boatman if he had seen or knew of two knights, one of whom wore red armour. 'Only a few weeks since, I carried two such as you describe,' the man answered. 'One indeed wore mail the colour of blood, the other plain armour. The one in red seemed greatly sorrowful, and the other possessed a wound that pained him greatly. They asked the way to a monastery on the island, and there I directed them.'

The two knights disembarked and the boatman, happy to be rid of the dark-faced Moor, left to return to the mainland. The knights made their way as instructed until they reached the monastery. Guerrehes hammered upon the door and called to any within to open up.

Shortly a lad came to answer and, looking askance at Morien, asked what they wanted.

'We are seeking two knights, Sir Perceval and Sir Aglovale. We would speak with either or with the holy men who dwell within.'

Bidding them wait, the boy departed. Soon another figure came into view. Tall and powerful he was, but his face was pale, and he moved with difficulty due to wounds that were not yet healed. But when he saw Sir Guerrehes he cried aloud, for this indeed was Sir Aglovale. The two greeted each other warmly, then the wounded man turned to Morien, who had remained silent all this while, staring in wonder at the man he knew to be his father. Aglovale marvelled at his appearance and asked him who he was and what he sought in that place.

Morien said: 'Sir, do you remember how, when you were seeking for Sir Lancelot, who had run mad, fifteen years ago, how you came to a land named Moraine, and there met a lady who was of Moorish blood. You loved her, it is said, and when you were forced to leave, promised to return and make her your wife.'

Startled, Sir Aglovale looked in wonder at the youth. 'Indeed, I remember,' he said. 'It was much to my grief that I failed to do as I had sworn. I rode long in search of Lancelot, but he had already returned to the court while I was away. After that, my brother Perceval had need of me as he does even now, greatly troubled as he is by his failure to find that which he seeks. I have long wondered about the fate of the lady I so much loved. I do not even know if she still lives. Have you word of her, Sir Knight – for I see that you too are of Moorish blood?'

'Indeed I do,' answered Morien. 'The lady still lives – or at least so she did when I saw her but a short time ago.' He paused and drew in his breath. 'She is my mother – and you, Sir Aglovale de Galles, are my father! I have come to bring you to where you may fulfil your vow.'

Then the two greeted each other as only those long lost and unknowing can. Any who saw their embraces and the joy they had in each other would have been warmed by the sight.

Then Aglovale invited them to come into the monastery to meet with Sir Perceval: 'Though I warn you that he is greatly saddened because of his failure to find the holy relic he seeks.'

When they came to the chamber where Sir Perceval was, they saw that it was as Aglovale had said. His face was hollow, and his eyes stared out at the world as though he saw only sorrow. Nonetheless, when he heard that Morien was his own brother's son and therefore his nephew, he became more cheerful and that night they took great delight in each other's company and shared the story of their adventures.

✛ ✛ ✛

IN THE MORNING Morien again asked Sir Aglovale when he would come with him back to Moraine, where he could at last marry his love and help recover the lands that had been taken from her.

Sir Aglovale spoke up at once, saying that he was eager to do as his son required of him, but that he must wait until he was fully recovered from the wounds that he had suffered. 'Once I am well,' he said, 'be assured I shall return to your mother and fulfil the promise I made so long ago.'

And though Morien was impatient to set out, yet he kept silent and assented to his father's wish. The four knights remained at the monastery another week until Sir Aglovale declared himself healed. And in that time Sir Perceval dreamed a great dream, in which he saw the Grail and learned that his brother knight, Sir Galahad, was destined to achieve this quest – but that he too, Perceval, would partake of this adventure and receive his own reward – as I have told in the story that precedes this.

Then they set forth and found a ship willing to carry them back to the land, and then on until they reached the hermitage from which they had departed, each to his own adventure, seemingly long since.

There to their great delight and wonder, they found Sir Lancelot and Sir Gawain recovering from wounds the former had received when he fought against the terrible beast. That night, as they ate and drank together, he told them how he had fared on his journey. For he had indeed discovered the hideous creature, riding through fields strewn with the bones of those it had slain. There, Sir Lancelot fought with it until it lay dead, receiving many wounds and suffering the poison the beast had carried in its jaws. Only a ring, gifted to him long since by a maiden of the faery kind, saved him from death, though he was greatly weakened from his battle. There Sir Gawain had found him and used his own healing skills to revive the great knight. Since then, they had remained at the monastery, while Lancelot recovered.

Now the three knights agreed to journey with Morien to the land of Moraine to recover the rights of the young knight's mother. And thus it fell out. Sir Perceval, renewed by his vision to take up the Quest again, and having shared word of Sir Galahad with his father Sir Lancelot, departed from them. Then Sir Aglovale, Sir Gawain, Sir Lancelot and Sir Morien set forth and went into the Moorish lands. There they stood firm with the youth as he laid claim to his mother's rights. At first those who had cast out both mother and son were set against them, but when they saw the strength of King Arthur's knights they gave way and agreed that if Aglovale and the lady were married, then all her lands and goods should be returned.

The tale speaks little of the reunion between Sir Aglovale and the lady, or of her delight at having her son returned to her. You may be certain that they were most happy, and thereafter Aglovale and his wife and son journeyed to Camelot the Golden and were welcomed by the king. Morien afterwards became a Knight of the Round Table and proved himself many times in battle and tourney. For the rest, Sir Gawain and the others set forth again upon the quest for the Grail, as had Sir Perceval. Of that story Master Thomas has told much – but not all, as you shall see, for there are stories that were unknown to him at that time, but which I have discovered and one of which I shall tell hereafter in this book.

———— ✠ ————

EXPLICIT THE TALE OF MORIEN.

INCIPIT THE ADVENTURES OF SONE DE NANSAY.

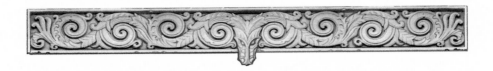

30: THE ADVENTURES OF SONE DE NANSAY

— ⊹ —

MASTER THOMAS WROTE MUCH ABOUT THE QUEST FOR THE GRAIL – OR 'SANKGREAL' AS HE NAMED IT. HE TELLS US THAT ALL THE KNIGHTS OF THE ROUND TABLE SET FORTH IN QUEST OF THE SACRED VESSEL BUT THAT ONLY THREE: SIR GALAHAD, SIR PERCEVAL, AND SIR BORS WERE SUCCESSFUL, AFTER WHICH THE GRAIL WAS WITHDRAWN FROM THIS WORLD INTO ANOTHER PLACE. PERHAPS BECAUSE HE POSSESSED TOO LITTLE TIME, OR CHOSE TO WRITE ONLY OF THESE THREE KNIGHTS, AS WELL AS SIR LANCELOT AND SIR GAWAIN, WHO FAILED IN THEIR ATTEMPT, HE MAKES LITTLE MENTION OF THE MANY OTHER KNIGHTS WHO SET FORTH FROM CAMELOT THE GOLDEN. MANY PERISHED OR WERE TURNED BACK, OTHERS CAME FROM FURTHER AWAY AND THEIR STORIES HAVE REMAINED UNTOLD. ONE SUCH IS THE STORY THAT TELLS OF EVENTS THAT TOOK PLACE AFTER THE QUEST, AND CONCERNS ONE SONE DE NANSAY, A GREAT KNIGHT WHOSE STORY IS LONG AND WHOSE LIFE BROUGHT HIM, TOWARDS ITS END, TO THE HIGHEST RANK AMONG MEN IN THIS WORLD.

⊹ ✠ ⊹

I WILL, THEN, TELL that part of his story that belongs with the accounts of the great quest, and which was first told by one who claimed to have lived for one hundred and five years. Whether this be true or not I cannot say, but the story he tells is remarkable.

Sone was the son of Henri of Nansay and Ydoine, daughter of Duke Mélone. He quickly learned to read and write and bent all his efforts to learning. He grew much and progressed well, being knowledgeable, courteous and handsome, and assuredly one of the finest-looking boys in the world, with many virtues. He learned with such application in infancy that he left four of his tutors behind, who were astonished by his intelligence. At fifteen years he took part in his first tournament and dazzled all who saw him. There he met and fell in love with Yde, the daughter of Baron Eudes. She, being a proud lady of great beauty, spurned Sone as both young and untried, and such was his despair that he left home and pursued the life of a wandering knight from that moment.

As he grew to full manhood, word of his prowess with sword and lance grew, and more than one noble lord, and even some kings, sought him out to join them. Wherever he went, if there was a tournament, he entered the lists and proved his prowess. Word reached King Arthur of this remarkable knight, whom he sought to join the Fellowship of the Round Table. But Sone refused – either because he was already serving elsewhere as a champion or had travelled far from Arthur's kingdom.

One day he found himself in Scotland, where he had heard of war brewing between the king of that land and the King of Norway. It happened that word of Sone's coming reached the ears of the Scottish queen, who was eager to meet him. Therefore he made his way to the court and, when he arrived, a lady-in-waiting remarked to the queen: 'Never can you have seen such a young lord. If it pleases you, go down and see how well he sits his steed. It is as if he were enchanted. He hardly seems a member of the human race, but more like an angel come down from heaven to inspect us.'

When the queen saw him, she declared that her lady had spoken truly. Sone dismounted on seeing the queen and her suite, passed his horse to a servant and approached her, kneeling at her feet. Finding him so pleasant to look at, she invited him to stand, looking upon him with pleasure. Then she asked: 'Tell us your name and where you were born, and what brings you here.'

'Madame, my name is Sone, and my country is called Alsace. I am a son of the Lord of Nansay, but my parents are dead, and my brother is lord of the domain.'

It happened that a knight was present, who had witnessed Sone's skill in a tournament. Recalling this, he told the queen about it, affirming that throughout the whole world there could not exist, in his opinion, one able to discharge himself with such ability.

At this the queen begged Sone to remain at court until her husband returned from a hunting expedition and, if he would, to take service in their fight against Norway. Sone bowed and promised to consider this request, but in his heart he knew that he would not, having heard only good things about King Alain of Norway, and nothing but bad about the Scottish king. As soon as he could he slipped away in the hours of darkness and took ship for Norway.

When the ship docked, Sone was noticed and word went quickly to the king, who, having heard of the young man's prowess, rode forth himself to meet him. When he saw the youth, he saw in him only the best and bravest of knights. He welcomed Sone warmly and invited him to come and dine.

When Sone entered, the great hall was lit up by his beauty. It was like the moon appearing in the midst of the stars, so greatly did Sone shine. The king's sons, Houdiant and Thomas, especially looked upon him as a friend and welcomed him with great respect.

The king also was very courteous and sat the three young men along with his barons at a table of honour. The king's sons were fascinated by Sone and kept him long at the table, drinking so much that each told stories no one else would have listened to. Indeed, they were so keen to talk that no one could hear anything else. The king's daughter, whose name was Odée, also watched Sone intently, believing him to be the bravest and most handsome man she had ever seen.

Sone, unused to such quantities of drink, kept for the most part silent, until Houdiant amiably told him: 'It is the way we pass the time here. Drink, eat, talk, threaten the absent; it is the custom of the country. If we rise too early all are offended.'

Then the king rose and took Sone and his sons to one side. He said: 'Welcome among us, dear sir. If it pleases you to stay, that would be useful in the perilous situation in which we find ourselves. The King of Scotland is driven with a desire for war and will soon attack us. He has sworn he will seize my two sons and marry my daughter to a peasant.'

Then the queen came, holding Odée by the hand. She courteously greeted Sone and gave him a magnificent gold ring saying: 'I give you this jewel through affection for you, but with this present I pray you, with a sincere heart, to keep company with my two sons. In times of danger remain with them as would a faithful friend.' She added, 'My daughter prays for that too.'

Sone bowed. 'Most willingly, madame,' he said. 'I will help as much as I may.' Odée blushed greatly at this, and from that moment thought of little else but the knight, while Sone also found himself much moved by her beauty.

✣ ✣ ✣

WITHIN WEEKS WORD came of a great army from Scotland that had landed on the shores of Norway and was preparing to march inland. When he heard this Sone begged to lead the king's army. King Alain agreed, sending his sons to accompany his new champion.

So it was that a great battle took place near the sea and, with Sone at its head, the Norwegians broke the Scottish army killing, it is said, as many as ten thousand, and capturing many more. But to everyone's sorrow, the king's two sons both fell in the battle. When he learned of this, the King of the Scots himself sent word asking that the war be settled by single combat. To this Alain, grieving the death of his sons, agreed. Word also came that the Scots had chosen a man named Aligos, who stood eleven feet tall and was judged one of the most powerful champions alive. Hearing this, Sone, mindful of his promise to the queen, and his failure to protect the brothers, begged once more to be allowed to represent Norway. So, it was agreed, with the date set for the combat twelve days hence.

Because this task was such a fearful one, and because he wanted to assuage the grief for his fallen sons, King Alain asked Sone to join him on a journey to a place of great sacredness. They set off in a party of only twenty men and the king kept Sone close beside him.

Their journey took them to a part of the country where few ever went, through valleys and mountains, in places that proved difficult to negotiate, until they came to grasslands near the foot of a mountain. Here the king made camp and the party rested until the evening. At midnight they moved on again, travelling till noon, making for the sea. Here, at some time in the past, a raised roadway had been built, leading out into the water. It was difficult to find, and many brave knights had come to grief there. But King Alain, knowing these lands well, went directly to where two rocks formed a gateway that led into the sea.

There the king drew his horn and sounded a call. Soon after a boat approached in which sat two monks. They appeared little pleased to see the small company, but when they saw the king their mood changed at once.

'Welcome sire, we hoped for your coming, since we heard you had suffered great grief and misfortune. Is there anything you need? Have you come to stay with us?'

'One could wish for nothing better,' replied the king.

'Then step aboard,' said one of the monks. 'The ferry will pick up your men and horses.'

The king and Sone stepped into the boat and the monks rowed them across the water to a small island. There, they saw a castle rising out of the living rock as though it had grown there. It stood in the open sea where no machine could hurl missiles at its crenellated walls. Four towers rose from either

corner, and in the centre, midway between them, one that surpassed the others. This contained a great hall, which seemed to Sone more sumptuous than anything he had seen in all his wandering.

When he was asked, in the name of God, why they had come, King Alain told them about Sone. 'He is a great warrior who has been sent to help us. Soon he will represent us all in single combat. It is for this reason that I have brought him hither, so that he may learn of the secrets you guard and hear the true tale of them. And so that he may be blessed by you and by God and so succeed against our great and terrible foe.'

Then the abbot himself came forward and said to the king: 'It is past noon, and a meal is ready. If it is your pleasure, we shall have it brought in.'

Tables were placed in a sheltered area that overlooked the outer wall and gave onto the sea. It was bounded by a carved balustrade of white marble upon which birds, animals and fish were carved, including ten leopards, each

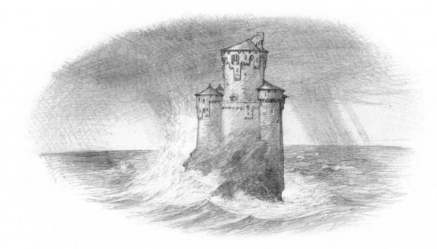

✢ *The Castle in the Sea* ✢

340

with a gaping mouth, whose heads turned ever to face the wind to produce agreeable harmonies. Anyone who wished to contemplate the sea could find no better place to be.

Three streams of water met close to the castle, welling up from the rock and flowing into the sea, mixing fresh water with salt. There swam so many fish that no amount of fishing could catch them all. Search the whole world and you would never find so solid a castle provided with such riches.

The abbot, the king and his knights were seated at tables of honour, while Sone took his place to one side where a seat had been reserved for him. The guests had a profusion of dishes to eat, enough to exhaust even those who served them.

After supper the king addressed the abbot, requesting that next morning the reliquaries which they protected could be opened up, so that all might pray and make confession. After which they would have to take their leave to return to the place where Sone was to fight the giant Aligos.

'We will hear your confessions willingly, sire, and intend to pray for you overnight. The perilous situation you have described calls for it and you will find us ready to invoke protection for both your champion and all the people of Norway.' Then to Sone he said: 'Brother, you will be fighting in the name of God, as you will discover, and tomorrow you shall see the great secret we have kept here these many years.'

You may be sure that Sone slept only briefly that night, for now, as well as the shadow of his coming battle, he fell to wondering about the secret the monks guarded and which required so mighty a castle to protect it.

✠ ✠ ✠

NEXT MORNING THE dawn bell was rung, and King Alain and Sone heard Mass at the church, chanted by the abbot himself. Then, still in his priestly garments, he stood before them all and told them the story that I repeat here. From it we learn more of the story of the Rich Fisher, which we saw in the story of Perceval.* It is my belief that had Master Thomas known of this, he would most certainly have included it in his book.

Thus the abbot said: 'Hear me, all who are present. As you may know, this castle was founded by none other than Joseph of Arimathea, who rests in one of the coffins nearby. On his deathbed, he asked for the story of his life to be written, and it is right that I should speak of it from the beginning, for all may take great strength from it.

'Joseph worked as a bailiff for seven years in the house of the Roman Governor of Galilea, Pontius Pilate, but he secretly revered Jesus Christ, who had preached the new religion. After seven years, on conclusion of his service, Joseph asked if he might have the body of Jesus as a gift.

'Pilate liked Joseph but thought him mad not to have asked for something better, though he did not refuse. For his part, Joseph felt well paid, for he believed Jesus to be a true king. He therefore placed the body in his own sepulchre – for which he was accused of going against the religion of the country.

'When these accusations were brought to Pilate, although he respected his former bailiff, he did not hesitate to render justice on him. For admitting his Christian faith Joseph was cast into a deep dungeon, filled with snakes, toads, and spiders. Enormous stones

---

* See 'The Elucidation of the Grail and the Story of Perceval' pp. 309–25

were rolled across the top, and it was then sealed.

'Being imprisoned in this terrible place troubled Joseph greatly, until Jesus appeared to him in a vision and offered him a wondrous vessel – that which is known as the Grail. The mere presence of this sacred thing removed the vermin, and softened the rocky floor, which now was easier to lie on than a fine woollen mattress. The place became fragrant and filled with light as bright as the sun.

'Forty years passed, and in all that time Joseph suffered neither hunger nor thirst. Nor did he show any sign of ageing, except that his hair and beard grew long. Then, in the reign of Vespasian, the emperor came to learn how Joseph had been incarcerated forty years ago. 'Take me there,' he said. The emperor had the stones removed and the opening completely cleared. From the cave came a light as bright as if the sun had risen; and such a sweet fragrance that all were overcome.

'Vespasian looked in and saw Joseph, and at once arranged to have him pulled up into the open air. In his arms, Joseph carried the vessel given him by Christ. All around people fell upon their knees and desired to kiss it. Any who were sick were immediately healed.

'With the wondrous vessel in his possession, Joseph now knocked down a wall and took out the holy lance with which Longinus had pierced the side of Christ. Joseph had previously hidden the lance in the wall, which was how he knew it was there. Now he honoured it and kept it with him.

'Now he felt the call to travel west and to spread the word of God. He went first to Syria, where he found an unattended ship near Ascalon. As he approached the vessel, a voice commanded him to come aboard, and to fear nothing.

'It was a good and solid craft, but though it left port as fast as any other craft, it had neither mast nor sail – a sight the inhabitants of Ascalon found miraculous. For several days the ship sailed on, until it arrived at last at Gaète, where Joseph disembarked. There he found a horse standing by with armour fine enough to suit the most valiant warrior.

'Accepting this gift, which he believed came from God, he crossed many countries as a valiant knight until he arrived in Norway. There he was welcomed and soon became greatly favoured. So respected was he that he led an army against the Saracens who occupied the land at that time and drove them out. He slew the Saracen king but spared his most beautiful daughter, with whom Joseph fell in love the moment he saw her. So great was his ardour – though it was not returned – that he had the girl baptized and married her. The truth was that she hated Joseph more than anyone because he had killed her father, but she hid this from him, biding her time for a day when she might be revenged.

'Now, because Norway was a kingdom, Joseph felt he ought to wear a crown. The lords of the country approved this, and he was crowned forthwith. His wife, who had by now borne him a child, was also crowned.

'Soon after this, by mischance he received a dreadful wound in the thigh, which he came to believe was a punishment from God for taking as wife a pagan princess. Not even the touch of the Grail could cure him, so he had the castle where we stand now built to preserve these sacred relics.

'Joseph had a boat in which he often went fishing, aided by a sailor who guided the boat to wherever he wanted to go. The fishing and the company of the sailor pleased him. Here he could forget his suffering, and because he thus fished his popular name spread everywhere: he was called the 'Fisher King' – a name that is known to this day.

'He led this life for many years until a knight came that could cure him – after which he lived but a short time. When he was on his deathbed, he appointed thirteen monks to serve in the tradition of the apostles, and thus we remain thirteen in this castle.'

Then the abbot turned to King Alain and told him that he held the kingdom of Norway from God, who would defend it against any who attacked. 'The Scots who have come here shall die or leave this land. And know for sure that whoever fights against Sone will die.'

Having told this marvellous account, much of which I have found in no other work, the abbot turned to the young knight and blessed him and said: 'Sone! God will aid you in your battle. I know this for certain.'

Then the abbot opened an ivory reliquary, ornamented with sculpted scenes, and took out the Grail. At once the whole castle was lit by a light as bright as the sun at noon. The abbot placed the Grail on the altar, then uncovered the Holy Lance of which you have heard. At its point drops of red blood formed and fell upon the earth, causing all there to marvel. The abbot then showed them two coffins, in one of which reposed the body of Joseph and in the other his son, Adam.

When they had marvelled at the relics, and prayed before them, King Alain declared that they must take their leave, since the time was growing near when Sone must encounter the giant Aligos. They went aboard the small craft and were taken by the monks back to their own ship, which in turn brought them

to Norway. From there they journeyed with haste to the place where the combat was to be held.

☩ ☩ ☩

THE BATTLE WHICH followed was terrible to behold. The giant Aligos was indeed eleven feet tall, and therefore too large to mount a horse, so that Sone was forced to fight him on foot. He seemed impervious to every blow that Sone struck him. Even when the knight managed to wound him, the giant simply shook his head and roared with pain but came on just as fiercely as ever. Several times he struck Sone, once almost breaking his arm when his huge sword struck the knight's shield. More than once, Sone found himself brought low, and must climb back to his feet before his opponent could deliver a killing blow. His armour grew quickly dinted by the repeated hammer blows of Aligos' sword.

But in the end, after several hours in which Sone only survived by means of his speed and agility, the giant began to slow. His huge frame, clad in a heavy breastplate and wielding a mighty sword, weighed him down and he began to tire. At last, seeing his opportunity and summoning all his strength, Sone leapt to one side, and before Aligos could swing towards him, severed the giant's sword arm. Then, as his opponent screamed in agony and blood fountained from his stump, Sone swung a mighty blow which severed the giant's head from his body. As Aligos fell dead, those who had been cheering both champions fell silent, both sides in awe of the knight's strength and skill.

Wearily, Sone retrieved the giant's head and took it to where the Scottish king sat at the head of his army. Sone laid the head at his feet and saluted the king, who knew in this moment that he had lost the war. Together, he and Sone went to where King Alain waited, and the Scottish king swore allegiance to him and promised never to return to the shores of Norway again.

Then the Norwegian army praised Sone mightily, cheering him until the very heavens rang with the sound of his name, and King Alain and he rode together back to the city. There, the king's daughter waited to greet them. She had eyes only for Sone and waited only until she could be alone with him. Then she poured out all her love for him, telling him that he owned her, body and soul, from that moment and that she would never love another.

When they heard this, both King Alain and his queen were delighted and promised Sone that, if he married Odée, he should inherit the kingdom since their sons were dead. Sone was greatly disturbed by this, for his thoughts were still upon his first great love, Yde – but of this he said nothing.

That evening a great feast was held in Sone's honour and to celebrate the ending of the war with Scotland. Later, when all had retired for the night, Odée came to Sone's room. She brought him a casket filled with gold and spoke again of her love for him. Sone, hiding his distress, for indeed he found the girl pleasing, spoke of his need to depart for his home to learn how his family had fared of late and to speak with them on many matters. Though Odée was saddened by this, before she left him Sone embraced her and promised to return.

✣ ✣ ✣

SONE RETURNED TO Nansay, where his family greeted him joyfully from his long wandering. News of his mighty battle in Norway, as well as his other great deeds, had already reached Alsace, and everyone wished to welcome him and hear of his adventures. But Yde had heard also of Odée. Sone rode to his home at Doncheri to see her, but she addressed him coldly, telling him he should return to his new love. This caused great hurt to Sone, and he went home full of anger and sorrow. There he learned that his brother, King Henri, had declared a great tournament to celebrate Sone's return to Nansay.

Preparations went ahead for this great contest, and Sone gave much attention to it to prevent himself from dwelling upon thoughts of Yde and Odée. The latter, meanwhile, had devised a plan to ensure that Sone did not forget her. She sent a small party of her most trusted companions, bearing with them a certain rare falcon, well trained in the art of hunting and most splendid in form. This was to be offered as a prize in the great tournament, to be awarded to him who did best in the jousts. In her heart Odée was certain that Sone would win the bird, but she commanded two of her women to accompany the party and instructed them how to behave and what to say.

As the date of the tournament approached, the king held a banquet to which all his nobles and barons were invited. Sone sat at his right hand, but Yde did not attend. Her heart had grown cold now towards Sone, and though he would speak nothing of it aloud, his own ardour had begun to cool.

It was at this moment that those sent by Odée, bringing the falcon, presented themselves at the gates. At first the guards were

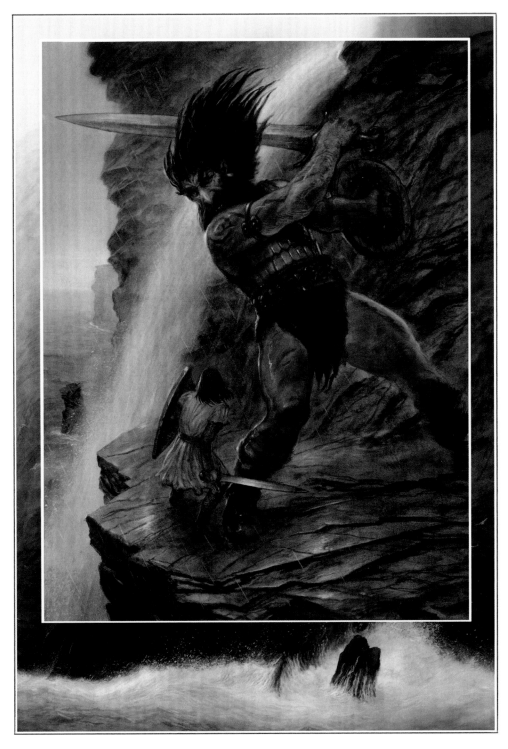

PLATE 9: *'The battle which followed was terrible to behold. The giant Aligos was indeed eleven feet tall'*

disinclined to allow them entrance, but one of Odée's women, a most fair and beautiful maiden named Papagai, asked to be allowed in, announcing that they brought a rare gift for the king.

Those who carried the falcon were allowed to enter. With them came a burly Breton named Celot, who slipped unnoticed into the company, mixing with the barons but closely following she who carried the falcon. Papagai advanced to where the king was seated.

Noticing Sone near the king, she flushed, and when Sone saw her, he too changed colour. This was solely on account of their great natural beauty, to which each reacted, but many of those looking on assumed it could be proof of an amorous liaison. Others, who could scarcely take their eyes from Papagai, noticed a second woman with her.

She was as ugly as her companion was fair, but Sone recognized her from the court of Norway. Her name was Orvale, and while he wondered greatly why she had come, he spoke politely to her and asked the king to honour her, as she was the daughter of a count. The king made both women welcome and commanded a knight to seat them at the table near him. 'Let us eat, friends,' he said, 'and we shall hear your news after.'

Everywhere knights were seated with their ladies. All looked at Papagai with wonder at her beauty, but Orvale was so hideous they could hardly bear to look at her. There was not a knight present, however tall, who could not have sheltered under her arm. She was equally proportioned save that she had a hump behind and one before that supported her chin. From the lump of the rear, she had fashioned an ear for her head. Her skin was darker than ink and she had a great beard and teeth so long that her upper lip was two

fingers distant from the lower. She had eyes bigger than those of a warhorse, and above them eyebrows three fingers wide.

She asked to be taken to where Sone sat at the table. He greeted her gently and made room for her to sit beside him. Then he asked after the King and Queen of Norway, and of course their daughter.

'She often weeps,' replied Orvale. 'On account of you, who has behaved so badly. You have taken her heart that she accorded you in good faith but acted unwisely by leaving her.'

'My dear friend,' answered Sone, 'eat, don't be angry. I promise to put to right any wrongs I have committed.'

'If you do so,' concluded Orvale, 'I think you will greatly profit from it.'

Orvale now gave Papagai the falcon, which sat upon her fist gracefully and elegantly. No better bird existed in the land at that time. She came before the king and declared: 'Hear, O King, you who are a great sovereign. We have come to you from afar and have brought you this falcon, the best that ever flew. The daughter of the King of Norway offers it to you, and asks in return for your judgement, having heard her cause, in a matter of great urgency to her.'

'I accept the falcon,' replied King Henri. 'And will hear the cause of your mistress.'

'Then pay attention,' continued Papagai, 'and let all be silent.'

Then she took up her harp, the finest that had ever been strung, and turning to the king, said: 'Sire, you will now hear a lay composed from the truth, telling the adventures of my lady. Then we will hear your judgement.' Then she struck the harp-strings and began the words of the lay. And the truth of this was that it had been composed by Odée, and in it she described her love for Sone and his promise to return to her.

All there listened with great attention, so fine was Papagai's playing and so beautiful her voice. Many wept openly, among them Sone himself, and all heard his name in the words of the song.

When she was done, Papagai declared: 'Dear King, this is my lady's just cause. Much more could I have sung, but it is not courteous to tell all. Now you must judge truly if your brother should marry so loyal and tender a queen, who would lose her life if she lost him. Since if he comes to her he will have the crown of Norway at his disposition, the kingdom and all the country want no more than the lady and her champion.'

When he heard this Sone's face changed colour. All saw how it was with him and as one person the whole court, along with King Henri, declared that Sone should marry Odée.

✣ ✣ ✣

SO IT WAS that Sone set forth again for Norway. Odée, meanwhile, thought of little else and ardently wished for his coming. Sick with love, she would climb up to the top of a tower, dressed in her most sumptuous attire, to scrutinize the distant horizon to catch sight of Sone's galley speeding on its way.

At length his ship was sighted, and word spread quickly through the port and the city beyond. As the news spread, Odée ordered all the sailors across the city to stay close and in great barques, nefs, galleys, sloops, transport barges, large and small fishing boats. Three-hundred vessels left port, filled with musical instruments. Trumpets, drums, symbols, tambourines, flageolets, sarrasin horns and those that were sounded for guests of honour. Great cornemuses, harps, psalteries, vielles, rotes and other instruments encouraged the dancers while conjurors performed magic tricks.

As soon as the galley carrying Sone arrived, they saluted it. The instruments started up, sounding joyously as new players joined in and the inhabitants of the city rejoiced. They had decorated the streets with banners, ornamented the doors, and carpeted the roads with flowers. All the bells rang through the breadth and length of the city. Not even white-haired old men and women failed to feel their hearts beat with joy, as all, great and small, ran to the port in jubilation.

As Sone's galley pulled in, he leapt from the ship and mounted a horse brought there for him. Without cloak or hood, so all could see him, he entered the city in triumph. The people bowed before him and prayed, hands joined in supplication, begging him to become their true lord and protect their kingdom.

Sone passed on to climb toward the castle. The queen mother herself came to meet him, held him in her arms and kissed him on the mouth, which touched him to the heart. Odée arrived after her mother and behaved calmly, not revealing how she truly felt. She welcomed her friend with her eyes and greeted him simply, saying: 'Sir, you are welcome as our sovereign, and if it pleases you to accept that title, you shall command all as our lord. I do not wish to hide that I have called you my love with a true heart, and from now on will act according to your will.'

When Sone heard this, he understood that he was about to learn something that would sadden him. And so it was. King Alain had died of a sudden chill taken while hunting, soon after Sone had departed for France. He mourned the passing of his friend and spoke gentle words to the queen and her daughter. Both thanked him for his kindness and spoke again of his impending acceptance of the kingship.

Thus matters proceeded. Servants brought Sone scarlet clothes trimmed with ermine; he was then taken before the people, who acclaimed his coming with the same enthusiasm that had met him at the port. Soon after, the bishop of the city arrived and spoke to all the crowd gathered outside the royal palace, reminding them that as King Alain was dead, the queen had agreed to give her daughter in marriage to Sone, thus allowing him to rule the land.

Then he asked if all agreed, and as one they cried: Yes! So the bishop asked Sone if he, too, was willing, and Sone gave his assent.

'Then I proclaim Sone our lord,' resumed the bishop. 'He will marry the princess and be crowned. Commit yourself to her before us all and she will do the same for you.' And with great delight the couple did as the bishop proposed, announcing their solemn engagement before the people, so that all rejoiced.

☩ ☩ ☩

IN THE MONTH that followed Sone was crowned, and his first command was that he wished to be married by the abbot of the island where he and King Alain had travelled, and that, if the holy man agreed, this should take place on the island itself. When he heard this, the abbot was glad and ordered a bell to be rung in celebration and sent word that he would do as Sone and Odée wished.

So it was that the new king and his bride

sailed to the mysterious island and there the abbot met them and made them welcome. He spoke to Sone quietly: 'Remember well, that as king you must also guard the Holy Lance that pierced the side of Christ and be the guardian of the Holy Grail.'

King Sone replied, 'I swear to it, and if it pleases God, and will carry it out while I live.'

Then the castle was prepared for the celebration, and the bells rang forth every hour in token of the marriage of Sone and Odée. The clerks intoned their chant while the abbot, dressed again in his priestly robes, began the ceremony. When all was ready the priest chanted over them and anointed them with holy oils and blessed them and declared them wed.

Once the service was ended, the Grail itself was brought forth and shown to all, also the Lance of Longinus and the cross containing a fragment of holy wood on which Jesus Christ was hung. The abbot kissed the Grail and gave it into the hands of Sone, who held it until the Mass was ended, at which time the abbot took the Grail and put it into its ivory reliquary.

Then Sone and his new bride went to the palace and sat at the table of honour. Both wore a crown, and white clothing according to the custom of the place. To the astonishment of many, the abbot changed his religious garments for ones of scarlet vermilion, reminding all that he was at the same time an abbot and a count.

At this moment lightning flashed and it began to thunder so violently that all thought the sky was about to fall on their heads. Such a storm was unleashed that it broke and tore down great trees, whose fragments struck the walls. The sea was so rough that it threw waves over the walls, covering much of the island with water in which goods floated. Many would have drowned had they not rushed to take shelter on the walls.

The storm became stronger and stronger, without the least respite, and Sone himself climbed to the walls with Odée at his side. Such a downpour of water fell on them that they were nearly washed into the sea. A day and a night the hurricane continued without ceasing. It lasted for three days and three nights during which no one there ate or drank, nor slept or rested.

On the dawn of the fourth day lightning struck the cemetery that lay beyond the walls of the castle, and there followed a clap of thunder so loud that it shook the whole island. Then the conflict ceased, and the hurricane was carried out to sea. The sky above cleared; the sun appeared and the light brought relief to all. The hurricane had gone but all the ships were lost, the storm having broken their rigging and sunk them.

The island was inundated with water, but there were so many conduits in the walls that it rapidly drained away. When the water had gone and the land cleared, a smell so foul spread across the island, causing all to feel sick and filling their hearts with fear. It came from the cemetery where the lightning had fallen. The people high on the walls were tired, having passed three days without sleep or rest, with nothing to eat or drink.

None dared approach the cemetery, not even Sone himself, but fortune saw to it that help was at hand. Having seen the terrible storm from the shore of the mainland, a certain brave sailor named Gratien set forth for the island in his ship, and when he came close, and smelled the dreadful stink, did not stop but came ashore and went himself to find what caused it.

In the cemetery he saw that the earth had been struck by lightning and that this had thrown up a tomb enclosing a corpse. The gravestone was completely broken, but the corpse, with flesh and body intact, lay with open mouth, from which the deadly stink seemed to come.

Though sick almost to death, Gratien dragged the body to the cliff top and threw it into the sea, at which the air became clear again and the sun shone from a blue sky.

From the top of the walls the new king and queen observed all that took place, and Odée, clinging to her husband's neck, begged that they should leave the place at once.

'My dear sweet love,' replied Sone, 'do not let us fail in our duty now.' They descended to the foot of the walls, where the monks were gathered. There they found the old queen mortally ill from the soaking and the stink, and that night she died.

Both Sone and Odée mourned her passing and prepared a tomb for her within the walls of the castle. Sone himself, along with the abbot, went together to the cemetery and saw the hole where the body had lain. The abbot went to where the tombstone that had marked the grave still stood and read the inscription. It showed that the grave had belonged to the wife of Joseph of Arimathea, whose pagan heart had never accepted the ways of her husband, and thus had remained untouched throughout the years. Her ill-will had caused the stink that had all but overwhelmed everyone who was there, until Gratien rid them of her tortured remains. For this the brave sailor was much praised and King Sone awarded him many favours.

So at last, the new king and queen returned to the mainland and soon after, accompanied by the abbot, set forth on a progress through the kingdom, seeking the promise of fealty from the people. And it is said that Sone ruled well, and in time rose to even greater power by the strength and honour he possessed. It is even said, though I know not if it be true, that he became Emperor of Rome in his later years, and that one of the children given him by Odée became pope. It is also told how, when his life was close to an end, Sone looked one last time into the Grail. which he had guarded for much of his life, and that, like Sir Galahad before him, he expired gently, and his spirit was taken up to heaven.

Such is the tale of Sone de Nansay, that I have told in the knowledge that Master Thomas would have been certain to include it in his mighty book, had he but known of it.

———— ⴲ ————

EXPLICIT LIBER QUARTUOR.
INCIPIT LIBER QUINQUE.

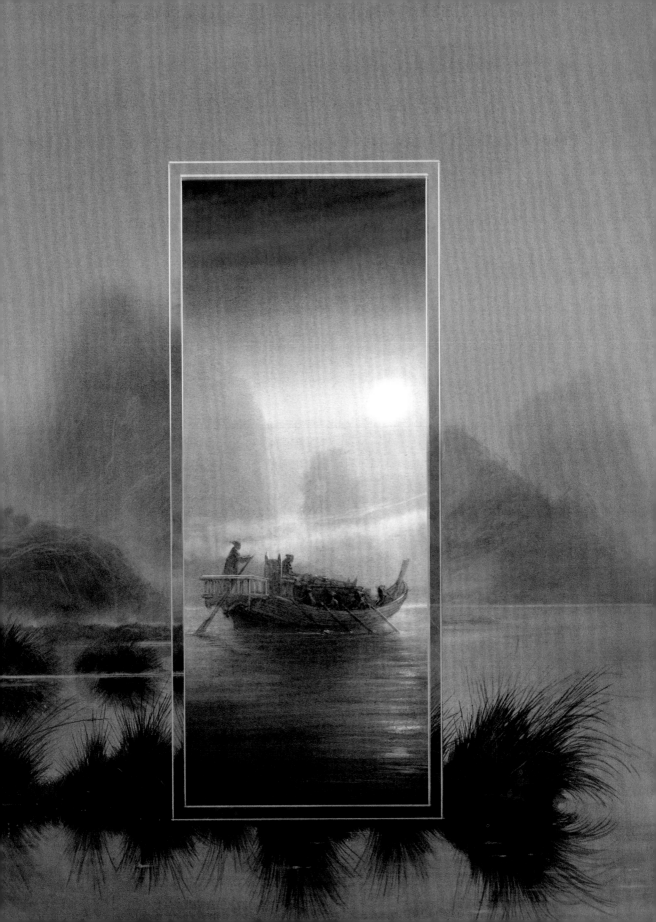

BOOK FIVE

THE ENDING
OF THE
ROUND TABLE

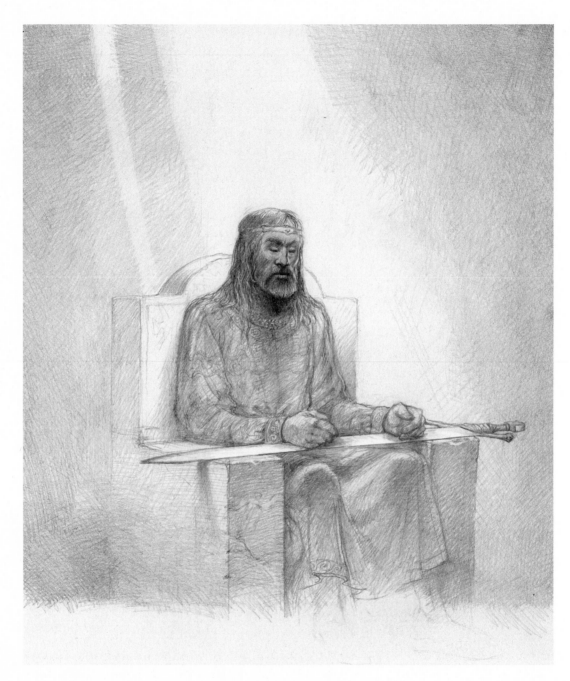

✦ *King Arthur in the Otherworld* ✦

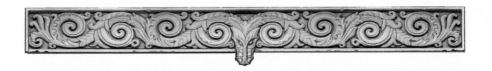

31: THE DEATH OF KING ARTHUR

✜

WHEN MASTER THOMAS CAME TO THE END OF HIS GREAT BOOK, TO WHICH I HAVE, WITH SOME TREPIDATION, SET MYSELF TO ADD THESE STORIES THAT HE DID NOT INCLUDE, HE GAVE US THE GREATEST ACCOUNT OF THE DEATH OF THE GREAT KING WHOSE LIFE AND DEEDS HE HAD SO WONDERFULLY CHRONICLED. FOR THIS REASON, THE BOOK WAS NAMED THE MORTE (THAT IS, THE DEATH) OF ARTHUR. CERTAIN IT IS THAT NO MAN NOW LIVING COULD WRITE A BETTER MEMORIAL THAN SIR THOMAS. HOWEVER, I HAVE BUT LATELY LEARNED OF TWO ACCOUNTS WHICH, THOUGH THEY CANNOT COME NEAR TO THE GLORY OF MASTER THOMAS'S PROSE, YET TELL OF EVENTS THAT HE DID NOT RECORD – FOR WHAT REASON I CANNOT SAY.

✜ ✜ ✜

THUS, I SHALL record these things here, though some speak of dreadful events that are perhaps best left unsaid. Only because of my desire to complete the work Sir Thomas left in some part unfinished will I do so, and may I be forgiven if I trespass too greatly upon his memory.

✜ ✜ ✜

IT IS TOLD, in certain of the works that I have read, that after the ending of the Great Quest, there was much mourning in the lands ruled by King Arthur – for, as many said, there were no adventures left to be enjoyed. Thus the Fellowship of the Round Table began to weaken, for just as many of the great knights had perished in the quest, or were lost to the world, ever wandering in lands not of this earth, so those who had returned were ill-at-ease and idle.

At last, several of the highest lords, including Sir Gawain and Sir Lancelot, came to King Arthur and spoke to him thus: 'Sire, you are assuredly the greatest king that has lived, and so all should follow you and do you service.

Merlin himself, who was never known to lie, foretold that one day you would rule over half the world. Indeed, you overcame the Emperor of Rome himself, and were crowned there in the holy city. Yet there are still those who do not pay you just honour – most of all the Kings of France and Spain. We have come to ask you to gather an army and to cross the sea, and to make war upon those who do not accept your rule.'

As those who have read Master Thomas's book know, these things took place long before the time of which the story tells here, where the Emperor Lucius was overcome and the king indeed crowned.* But I bid you put from your minds for this brief time the story that tells how Arthur and Gawain made war upon Sir Lancelot, because of the death of Sir Gareth, Gawain's brother, when Lancelot rescued Queen Guinevere from the flames to which she was condemned.

Here is a different tale. For when he heard the plea that Gawain and Lancelot made, and how many other noble lords and knights felt the same, King Arthur called for messages to be sent throughout the land, inviting those who would join him in a war against the French and the Spanish, to come to Camelot the Golden. Within weeks many noble lords answered his call, so that soon there were more than ten thousand gathered in readiness for war.

Then King Arthur called upon his son, Mordred, to guard the kingdom in his absence and prepared to take ship. Having crossed the water, the army marched inland and so entered the lands of the French king, whose name was Flories, and who, when he heard how King Arthur came against him in war,

summoned his own army. But even while his lords and knights assembled, he sent a letter to King Arthur.

> 'Noble Sire, I promise that you will rue the day when you came against me. But for the sake of all who ride with us, great knights and lords, and common men alike, I ask if you will attempt to settle this war in single combat, king against king, my body against yours.'

When King Arthur read this, he was silent for a time, for in truth the years had begun to weigh upon him, and he knew that King Flories was younger than he. Yet in his heart there was kindled a spark that swiftly became a flame, that he longed to ride again in battle against an honourable foe. So, though both Sir Gawain and Sir Lancelot, as well as many other knights, begged him not to accept the French king's words, King Arthur declared that three days hence he would meet with his opponent in the field where the two armies were already assembled, and there, before all, he would fight for the right of conquest.

So it was that on the third day King Arthur put on his splendid armour and chose the finest mount he had and rode out onto the field. There, King Flories came also, and there was much sounding of trumpets from either camp, until the very heavens shook with the sound.

The two kings set their lances in rest and came together. Both shattered their spears but made no damage to each other. Twice more they fought thus, and at the end neither had the advantage. So they both dismounted and drew their swords and came together. King Arthur had his mighty sword, Excalibur, with which he defended himself fiercely. Yet

---

* See *Le Morte D'Arthur*, Book V Ch. xii.

it was King Flories who struck the first telling blows, cutting through King Arthur's hauberk, and wounding him in the side. And with another blow he cut into the king's leg and sliced away some of the flesh from the bone.

All those on the British side saw that King Arthur was wounded and were greatly afraid. But the king drew upon all his strength, and wielding Excalibur he cut first through the French king's shield and into his arm. And when Flories cried aloud and fell back, King Arthur struck him upon the helm, which fell from his head along with locks of his hair. Now King Arthur had the advantage, and struck again so that Flories fell back, blinded by blood that flowed from a wound in his temple. And King Arthur made a great effort and struck him again, so that he fell to the earth, dead.

Then there was great rejoicing from the Britons, and much sorrow and mourning from the French. But thus warfare was saved for that time, and the French nobles came to pay homage to King Arthur.

Now many of the Knights of the Round Table and other noble lords came to Arthur and begged that he would lead them into Spain, to overcome his enemies there. But Arthur declared that he had had enough of war and would return home. Even as he spoke of this, a messenger came who told him how Mordred had risen against his father and had taken Queen Guinevere prisoner. When he heard this the king sought at once to return, and now all were greatly angered against Mordred and sought his death. The army turned about and left the French kingdom in the care of a British noble, while all the rest returned home.

All who have read Master Thomas's book will know well what followed, so I shall not write it here, except to say that in the great battle of Camlann Mordred fell to Arthur's blade, but that the king himself received a mortal wound. What followed is told only briefly by Master Thomas, who said that he could not say whether King Arthur was dead or not, or whether he passed, by the will of our Lord, into another place. Yet in the story that I have found, and that I have told here, it is said very clearly that the king was taken to Avalon, to be healed of his wounds, and that since that time he has been seen hunting in the Great Wood, with a pack of hounds whose cries were heard by all. Of this the story speaks no more, but I may call to witness one other, the bard Taliesin, who visited Merlin at the time when he ran mad in the forest.* There the two spoke at length concerning the fate of the king, and Taliesin told a different tale: of how he had been present at the last battle and how he had helped carry the wounded king to a sheltered cove where a small boat lay at anchor. 'We took him to the island of Avalon, in a boat steered by the wise Barinthus, who knows all the ways of the tides and winds. There a great lady laid him in her own bed, hung round with gold and silk, and examined his wounds. She said that he would recover if he remained with her for a long time.'

And Merlin answered: 'How terrible has been the star of the land since that day!'

'Perhaps we should send a messenger to Arthur, begging him to return,' answered Taliesin.

'That may not be,' said Merlin. 'One who has passed to Avalon may not be recalled in his own lifetime.'

And yet, there is one more account that

---

* See 'The Coming of Merlin' pp. 3–11

I have found, and this will I tell now, for it is indeed a wondrous tale, which to my certain knowledge few have heard. It can only bring joy to those who believe that the great king is indeed not dead but may one day return to protect his land in time of need.

EXPLICIT THE DEATH OF KING ARTHUR.
HERE BEGINS THE VOYAGE TO AVALON.

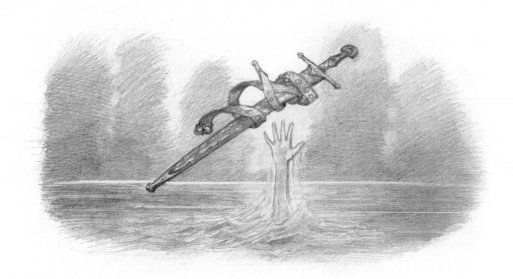

⤍ *Excalibur* ⤎

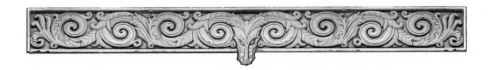

32: THE VOYAGE TO AVALON

✠

HE WHO TELLS THIS STORY IS NAMED GUILLAUME DE TOERELLA. HE WRITES AS ONE WHO SAW THESE THINGS WITH HIS OWN EYES – AND WHO AM I TO DISBELIEVE HIM? THE TALE HE TELLS IS WONDROUS AND STRANGE, BUT WITHIN IT LIES MUCH THAT I BELIEVE TO BE TRUE. THEREFORE, I WILL TELL IT AS HE DID, IN HIS OWN WORDS, THAT I HAVE COPIED FAITHFULLY AND, I HOPE, WITHOUT ERROR.

✠ ✠ ✠

ON THE MORNING of Midsummer's Day, I went riding, enjoying the wind on my face and the purity of the air. So eager was my steed that I could scarcely hold him in check, so determined he was to gallop. I gave him his head and let him run where he would. At last, he began to tire, and finding myself by a river, I reined in and dismounted, giving my horse time to drink. There I saw how, a little way off, the river emptied into the sea, and as I looked, I saw a strange sight. At the edge of the water, there lay a great creature – one that is, I believe, called a whale.

So great was my desire to see more of this beast, that I came closer to it, and as I did so it seemed that I heard it speak within my mind, and that it invited me to climb upon its back. At first I was fearful, but it seemed to me that the creature was gentle, and so I pulled myself up its great sides until I stood upon its back. So huge it was that I could see as far as ten leagues in each direction. Then, as I wondered at this, the beast began to swim away from the shore towards the deep sea. Fearful for my life, I clung to its back, which was so ridged that I found places to hold on.

Thus we went together, the creature and I, across the wild sea, past many lands I would have wished to explore, until at last the great beast came to another shore where waters struck the rocks with a great noise. Here the whale stopped and with much relief, I climbed down from its back and gladly walked on the earth again.

By this time, it had grown dark, so that I could scarcely see where I had come. Then I saw where a light shone out in the darkness, and to this I made my way. There I saw a most remarkable thing: a great tree rose out of the earth, and in its branches coiled a huge serpent. On its head, like a crown, sat a great ruby, and from this came the light. By this I saw a wide meadow, where grew many beauteous flowers. The perfume of these was so delightful that my head swam. I could not tell what kind of tree it was before which I stood, but its branches were laden with fruit, in shape like oranges or tangerines, but of a different colour. By this time I was so hungry, having not eaten since the morning, that I took some of the fruit and ate it. How wonderful it tasted! Like nothing I have had before or since. Then I noticed that at the foot of the tree was set a stone basin, filled with fresh clear water. Of this I drank my fill, noticing that no matter how much I took, the level of water remained exactly the same.

As I stood thus, marvelling at the strangeness of this place, I heard a voice addressing me. I realized that it was the serpent itself that spoke, and though this was most strange, I heard it address me by name: 'Guillaume, you have come here by a wondrous route and not of your own choosing. Therefore, I will tell you that you are on the enchanted isle of Avalon. Here lives Morgan le Fay, and my master, King Arthur.'

Greatly amazed I was to hear this, for as all know, the great King Arthur was taken from the field of war and sailed in a magical barge to another land. It seemed that, by some miracle, I had come to this very place. But at this moment I began to feel a great sleep coming upon me, and I lay down on the grass amid the wonderfully scented flowers, and so fell asleep.

In the morning the song of birds awoke me, and I listened with delight to these as I rose and washed myself with water from the stone basin and quenched my thirst. All around me, the earth was clad with plants of green and gold, at which I marvelled greatly. Then I remembered what the serpent had told me of the place, and of King Arthur, and so I began to search for any kind of habitation – tower, palace, or house. At first I could see nothing, then I came to where a beautiful palfrey stood, its harness the most fine I had ever seen. The steed was hung about with cloth of gold on which were embroidered scenes of love. There I saw Tristan and Isolt, Pyramus and Thisbe, Floris and Blanchfleur, Paris and Helen, and many more, while on its harness were bells of gold and silver which chimed sweetly when it moved.

I clambered upon the back of this steed and urged it to go forward. But though I pulled upon the reins, it refused to go in any direction but that which it wished to. So I gave it its head and allowed it to go where it would.

More marvellous was that place than any I have ever seen, so rich was it, clad in flowers and trees of the most marvellous kind, threaded by silver streams, patched with fields of wheat and barley of the most wondrous kind.

I rode on for a time, until I saw two dogs coming towards me. To my amazement they came gambolling to me and showed such affection that it was as if they had known me for a long time. Then I knew that I was in a place of great enhancements, and I followed the dogs until I saw where a sparrowhawk was perched upon a branch. It looked at me with its golden eyes and I felt that it knew me as had the dogs, though I had never seen any of them before.

Then I rode onward for a time until I found myself in a garden where many great trees grew, all of them the same size and height.

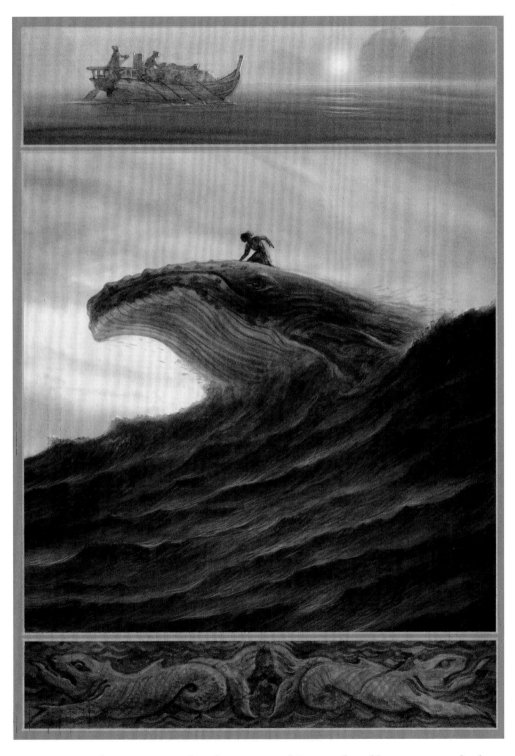

PLATE 10: *'Thus we went together, the creature and I, across the wild sea, past many lands I would have wished to explore'*

Amid these was set a palace of such beauty that I believe it would have rivalled Solomon's temple. Its walls were adorned with jasper, both yellow and green, held together by bands of silver. The entrance was tall and supported by arches of crystal. The doors were of ebony, decorated in gold.

The palfrey stopped before the gates and would go no further. 'Is this where I am meant to be?' I said aloud. At that moment a most beautiful maiden, who seemed no more than sixteen years of age, approached. She wore a dress of black samite, quite plain, without any adornment. Her skin was pale and her hair red.

'Welcome, Guillaume,' she said. 'You are come here by my will.'

'Of all the wonders I have seen in this place,' I answered, 'yet there is one thing I desire more than anything to know – if you have word of King Arthur, of whom the serpent in the great tree told me? And if it please you I would know your name?'

'When King Arthur ruled in Britain I was known as Morgan le Fay. You shall call me by that name.'

Seeing my amazement, the maiden smiled. 'As to my lord and dear brother Arthur, he is indeed here. You will find him in the palace – but I must tell you that a great melancholy has fallen upon him of late. You may find him less good company than you expect. Nor can I do anything to heal him of this, for the strongest magic I possess has no effect.'

'My lady, just to see the great king would be more than enough, though I am sorry to hear of his sorrow.'

'Then enter. You will see what you wish to see.'

So having placed the sparrowhawk on the pommel of the palfrey's saddle, bade the dogs to stay where they were, and tethered the mount to a post, I entered the palace.

I knew at once that it was of no earthly design, since no man then living, save perhaps Merlin himself, could have built it. On its walls and in windows made of stained glass, were displayed all the deeds of the Round Table Knights. All were here, from Gawain to Palomides, Lancelot to Perceval and Bors, who were with Galahad at the finding of the Grail. All these and more that I will not list here were depicted in that wondrous place.

Despite these wonders I could see no living thing other than she who brought me there. 'Why can I not see the king or those who serve him?' I asked. 'Surely such a great lord as he must have many servants?'

At this Morgan le Fay smiled. 'You cannot see him, or any of those who serve us here, because you have not been told how. This will I do.'

Then she raised her hand and I saw that she wore a great ring upon her finger, and that the jewel set within it flashed and flamed like a star.

'You must look through this stone and you will see all that you wish to see,' said the lady. Then she took the ring from her finger and gave it to me.

Heavy it was and seemed warm to me. I lifted it to my eye, and there I saw a great wonder, For the scales that had covered my eyes fell away, and I was able to see all that was there. On a bed hung with silken coverings sewn with gold and silver, sat a man who seemed no more than thirty-three years of age. He seemed sunk in deepest melancholy, as he sat, staring at a mighty sword in his lap.

'Is this truly the great king?' I asked.

The Lady Morgan responded that it was, at which I asked if I could approach and again the lady nodded. So, I came and stood before the great king, wondering greatly that he seemed like other men. I heard him speak, as if to his sword: 'Excalibur! Such a sad pass you have brought me to. All my years as king, sending forth my knights in search of wrongs to right, gentlewomen to protect, evils to destroy. Now I am come to this! How much I regret going aboard the ship that carried me here! How I long to return to the world!'

At this moment I must have made some sound, for the king looked up. 'Who are you?' he cried aloud. 'Where have you come from?'

'Sire,' I said, falling to my knees. 'I am called Guillaume de Toerella, and I am come by chance and strange wonder to this place.' Then I told him all that had occurred. When he had listened to what I had to say, the king looked at me sadly. 'You are welcome here,' he said. 'Though I can tell you little or nothing of where we are.'

He turned then to Morgan. 'Lady, I do not remember anything of my coming here, nor how it is that I have my sword again.'

'My lord,' said Morgan. 'You are in Avalon, which is my realm, to heal yourself of your wounds. As to the sword, when it was returned to the waters by your command, I received it and brought it here to you.'

'It seems to me that I have slept for a long while,' said the king. 'Tell me, Guillaume of Toerella, what do men say of me now in the world?'

'My lord,' I said. 'They speak of you as one of the greatest kings of the world, and the stories of your knights are told through all the lands. I myself have heard many of these told in the halls of my own country.'

Then I told him all the story that I had heard of the great battle at Camlann field and of all that followed, and I spoke of the great

tomb that was erected in Britain, that said it was his own.

At this the king looked sadder than ever, so it was with great boldness that I said: 'May I ask a question of you, my lord? Are you truly that very King Arthur who is expected, and by what manner are you made so young again, for I am told that you were full of years before you fell at Camlann field?'

'I am indeed he who was King of Britain and established the Round Table at Camelot the Golden and sent my knights forth into the world in search of wrongs to right. I even saw them depart in search of the Grail – from the quest for which so few returned. As to how I come to seem so young, that is easily told, though I do not understand it. After I went aboard the ship that brought me here, I began at once to heal, so that when I arrived here, I was whole again. Then this lady brought me to a fountain and bade me unarm myself and enter it naked. This I did, and when I emerged, I was as you see me now. The years had fallen from me like leaves from a tree, and I was filled with vigour. Now, to my great wonder I am given to drink each day from the Holy Grail itself, which resides now in the castle guarded by my knight Sir Perceval. I do not feel hunger or thirst, nor do I grow any older. But time does not run in this place as it does in the world outside, so that I do not know how many years have passed since I came here.'

Then I told the king how much time had passed since he had been last seen upon the earth – though there were those who said they had heard him hunting in the Great Wood.

'How I wish that it were so,' said Arthur, and it seemed to me that he wept a little, to hear these things. Then he looked again at the sword which he still held, and stood suddenly and proffered it to me, hilt foremost, while he held the blade between his hands. At first, I was afraid to touch the blade, but the king smiled and nodded, and I reached out and touched the hilt. And in that moment, it seemed to me that I beheld a vision of the world, with all its terrors and sicknesses. There I saw men without honour and others that sought only to raise themselves to power. Gone were the days of Arthur, when the Fellowship of the Round Table kept watch over the land and brought peace and kindness to all. Now there was but greed and rapine in every land.

Then I too wept, as had the king, for I understood that the world had fallen into shadow and that one such as he was sorely needed. I let my hands fall from the hilt of Excalibur, for I could no longer bear to see these things. And King Arthur took back the sword and sat down again upon the bed and looked neither at me nor the Lady Morgan, but rather at things only he could see.

So things stood for a while, until I was moved to say, out of pity for the king: 'Men wait still for your return to the world beyond this place. Tell me, Lord, will you come forth to lead us again?'

King Arthur looked at me and said: 'I cannot say for certain, but it may be that the day will come when I may depart this place and be with my fellows again, for such is my greatest wish.'

Then Morgan took me to one side and told me: 'It is time for you to leave. I will walk with you to where the palfrey waits and beyond that to the great creature – who is indeed a woman enchanted into that shape that serves me well. But know that you have my gratitude as well as that of the king, for you have

opened his mind to who he was, and that he is still needed in the world. It is for this reason that I brought you here and that now I shall send you back.'

So I took my leave of King Arthur, though truth to tell he seemed no longer to see me, and followed the enchantress back to where the palfrey waited, with the sparrowhawk perched on its saddle and the dogs sitting by its feet. And indeed, they seemed pleased to see me, as though I had been their master for many years.

'Go well, Guillaume de Toerella,' said Morgan. 'Remember these things that you have seen and write them down, so that others may know the truth.'

Thus it was that I left the island of Avalon, returning to the shore where I found the great whale waiting for me. Once again, I climbed upon its back, and there the two dogs joined me, seeming happy to ride there with me, and so we were carried across the sea until we reached my own land. There, my mount awaited me as though I had been gone but a few hours – and indeed it seemed that time had all but ceased to move while I was in that other place.

As for the dogs that had been with me on

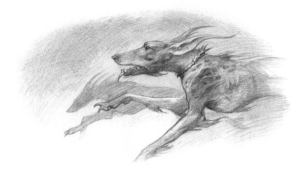

→ *The Hounds of Avalon* ←

the island, they stayed with me and became champions of the hunt.

I have written all that took place in that time, and of the words I spoke to King Arthur, and of his words to me, and all else. Even now, I am not sure if this was more than a dream, yet in my heart I believe that the great king will yet return and walk among us yet again and guide us into less troubled times.

☩ ☩ ☩

THUS, I TOO conclude this book, which I have written down in honour of Master Thomas Malory and which contains stories omitted from his great work. I hope that, wherever his spirit may be, he will look with kindness on my words, and know that his writing is still read in many lands, and that it will continue to be so, by many, for years to come. Other tales there are, as I have discovered only of late, and if I am permitted, I shall gather these together at another time.

———— ☩ ————

EXPLICIT THE GREAT BOOK OF KING ARTHUR AND THE KNIGHTS OF THE ROUND TABLE.

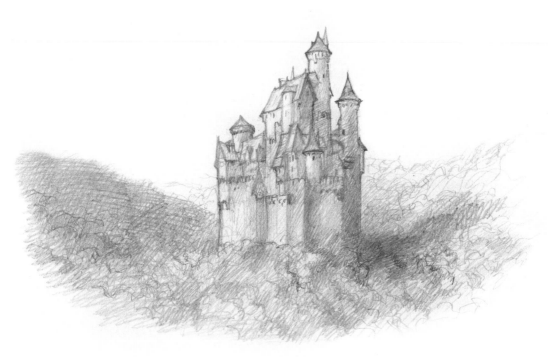

✦ *The Castle in the Forest* ✦

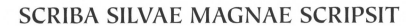
SCRIBA SILVAE MAGNAE SCRIPSIT

NOTES AND SOURCES

BOOK ONE: THE BOOK OF MERLIN

1: The Coming of Merlin

The eleventh-century cleric Geoffrey of Monmouth is best remembered for his great book *Historia Regum Britanniae* (The History of the Kings of Britain), which was something of a 'best-seller' in its time. It was the first book to attempt a full recreation of the life and deeds of Arthur, and it set the seal upon the outpouring of Arthurian literature which followed throughout the next four hundred years. But it is often forgotten that Geoffrey wrote another book, the *Vita Merlini* or Life of Merlin. He had already compiled a series of remarkable prophecies, collected from oral traditions, as the *Prophecies of Merlin*, and incorporated this, along with the story of Merlin's encounter with the tyrant Vortigern, in the *Historia*. Now, however, he turned his attention to the native legends dealing with the figure of Merlin (or Myrddin) in Wales. These tell a very different story to that of the better-known Merlin of Arthurian Romance, and suggest that there was a separate figure whose life became drawn into the Arthurian world after Geoffrey's stories were published. The version included here is, as far as I am aware, the first modern retelling. Geoffrey's original text is a Latin poem of 1,529 lines. I have adapted this freely and omitted many details which hold up the story. Thus, there are prophecies and at least one repetitive incident in which Merlin cures another wild man who seems merely a duplicate of himself. The character of Ganeida, Merlin's sister, may well be the original of the later Nimue. To the disapproving minds of the medieval scribes, the idea of a brother and sister living together in the woods smacked of incest and it was probably this that gave rise to the tale of Merlin being seduced by the lovely young fairy woman as she appears in Malory and elsewhere.

There are a number of fascinating themes in this text, including the famous motif of the threefold death, as predicted by Merlin for the youth who does indeed meet his death in three different ways. Behind this lies a much older form of sacrifice as practised by the Celts, in which a chosen victim was stabbed, strangled, and drowned in a bog. For a fuller treatment of all this and a breakdown of the hidden meanings within the text see R.J. Stewart: *The Mystic Life of Merlin* and *The Prophetic Vision of Merlin* (Arkana, 1986); and for more about Nimue and Ganeida, *Ladies of the Lake* by Caitlín & John Matthews (Thorsons, 1991). The original text has been translated several times, by J.J. Parry as *Vita Merlini* (University of Illinois Press, 1925) and by Basil Clarke as *The Life of Merlin* (University of Wales Press, 1973). A more recent translation by Mark Walker is *Geoffrey of Monmouth's Life of Merlin: A New Verse Translation* (Amberley Books, 2011). I have referred extensively to all these versions in making my own.

2: The Story of Avenable

This story is found in several different versions. The first, on which this retelling is based, is contained within the *English Prose Merlin* first edited by Henry B. Wheatley between 1865 and 1899 (*Merlin or the Early History of King Arthur*, 4 vols, Early English Text Society [London: Kegan Paul, Trench, Tubner, reprinted New York: Greenwood Press, 1969]). The second, more elaborate version appears within the thirteenth-century Arthurian romance, *Silence*, which was only recently discovered and has now been translated by Sara Roche-Mahdi (East Lansing: Colleagues Press, 1992). The latter is by far the longest version, but I have opted for the English version on the grounds that it reads better and requires less knowledge of events before the beginning of the story. Nonetheless I would strongly recommend a reading of *Silence* since this is a powerful and charming romance which may be considered one of the first feminist novels. Its author, who is named Heldris of Cornwall in the manuscript, may in fact have been a woman, despite the fact of referring to himself as 'Master' Heldris throughout. The story, which tells the tale of a woman brought up as a boy, includes some wonderful scenes, and a long and fascinating discussion between the allegorical figures of 'Nature' and 'Nurture' as to whether the forming of a character depends on the natural gender of the child, or its nurturing or upbringing – a topic of considerable interest in our own time. The character of Silence herself, who is called Avenable or Grisandole in the English text, is that of a strong-minded individual, who carves out a career in a man's world through her skill, strength, and native wit. More recently, *The Story of Silence*, a novel based on the original text by Alex Myers, was published in 2020.

Of course, the most interesting aspect of this story is the part dealing with Merlin, the story of his laughter, and his ability to transform himself into a stag. All are drawn from much earlier, Celtic material, including some early poems attributed to Merlin himself, and the famous *Vita Merlini* of Geoffrey of Monmouth.

The only surviving version of the 'English Merlin' is now in Cambridge University Library (FF III ii). As well as Wheatley's edition, from which I have worked in my own retelling, there is an extract which includes the Grisandole story, in *The Romance of Merlin*, edited by Peter Goodrich (Garland Publishing, 1990). I have included the Wheatley text in full, both in my *Arthurian Reader* (Thorsons, 1991) and in *Merlin Through the Ages* edited with R.J. Stewart (Cassell, 1994). A very different, fictionalized version, told from the point of view of Merlin, appeared in the anthology *Merlin and Woman*, edited by R.J. Stewart (Blandford Press, 1988) and in an extended version in *The Song of Arthur* (Quest Books, 2002). A fascinating breakdown of the many versions of this story, which are to be found as far away as India and China, can be found in a long essay by Lucy Allen Paton: 'The Story of Grisandole: A Study in the Legend of Merlin' (*Publications of the Modern Language Society of America*, vol. XXII, [1907] pp. 243–282).

3: Merlin and the Dragons

There are two accounts on which this story is based. One is found in the *Historia Brittonum* by a ninth-century Welsh monk named Nennius. The other is in Geoffrey of Monmouth's celebrated *Historia Regum Britanniae*. Here I have amalgamated the two versions to form a more complete whole. Dinas Emrys, where the scene of the battle between the two serpents takes place, is situated not far from Beddgelert in Gwynedd, north-west Wales. Ruins still crown the hill which date from the fifth–sixth centuries – suggesting there may well be a germ of truth behind the idea of Vortigern's tower. Vortigern himself came to power in the fifth century. He was probably a native British warlord, though the early historian Bede calls him 'King of the Britons'. He is best remembered in these early sources for having invited Saxon mercenaries into Britain to help defend the country against the Picts, who were invading from the north. As payment they demanded lands in Britain then sent for their families and more warriors who became invaders. The sixth-century Arthur is believed to have brought together scattered British tribes to fight against the Saxons – pinning them down on the coast long enough for them to become settlers rather than invaders. The story of Merlin and the Dragons seems to have arisen from folklore concerning the area. Merlin himself is referred to as Emrys in older records and this probably led to the association with the site. For more information, see my *Book of Merlin* (Amberley Books, 2019). For the original texts on which the story told here is based see: *Nennius: British History and the Welsh Annals* edited and translated by John Morris (Phillimore / Rowman & Littlefield, 1980) and *The History of the Kings of Britain* translated by Lewis Thorpe (Penguin Classics, 1973).

BOOK TWO: THE BOOK OF THE ROUND TABLE

4: The Vows of King Arthur and His Knights

The tale known as *The Avowing of King Arthur, Sir Gawain, Sir Kay and Baldwin of Britain* exists in a single manuscript, the Liverpool Ireland MS now in Geneva. This dates from some time after 1450, though the poem itself was probably written earlier. Like 'The Adventures at Tarn Wathelyn' (pp. 260–5) and the more familiar 'Wedding of Sir Gawain and the Lady Ragnall' (pp. 299–305) it is written in a Middle English dialect which suggests it was composed by a poet living in the West Midlands. It is some 1,148 lines in length and full of lively description and passages of action which still read well today.

The story it tells is really several tales bound together by the device of the multiple vow. This theme is well known throughout medieval tradition, including several other Arthurian tales such as 'The Wedding of Sir Gawain and the Lady Ragnall', 'The Carle of Carlisle' and the famous *Gawain and the Green Knight*. All these illustrate, in their own way, the importance of the vow, which was not taken lightly and was seldom, if ever, reneged upon.

The theme of Arthur's pursuit of the boar goes back to Celtic myth, where, in the old Welsh tale of *Culhwch & Olwen* from the *Mabinogion*, not only Arthur but his entire band of heroes pursues the mighty Twrch Trwyth, a boar of such mythic stature that it destroys half the country before it is finally brought to bay. In the story given here, there is a wonderfully realistic account of the battle between the king and the boar which could only have been written by someone who had taken part in such hunts. The boar was certainly a worthy and fearsome opponent at the time when the poem was written, since boars were larger and fiercer than their current descendants, weighing in at around 300 pounds and often measuring four feet in height. The seeming exaggeration of the beast which is described as 'taller than a horse' in this poem, is thus not so far from the truth.

The knight encountered by Kay and Gawain, who is named Menealfe in this story, may represent a lingering echo from a more otherworldly characteristic once carried by the story before it was written down by its rather pious author. Menealfe can mean 'Elf-Man', or even, as suggested by Nirmal Dass, derive from classical Greek, meaning 'he incurs the wrath'. If the former, the knight has certainly lost any supernatural qualities such a name might lead us to expect.

The three knights who accompany Arthur include the familiar Gawain and Kay and the less well-known Baldwin, who actually carries the weight of the story. Baldwin appears elsewhere in another Middle English poem: *Sir Gawain and the Carle of Carlisle* (see pp. 277–82) where he is referred to as 'Bishop Baldwin'. As Louis Hall points out, 'In this last tale the bishop acts like a knight, but here the knight talks like a bishop' (*Knightly Tales of Sir Gawain*).

The *exemplum* (literally 'examples') given by Baldwin are hard to swallow in this day and age – especially the first, in which Baldwin seems to be saying that if women are kept busy, they remain submissive, but if they are allowed too much freedom or idleness they may well get up to evil! Not many readers would stomach this kind of sexist remark today, but we have to remember that in the Middle Ages the custom was different, and women were – by and large – depicted as second-class citizens or, by the Church, as tools of the devil.

Perhaps the only way to interpret the tale for a modern audience is to see Baldwin's remarks as an ironic comment on the lives and mores of his peers. Indeed, none of the knights save Baldwin himself come off very well in this story. Arthur is shown as an irreverent prankster, Kay as a boastful coward, and Gawain, though he deports himself well, is little more than a cipher of knightly excellence. Baldwin, by comparison, towers over the rest. He is a more rounded character, with humour, wisdom, and manly courage. Perhaps his earlier portrayal as a bishop had something to do with this, since despite the changes which characters regularly undergo in the Arthurian legends, they frequently carry over aspects of their earlier incarnations into later texts. Baldwin's stories, as he tells them, are more universal, and carry a powerful charge of wisdom.

However one feels about any of this, the tale moves along briskly and ends with a well-rounded period. It is a story rooted very much in this world, with a minimum of magical details of the kind found in most Arthurian texts. As a story of four boastful men, it can amuse us; as a piece of the pattern which threads the Arthurian mythos, it is exciting and rich in detail.

Editions include that of W.H. French and C.B. Hale's *Middle English Metrical Romances* (New York: Russell & Russell, 1930) and more recently by Roger Dahood as *The Avowing of King Arthur* (New York: Garland, 1984). There is also an excellent verse translation by Nirmal Dass (University Press of America, 1987). I have used mostly French and Hale, augmented by Louis B. Hall's excellent prose rendition in his *The Knightly Tales of Sir Gawain* (Chicago: Nelson Hall, 1976).

5: The Knight of the Parrot

Le Chevalier du Papegau (The Knight of the Parrot) is that rare thing, an Arthurian satire. Others do exist, such as the thirteenth-century Gawain romance *Hunbaut*, but by and large the writers of these stories took their subject seriously. The anonymous author of the story retold here takes the opportunity to poke fun at the concept of chivalry. Not that he was altogether against the institution, as we can see from Arthur's early remarks on the subject to the Merciless Lion. But this is balanced by his later behaviour when he strikes the Lady of the Blonde Hair for causing him to lose face in the tournament. The excuse – you asked me to behave like a bad knight, well I'm still doing it! – is a thin one by medieval or modern standards but reflects the attitude towards women at the time. I chose to omit this part of the tale on the grounds that it presents Arthur in a less than glamorous light and against the traditional values he normally represents.

The parrot itself seems to have served as a device through which the author could put a more rational and ironic point of view, and the story is unusual on two further counts: the fact that it takes place at the beginning of Arthur's reign, and that it features him as a hero. Generally, the best-known stories of this genre tend to focus on later periods, and they very seldom feature Arthur as anything other than a figurehead who sets the ball rolling by sending forth one of his knights in response to the usual distressed damsel. Here, however, Arthur takes the lead from the beginning, and shows himself to be every bit as worthy a knight as any of the great Round Table Fellowship.

Despite the comedic passages – mostly provided by the parrot – the story is in fact a very archetypical one. Arthur faces a whole range of tests and trials, ranging from serpents to wild women, to sword bridges and crushing wheels. He also encounters a helpful ghost, one of the few in Arthurian tradition (for another see 'The Adventures at Tarn Wathelyn' pp. 260–5). He overcomes them all with the usual amount of sweat, bravery, and occasional magical help. A succession of distressed damsels is on hand to keep him busy and, overall, he fares well and provides the reader with enough to keep him or her entertained throughout a lengthy text.

I have made two abridgements to the story. In the first I have omitted Arthur's encounter with two giants, in part to save space and because this holds up the action. The episode occurs between Arthur's initial fight outside the Amorous Castle and his continuing mission to find the Perilous Castle and defeat the marshal. The second cut comes near to the end, when after he has successfully overcome all opposition and reached the Perilous Castle a further series of adventures takes place which adds little to the story. I have generally tidied up the ending also, to give a tighter and more fitting resolution to the story. Those who wish to read either the omitted passages or the ending given by the original storyteller, are referred to the translation of Thomas Vesce mentioned below.

A word about the names of the characters. They all have very symbolic names which serve to identify them by type rather than character. Thus, the women have names like The Lady of the Blonde Hair, the wonderfully named Beauty Without Villainy, and Arthur encounters The Amorous Knight of the Savage Castle, and the Count of the Amorous City – not to mention the Merciless Lion. These are all part and parcel of the medieval storyteller's art and were intended to describe characteristics rather than characters. I chose to replace them here with names chosen from the many lesser characters in other stories simply to distinguish them from each other.

The romance exists in a single manuscript in the National Library of Paris (BN, fr.2154). This is a text copied in the fifteenth or sixteenth centuries, but both its recent translator, Thomas E. Vesce, and its only editor, Ferdinand Heuckenkamp, agree that the original version of the story dates from the late thirteenth century. It certainly suggests a knowledge of several of the romances by Chrétien de Troyes, including *Erec and Enide*, *Lancelot* and *Perceval*, from which several episodes in *Le Chevalier* appear to have been borrowed. However, there is a freshness and originality about the romance which mark out its author as having a mind of his own and a very independent viewpoint.

The only edition, by Ferdinand Heuckenkamp, was published in Halle by M. Niemeyer in 1896, and the work has only recently been translated by Thomas Vesce as *The Knight of the Parrot* (New York & London: Garland Publishing, 1986). I have used this text throughout and am indebted to Professor Vesce for his work in making this story available in English.

6: How Sir Lancelot Earned his Name

In this tale we find a somewhat different story to that normally associated with the great French knight. The more usual version, told in such works as the thirteenth-century *Prose Lancelot* or Chrétien de Troyes' twelfth-century poem, *Lancelot, or the Knight of the Cart*, emphasises the hero's illicit passion for Arthur's queen, as well as his great personal strength and prowess. *Lanzalet*, which was written by a Swiss knight named Ulrich von Zatzikhoven in c.1194, very possibly represents an earlier phase in the development of Lancelot's history, when he was still an unknown, errant knight. Here, he meets and falls in love with (and ultimately marries) another lady, while of the Guinevere story there is no trace – although the hero does become the queen's champion. In the version I give here, I have amended the close of the story to better fit the overall arc of the book; and for the same reason I have given it my own title.

Lanzalet, the source of this story, is, to my mind, one of the best of the many Arthurian tales surviving from the period in which they were first becoming popular among a courtly audience. It has shape, style and pace and is generally written in an engaging and occasionally witty style, which is in marked contrast to some of the more worthy romances which nowadays make dull reading.

There are some marvellous scenes and descriptions in it, which I have tried to capture as best I can. Notably there is the account of the tournament in which Lanzalet disguises himself in different coloured armour (a theme which was adapted by several later storytellers, but nowhere as well as here). Beside this I would place the descriptions of Iweret's castle, the Beautiful Forest, perhaps images of an Earthly Paradise, and the marvellous tent with its magic mirror. All of these could so easily be seen as stock devices within the medieval romance tradition, but here they are used to good effect more rarely found among the later retellings.

The whole episode of Lanzalet's meeting with Iweret at the fountain in Beforet, is a classic example of this kind of adventure, and the exchange between the two knights bears all the signs of a ritual question and response. In addition, the psychology and motivation of the characters is as good as anything I have found in these tales, where very often characters act with no reason other than the author's desire to keep the story moving!

I have chosen to retell only the first half of the poem here, since the rest is little more than a string of further adventures, and the real story, ending with Lanzalet's discovery of his name, and his love for Yblis, seems to end here. I have chosen to adopt more familiar spellings of the names ('Ban' for Lanzalet's father, rather than 'Pant' as in the original) and Lancelot rather than Lanzalet, and so on, and have replaced some of the place-names also, for the sake of unity within this volume.

The original text is found in two incomplete manuscripts and two fragments, edited, in the original German, by Karl A. Hahn: *Lanzalet, eine Erahlung* (Frankfurt: Bronner, 1845). It has been translated only once, in an excellent version by Kenneth G.T. Webster, which has extensive notes by the great Arthurian scholar Roger Sherman Loomis (New York: Columbia University Press, 1951). I have followed this version entirely in my own retelling.

Those who wish to read the entire story are recommended to seek out this edition, which makes excellent reading. There is as yet little background reading in English; however, one of the best commentaries remains that of Ernst Soudek: 'Suspense in the Early Arthurian Epic: An Introduction to Ulrich von Zatzikhoven's Lanzalet' in his *Studies in the Lancelot Legend* (Houston: Rice University Press, 1972). Another, much shorter, account can be found in *Ladies of the Lake* by Caitlín and John Matthews (HarperCollins, 1992).

7: The Tale of Palomides and the Questing Beast

This was one of the most difficult tales to uncover. There is virtually no complete account of it in any single text and I had to go, in the end, to five different sources to put together the pieces. Most of it is to be found in the various accounts of the Tristan saga, which is omitted here because of its extreme prolixity and a certain degree of overlap with the Lancelot saga. Malory's version is, to be honest, one of the least exciting parts of the *Morte* – an endless recital of tournaments and fights, which make for dull reading today. Instead, I turned to *The Tavola Rotonda* (Round Table) a huge Italian epic which parallels that of Malory to some extent. It was brilliantly translated by Anne Shaver (*Medieval Texts and Studies*, New York: Binghampton, 1983). I also made use of two other Tristan texts: *Tristano Riccardiano* trans. by F. Regina Psaki (D.S. Brewer, 2006) and *Tristano Panciatichiano* trans. by Gloria Allaire (D.S. Brewer, 2002). I also found an excellent retelling by Brian Kennedy Cook: *The Quest of the Beast* (Edmund Ward, 1957), which is mostly a reworking of Malory but adds materials from other resources in much the same way as I have done here. Palomides is significant in that he and his brothers, Safere and Segwarides, are almost the only Saracen (Muslim) knights to be included in the roll call of the Round Table. At a time when these were considered the greatest enemy of Christianity, this is unusual, especially since the other two men are baptized but Palomides is not. His long-standing love for Iseult, mistress of Tristan, and the friendship/animosity between the two men is a fascinating tale on its own, and one which I hope to return to in another volume.

8: The Adventure of the Fair Unknown

The story of the Fair Unknown appears in several versions and in more than one language. In English the text is called *Libeaus Desconus*, in French it becomes *Le Bel Inconnu*. The story it tells, of the adventures of the famous son of a famous father who must prove his abilities whilst labouring under an alias or nickname, is a frequent theme in Arthurian legends. One of the most famous of these is Malory's 'Tale of Sir Gareth', which forms an extended and largely separate episode within the pages of *Le Morte D'Arthur*. Malory almost certainly knew one of the versions of the Fair Unknown story, though he made several changes to it and gave it an overall coherence which its fellows lack.

The version I have followed here is that of *Le Bel Inconnu*, attributed to Renaut de Bage or Renals de Biauju, of whom nothing much is known beyond the few clues he gives in the text itself. He may have been a member of the influential Bage family, and if this identification holds up the romance was probably written some time between 1191 and 1250. More precisely than this we cannot say.

The story betrays the influence of Chrétien de Troyes, as well as the *Lai du Lanval* of Marie de France (see 'The Tale of Sir Lanval' pp. 103–7) and the first and second *Continuations* of the French *Perceval*. References to famous knights of the Round Table such as Gawain, Lancelot, Sagramore, Kay, Yvain and others betray Renaut's wide reading, and the romance is dotted with exquisite detail of the costumes and customs of the twelfth and early thirteenth centuries. The author never fails to spend as long as possible (without holding up the action) on descriptions of buildings, clothing, food and song. The scene where the Fair Unknown reaches his goal, the enchanted city of the Golden Isle, and there encounters the similarly enchanted *jongleurs* (singers) produces an array of nearly every musical instrument in current usage at this period, and there is indeed a strong musical influence running through the whole work.

Renaut was clearly a follower of the School of Courtly Love, which placed women on pedestals and extolled the virtues of adultery. His frequent pleas to the figure of Love herself make it clear that he saw himself as a lover in the Courtly fashion. The curious and some would say unsatisfactory ending of the romance, in which Renaut refuses to tell us anything more about his hero until he has held his own (lost or rejecting) lover naked in his arms again, suggests a personal story underlying the one which is being told.

In particular, the portrait of the Lady White Hands (perhaps named after Tristan's ill-starred wife) is interesting, since she clearly began life as a faery woman, and had been adapted to become a mysterious woman well versed in magic and the seven liberal arts – an education which would have been denied to most women at the time Renaut was writing. The fact that she knows her fate but does nothing to prevent it may seem unsatisfactory to modern readers but is very much in keeping with the custom of the time, when otherworldly women are seen as being unconcerned with mortal pursuits.

The realm of the Isle d'or (Isle of Gold), over which she rules, is itself clearly an otherworldly dwelling. The palisade of sharpened stakes, bearing the heads of slain heroes, and the custom of the challenger who must replace the reigning champion if he succeeds in defeating him, are enough to show this. Both are common themes in Arthurian story, and always indicate the presence of supernatural events or places. Likewise, the episode of the Terrible Kiss (the *Fier Baser* as it is called in other romances) appears in several texts. Generally, the serpent would have had the head or face of a beautiful woman, but Renaut chooses to make it a serpent pure and simple – though no less fearsome for that.

Other notable episodes are those in which the Fair Unknown hesitates to enter the Lady White Hands' chamber and, when he does decide to do so, is presented with several fearsome tests – such as a raging torrent or toppling walls – which turn out to be illusions. All of which helps reinforce the otherworldly nature of the story.

'The Fair Unknown' is a long work, numbering 6,266 lines. I have resisted the temptation to omit some of the adventures because they all prove to have been foreseen and to have a bearing on later events. The teller's skill in keeping the attention of the listener alert over such a long work bears out his ability as a poet – though most readers would find him dull and jingly by today's standards. But his delight in the story, and the way that he plays with the literary conventions of the time – attributing the same features to more than one of his fair heroines in a deliberate attempt to illustrate his hero's confusion, show him to have been both well-read and no slouch at his craft.

There have been three editions of the text, all of them in French and all generally superseded by the recent publication by Karen Fosco, admirably translated by Coleen P. Donagher. (Garland Press, 1992). I have used this edition throughout, with occasional reference to the introduction and notes by Williams G. Perrie in his edition of 1939 (Oxford: Fox, Jones, 1915). In addition, I borrowed a few details from the English poem of *Libeaus Desconus* by William of Chester, whose wonderful descriptions of plants, armour and beautiful women could not be gainsaid. The best version of this is found in *Sir Cleges. Sir Libeaus Desconus: Two Old English Metrical Romances, Rendered into Prose* by Jessie L. Weston (David Nutt, 1902).

9: The Tale of Sir Lanval

'Lanval' is one of a series of *Lais* (stories) written by a twelfth-century poet who wrote under the name Marie de France. Her work is characterized by a mixture of the romantic and the down-to-earth, of magic and human passion which far outstrips the confines of the Courtly Love ethic from which she was nominally writing. Her stories are all of love and were written for a courtly audience in both France and England. She was highly literate in a time when learning was not encouraged in women. Nothing more is known of her than that she apparently lived in England and may have dedicated her collection of stories to Henry II. Apart from the *Lais* she also composed a group of fables and a version of the legend of St Patrick. The only complete text of the *Lais* is found in a manuscript preserved in London, B.L. Harley 978.

The story of Lanval belongs to a group of tales which deal with the theme of the Faery Lover. Typically, a mysterious woman (or man) appears, forms a liaison with a mortal, then vanishes again, often stipulating that no one must know about her on pain of losing her. Similar stories are frequently told of

Gawain. In common with most of the stories in Marie's collection, the origins are in Celtic myth, hence the appearance of this tale here among the early stories. She seems to have either heard the stories being recited by wandering Breton storytellers, or to have had access to an earlier group of such tales which she chose to turn into verse.

Somewhat unusual is the portrayal of Guinevere as an unfaithful wife. Elsewhere, of course, her affair with Lancelot was well known, but in most versions in which this is mentioned it is stated that other than this both were faithful to each other. In 'Lanval' Guinevere not only propositions the hero, but when he refuses her, acts in a thoroughly unpleasant manner, suggesting that he had approached her, and accusing him of insulting her. The way in which Lanval extricates himself from this decidedly awkward situation is powerfully portrayed, and his last-minute rescue makes a fitting conclusion to this brief but fascinating tale.

The *Lais* have been often edited, but rarely translated until recent times, which have seen several new versions appearing. The best of these is the translation by Glyn Burgess and Keith Busby, *The Lais of Marie de France* (Penguin Books, 1986), which I have used for my own retelling. Earlier versions are by Eugene Mason, *French Medieval Romances from the Lays of Marie de France* (London & New York: Dent/Dutton, 1911), which gives a less accurate account, and *The Lais of Marie de France* translated in verse by Robert Hanning and Joan Ferrante (New York: Dutton, 1978).

10: The Adventures of Meriadoc, Prince of Cambria

The Historia Meridaoci, Regis Cambrie (History of Meriadoc, King of Cambria) is one of a handful of surviving Arthurian romances written in Latin. The most famous of these remains Geoffrey of Monmouth's *Historia Regum Britanniae* (History of the Kings of Britain) and his *Vita Merlini* (Life of Merlin), which did much to set the pattern for Arthurian writing during the eleventh and twelfth centuries. *Meridaoci* and its companion piece *De Ortu Waluuanii, nepotis Arturi* (The Rise of Gawain, Nephew of Arthur [pp. 235–47]), are unusual in that they tell stories which appear nowhere else, whereas the narrative structure of Geoffrey's work continued to be picked over throughout the remainder of the Middle Ages, generating numerous copies, versions, and translations which added significantly to the corpus of Arthurian literature in general. Yet both these stories remained almost completely unknown until they were recently edited and translated by Mildred Leake Day from the unique manuscripts (Cotton Faustina B VI, and Bodleian Rawlinson B 149) in the British Library and the Bodleian Library respectively.

What makes them unique as Arthurian stories is the blend of factual, historically detailed narrative with the touch of otherworldliness which is more common to the Matter of Britain. Much of the story of Meriadoc and his sister Orwen concerns the plot against their father, King Caradoc, and their subsequent upbringing in a cave by Ivor the Huntsman. However, after a brief episode in which Meriadoc regains his title, avenges himself on his father's killer, and sets out on a career of adventure, the texture of the story becomes suddenly otherworldly in character, with mysterious castles which appear and disappear, beautiful faery ladies, and strange adventures out of time. The effect of this is to make the otherworldly adventures even more powerful, coming as they do on the heels of a detailed description of siege warfare (much abbreviated in my retelling).

The story proceeds with great pace and panache, as Meriadoc rises to ever greater heights, only to be cast down at the very pinnacle of his career. The story of his triumphal return, his marriage and inheritance make for a rich and entertaining story which blends some of the best elements of Arthurian romance with a strong touch of Roman epic.

There is also, as with so many of the Arthurian tales, a strong Celtic element underlying the text. In the episode where Meriadoc's men enter the strange castle in search of shelter and are overcome by an inexplicable sense of fear which roots them to the spot, this is strongly reminiscent of the story of Fionn mac Cumhail, the Irish Hero, who with his men enters the Hostel of the Quicken Tree and are similarly frozen, before being attacked by an otherworldly figure not unlike the monstrous churl of the kitchen who subsequently attacks Meriadoc while he is in search of food. (A theme also found in 'The Tale of Gorlagros and Gawain', pp. 266–76.)

I have very slightly amended the ending of the story, since in the original it stops short and leaves some untidy ends. It seemed appropriate to bring Meriadoc home at the end of his great adventure, unlike the text which simply records his illustrious descendants. I am especially grateful to Mildred Leake Day for making this text accessible. I have worked from her edition and translation exclusively. (*The Story of Meriadoc, King of Cambria* ed. and trans. by Mildred Leake Day, Garland Publishing, 1988, later included in *Latin Arthurian Literature* edited by Mildred Leake Day, Boydell & Brewer, 2005.)

11: The Tale of Guingamor and Guerrehes

The story told here actually derives from two separate texts. One is the Breton *Lai* of *Guingamor* dating from c.1185 and the second from part of the First Continuation to the Old French *Story of the Grail* by Chrétien de Troyes.

THE GREAT BOOK OF KING ARTHUR

Attributed to Gautier de Danaans and dating from approximately 1190 to 1200, this attempts to extend and complete the story left unfinished by Chrétien at his death. In connecting the two stories I am following the lead of Professor Dell R. Skeels, whose translation of the two stories was published in *The Anthropologist Looks at Myth* (Austin, TX & London: University of Texas Press, 1966).

Originally, the two stories were probably part of a longer tale, told by one of the many wandering Breton *conteurs* who preserved and disseminated so much of Arthurian literature. At some point, the second part, concerning Guerrehes, became detached, to resurface again in the longer Second Continuation, itself an episodic work with little real connection to Chrétien's original poem. Yet, the tales require a knowledge of each other to explain their motivation and indeed to make sense of their complex symbolic frame of reference. The Guerrehes story, in particular, makes little real sense without the existence of the Guingamor story, which both sets the scene and establishes the relationship between the human and otherworldly characters.

In the first half of the story, Guingamor pursues a mythical white boar, which leads him, ultimately, into the Otherworld. This has been duly noted for its similarity with the hunting of the great boar Twrch Trwyth in the old Welsh Arthurian story 'Culhwch and Olwen' in which Arthur and his heroes assist the young Culhwch to win the hand of a giant's daughter and in the process hunt the great boar across most of Wales.

In fact, this is only one of several borrowings in the present text from more ancient traditional material concerning the relationship of mortals and the people of Faery. The last part of Guingamor's name, like that of King Brangamor in the latter half of the tale, both derive from the French word *mort* (death) and it is evident, as Dr Skeels has pointed out, that the latter 'has inherited, both in name and actuality, mortality or death from his father, Guingamor'. He adds: 'It is the task of Guerrehes to remove the infection of death from his father.' This much is evident, though unstated, in the work itself. At the end, the mysterious faery woman from the island tells King Arthur that 'a miracle will happen in his court' once the body of the dead king is returned. Since Guingamor himself, though impossibly aged from his three-hundred-year sojourn in the Otherworld, is apparently able to father a child on his faery mistress, and must therefore have been restored after his return there, it is not beyond the bounds of possibility that the 'miracle' would constitute the restoration to life of the dead King Brangamor.

In telling this story I have resorted, more than usually, to a degree of 'restoration'. This is purely to strengthen the ties between the two halves of the tale, which are less satisfactorily connected in the original texts. For example, I have suggested that the king to whom the charcoal burner relates the story of Guingamor was in fact Arthur, since this seems more than likely from the internal evidence of the stories, though he is not named at all in the original text of 'Guingamor'. Other than this, however, I have allowed the tale to speak for itself, since it is, anyway, a remarkably modern-sounding text, in which the characters, though not always clearly motivated, behave in a way consistent with the story itself.

Like many of the tales retold in this book, 'Guingamor and Guerrehes' is very clearly Celtic in origin. The description of the Otherworld, with its magical fountain, its strange castles and the miniature knight who gives Guerrehes so much sorrow, all derive ultimately from Celtic sources. The presence of two names containing the prefix 'Bran' strengthens this further, since Bran began life as a Celtic deity, whose story influences the whole of Arthurian literature and tradition to a marked degree. (See Helain Newstead *Bran the Blessed in Arthurian Literature* Columbia University Press, 1939, for a full analysis.)

There are obvious parallels between this story and the Grail myth, to which only the 'Guerrehes' story is attached by reason of its presence within the First Continuation. In particular, we might instance the whole matter of the spearhead, clearly a magical talisman of some kind, which must be first removed from the wound in the dead knight's chest and then driven into the breast of the evil knight in an exact imitation of the earlier blow. This recalls the Dolorous Stroke in the Grail story, where the Grail King, Pelleam, is wounded in the genitals by a spear which is one of the 'Hallows', the four sacred objects which are part of the Grail mystery. Given that the original wounded king was himself Bran the Blessed, together with the fact that Pelleam can only be cured by the same spear that wounded him, we can see several striking parallels between the 'Guerrehes' story and the Grail myths.

The hero of the 'Guerrehes' story is called Gaheres in *Le Morte D'Arthur* and is one of the four brothers who form the Orkney clan – Gawain, Gareth and Agravain being the other three. He is a somewhat shadowy figure both in Malory and in the longer *Vulgate Cycle* from which the later author drew his story; in our story he has a far more pronounced role. The similarity between the names Guingamor and Guinglain (see 'The Adventure of the Fair Unknown', pp. 87–102) who is Gawain's son by a faery woman, suggests that, at some point, the story may have been related to the elder brother, though no trace of this remains extant.

'Guingamor' is edited by Gaston Paris in *Romania* vol VIII (1897) pp. 50–59, and 'Guerrehes' by William Roach and Robert Ivy in vol II of *The Continuations of the Old French Perceval of Chrétien de Troyes* (Philadelphia, 1950). I have used Professor Skeel's translation to complete my own version and have consulted Roach and Ivy for the background to the texts.

12: The Adventures of Eagle-Boy

'The Adventures of Eagle-Boy', or *Eachtra Mhacaoiimh an Iolair*, is another product of the late-flowering of Arthurian Romances in Ireland. Dating from the end of the fifteenth or early sixteenth centuries, it draws heavily on the life of Guillaume of Palerne, who is similarly carried off by an animal and returns later to avenge his wronged mother. 'Eagle-Boy' is ascribed to one Brian O'Corcoran, who says, at the beginning of the manuscript, that he got it from a gentleman who had heard the tale told in French. This story may have been a non-Arthurian romance called *Sir Eglamour of Artois*, which certainly follows the line of the present story to a considerable degree. 'Eagle-Boy' is a long and prolix tale, filled with decoration and wordplay which is of little interest to modern readers. I have therefore treated it more freely than most of the texts retold here, cutting several adventures, and abridging the very detailed descriptions down to a more reasonable length. However, the tale does follow the course of the original in most instances, and this is, as far as I am aware, the first time it has been retold for a popular audience. The author obviously knew some Arthurian stories, as he peppers the tale with references to Camelot (where however the king lives in 'the Red Hall' a borrowing from the Ulster saga) and the famous custom that the king shall not eat until he had heard of a wonder.

The story is found in twenty manuscripts, suggesting that it was popular. It was edited in Irish by E.W. Digby and J.H. Lloyd (Dublin: Hodges & Figgis, 1912) and translated by R.A.S. Macalister in *Two Irish Arthurian Romances* (London: Irish Text Society, 1908).

13: The Story of Caradoc of the Strong Arm

The *Livre du Caradoc* is part of a much longer romance, or series of romances, grouped under the general heading of *The Continuations of the Old French Perceval* (edited by William Roach and Robert H. Ivy, Philadelphia, 1950). Despite this it is clearly intended to form a complete tale on its own, narrating the history of its hero from birth to establishment as a successful Round Table knight. The poem forms part of the *First Continuation*, which itself exists in three different versions, generally called the Short, the Long, and the Mixed. These versions vary in length between 3,300 and 5,000 lines, suggesting that each was copied by a different hand from a single source. Each author sought to add or expand the details of the story. Thus, the longer version contains a version of the *Story of the Horn*, as well as the episode of the Beheading Game, better known from its most famous retelling in the fourteenth-century poem *Sir Gawain and the Green Knight*. Since that story is not included here, I wanted to make use of this more vestigial version of the challenge.

Caradoc himself is, as his name would suggest, of Welsh origin, and is almost certainly the same character who appears in Celtic literature as Caradoc *Vreichvras* (Strong Arm), the son of Llyr Marini and Tegau Eufron. It is probable that the episode of the poem which includes the hero's acquisition of the serpent attached to his body, causing him to have a 'shrunken arm' (Briefbras), derives from a misunderstanding of this epithet. In Welsh tradition Caradoc is a legendary or semi-legendary ancestor of the house of Morganwg, while history claims him as the founder of the kingdom of Gwent some time around the fifth century. This makes him slightly earlier than Arthur and may well be another example of the way in which the heroic war-leader subsumed many earlier heroes as part of his fabled war-band. I have omitted the final episode of the poem, which repeats the story of the magical testing horn, and because it seems like an unnecessary addition to the tale, which really ends with Caradoc's healing. I have added one suggestion to the end, which is not in the original text – that Guinier's title was 'gold-breast'. This idea derives from the fact that Caradoc's mother is called this in the Welsh tradition and seems a reasonable supposition.

The story itself is one of the finest of its kind I have come across, and it is astonishing that it has remained so little known until now. The psychological motivation of the characters is far more developed than usual in these romances, and the whole story of Caradoc's strange birth and the subsequent treatment of his mother, ranks among the finest pieces of storytelling in the entire Arthurian corpus. Even the oft-repeated theme of the beheading game is more clearly explained herein, and the general drive of the story keeps one guessing throughout, with far less of the stock situation than is usually found in these romances. Where such episodes do enter, they are made skilful use of. In all, the story seems to me to echo many themes from Celtic tradition, skilfully woven into a medieval romance by the anonymous author.

The poem has only recently been translated in its entirety by Ross G. Arthur in his *Three Arthurian Romances* (J. M. Dent: Everyman Editions, 1996) and I have made use of this in preparing my own version. The episode of the Beheading Test was translated by Elizabeth Brewer and can be found in her excellent collection of Gawain material: *Sir Gawain and the Green Knight: Sources and Analogues*. (D.S. Brewer, 1992). The notes to the edition of the *Continuations* by Roach and Ivy are of great value when it comes to understanding the background of the work. The only critical study which has appeared to date is by Marguerite Rossi: 'Sur l'épisode de Cradoc de la Continuation Gauvain' in *Mélanges de langue et littérature françaises du Moyen Âge et de la Renaissance offerts*

THE GREAT BOOK OF KING ARTHUR

à Charles Foulon Charles Foulon. vol 2, Rennes: Marche Romane, 1980. Nigel Bryant, in his fabulously rich collection, *The Complete Story of the Grail*, does not include this story, but his discussion of the other texts is admirable in setting the story of Caradoc in relation to the other Continuations.

14: The Adventures of Melora and Orlando

'The Adventures of Melora and Orlando' (*Eachtra Mhelora agus Orlando*) survives in three manuscripts, all of which date from between the sixteenth and seventeenth centuries. This is a comparatively late date – as in the case of 'The Visit of the Grey-Hammed Lady' (see pp. 177–87), yet it draws heavily on earlier stories from Celtic tradition, as well as medieval romance – in particular Ariosto's epic of Charlemagne, *Orlando Furioso* – and folk lore. It is a complex and varied tale which has more incident in it than many of the more well-known Arthurian romances. It is unusual in that it represents King Arthur as having a daughter (a rare event, which occurs hardly anywhere else in the literature) – as spirited a princess as any king might wish for – who makes a resourceful and attractive heroine. Another interesting detail is the inclusion of the Lance of Longinus, as a thoroughgoing Celtic magical weapon resembling the Spear of Lugh, which is in fact known to have influenced the image of the spear as it appears in Arthurian, and especially Grail, literature. The other two treasures – the green stone and the oil – may well represent an even older strata of material, though it must also be said that these objects may be the product of Christian legends such as the Oil of Mercy. Be that as it may, there is a strong underlay of Pagan tradition within this story: Merlin's appearance as the one-eyed, one-armed, one-legged creature recalls several such beings – the Giant Herdsman in the Medieval Welsh Arthurian tale of *Owein & Luned* being the best known – but nowhere else as far as I am aware does Merlin appear in this guise – nor indeed is he elsewhere represented in such a negative light. (Because of this, and for the sake of consistency, I felt compelled to add a brief final coda to the story which suggests that Merlin's part in the story was less negative than it appeared.) Mador, the unfortunate adversary in the story, may be a variation of Mador de la Porte, who appears briefly towards the end of *Le Morte D'Arthur* as one of the cronies of the evil Mordred. But the heart of the story undoubtedly derives from the great medieval Italian epic *Orlando Furioso*. There, in Cantos III–IV, we hear how the female knight Bradament rescues Rogero from the castle of Atlantis by acquiring the magical ring of the King of Africa. The anonymous author of 'Melora and Orlando' seems to have taken this basic storyline and mixed it with the much older Irish tale of *Aiden Clainne Tuiueann* (*The Fate of the Children of Tuireann*) in which we find another story of quest for sacred or magical objects which will release the main protagonists from enchantment. The other interesting character in the story is the evil hag employed by Merlin to hold Orlando in prison and to steal his powers of speech. Called simply the Destroying One (or as I have here called her, the Destroyer) she is black, ancient, hideous, and evil. She resembles a number of such hag-like figures, one of the most prominent being the hideous woman in 'The Wedding of Sir Gawain and the Lady Ragnall' (who is afterwards proven to be a beauty under enchantment) and the 'mother' of Sir Bercilak's wife in *Sir Gawain & the Green Knight*, who turns out to be Morgan le Fay in disguise. It is probable that the author of 'Melora and Orlando' was thinking of one of these, and that he maybe thought she embodied the negative aspects of Morgan (who is known in Irish tradition as the Morrigan), here working alongside Merlin, though in most stories the two are deadly adversaries.

There is sufficient reworking in the story as a whole to suggest that the author had a fairly wide knowledge of Arthurian literature, but sought to change and reshape it to better fit with the taste of his time. I am especially glad to be able to include it here, in what is the first modern retelling since Connor P. Hartnet's translation in his thesis *Irish Arthurian Literature* (New York: University Thesis, 1973).

15: The Visit of the Grey-Hammed Lady

The fifteenth century saw something of an outburst of Arthurian literature in Ireland. Previously there had been little interest in the figure of Arthur, who was, after all, a British Celt, and there were enough cycles of epic adventures featuring Irish heroes to more than satisfy the deepest craving for mythical stories. However, with the expansion of awareness of world literature which took place around this time, the Irish bards and storytellers responded to a general interest in Arthurian matters, producing at least four tales set in their own, very idiosyncratic Arthurian universe. This story, *Sgél Isgaide Léthe* (The Visit of Grey-Ham), is found in two manuscripts, one in the British Museum (MS Egerton 1781) dating from around 1484–7 and another in Oxford (MS Rawlinson B 477) completed after 1678. The story owes a good deal to a medieval English romance, *Partonope of Blois*, but it is, for all that, possessed of an imaginative flair which is seldom found outside Celtic literature. It displays all the qualities one would expect from literature originating in Ireland at this time and earlier – colour, richness, humour, adventure and an impressive use of language and metaphor. Essentially it tells the story of a test of honesty which leads in the second part to a visit of Arthur and his men to the Otherworld. As well as *Partonope* it draws heavily on traditional Celtic material such as

'The Chase of Sliabh Cuileann' where we hear of the hero Fionn chasing a deer which afterwards proved to be a woman; or 'Oisin in the Land of Youth', where the hero acquires a faery mistress who swears him to secrecy. Voyages to the Otherworld such as the one described here are common throughout Celtic literature, and in several instances the obtaining of new wives for the heroes of the story are to be found in stories such as 'The Wasting Sickness of Cuchulainn' and the various *Immrama* or Voyage tales of which there are a number in Irish literature (see *The Encyclopaedia of Celtic Myth & Legend* by John & Caitlín Matthews, Rider, 2003).

On a first reading the story seems confused. At times it reads like two stories loosely attached, at others it seems to wander off the track and never return to it. The whole 'reason' given by the Deer-Woman and her foster-father for coming to Camelot seems to have nothing to do with the story, and the opening material relating to the Gascon Lad gets dropped once the main arc of the story is under way. I have chosen to make a few changes in this text, basing my assumptions on other Celtic tales which seem to have influenced this version. Thus, I have changed the name of the Otherworld place where Arthur and his men find new wives from the 'Monastery' of the Dead – almost certainly an effort on the part of the author to Christianize the story – to the 'House' of the Dead, which is more in keeping with Celtic tales of this kind. I have also abbreviated some of the poems which, though wonderful, detract from the plot of the story. Additionally, I have omitted the sub-plot relating to the marriage opportunities of the Deer-Woman's brother, which goes nowhere and seems to contradict the main storyline. I have also suggested an ending which brings us back to the beginning and ties up some of the loose ends. In the original, Arthur and his men go home with the faery women whom they met in the Otherworld and do not return to their wives. Even Arthur, though it is not especially mentioned, presumably remained with his faery bride and abandons Guinevere. This is such a marked divergence from the more familiar medieval romances that I felt it was necessary to change it. I did this out of concern for the general reader who would have ended up more confused than edified but may in the process have missed the finer qualities of the story.

The translation is taken, along with others here, from the wonderful collection by Connor P. Hartnet in his thesis *Irish Arthurian Literature* (New York University Thesis, 1973).

16: The Story of Tyolet

'Tyolet' belongs to the genre of works called *Lais* – short, usually romantic poems intended for a courtly audience, but which often preserve material from an earlier period. It is these brief tales which constitute the raw material from which the great epic cycles of Arthurian romance were formed, and many of the stories told in this form turn up again, usually in a hugely extended and elaborated way, in the later romances.

Thus, we can see echoes of the boyhood of the Grail hero Perceval in the story of Tyolet, while a thoroughly muddled version of the main story turns up, with Lancelot as the hero, in the vast Vulgate Cycle. It is generally acknowledged by the majority of scholars, that these *Lais* – especially the ones which originated in Brittany, as well as those by the acknowledged mistress of the *Lai*, Marie de France – contain an extensive amount of Celtic material. They may well, indeed, be the descendants of the original stories, carried overseas by the Celtic bards fleeing from the Saxon invaders after the disappearance of Arthur in the sixth century. Planted in the fertile soil of Normandy, these tales later returned to Britain, in the guise of the new courtly literature, in the eleventh century, and formed the basis of subsequent Arthurian epics.

Tyolet does not appear as a character in any other Arthurian tale, though as noted above elements of his story re-appear in different guises in various later romances. Indeed, it seems more than likely that the original story which inspired the anonymous author may have been the same as that upon which Chrétien de Troyes based his story of *Perceval*. Tyolet, however, retains details which are missing from the latter, such as the teaching of the youth by a faery woman, and the transformation of the stag into a knight. The exchange between Tyolet and this character is both comedic and archetypal and may indeed derive from a far more ancient question and answer sequence. The episode in which the hero gives the spoils of his adventure to another, who then claims it for himself, is found in the romances of Tristan among others.

The text, which dates from the thirteenth century, has been edited several times, notably by Gaston Paris in *Romania* 8 (1879) pp. 40–50. I have used the translation of J.L. Weston in her *Guingamore, Lanval, Tyolet, Bisclavaret: Four Lais Rendered into English Prose.* (London: David Nutt, 1900). An interesting commentary by Herman Braet, 'Tyolet/Perceval: the Father Quest' can be found in *An Arthurian Tapestry: Essays Presented to Lewis Thorpe* (Glasgow: French Department of the University, 1981).

17: The Story of Jaufre and the Great Lamentation

Jaufre is the only surviving Arthurian romance written in Occitan, a medieval dialect spoken throughout Southern and Southwestern France. It has been dated from as early as 1180 to as late as 1225 and seems to have influenced Chrétien de Troyes in the creation of his Arthurian works, in which Jaufre is called Griflet.

In this guise the hero makes an appearance in several other Arthurian stories, including *The Boy and the Mantle*, the *Lancelot-Grail Cycle* and of course Malory, where he is called Griflet le Fils de Do (Griflet the Son of God) an intriguing title which has been taken to indicate that Griflet in fact descends from the Celtic hero Gilfaethwy the son of Do. Do, however, is a Celtic Goddess rather than a god, and the change in gender is probably a reflection of the changing attitudes of the medieval world towards the earlier, pagan roots of the legends. In the *Lancelot-Grail* version of the death of Arthur, it is Griflet, rather than the more usual Bedivere, who is entrusted with the task of returning the magical sword Excalibur to the water. This suggests that he may once have been a far more important figure in the legends, and taken with his appearances in both Chrétien and Malory, it is even possible to reconstruct a biography of his life and adventures.

As well as being an exciting tale, Jaufre is also that comparatively rare thing in Arthurian epics, a comedy. Though there are genuinely dramatic episodes (such as that with the lepers) much of the story is taken up with somewhat tongue-in-cheek adventures which burlesques the more familiar aspects of Chivalry. In particular, the episode of Arthur and the wizard disguised as a beast seems to me one of the best comic scenes in the genre.

In contrast to this, the whole theme of the mysterious lamentations at the castle of Monbrun is fascinating and seems almost like a reflection of the Grail story, save that here there is a question which must not be asked, rather than one that should. The appearance, too, of the leper's hideous mother, not only ties up two parts of the story very neatly but is also reminiscent of the appearance of the loathly lady, who so often comes to urge on and further test the knights who seek the Grail. In all there is some evidence to suggest that the author knew an earlier story on which Chrétien de Troyes may also have drawn when he composed his poem of the Grail.

In retelling the story, I have simplified it considerably, as well as omitting several episodes. The end of the poem drags out the action long after it has really ended, and this I have severely curtailed. For the rest I have tried to retain the curious blend of humour and excitement, passion, and cruelty, which is a feature of this very fine romance.

'Jaufre' exists in two manuscripts, extending to some 11,000 lines of rhyming couplets. Both are held by the Bibliothèque National (BNB Francis 2164, which dates from around 1300, and BNB Fr.12571, which is a copy by a fourteenth-century Italian scribe). It was edited by Clovis Brunel as *Jaufre: Roman Arthurien en Ancien Provencal* (Paris: Picard, 1943) and has been translated three times, once by Alfred Elwes in 1856 (*Jaufre the Knight and the Fair Brunnisend*, London: reprinted by Newcastle Publishing, 1979) again by Vernon Ives in 1935, and most recently by Ross G. Arthur as *Jaufre: An Occitan*

Arthurian Romance (New York & London: Garland Publishing, 1992). I have made use of the first and third of these in preparing my own version. One of the most enlightening commentaries on the poem is by Suzanne Fleishman: 'Jaufre, or Chivalry Askew: Social Overtones of Parody in Arthurian Romance' in *Viator* 12 (1981) pp.101–129. An adaptation, available as an audio production, has recently been completed by Anne Lister, and can be heard at https://anchor.fm/anne-lister. The thesis by Margaret Anne Purbrick, *The Medieval Romance of Jaufre: A Storyteller's Perspective*, Cardiff University, 2019, is available at ORCA.cf.ac.uk.

18: The Tale of Sir Marrok and the Wolf

This is one of those stories which was clearly in circulation at the time that Malory was writing his epic. Although he mentions it in the *Morte*, in book 19 chapter 2, where he writes: '*Sir Marrok, the good knight that was betrayed with his wife, for she made him seven years a werewolf,*' the tale itself is not told. It simply appears when Marrok is listed among many knights of the Round Table. I thought it was appropriate to supply that missing story in this follow-up to Malory's great work. This version comes from the French *Lais* of Marie de France, where it is called *Bisclavaret*. It's unusual because the figure of the werewolf was generally considered to be evil and abhorrent, whereas in this instance Sir Marrok is regarded as a hero. The translation on which my account is based is that of Jessie L. Weston in *Guingamor, Launfal*, (London: David Nutt, 1900). Miss Weston points out several parallels in Celtic faerytale tradition such as the 'Morraha' included by Joseph Jacobs in his collection *More Celtic Fairy Tales* (London: David Nutt, 1895). Another possible similarity is a tale published in the *Scottish Celtic Review* for 1880, known as 'How the great Tuairisgeal was put to Death' – though here it is a witch's spells which cause the transformation. In neither of the versions are Marrok's wife or the knight whom she later marries named, therefore I chose to call them Alys and Jocelyn to give more colour to the story. It is possible that the name *Morraha* may have influenced that of Marrok, who is unknown elsewhere.

19: The Tale of Sir Torec and the Circlet of Gold

This is one of several stories interpolated into a Dutch translation of a series of linked French texts dealing with Lancelot and the death of Arthur. They were compiled around 1320 in Brabant by a nameless scribe who may have added materials of his own to those of the author of the work, Jacob von Maelent.

Jacob himself probably took the ideas for this story from an earlier French text called *Torrez, The Knight of Golden Circlet*, written in the thirteenth century but no longer extant. Of all the stories retold here, this required the most restyling. The original is long, prolix and winds about, drawing in the adventures of other knights and their ladies, with often confused (and confusing) results. I chose to omit the long side-track into the adventures of Melions and his battles with ogres, and to abridge the lengthy disquisitions on love and morality expounded to Torec at the White Castle. Those wishing to explore these or to follow the interwoven stories can read them in English in the collection: *Dutch Romances III Five Interpolated Romances from the Lancelot Compilation* edited by David F. Johnson and Geert H. M. Claassens (D.S. Brewer, 2003). I wanted to include this tale because it contains elements not found elsewhere, such as the behaviour (not exactly chivalric) by Arthur himself, and an unusually critical view of the Round Table Fellowship.

BOOK THREE: THE BOOK OF SIR GAWAIN

20: The Rise of Sir Gawain

De Ortu Waluuanii nepotis Arturi, or *The Rise of Gawain, Nephew of Arthur*, is one of the few surviving Arthurian romances (excluding pseudo-historical works such as Geoffrey of Monmouth's *Historia Regum Britanniae*) written in Latin. It dates from the end of the twelfth century, although the unique manuscript, Cotton Faustina B, held by the British Museum, dates from the beginning of the fourteenth century. It had been attributed, with some caution, to a writer named Robert of Mont St. Michel, a Benedictine abbot from the school of Bec, who is the author of several theological works.

The story it tells is unique in the annals of Arthuriana, in that it describes Gawain's whole career, from birth to his establishment as Arthur's nephew – a fact which, as the title suggests, was an important aspect of the story, even though he is not officially recognized as such until the end of the romance. For the rest, Gawain's visit to Rome, and his meteoric rise to fame and fortune, makes a fascinating tale with many original and interesting facets. To my mind it further demonstrates a fact which is already evidenced in the surviving stories which feature Gawain – namely that his position as an Arthurian hero was at one time pre-eminent, far above that of Lancelot or Galahad or any of the better-known knights of the Round Table. Gawain indeed remains a central character in the drama of Arthur's days, but he becomes steadily demoted until, by the time Sir Thomas Malory composed his book, the character of the king's nephew had been debased to little better than a lecher and murderer. I have traced the course of this descent in my book *Gawain, Knight of the Goddess* (Inner Traditions, 2003), pointing out there that the systematic blackening of Gawain's character derives from his long-term association with paganism. Thus, his devotion to the Great Goddess, and through her to all women, becomes, in the hands of the monkish writers of the medieval Arthurian romances, a very human, libidinous trend, which put Gawain beyond the pale. (The fact that Lancelot is the lover of Queen Guinevere receives less attention despite this.)

In the *De Ortu* none of this stigma is present. It is, to my mind, one of the most modern sounding tales in this collection. It required very little emendation to bring it into line with the rest of the Gawain stories. Gawain is, purely and simply, a hero par excellence, whose natural inheritance shines through his lowly upbringing, and proves that 'blood will out'. There is something, too, about the message which reaches Gawain and sends him back to Britain as he is about to assume the highest office, which smacks of a genuine historical tradition. If, as has been suggested by other authorities over the years, the Romano-British people did send to Rome for help against the Saxons, it would have been just such a response which might have gone out from the empire to its old colony. Though we have no direct evidence for this, it makes a fitting climax to a powerful story.

I have compressed part of the action considerably to be able to include the whole of the story. In particular the sea battle, which is long and fascinating, has had to be much abridged. It contains a detailed and fascinating account of medieval maritime warfare, including several pages on the making and uses of 'Greek Fire', an early incendiary device which was often used to turn the tide of victory in such conflicts. Indeed, the author shows some not-inconsiderable knowledge of siege warfare as well as battle at sea, a fact which seems to give the lie to the suggested author being an ecclesiastic.

The text was first edited by J.D. Bruce in 1898 ('De Ortu Waluuanii': *The Publications of the Modern Language Association* vol 13, pp. 365–455. Its most recent editor, Mildred Leake Day, also included an excellent translation, which I have followed in making my own rendition of the story. (*The Rise of Gawain, Nephew of Arthur*, New York & London: Garland Publishing, 1984.)

21: Sir Gawain and the Crop-Eared Dog

Eachtra an Mhadra Mhaoil (The Story of the Crop-Eared Dog) is one of several remarkable Arthurian stories written in medieval Irish and dating from the fifteenth or sixteenth centuries. They are virtually unique for several reasons, the most important being that they encapsulate an entire world of Celtic storytelling in an Arthurian format. It seems unlikely that there was ever a large-scale Irish tradition of Arthurian stories, since Arthur was first and foremost a British hero. However, he was also perceived as a Celt, and this meant that in a Celtic-speaking culture such as Ireland it was inevitable that his deeds should be celebrated. But what deeds! Nowhere else, in all the vast architecture of the Arthurian mythos which has survived, was the court described in quite this way. Right from the start, where Arthur is invoked as 'King Arthur, son of Iubhar (Uther), son of Ambrose, son of Constantine', who convenes a hunting expedition 'in the Dangerous Forest, on the Plain of Wonders', we can see coming together two great storytelling styles: the ornate, magical work of the Celtic bards, and the rich imaginative world of the medieval romancers. Nor is one disappointed by what follows, a sensational, wild, extraordinary tale of magic and adventure which few – if any – of the Norman and Anglo-Norman writers was destined to achieve. Some of this exuberant quality, reluctantly, I had to moderate to bring it in line with the remaining tales in this collection.

Though these texts are late in composition, dating from the fifteenth to sixteenth centuries, they reflect a much earlier strand of Celtic storytelling. So far, no precise analogies have come to light for either 'The Story of the Crop-Eared Dog' or its companion piece, 'The Adventures of Eagle-Boy' (pp. 141–9). A third Irish text, *Ceilidhe Iosgaide Leithe* or 'The Visit of the Grey-Hammed Lady' (pp. 177–87), owes more to the ancient Faery tradition of Ireland than to Arthurian literature. It may well, as has been suggested by several other scholars, have had its Arthurian content grafted onto an older tale. A fourth story, *Eachtra an Amadán Mor*, or 'The Story of the Great Fool', is a direct echo of the Perceval story. Certainly, in the present tale, the fantastic islands, each with its own guardian or champion, seem to derive from a form of Celtic tale known as *Immrama* or Voyages. Here it has been superimposed on the typical knightly exploit where the hero meets with a different adventure at every turn of the road or clearing in the forest. Whatever the truth, these stories make for fascinating reading, and open a window onto a whole new dimension of Arthurian tales.

For this reason, I am especially glad to include this story here, and would encourage any interested reader to seek out the original text, in the edition and translation by R.A.S. Macalister (Early Irish Text Society, 1910). Though this makes for an interesting read, it is far from accurate, and should be supplemented by the work of Connor P. Hartnett: *Irish Arthurian Literature* (New York University, 1973). Hartnett corrects several errors made by Macalister, such as the mistranslation of the name Gawain into Galahad, which is corrected throughout in my version. As in the other tales from this source, I have made a few minor changes, using Camelot the Golden, as throughout the book, for Arthur's central court. In the original it is called, in Celtic style 'The Fort of the Red Hall', but this stood out so much that I felt it was necessary to change it for the sake of coherence. In addition, I deleted the reference to Gawain marrying the King of Sorcha's daughter, as Gawain really does have too many wives in this collection, and the marriage added nothing essential to the story.

22: The Adventures at Tarn Wathelyn

This is really two stories, loosely connected by thematic resonances and by their setting – the haunted tarn (a small mountain lake) known as Wathelyn. It includes one of several appearances by a ghost to be found in Arthurian literature; including the grisly phantoms encountered by Sir Lancelot in the Chapel Perilous, and the appearance of the ghost of Sir Gawain himself to Arthur before the battle of Camlann. All are different from the kind of ghost we are used to reading about today. Modern ghosts are primarily psychological in kind, where their medieval counterparts existed as a perfectly natural phenomenon (though no less frightening for that) whose task was to foretell the future and induce a feeling of repentance in the hearts of those to whom they appeared. In this instance the ghost very precisely predicts the final conflict between Arthur and Mordred (the child who will become a man carrying a black shield with a silver saltire upon it) and Gawain's own death amid the rocky landscape of the Cornish coast.

Gawain, himself, was one of the most renowned of Arthur's knights throughout much of the period of the popularity of Arthurian literature. He is also one of the oldest of whom we have any knowledge. He appears in Celtic tradition as Gwalchmai (the Hawk of May) and is renowned for his skills and daring. Until the coming of the French knight, Sir Lancelot, he was the foremost hero of the Round Table, and, as in this story, the favoured knight of Queen Guinevere.

Nothing more is known of the queen's mother, or indeed of the promise she is said to have broken, though it is more than likely that the anonymous poet who penned this romance may well have known other stories that have since been lost. There is certainly a good chance that he had read 'The Wedding of Sir Gawain and the Lady Ragnall' (pp. 299–305), since the premise that Arthur has given other people's lands to his favourite nephew is repeated in both works.

The original text dates from the fifteenth century. It was written in alliterative verse, in a northern dialect of Middle English, and is preserved in four manuscript copies, notably that now found in the library of Lincoln Cathedral. It has been edited three times: once by Sir Frederic Madden in his

Syr Gawayne (London: Richard & John Taylor, 1839), again by F.J. Amours in *Scottish Alliterative Poems in Riming Stanzas* (Edinburgh: Scottish Text Society, 1897), and again by R.J. Gates for the University of Pennsylvania Press in 1969. It was transliterated into modern English by Louis B. Hall in his *The Knightly Tales of Sir Gawain* (Chicago: Nelson Hall, 1976). I have looked at all four versions in preparing this retelling but have relied primarily on that of Dr Hall.

23: The Tale of Gorlagros and Gawain

This is an unusual as well as powerful tale, which has at its heart a particularly medieval subject – that of fealty. According to the feudal laws of the time a knight could not be his own master, but inevitably owed allegiance to a king or a lesser nobleman, who was his 'liege lord'. This meant, effectively, binding oneself to an overlord, offering him service by bearing arms and fighting alongside him in time of war, or by representing him as a champion. Even mercenaries, who had no specific allegiance, sold their skills as fighting men to whichever lord required them. In return the lord offered the protection of his name and power, as well as providing weapons and armour – no small expense at the time.

In the story which follows, therefore, when Arthur and his knights encounter a lord who owes allegiance to no one they are understandably shocked, and Arthur is at once determined – in a manner which we might well find unreasonable today – to go to war over the matter, essentially bringing the errant Gorlagros to heel. This in turn provokes a decision on the part of Gawain, which is a test even of his honour – so often remarked upon in the stories in which he is a major character.

In our time the desire for freedom of the individual is generally upheld at any cost. But here the story turns not so much on Gorlagros' refusal to bend the knee to Arthur, as on the way Gawain and he resolve the problem which faces them. In the event, neither lose their honour – or their lives, as they might so easily have done. In essence the bond of fealty was a mutual one, and in acting as he does Gorlagros is breaking the bond between himself and his people. They, in turn, have the right to reject him.

The resolution of all this is skilfully handled by the anonymous author, who seems to have hailed from lowland Scotland. The single manuscript in which the story exists dates from around 1508 and is today held by the National Library of Scotland. This makes it one of the latest Arthurian romances included here, and as such it displays a considerable grasp of the concept of fealty, which was already beginning to lose its importance by this date, being reduced to little more than a monetary contract between the lord and the knights in his employment.

The story as we have it derives from an episode in the first continuation to Chrétien de Troyes' poem *Perceval*, usually attributed to Wauchier de Danaans. This episode, concerning the visit to the Orgellous (Proud) Castle and the defeat of a character known as the Rich Soudoier, may itself have derived from an earlier source. The character appears again in 'The Elucidation' (see pp. 309–25). Nor should one overlook the possible influence of the Gawain texts written in and around the area of the Midlands from the twelfth to the fourteenth centuries.

Here, as so often in related texts, we find the inevitable comparison between the blustering Sir Kay and the noble Gawain. The episode in which Kay steals food from the hall of the first castle they encounter is similar to occasions in several other stories where he acts in an impulsive or overbearing manner – usually with unfortunate results, since Kay always comes off the worst and has to be rescued by his comrades. In the present story, of course, he does redeem himself, by overcoming another knight and capturing him.

How much originality can be attributed to the author of this text is, as almost always with medieval texts, difficult to say. He writes with a seemingly wide knowledge of arms, armour, and siege-warfare – some of which is present within the episodes of Chrétien's poem. The characters speak with the authentic voices of their time, and I have not attempted to update them too much – allowing them rather to speak for themselves.

'Gorlagros and Gawain' has been edited several times, including in the incomparable *Syr Gawayne* of Sir Frederic Madden (London, 1939; reprinted by AMS Press, N.Y. 1971), and F.J. Amours' *Scottish Alliterative Poems in Riming Stanzas* (Edinburgh: Blackwood, 1897). As so often, the best modern rendition is by Louis B. Hall in his *Knightly Tales of Sir Gawain* (Chicago: Nelson Hall, 1976). A detailed examination of the story and its relationship to the Chrétien continuation was made by Paul J. Ketrick in *The Relation of Gorlagros and Gawane to the Old French Perceval* (Washington, D.C.: Catholic University of America Press, 1931).

24: Sir Gawain and the Carle of Carlisle

The many tales that have survived which feature Gawain as the hero bear testimony to the importance of his character throughout the early stages of the Arthurian cycle. Before Lancelot became the premier hero of the later medieval epics, Gawain was the first of Arthur's knights. As the king's nephew, and the son of a king, he had a privileged place at the court, and was besides recognized as a champion of great power. He was also noted for his courtesy, and for his love of women – a fact which later caused him to be dubbed a libertine. Indeed, as Lancelot's star rose so Gawain's fell, though the reasons for this go deeper than the fickle wind of fashion. The later writers of the Arthurian cycle, who sought to Christianize what were, essentially, pagan stories, recognized in Gawain the last of an older breed of heroes dedicated to the service of a goddess rather than a god. The two greatest tales in which he featured, *Sir Gawain and the Green Knight* and 'The Wedding of Gawain and the Lady Ragnall' (see below), both told stories which showed Gawain as a Knight of the Goddess, despite a veneer of Christian symbolism placed there by the medieval authors. It was this which caused Gawain to be steadily demoted from the premier hero of the Round Table to a blustering braggart and even a murderer, in which guise he sometimes appears in Malory's version of the cycle. It was for this reason, perhaps, that the two shorter Gawain stories included here (see also 'Gorlagros and Gawain', pp. 266–76) were omitted from *Le Morte D'Arthur* – though Malory may simply not have known them.

The two other heroes who appear in this story are not only important in their own right but serve as contrast to Gawain. The first of these is Sir Kay, who, like Gawain, was once both better known and better liked than in his later incarnations. He is listed among the first of Arthur's heroes in the early Celtic stories, and in 'Culhwch and Olwen' from the great Welsh myth-book *The Mabinogion*. He has a remarkable set of abilities, including being able to hold his breath under water for nine nights and nine days, and being able to go without sleep for as long. In Malory's version of the stories, he is a blusterer and a fool, mean-spirited and ill-natured. In the story told here he is somewhere between the two, capable of courage but contrasted by his failure with the more courageous Gawain.

The third of the trio of heroes, Bishop Baldwin, is almost certainly the same as the 'Sir Baldwin of Britain' who features in 'The Vows of King Arthur and his Knights' (see above) where he again serves as a foil to the more aggressively inclined knights. Though he is, as he reminds the Carle in the story, 'in holy orders' he is a knight as well and follows all the adventurous pursuits of a knight. In the older Welsh stories, he is known as 'Bishop Bidwini', an indication of his long-standing association with the Arthurian cycles.

As for the 'Carle', he is really one of several such characters who appear scattered throughout the Arthurian corpus – generally as bold, rough-natured fellows who will just as soon deliver a buffet as a gift, and who possess some magical attributes. The word 'carl' is borrowed from Old Norse and meant simply 'man'; in English it becomes synonymous with the word 'churl' (from which we have 'churlish'). In the story given here he is under a spell in much the same way as the Green Knight or Sir Gromer Somer Jour are in the two great Gawain romances named above. In each case the villain is exonerated from his previous behaviour when all is finally explained.

The story which follows here is a small masterpiece of storytelling excellence, which preserves Gawain's original qualities as a hero, and as a courtly knight, contrasting him favourably with both Kay and the Bishop. The story also contains some of the elements of the Green Knight story, both in the episode of the beheading of the Carle and in the feelings evinced by Gawain for his host's wife. Her behaviour, and that of his daughter, may seem odd or even repugnant to us today, but faithfully reflects the power of men over their wives and children in the Middle Ages.

The main version used here is an anonymous text composed somewhere between 1450 and 1470, which also exists in a later, sixteenth-century reworking. The episode of the beheading, which is missing from the fifteenth-century text, is here restored from this version, which in fact retains several features that are clearly from an older text. Both versions have been used in the writing of the story given here (see also 'The Mule Without a Bridle', pp. 291–8).

The best edition of 'The Carle' is that by Donald Sands in his *Middle English Verse Romances* (New York: Reinhart & Winston, 1966). It had been translated by Professor Louis B. Hall in his admirable collection *The Knightly Tales of Sir Gawain*, and the two versions were edited by Auvo Kurvinen in *Sir Gawain and the Carle of Carlisle in Two Versions* (Helsinki: Annales Academiae Scientiarum Fennicae. Series B 71.2., 1951). There is a good commentary on the story by Robert W. Ackerman in *Arthurian Literature in the Middle Ages* edited by R.S. Loomis (Oxford: Clarendon Press, 1959, pp. 493–5). For more about Gawain and his pagan origins, see my *Gawain, Knight of the Goddess* (Inner Traditions, 2002).

25: The Knight With the Enchanted Sword

The Knight with the Sword, or *Le Chevalier a L'Epée*, is one of several shorter romances featuring Gawain included here. Most of these establish the hero as someone with a particular devotion to women – or, as some would have it, as a 'ladies' man'. The fact that this hides a deeper theme, in which Gawain serves a more archetypal representation of the feminine – the Goddess – is demonstrated in several texts in which Gawain features as the hero. In *Le Chevalier a L'Epée* the story seems weighted somewhat towards the masculine view, but this is really no more than an expression of the medieval attitude towards women, who were seen as little more than chattels to be passed from hand to hand according to the requirements of their male relatives. As the poem's most recent translator, Ross G. Arthur, has wisely remarked: '... we need only imagine what the heroine's life was like before she met Gawain, and what happened to her after they parted ... and what would have happened to Gawain if it were not for the help she gave him,' to understand the real drift of the story.

Much of what happens here may seem odd to us today but is mostly dictated by the manners and customs of the time. It was quite common for knights to dispute over a woman and for her to be passed like a chattel from one to the other after a fight to see who was the strongest. The episode of the Perilous Bed, which features in this romance, is a widespread motif that appears in several other surviving romances, including the *Perceval* of Chrétien de Troyes and the famous *Lancelot-Grail* cycle of romances. The same episode occurs in 'How Sir Lancelot Earned his Name' (based on the *Lanzalet* of Ulrich von Zatzikhoven pp. 55–77). There the outcome is somewhat different, and I have included both versions for the sake of completeness. In most instances the hero involved is Gawain, which leads one to suppose that this was a well-established tradition, possibly pre-dating the medieval texts in which it appears. As so often in these tales, the lord of the castle is nameless, as is his daughter; therefore, I have given them names drawn from other Arthurian sources to make it easier to identify them.

The poem dates from the early thirteenth century and is attributed to an author who signs himself Paien de Maisieres and who may also be the writer of another short Gawain romance included here: 'The Mule Without A Bridle' (pp. 291–8). It has been edited several times, most notably by Edward C. Armstrong: *Le Chevalier a L'Epée* (Baltimore: Murphy, 1900) and R.C. Johnson and D.D.R. Owen in *Two Old French Gauvain Romances* (Edinburgh & London: Scottish Academic Press, 1972). Two translations have appeared to date: one in *From Cuchulainn to Gawain* by Elizabeth Brewer (D.S. Brewer, 1973); and the most recent by Ross G. Arthur in *Three Arthurian Romances* (J.M. Dent, 1996), both of which I have made use of in my own version.

26: The Mule Without A Bridle

The story of *La Mule Sans Frein* (The Mule Without a Bridle) was written in Old French and is attributed to one Paien, or Pagan, de Maisieres, sometimes assumed to be a pseudonym which parodies the name of the great French Arthurian poet, Chrétien de Troyes. It exists in a single manuscript which also contains another, somewhat similar romance, *Le Chevalier a L'Epee* (The Knight with the Enchanted Sword, see pp. 283–90). Both are brief and have a satirical bent which pokes fun at the more serious chivalric romances of Chrétien and his followers.

Yet, despite its frivolous-seeming story, it in fact hides a more serious theme, that of sovereignty over the land – an important theme in Arthurian romance, which dates back to Celtic times. Essentially this theme revolves around the relationship between the king and the land, described in Celtic tradition as an almost symbiotic connection between the ruler and the spirit of the place over which he rules. Only kings who are perfect in body can rule – thus for instance when the Irish king, Nuadh, loses a hand, which is replaced by a silver one, he can no longer be king. Gawain, who is Arthur's nephew, and often his representative, is here depicted as securing a bridle which gives him the right to rule over the lands owned by the girl with the mule, and which also gives him power over animals. (I have discussed this at greater length in my book, *Gawain, Knight of the Goddess*, Inner Traditions, 2002).

The setting of the adventure itself is very clearly an Otherworldly one. The valley with the wild beasts, the place of scorpions, and finally the castle itself with its revolving walls and strange inhabitants – the churl who offers to play the Beheading Game with Gawain, the lions and dragons and the obviously faery lady – all make this apparent. The episode of the beheading is of particular interest as it marks a very different account of this ancient theme, which is best known from the version found in *Sir Gawain and the Green Knight*, but which in all probability derives from an older Celtic text, *Bricriu's Feast*, in which a remarkably similar event takes place, where the protagonists are the great Irish hero Cuchulainn, and the trickster (*bachlach*), Bricriu. A full account of this, and other, analogies will be found in Elizabeth Brewer's book on the subject (see below).

In its present form the story ends rather abruptly and perhaps even unsatisfactorily. One feels that Gawain ought to have married either the girl with the mule, or her mistress, but since both are faery beings and Gawain is known to have had liaisons with several other such magical women, this might be the reason for it. In any case, Gawain is depicted in his most heroic guise, contrasted as so often with the foolish and cowardly Kay (see 'The Vows of King Arthur and His Knights', pp. 27–35).

The episode of the people who suddenly appear rejoicing in the streets at the end is reminiscent of the Grail story, where the land and people are healed by the achieving of the Grail adventure. One may also compare it to Lancelot's visit to the home of the Grail king in Malory, where the hero rescues a woman from a boiling bath and emerges to a tumultuous reception. In addition, there is the curious fact that both the knight with whom Gawain fights, and who is apparently healed by his efforts, and the lady of the castle, are both discovered lying in bed. This recalls the wounded king episode in the Grail romances, where the king also lies on a bed and is only healed when the Grail-winners ask the famous 'question', which releases the spell binding both king and land in thrall.

The text has been edited twice. Once by B. Orlowski (*La Demoiselle a la Mule*, Paris, 1911) and again in *Two Old French Gauvain Romances* by R.C. Johnston and D.D.R. Owen (Scottish Academic Press, 1972). It was translated into rather curious verse form by M. Le Grand in *Fabliaux or Tales Abridged from French Manuscripts* (London, 1815), and more recently in prose by Elizabeth Brewer in *Sir Gawain and the Green Knight: Sources and Analogues* (D.S. Brewer, 1992.) I have made use of several of these versions in my own retelling.

27: The Wedding of Sir Gawain and the Lady Ragnall

This is one of the most famous of the independent Arthurian tales and probably does not deserve the appellation 'forgotten'. It forms the basis for Chaucer's 'Wife of Bath's tale', and while in that retelling the hero has no name, the setting is still Arthurian. By all accounts it is an extraordinary story which deserves to be better known. It also makes a welcome alternative to the misogynistic tales such as 'The Vows of King Arthur and His Knights' (pp. 27–35).

Though it has been often retold in recent years, frequently as a feminist parable, I have avoided any interpretation within the story itself and have told it 'straight', very much as it was written by the original anonymous author some time in the middle of the fifteenth century, making it one of the few stories retold here which may be later than Malory's *Morte D'Arthur*. (Some critics believe it may have been penned by Malory himself, though this is unlikely.)

There is much within the text which bears comment. The attitude of the day which saw women as chattel, and linked them to their husbands as status symbols, is challenged throughout. Ragnall makes her own choice of husband, selecting Sir Gawain, the most famous and best-loved knight of the Round Table, with a reputation for courtesy and for his numerous relationships with women. Indeed, this service to all womanhood gained him the reputation of a womanizer, and he is portrayed as such in many of the later romances in which he appears. The reason for this seems to have been that, as a Celtic hero, Gawain (or as he is known there, Gwalchmai, the Hawk of May) was a champion of the Goddess and therefore of all women. To the disapproving minds of the medieval chroniclers and romancers, this made him not only a pagan but also dangerous, and their reaction was to systematically blacken his name. I have dealt with this at some length in my book *Gawain, Knight of the Goddess* (Inner Traditions, 2002) and recommend readers to this for a more detailed account.

Ragnall herself is a fascinating character, independent and determined and possessed of an earthy sense of humour, despite her perilous situation. If either Arthur or Gawain had refused her offer, she might have been condemned to perpetual ugliness, but her confidence in their chivalrous nature proves well founded. It is probable, from evidence found elsewhere, that she was, at one point, a faery woman, who sought to test the king and his nephew. As is often the way in such instances, the bride later vanishes, returning to Faery after several years (see 'The Tale of Sir Lanval', pp. 103–7). In this version of the story she simply dies, having given birth to Gawain's son, Guinglain, who is of course the hero of 'The Adventure of the Fair Unknown' (pp. 87–102) where he is clearly stated to have been the offspring of Gawain's love for a faery, or fay.

The answer to the question, 'What is it women desire most?', is here given as 'sovereignty'. In the text this is elaborated to mean more simply 'power over men', but I have chosen to preserve the older interpretation of the word, since this itself links Ragnall to an even older figure, Lady Sovereignty. In ancient Celtic myth she is the *genia loci* of the land, a personification of the spiritual presence of the earth. No king could ascend to the rulership of the land until he had encountered her, sometimes being challenged to kiss or sleep with her in hideous form – at which point she turned into a beautiful woman just as Ragnall does in the story given here.

In other versions of the story, particularly the ballad version found in Bishop Percy's *Reliques of Ancient English Poetry* (George Routledge, 1857) the cause of Ragnall's state and Gromer's animosity towards Arthur is attributed to the arch-villainess of Arthurian tradition, Morgan le Fay. As a woman of faery blood herself and a lineal descendant of the Irish battle-goddess, Morrigan, she has a firmly grounded enmity with both Gawain and Arthur. In the most famous Gawain story, concerning his encounter with the Green Knight, she is again said to be the driving force behind the attack. Here, she appears as a hideous old woman, while the Green Knight himself bears more than a little resemblance to Gromer Somer Jour. That both these characters derive from more ancient ancestors than is apparent in the medieval poems is evidenced in both the works. In *Gawain and the Green Knight*, the challenger bears a holly bough in his hand and dresses entirely in green, marking him out clearly enough as a type of Winter King. In Gromer's case, though his behaviour in the poem makes him no more than a challenger of a kind frequently encountered in Arthurian literature, his name suggests that he was once much more. Gromer Somer Jour may be translated as meaning 'Man of the Summer's Day' making him the polar opposite of the Green Knight, Summer Lord to the other's Winter King.

Behind both stories lies an ancient tale of the struggle of the kings of Summer and Winter for the hand of the Spring Maiden – here represented by Ragnall, who like her ancestor, Lady Sovereignty, represents the land in its barren, sleeping, wintry mode, which can be awoken to the beauty of spring by the love and trust of Gawain, who in Celtic tradition is himself a solar hero. It seemed appropriate to invoke this idea in this story.

The text of 'The Wedding of Sir Gawain and the Lady Ragnall' has been edited several times, notably by B.J. Whiting in *Sources and Analogues of Chaucer's*

Canterbury Tales ed. W.F. Bryan and G. Dempster. (New York: Humanities Press, 1958, pp. 242–64) and by Donald B. Sands in *Middle English Verse Romances* (Holt, Reinhart, and Winston, 1966). A 'modern spelling' edition, with useful notes and commentary by John Witherington, was published by the Department of English, Lancaster University, 1991. Variants of the story are to be found in Frederick Madden's *Syr Gawayne*, (New York: AMS Press, 1971; original edition Edinburgh, 1839). For a detailed discussion of Ragnall's role in Arthurian legend and tradition see *The Ladies of the Lake* by Caitlín and John Matthews (Thorsons, 1992).

BOOK FOUR: THE BOOK OF THE GRAIL

28: The Elucidation of the Grail and the Story of Sir Perceval

This story is drawn from two separate texts: the *Didot Perceval*, dating from the thirteenth century, and the anonymous *L'Elucidation*, composed around 1195. I have given myself more licence than with most of the stories included here in order to bring in some of the elements lacking in Malory's account. Those wishing to know more about the mysterious *L'Elucidation*, which raises a whole raft of ideas concerning the origin and meaning of the Grail myth, are directed to *The Lost Book of the Grail* by John and Caitlín Matthews and Gareth Knight (Inner Traditions, 2018), which also includes the first full and accurate translation of the text. Another version of this is included in Nigel Bryant's collection: *The Complete Story of the Grail* (D.S. Brewer, 2018).

Accounts of the Grail quest are numerous and vary considerably in quality and intent. Malory gives us one of the fullest and most elaborate accounts in his book, while *The Story of the Grail* by the twelfth-century French poet Chrétien de Troyes is a bare bones retelling of an older, possibly Hebrew source. The multi-volume *Lancelot-Grail* Cycle, written not long after, and which furnished much of Malory's version, sets the entire Arthurian story against the background of the Grail, interpreting it in a wholly theological way. Malory stripped out most of the theology and kept the magical and spiritual essence of the story. He also followed the lines of the French epic in replacing the original Grail winner, Perceval, with the saintly Galahad, son of Lancelot. Other versions vary from the highly charged and symbolically overweighed *Parzifal* of Wolfram von Eschenbach to the elliptical *Diu Crone* of Heinrich von dem Türlin.

Falling somewhere between all of these is *The Prose Perceval*, more generally known as the *Didot Perceval* after one of the manuscript's early owners. This is a masterly abridgement of the vast tale into a brief but telling story, full of mystery and magic. It describes the coming of the Grail, the effect this had on the Arthurian world, tells some of Perceval's adventures, and ends with a brief rendition of the *Mort Artu* or Death of Arthur, which I have used in the penultimate story in this book. I have chosen to extract parts from all these sections, abridging them in places to tell the story both economically and clearly. I have also, as mentioned in the previous note, added details intended to link the story more directly to the *L'Elucidation* which precedes it here. This gives a quite different version of the story to that included by Malory.

In essence, the story is about contrasts and tells how a simple youth (Perceval) discovers the ways of the world and the spirit. His many failures are balanced by his final success – though, uniquely within this corpus of material, he is helped somewhat by Merlin, who is very much a behind-the-scenes operator in this tale. The text is also unusual in that it describes the Grail as emitting music, and in referring to the mysterious 'enchantments' which lie over Britain until the Grail is found. I have made this only affect the Wasteland, since this can be seen as a metaphor for the whole of Arthur's kingdom. I have also reduced several of the more overt Christian references to better suit the more mystical tone of the tale overall. The mention of Merlin's retirement to his *'esplumoir'* is also interesting. This word has no exact meaning but seems to relate to the word for a 'moulting cage' for birds of prey. It suggests that the mage retires to 'moult', or leave behind the ways of the world, and to watch from within all that takes place outside. This concept, though hinted at in other texts, is nowhere more clearly stated than here. The basis of the story springs from Merlin's retirement to his observatory, as chronicled in 'The Coming of Merlin' (pp. 3–11).

The text dates from some time between 1190 and 1215 and exists in two dissimilar versions, which nonetheless tell more or less the same story. The version used here is that of the E manuscript, which was translated by Dell Skeels as *The Romance of Perceval in Prose* (Seattle and London: Washington University Press, 1966). Professor Skeels' introduction and notes have been very useful in preparing this version, as has the commentary of Albert Pauphilet, 'Le Roman en Prose de Perceval', contained in *Mélanges d'histoire du Moyen Âge offerts à M. Ferdinand Lot* (Paris: Champion, 1925). The best edition to date of the original text is that of William Roach: *The Didot Perceval* (Philadelphia: University of Pennsylvania Press, 1941), which includes both versions of the text.

29: The Tale of Morien

'The Tale of Morien' is one of the more complex stories included here. It is also a most unusual tale, which suggests a far less racially biased account of the hero (one of a tiny handful of knights of colour to be found in the Arthurian cycle). The anonymous author goes out of his way to show how the ordinary people fear and suspect Morien – who is of Moorish descent and described as 'black as a burned brand') – as a demon from Hell; while the Arthurian knights such as Gawain, Lancelot and Guerrehes treat him as a normal man and a noble knight. The story belongs to a unique collection dating from the beginning of the fourteenth century and therefore predating Malory, which forms what is nowadays known as *The Dutch Lancelot*. This is a close translation of the great collection of the *Lancelot-Grail* (formally the *Vulgate Cycle*), which tells the story of the Grail Quest in detail. This was itself the foundation for Malory's own retelling – though he edited out the vast wealth of theological commentary which more than doubles the length of the various stories. 'Morien' is not found elsewhere, and we have no idea where it originated, or indeed when, though internal references suggest it might have been in the thirteenth century, not least of which is borne out by the fact that the story is written in verse rather than prose, as were most of the earlier romances. The story is a lengthy one – extending to some 5,000 lines in the original, and I was forced (reluctantly) to make several cuts to include it here. By summarizing the adventures of Gawain and Lancelot (which would make excellent stand-alone stories) I was able to explore the story of Morien's search for his father in greater depths. The poem alone seems to be responsible for the change from Perceval to Aglovale as the hero's progenitor since, as the author states at the beginning of his poem, Perceval died a virgin so could not have produced a son. There is something really warm-hearted about this work, and I am glad to have been able to include it here. The only full translation to date was made by Jessie L. Weston (as *The Romance of Morien*, D. Nutt, London, 1901) in a somewhat antique style which is hard to read with enjoyment today. I drew upon this almost entirely for my own version, but also found a great deal of helpful material (as well as some excellent translations from the original) in *An Unlikely Hero: The Romance of Moriaen and Racial Discursivity in the Middle Ages*, a thesis delivered by Erik Hendrix in 2014. The great expert on Dutch Arthurian romance, Bart Besamusca, provides the best in-depth study of this (and other Dutch romances) in *Walewein, Moriaen en de Ridder metter mouwen* (Uitgeverij Verloren, Hilversum, 1993).

30: The Adventures of Sone de Nansay

The little-known text of 'Sone de Nansay' was written some time between the end of the thirteenth and beginning of the fourteenth centuries by an anonymous author. It is found in a single manuscript in the Royal Library of Turin, Italy (Ms. 1626) as part of a collection of chivalric and Arthurian tales, including Chrétien de Troyes' *Cligès*. Written in medieval French, the copy was made some time during the mid-fourteenth century, but the poem of *Sone* itself dates from somewhat earlier. It consists of some 21,321 lines, with a lacuna of some 2,400 lines, the result of fire damage, the contents of which can be inferred from the remainder of the work. *Sone* is said to derive from the German name, *Sueno*, while *Nansay* is probably *Nanbsheim*, near Neuf-Brisach in north-eastern France. The story has received little attention until now, due in part to its length and the dismissive comments of the first scholars to notice it, who termed it prolix and lacking in skill, as well as failing to grasp the nature of the Grail material, which was seen as having been 'inserted' into the romance in a clumsy way. In fact, a great deal of the poem is taken up with the Grail story, with its titular hero's life being compared to that of the first Grail guardian, Joseph of Arimathea. It also adds many important details to the Grail myth, especially in its description of the building where the sacred relic is kept. This is the only part of the poem to receive any attention until now, as it has been recognized as containing many subtle references within the work that add to our understanding of the Grail myth. The only full-length study of the poem in English to date is by Kruger Normand in a PhD dissertation submitted in 1975 to the University of Pennsylvania. Normand categorizes the work as 'ancestral and biographical' since it describes the life of the hero from birth to death and deals both with his antecedents and successors. I am grateful to Dr. Normand for providing the most detailed summary of the work, which helped in my own reconstruction of various elements of the story here. I am also grateful to Gareth Knight, who translated extensive sections of the work in the book we wrote together: *Temples of the Grail* (Llewellyn, 2018). The tale is long and winds around considerably as the hero journeys across parts of Europe, Scandinavia, Ireland, and Scotland. Here, I have focussed on the passages dealing with the continuing story of the Grail after the story told in Malory, the *Lancelot-Grail*, and others. No other text of which I am aware covers this period and it seemed a perfect way to extend the usual accounts of the quest. It is also unusual in making Joseph of Arimathea, described as a guardian of the Grail in many versions of the story, a warrior. Just two editions of the work have appeared to date: the first by Moritz Goldschmidt in 1899 and a more recent edition by Claude Lachet in 2014. Until such time as a full translation into English appears, the longest extracts are in *Temples of the Grail* by Gareth Knight and myself.

BOOK FIVE: THE ENDING OF THE ROUND TABLE

31/32: The Death of Arthur and The Voyage to Avalon

The last story in the book is really two stories, drawn from different sources. It seemed important to end, as did Malory, with the passing of the king, but I wanted to tell a variant account of that last battle and tell the story of what came after. For the first part, I turned again to the *Didot Perceval* (see 'The Elucidation of the Grail and the Story of Perceval' above). Written between 1190 and 1215, this is a greatly abbreviated account of the adventures of Perceval's quest for the Grail, and furnished parts of that story told here (pp. 311–25). From this I took the briefest account of Arthur's passing, quoting also, briefly, from the *Vita Merlini*, which furnished the story with which this book begins. To follow this, I turned to an extraordinary and largely unknown fourteenth-century romance called *La Faula* (A Fable), the only surviving Arthurian romance written in Catalan (though Arthur and Morgan le Fay both speak in French) by Guillaume de Toerella (1348–?). It gives an account of a journey to the isle of Avalon, where the narrator meets the restored King Arthur, who is bemoaning his state of immortality and wishing to return to the outer world. This is a unique story, which has remained unavailable to all but speakers of Catalan until its recent translation into Italian and French. Thanks to Dr. Maria Mariola Glavan for allowing me access to her translation-in-progress, which enabled me to write my own version. I am hugely grateful to Dr. Glavan and to Dr. Kresimir Vukovic, for their assistance in this – though neither should be held responsible for the version which appears here.

As with all the stories retold in this collection, I have allowed myself freedom to reshape, and occasionally add, to the existing story. This, as stated before, is to permit the weaving of the stories into something like a coherent narrative – much as Caxton did with Malory's original text. For those wishing to follow up on the story as it appears in the original, until such time as a full English translation appears, you are recommended to the excellent edition and modern French translation prepared by Michel Adroher in *La Faula: Le roi Arthur en Méditerranée* (UGA Editions, 2020). (An Italian version is available as *La Favola*, Carocci, 2004.) The best translation of the *Didot Perceval* is still that made by Dell Skeels as *The Romance of Perceval in Prose* (University of Washington Press, 1966).

FURTHER READING

The sources for the individual stories included above are given within the notes for each text. What follows is a brief, eclectic list of additional titles, other texts, as well as more general studies, intended to assist the interested reader in finding his or her way through the labyrinth of Arthurian lore and literature.

Adams, Max, *The First Kingdom* (London: Head of Zeus, 2021)

Barber, Richard, *King Arthur, Hero and Legend* (Suffolk: Boydell Press, 1986)

Bromwich, Rachel, *Triodd Ynys Prydein* (The Welsh Triads) (Cardiff: University of Wales Press, 1977)

Bromwich, Rachel, A.O.H. Jarman & B. F. Roberts eds, *The Arthur of the Welsh* (Cardiff: University of Wales Press, 1993)

Bryant, Nigel (trans.), *The Complete Story of the Grail: Chrétien's Perceval and its Continuations* (Cambridge: D.S. Brewer, 2011)

Chrétien de Troyes, *Perceval, or the Story of the Grail*, trans. Nigel Bryant (Cambridge: D.S. Brewer, 1982)

Darrah, John, *Paganism in Arthurian Romance* (Suffolk: Boydell Press, 1994)

Geoffrey of Monmouth, *History of the Kings of Britain,* trans. Lewis Thorp (London: Penguin Books, 1966)

Goodrich, Peter (ed.), *The Romance of Merlin* (London & New York: Garland Publishing, 1990)

Guest, Charlotte, *The Mabinogion* (London: Dent, Everyman's Library, 1906)

Lacey, Norris J. et al. (trans.), *The Lancelot-Grail* (10 vols): *The Old French Arthurian Vulgate and Post-Vulgate in Translation* (Cambridge: D.S. Brewer, 2010)

Logorio, Valerie & Mildred Leake Day, *King Arthur Through the Ages* (2 vols) (London & New York: Garland Publishing, 1990)

Loomis, R.S., *The Grail: From Celtic Myth to Christian Symbol* (Cardiff: University of Wales Press, 1963)

Markale, Jean, *King Arthur King of Kings* (London: Gordon & Cremonesi, 1977)

Matthews, Caitlín, *King Arthur & the Goddess of the Land* (Rochester, VT: Inner Traditions, 2002)

——, *Mabon & the Guardians of Celtic Britain* (Rochester, VT: Inner Traditions, 2002)

Matthews, Caitlín & John Matthews, *The Arthurian Book of Days* (London: Sidgwick & Jackson/New York: St Martins, 1990)

——, *The Complete King Arthur* (Rochester, VT: Inner Traditions, 2018)

——, *Ladies of the Lake* (Wellingborough: Aquarian Press, 1992)

Matthews, John, *An Arthurian Reader* (Wellingborough: Aquarian Press, 1988)

——, *At the Table of the Grail* (London: Watkins Publishing, 2002)

——, *Gawain, Knight of the Goddess* (Rochester, VT: Inner Traditions, 2002)

——, *The Grail: Quest for the Eternal* (London: Thames & Hudson, 1981; Crossroads, 1990)

——, *King Arthur: from Dark Age Warrior to Medieval King* (London: Carlton Books, 2003)

Matthews, John and Gareth Knight, *Temples of the Grail* (Woodbury, MN: Llewellyn, 2018)

Morris, John, *The Age of Arthur* (London: Weidenfeld & Nicolson, 1973)

Stewart, R.J., *The Prophetic Life of Merlin* (London: Arkana, 1986)

Tolstoy, Nikolai, *The Quest for Merlin* (London: Hamish Hamilton, 1985)

Venning, Timothy, *The King Arthur Mysteries* (London: Pen & Sword History, 2021)

von Eschenbach, Wolfram, *Parzival,* trans. A.T. Hatto (London: Penguin Books, 1980)